SEVEN SEAS ENTERTAINMENT PRESENTS

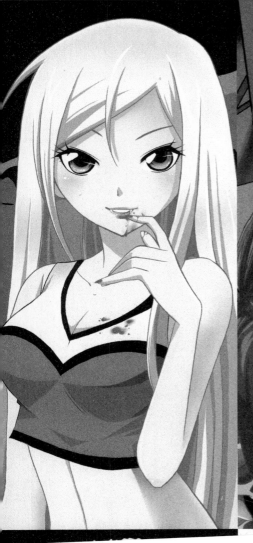

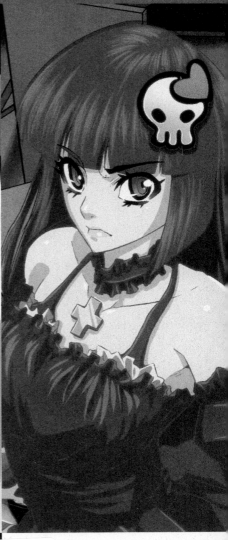

RANORMAL
Mystery Squad

by
Arnold

art by
Comipa & Ian Cang

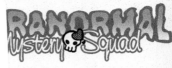

VAMPIRE
CHEERLEADERS
MONSTER MASH COLLECTION

stories by **Adam Arnold**
art by **Shiei, Comipa, & Ian Cang**

STAFF CREDITS

lettering & design	**Nicky Lim**
p.m.s. art assists & tones	**Jaimee delos Santos, Mark Henry Bustamante, Ian Olympia**
v.c. tones	**Ludwig Sacramento**
copy editor	**Shanti Whitesides**
editor	**Alexis Roberts**
publisher	**Jason DeAngelis Seven Seas Entertainment**

ISBN: 978-1-935934-74-5

Printed in the USA

First Printing: June 2012

10 9 8 7 6 5 4 3 2 1

FOLLOW US ONLINE: **www.gomanga.com**

READING DIRECTIONS

This book reads from *right to left*, Japanese style. If this is your first time reading manga, you start reading from the top right panel on each page and take it from there. If you get lost, just follow the numbered diagram here. It may seem backwards at first, but you'll get the hang of it! Have fun!!

VAMPIRE CHEERLEADERS

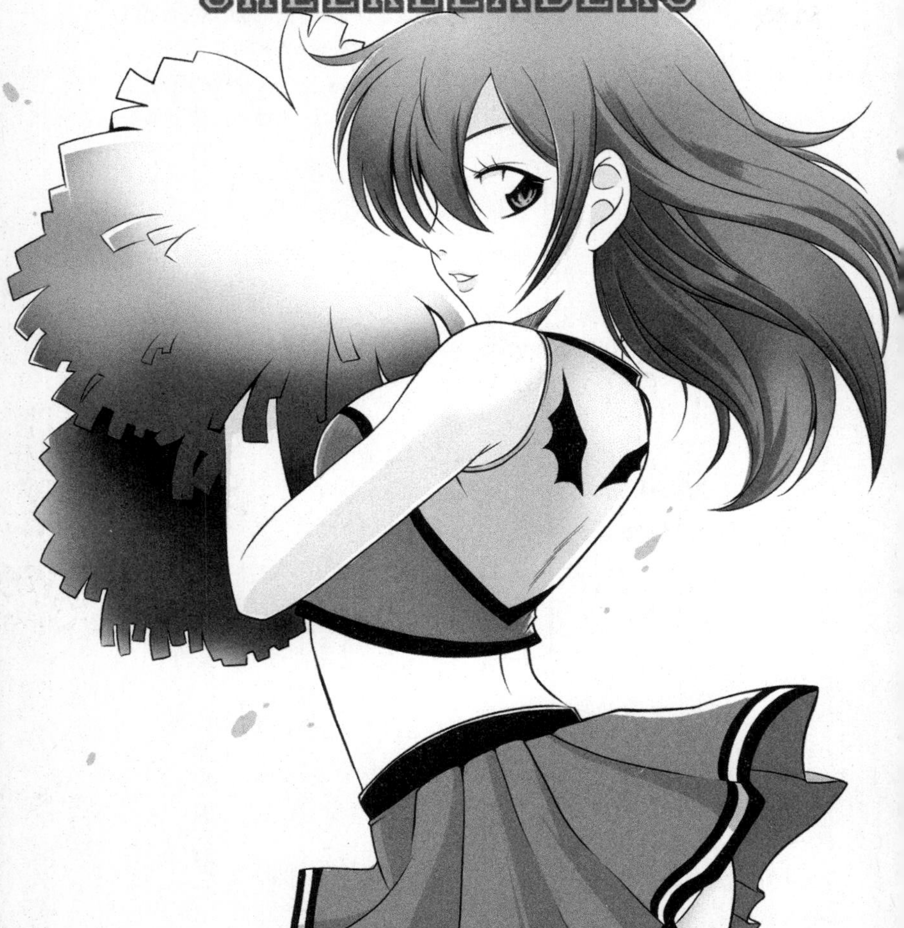

"FANG SERVICE"

STORY ADAM ARNOLD / ART SHIEI

VAMPIRE

CHEERLEADERS

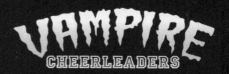

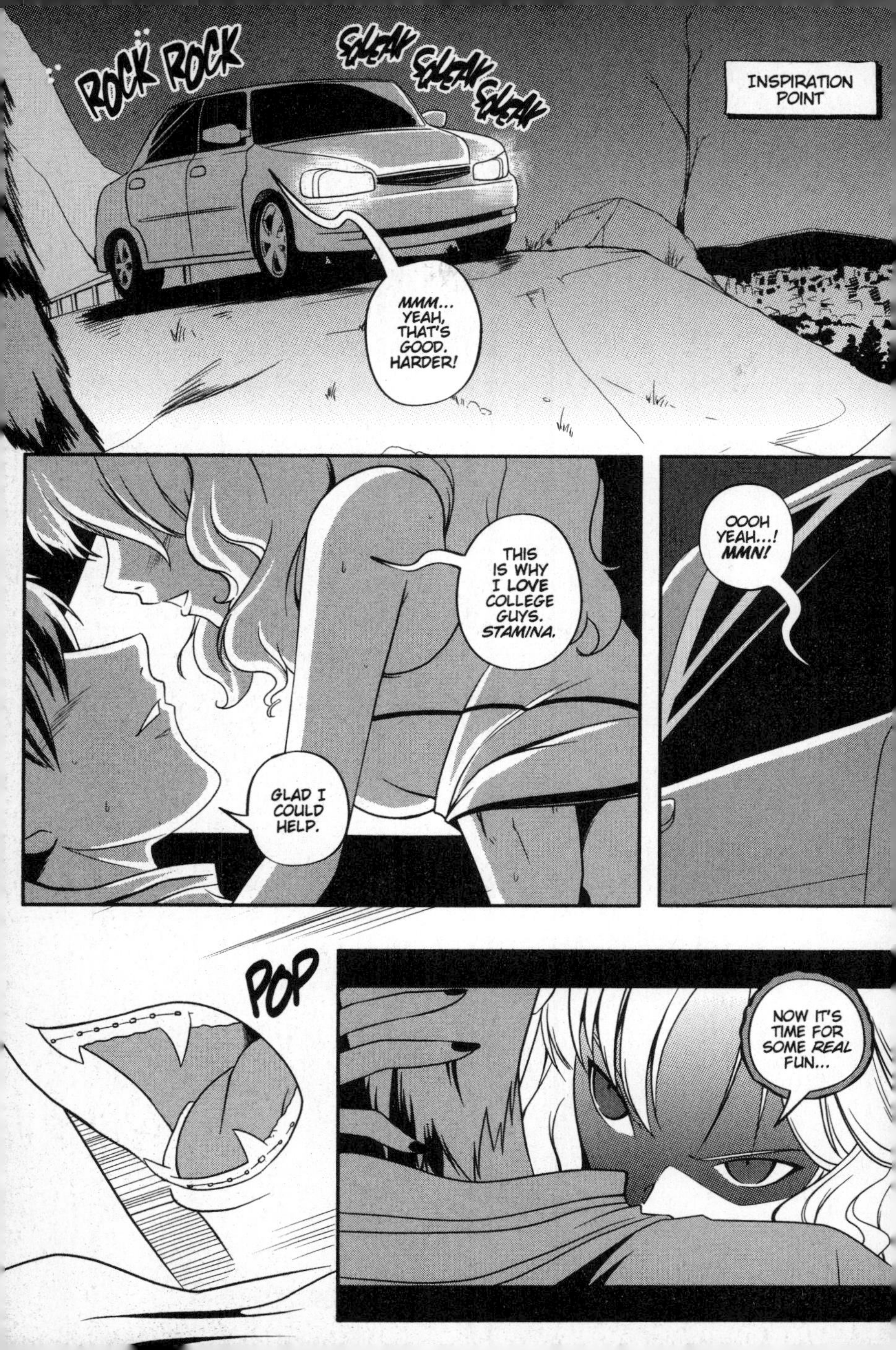
INSPIRATION POINT
SQUEAK SQUEAK SQUEAK
ROCK ROCK
MMM... YEAH, THAT'S GOOD. HARDER!
OOOH YEAH...! *MMN!*
THIS IS WHY I LOVE COLLEGE GUYS. *STAMINA.*
GLAD I COULD HELP.
NOW IT'S TIME FOR SOME *REAL* FUN...
POP

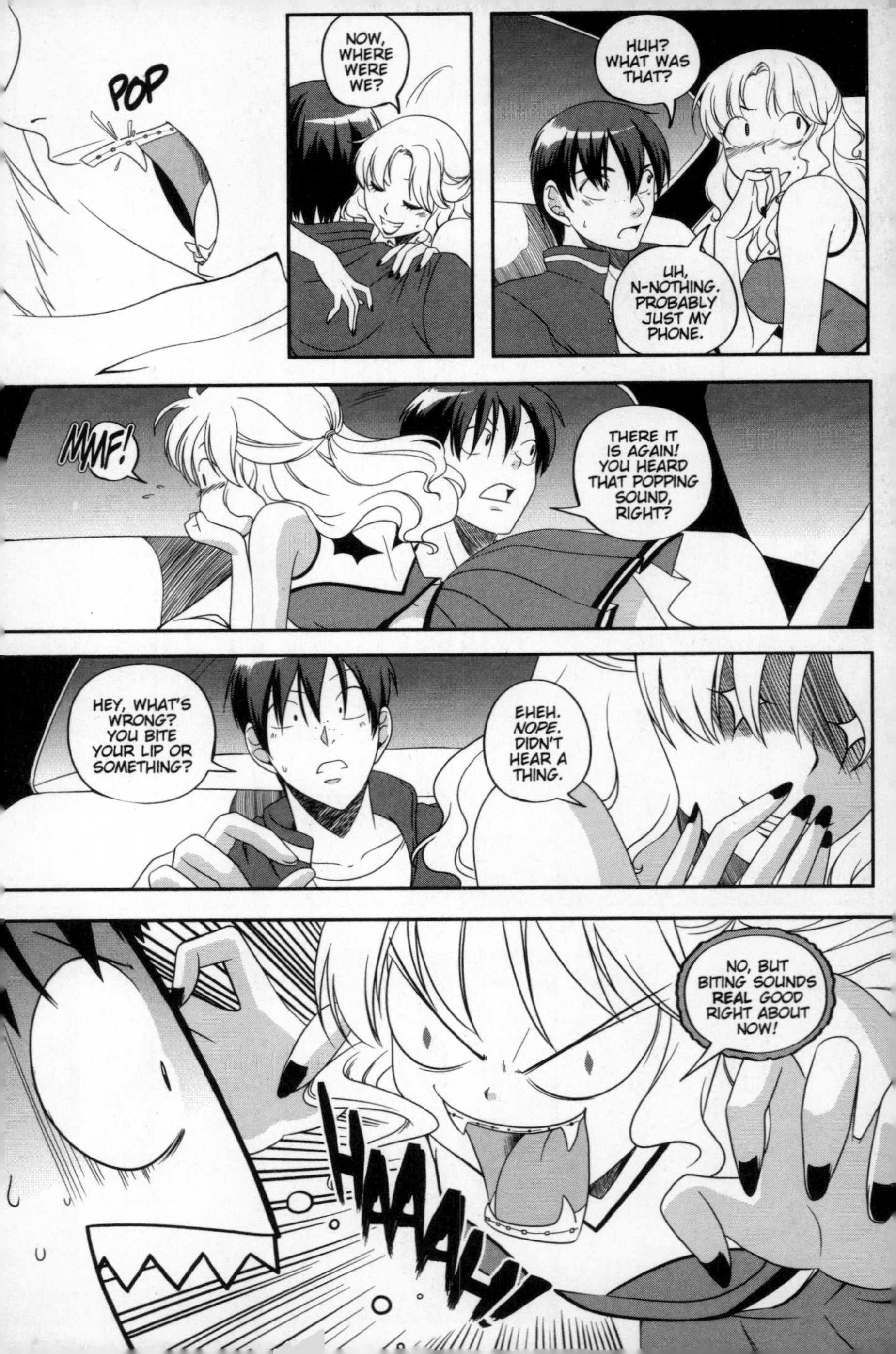
HUH? WHAT WAS THAT?
UH, N-NOTHING. PROBABLY JUST MY PHONE.
NOW, WHERE WERE WE?
POP
THERE IT IS AGAIN! YOU HEARD THAT POPPING SOUND, RIGHT?
MMF!
EHEH. *NOPE.* DIDN'T HEAR A THING.
HEY, WHAT'S WRONG? YOU BITE YOUR LIP OR SOMETHING?
NO, BUT BITING SOUNDS REAL GOOD RIGHT ABOUT NOW!
HAAAH!!

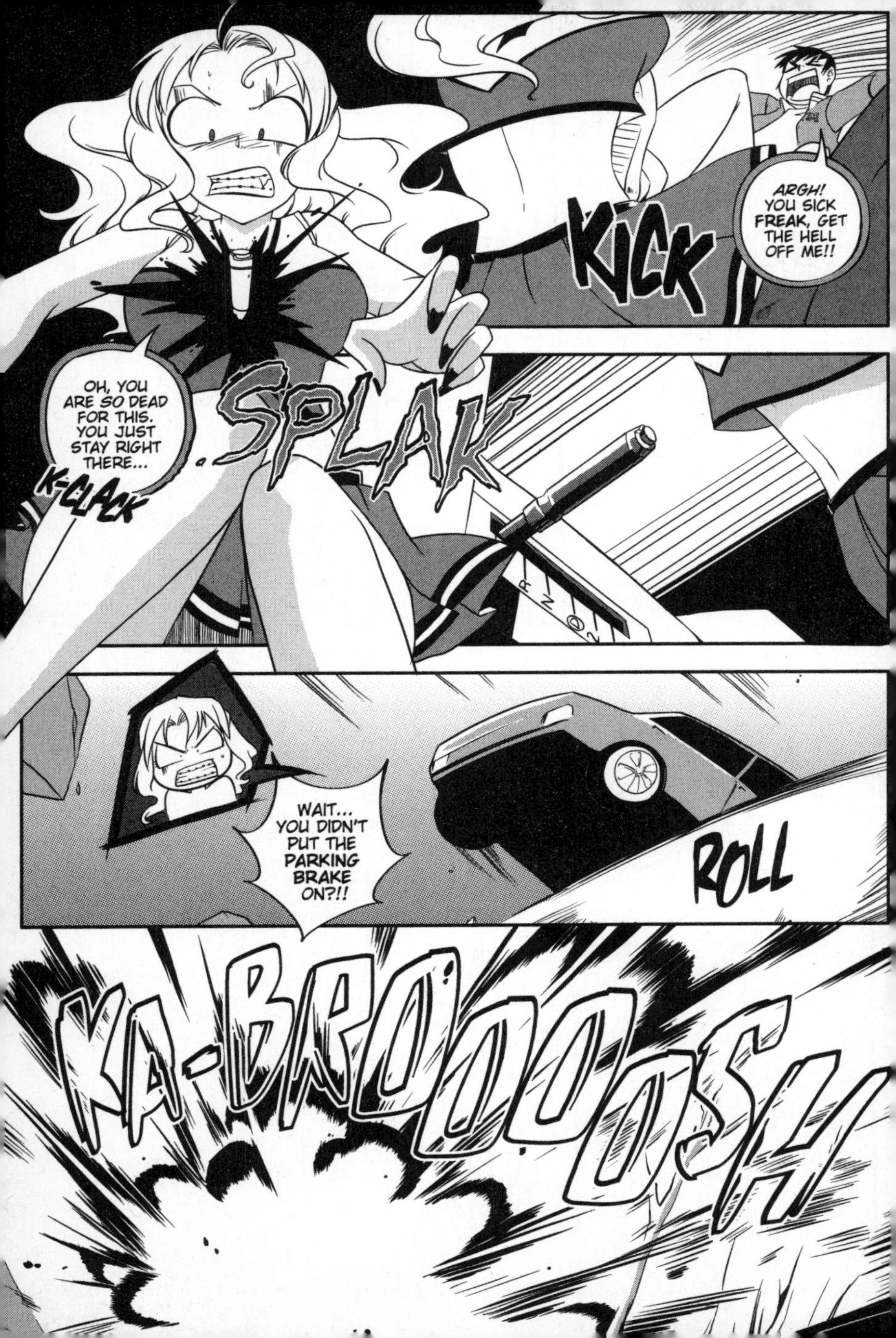
ARGH! YOU SICK FREAK, GET THE HELL OFF ME!!
KICK
SPLAK
OH, YOU ARE SO DEAD FOR THIS. YOU JUST STAY RIGHT THERE...
K-CLACK
WAIT... YOU DIDN'T PUT THE PARKING BRAKE ON?!!
ROLL
KA-BROOOOOSH

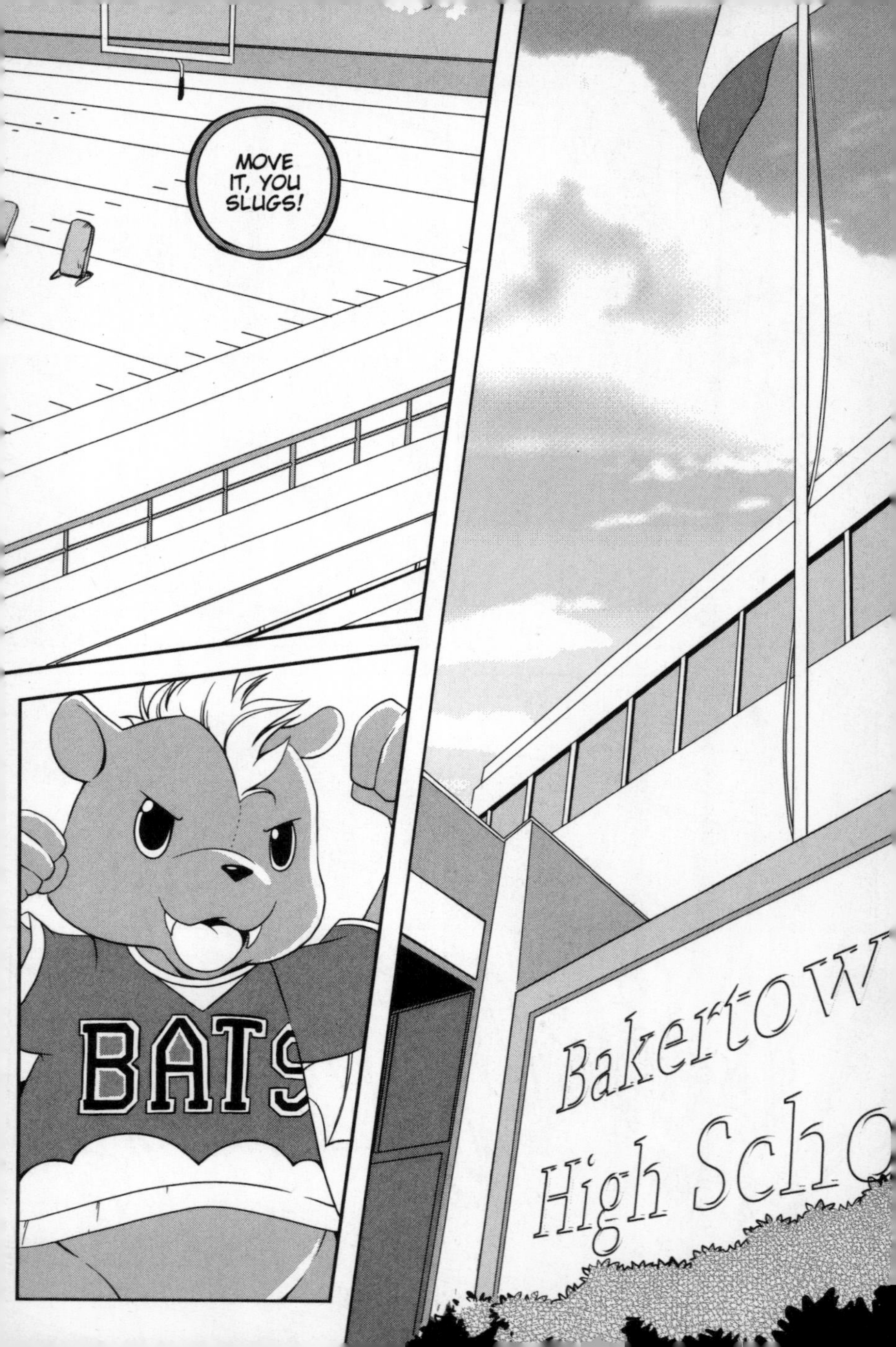
MOVE IT, YOU SLUGS!
BATS

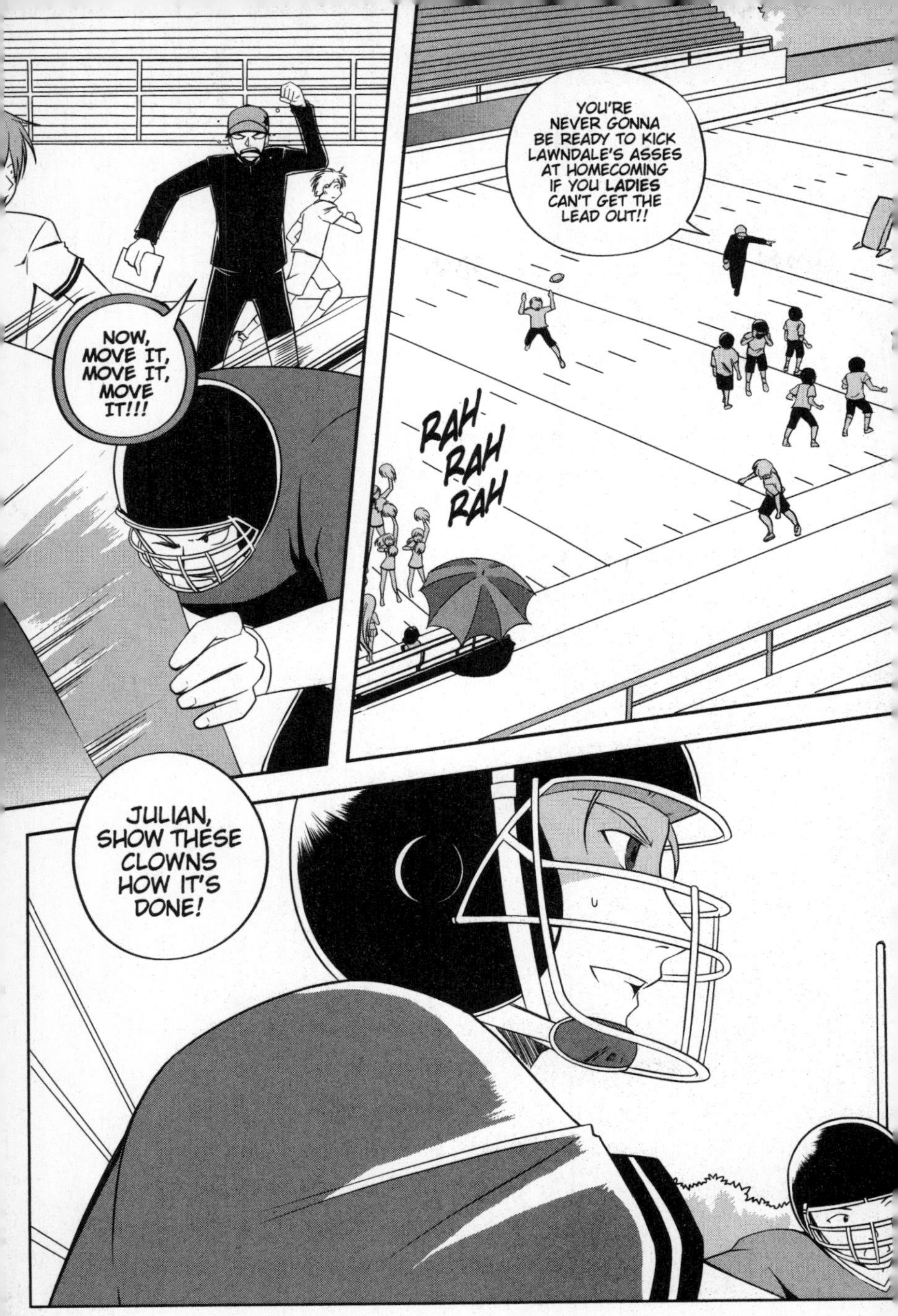
YOU'RE NEVER GONNA BE READY TO KICK LAWNDALE'S ASSES AT HOMECOMING IF YOU LADIES CAN'T GET THE LEAD OUT!!
RAH RAH RAH
NOW, MOVE IT, MOVE IT, MOVE IT!!!
JULIAN, SHOW THESE CLOWNS HOW IT'S DONE!

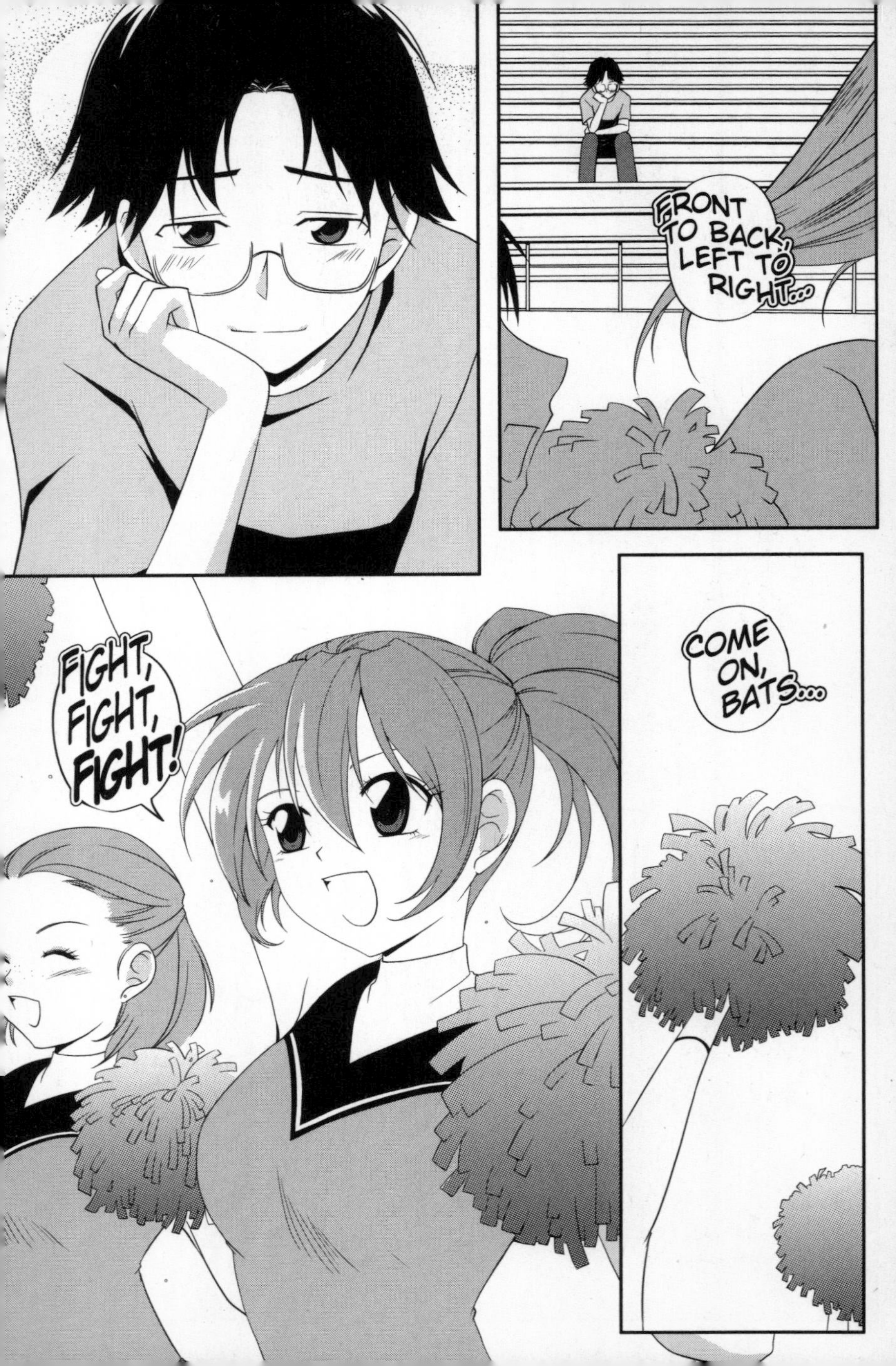
FRONT TO BACK, LEFT TO RIGHT...
COME ON, BATS...
FIGHT, FIGHT, FIGHT!

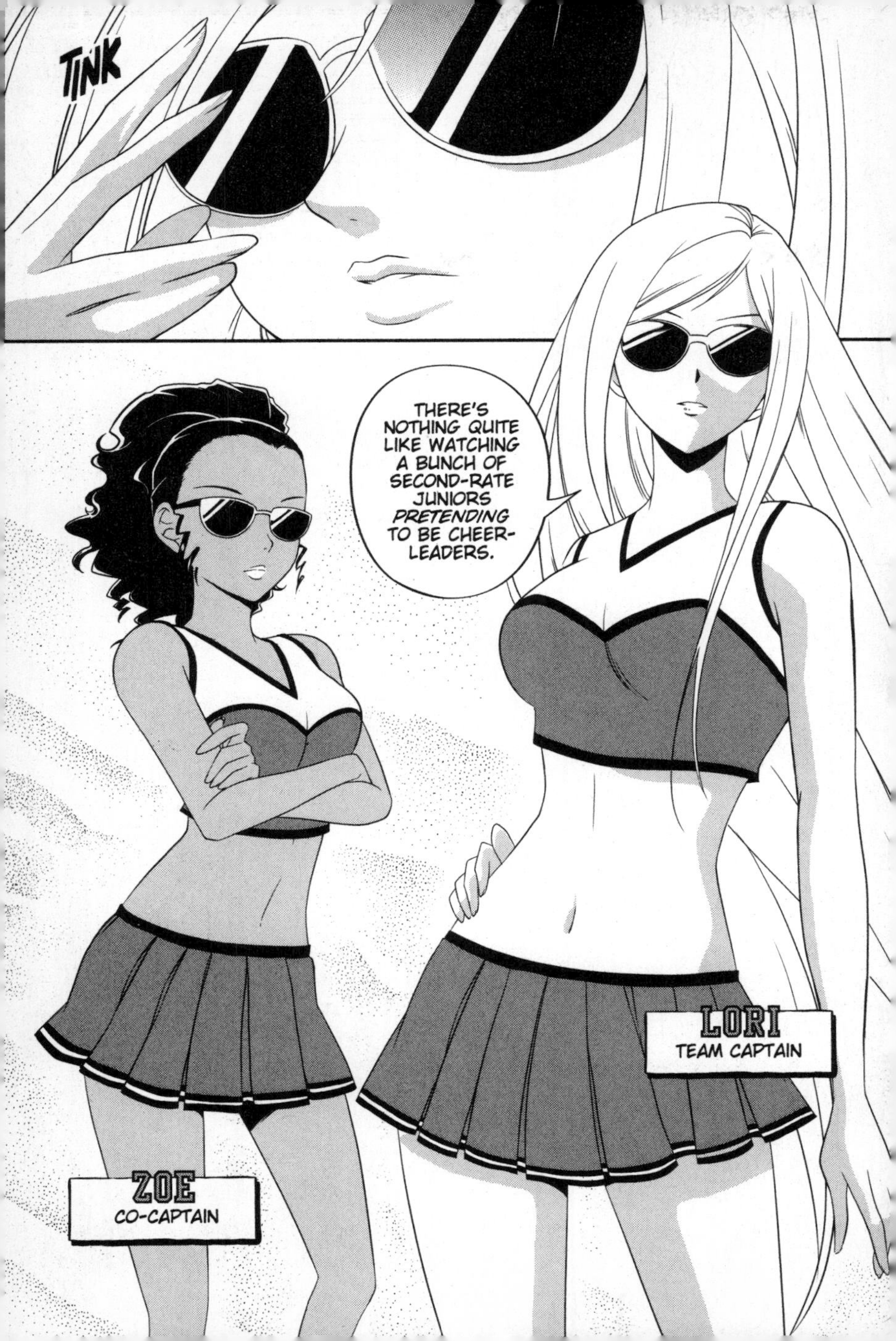
TINK
THERE'S NOTHING QUITE LIKE WATCHING A BUNCH OF SECOND-RATE JUNIORS *PRETENDING* TO BE CHEER-LEADERS.
LORI
TEAM CAPTAIN
ZOE
CO-CAPTAIN

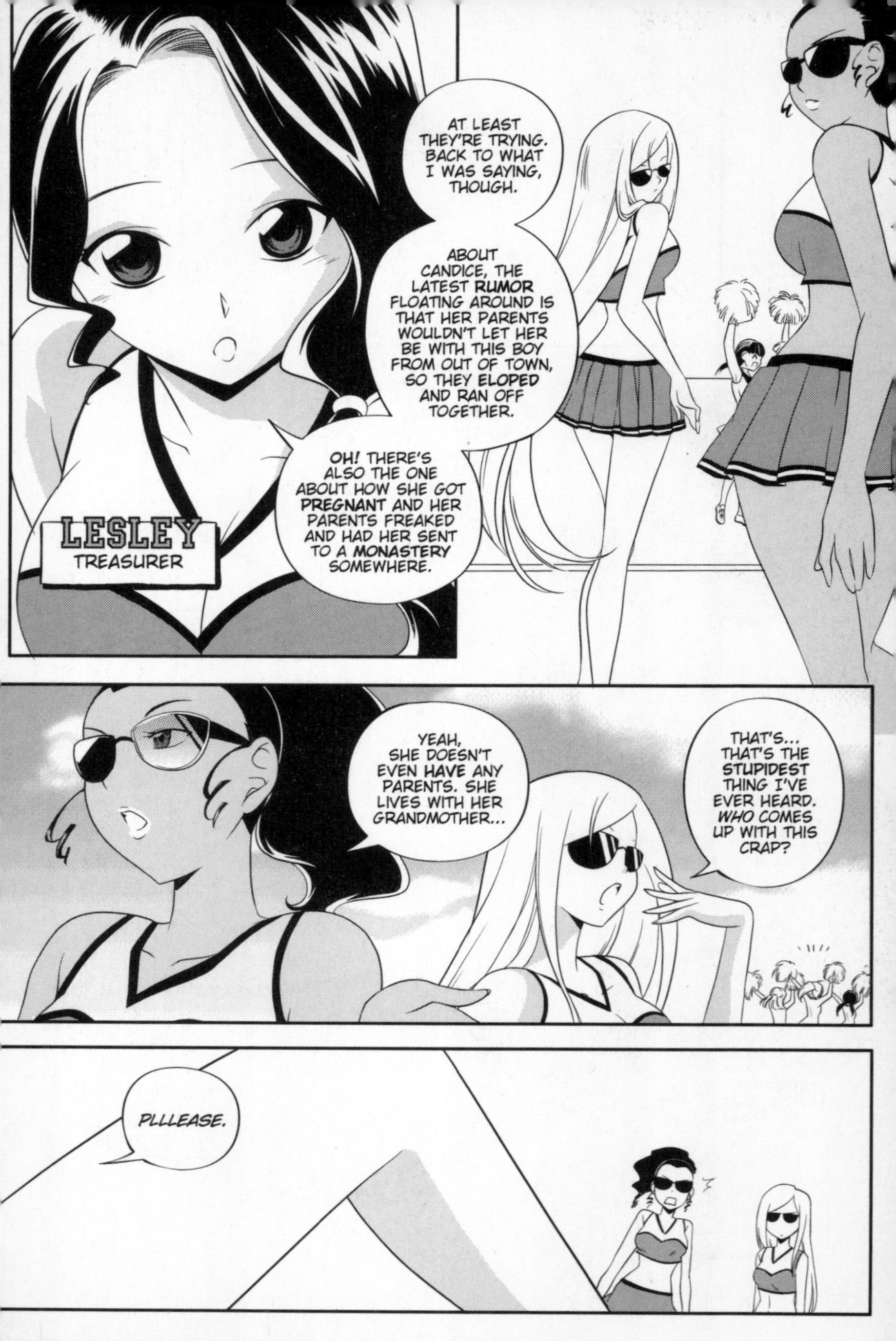
AT LEAST THEY'RE TRYING. BACK TO WHAT I WAS SAYING, THOUGH.
ABOUT CANDICE, THE LATEST RUMOR FLOATING AROUND IS THAT HER PARENTS WOULDN'T LET HER BE WITH THIS BOY FROM OUT OF TOWN, SO THEY ELOPED AND RAN OFF TOGETHER.
OH! THERE'S ALSO THE ONE ABOUT HOW SHE GOT PREGNANT AND HER PARENTS FREAKED AND HAD HER SENT TO A MONASTERY SOMEWHERE.
LESLEY
TREASURER
THAT'S... THAT'S THE STUPIDEST THING I'VE EVER HEARD. WHO COMES UP WITH THIS CRAP?
YEAH, SHE DOESN'T EVEN HAVE ANY PARENTS. SHE LIVES WITH HER GRANDMOTHER...
PLLLEASE.

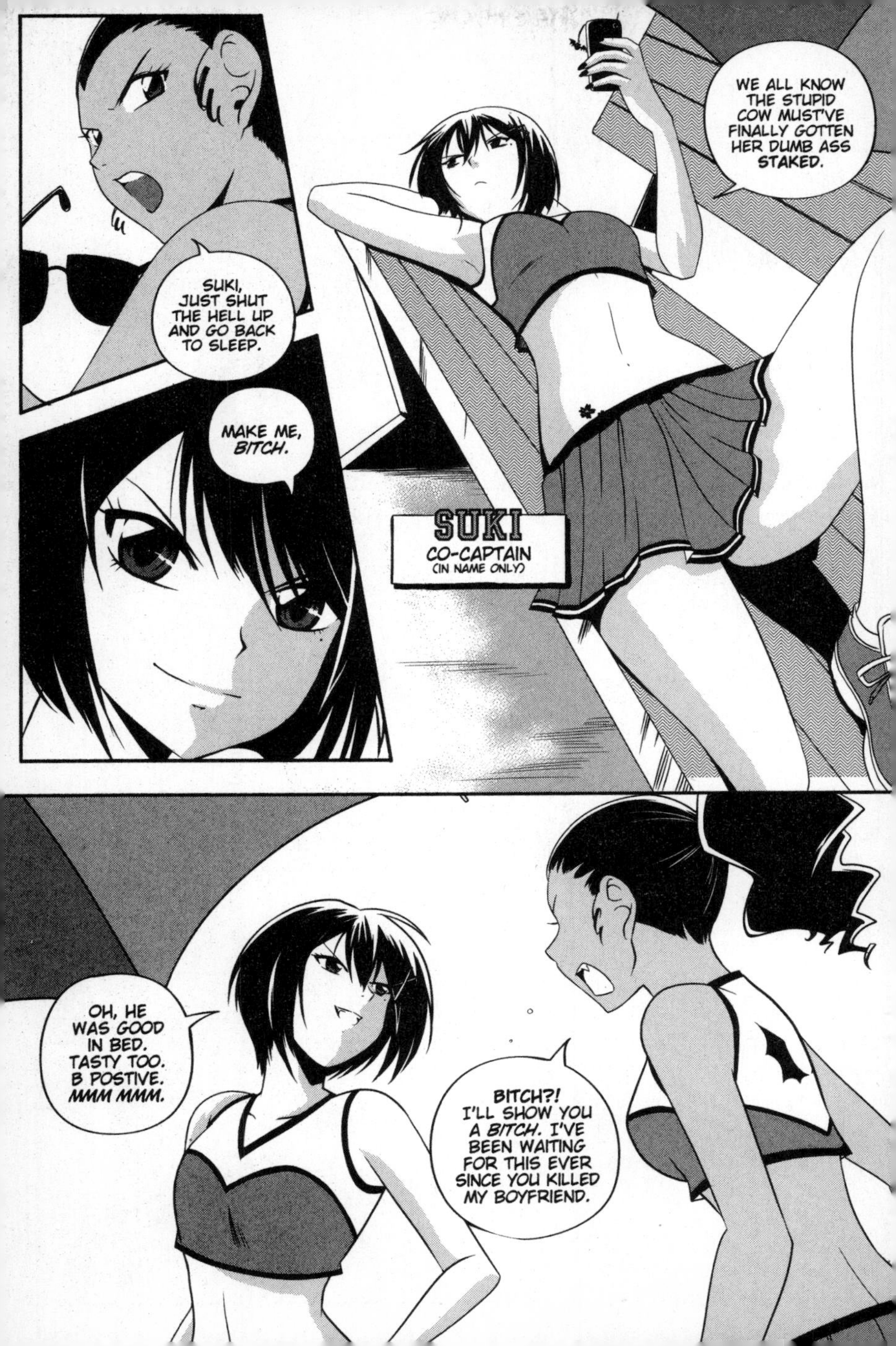
WE ALL KNOW THE STUPID COW MUST'VE FINALLY GOTTEN HER DUMB ASS STAKED.
SUKI
CO-CAPTAIN
(IN NAME ONLY)
SUKI, JUST SHUT THE HELL UP AND GO BACK TO SLEEP.
MAKE ME, *BITCH*.
BITCH?! I'LL SHOW YOU A *BITCH*. I'VE BEEN WAITING FOR THIS EVER SINCE YOU KILLED MY BOYFRIEND.
OH, HE WAS GOOD IN BED. TASTY TOO. B POSTIVE. ***MMM MMM.***

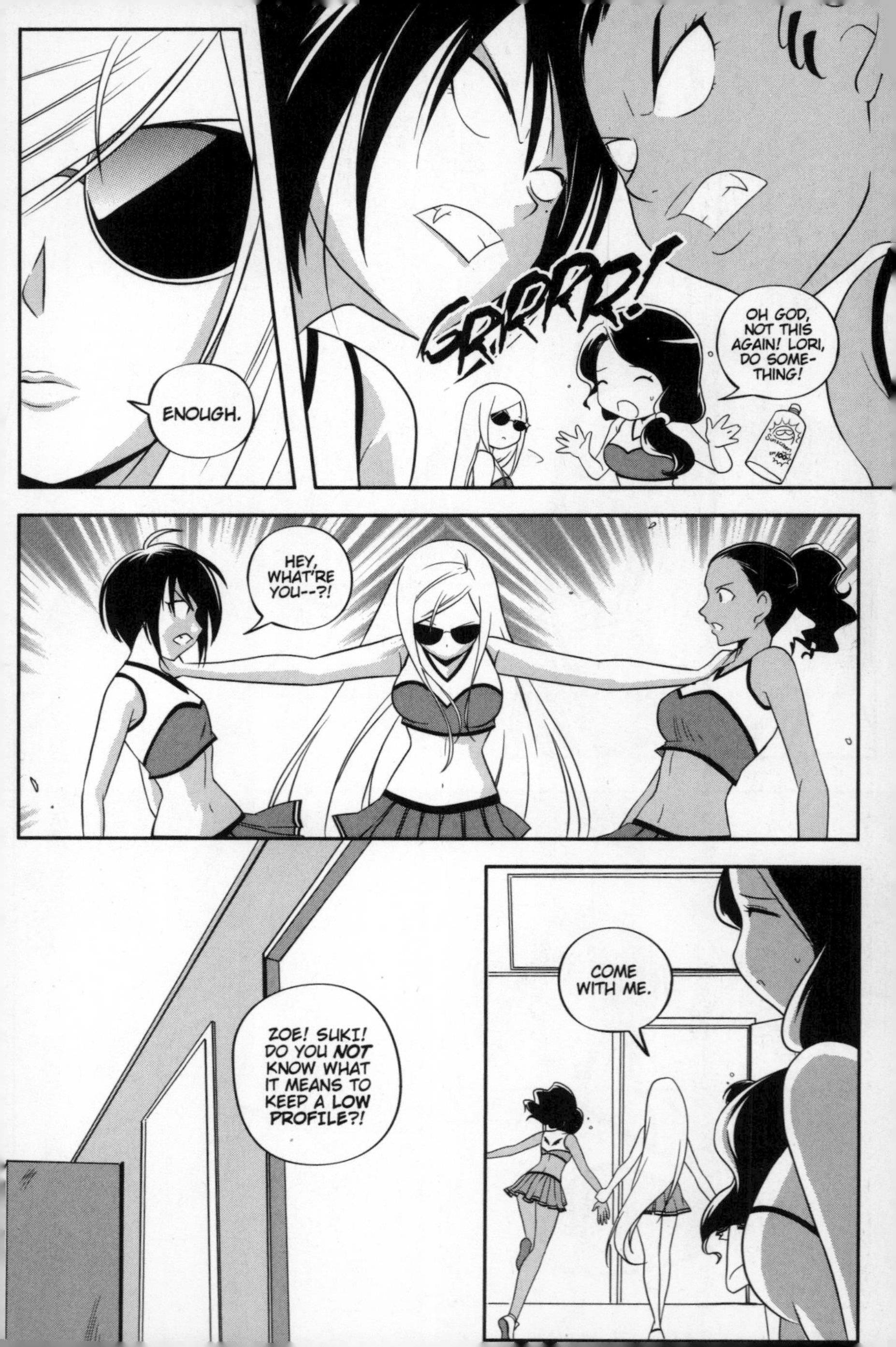
OH GOD, NOT THIS AGAIN! LORI, DO SOME-THING!
GRRRR!
ENOUGH.
HEY, WHAT'RE YOU--?!
COME WITH ME.
ZOE! SUKI! DO YOU **NOT** KNOW WHAT IT MEANS TO KEEP A LOW PROFILE?!

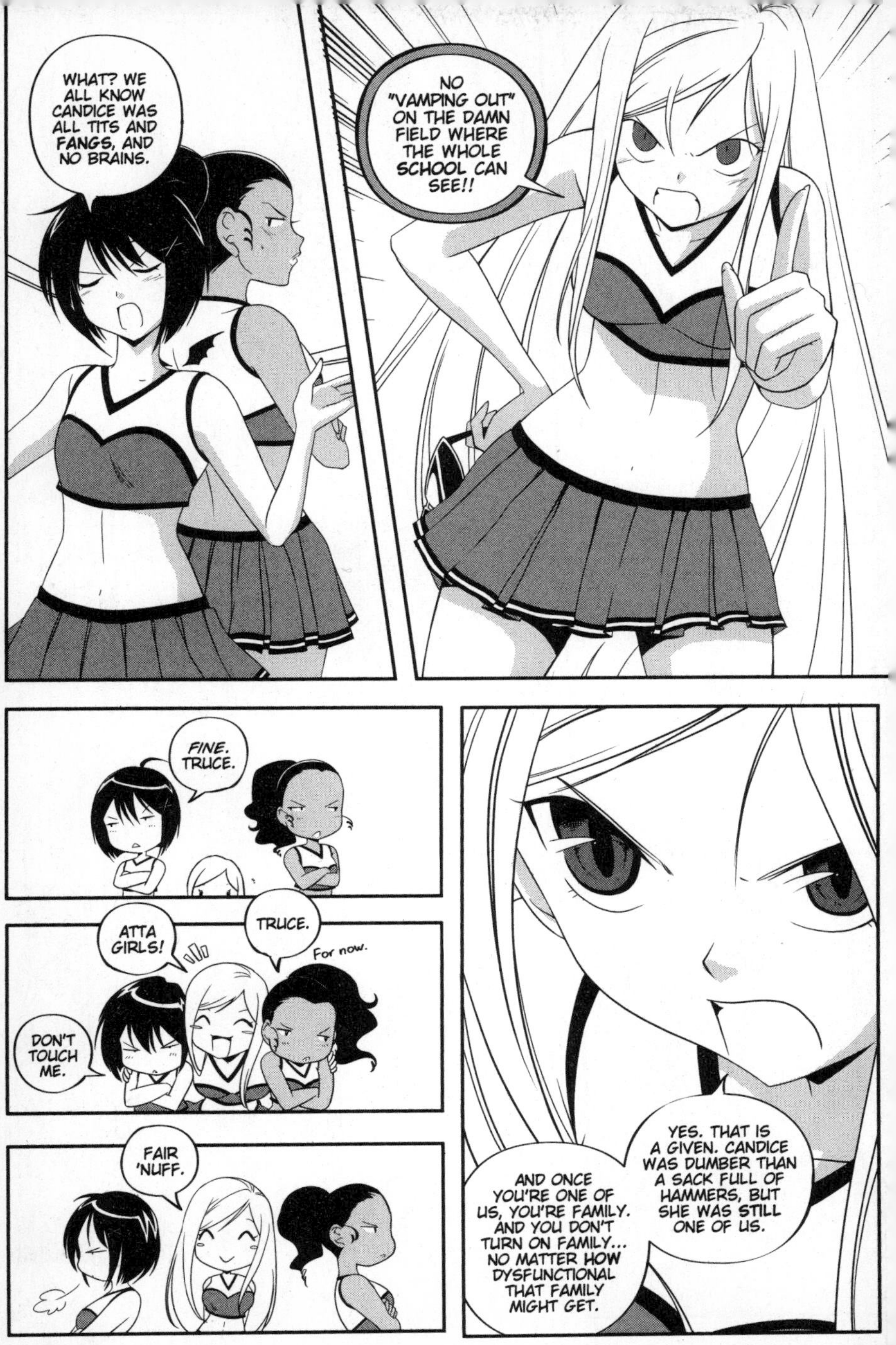
NO "VAMPING OUT" ON THE DAMN FIELD WHERE THE WHOLE SCHOOL CAN SEE!!
WHAT? WE ALL KNOW CANDICE WAS ALL TITS AND FANGS, AND NO BRAINS.
YES. THAT IS A GIVEN. CANDICE WAS DUMBER THAN A SACK FULL OF HAMMERS, BUT SHE WAS STILL ONE OF US.
AND ONCE YOU'RE ONE OF US, YOU'RE FAMILY. AND YOU DON'T TURN ON FAMILY... NO MATTER HOW DYSFUNCTIONAL THAT FAMILY MIGHT GET.
FINE. TRUCE.
TRUCE.
For now.
ATTA GIRLS!
DON'T TOUCH ME.
FAIR 'NUFF.

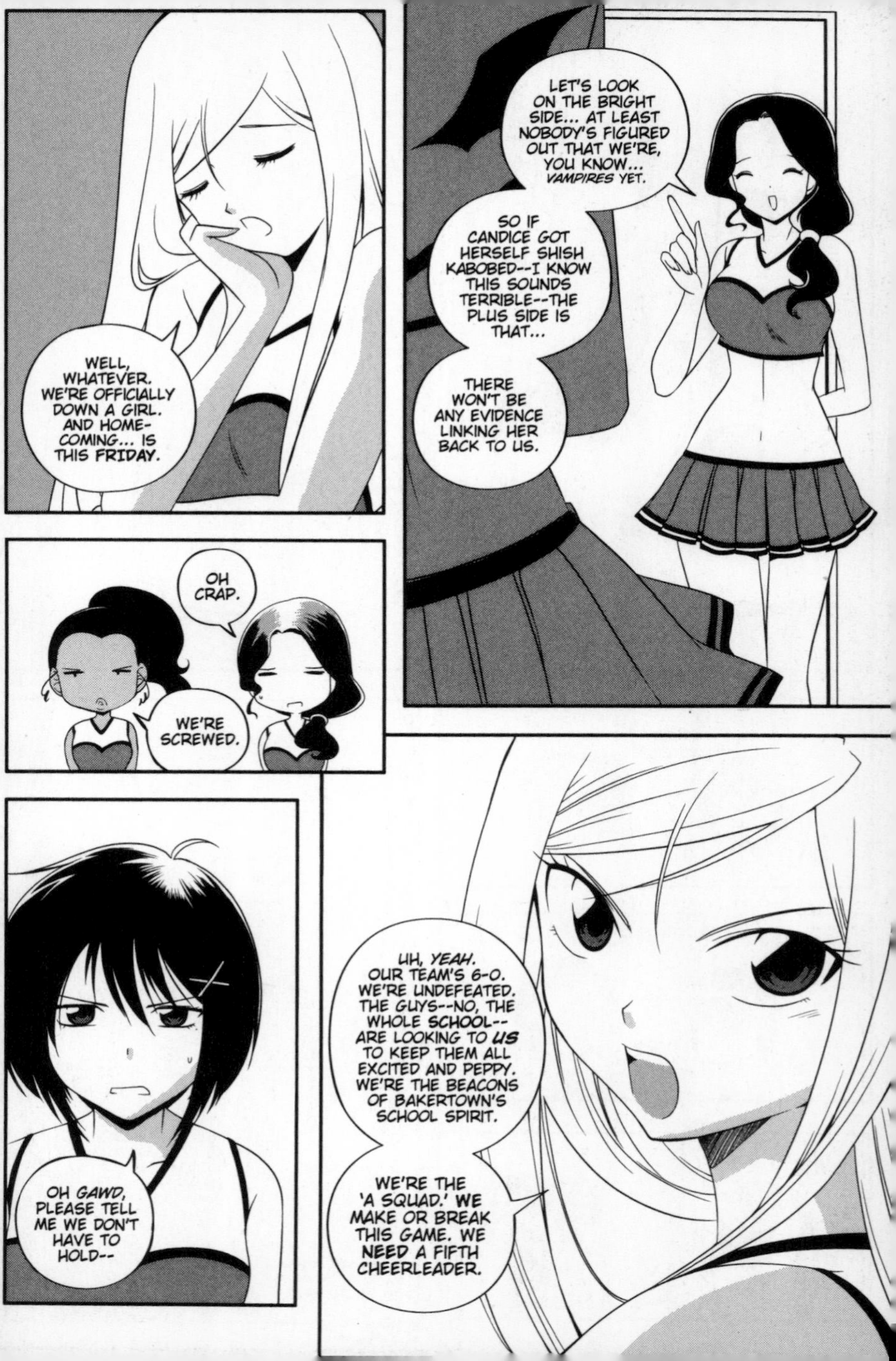

LET'S LOOK ON THE BRIGHT SIDE... AT LEAST NOBODY'S FIGURED OUT THAT WE'RE, YOU KNOW... *VAMPIRES* YET.
SO IF CANDICE GOT HERSELF SHISH KABOBED--I KNOW THIS SOUNDS TERRIBLE--THE PLUS SIDE IS THAT...
THERE WON'T BE ANY EVIDENCE LINKING HER BACK TO US.
WELL, WHATEVER. WE'RE OFFICIALLY DOWN A GIRL. AND HOME-COMING... IS THIS **FRIDAY**.
OH CRAP.
WE'RE SCREWED.
UH, *YEAH*. OUR TEAM'S 6-0. WE'RE UNDEFEATED. THE GUYS--NO, THE WHOLE **SCHOOL**--ARE LOOKING TO ***US*** TO KEEP THEM ALL EXCITED AND PEPPY. WE'RE THE BEACONS OF BAKERTOWN'S SCHOOL SPIRIT.
WE'RE THE 'A SQUAD.' **WE** MAKE OR BREAK THIS GAME. WE **NEED** A FIFTH CHEERLEADER.
OH *GAWD*, PLEASE TELL ME WE DON'T HAVE TO HOLD--

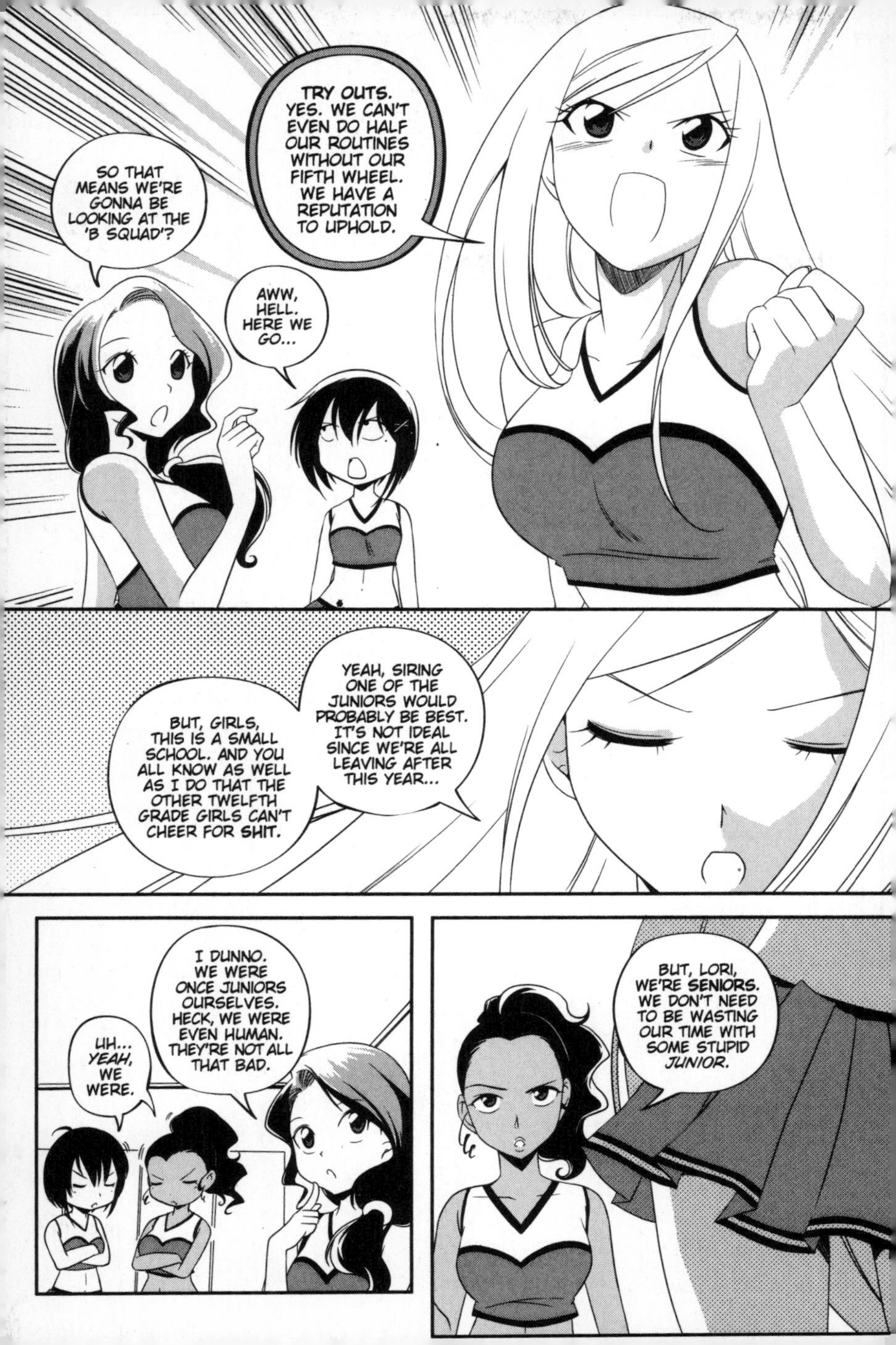
TRY OUTS. YES. WE CAN'T EVEN DO HALF OUR ROUTINES WITHOUT OUR FIFTH WHEEL. WE HAVE A REPUTATION TO UPHOLD.
SO THAT MEANS WE'RE GONNA BE LOOKING AT THE 'B SQUAD'?
AWW, HELL. HERE WE GO...
YEAH, SIRING ONE OF THE JUNIORS WOULD PROBABLY BE BEST. IT'S NOT IDEAL SINCE WE'RE ALL LEAVING AFTER THIS YEAR...
BUT, GIRLS, THIS IS A SMALL SCHOOL. AND YOU ALL KNOW AS WELL AS I DO THAT THE OTHER TWELFTH GRADE GIRLS CAN'T CHEER FOR **SHIT**.
BUT, LORI, WE'RE **SENIORS**. WE DON'T NEED TO BE WASTING OUR TIME WITH SOME STUPID *JUNIOR*.
I DUNNO. WE WERE ONCE JUNIORS OURSELVES. HECK, WE WERE EVEN HUMAN. THEY'RE NOT ALL THAT BAD.
UH... *YEAH,* WE WERE.

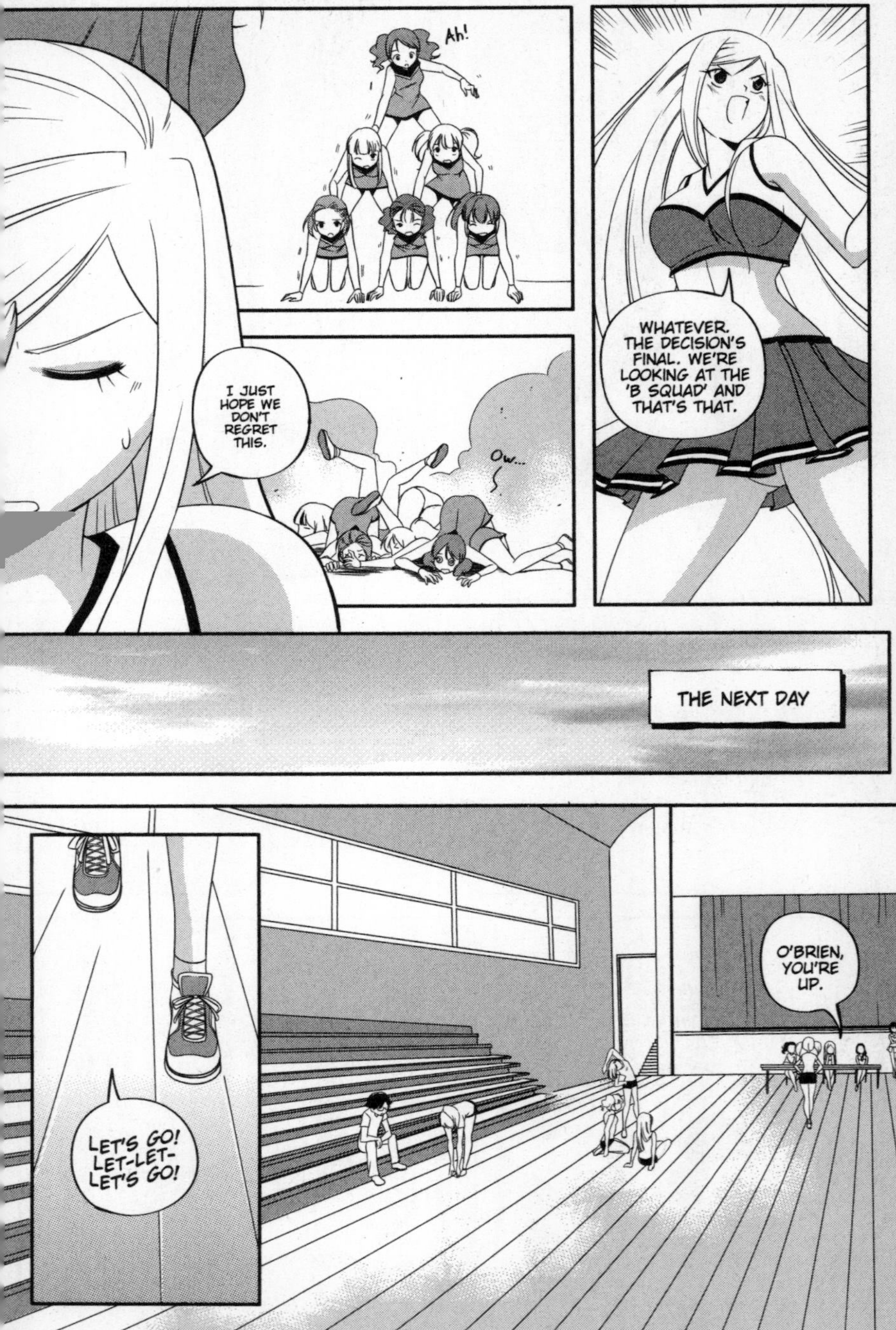
WHATEVER. THE DECISION'S FINAL. WE'RE LOOKING AT THE 'B SQUAD' AND THAT'S THAT.
Ah!
Ow...
I JUST HOPE WE DON'T REGRET THIS.
THE NEXT DAY
O'BRIEN, YOU'RE UP.
LET'S GO! LET-LET-LET'S GO!

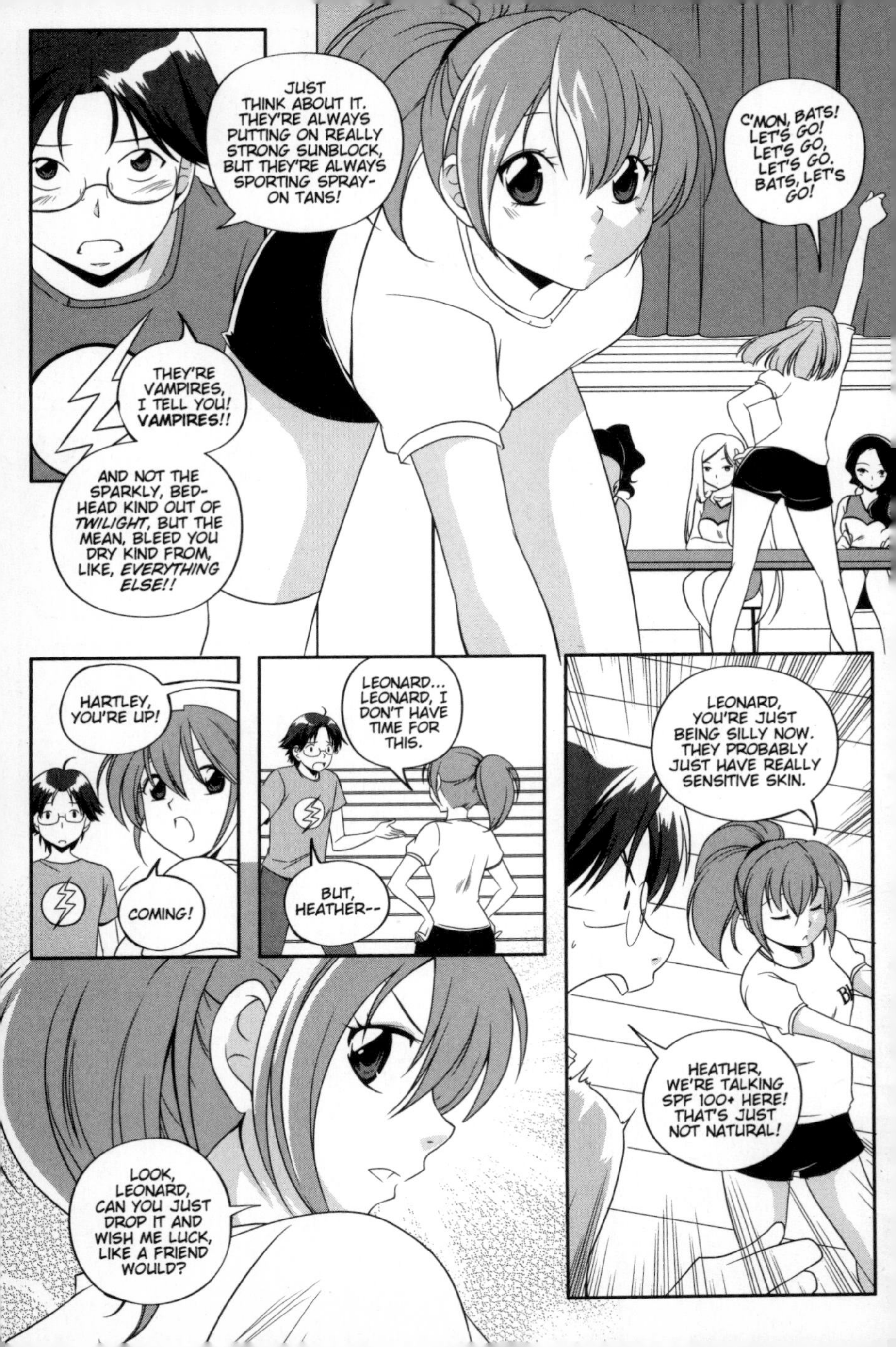
C'MON, BATS! LET'S GO! LET'S GO, LET'S GO. BATS, LET'S GO!
JUST THINK ABOUT IT. THEY'RE ALWAYS PUTTING ON REALLY STRONG SUNBLOCK, BUT THEY'RE ALWAYS SPORTING SPRAY-ON TANS!
THEY'RE VAMPIRES, I TELL YOU! **VAMPIRES!!**
AND NOT THE SPARKLY, BED-HEAD KIND OUT OF *TWILIGHT*, BUT THE MEAN, BLEED YOU DRY KIND FROM, LIKE, *EVERYTHING ELSE!!*
LEONARD, YOU'RE JUST BEING SILLY NOW. THEY PROBABLY JUST HAVE REALLY SENSITIVE SKIN.
HEATHER, WE'RE TALKING SPF 100+ HERE! THAT'S JUST NOT NATURAL!
LEONARD... LEONARD, I DON'T HAVE TIME FOR THIS.
BUT, HEATHER--
HARTLEY, YOU'RE UP!
COMING!
LOOK, LEONARD, CAN YOU JUST DROP IT AND WISH ME LUCK, LIKE A FRIEND WOULD?

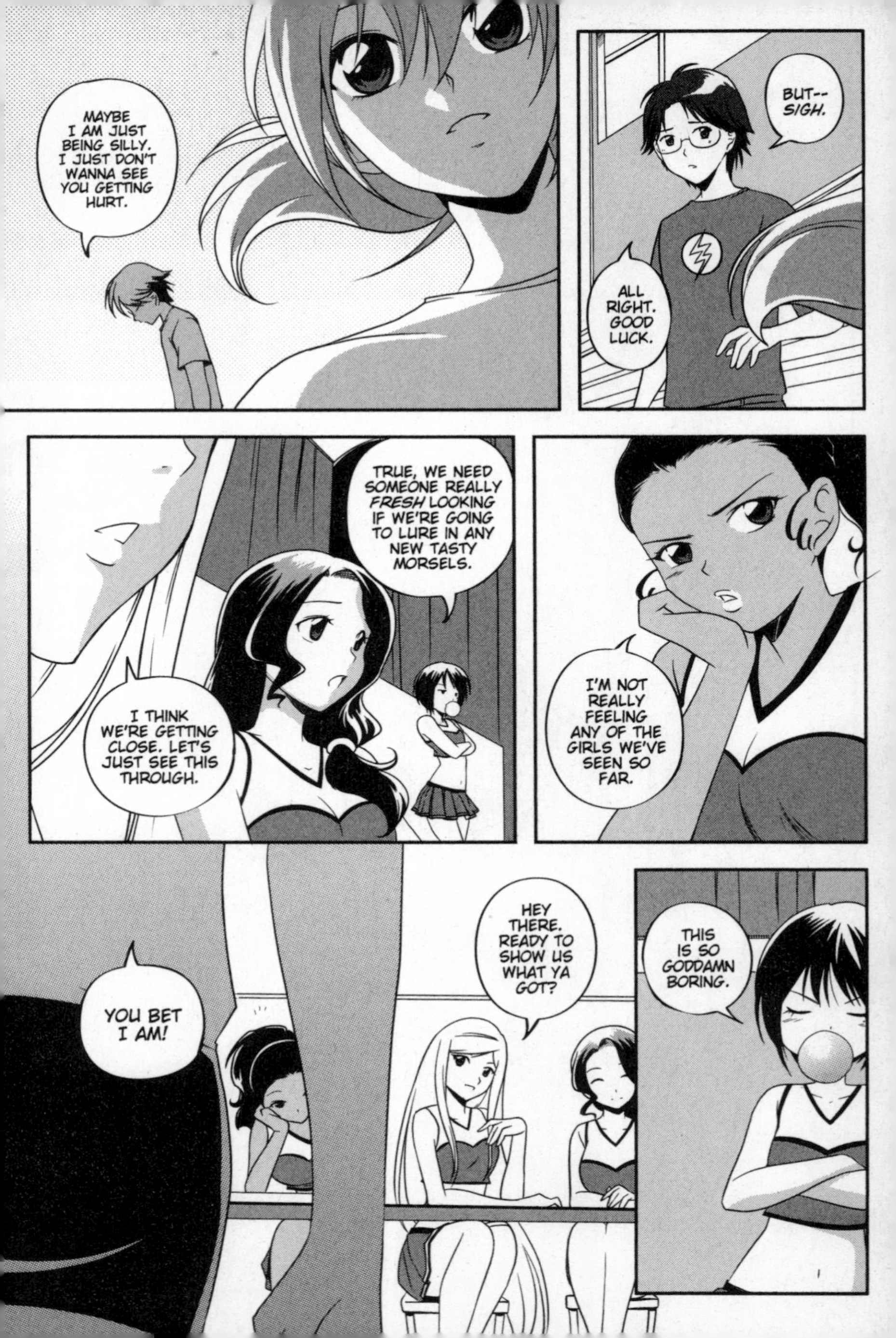
BUT-- SIGH.
ALL RIGHT. GOOD LUCK.
MAYBE I AM JUST BEING SILLY. I JUST DON'T WANNA SEE YOU GETTING HURT.
I'M NOT REALLY FEELING ANY OF THE GIRLS WE'VE SEEN SO FAR.
TRUE, WE NEED SOMEONE REALLY *FRESH* LOOKING IF WE'RE GOING TO LURE IN ANY NEW TASTY MORSELS.
I THINK WE'RE GETTING CLOSE. LET'S JUST SEE THIS THROUGH.
THIS IS SO GODDAMN BORING.
HEY THERE. READY TO SHOW US WHAT YA GOT?
YOU BET I AM!

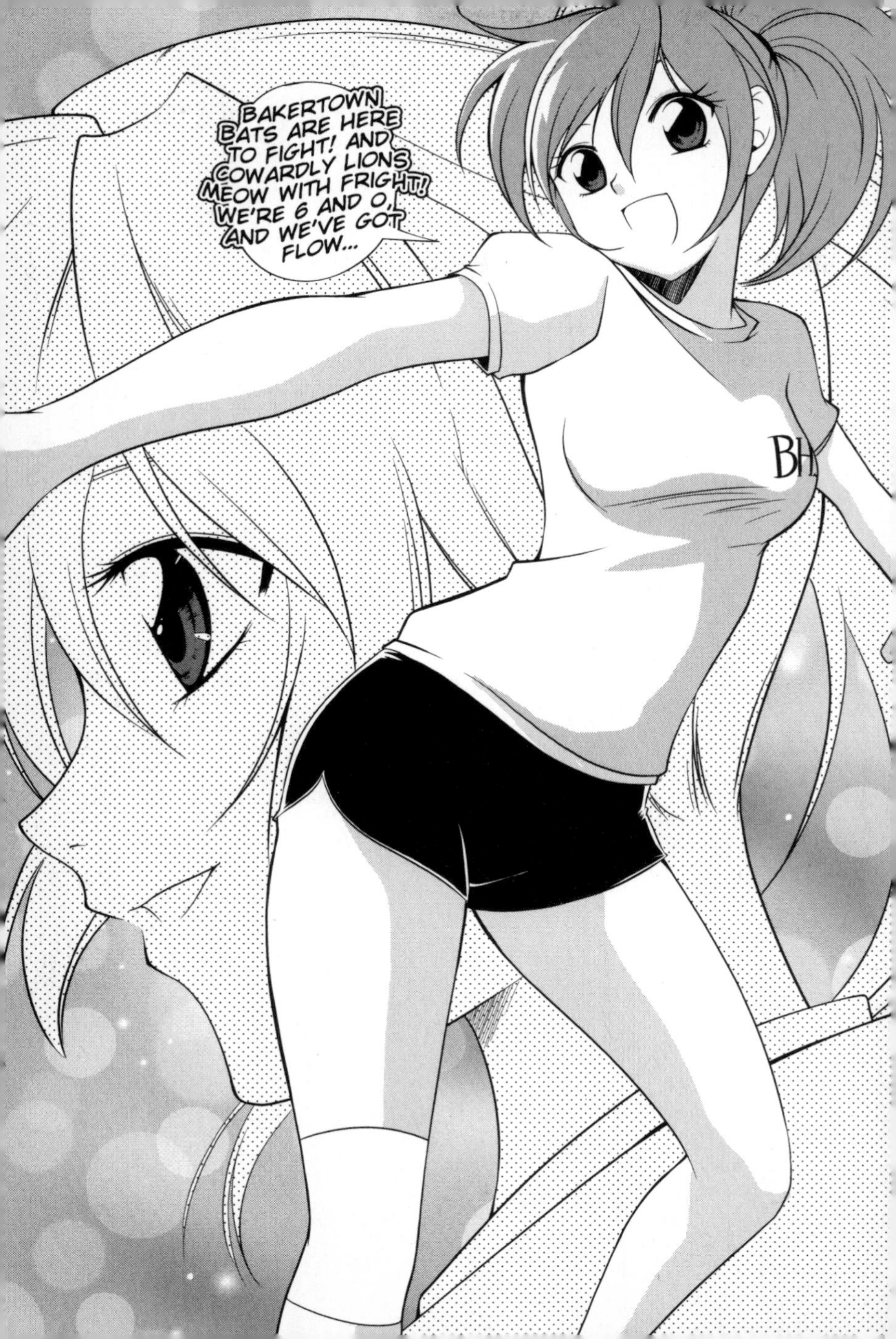
BAKERTOWN BATS ARE HERE TO FIGHT! AND COWARDLY LIONS MEOW WITH FRIGHT! WE'RE 6 AND 0, AND WE'VE GOT FLOW...
BH

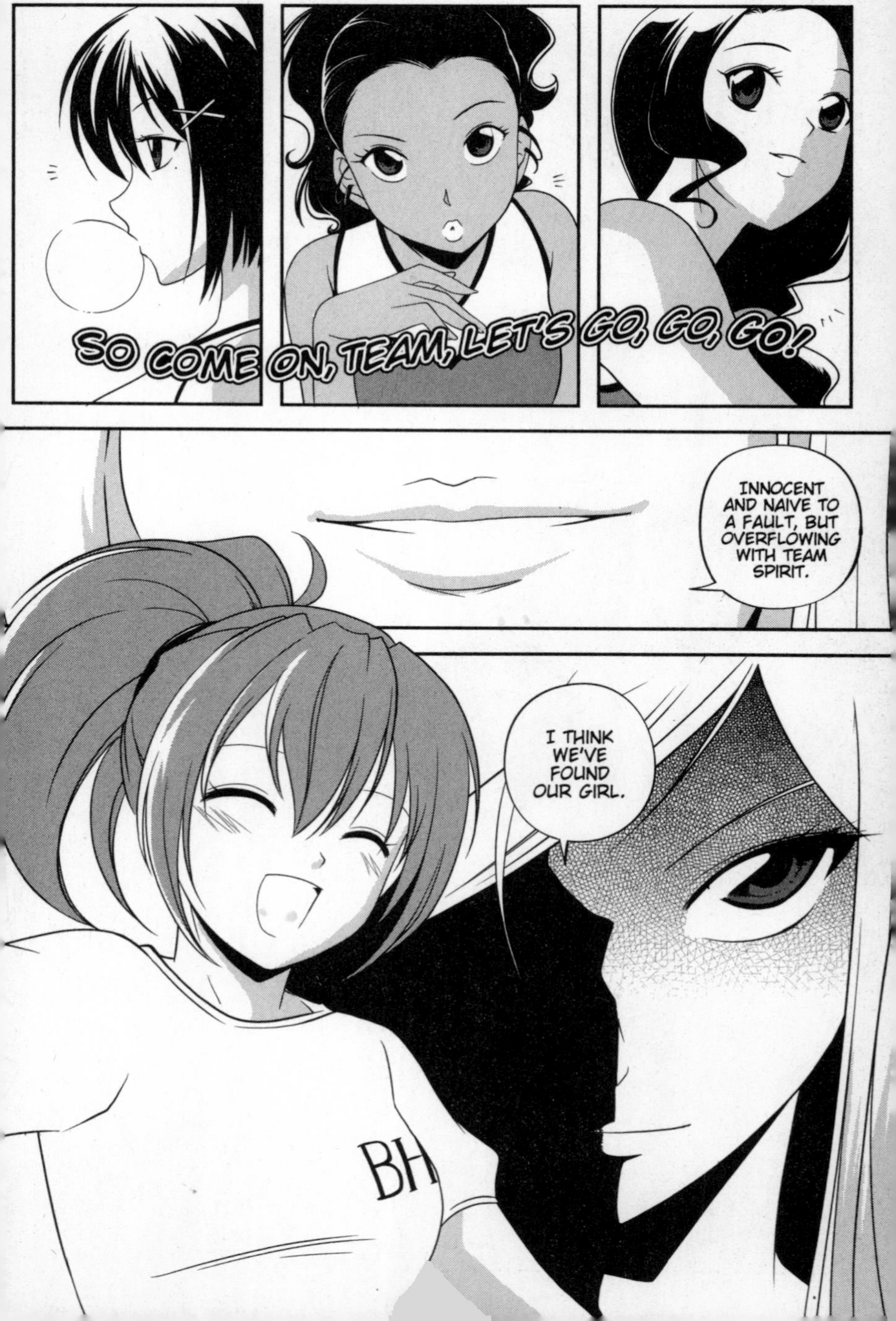
SO COME ON, TEAM, LET'S GO, GO, GO!
INNOCENT AND NAIVE TO A FAULT, BUT OVERFLOWING WITH TEAM SPIRIT.
I THINK WE'VE FOUND OUR GIRL.
BH

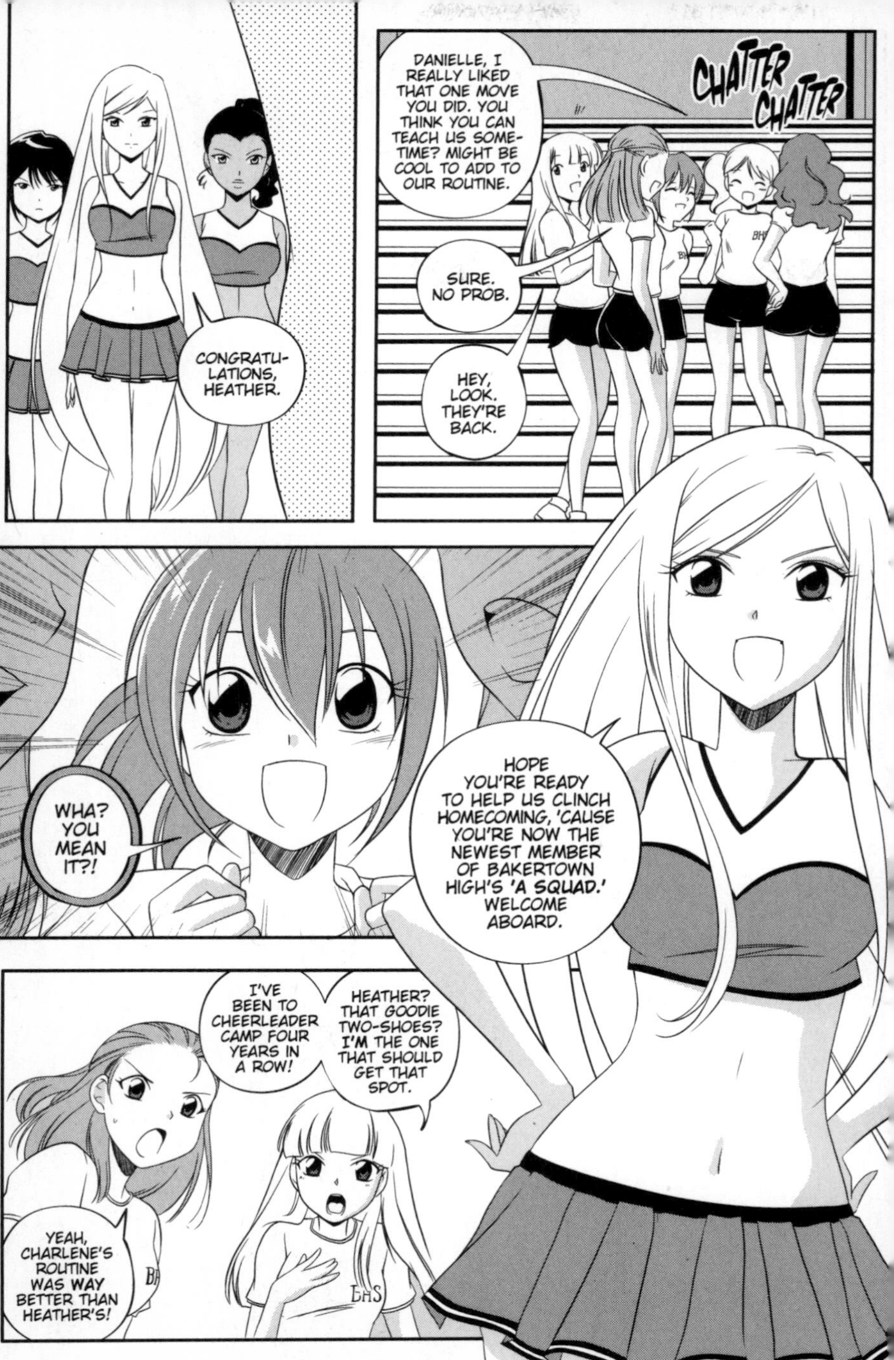
CHATTER CHATTER
DANIELLE, I REALLY LIKED THAT ONE MOVE YOU DID. YOU THINK YOU CAN TEACH US SOME-TIME? MIGHT BE COOL TO ADD TO OUR ROUTINE.
SURE. NO PROB.
HEY, LOOK. THEY'RE BACK.
CONGRATU-LATIONS, HEATHER.
HOPE YOU'RE READY TO HELP US CLINCH HOMECOMING, 'CAUSE YOU'RE NOW THE NEWEST MEMBER OF BAKERTOWN HIGH'S **'A SQUAD.'** WELCOME ABOARD.
WHA? YOU MEAN IT?!
HEATHER? THAT GOODIE TWO-SHOES? *I'M* THE ONE THAT SHOULD GET THAT SPOT.
I'VE BEEN TO CHEERLEADER CAMP FOUR YEARS IN A ROW!
YEAH, CHARLENE'S ROUTINE WAS WAY BETTER THAN HEATHER'S!

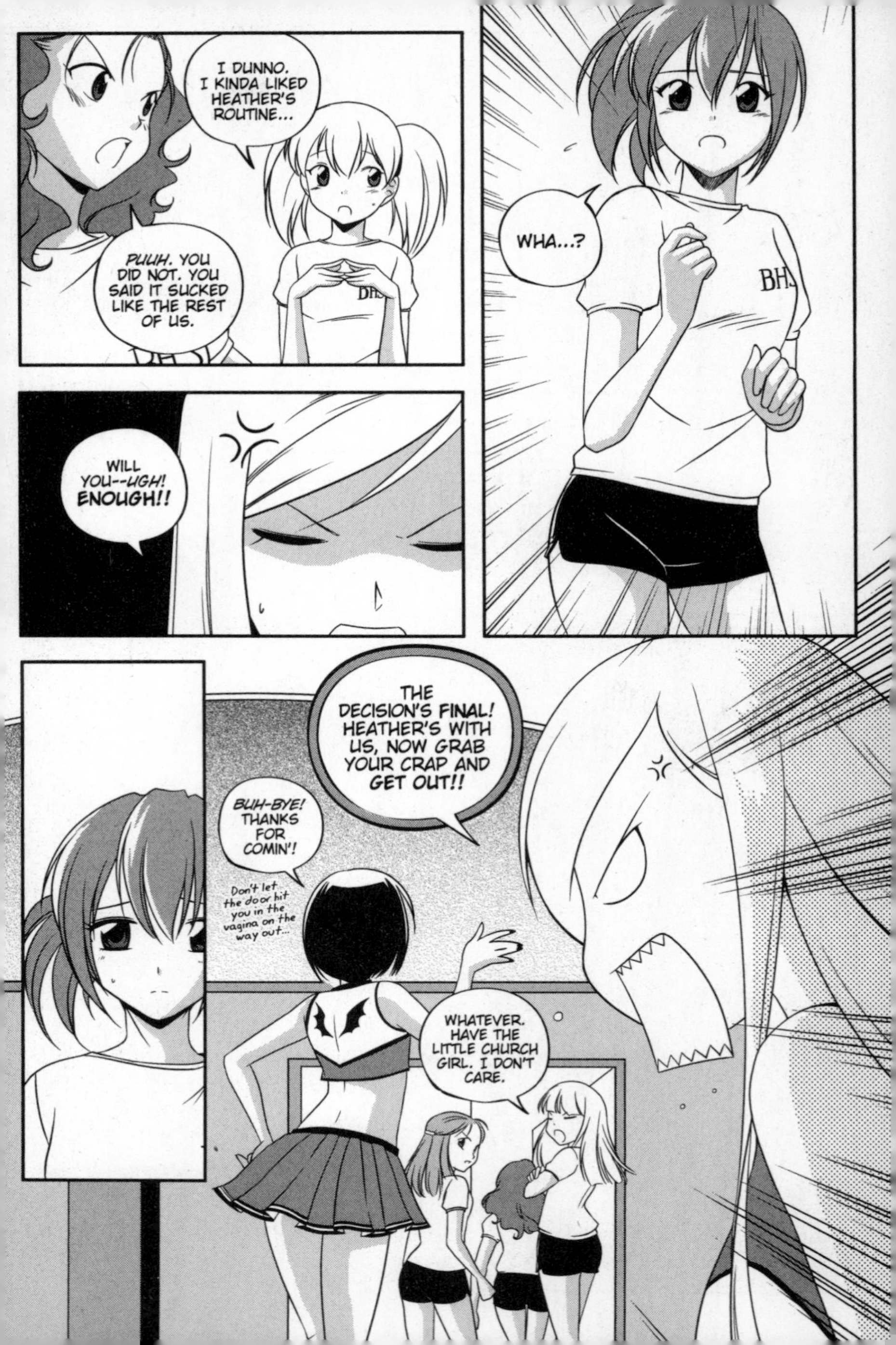
WHA...?
I DUNNO. I KINDA LIKED HEATHER'S ROUTINE...
PUUH. YOU DID NOT. YOU SAID IT SUCKED LIKE THE REST OF US.
WILL YOU--*UGH*! **ENOUGH!!**
THE DECISION'S **FINAL**! HEATHER'S WITH US, NOW GRAB YOUR CRAP AND **GET OUT!!**
BUH-BYE! THANKS FOR COMIN'!
Don't let the door hit you in the vagina on the way out...
WHATEVER. HAVE THE LITTLE CHURCH GIRL. I DON'T CARE.

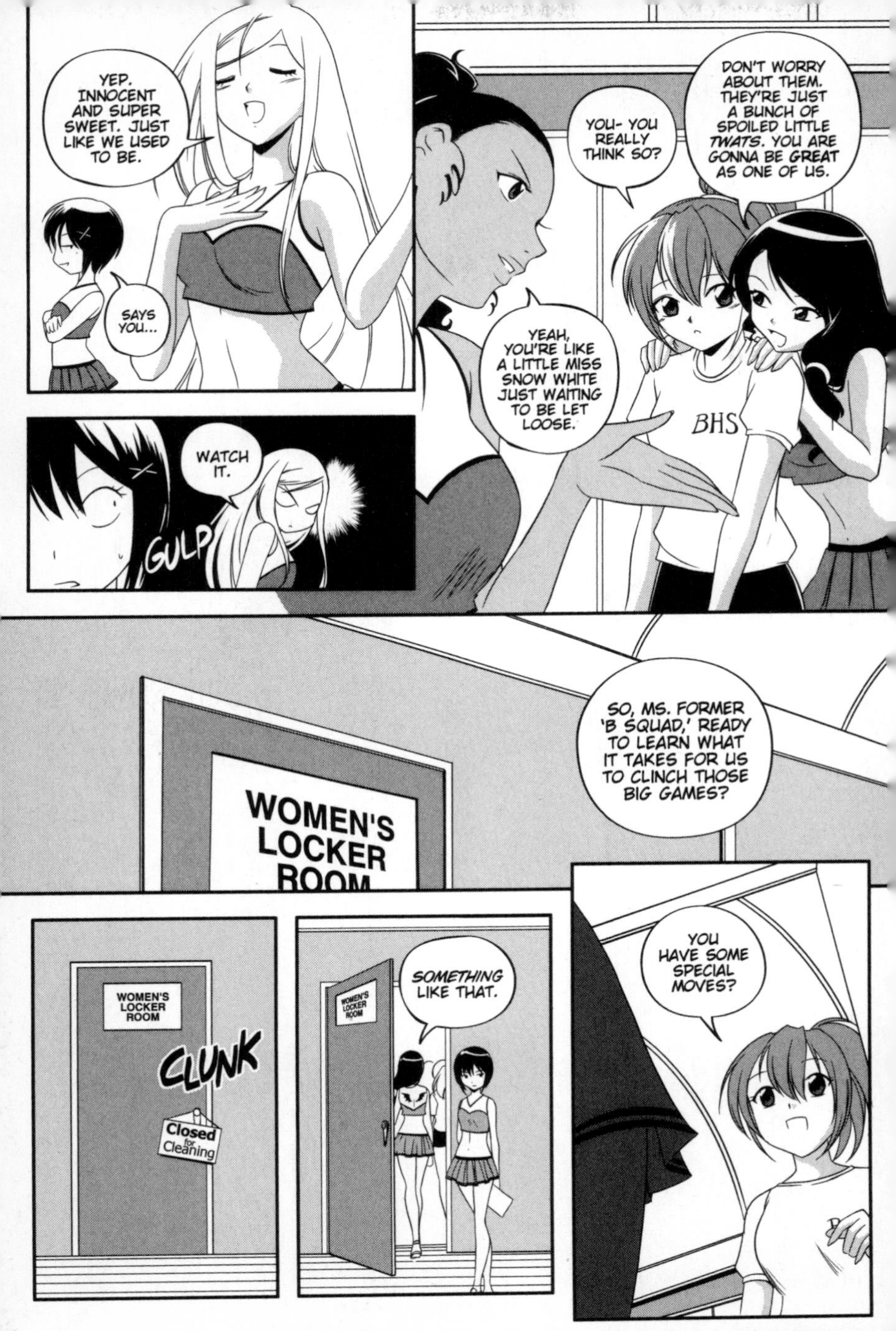
DON'T WORRY ABOUT THEM. THEY'RE JUST A BUNCH OF SPOILED LITTLE *TWATS*. YOU ARE GONNA BE **GREAT** AS ONE OF US.
YOU- YOU REALLY THINK SO?
YEAH, YOU'RE LIKE A LITTLE MISS SNOW WHITE JUST WAITING TO BE LET LOOSE.
BHS
YEP. INNOCENT AND SUPER SWEET. JUST LIKE WE USED TO BE.
SAYS YOU...
WATCH IT.
GULP
SO, MS. FORMER 'B SQUAD,' READY TO LEARN WHAT IT TAKES FOR US TO CLINCH THOSE BIG GAMES?
WOMEN'S LOCKER ROOM
YOU HAVE SOME SPECIAL MOVES?
WOMEN'S LOCKER ROOM
SOMETHING LIKE THAT.
WOMEN'S LOCKER ROOM
CLUNK
Closed for Cleaning

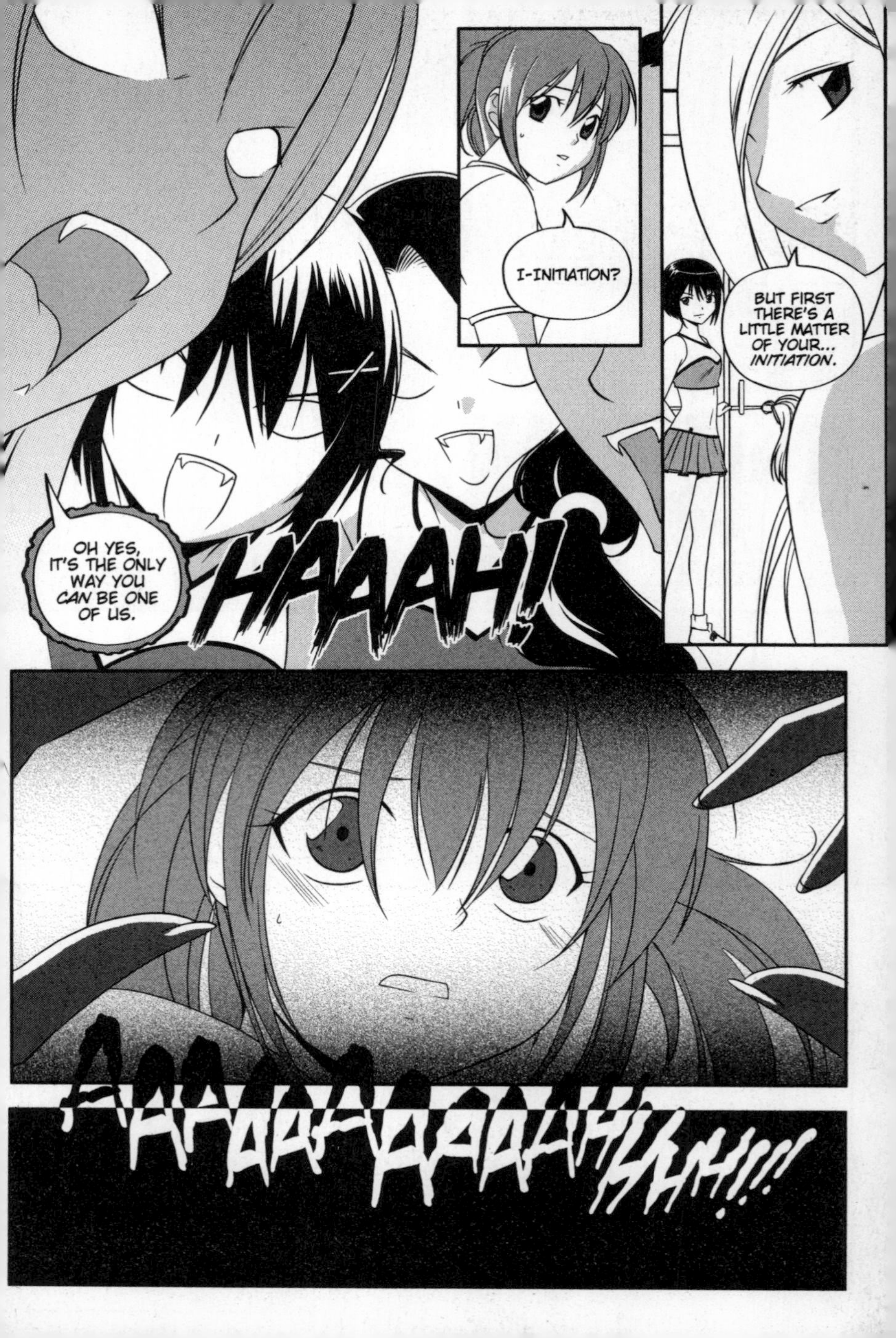
BUT FIRST THERE'S A LITTLE MATTER OF YOUR... *INITIATION*.
I-INITIATION?
OH YES, IT'S THE ONLY WAY YOU CAN BE ONE OF US.
HAAAH!
AAAAA-AAAAAHHHH!!!

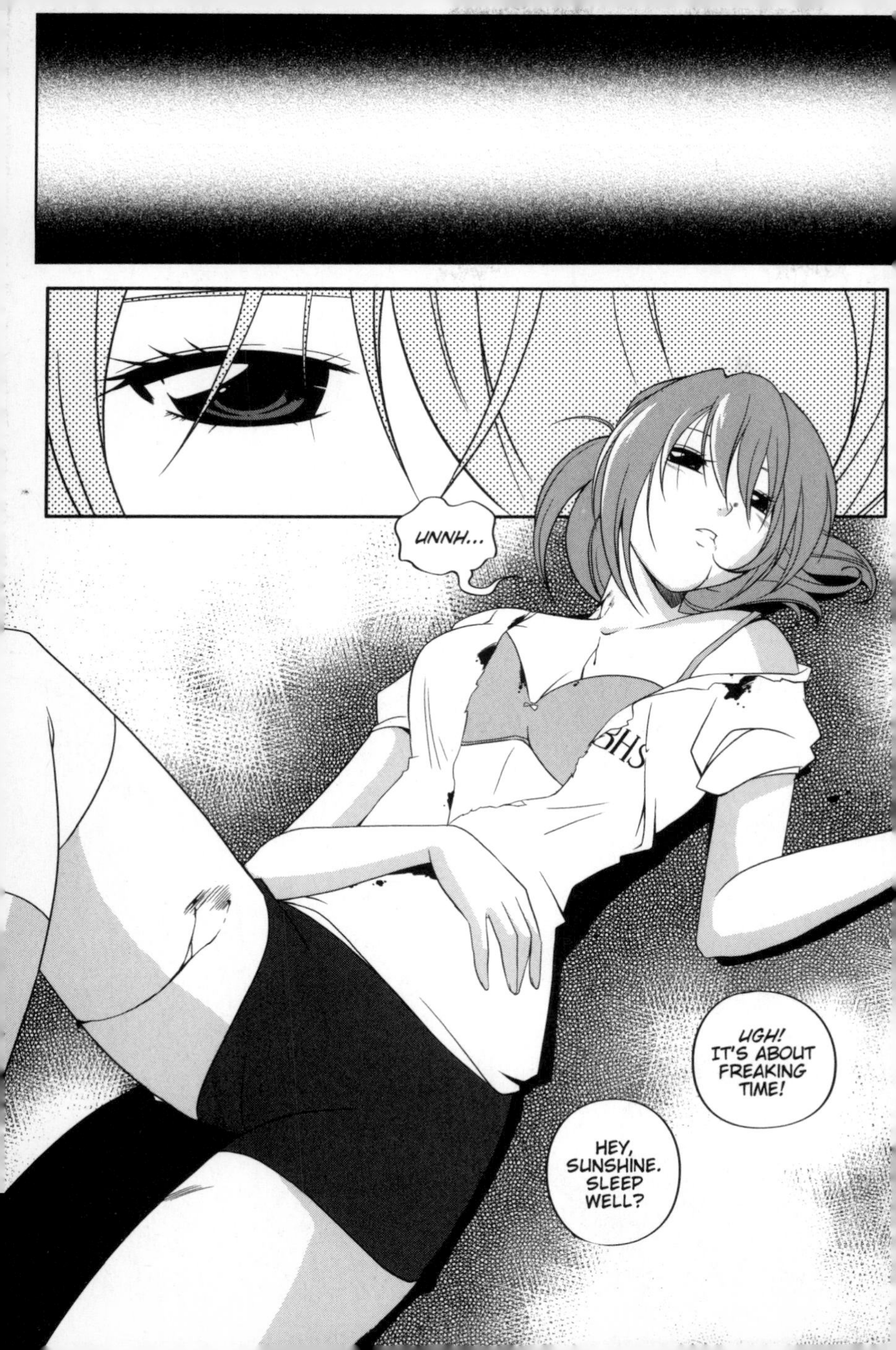
UNNH...
UGH! IT'S ABOUT FREAKING TIME!
HEY, SUNSHINE. SLEEP WELL?

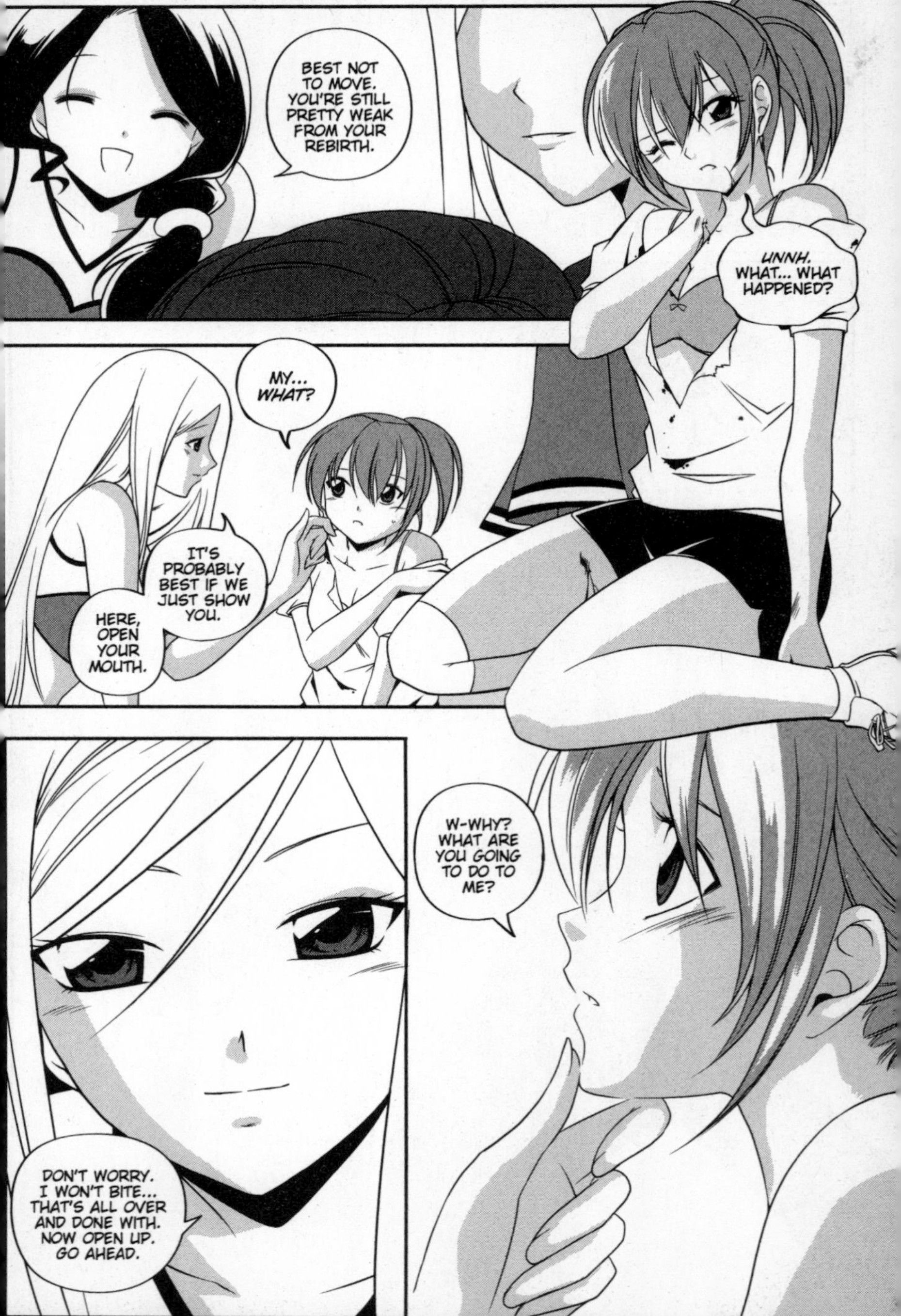
UNNH. WHAT... WHAT HAPPENED?
BEST NOT TO MOVE. YOU'RE STILL PRETTY WEAK FROM YOUR REBIRTH.
MY... WHAT?
IT'S PROBABLY BEST IF WE JUST SHOW YOU.
HERE, OPEN YOUR MOUTH.
W-WHY? WHAT ARE YOU GOING TO DO TO ME?
DON'T WORRY. I WON'T BITE... THAT'S ALL OVER AND DONE WITH. NOW OPEN UP. GO AHEAD.

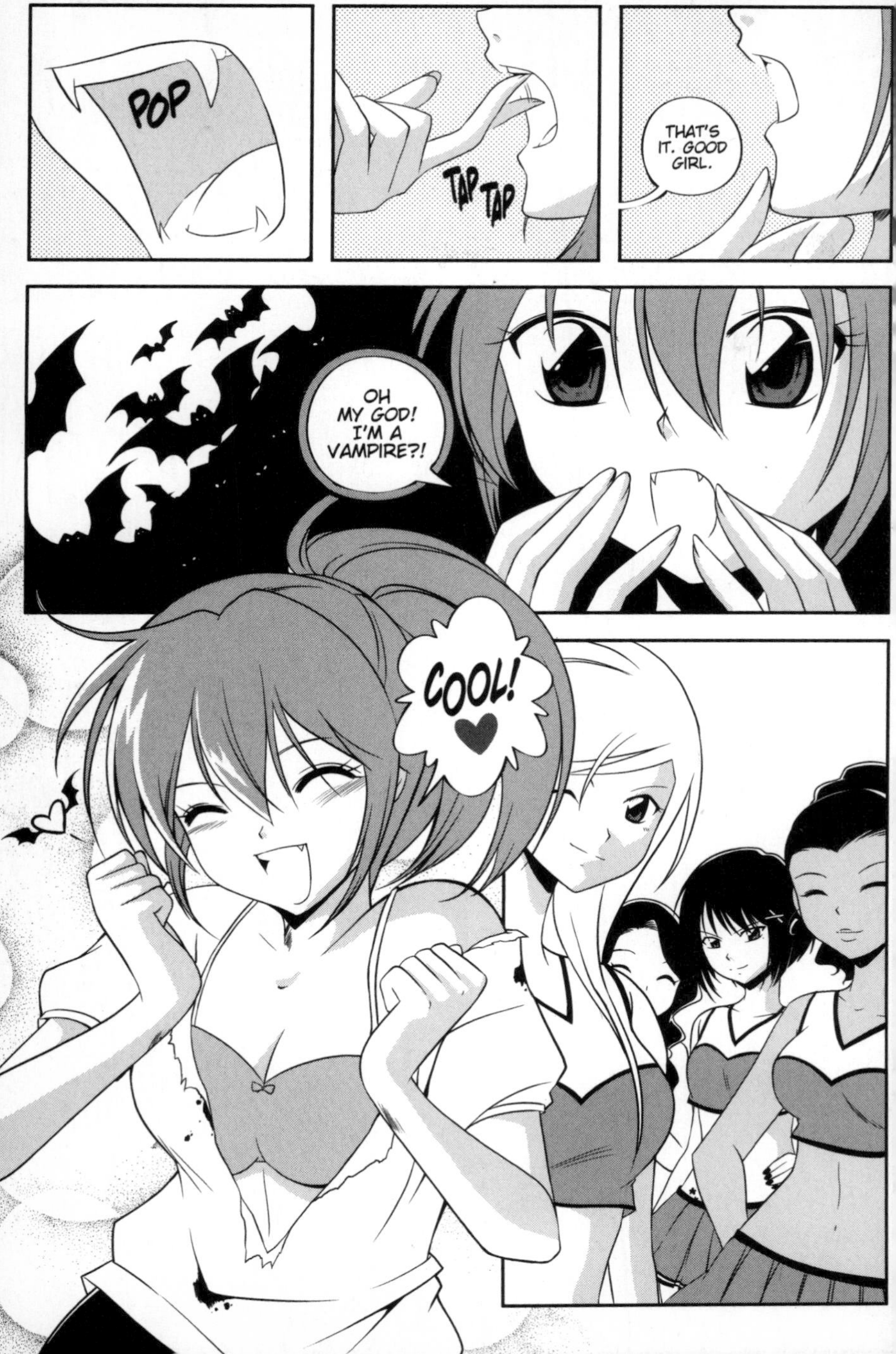

THAT'S IT. GOOD GIRL.
TAP TAP
POP
OH MY GOD! I'M A VAMPIRE?!
COOL!

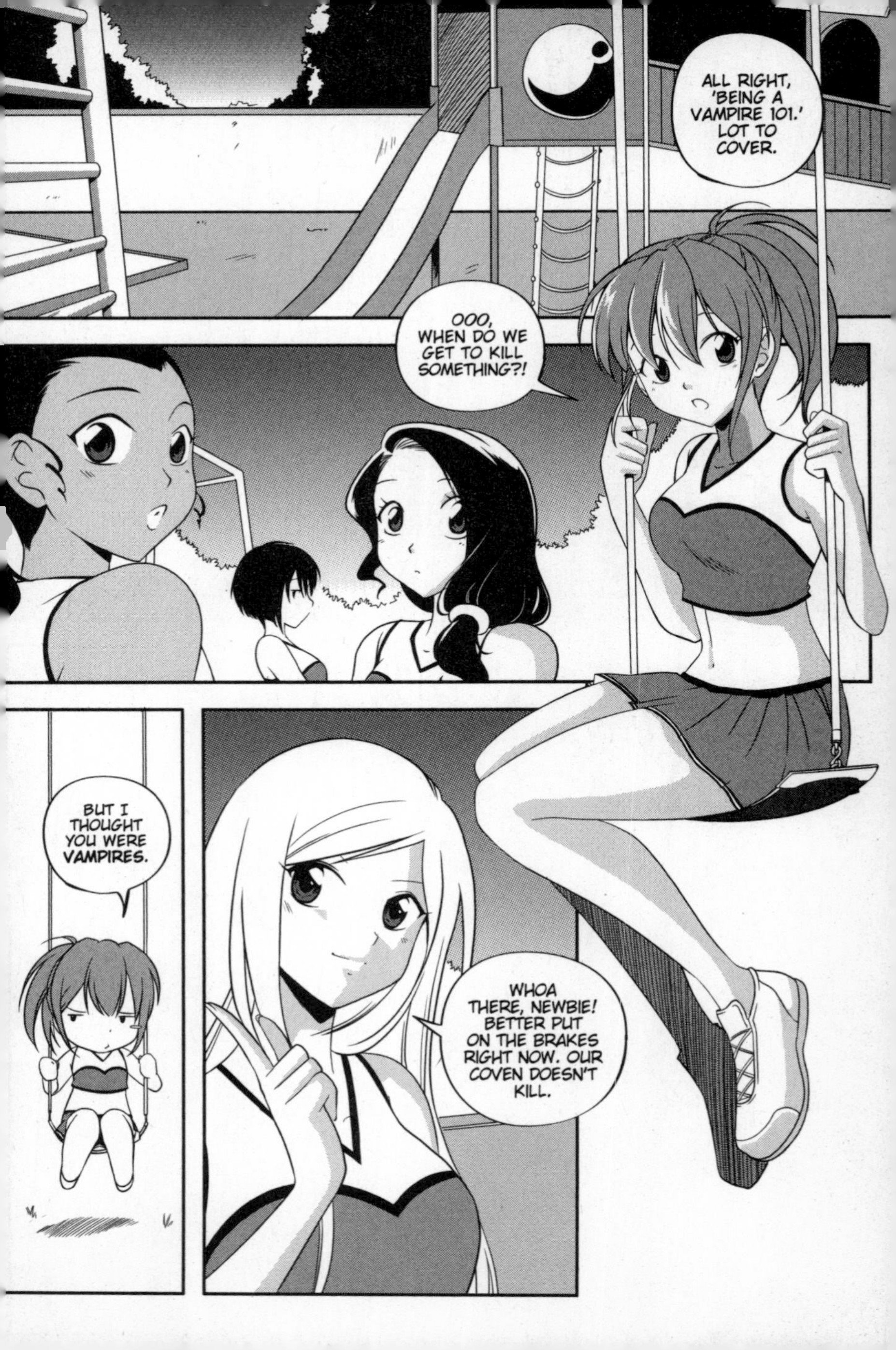
ALL RIGHT, 'BEING A VAMPIRE 101.' LOT TO COVER.
OOO, WHEN DO WE GET TO KILL SOMETHING?!
WHOA THERE, NEWBIE! BETTER PUT ON THE BRAKES RIGHT NOW. OUR COVEN DOESN'T KILL.
BUT I THOUGHT YOU WERE VAMPIRES.

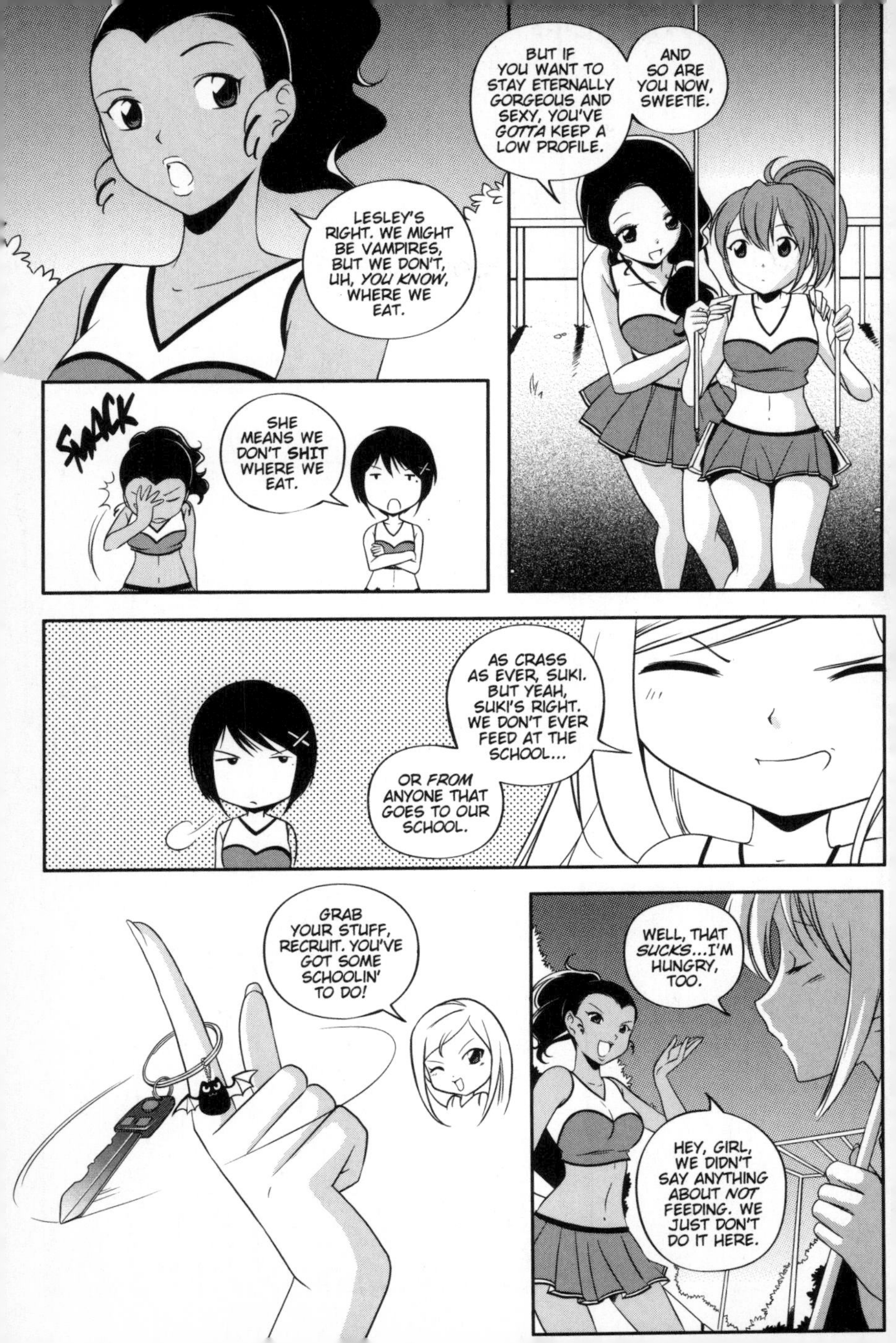
AND SO ARE YOU NOW, SWEETIE.
BUT IF YOU WANT TO STAY ETERNALLY GORGEOUS AND SEXY, YOU'VE *GOTTA* KEEP A LOW PROFILE.
LESLEY'S RIGHT. WE MIGHT BE VAMPIRES, BUT WE DON'T, UH, *YOU KNOW*, WHERE WE EAT.
SMACK
SHE MEANS WE DON'T **SHIT** WHERE WE EAT.
AS CRASS AS EVER, SUKI. BUT YEAH, SUKI'S RIGHT. WE DON'T EVER FEED AT THE SCHOOL...
OR *FROM* ANYONE THAT GOES TO OUR SCHOOL.
WELL, THAT *SUCKS*...I'M HUNGRY, TOO.
HEY, GIRL, WE DIDN'T SAY ANYTHING ABOUT *NOT* FEEDING. WE JUST DON'T DO IT HERE.
GRAB YOUR STUFF, RECRUIT. YOU'VE GOT SOME SCHOOLIN' TO DO!

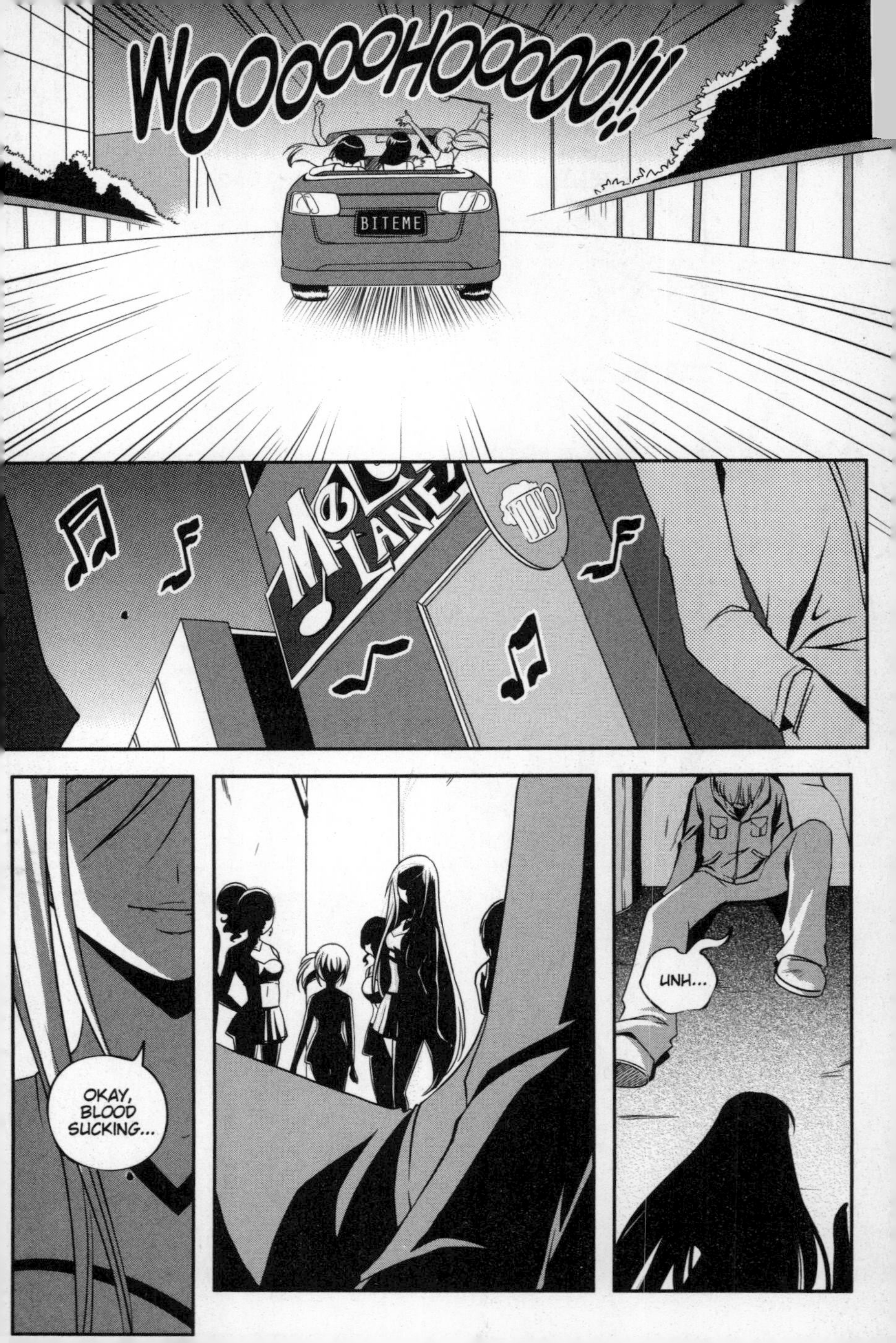
WOOOOHOOOOOO!!!
BITEME
UNH...
OKAY, BLOOD SUCKING...

IT'S JUST LIKE MRS. HEATH SAID IN HEALTH CLASS. MEN HAVE TWELVE PINTS OF BLOOD AND LADIES HAVE TEN.
YOU DRINK MORE THAN FOUR PINTS AND YOU'VE GOT A CORPSE ON YOUR HANDS. AND BELIEVE ME, ONE CORPSE LEADS TO MORE CORPSES, WHICH LEADS TO A BOATLOAD OF TROUBLE.
TA-DA
SAYS, YOU.
SUKI, SHHH!
SINCE WE WANT TO KEEP OURSELVES WELL UNDER THE RADAR, ONLY DRINK A MAX OF TWO PINTS.
JUST LIKE GIVING BLOOD. WEAK AND WOBBLY AS HELL, BUT NOTHING A BAG OF CHOCOLATE CHIP COOKIES WON'T CURE.
RAR!
GOT IT. TWO PINTS. NO CORPSES. WEAK BUT NOT HOSPITALIZED. CAN I EAT 'IM ALREADY?!
NOT SO FAST.
YEAH, YOU'VE GOTTA GET YOUR TECHNIQUE DOWN FIRST. HERE, PRACTICE ON THIS MELON.
SERIOUSLY?!!

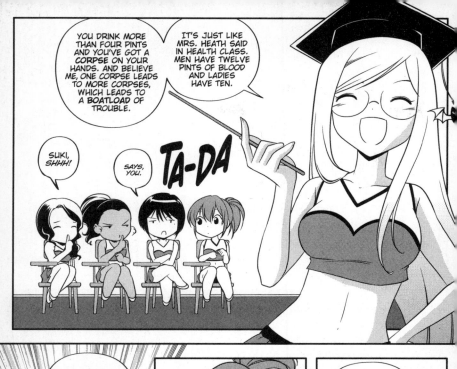

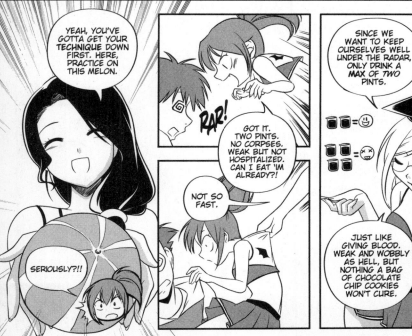

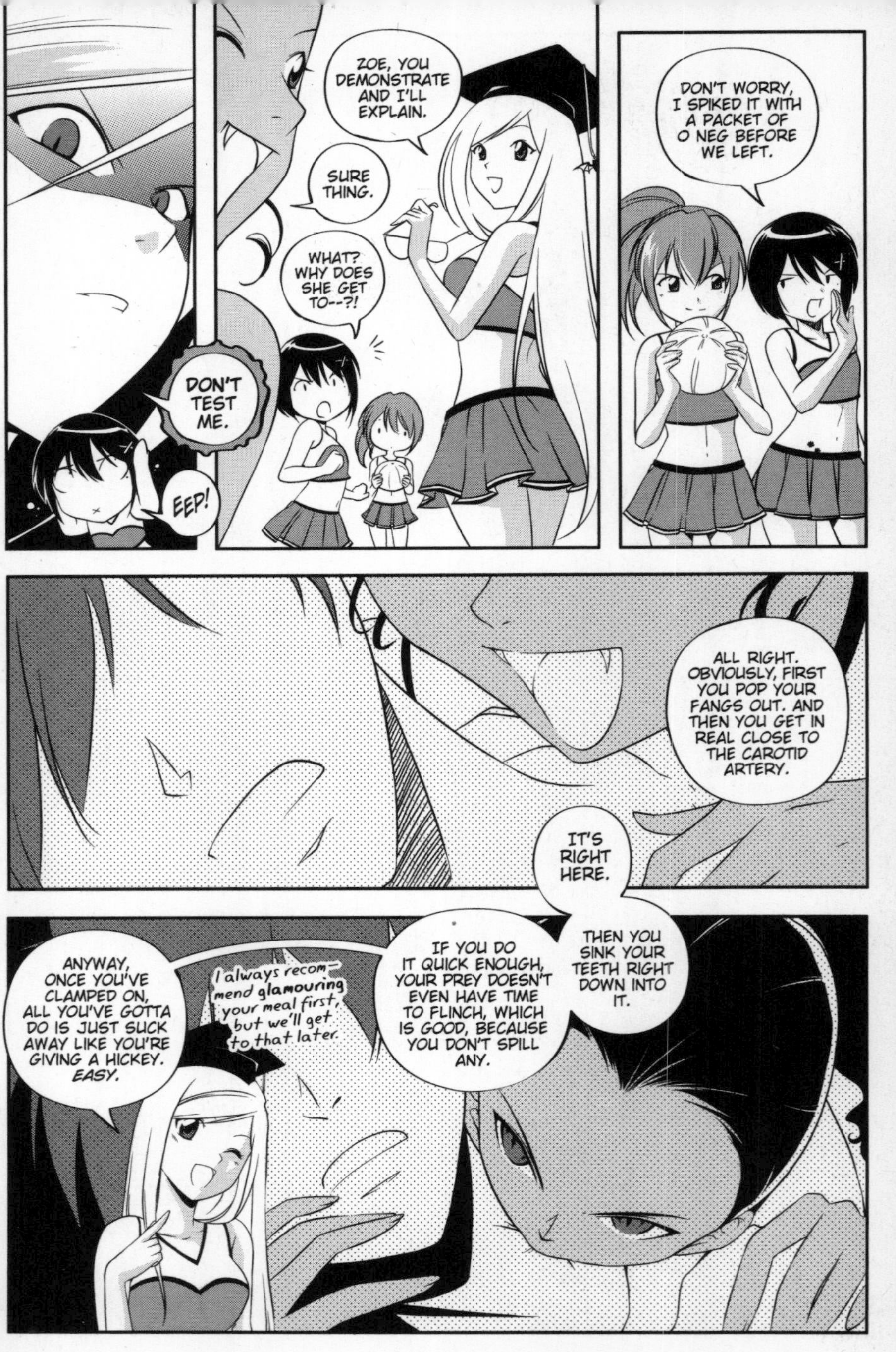
DON'T WORRY, I SPIKED IT WITH A PACKET OF O NEG BEFORE WE LEFT.
ZOE, YOU DEMONSTRATE AND I'LL EXPLAIN.
SURE THING.
WHAT? WHY DOES SHE GET TO--?!
DON'T TEST ME.
EEP!
ALL RIGHT. OBVIOUSLY, FIRST YOU POP YOUR FANGS OUT. AND THEN YOU GET IN REAL CLOSE TO THE CAROTID ARTERY.
IT'S RIGHT HERE.
THEN YOU SINK YOUR TEETH RIGHT DOWN INTO IT.
IF YOU DO IT QUICK ENOUGH, YOUR PREY DOESN'T EVEN HAVE TIME TO FLINCH, WHICH IS GOOD, BECAUSE YOU DON'T SPILL ANY.
I always recom-mend glamouring your meal first, but we'll get to that later.
ANYWAY, ONCE YOU'VE CLAMPED ON, ALL YOU'VE GOTTA DO IS JUST SUCK AWAY LIKE YOU'RE GIVING A HICKEY. EASY.

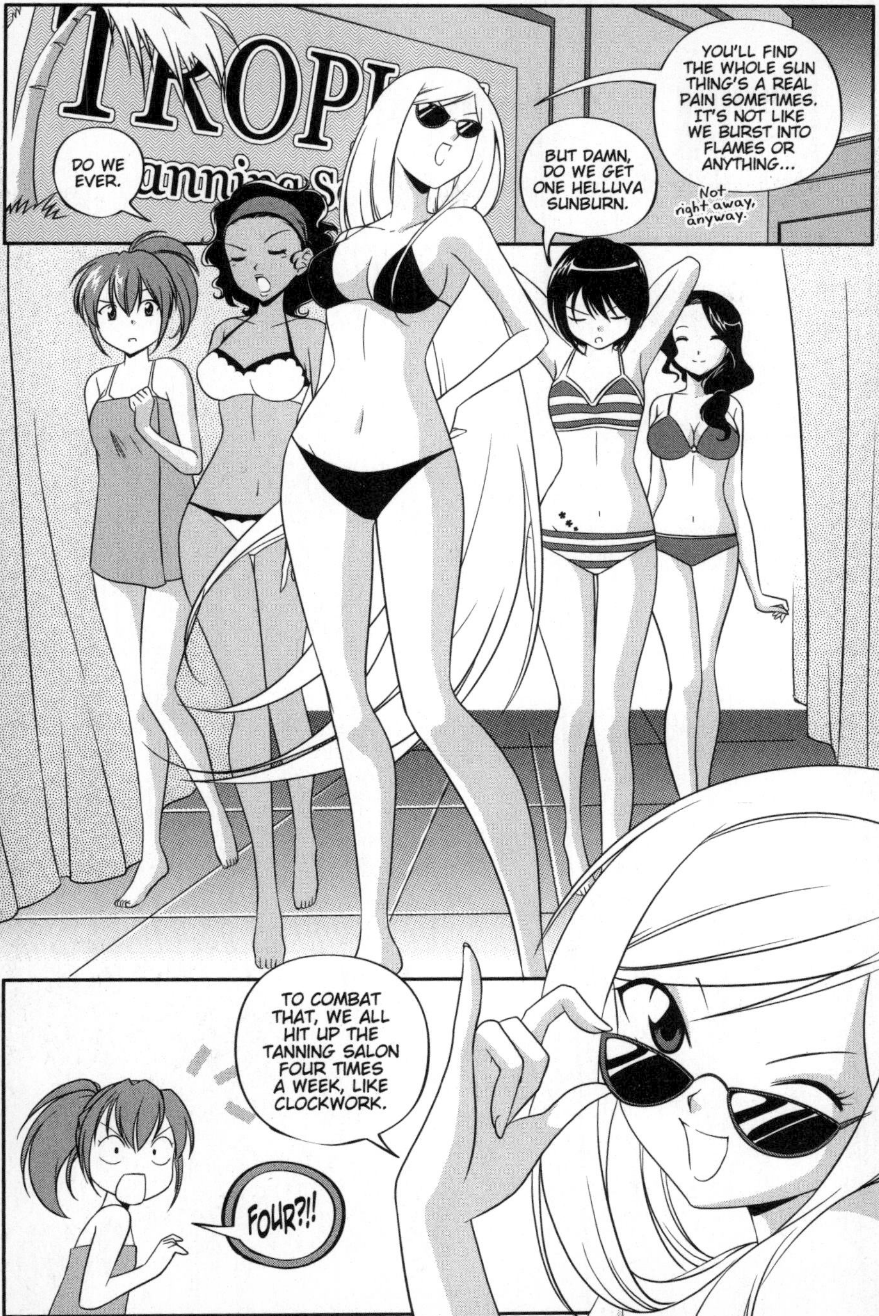
YOU'LL FIND THE WHOLE SUN THING'S A REAL PAIN SOMETIMES. IT'S NOT LIKE WE BURST INTO FLAMES OR ANYTHING...
Not right away, anyway.
BUT DAMN, DO WE GET ONE HELLUVA SUNBURN.
DO WE EVER.
TO COMBAT THAT, WE ALL HIT UP THE TANNING SALON FOUR TIMES A WEEK, LIKE CLOCKWORK.
FOUR?!!

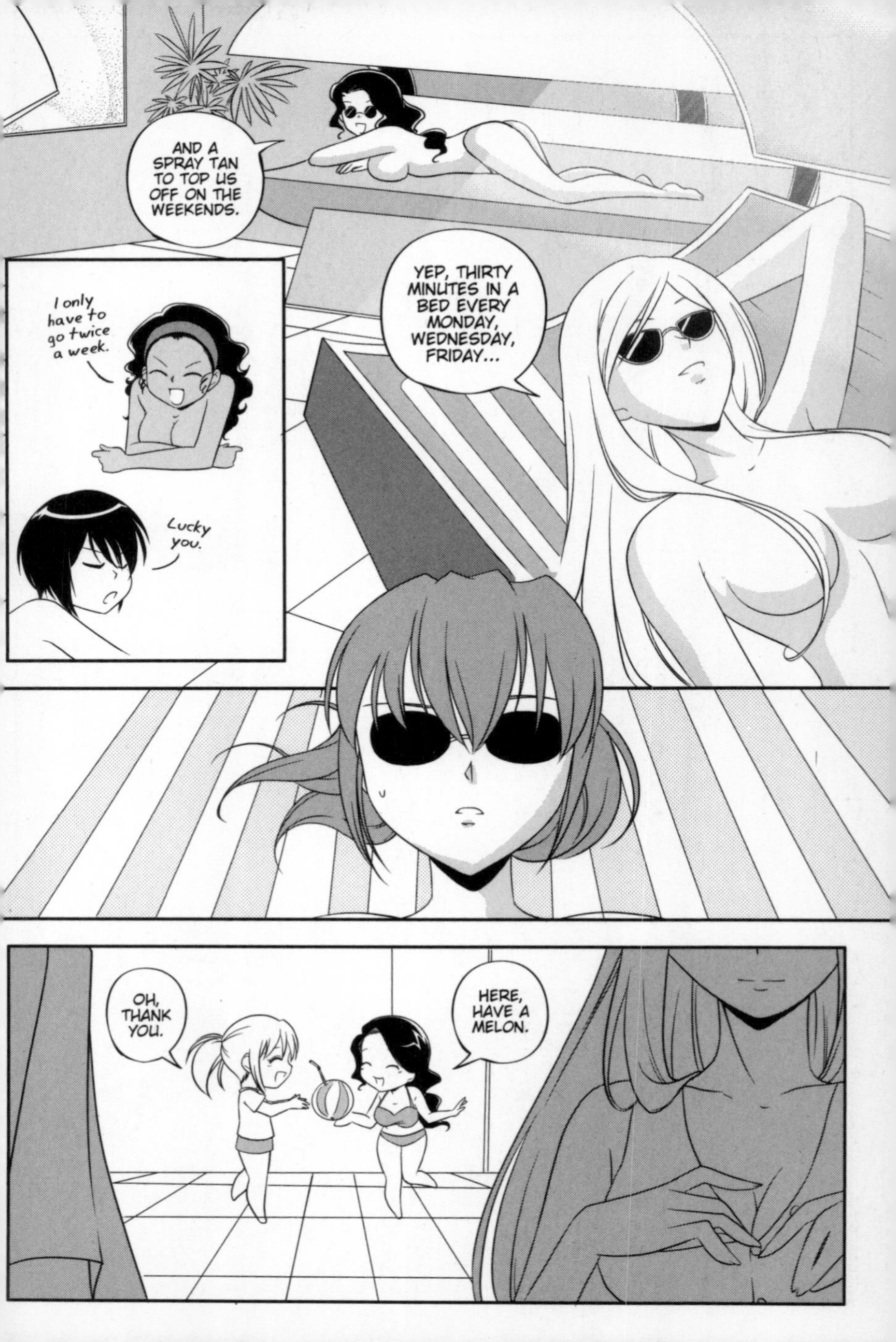
YEP, THIRTY MINUTES IN A BED EVERY MONDAY, WEDNESDAY, FRIDAY...
AND A SPRAY TAN TO TOP US OFF ON THE WEEKENDS.
I only have to go twice a week.
Lucky you.
HERE, HAVE A MELON.
OH, THANK YOU.

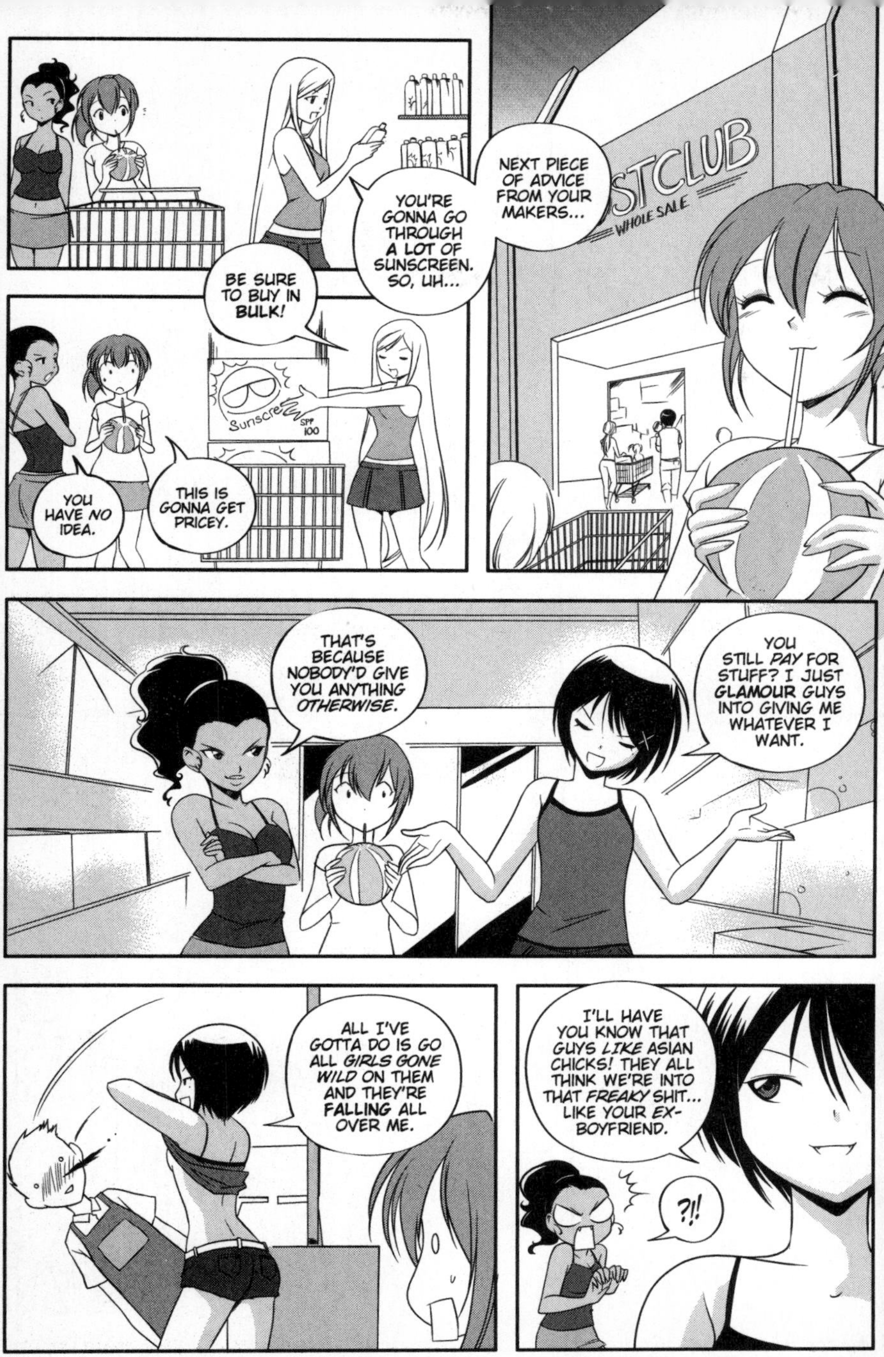
STCLUB
WHOLE SALE
NEXT PIECE OF ADVICE FROM YOUR MAKERS...
YOU'RE GONNA GO THROUGH A LOT OF SUNSCREEN. SO, UH...
BE SURE TO BUY IN BULK!
Sunscreen SPF 100
THIS IS GONNA GET PRICEY.
YOU HAVE NO IDEA.
YOU STILL PAY FOR STUFF? I JUST GLAMOUR GUYS INTO GIVING ME WHATEVER I WANT.
THAT'S BECAUSE NOBODY'D GIVE YOU ANYTHING OTHERWISE.
I'LL HAVE YOU KNOW THAT GUYS LIKE ASIAN CHICKS! THEY ALL THINK WE'RE INTO THAT FREAKY SHIT... LIKE YOUR EX-BOYFRIEND.
?!!
ALL I'VE GOTTA DO IS GO ALL GIRLS GONE WILD ON THEM AND THEY'RE FALLING ALL OVER ME.

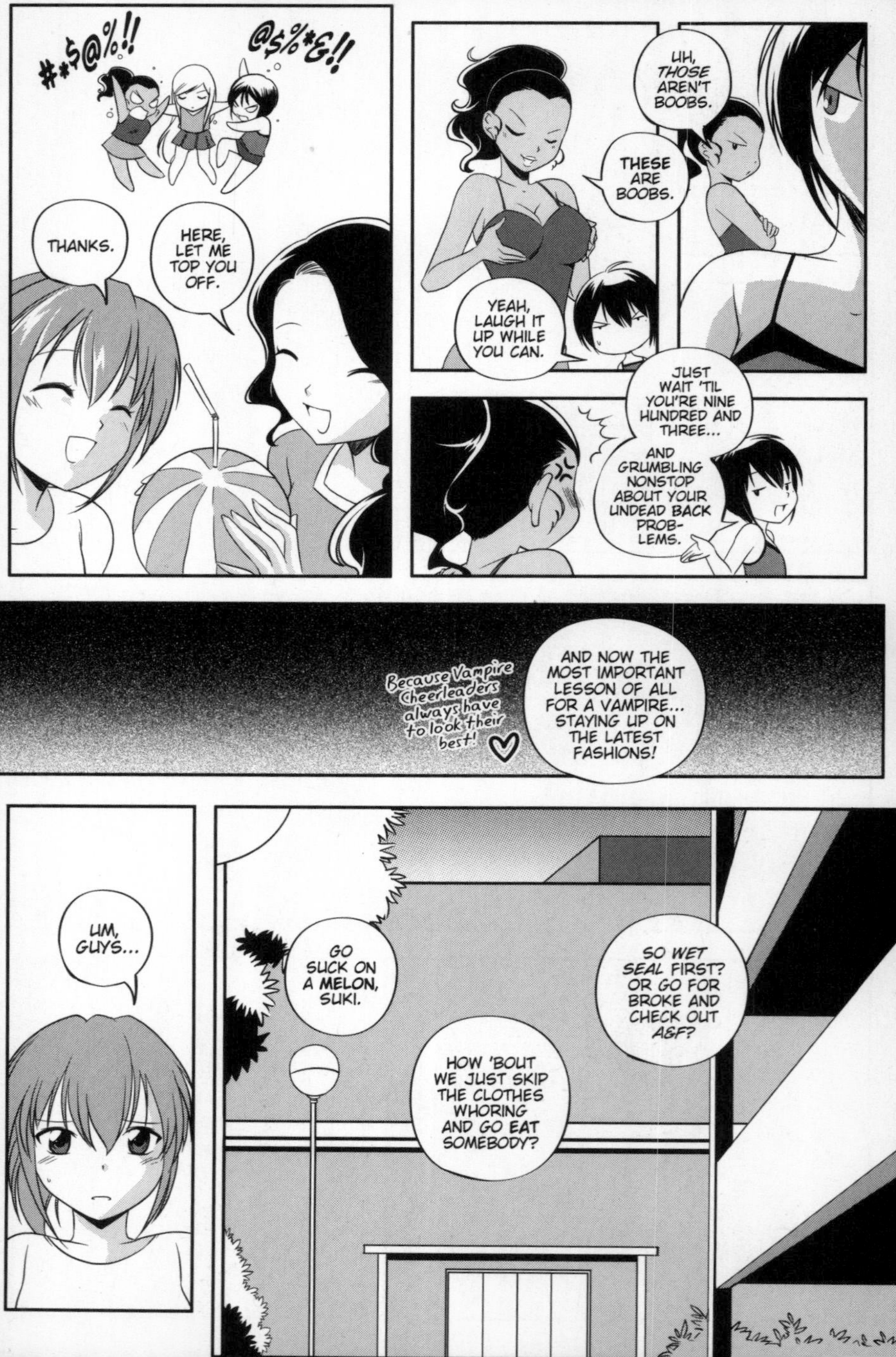
UH, *THOSE* AREN'T BOOBS.
THESE ARE BOOBS.
YEAH, LAUGH IT UP WHILE YOU CAN.
JUST WAIT 'TIL YOU'RE NINE HUNDRED AND THREE...
AND GRUMBLING NONSTOP ABOUT YOUR UNDEAD BACK PROB-LEMS.
@$%*&!!
#*$@%!!
HERE, LET ME TOP YOU OFF.
THANKS.
AND NOW THE MOST IMPORTANT LESSON OF ALL FOR A VAMPIRE... STAYING UP ON THE LATEST FASHIONS!
Because Vampire Cheerleaders always have to look their best! ♡
SO *WET SEAL* FIRST? OR GO FOR BROKE AND CHECK OUT *A&F*?
GO SUCK ON A MELON, SUKI.
HOW 'BOUT WE JUST SKIP THE CLOTHES WHORING AND GO EAT SOMEBODY?
UM, GUYS...

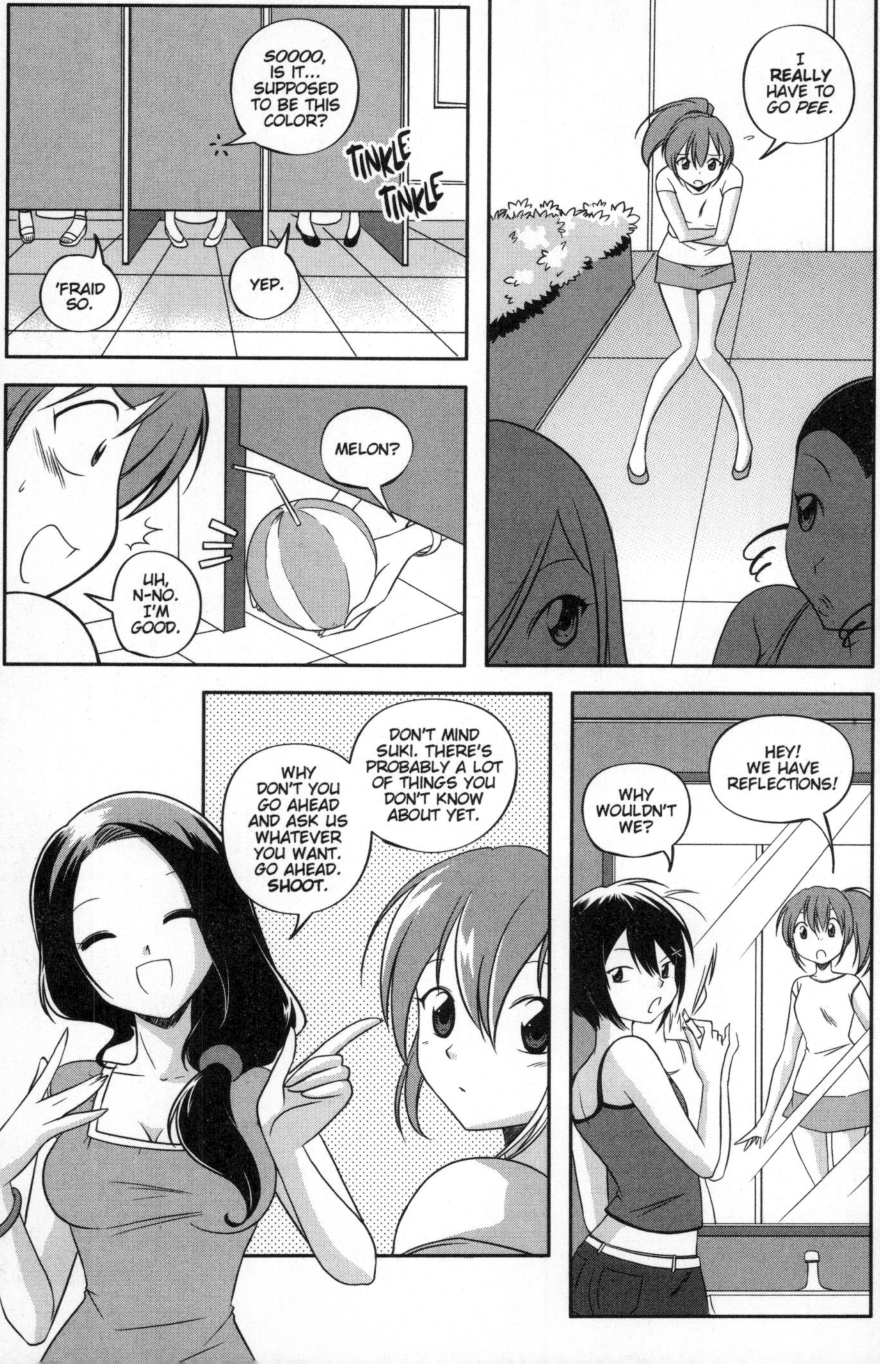
I REALLY HAVE TO GO PEE.
SOOOO, IS IT... SUPPOSED TO BE THIS COLOR?
TINKLE TINKLE
YEP.
'FRAID SO.
MELON?
UH, N-NO. I'M GOOD.
HEY! WE HAVE REFLECTIONS!
WHY WOULDN'T WE?
DON'T MIND SUKI. THERE'S PROBABLY A LOT OF THINGS YOU DON'T KNOW ABOUT YET.
WHY DON'T YOU GO AHEAD AND ASK US WHATEVER YOU WANT. GO AHEAD. SHOOT.

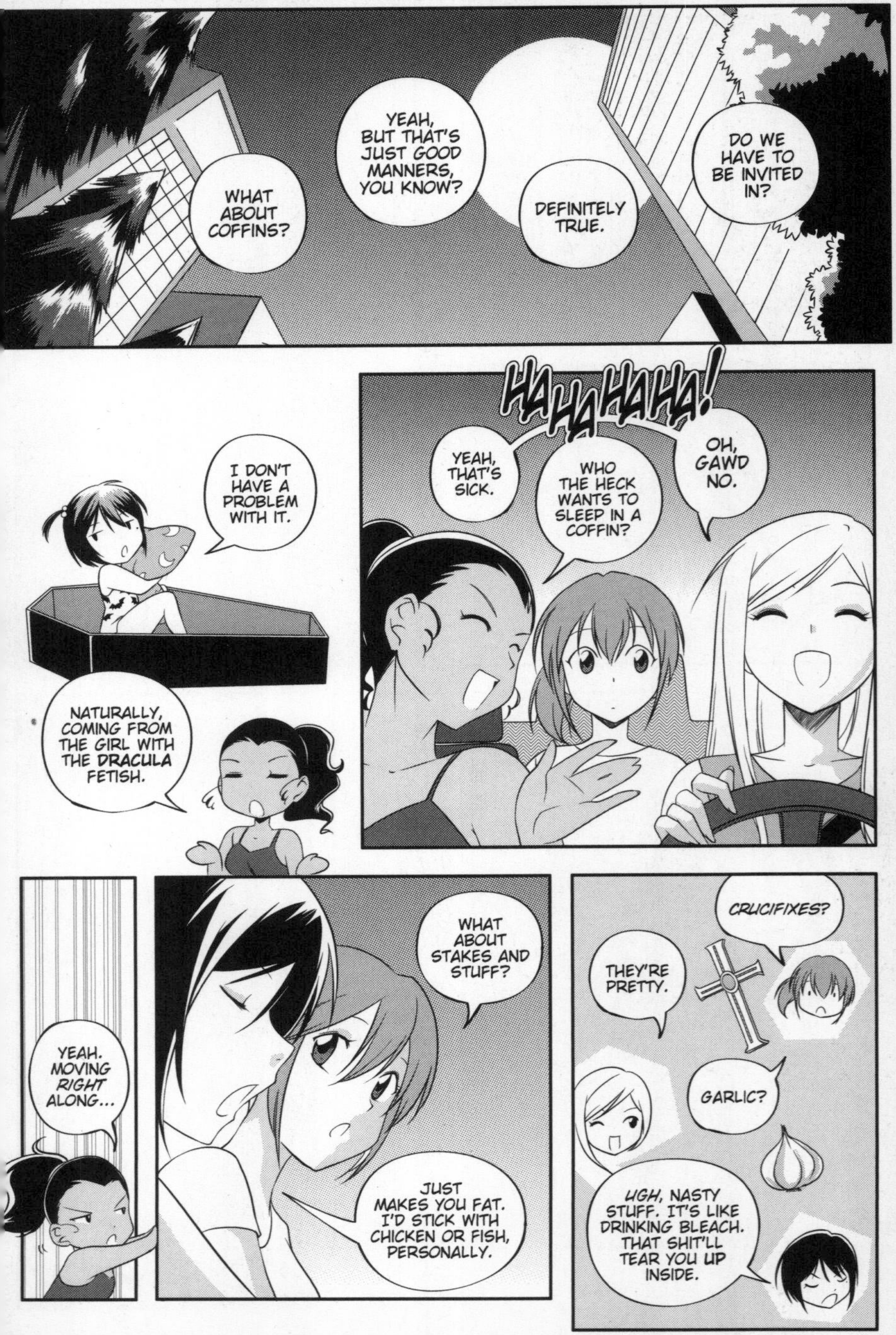
DO WE HAVE TO BE INVITED IN?
DEFINITELY TRUE.
YEAH, BUT THAT'S JUST GOOD MANNERS, YOU KNOW?
WHAT ABOUT COFFINS?
HAHAHAHAHA!
OH, GAWD NO.
WHO THE HECK WANTS TO SLEEP IN A COFFIN?
YEAH, THAT'S SICK.
I DON'T HAVE A PROBLEM WITH IT.
NATURALLY, COMING FROM THE GIRL WITH THE **DRACULA** FETISH.
CRUCIFIXES?
THEY'RE PRETTY.
GARLIC?
UGH, NASTY STUFF. IT'S LIKE DRINKING BLEACH. THAT SHIT'LL TEAR YOU UP INSIDE.
WHAT ABOUT STAKES AND STUFF?
JUST MAKES YOU FAT. I'D STICK WITH CHICKEN OR FISH, PERSONALLY.
YEAH. MOVING *RIGHT* ALONG...

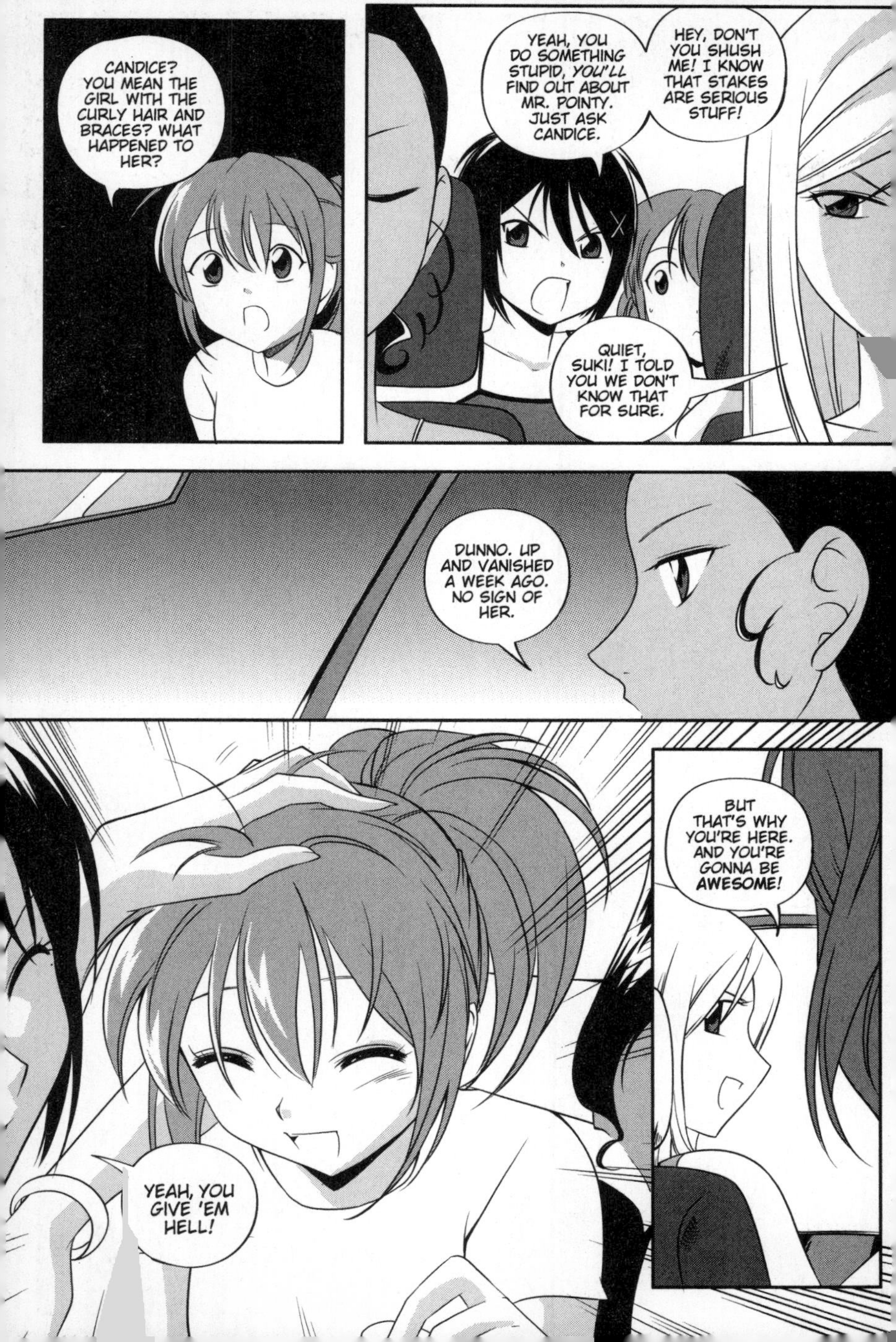
HEY, DON'T YOU SHUSH ME! I KNOW THAT STAKES ARE SERIOUS STUFF!
YEAH, YOU DO SOMETHING STUPID, *YOU'LL* FIND OUT ABOUT MR. POINTY. JUST ASK CANDICE.
QUIET, SUKI! I TOLD YOU WE DON'T KNOW THAT FOR SURE.
CANDICE? YOU MEAN THE GIRL WITH THE CURLY HAIR AND BRACES? WHAT HAPPENED TO HER?
DUNNO. UP AND VANISHED A WEEK AGO. NO SIGN OF HER.
BUT THAT'S WHY YOU'RE HERE. AND YOU'RE GONNA BE **AWESOME!**
YEAH, YOU GIVE 'EM HELL!

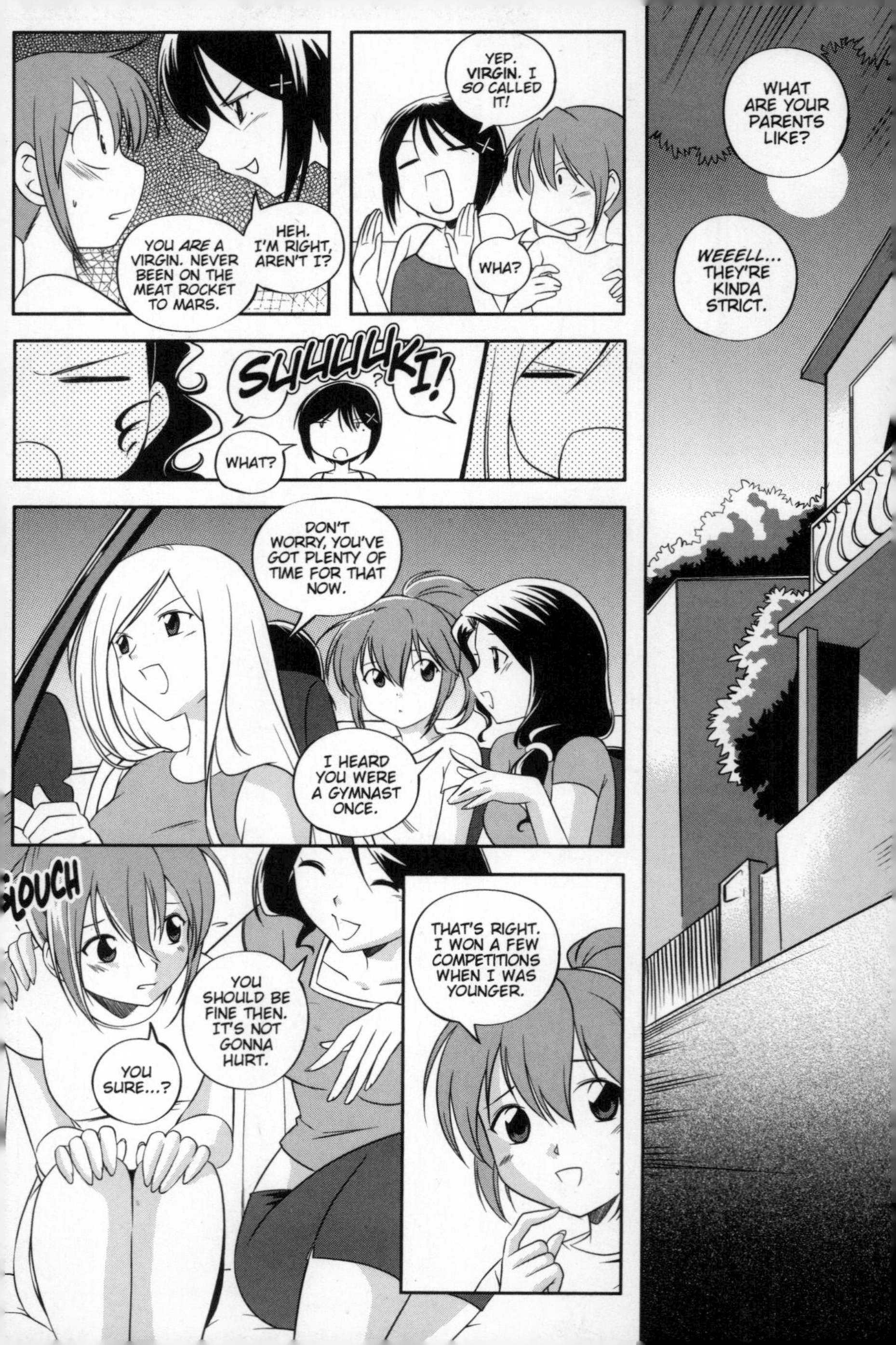
WHAT ARE YOUR PARENTS LIKE?
WEEELL... THEY'RE KINDA STRICT.
YEP. VIRGIN. I SO CALLED IT!
WHA?
HEH. I'M RIGHT, AREN'T I?
YOU ARE A VIRGIN. NEVER BEEN ON THE MEAT ROCKET TO MARS.
SUUUUKI!
WHAT?
DON'T WORRY, YOU'VE GOT PLENTY OF TIME FOR THAT NOW.
I HEARD YOU WERE A GYMNAST ONCE.
THAT'S RIGHT. I WON A FEW COMPETITIONS WHEN I WAS YOUNGER.
LOUCH
YOU SHOULD BE FINE THEN. IT'S NOT GONNA HURT.
YOU SURE...?

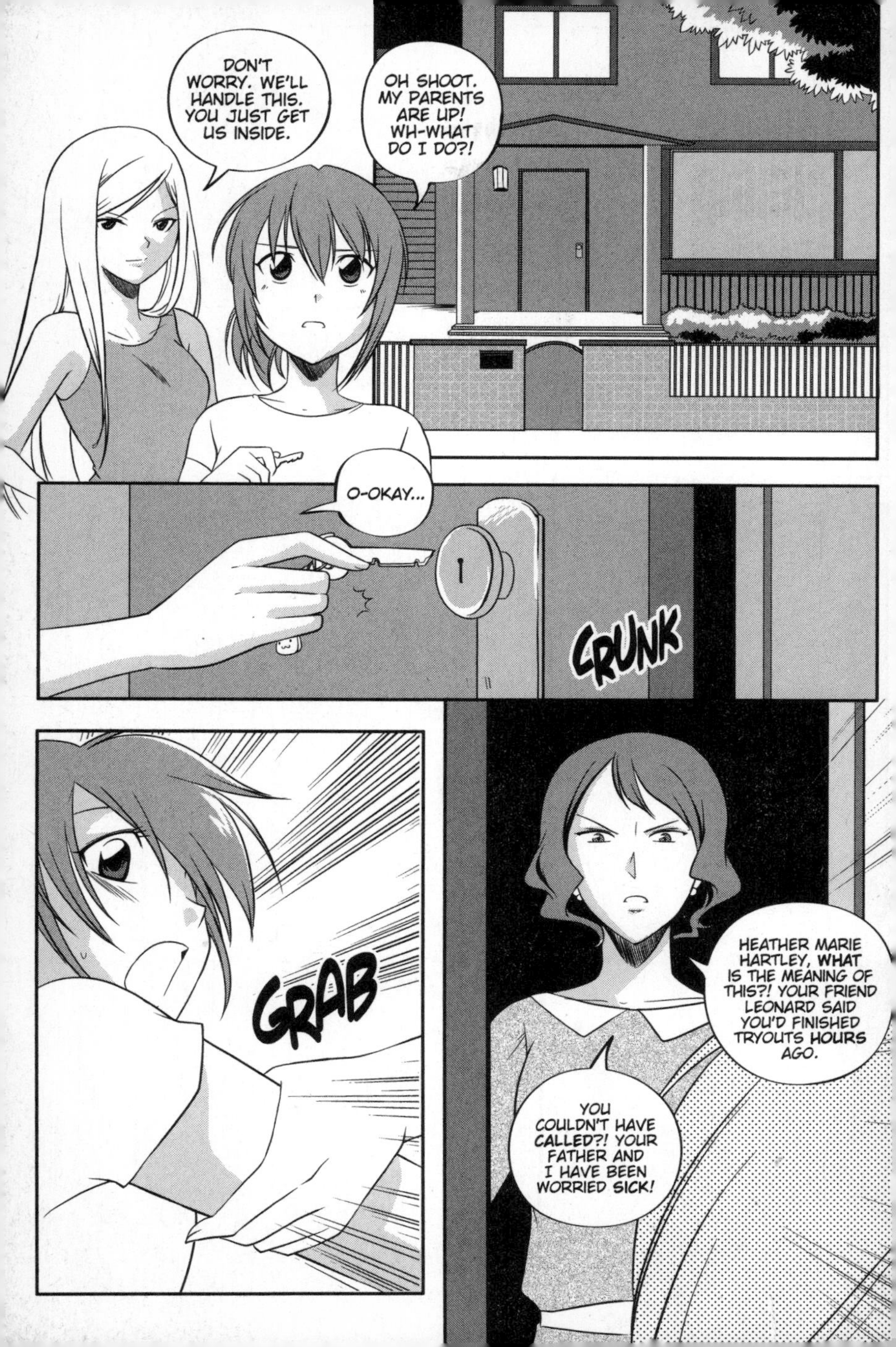
OH SHOOT. MY PARENTS ARE UP! WH-WHAT DO I DO?!
DON'T WORRY. WE'LL HANDLE THIS. YOU JUST GET US INSIDE.
O-OKAY...
CRUNK
HEATHER MARIE HARTLEY, WHAT IS THE MEANING OF THIS?! YOUR FRIEND LEONARD SAID YOU'D FINISHED TRYOUTS HOURS AGO.
YOU COULDN'T HAVE CALLED?! YOUR FATHER AND I HAVE BEEN WORRIED SICK!
GRAB

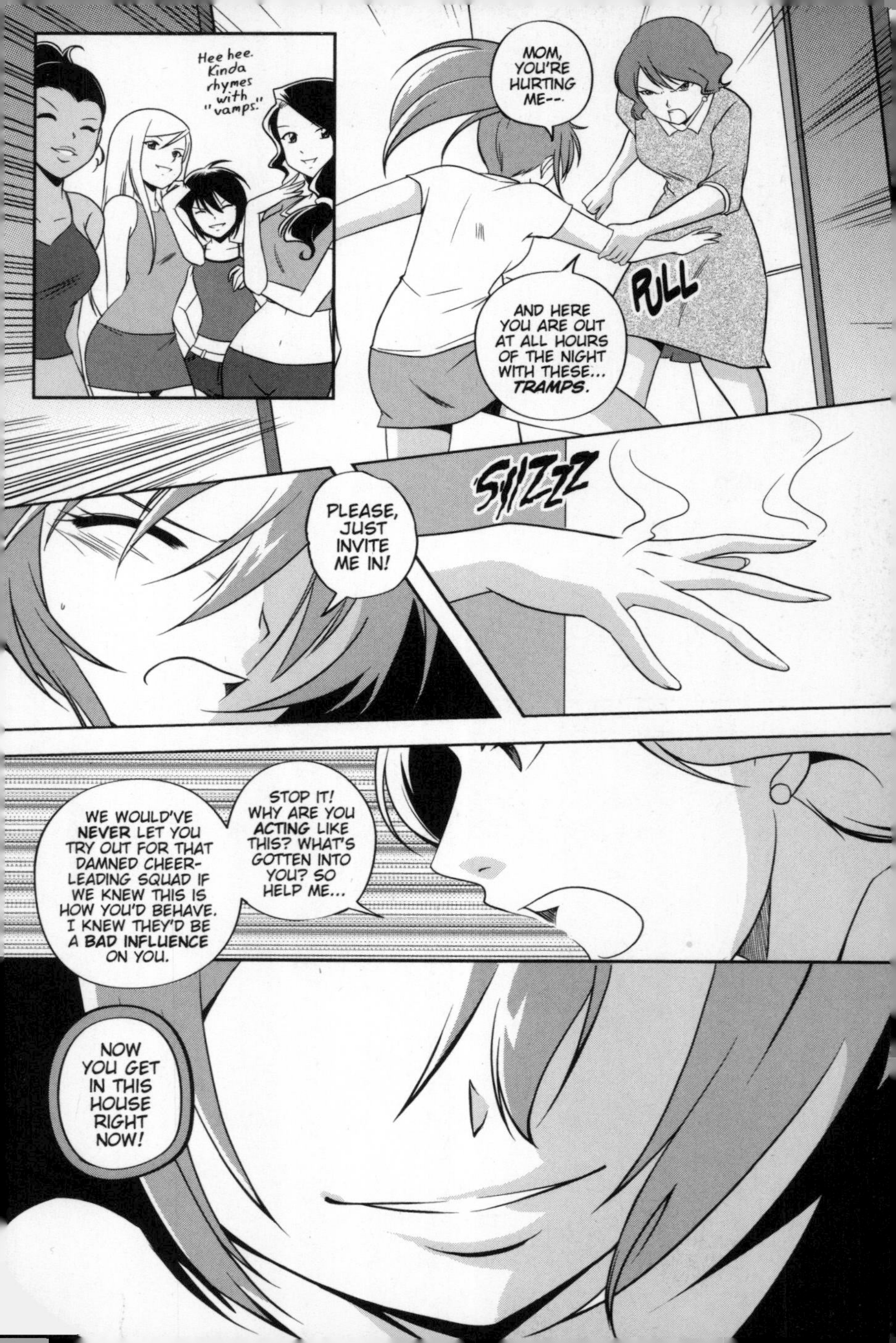
MOM, YOU'RE HURTING ME--.
PULL
AND HERE YOU ARE OUT AT ALL HOURS OF THE NIGHT WITH THESE... TRAMPS.
Hee hee. Kinda rhymes with "vamps."
SWIZZZ
PLEASE, JUST INVITE ME IN!
STOP IT! WHY ARE YOU ACTING LIKE THIS? WHAT'S GOTTEN INTO YOU? SO HELP ME...
WE WOULD'VE NEVER LET YOU TRY OUT FOR THAT DAMNED CHEER-LEADING SQUAD IF WE KNEW THIS IS HOW YOU'D BEHAVE. I KNEW THEY'D BE A BAD INFLUENCE ON YOU.
NOW YOU GET IN THIS HOUSE RIGHT NOW!

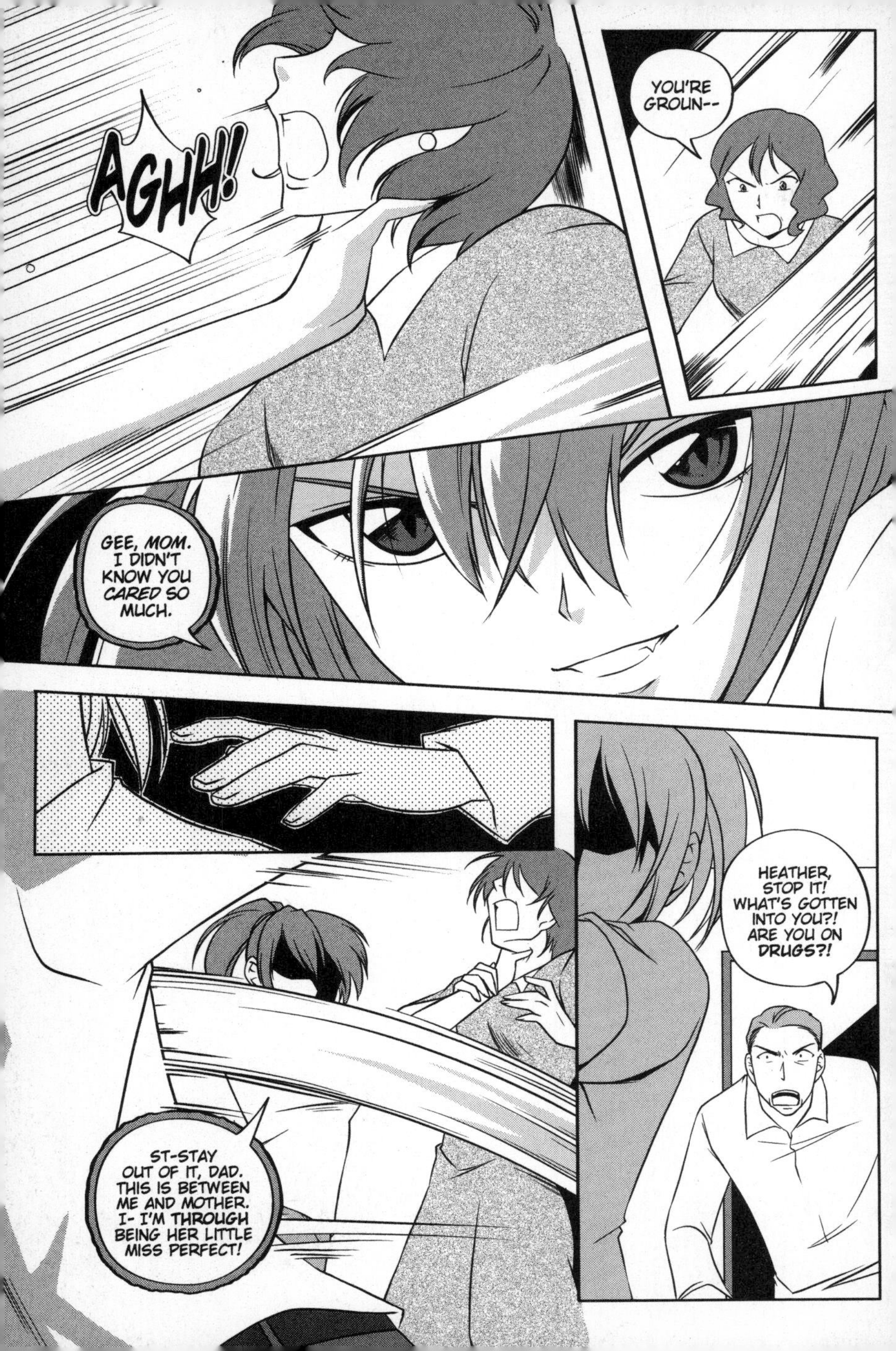
YOU'RE GROUN--
AGHH!
GEE, MOM. I DIDN'T KNOW YOU CARED SO MUCH.
HEATHER, STOP IT! WHAT'S GOTTEN INTO YOU?! ARE YOU ON DRUGS?!
ST-STAY OUT OF IT, DAD. THIS IS BETWEEN ME AND MOTHER. I- I'M THROUGH BEING HER LITTLE MISS PERFECT!

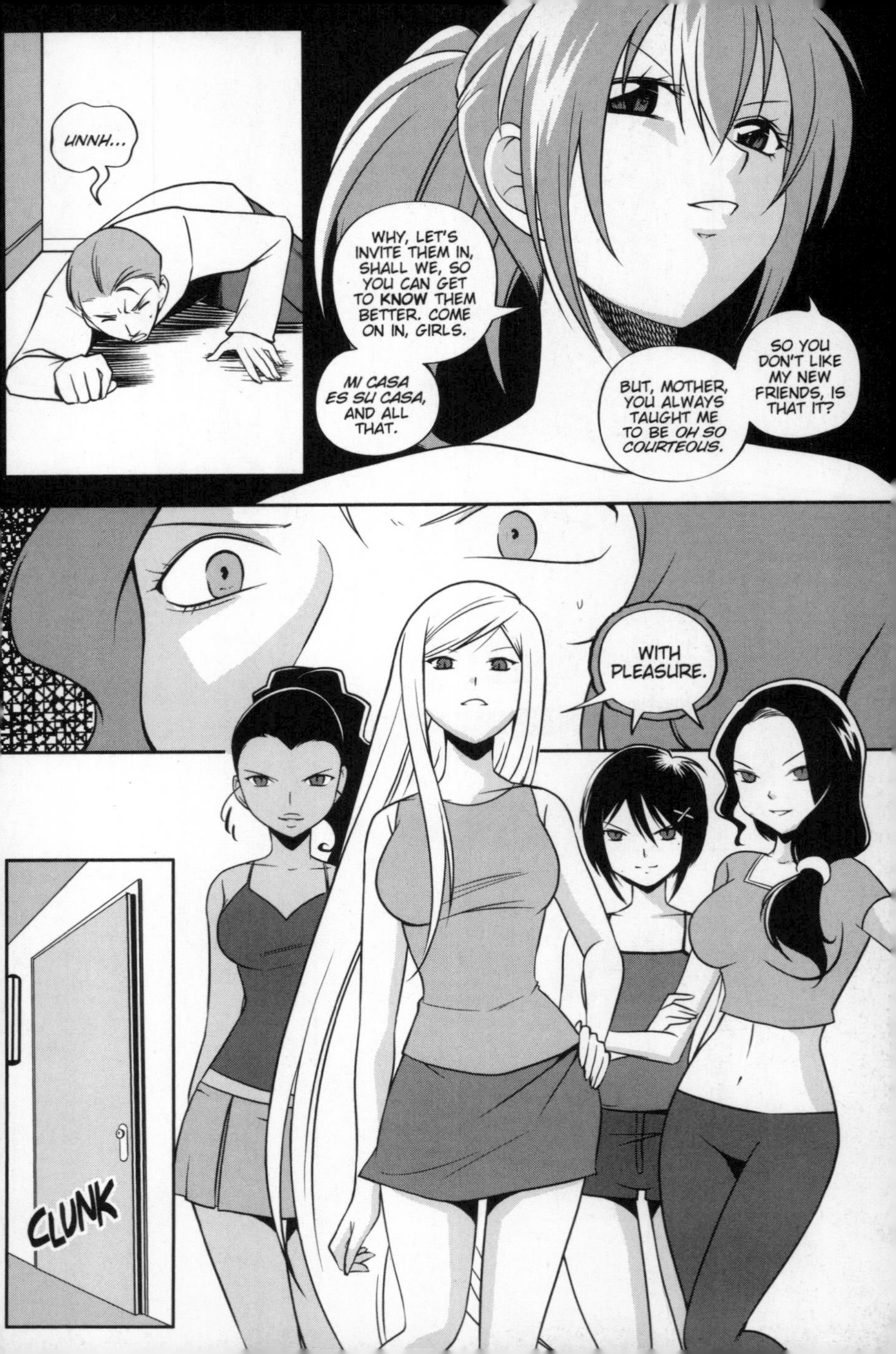
SO YOU DON'T LIKE MY NEW FRIENDS, IS THAT IT?
BUT, MOTHER, YOU ALWAYS TAUGHT ME TO BE *OH SO COURTEOUS*.
WHY, LET'S INVITE THEM IN, SHALL WE, SO YOU CAN GET TO **KNOW** THEM BETTER. COME ON IN, GIRLS.
MI CASA ES SU CASA, AND ALL THAT.
UNNH...
WITH PLEASURE.
CLUNK

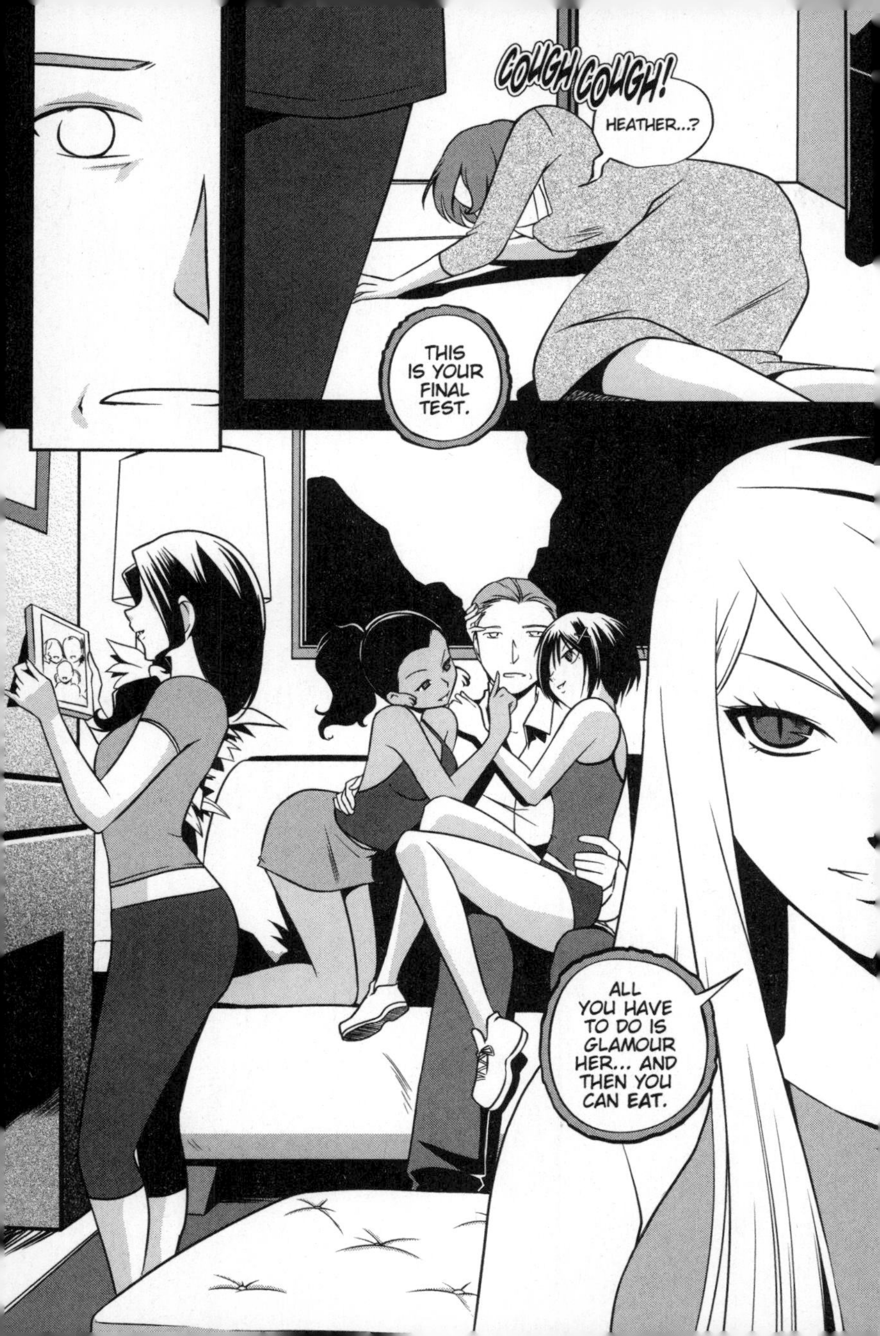
COUGH COUGH!
HEATHER...?
THIS IS YOUR FINAL TEST.
ALL YOU HAVE TO DO IS GLAMOUR HER... AND THEN YOU CAN EAT.

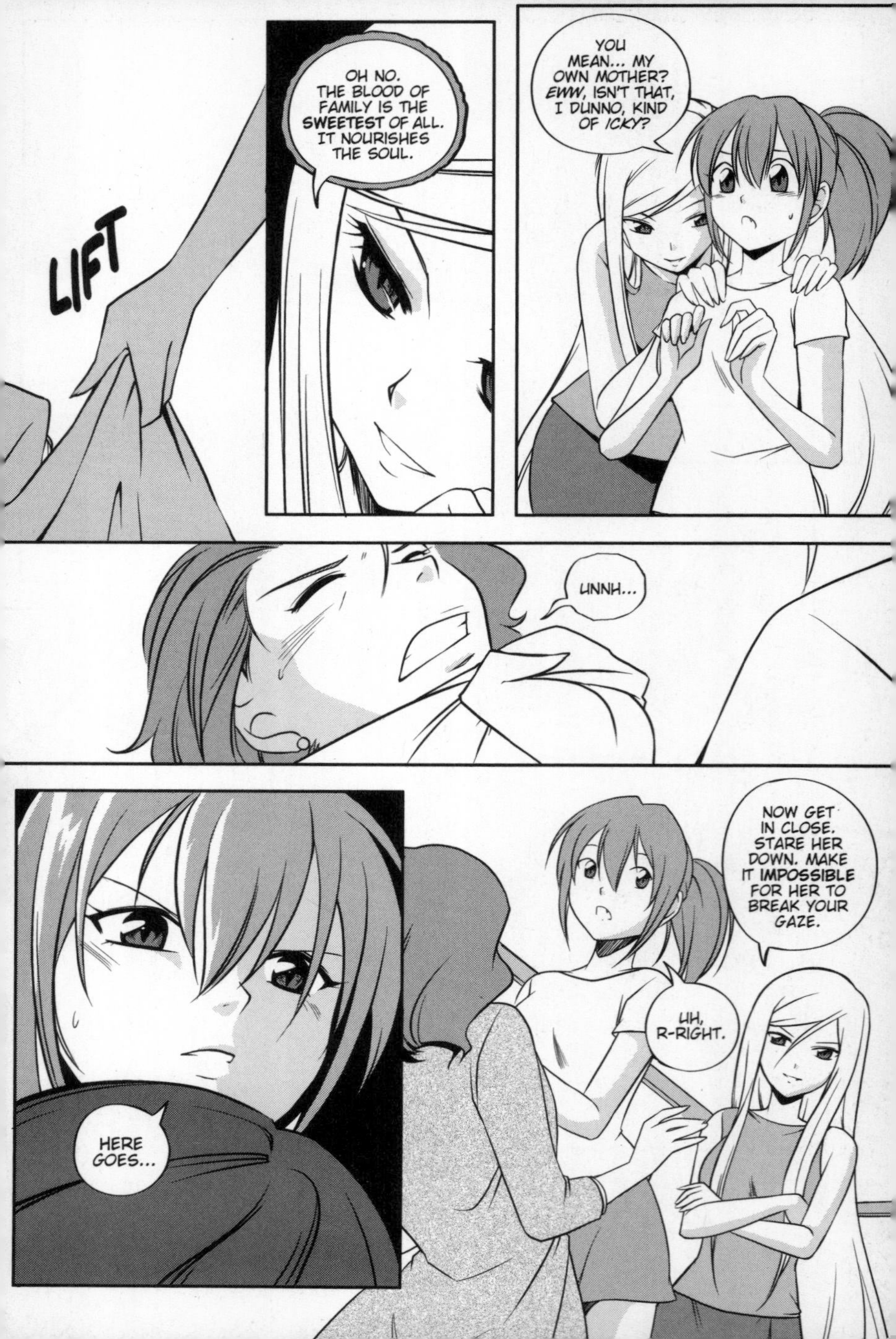
YOU MEAN... MY OWN MOTHER? EWW, ISN'T THAT, I DUNNO, KIND OF ICKY?
OH NO. THE BLOOD OF FAMILY IS THE SWEETEST OF ALL. IT NOURISHES THE SOUL.
LIFT
UNNH...
NOW GET IN CLOSE. STARE HER DOWN. MAKE IT IMPOSSIBLE FOR HER TO BREAK YOUR GAZE.
UH, R-RIGHT.
HERE GOES...

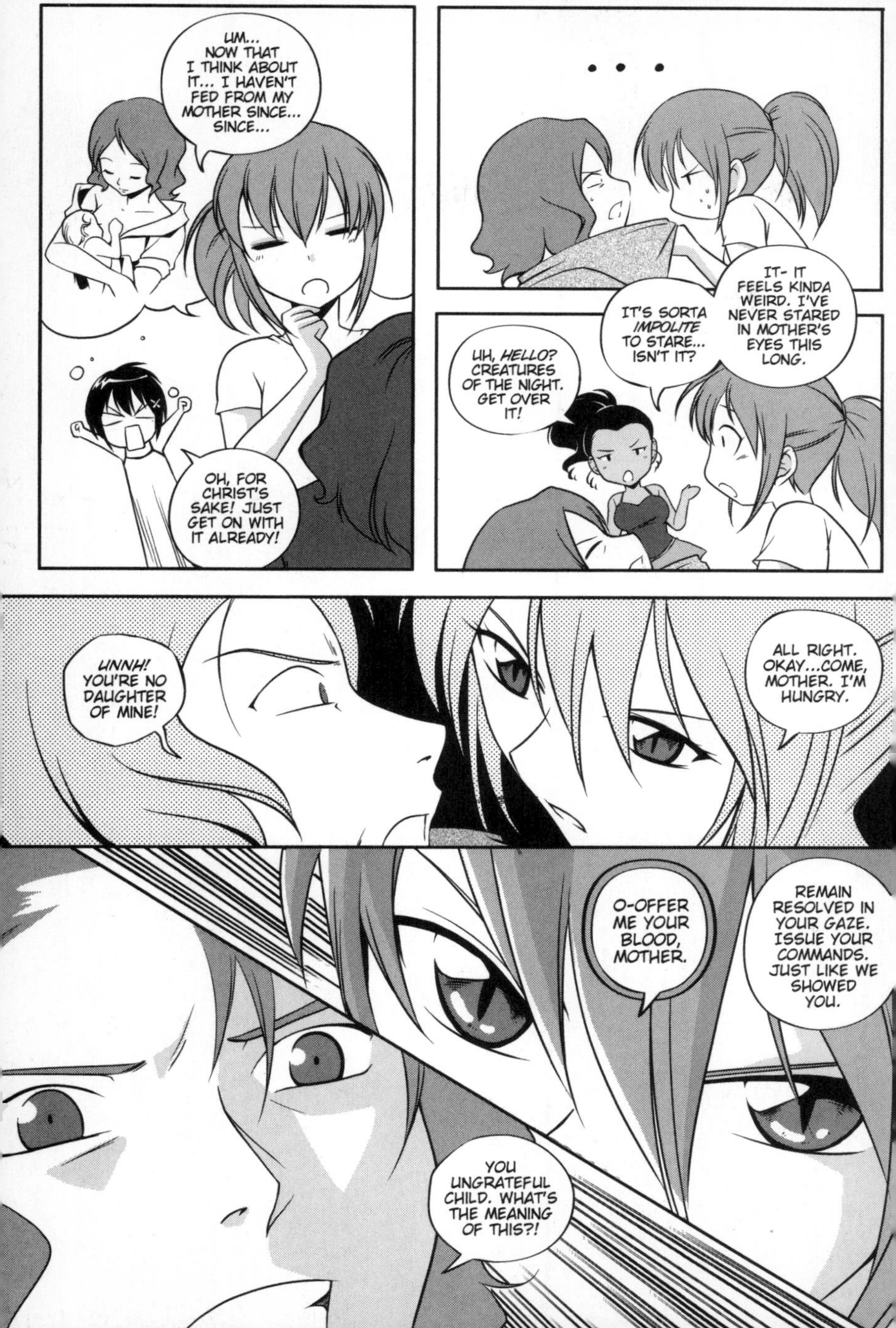
• • •
IT- IT FEELS KINDA WEIRD. I'VE NEVER STARED IN MOTHER'S EYES THIS LONG.
IT'S SORTA *IMPOLITE* TO STARE... ISN'T IT?
UH, *HELLO*? CREATURES OF THE NIGHT. GET OVER IT!
UM... NOW THAT I THINK ABOUT IT... I HAVEN'T FED FROM MY MOTHER SINCE... SINCE...
OH, FOR CHRIST'S SAKE! JUST GET ON WITH IT ALREADY!
ALL RIGHT. OKAY...COME, MOTHER. I'M HUNGRY.
UNNH! YOU'RE NO DAUGHTER OF MINE!
REMAIN RESOLVED IN YOUR GAZE. ISSUE YOUR COMMANDS. JUST LIKE WE SHOWED YOU.
O-OFFER ME YOUR BLOOD, MOTHER.
YOU UNGRATEFUL CHILD. WHAT'S THE MEANING OF THIS?!

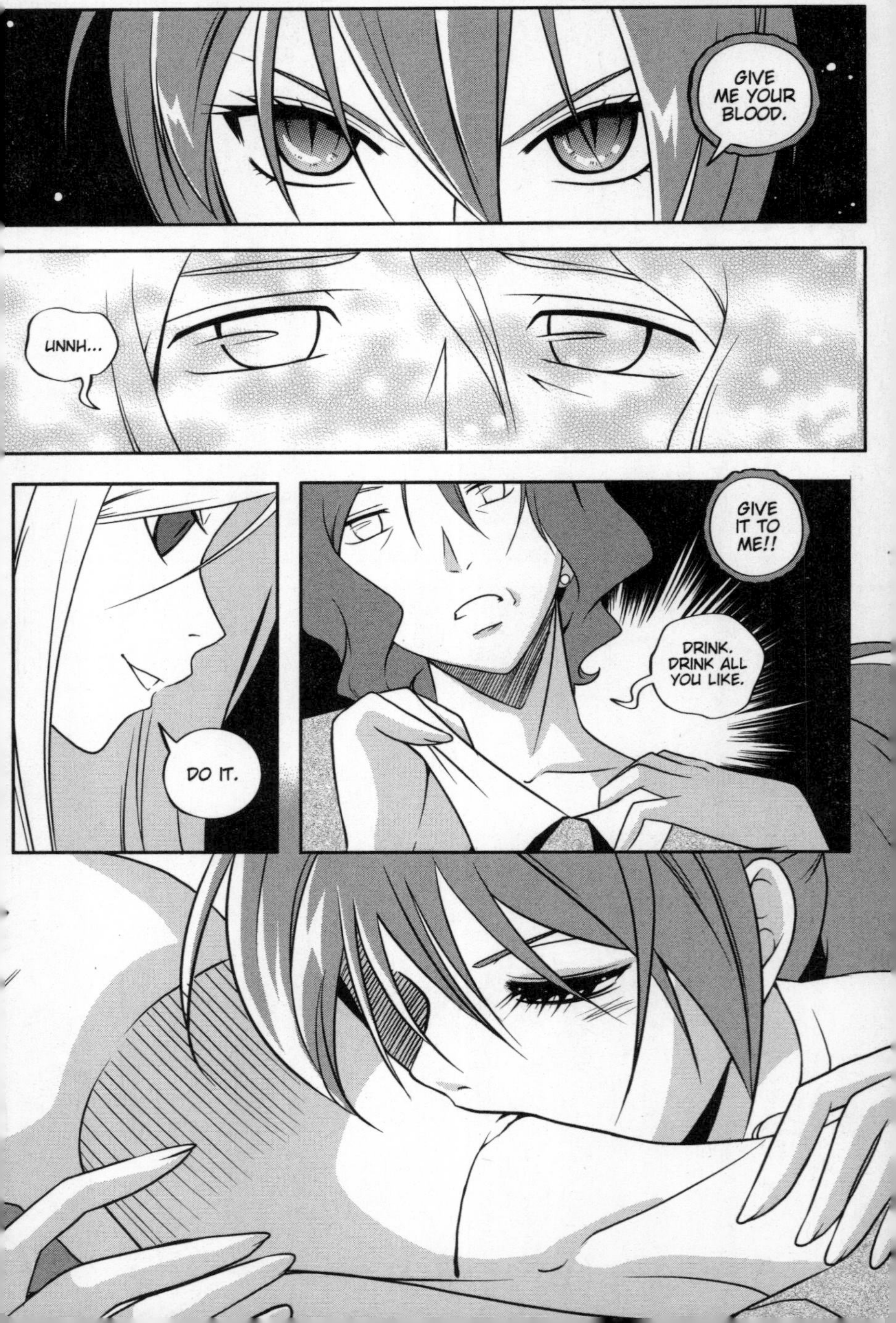
GIVE ME YOUR BLOOD.
UNNH...
GIVE IT TO ME!!
DRINK. DRINK ALL YOU LIKE.
DO IT.

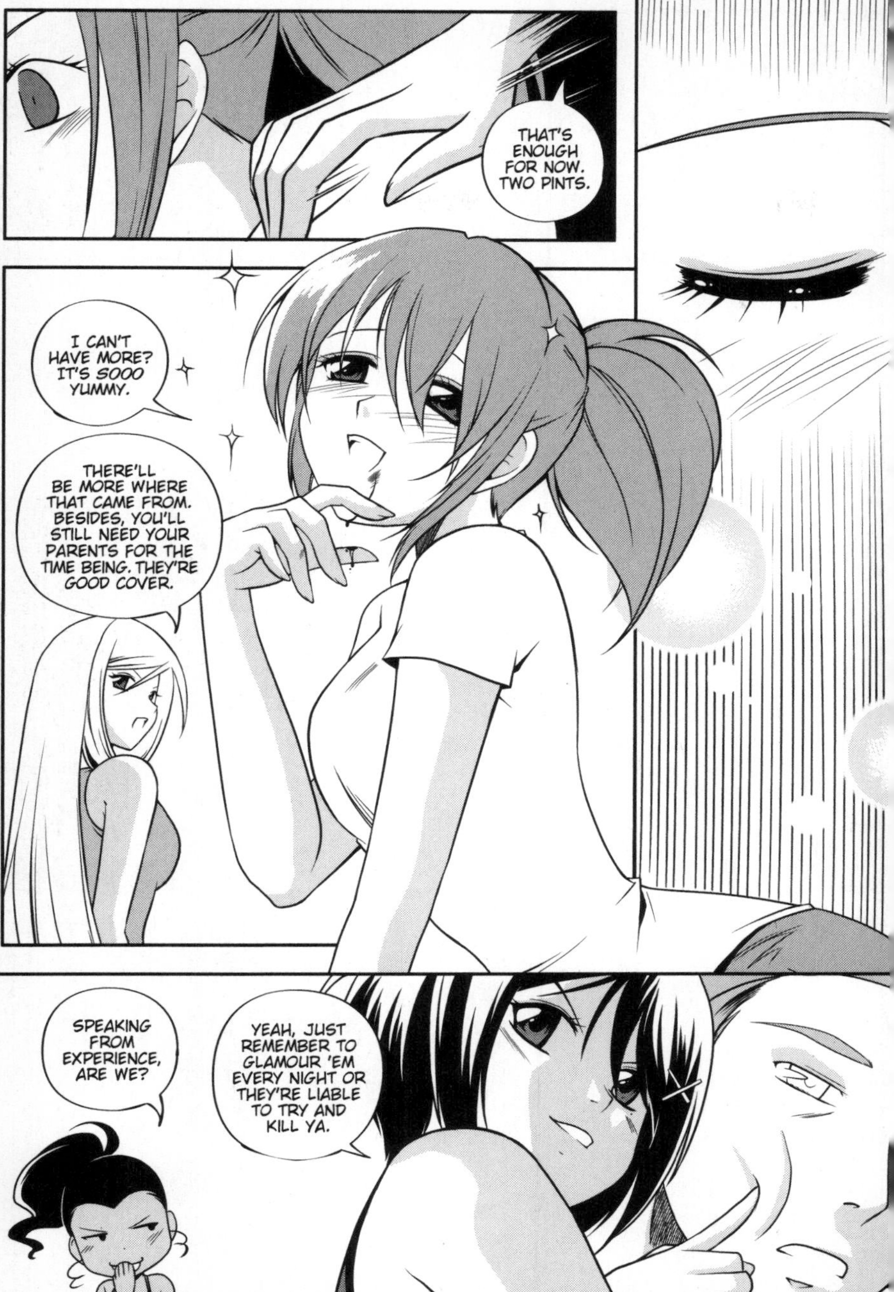
THAT'S ENOUGH FOR NOW. TWO PINTS.
I CAN'T HAVE MORE? IT'S SOOO YUMMY.
THERE'LL BE MORE WHERE THAT CAME FROM. BESIDES, YOU'LL STILL NEED YOUR PARENTS FOR THE TIME BEING. THEY'RE GOOD COVER.
YEAH, JUST REMEMBER TO GLAMOUR 'EM EVERY NIGHT OR THEY'RE LIABLE TO TRY AND KILL YA.
SPEAKING FROM EXPERIENCE, ARE WE?

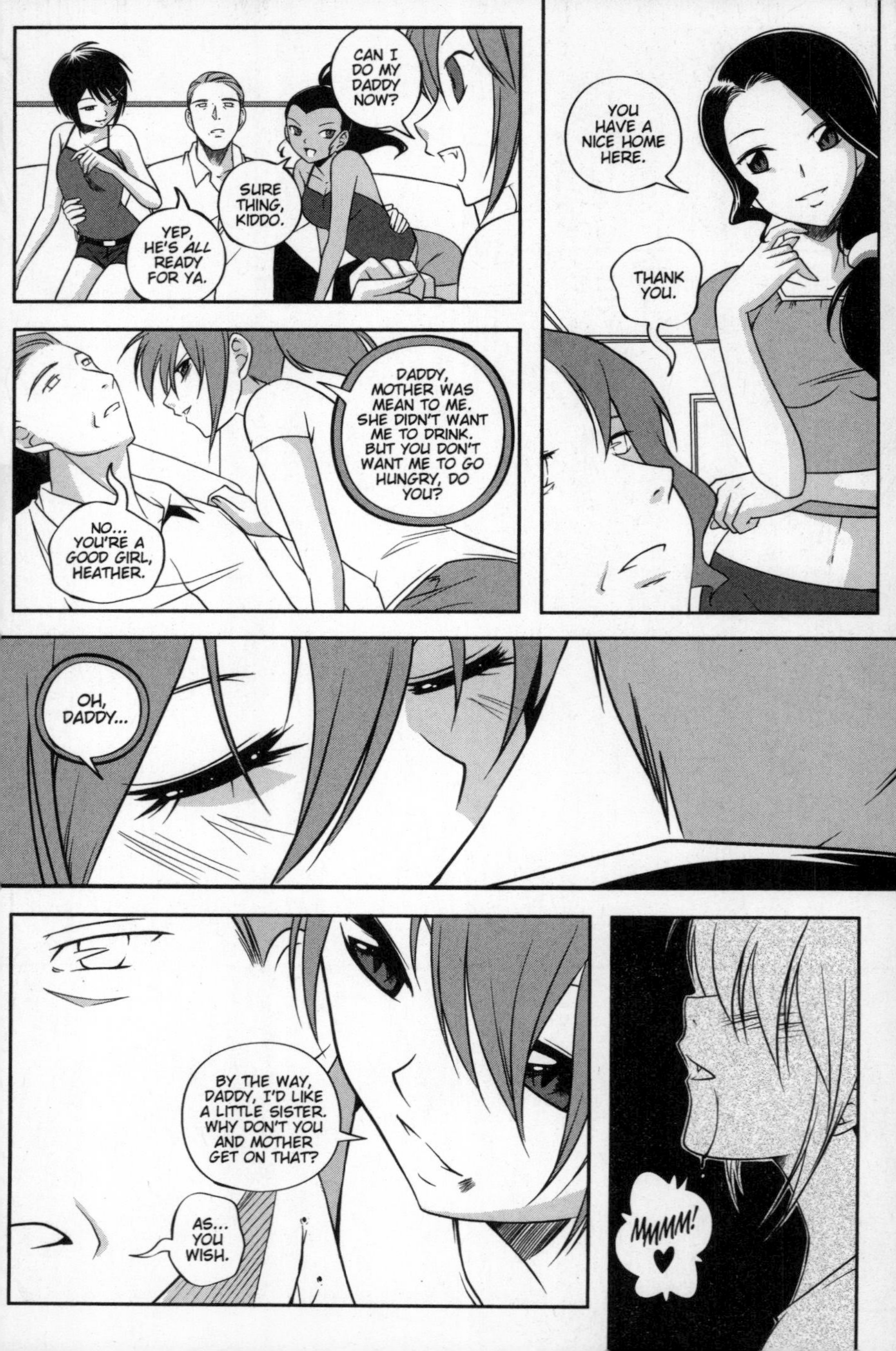
YOU HAVE A NICE HOME HERE.
THANK YOU.
CAN I DO MY DADDY NOW?
SURE THING, KIDDO.
YEP, HE'S ALL READY FOR YA.
DADDY, MOTHER WAS MEAN TO ME. SHE DIDN'T WANT ME TO DRINK. BUT YOU DON'T WANT ME TO GO HUNGRY, DO YOU?
NO... YOU'RE A GOOD GIRL, HEATHER.
OH, DADDY...
MMMM! ♥
BY THE WAY, DADDY, I'D LIKE A LITTLE SISTER. WHY DON'T YOU AND MOTHER GET ON THAT?
AS... YOU WISH.

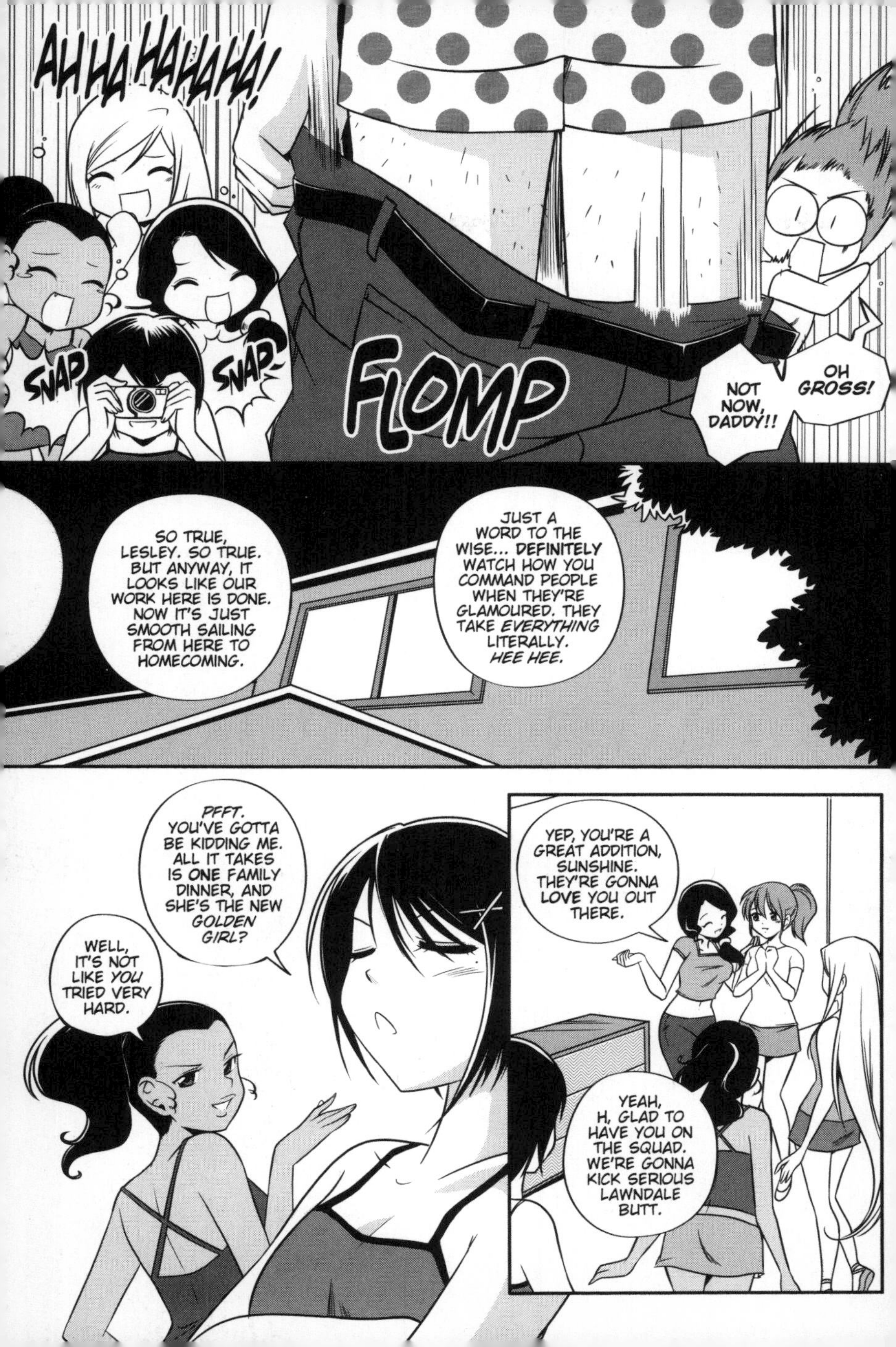
OH GROSS!
NOT NOW, DADDY!!
AH HA HAHAHA!
FLOMP
SNAP
SNAP
JUST A WORD TO THE WISE... DEFINITELY WATCH HOW YOU COMMAND PEOPLE WHEN THEY'RE GLAMOURED. THEY TAKE *EVERYTHING* LITERALLY. *HEE HEE.*
SO TRUE, LESLEY. SO TRUE. BUT ANYWAY, IT LOOKS LIKE OUR WORK HERE IS DONE. NOW IT'S JUST SMOOTH SAILING FROM HERE TO HOMECOMING.
YEP, YOU'RE A GREAT ADDITION, SUNSHINE. THEY'RE GONNA LOVE YOU OUT THERE.
YEAH, H, GLAD TO HAVE YOU ON THE SQUAD. WE'RE GONNA KICK SERIOUS LAWNDALE BUTT.
PFFT. YOU'VE GOTTA BE KIDDING ME. ALL IT TAKES IS ONE FAMILY DINNER, AND SHE'S THE NEW *GOLDEN GIRL?*
WELL, IT'S NOT LIKE *YOU* TRIED VERY HARD.

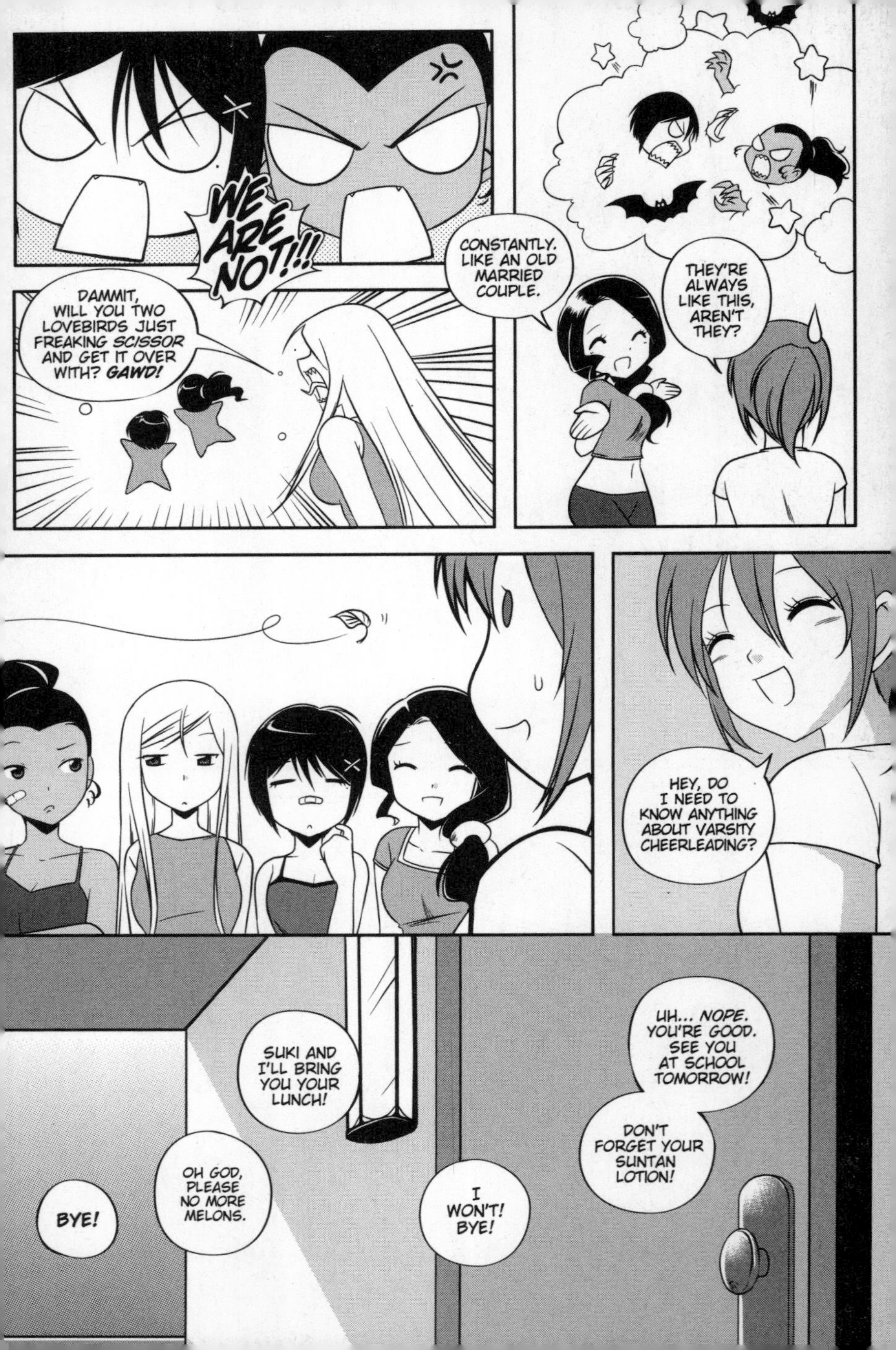
THEY'RE ALWAYS LIKE THIS, AREN'T THEY?
CONSTANTLY. LIKE AN OLD MARRIED COUPLE.
WE ARE NOT!!!
DAMMIT, WILL YOU TWO LOVEBIRDS JUST FREAKING *SCISSOR* AND GET IT OVER WITH? **GAWD!**
HEY, DO I NEED TO KNOW ANYTHING ABOUT VARSITY CHEERLEADING?
UH... *NOPE.* YOU'RE GOOD. SEE YOU AT SCHOOL TOMORROW!
DON'T FORGET YOUR SUNTAN LOTION!
SUKI AND I'LL BRING YOU YOUR LUNCH!
I WON'T! BYE!
OH GOD, PLEASE NO MORE MELONS.
BYE!

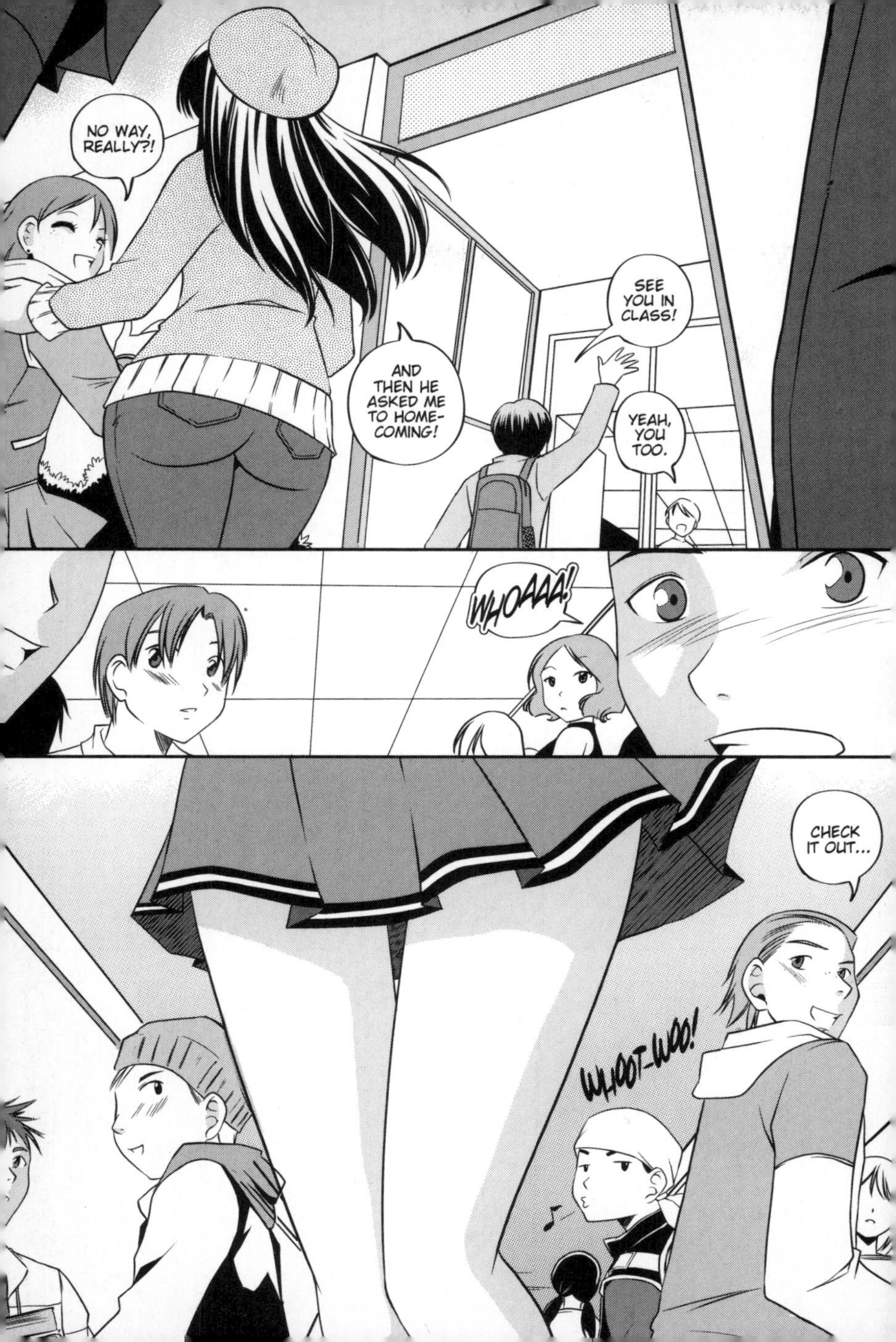
SEE YOU IN CLASS!
YEAH, YOU TOO.
AND THEN HE ASKED ME TO HOME-COMING!
NO WAY, REALLY?!
WHOAAA!
CHECK IT OUT...
WHOOT-WOO!

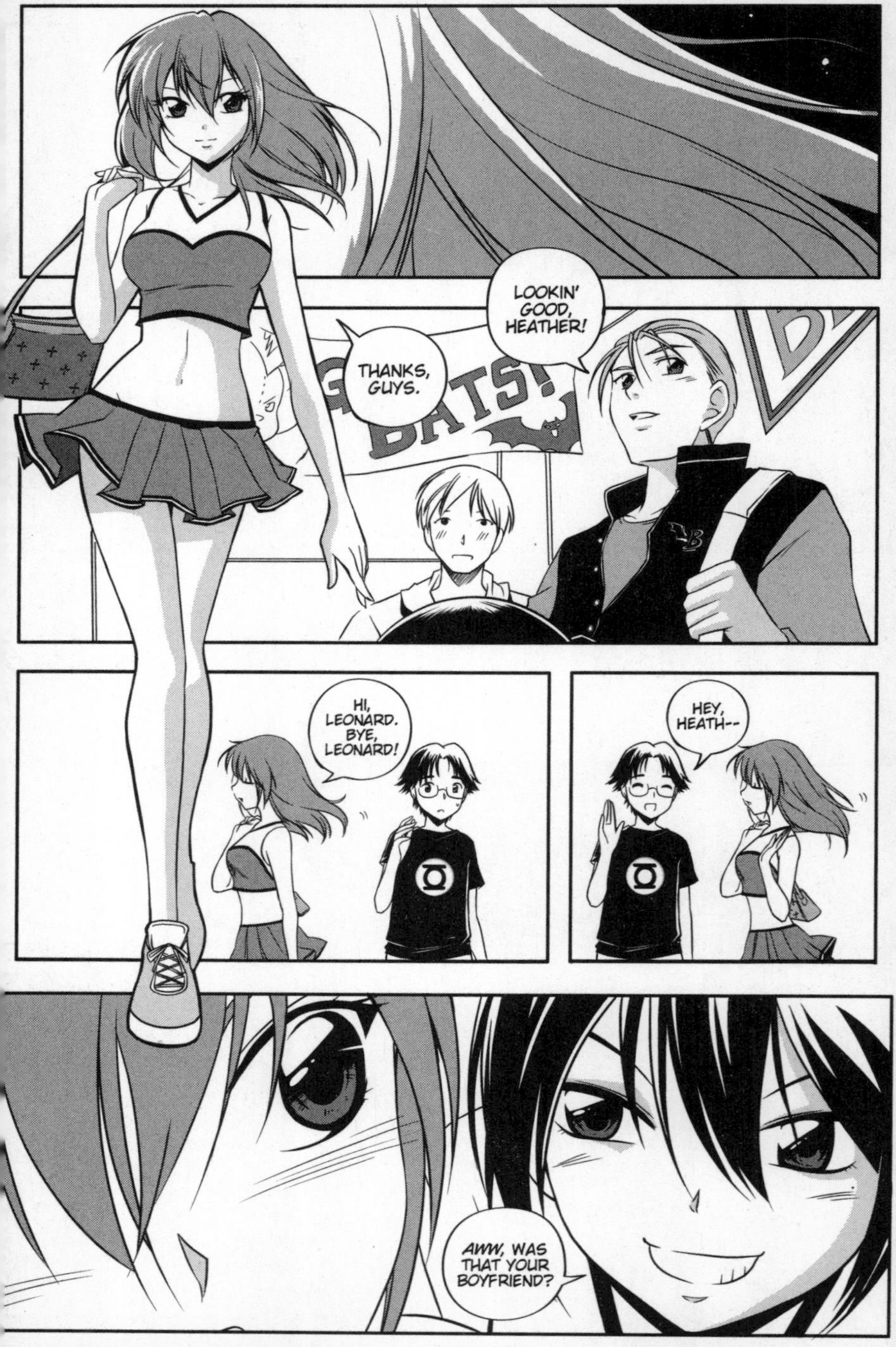
LOOKIN' GOOD, HEATHER!
THANKS, GUYS.
BATS!
HEY, HEATH--
HI, LEONARD. BYE, LEONARD!
AWW, WAS THAT YOUR BOYFRIEND?

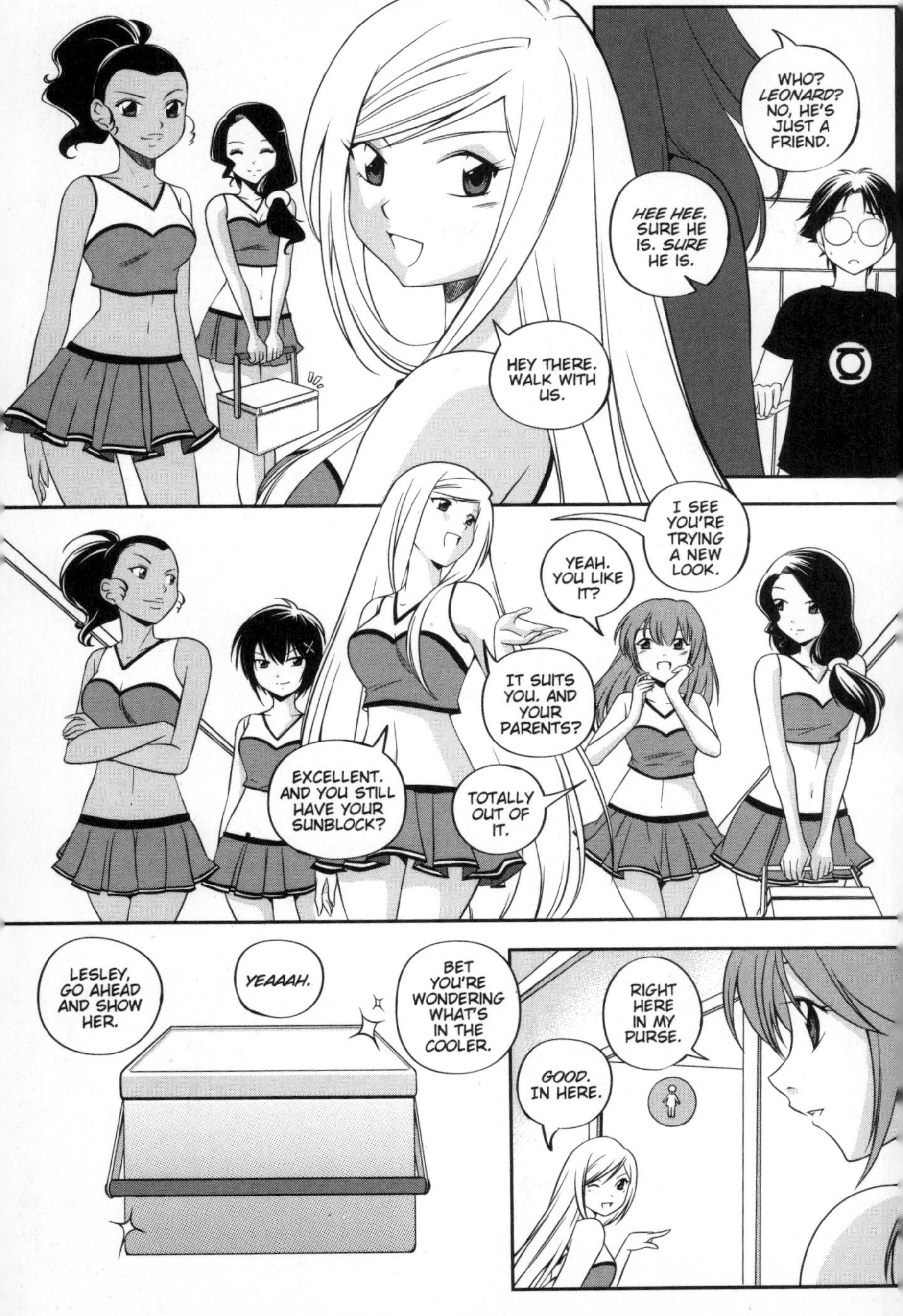
WHO? LEONARD? NO, HE'S JUST A FRIEND.
HEE HEE. SURE HE IS. SURE HE IS.
HEY THERE. WALK WITH US.
I SEE YOU'RE TRYING A NEW LOOK.
YEAH. YOU LIKE IT?
IT SUITS YOU. AND YOUR PARENTS?
TOTALLY OUT OF IT.
EXCELLENT. AND YOU STILL HAVE YOUR SUNBLOCK?
RIGHT HERE IN MY PURSE.
GOOD. IN HERE.
BET YOU'RE WONDERING WHAT'S IN THE COOLER.
YEAAAH.
LESLEY, GO AHEAD AND SHOW HER.

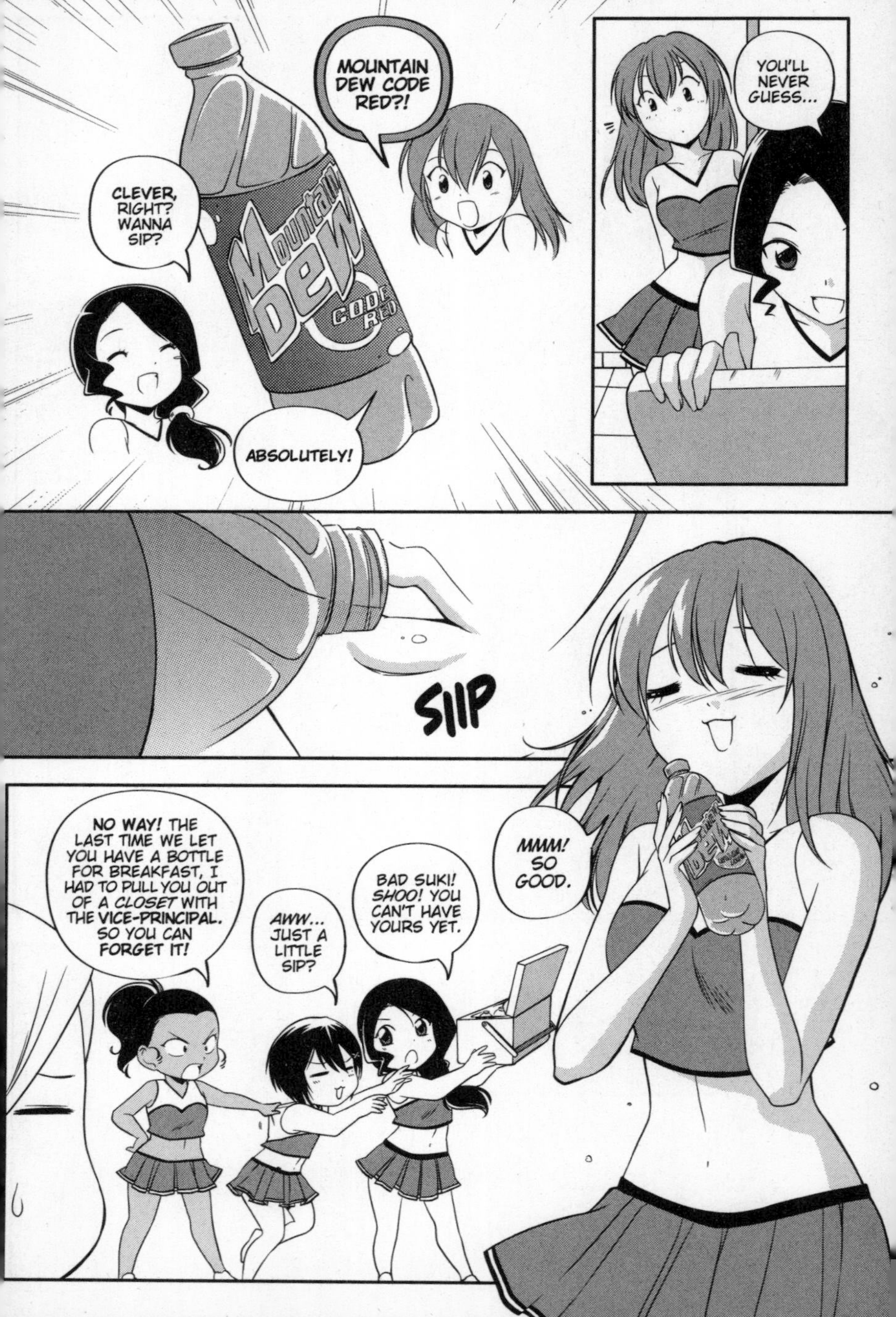
YOU'LL NEVER GUESS...
MOUNTAIN DEW CODE RED?!
CLEVER, RIGHT? WANNA SIP?
Mountain Dew
CODE RED
ABSOLUTELY!
SIIP
MMM! SO GOOD.
BAD SUKI! SHOO! YOU CAN'T HAVE YOURS YET.
AWW... JUST A LITTLE SIP?
NO WAY! THE LAST TIME WE LET YOU HAVE A BOTTLE FOR BREAKFAST, I HAD TO PULL YOU OUT OF A CLOSET WITH THE VICE-PRINCIPAL. SO YOU CAN FORGET IT!

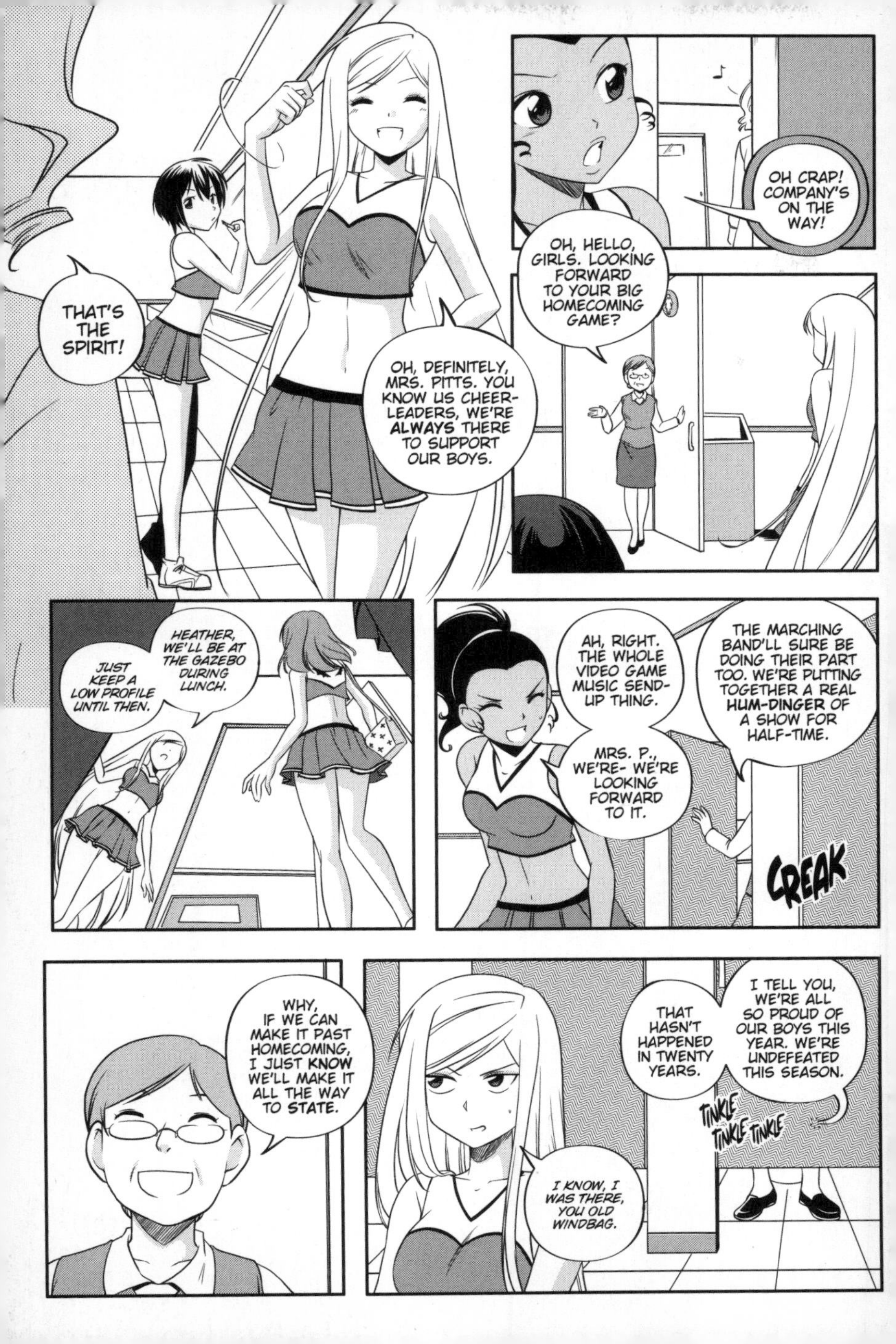
OH CRAP! COMPANY'S ON THE WAY!
OH, HELLO, GIRLS. LOOKING FORWARD TO YOUR BIG HOMECOMING GAME?
OH, DEFINITELY, MRS. PITTS. YOU KNOW US CHEER-LEADERS, WE'RE **ALWAYS** THERE TO SUPPORT OUR BOYS.
THAT'S THE SPIRIT!
THE MARCHING BAND'LL SURE BE DOING THEIR PART TOO. WE'RE PUTTING TOGETHER A REAL **HUM-DINGER** OF A SHOW FOR HALF-TIME.
AH, RIGHT. THE WHOLE VIDEO GAME MUSIC SEND-UP THING.
MRS. P., WE'RE- WE'RE LOOKING FORWARD TO IT.
CREAK
HEATHER, WE'LL BE AT THE GAZEBO DURING LUNCH.
JUST KEEP A LOW PROFILE UNTIL THEN.
I TELL YOU, WE'RE ALL SO PROUD OF OUR BOYS THIS YEAR. WE'RE UNDEFEATED THIS SEASON.
THAT HASN'T HAPPENED IN TWENTY YEARS.
TINKLE TINKLE TINKLE
I KNOW, I WAS THERE, YOU OLD WINDBAG.
WHY, IF WE CAN MAKE IT PAST HOMECOMING, I JUST **KNOW** WE'LL MAKE IT ALL THE WAY TO **STATE**.

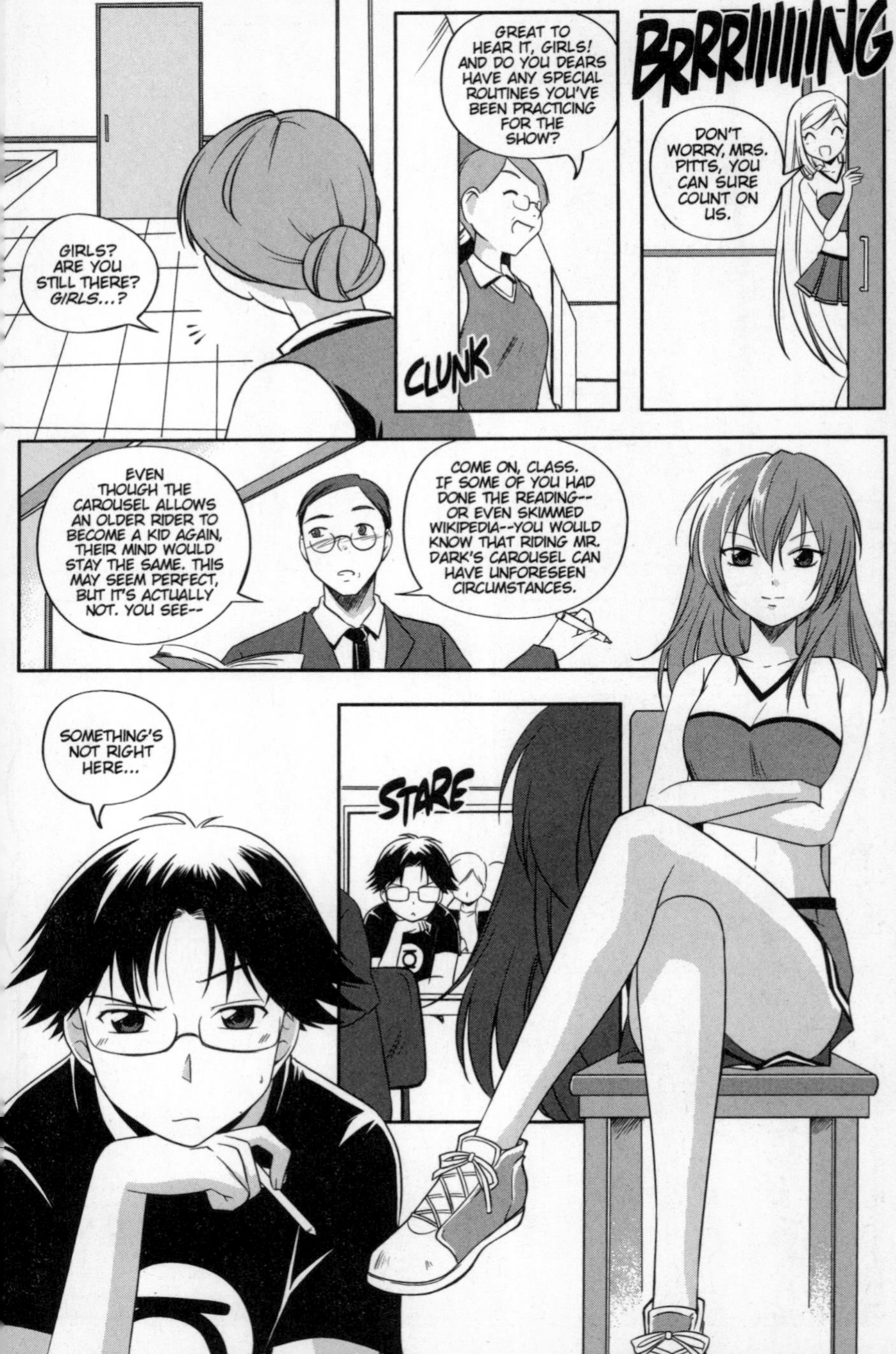
BRRRIIIIIING
DON'T WORRY, MRS. PITTS, YOU CAN SURE COUNT ON US.
GREAT TO HEAR IT, GIRLS! AND DO YOU DEARS HAVE ANY SPECIAL ROUTINES YOU'VE BEEN PRACTICING FOR THE SHOW?
CLUNK
GIRLS? ARE YOU STILL THERE? GIRLS...?
COME ON, CLASS. IF SOME OF YOU HAD DONE THE READING--OR EVEN SKIMMED WIKIPEDIA--YOU WOULD KNOW THAT RIDING MR. DARK'S CAROUSEL CAN HAVE UNFORESEEN CIRCUMSTANCES.
EVEN THOUGH THE CAROUSEL ALLOWS AN OLDER RIDER TO BECOME A KID AGAIN, THEIR MIND WOULD STAY THE SAME. THIS MAY SEEM PERFECT, BUT IT'S ACTUALLY NOT. YOU SEE--
STARE
SOMETHING'S NOT RIGHT HERE...

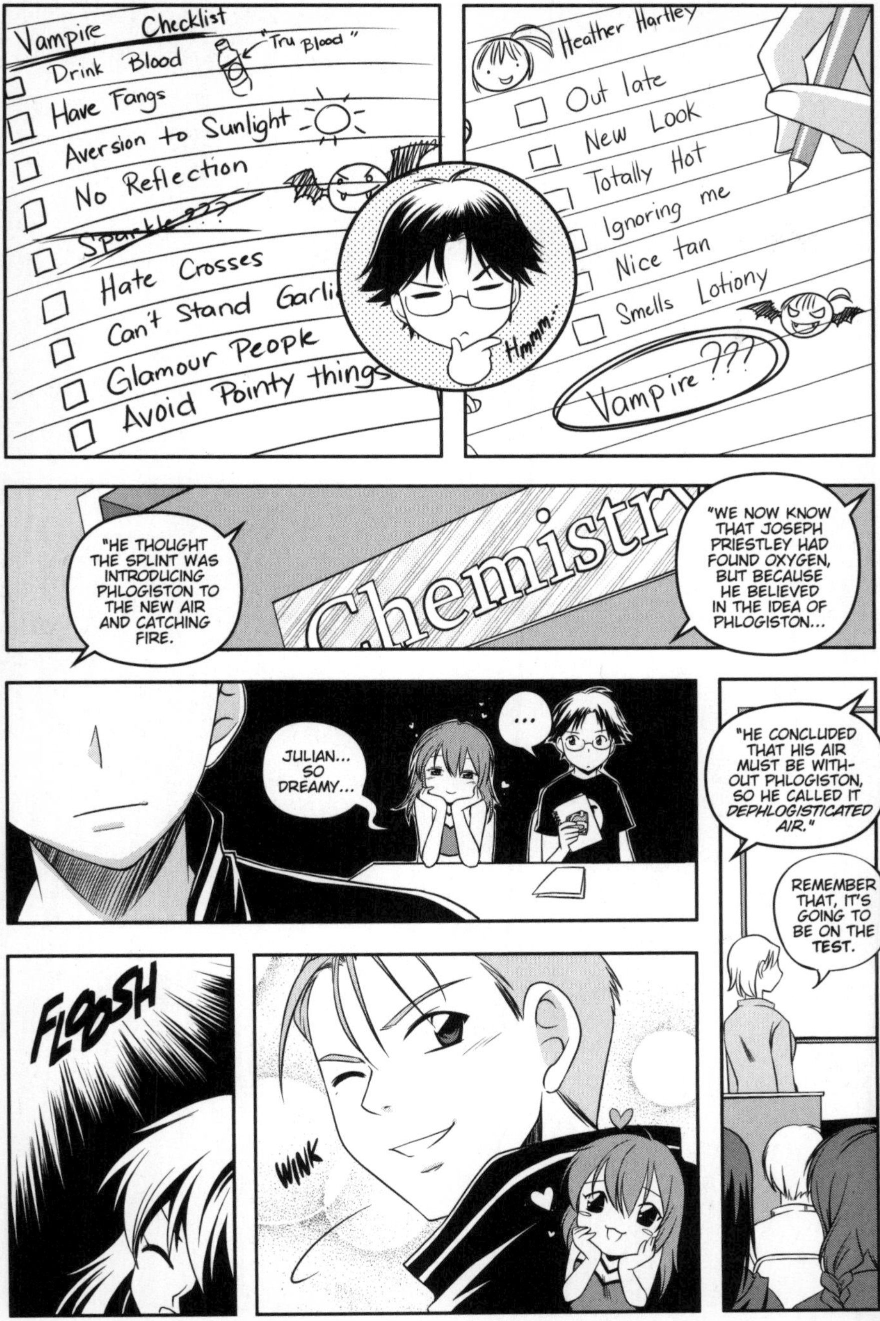

Heather Hartley
Out late
New Look
Totally Hot
Ignoring me
Nice tan
Smells Lotiony
Vampire ???
Hmmm...
Vampire Checklist
Drink Blood
"Tru Blood"
Have Fangs
Aversion to Sunlight
No Reflection
~~Sparkle???~~
Hate Crosses
Can't Stand Garli
Glamour People
Avoid Pointy things
Chemistry
"WE NOW KNOW THAT JOSEPH PRIESTLEY HAD FOUND OXYGEN, BUT BECAUSE HE BELIEVED IN THE IDEA OF PHLOGISTON...
"HE THOUGHT THE SPLINT WAS INTRODUCING PHLOGISTON TO THE NEW AIR AND CATCHING FIRE.
"HE CONCLUDED THAT HIS AIR MUST BE WITH-OUT PHLOGISTON, SO HE CALLED IT *DEPHLOGISTICATED AIR.*"
REMEMBER THAT, IT'S GOING TO BE ON THE TEST.
...
JULIAN... SO DREAMY...
WINK
FLOOSH

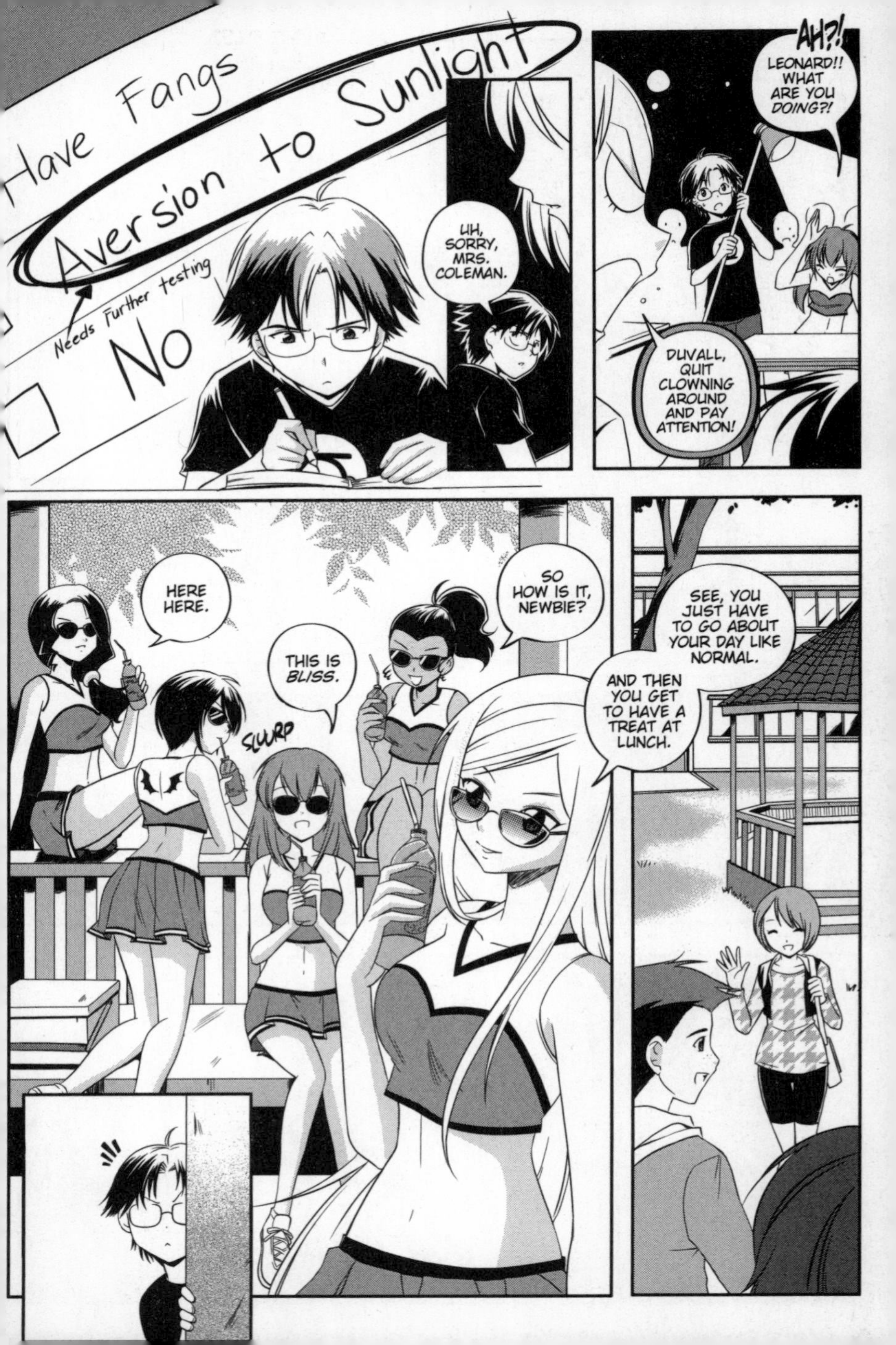
AH?!
LEONARD!! WHAT ARE YOU DOING?!
DUVALL, QUIT CLOWNING AROUND AND PAY ATTENTION!
UH, SORRY, MRS. COLEMAN.
Have Fangs
Aversion to Sunlight
Needs Further testing
No
SEE, YOU JUST HAVE TO GO ABOUT YOUR DAY LIKE NORMAL.
AND THEN YOU GET TO HAVE A TREAT AT LUNCH.
SO HOW IS IT, NEWBIE?
THIS IS BLISS.
HERE HERE.
SLURP

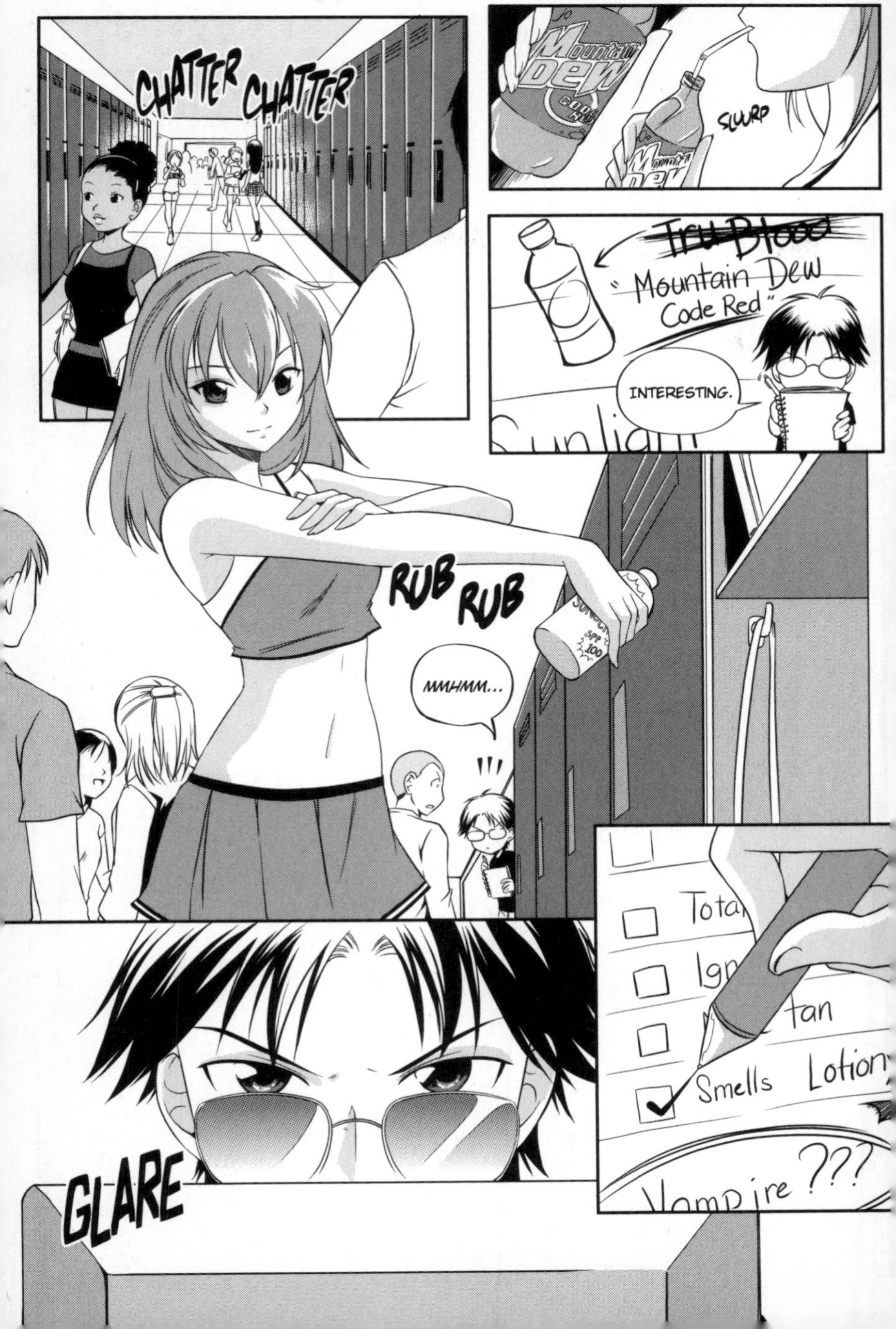
SLUURP
Tru Blood
"Mountain Dew Code Red"
INTERESTING.
CHATTER CHATTER
RUB RUB
MMHMM...
!!!
tan
Smells Lotion
Vampire ???
GLARE

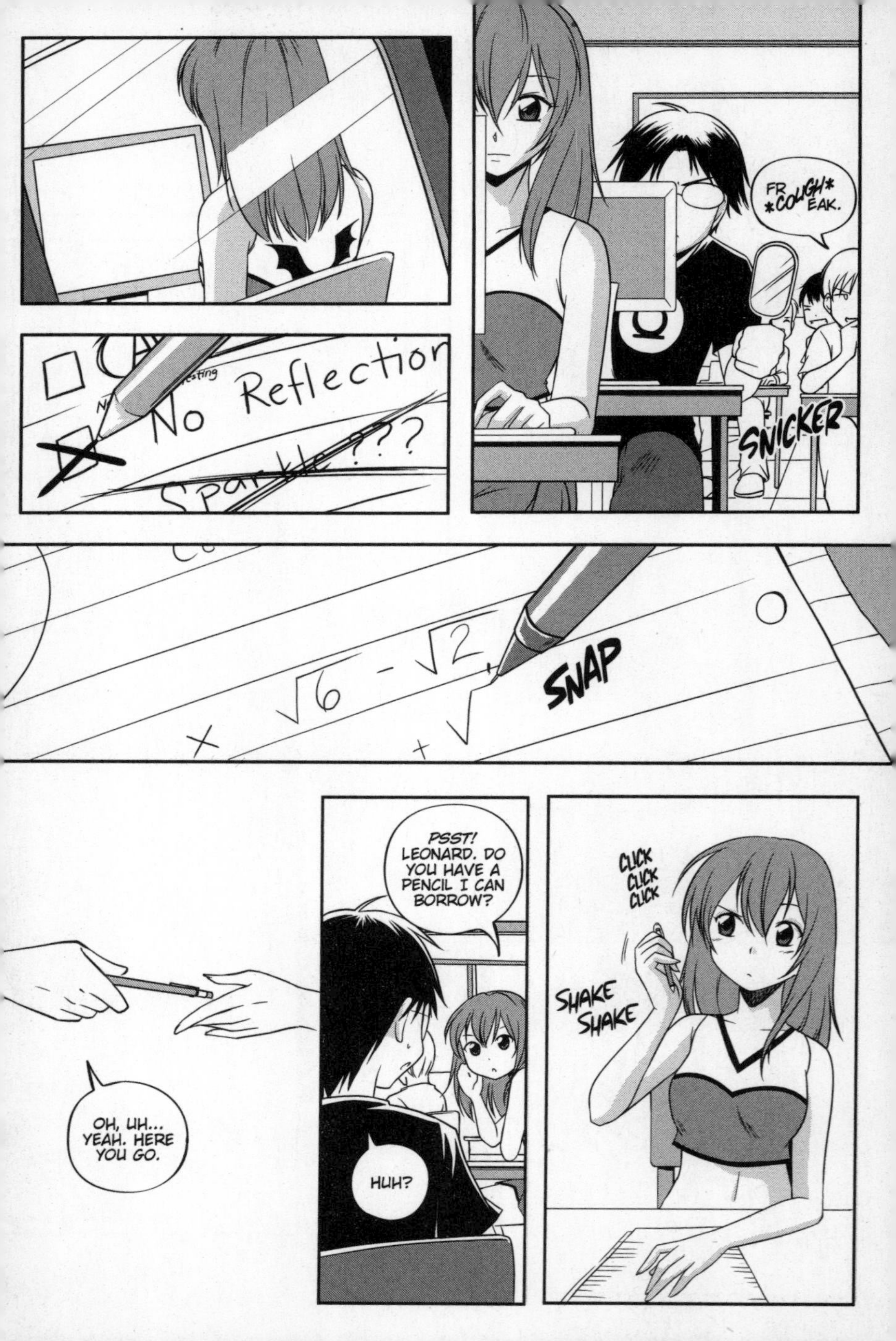
FR *COUGH* EAK.
SNICKER
No Reflection
Sparkle???
SNAP
CLICK CLICK CLICK
SHAKE SHAKE
PSST! LEONARD. DO YOU HAVE A PENCIL I CAN BORROW?
HUH?
OH, UH... YEAH. HERE YOU GO.

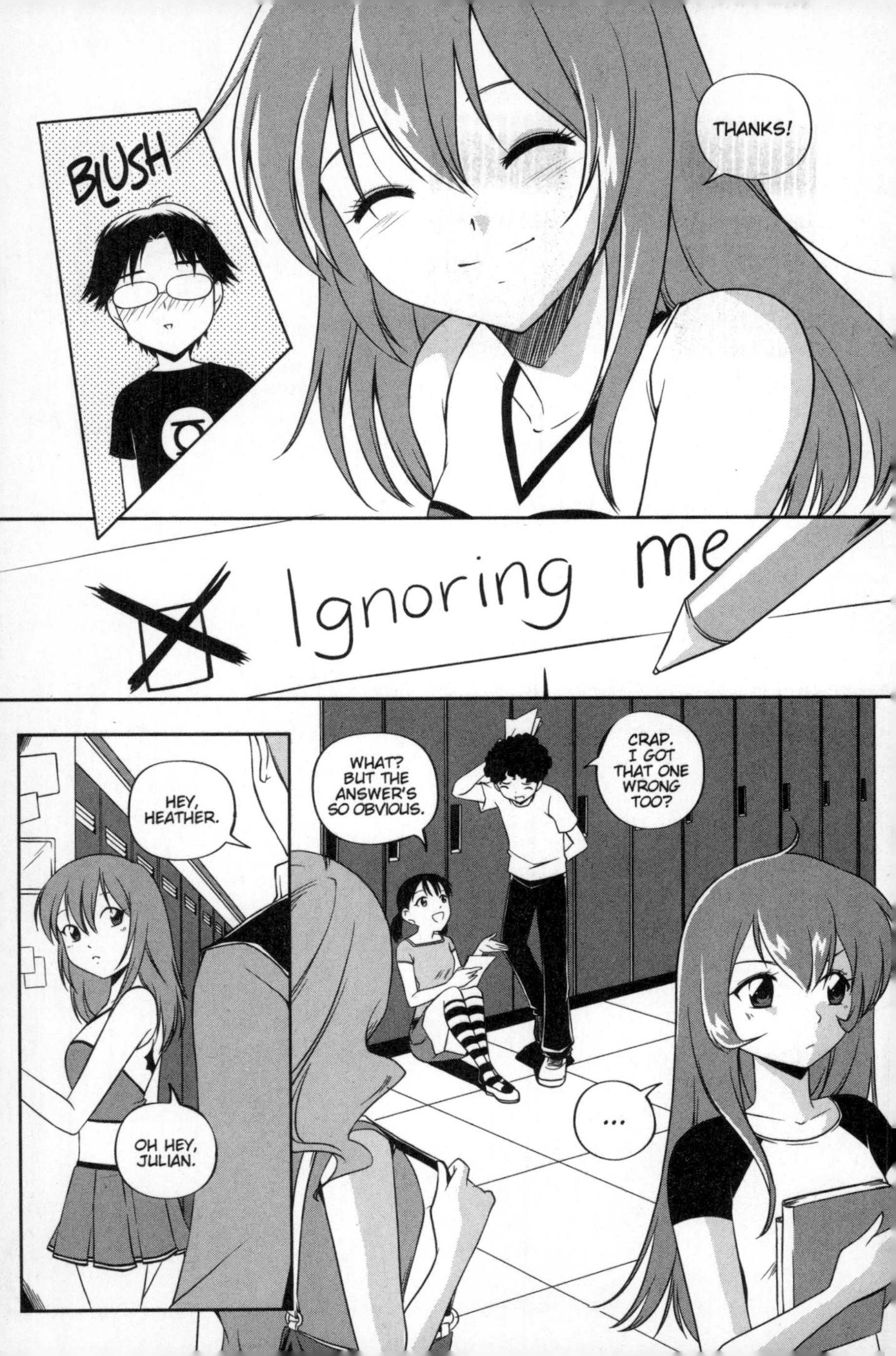
THANKS!
BLUSH
Ignoring me
CRAP. I GOT THAT ONE WRONG TOO?
WHAT? BUT THE ANSWER'S SO OBVIOUS.
...
HEY, HEATHER.
OH HEY, JULIAN.

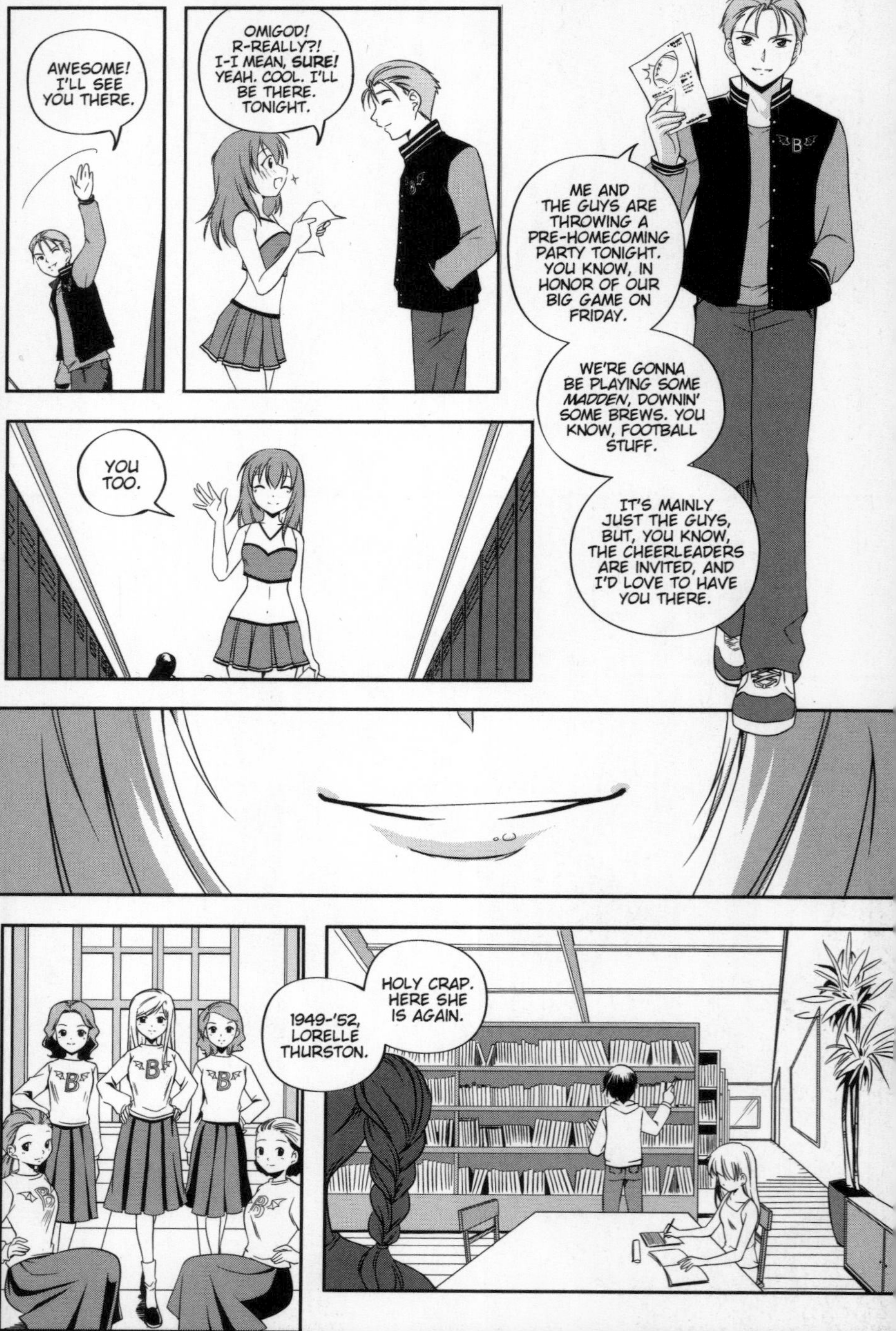
ME AND THE GUYS ARE THROWING A PRE-HOMECOMING PARTY TONIGHT. YOU KNOW, IN HONOR OF OUR BIG GAME ON FRIDAY.
WE'RE GONNA BE PLAYING SOME *MADDEN*, DOWNIN' SOME BREWS. YOU KNOW, FOOTBALL STUFF.
IT'S MAINLY JUST THE GUYS, BUT, YOU KNOW, THE CHEERLEADERS ARE INVITED, AND I'D LOVE TO HAVE YOU THERE.
OMIGOD! R-REALLY?! I-I MEAN, SURE! YEAH. COOL. I'LL BE THERE. TONIGHT.
AWESOME! I'LL SEE YOU THERE.
YOU TOO.
HOLY CRAP. HERE SHE IS AGAIN.
1949-'52, LORELLE THURSTON.

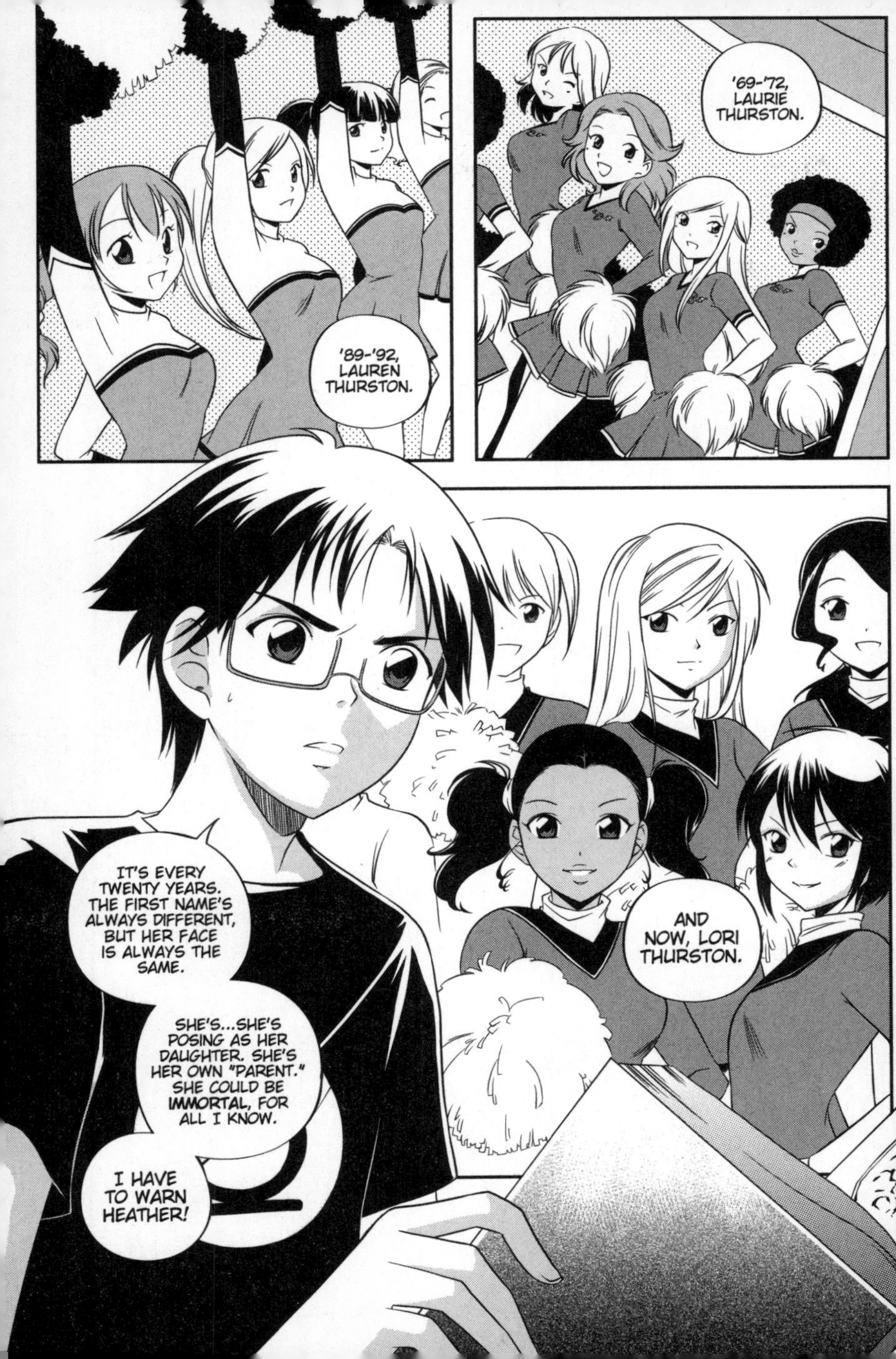
'69-'72, LAURIE THURSTON.
'89-'92, LAUREN THURSTON.
AND NOW, LORI THURSTON.
IT'S EVERY TWENTY YEARS. THE FIRST NAME'S ALWAYS DIFFERENT, BUT HER FACE IS ALWAYS THE SAME.
SHE'S...SHE'S POSING AS HER DAUGHTER. SHE'S HER OWN "PARENT." SHE COULD BE **IMMORTAL**, FOR ALL I KNOW.
I HAVE TO WARN HEATHER!

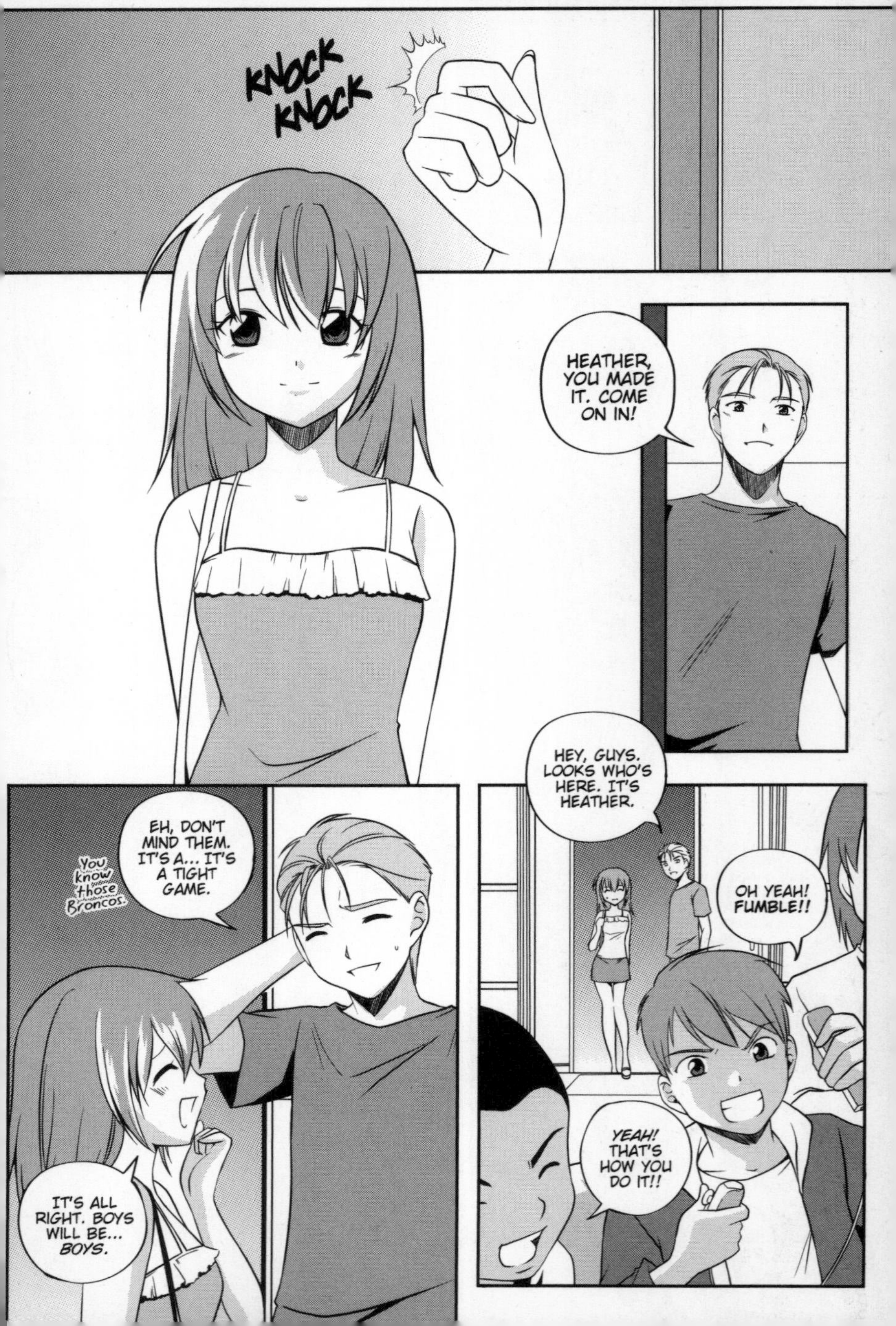

KNOCK KNOCK
HEATHER, YOU MADE IT. COME ON IN!
HEY, GUYS. LOOKS WHO'S HERE. IT'S HEATHER.
OH YEAH! FUMBLE!!
YEAH! THAT'S HOW YOU DO IT!!
EH, DON'T MIND THEM. IT'S A... IT'S A TIGHT GAME.
You know those Broncos.
IT'S ALL RIGHT. BOYS WILL BE... BOYS.

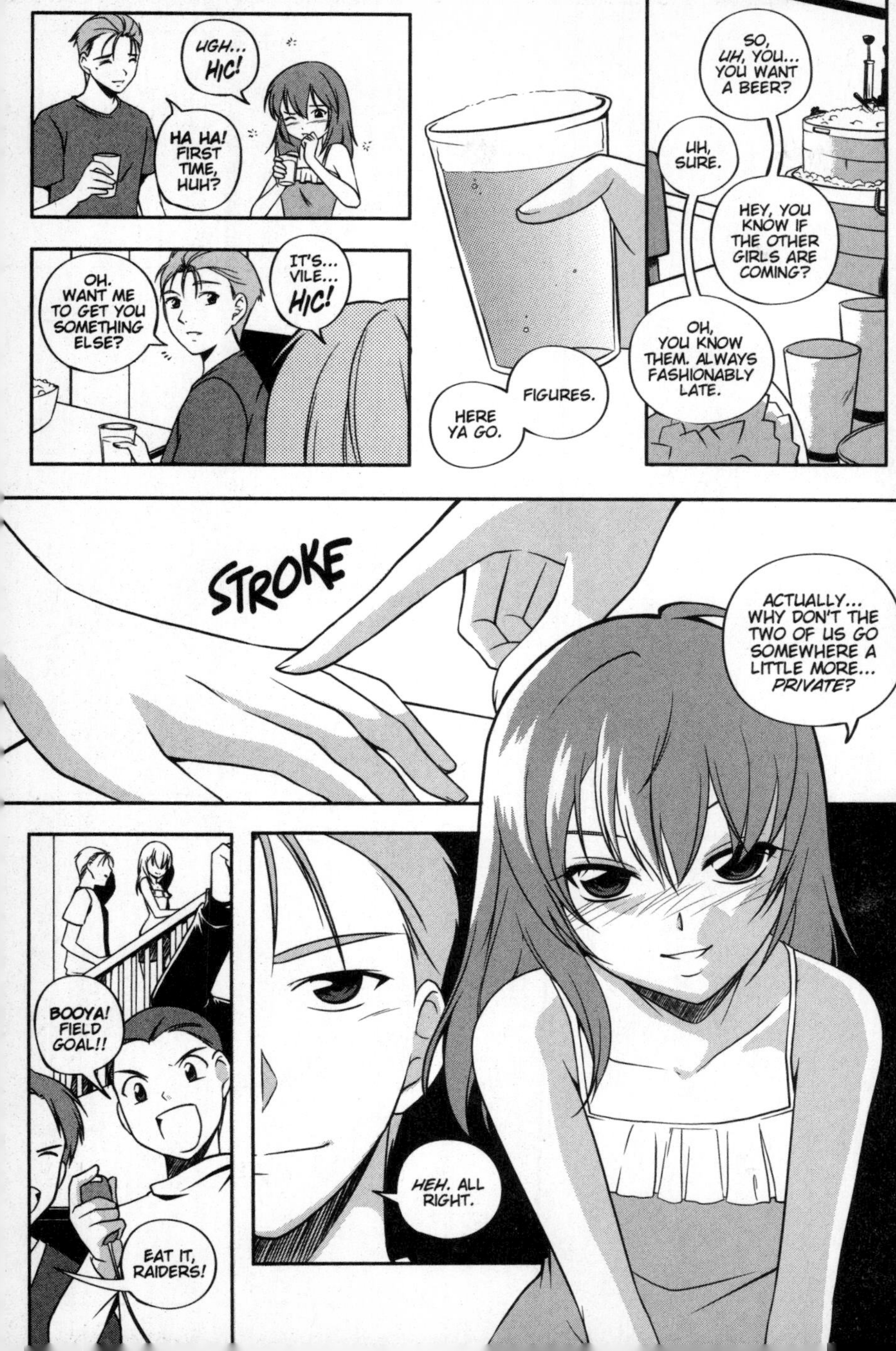

SO, UH, YOU... YOU WANT A BEER?
UH, SURE.
HEY, YOU KNOW IF THE OTHER GIRLS ARE COMING?
OH, YOU KNOW THEM. ALWAYS FASHIONABLY LATE.
FIGURES.
HERE YA GO.
UGH... HIC!
HA HA! FIRST TIME, HUH?
IT'S... VILE... HIC!
OH. WANT ME TO GET YOU SOMETHING ELSE?
STROKE
ACTUALLY... WHY DON'T THE TWO OF US GO SOMEWHERE A LITTLE MORE... *PRIVATE?*
HEH. ALL RIGHT.
BOOYA! FIELD GOAL!!
EAT IT, RAIDERS!

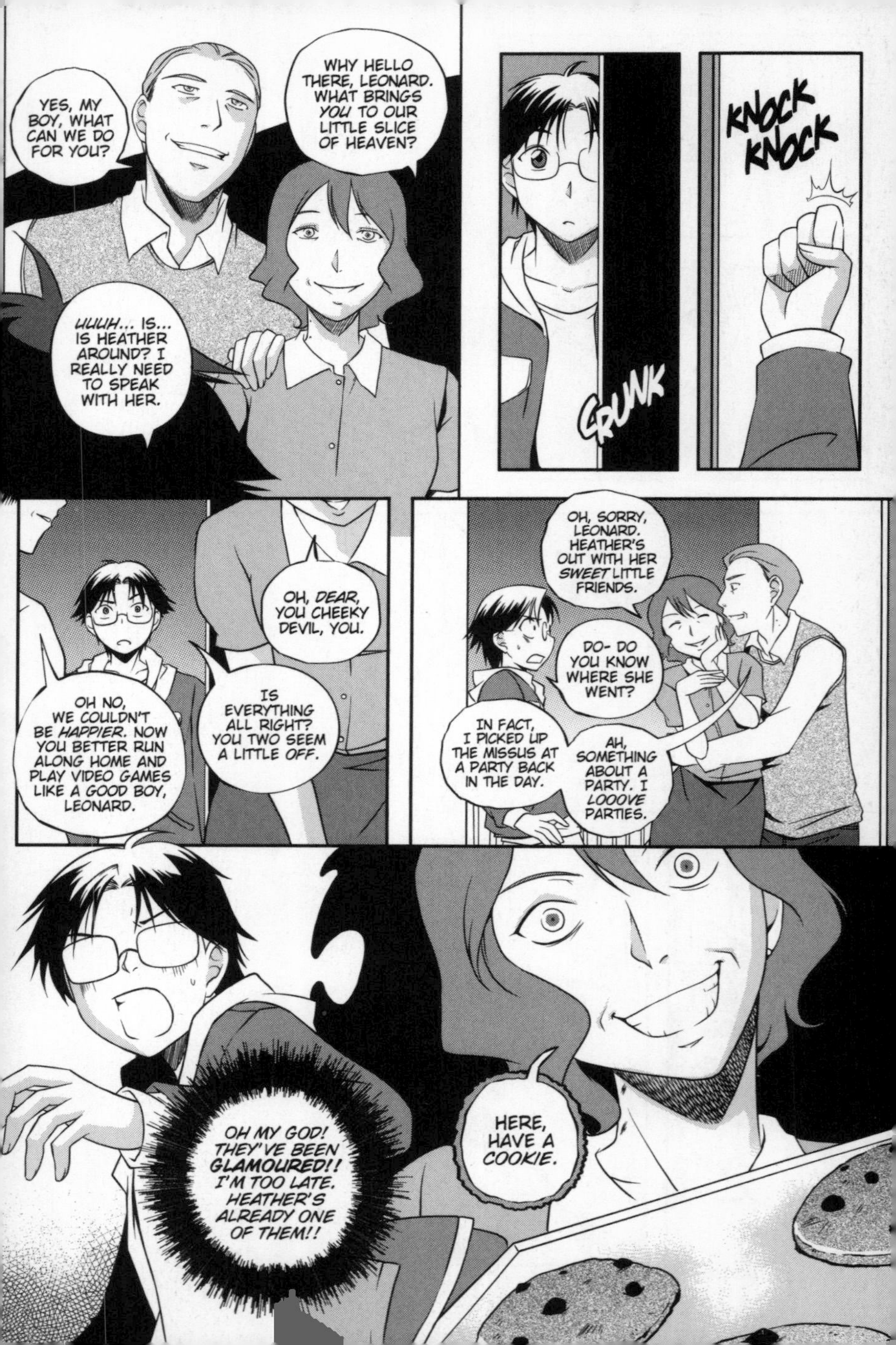

KNOCK KNOCK
CRUNK
WHY HELLO THERE, LEONARD. WHAT BRINGS YOU TO OUR LITTLE SLICE OF HEAVEN?
YES, MY BOY, WHAT CAN WE DO FOR YOU?
UUUH... IS... IS HEATHER AROUND? I REALLY NEED TO SPEAK WITH HER.
OH, SORRY, LEONARD. HEATHER'S OUT WITH HER SWEET LITTLE FRIENDS.
DO- DO YOU KNOW WHERE SHE WENT?
AH, SOMETHING ABOUT A PARTY. I LOOOVE PARTIES.
IN FACT, I PICKED UP THE MISSUS AT A PARTY BACK IN THE DAY.
OH, DEAR, YOU CHEEKY DEVIL, YOU.
IS EVERYTHING ALL RIGHT? YOU TWO SEEM A LITTLE OFF.
OH NO, WE COULDN'T BE HAPPIER. NOW YOU BETTER RUN ALONG HOME AND PLAY VIDEO GAMES LIKE A GOOD BOY, LEONARD.
HERE, HAVE A COOKIE.
OH MY GOD! THEY'VE BEEN GLAMOURED!! I'M TOO LATE. HEATHER'S ALREADY ONE OF THEM!!

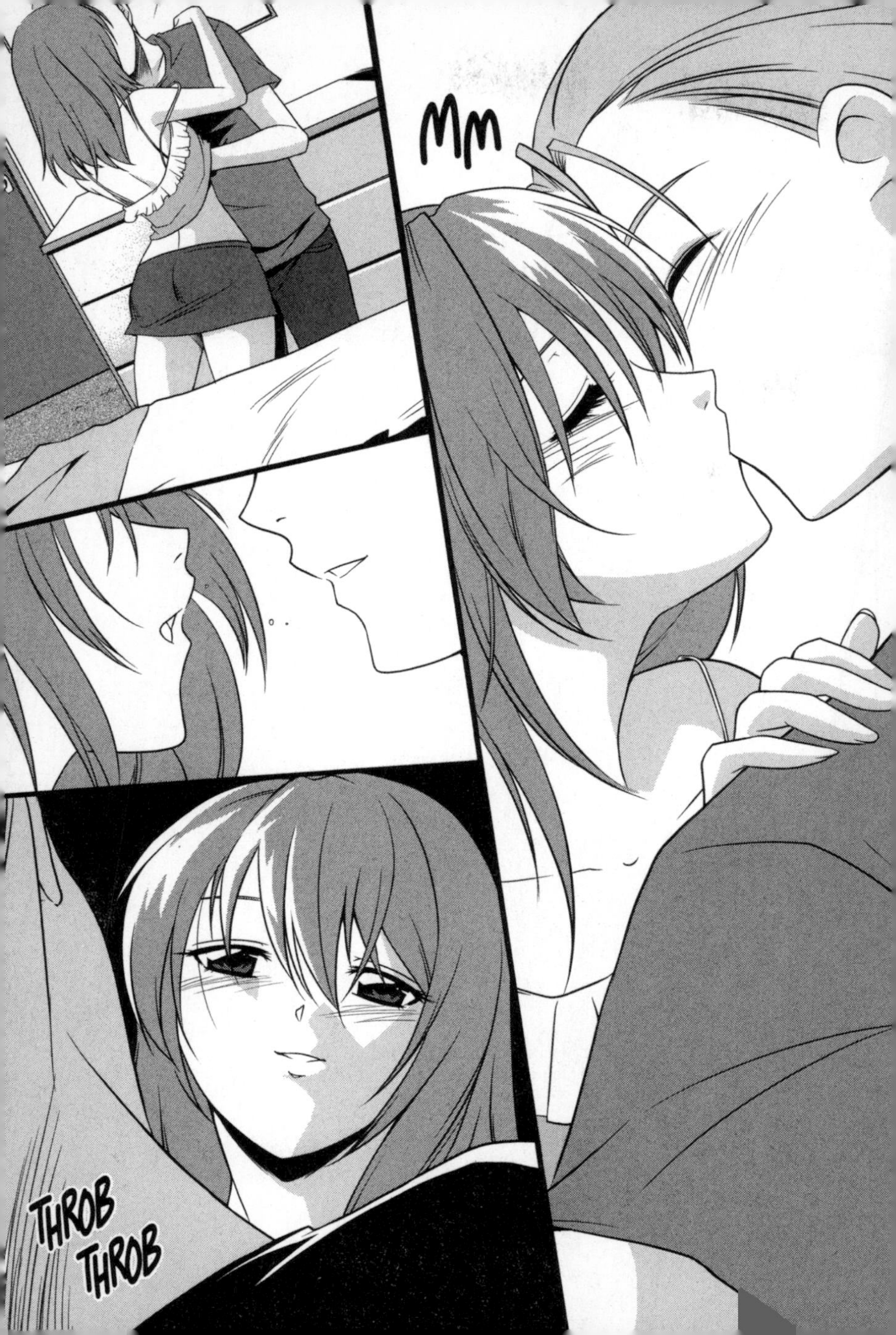
MM
THROB THROB

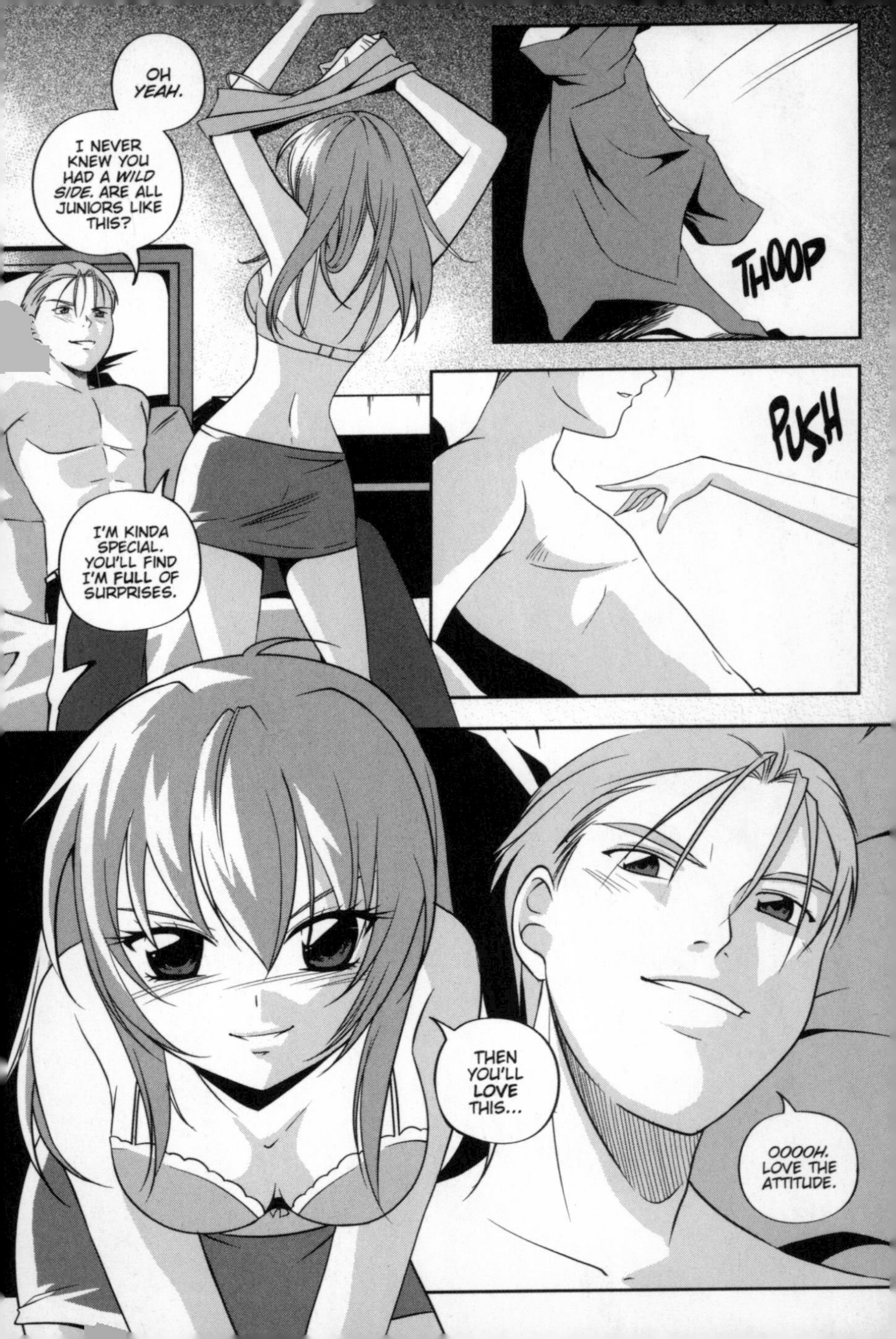
THOOP
PUSH
OH YEAH.
I NEVER KNEW YOU HAD A WILD SIDE. ARE ALL JUNIORS LIKE THIS?
I'M KINDA SPECIAL. YOU'LL FIND I'M FULL OF SURPRISES.
THEN YOU'LL LOVE THIS...
OOOOH. LOVE THE ATTITUDE.

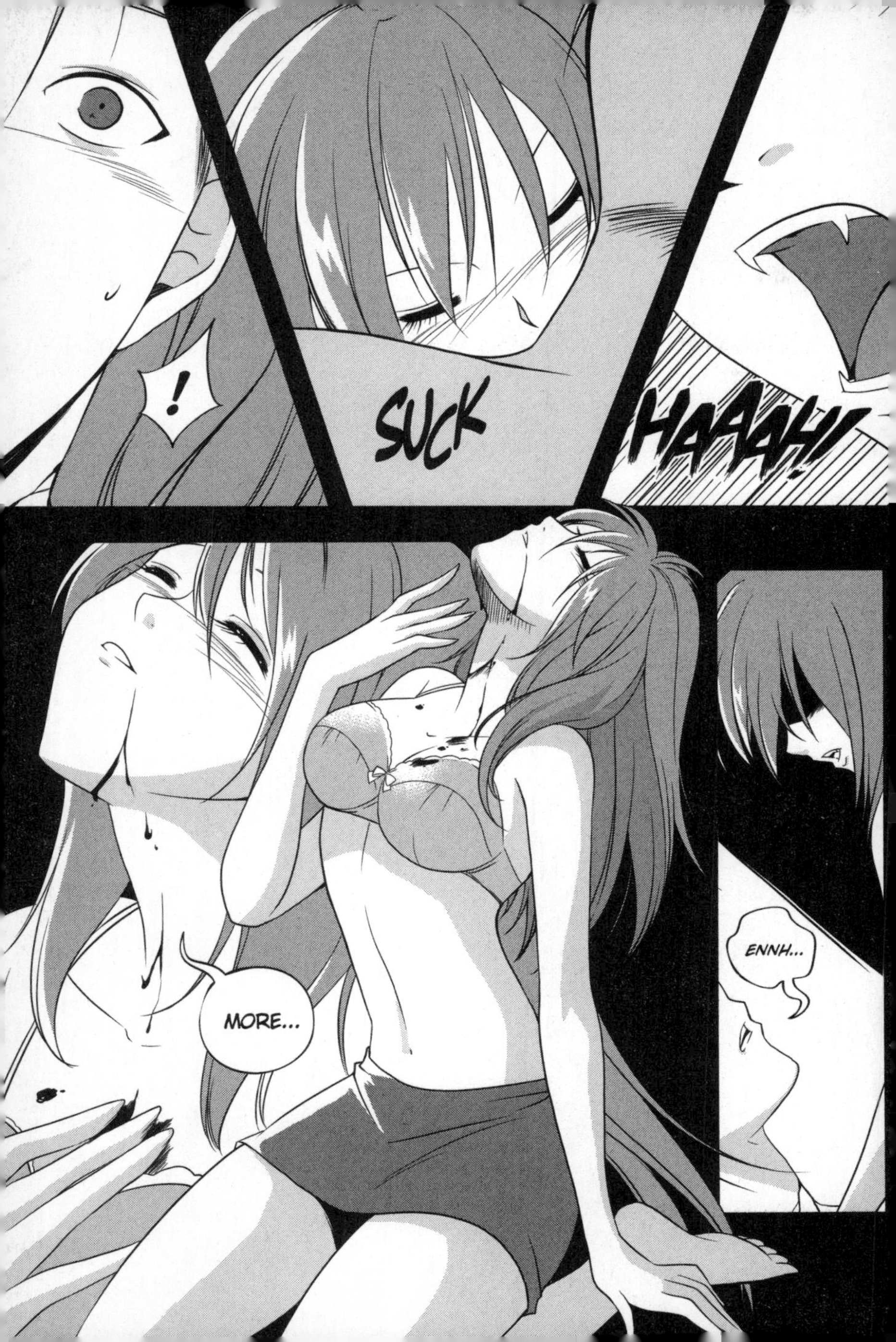
HAAAH!
SUCK
!
ENNH...
MORE...

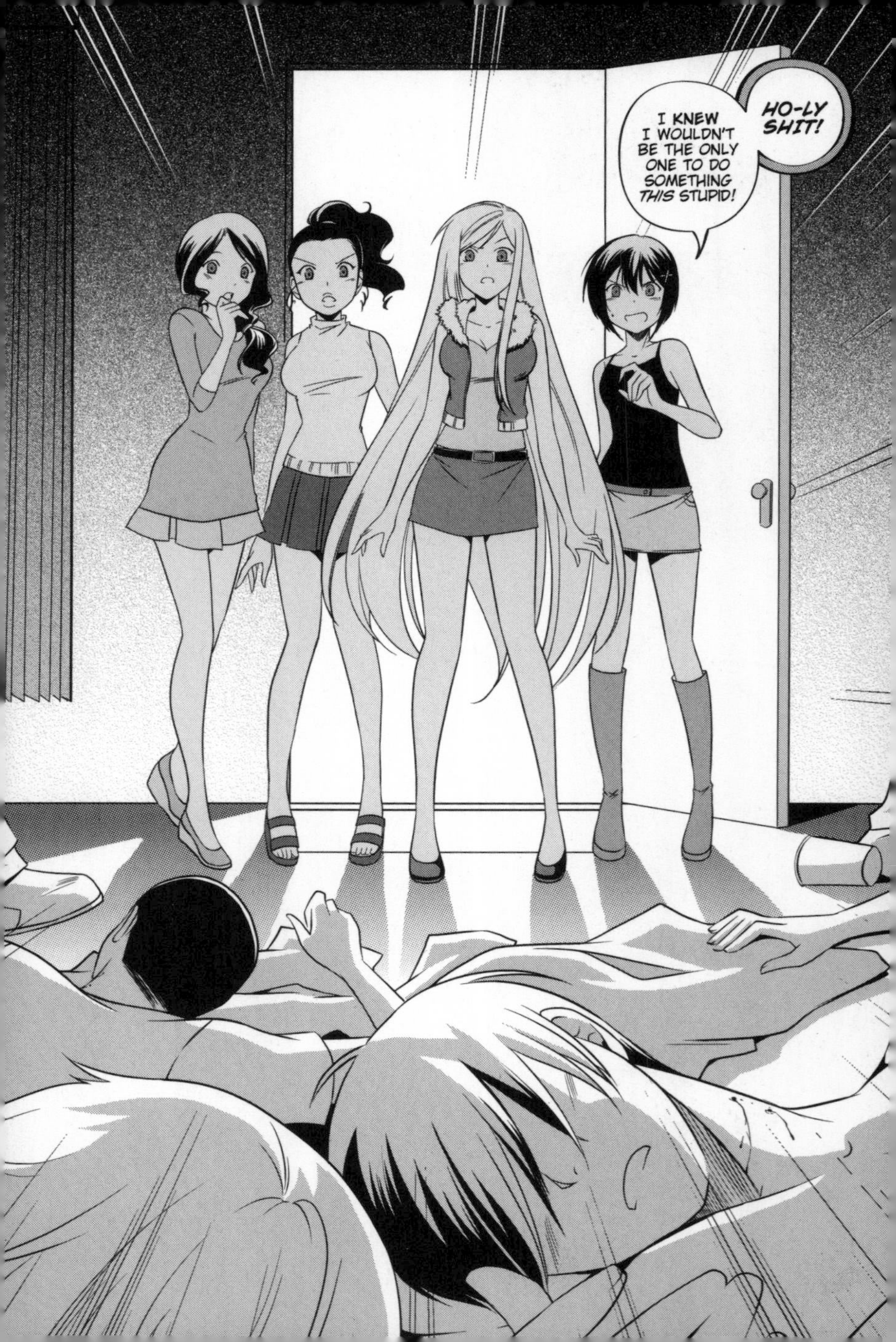
HO-LY SHIT!
I KNEW I WOULDN'T BE THE ONLY ONE TO DO SOMETHING THIS STUPID!

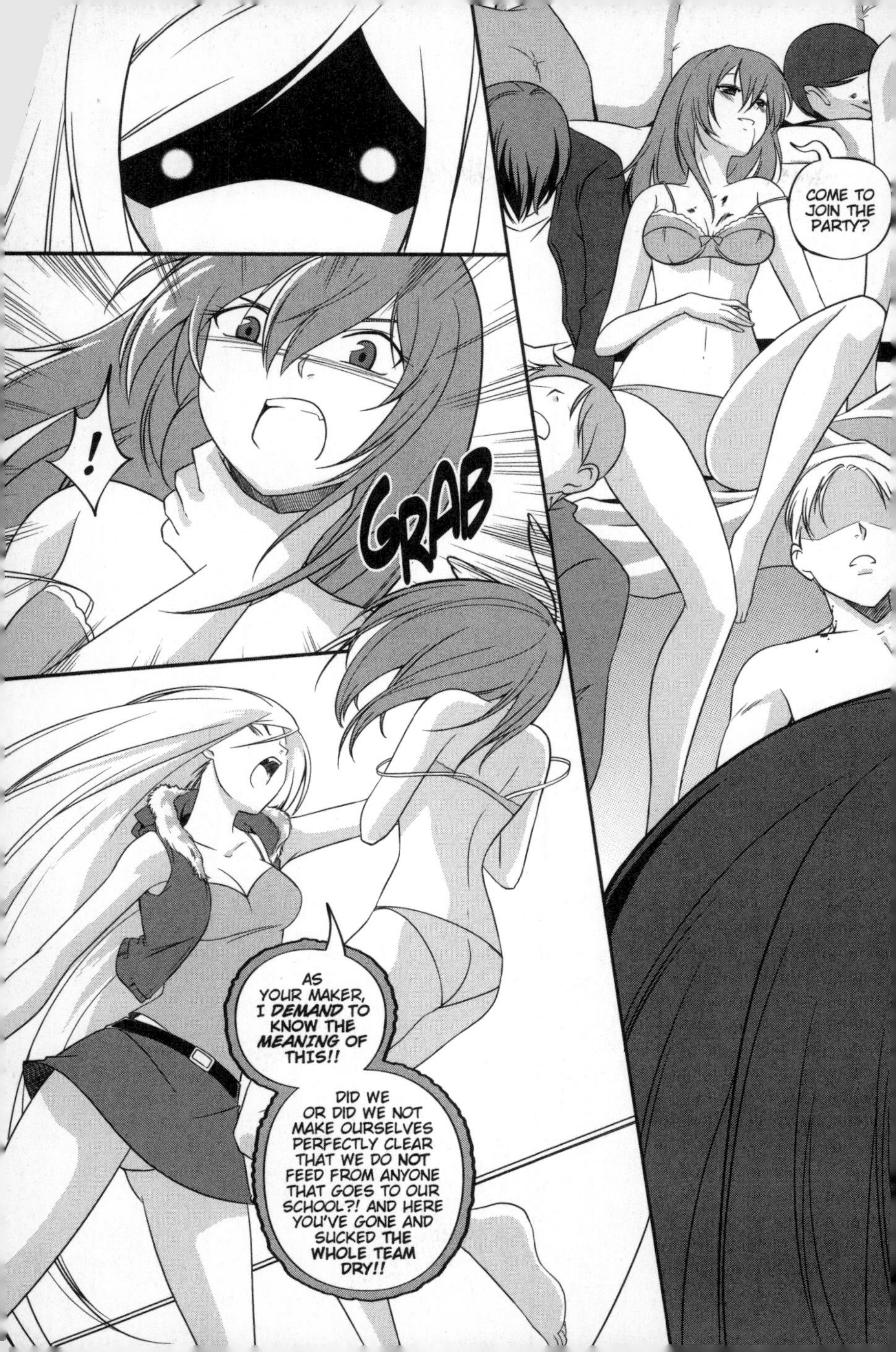
COME TO JOIN THE PARTY?
!
GRAB
AS YOUR MAKER, I *DEMAND* TO KNOW THE *MEANING* OF THIS!!
DID WE OR DID WE NOT MAKE OURSELVES PERFECTLY CLEAR THAT WE DO **NOT** FEED FROM ANYONE THAT GOES TO OUR SCHOOL?! AND HERE YOU'VE GONE AND SUCKED THE **WHOLE TEAM** DRY!!

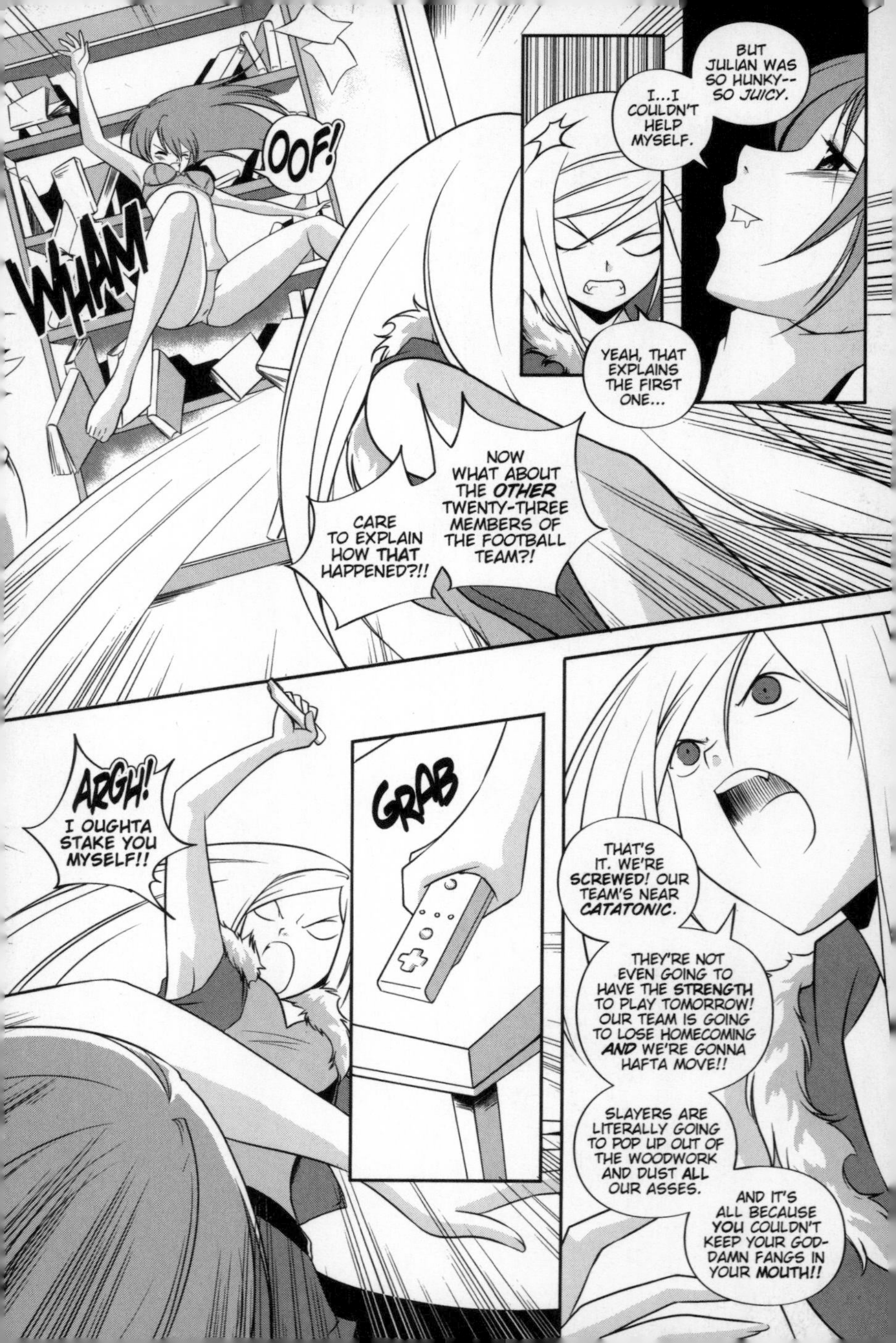
BUT JULIAN WAS SO HUNKY-- SO JUICY.
I...I COULDN'T HELP MYSELF.
YEAH, THAT EXPLAINS THE FIRST ONE...
NOW WHAT ABOUT THE OTHER TWENTY-THREE MEMBERS OF THE FOOTBALL TEAM?!
CARE TO EXPLAIN HOW THAT HAPPENED?!!
OOF!
WHAM
THAT'S IT. WE'RE SCREWED! OUR TEAM'S NEAR CATATONIC.
THEY'RE NOT EVEN GOING TO HAVE THE STRENGTH TO PLAY TOMORROW! OUR TEAM IS GOING TO LOSE HOMECOMING AND WE'RE GONNA HAFTA MOVE!!
SLAYERS ARE LITERALLY GOING TO POP UP OUT OF THE WOODWORK AND DUST ALL OUR ASSES.
AND IT'S ALL BECAUSE YOU COULDN'T KEEP YOUR GOD-DAMN FANGS IN YOUR MOUTH!!
GRAB
ARGH! I OUGHTA STAKE YOU MYSELF!!

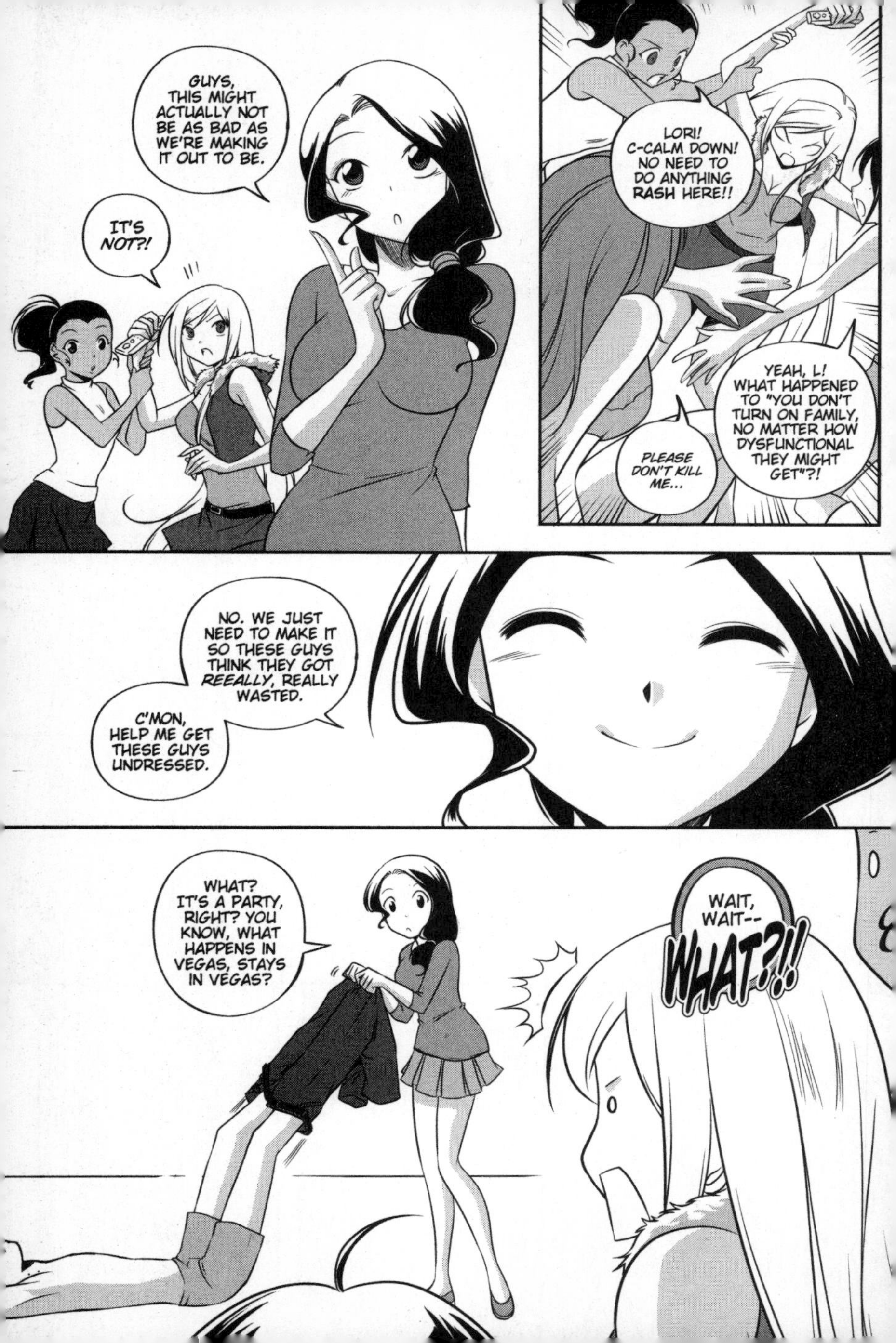
LORI! C-CALM DOWN! NO NEED TO DO ANYTHING RASH HERE!!
YEAH, L! WHAT HAPPENED TO "YOU DON'T TURN ON FAMILY, NO MATTER HOW DYSFUNCTIONAL THEY MIGHT GET"?!
PLEASE DON'T KILL ME...
GUYS, THIS MIGHT ACTUALLY NOT BE AS BAD AS WE'RE MAKING IT OUT TO BE.
IT'S NOT?!
NO. WE JUST NEED TO MAKE IT SO THESE GUYS THINK THEY GOT REEALLY, REALLY WASTED.
C'MON, HELP ME GET THESE GUYS UNDRESSED.
WAIT, WAIT--
WHAT?!!
WHAT? IT'S A PARTY, RIGHT? YOU KNOW, WHAT HAPPENS IN VEGAS, STAYS IN VEGAS?

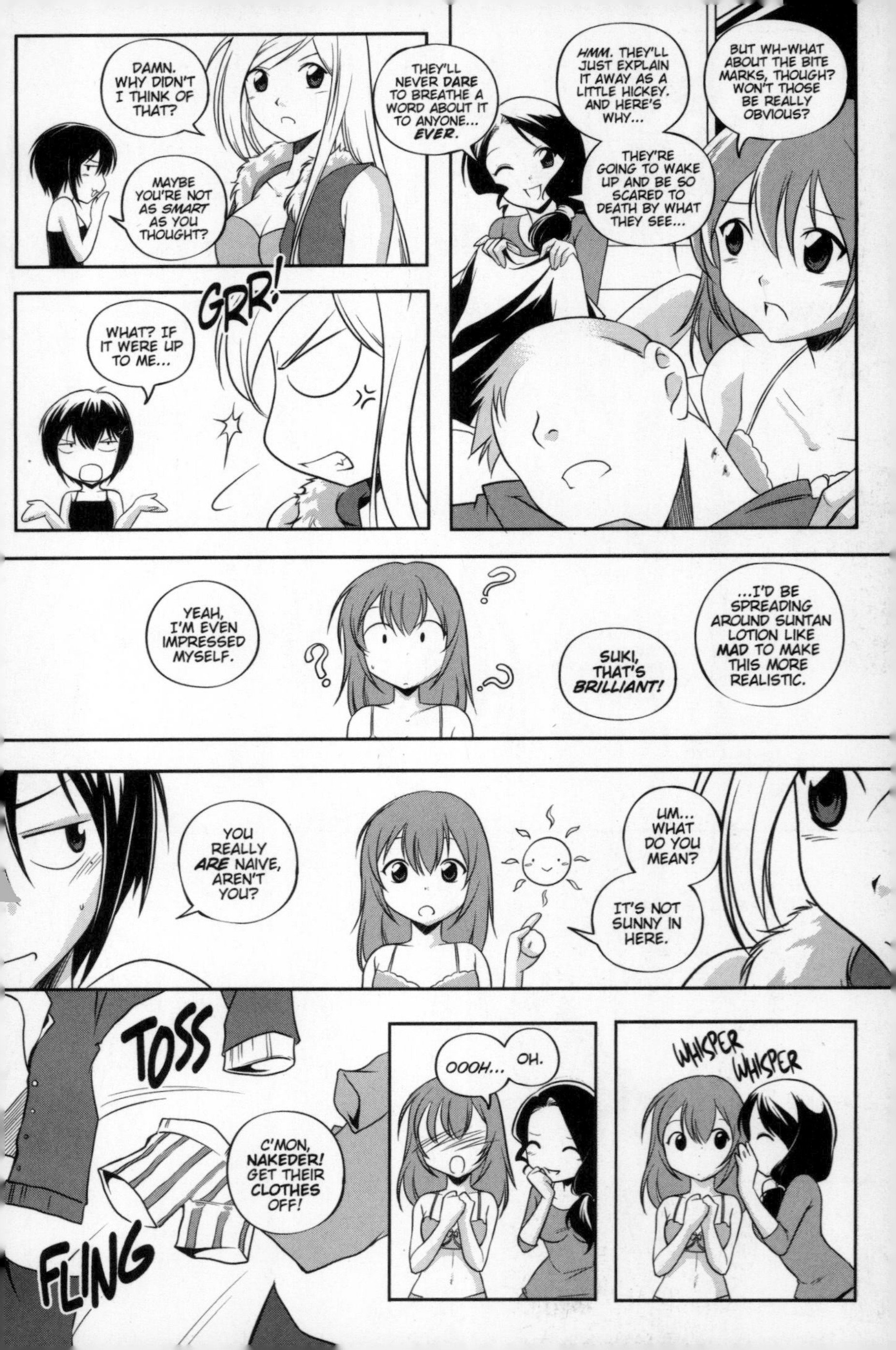
BUT WH-WHAT ABOUT THE BITE MARKS, THOUGH? WON'T THOSE BE REALLY OBVIOUS?
HMM. THEY'LL JUST EXPLAIN IT AWAY AS A LITTLE HICKEY. AND HERE'S WHY...
THEY'RE GOING TO WAKE UP AND BE SO SCARED TO DEATH BY WHAT THEY SEE...
THEY'LL NEVER **DARE** TO BREATHE A WORD ABOUT IT TO ANYONE... ***EVER.***
DAMN. WHY DIDN'T I THINK OF THAT?
MAYBE YOU'RE NOT AS *SMART* AS YOU THOUGHT?
GRR!
WHAT? IF IT WERE UP TO ME...
...I'D BE SPREADING AROUND SUNTAN LOTION LIKE **MAD** TO MAKE THIS MORE REALISTIC.
SUKI, THAT'S *BRILLIANT!*
YEAH, I'M EVEN IMPRESSED MYSELF.
UM... WHAT DO YOU MEAN?
IT'S NOT SUNNY IN HERE.
YOU REALLY ***ARE*** NAIVE, AREN'T YOU?
WHISPER WHISPER
OOOH... OH.
TOSS
C'MON, **NAKEDER!** GET THEIR **CLOTHES** OFF!
FLING

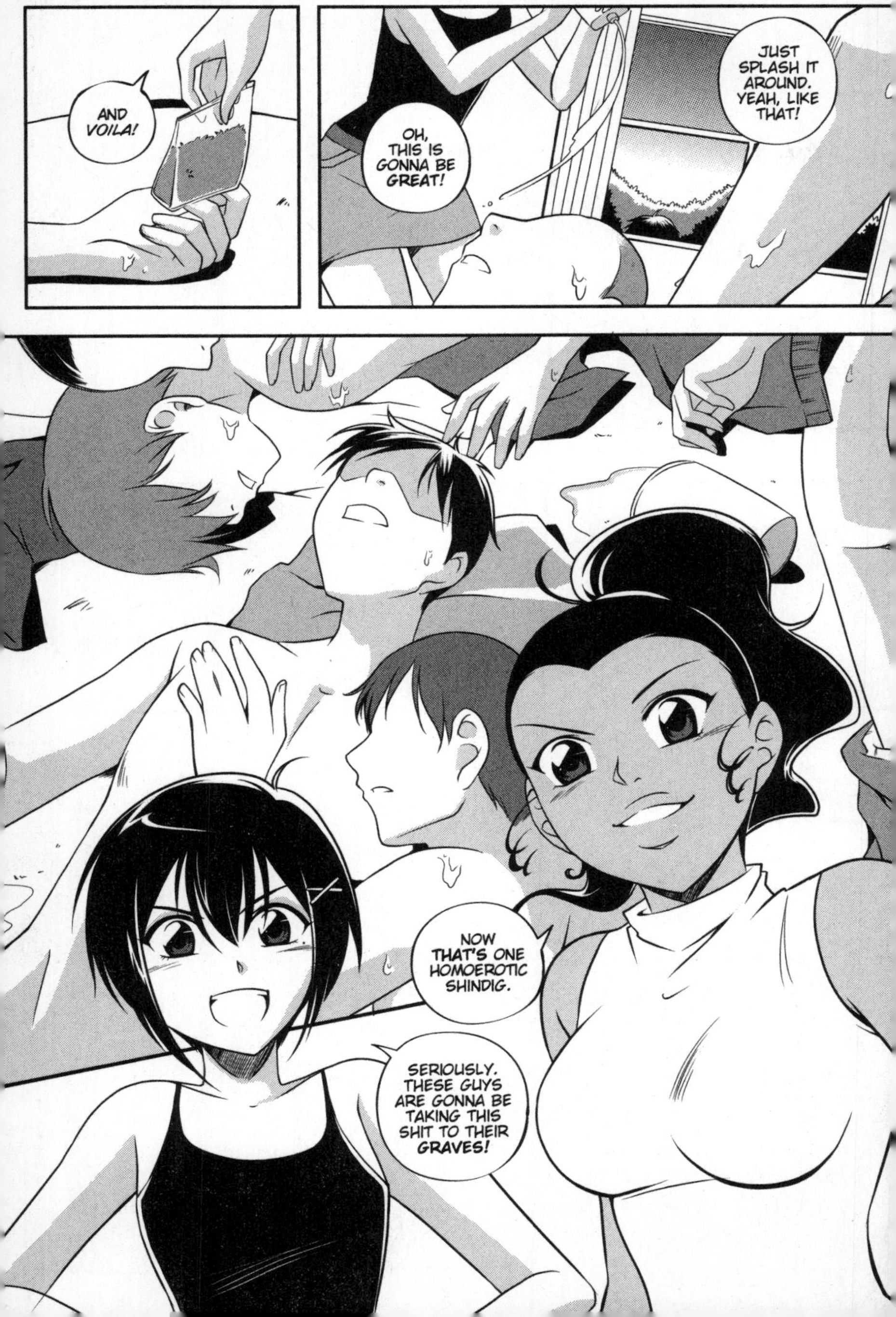
JUST SPLASH IT AROUND. YEAH, LIKE THAT!
OH, THIS IS GONNA BE GREAT!
AND *VOILA!*
NOW **THAT'S** ONE HOMOEROTIC SHINDIG.
SERIOUSLY. THESE GUYS ARE GONNA BE TAKING THIS SHIT TO THEIR **GRAVES!**

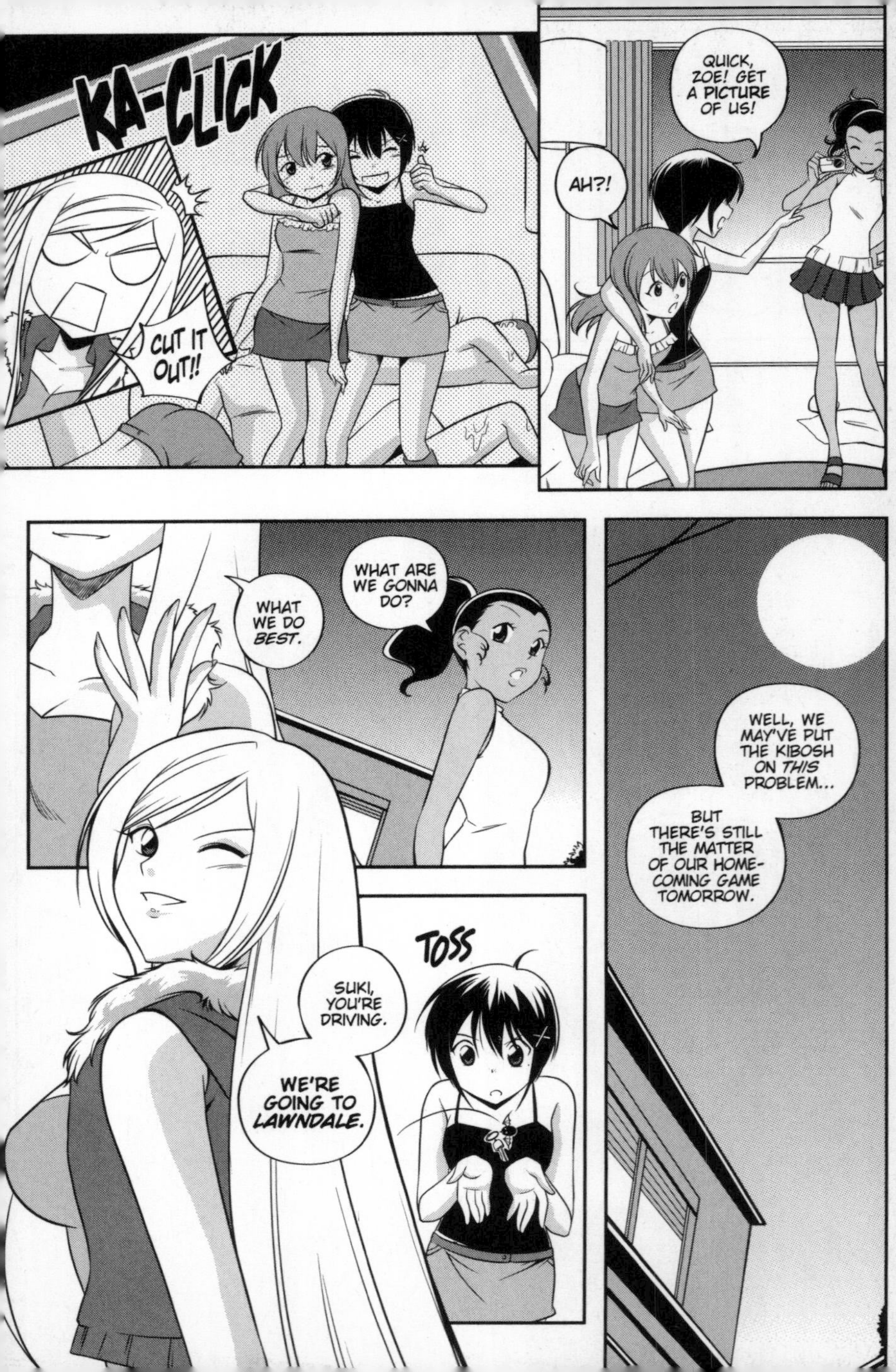
QUICK, ZOE! GET A PICTURE OF US!
AH?!
KA-CLICK
CUT IT OUT!!
WELL, WE MAY'VE PUT THE KIBOSH ON *THIS* PROBLEM...
BUT THERE'S STILL THE MATTER OF OUR HOME-COMING GAME TOMORROW.
WHAT ARE WE GONNA DO?
WHAT WE DO *BEST*.
TOSS
SUKI, YOU'RE DRIVING.
WE'RE GOING TO *LAWNDALE*.

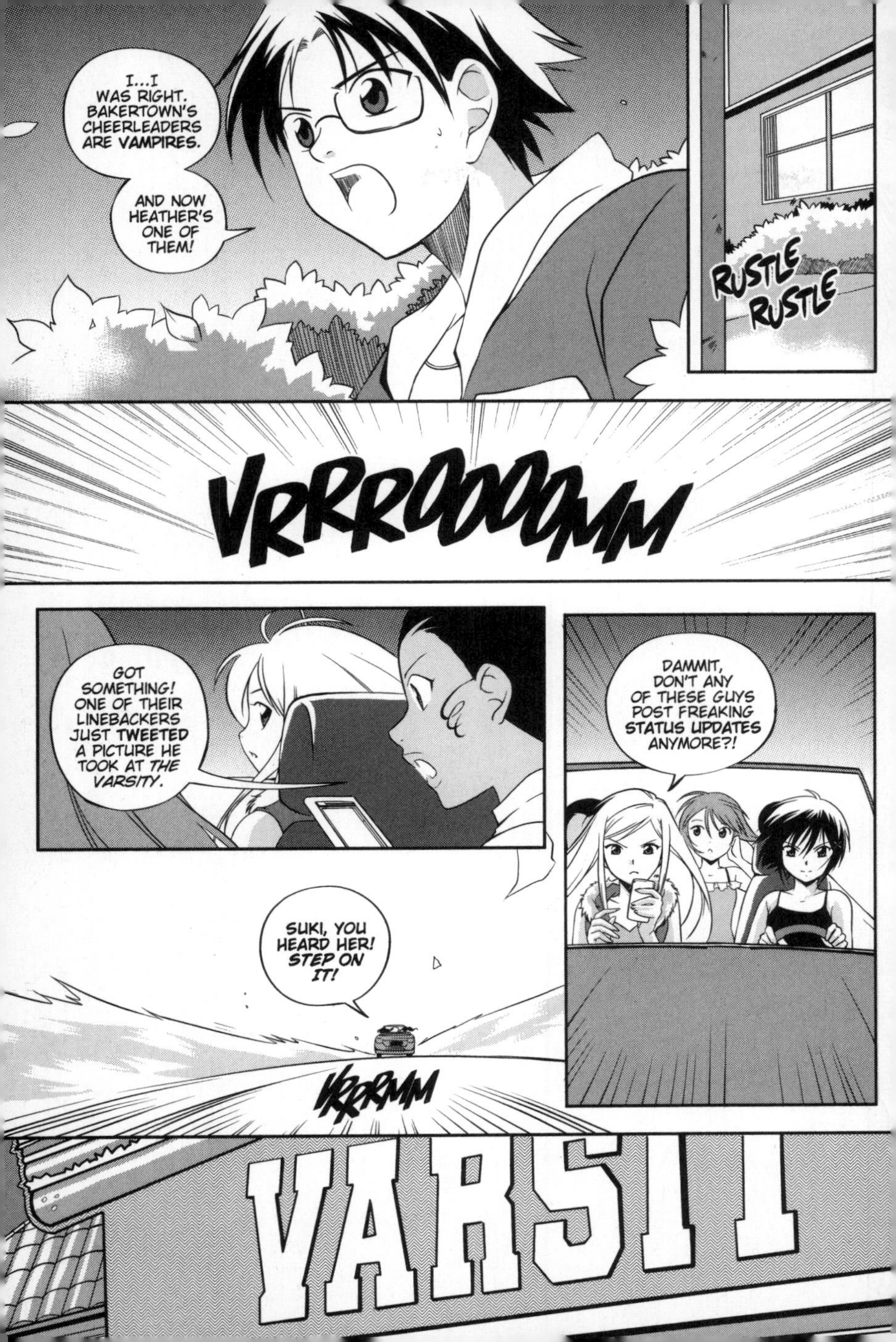
RUSTLE RUSTLE
I...I WAS RIGHT. BAKERTOWN'S CHEERLEADERS ARE VAMPIRES.
AND NOW HEATHER'S ONE OF THEM!
VRRROOOOMM
DAMMIT, DON'T ANY OF THESE GUYS POST FREAKING STATUS UPDATES ANYMORE?!
GOT SOMETHING! ONE OF THEIR LINEBACKERS JUST TWEETED A PICTURE HE TOOK AT THE VARSITY.
SUKI, YOU HEARD HER! STEP ON IT!
VRRRMM
VARSIT

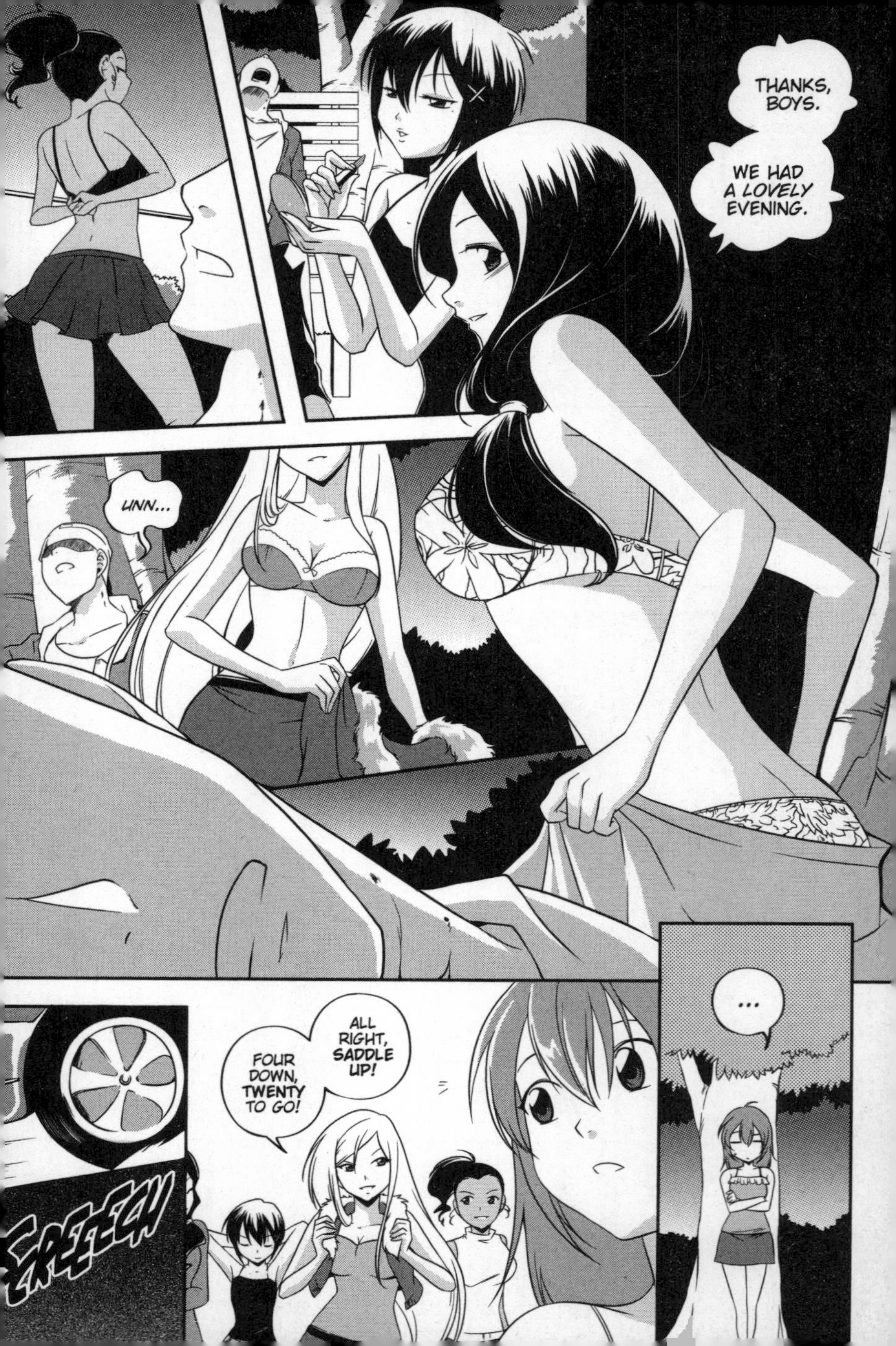
THANKS, BOYS.
WE HAD A *LOVELY* EVENING.
UNN...
...
ALL RIGHT, SADDLE UP!
FOUR DOWN, TWENTY TO GO!
SCREEECH

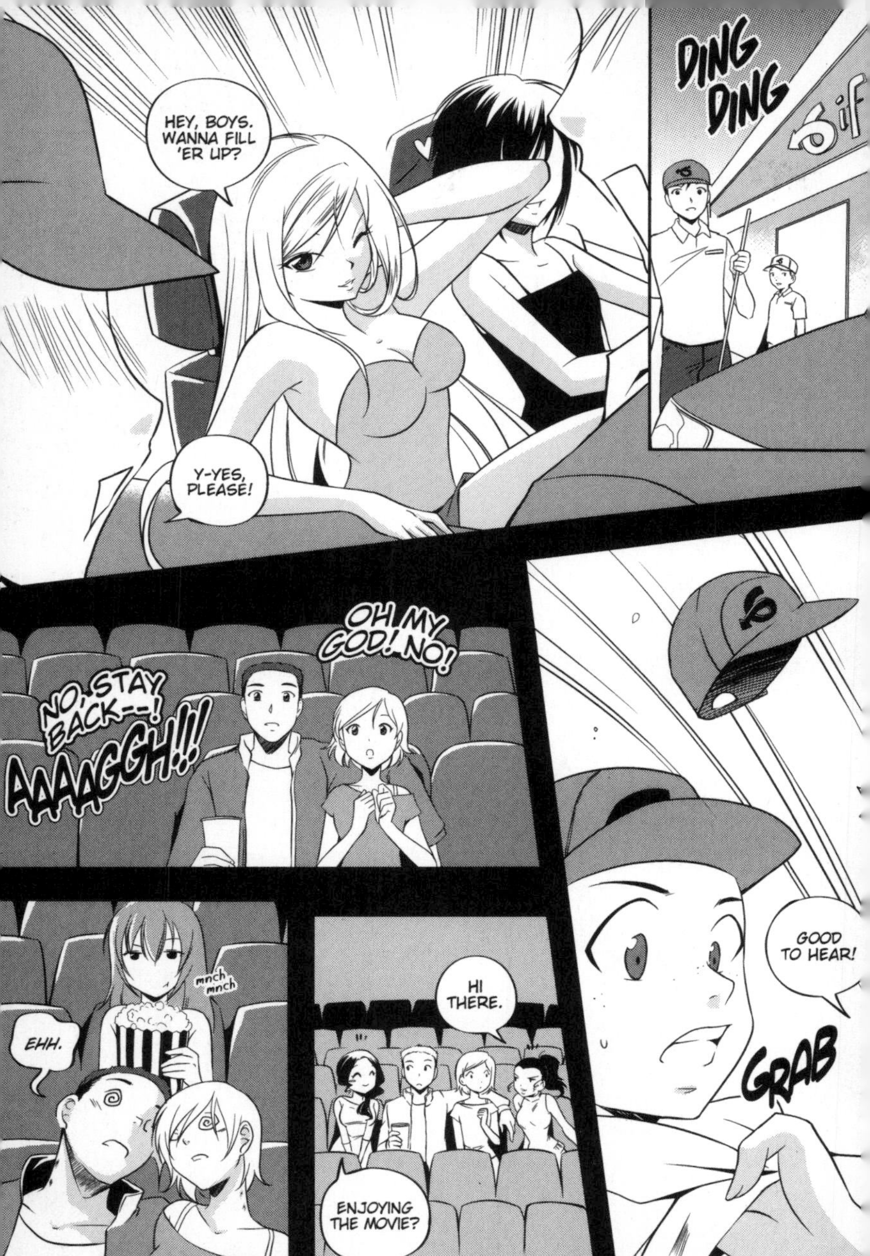
DING DING
HEY, BOYS. WANNA FILL 'ER UP?
Y-YES, PLEASE!
GOOD TO HEAR!
GRAB
OH MY GOD! NO!
NO, STAY BACK--!
AAAAGGH!!!
HI THERE.
ENJOYING THE MOVIE?
mnch mnch
EHH.

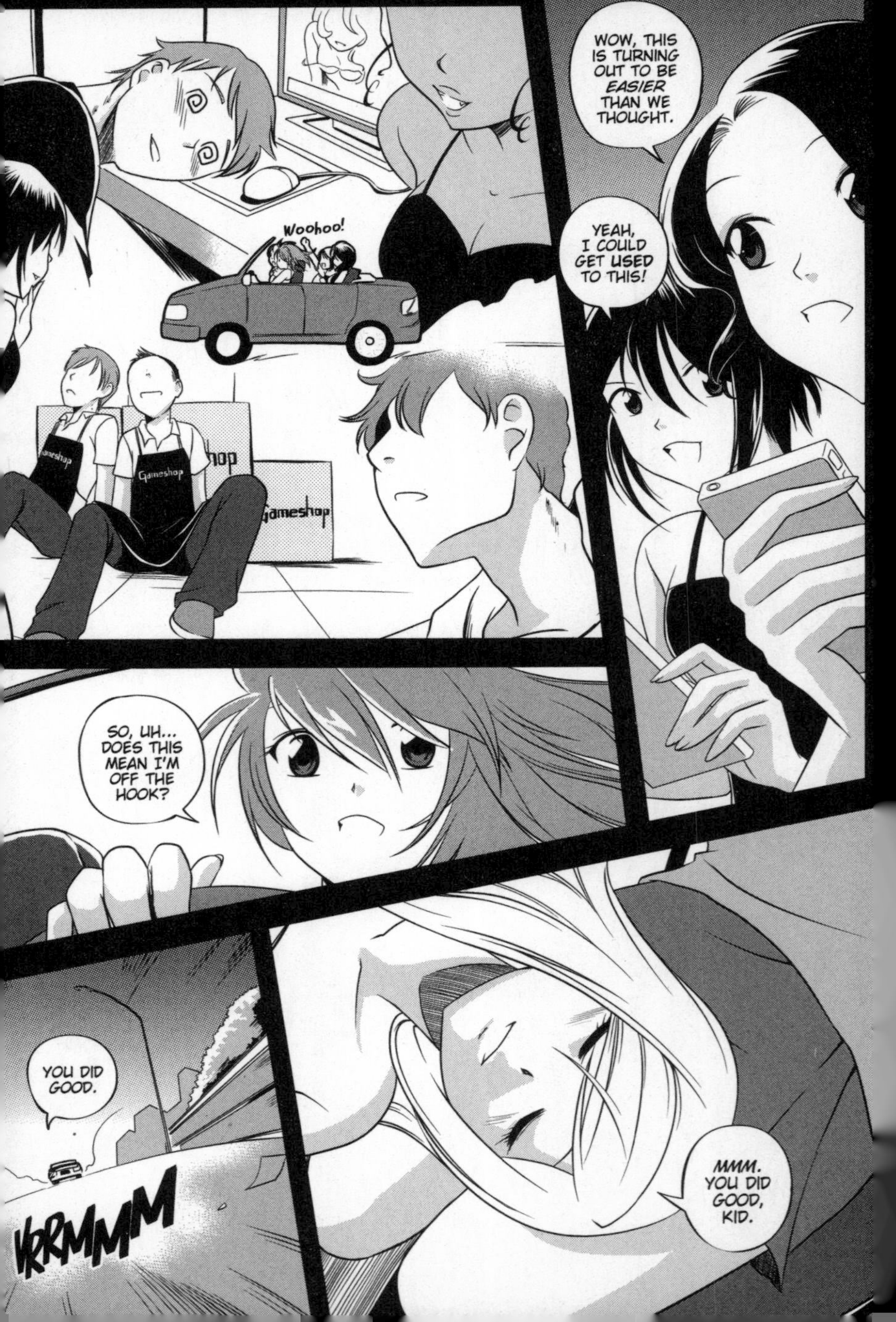

WOW, THIS IS TURNING OUT TO BE *EASIER* THAN WE THOUGHT.
YEAH, I COULD GET USED TO THIS!
Woohoo!
Gameshop
Gameshop
Gameshop
SO, UH... DOES THIS MEAN I'M OFF THE HOOK?
MMM. YOU DID GOOD, KID.
YOU DID GOOD.
VRRMMM

CLOP CLOP

STAGGER

STUMBLE

NN...

ACK?!

UUHH...

UNNNH...

HEH.

ROOOAR!

HEY, LIONS, ARE YOU THERE? RAISE YOUR PAWS IN THE AIR!

SHOW YOUR PRIDE! GOLD & RED!! PUT THESE BATSIES RIGHT TO BED!

DO IT RIGHT! ROAR! ROAR!

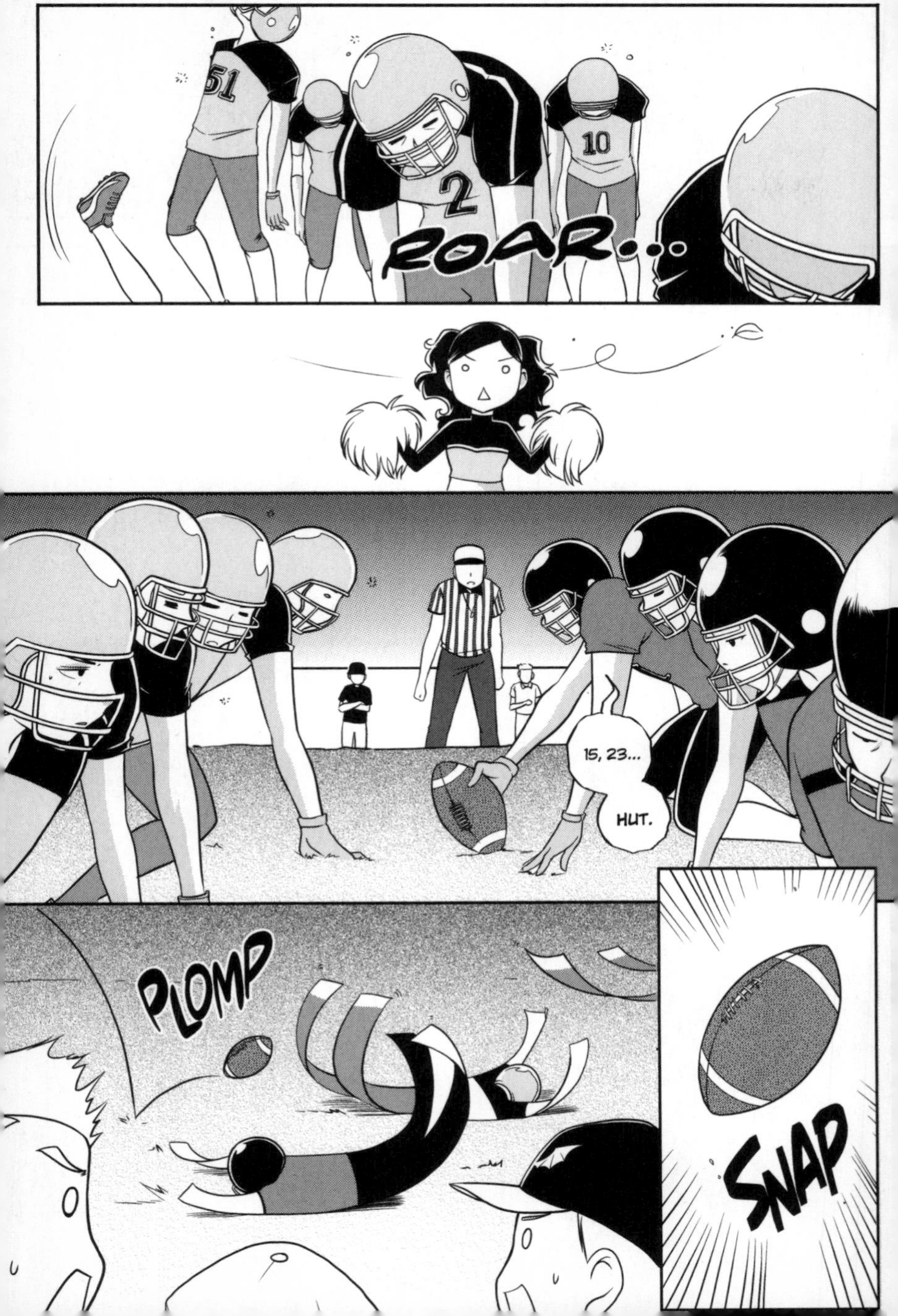
ROAR...
15, 23...
HUT.
SNAP
PLOMP

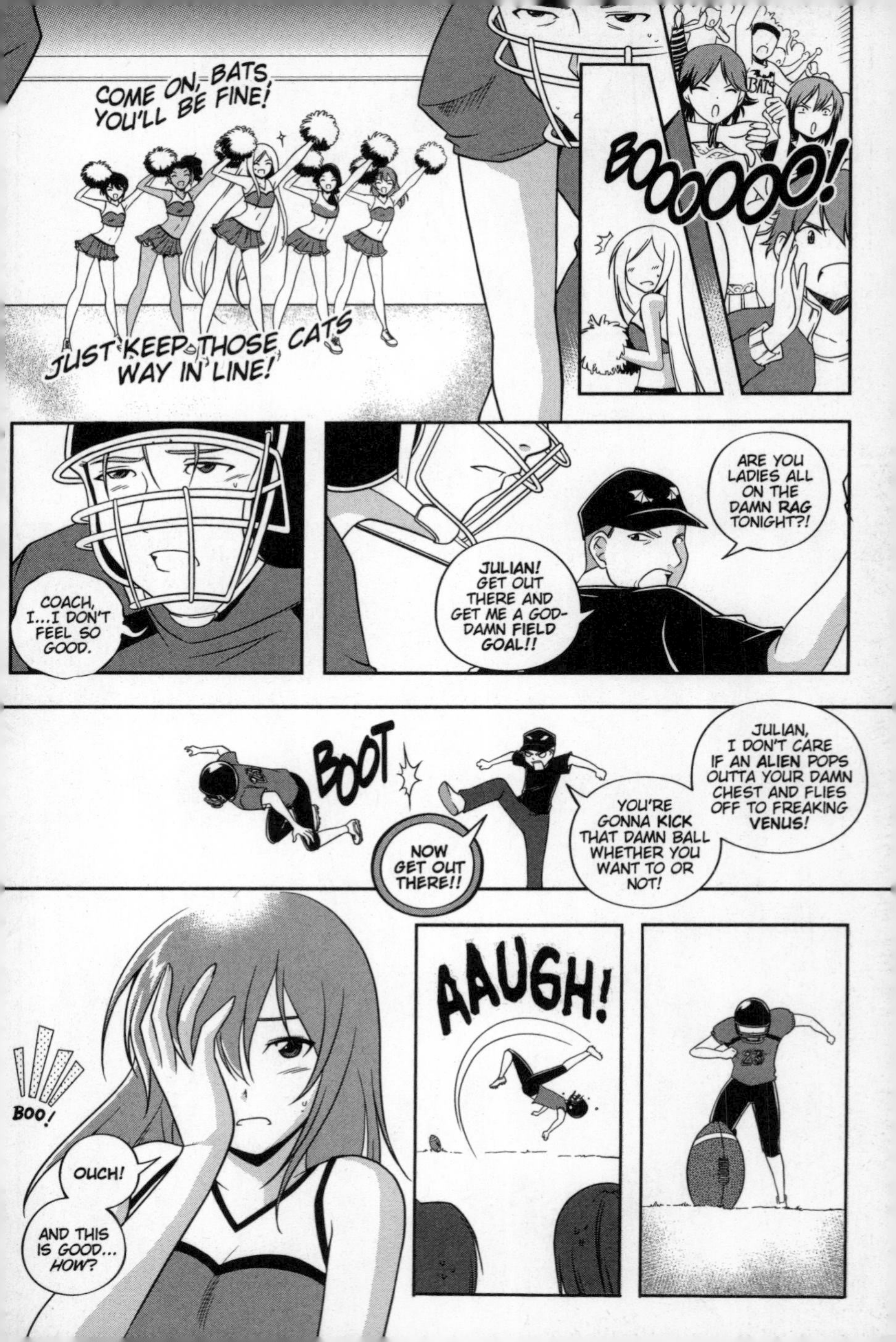
BOOOOOOO!
COME ON, BATS, YOU'LL BE FINE!
JUST KEEP THOSE CATS WAY IN LINE!
ARE YOU LADIES ALL ON THE DAMN RAG TONIGHT?!
JULIAN! GET OUT THERE AND GET ME A GOD-DAMN FIELD GOAL!!
COACH, I...I DON'T FEEL SO GOOD.
JULIAN, I DON'T CARE IF AN ALIEN POPS OUTTA YOUR DAMN CHEST AND FLIES OFF TO FREAKING VENUS!
YOU'RE GONNA KICK THAT DAMN BALL WHETHER YOU WANT TO OR NOT!
NOW GET OUT THERE!!
BOOT
AAUGH!
BOO!
OUCH!
AND THIS IS GOOD... HOW?

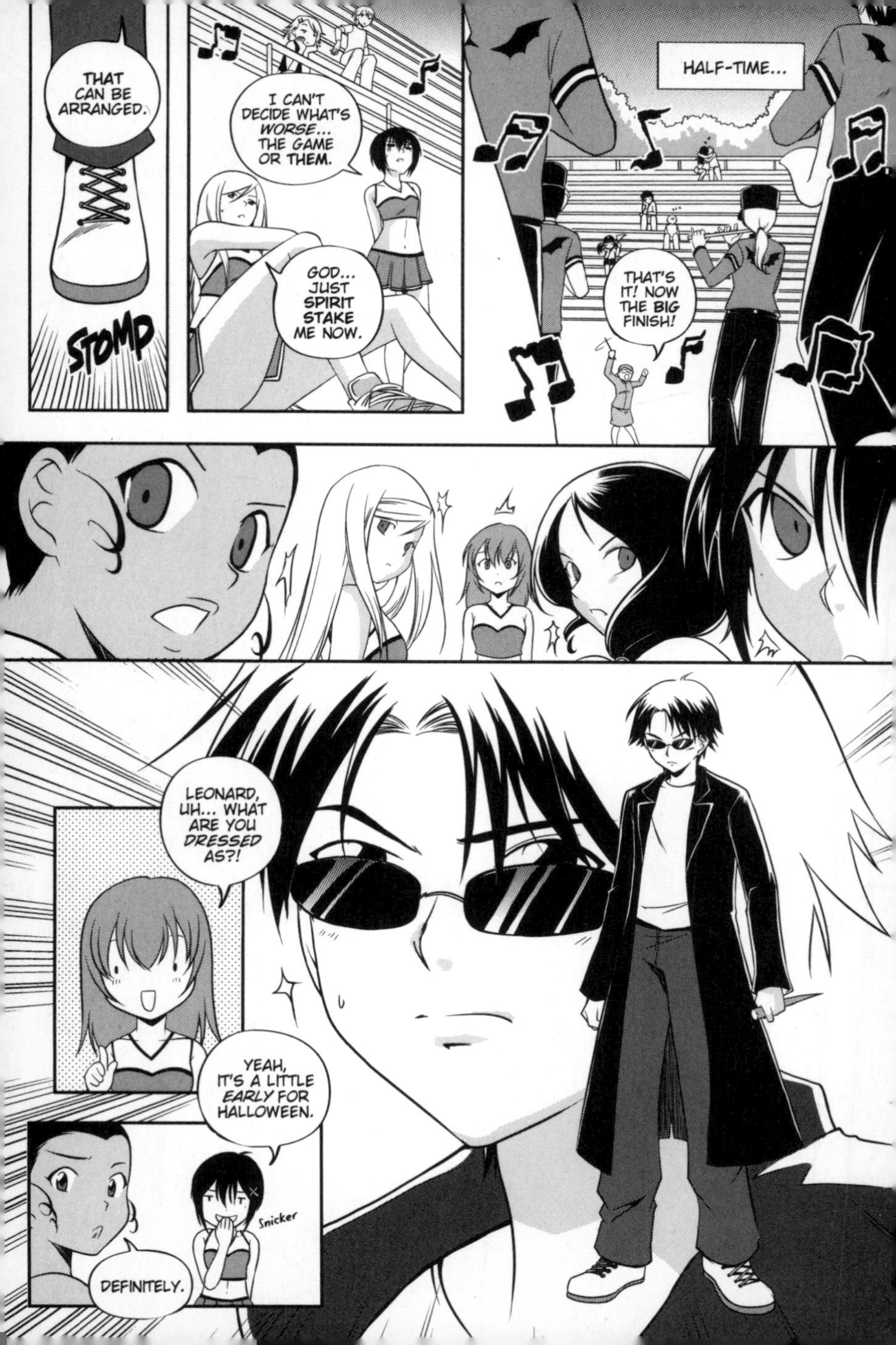
HALF-TIME...
THAT'S IT! NOW THE BIG FINISH!
I CAN'T DECIDE WHAT'S *WORSE*... THE GAME OR THEM.
GOD... JUST SPIRIT STAKE ME NOW.
THAT CAN BE ARRANGED.
STOMP
LEONARD, UH... WHAT ARE YOU *DRESSED* AS?!
YEAH, IT'S A LITTLE *EARLY* FOR HALLOWEEN.
Snicker
DEFINITELY.

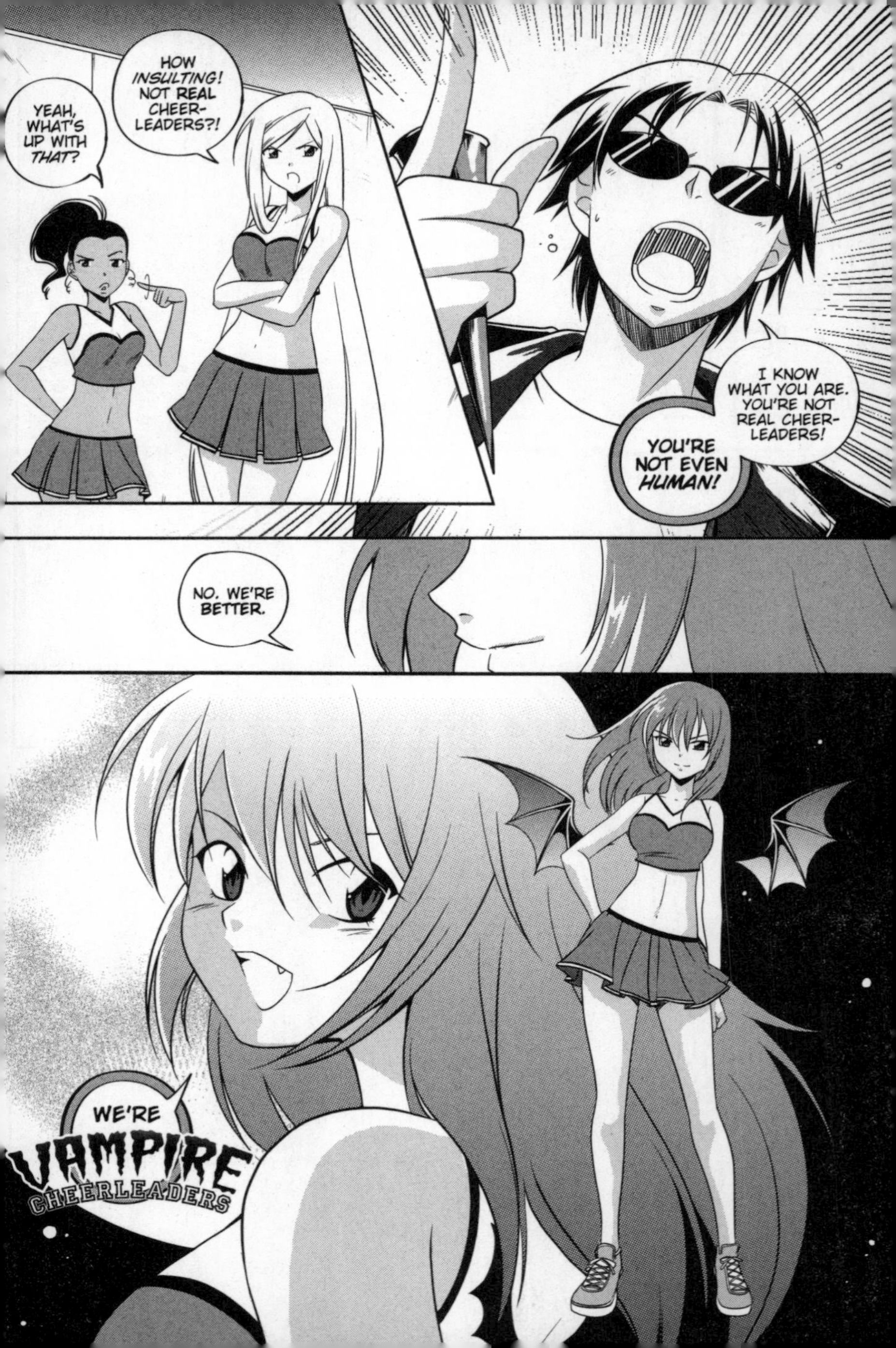
I KNOW WHAT YOU ARE. YOU'RE NOT REAL CHEER-LEADERS!
YOU'RE NOT EVEN *HUMAN!*
HOW *INSULTING!* NOT REAL CHEER-LEADERS?!
YEAH, WHAT'S UP WITH *THAT?*
NO. WE'RE BETTER.
WE'RE
VAMPIRE CHEERLEADERS

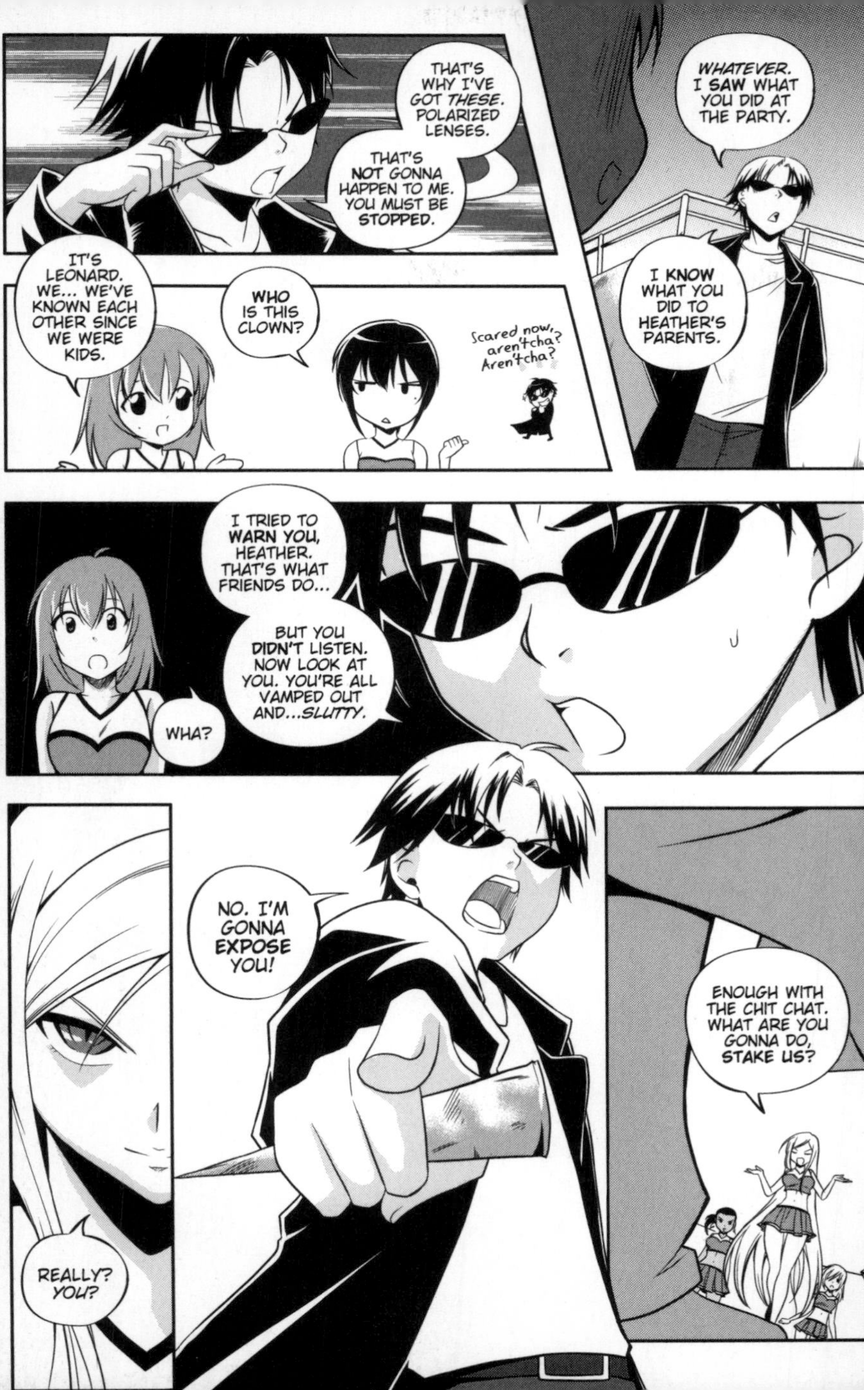
WHATEVER. I SAW WHAT YOU DID AT THE PARTY.
I KNOW WHAT YOU DID TO HEATHER'S PARENTS.
THAT'S WHY I'VE GOT THESE. POLARIZED LENSES.
THAT'S NOT GONNA HAPPEN TO ME. YOU MUST BE STOPPED.
WHO IS THIS CLOWN?
IT'S LEONARD. WE... WE'VE KNOWN EACH OTHER SINCE WE WERE KIDS.
Scared now, aren'tcha? Aren'tcha?
I TRIED TO WARN YOU, HEATHER. THAT'S WHAT FRIENDS DO...
BUT YOU DIDN'T LISTEN. NOW LOOK AT YOU. YOU'RE ALL VAMPED OUT AND...SLUTTY.
WHA?
ENOUGH WITH THE CHIT CHAT. WHAT ARE YOU GONNA DO, STAKE US?
NO. I'M GONNA EXPOSE YOU!
REALLY? YOU?

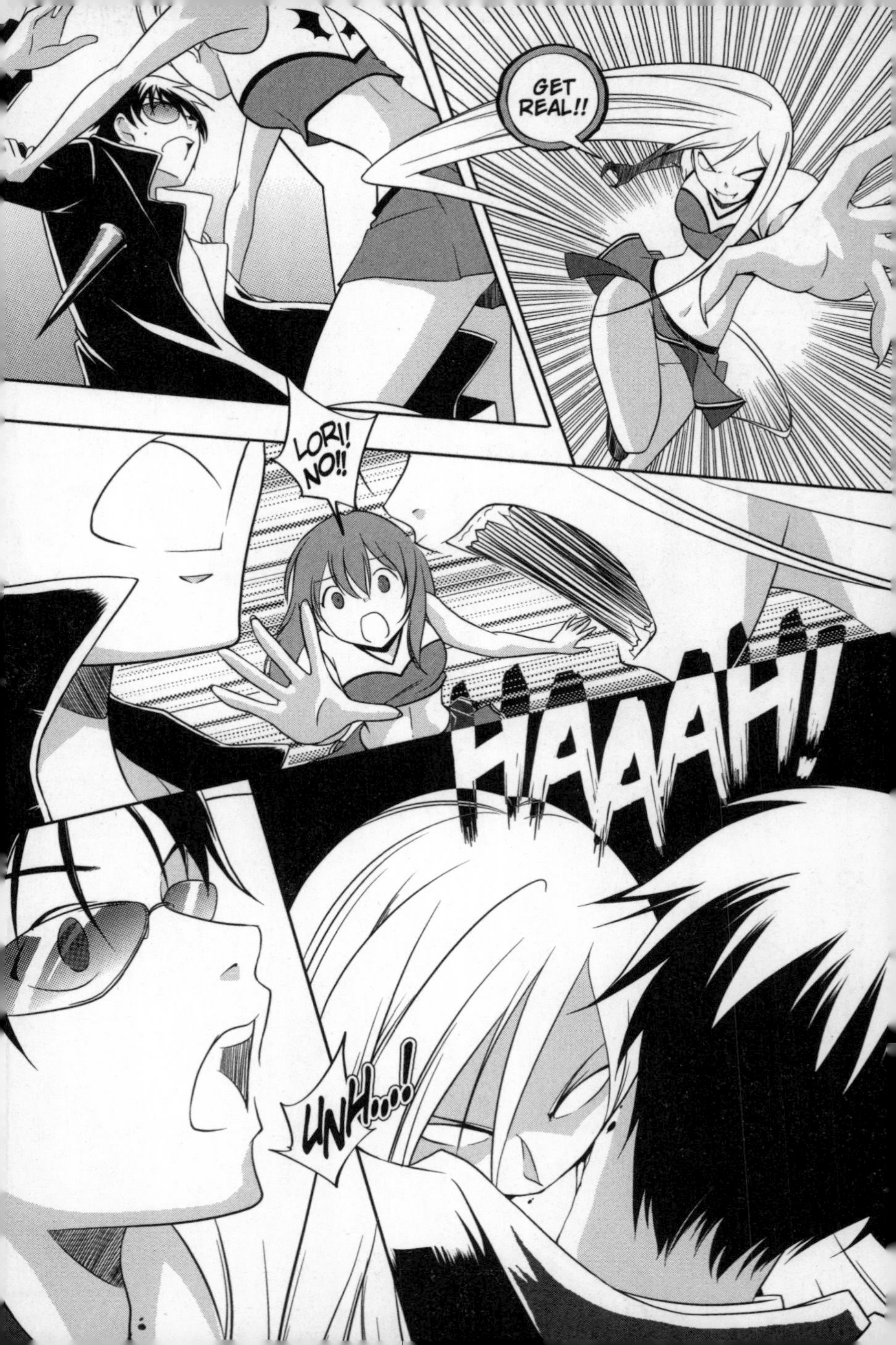
GET REAL!!
LORI! NO!!
HAAAH!
UNH...!

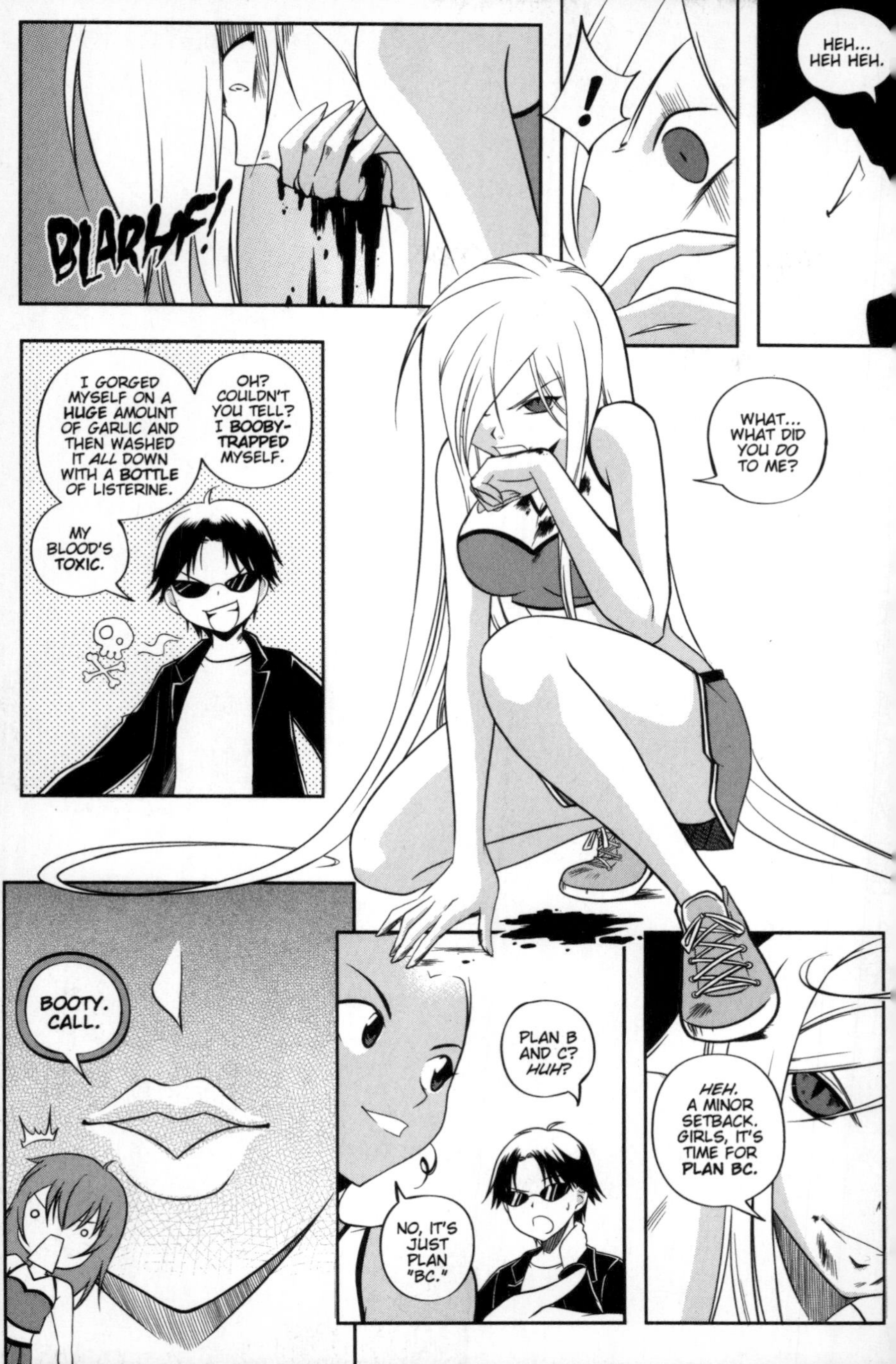
HEH... HEH HEH.
!
BLARHF!
WHAT... WHAT DID YOU DO TO ME?
OH? COULDN'T YOU TELL? I BOOBY-TRAPPED MYSELF.
I GORGED MYSELF ON A HUGE AMOUNT OF GARLIC AND THEN WASHED IT ALL DOWN WITH A BOTTLE OF LISTERINE.
MY BLOOD'S TOXIC.
HEH. A MINOR SETBACK. GIRLS, IT'S TIME FOR PLAN BC.
PLAN B AND C? HUH?
NO, IT'S JUST PLAN "BC."
BOOTY. CALL.

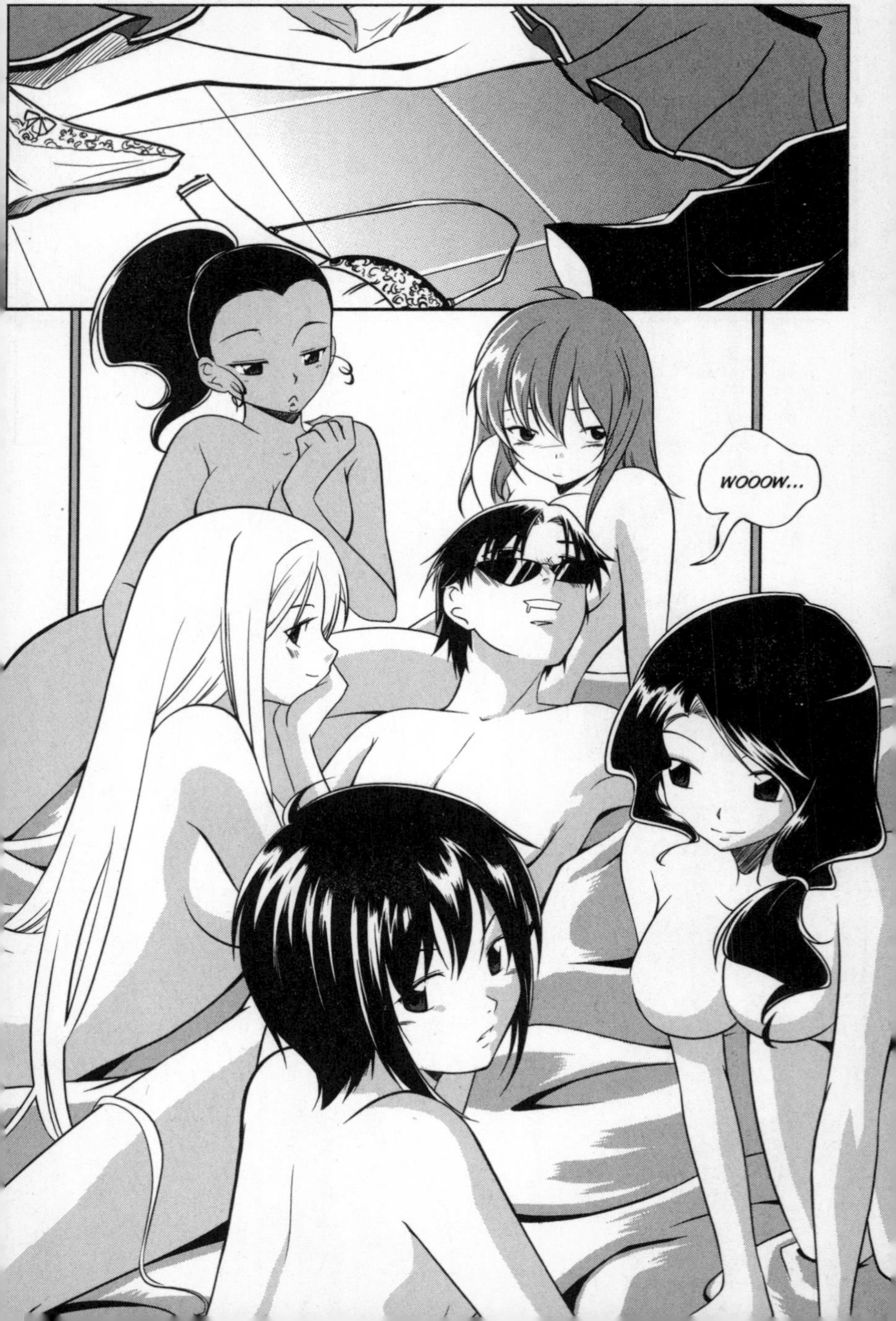
WOOOW...

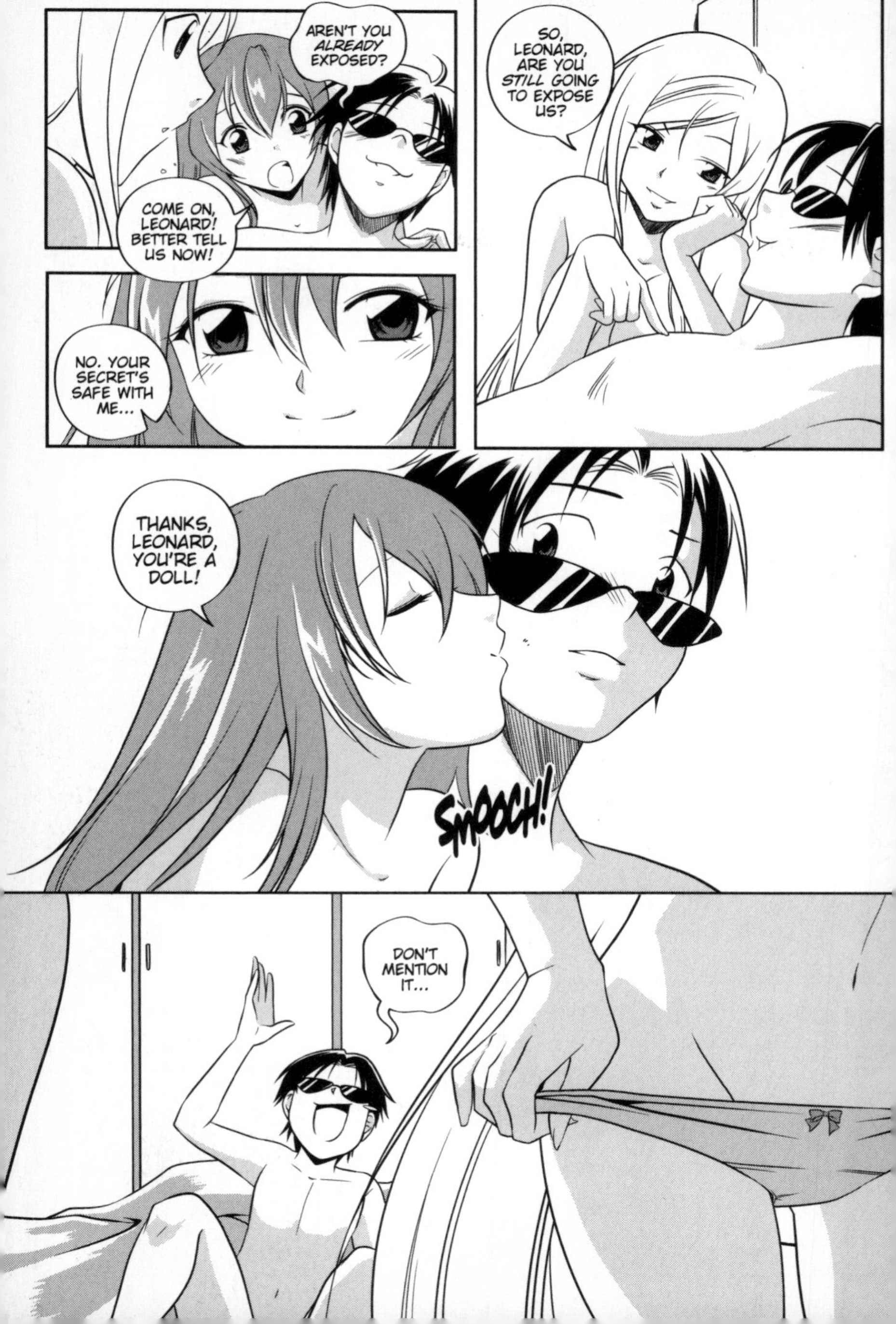
SO, LEONARD, ARE YOU *STILL* GOING TO EXPOSE US?
AREN'T YOU *ALREADY* EXPOSED?
COME ON, LEONARD! BETTER TELL US NOW!
NO. YOUR SECRET'S SAFE WITH ME...
THANKS, LEONARD, YOU'RE A DOLL!
SMOOCH!
DON'T MENTION IT...

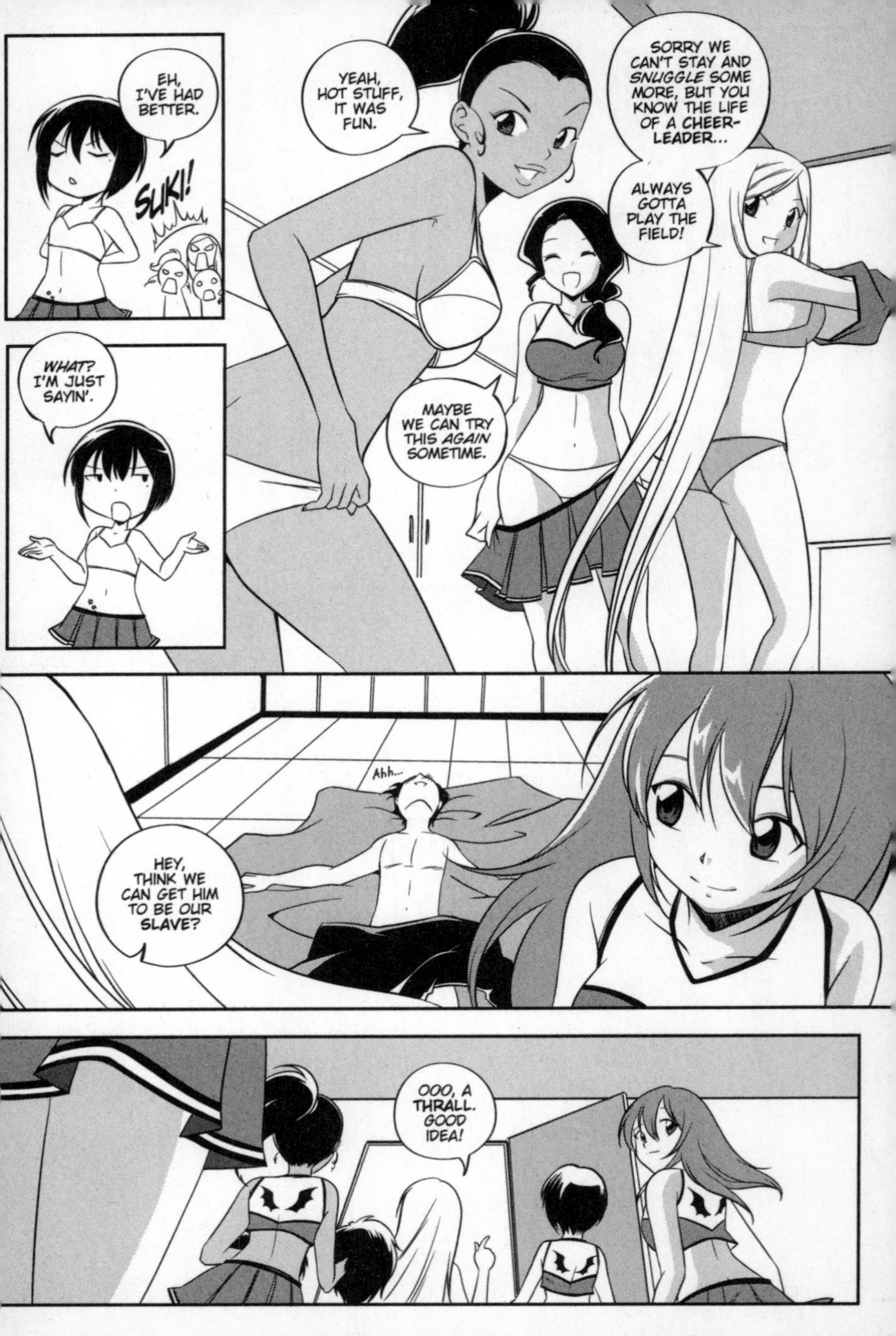
SORRY WE CAN'T STAY AND SNUGGLE SOME MORE, BUT YOU KNOW THE LIFE OF A CHEER-LEADER...
YEAH, HOT STUFF, IT WAS FUN.
ALWAYS GOTTA PLAY THE FIELD!
MAYBE WE CAN TRY THIS AGAIN SOMETIME.
EH, I'VE HAD BETTER.
SUKI!
WHAT? I'M JUST SAYIN'.
Ahh...
HEY, THINK WE CAN GET HIM TO BE OUR SLAVE?
OOO, A THRALL. GOOD IDEA!

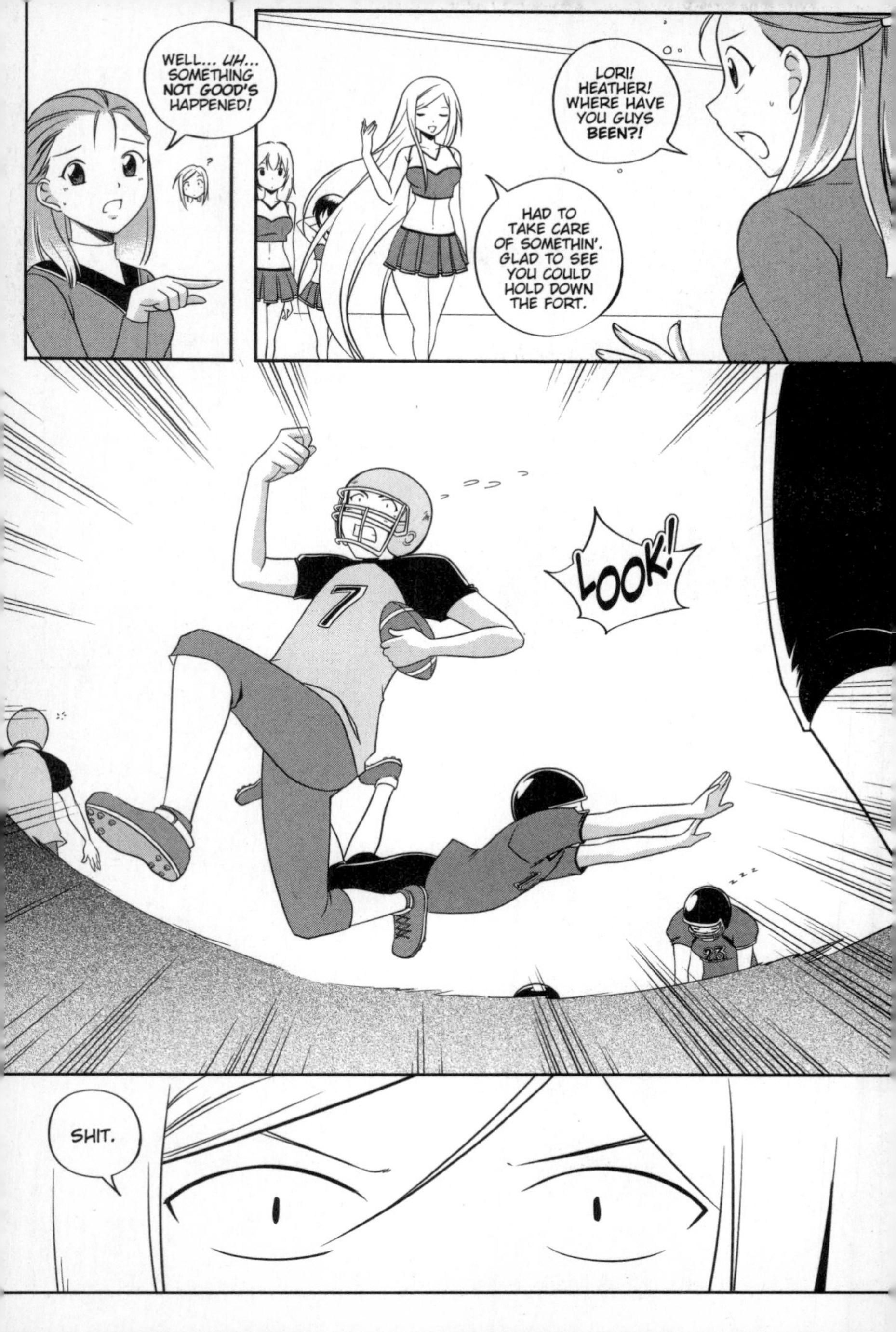
LORI! HEATHER! WHERE HAVE YOU GUYS BEEN?!
HAD TO TAKE CARE OF SOMETHIN'. GLAD TO SEE YOU COULD HOLD DOWN THE FORT.
WELL... *UH*... SOMETHING NOT GOOD'S HAPPENED!
?
LOOK!
SHIT.

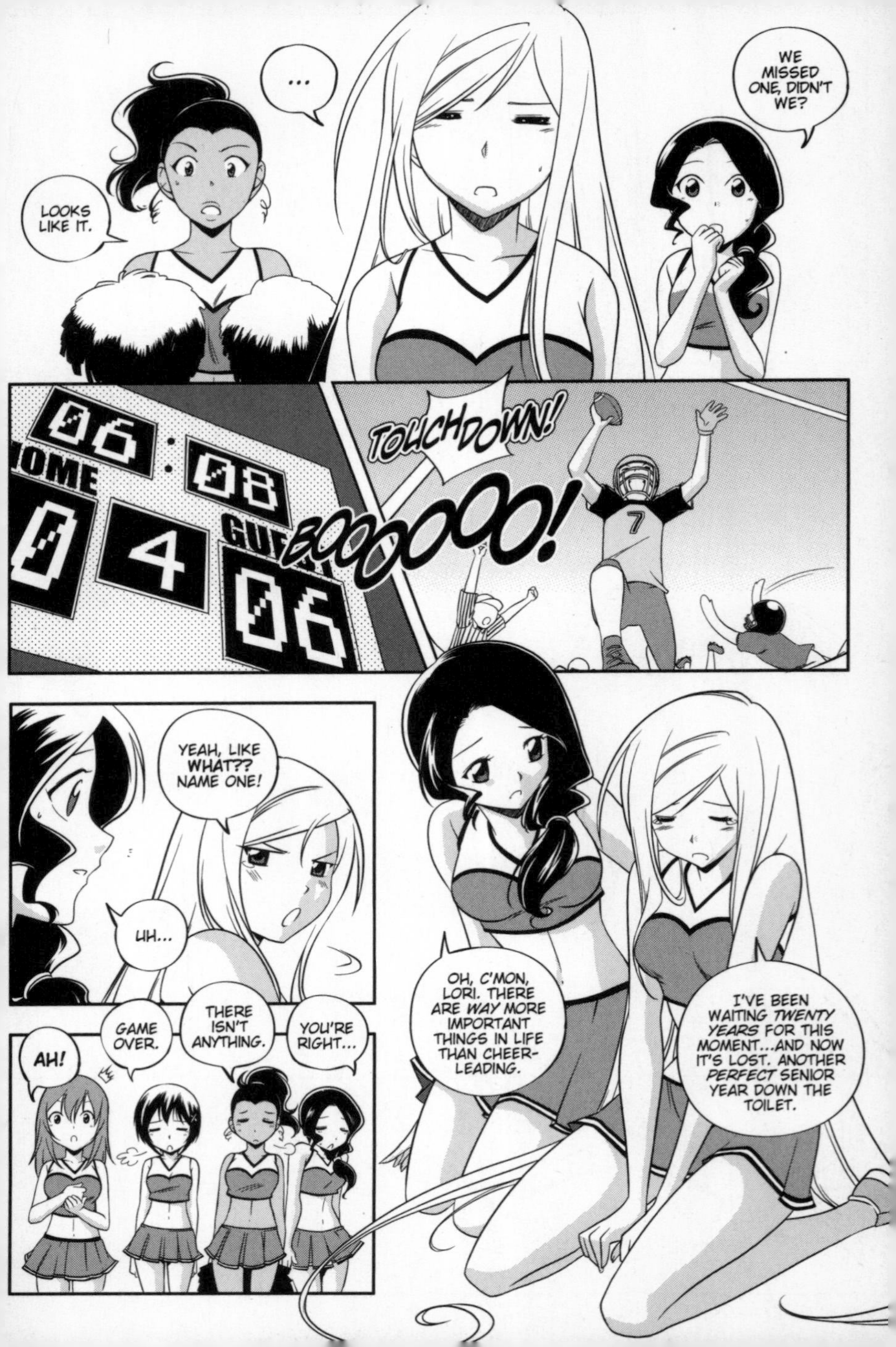
WE MISSED ONE, DIDN'T WE?
...
LOOKS LIKE IT.
TOUCHDOWN!
BOOOOOOO!
I'VE BEEN WAITING *TWENTY YEARS* FOR THIS MOMENT...AND NOW IT'S LOST. ANOTHER *PERFECT* SENIOR YEAR DOWN THE TOILET.
OH, C'MON, LORI. THERE ARE *WAY* MORE IMPORTANT THINGS IN LIFE THAN CHEER-LEADING.
YEAH, LIKE **WHAT??** NAME ONE!
UH...
YOU'RE RIGHT...
THERE ISN'T ANYTHING.
GAME OVER.
AH!

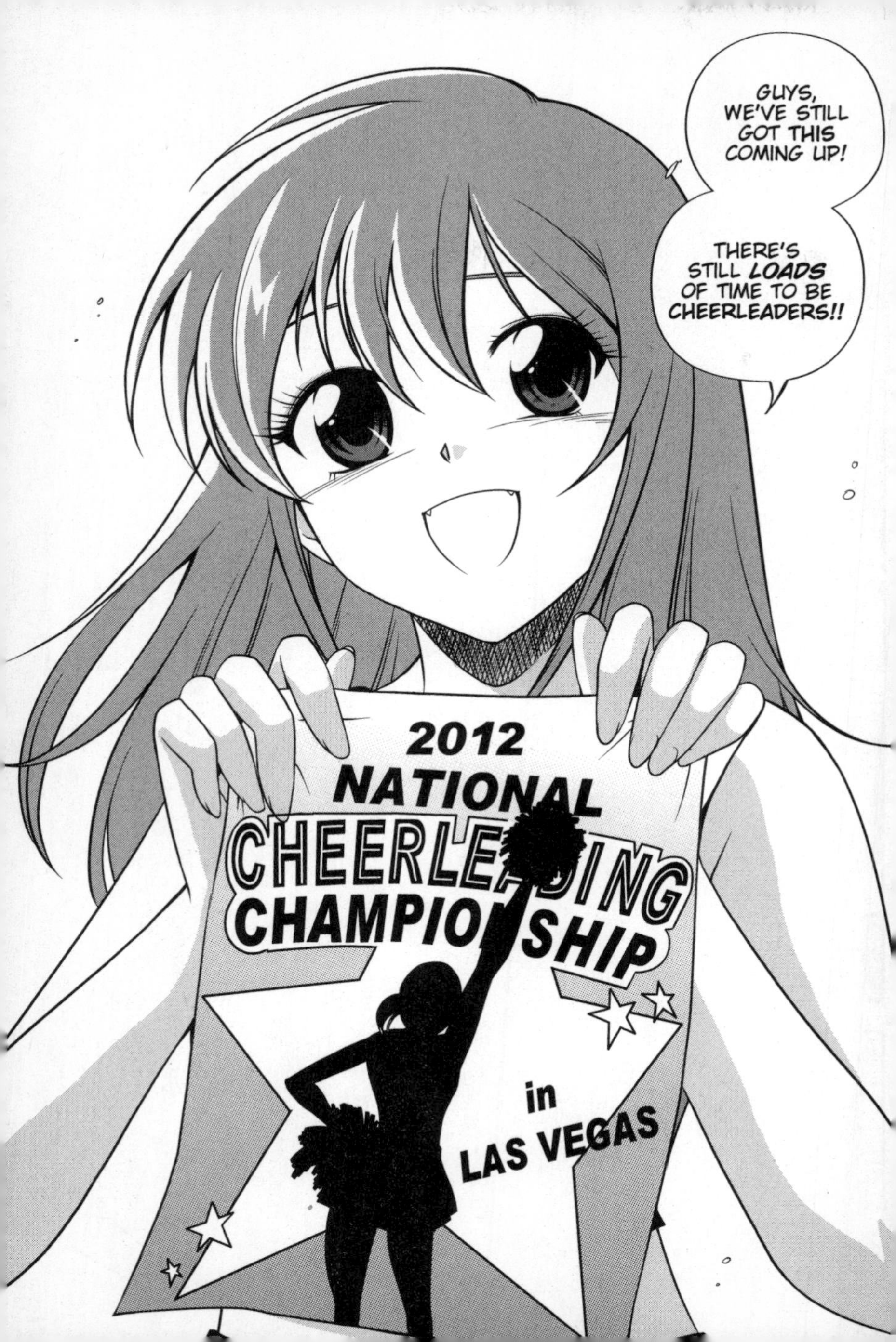
GUYS, WE'VE STILL GOT THIS COMING UP!
THERE'S STILL LOADS OF TIME TO BE CHEERLEADERS!!
2012 NATIONAL CHEERLEADING CHAMPIONSHIP in LAS VEGAS

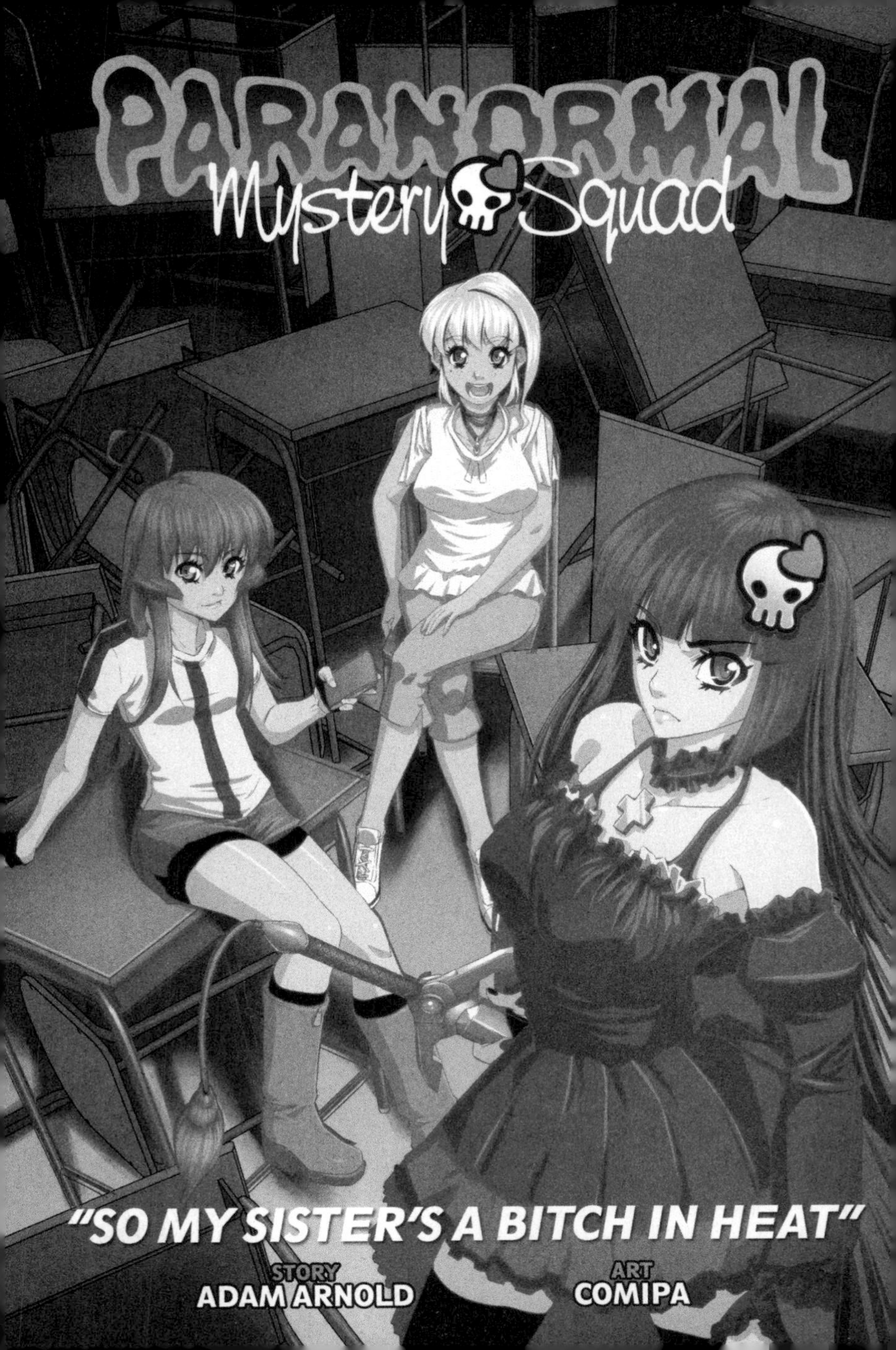
PARANORMAL
Mystery Squad
"SO MY SISTER'S A BITCH IN HEAT"
STORY
ADAM ARNOLD
ART
COMIPA

PARANORMAL
Mystery Squad

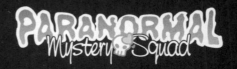

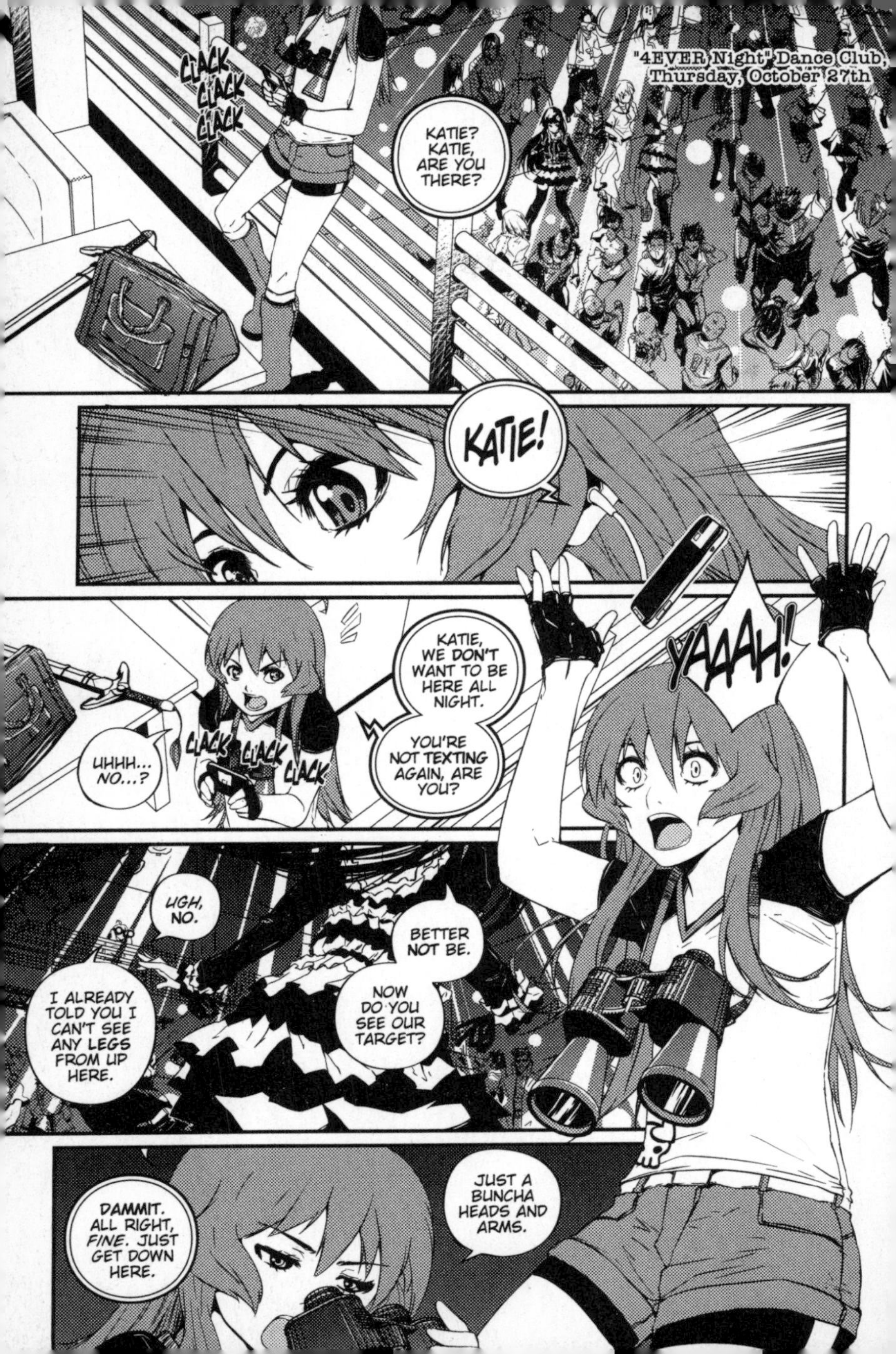
"4EVER Night" Dance Club,
Thursday, October 27th
KATIE? KATIE, ARE YOU THERE?
CLACK CLACK CLACK
KATIE!
YAAAH!
KATIE, WE DON'T WANT TO BE HERE ALL NIGHT.
YOU'RE NOT TEXTING AGAIN, ARE YOU?
CLACK CLACK CLACK
UHHH... NO...?
BETTER NOT BE.
NOW DO YOU SEE OUR TARGET?
UGH, NO.
I ALREADY TOLD YOU I CAN'T SEE ANY LEGS FROM UP HERE.
JUST A BUNCHA HEADS AND ARMS.
DAMMIT. ALL RIGHT, *FINE*. JUST GET DOWN HERE.

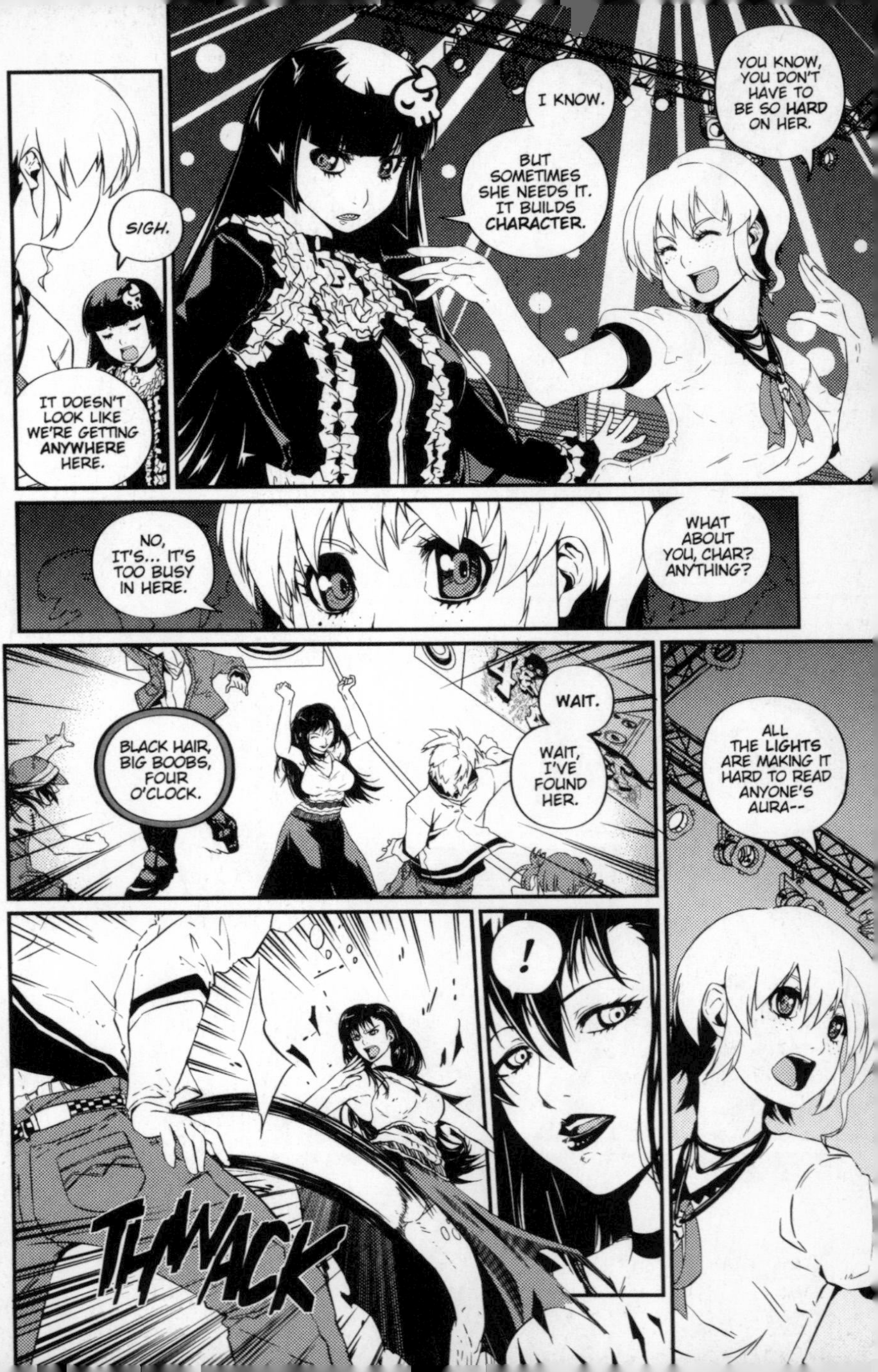
YOU KNOW, YOU DON'T HAVE TO BE SO HARD ON HER.
I KNOW.
BUT SOMETIMES SHE NEEDS IT. IT BUILDS CHARACTER.
SIGH.
IT DOESN'T LOOK LIKE WE'RE GETTING ANYWHERE HERE.
WHAT ABOUT YOU, CHAR? ANYTHING?
NO, IT'S... IT'S TOO BUSY IN HERE.
ALL THE LIGHTS ARE MAKING IT HARD TO READ ANYONE'S AURA--
WAIT.
WAIT, I'VE FOUND HER.
BLACK HAIR, BIG BOOBS, FOUR O'CLOCK.
!
THWACK

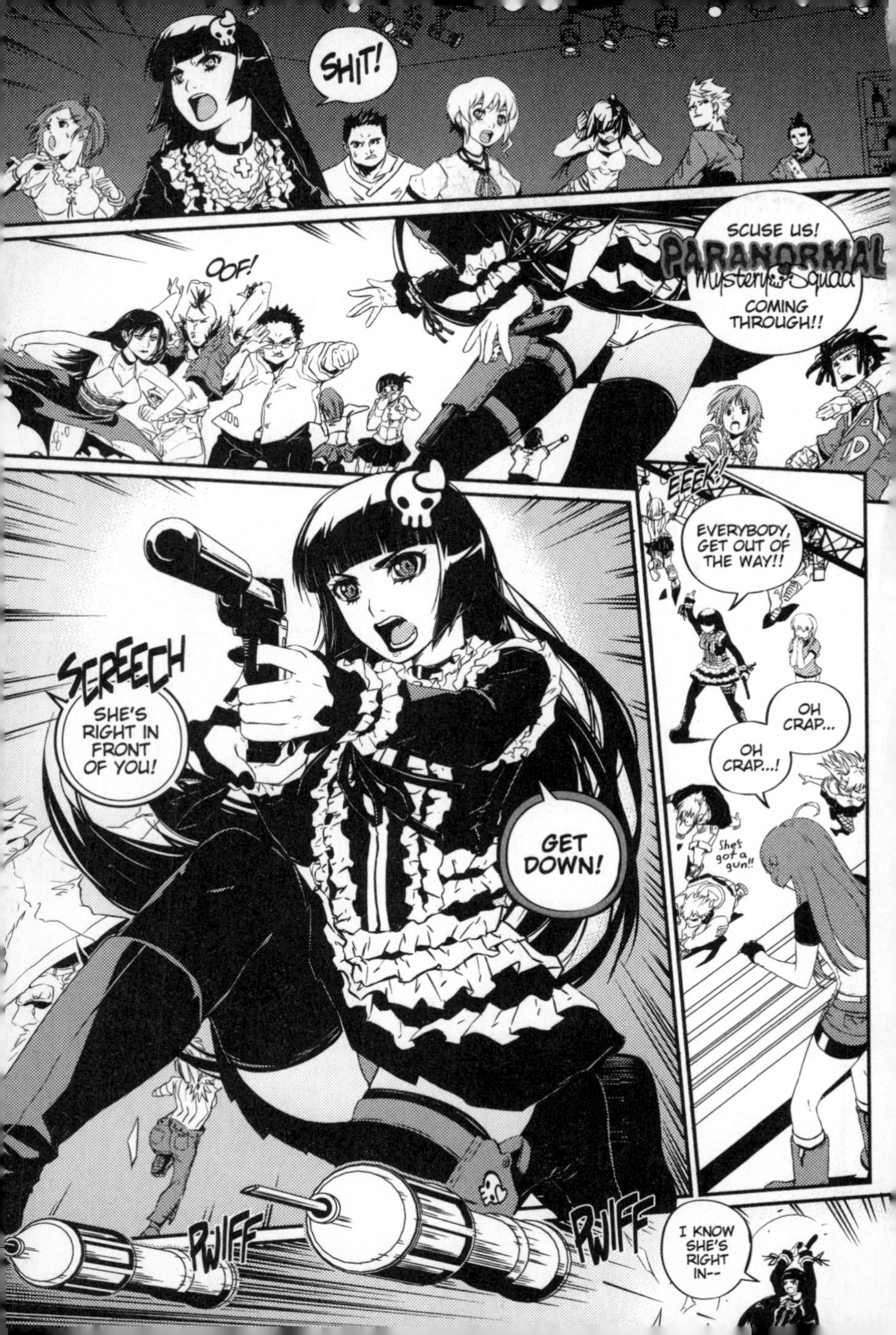
SHIT!
SCUSE US! PARANORMAL Mystery Squad COMING THROUGH!!
OOF!
EEEK!
EVERYBODY, GET OUT OF THE WAY!!
OH CRAP...
OH CRAP...!
She's got a gun!!
I KNOW SHE'S RIGHT IN--
SCREECH
SHE'S RIGHT IN FRONT OF YOU!
GET DOWN!
PWIFF
PWIFF

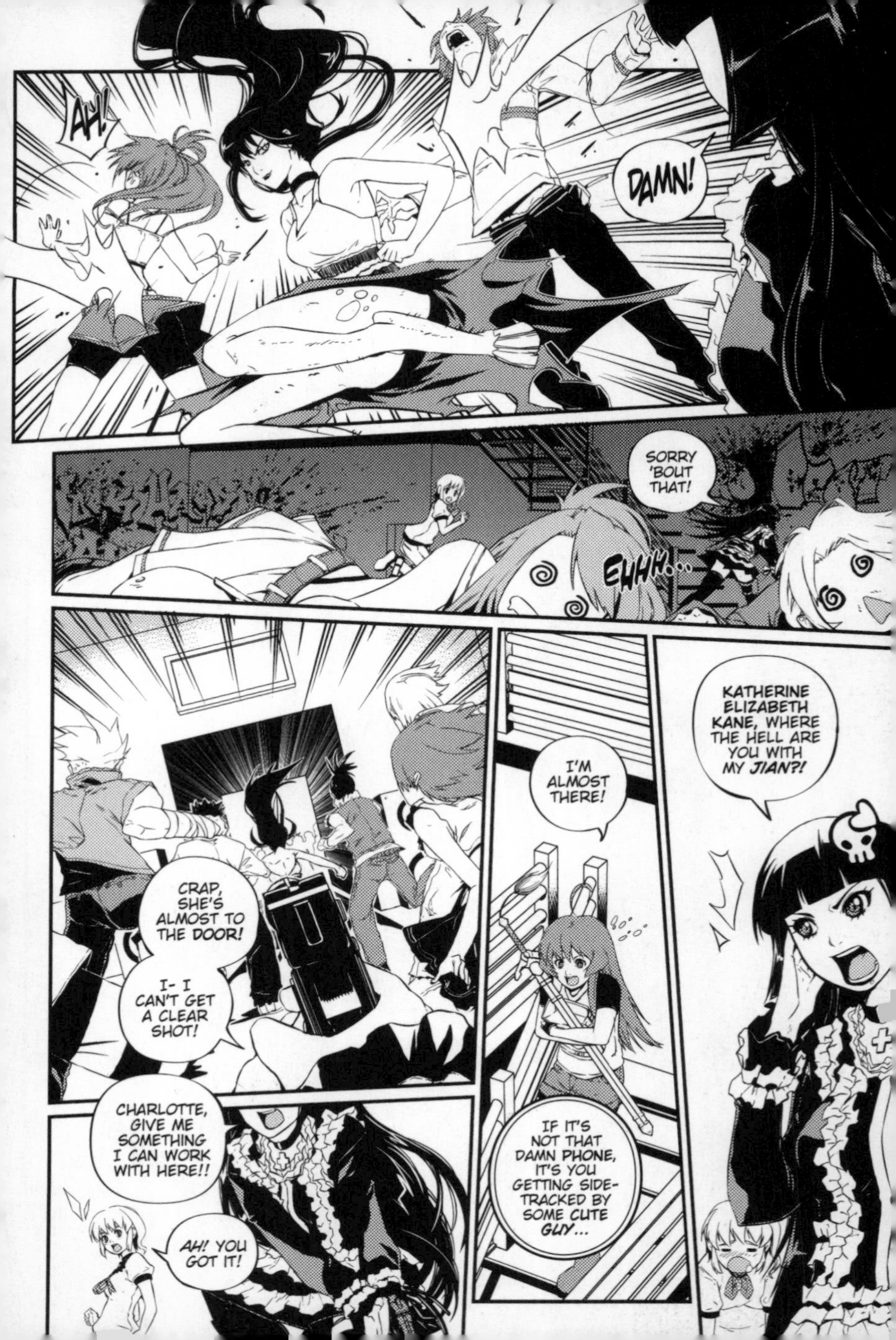
DAMN!
AH!
SORRY 'BOUT THAT!
EHHH...
KATHERINE ELIZABETH KANE, WHERE THE HELL ARE YOU WITH MY *JIAN?!*
I'M ALMOST THERE!
IF IT'S NOT THAT DAMN PHONE, IT'S YOU GETTING SIDE-TRACKED BY SOME CUTE *GUY*...
CRAP, SHE'S ALMOST TO THE *DOOR!*
I- I CAN'T GET A CLEAR SHOT!
CHARLOTTE, GIVE ME SOMETHING I CAN WORK WITH HERE!!
AH! YOU GOT IT!

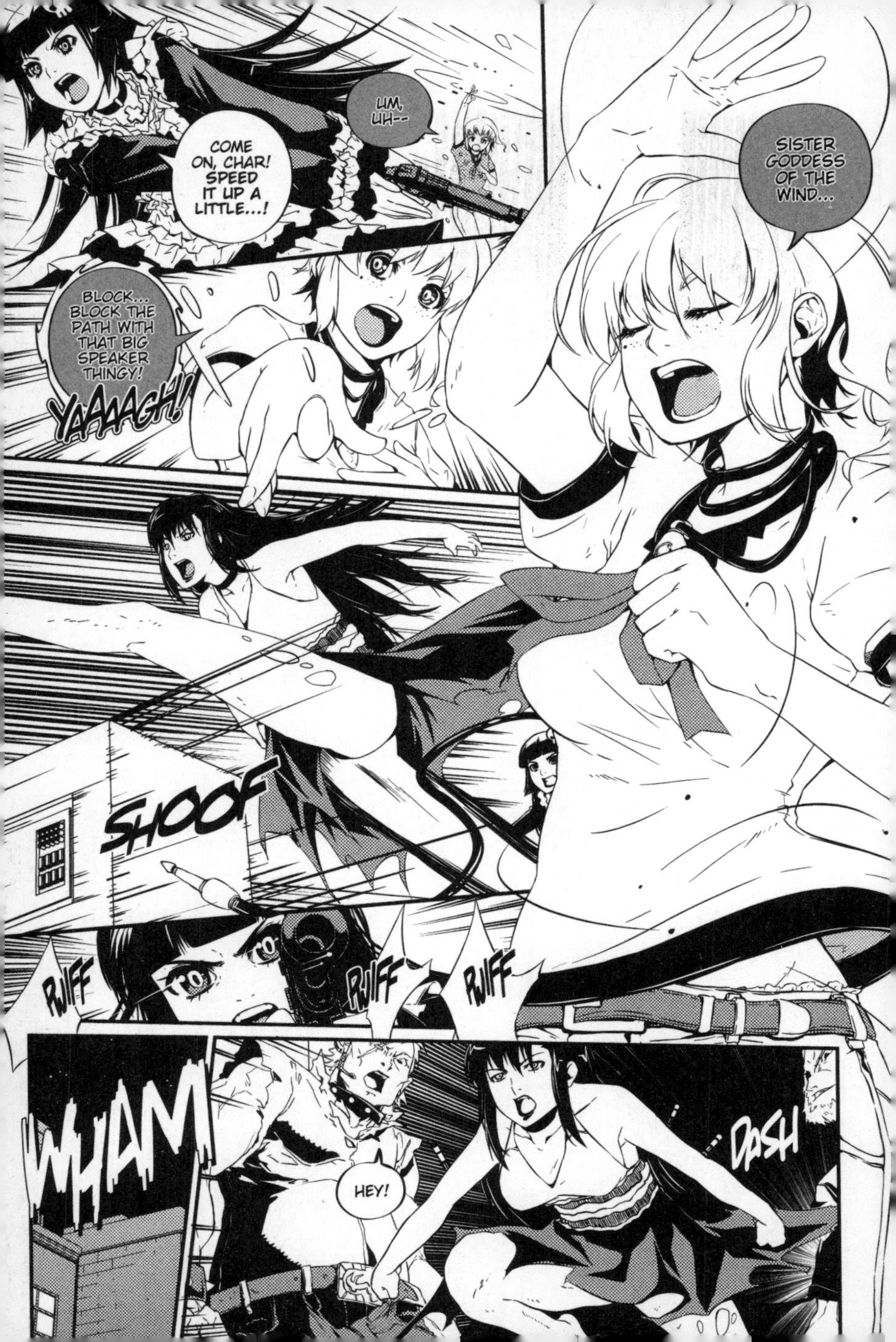
SISTER GODDESS OF THE WIND...
UM, UH--
COME ON, CHAR! SPEED IT UP A LITTLE...!
BLOCK... BLOCK THE PATH WITH THAT BIG SPEAKER THINGY!
YAAAAGH!
SHOOF
PWIFF
PWIFF
PWIFF
DASH
HEY!
WHAM

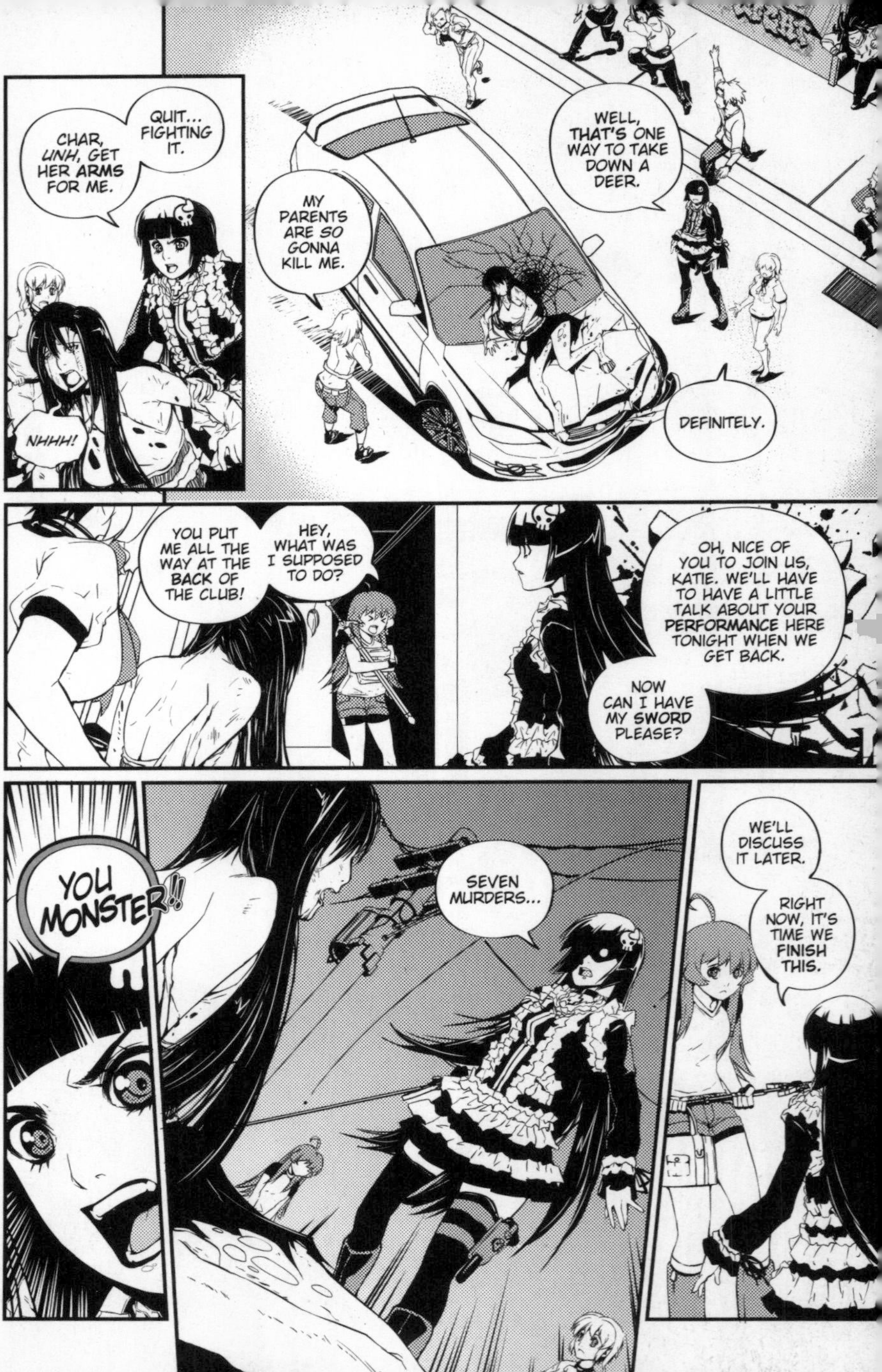
WELL, THAT'S ONE WAY TO TAKE DOWN A DEER.
MY PARENTS ARE SO GONNA KILL ME.
DEFINITELY.
QUIT... FIGHTING IT.
CHAR, UNH, GET HER ARMS FOR ME.
NHHH!
OH, NICE OF YOU TO JOIN US, KATIE. WE'LL HAVE TO HAVE A LITTLE TALK ABOUT YOUR PERFORMANCE HERE TONIGHT WHEN WE GET BACK.
NOW CAN I HAVE MY SWORD PLEASE?
HEY, WHAT WAS I SUPPOSED TO DO?
YOU PUT ME ALL THE WAY AT THE BACK OF THE CLUB!
WE'LL DISCUSS IT LATER.
RIGHT NOW, IT'S TIME WE FINISH THIS.
SEVEN MURDERS...
YOU MONSTER!!

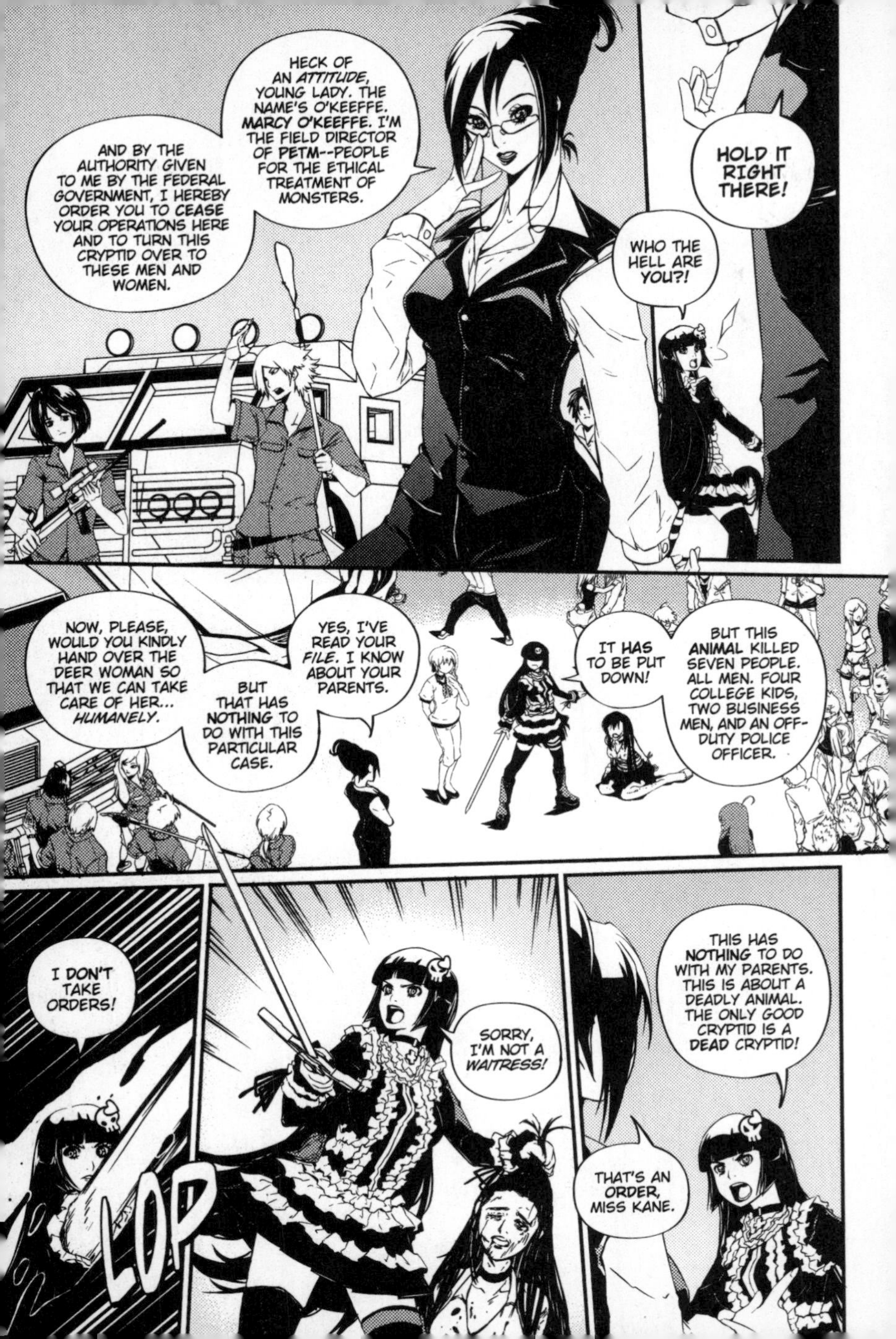
HOLD IT RIGHT THERE!
WHO THE HELL ARE *YOU*?!
HECK OF AN *ATTITUDE*, YOUNG LADY. THE NAME'S O'KEEFFE. **MARCY O'KEEFFE**. I'M THE FIELD DIRECTOR OF **PETM**--PEOPLE FOR THE ETHICAL TREATMENT OF MONSTERS.
AND BY THE AUTHORITY GIVEN TO ME BY THE FEDERAL GOVERNMENT, I HEREBY ORDER YOU TO **CEASE** YOUR OPERATIONS HERE AND TO TURN THIS CRYPTID OVER TO THESE MEN AND WOMEN.
BUT THIS **ANIMAL** KILLED SEVEN PEOPLE. ALL MEN. FOUR COLLEGE KIDS, TWO BUSINESS MEN, AND AN OFF-DUTY POLICE OFFICER.
IT **HAS** TO BE PUT *DOWN*!
YES, I'VE READ YOUR *FILE*. I KNOW ABOUT YOUR PARENTS.
BUT THAT HAS **NOTHING** TO DO WITH THIS PARTICULAR CASE.
NOW, PLEASE, WOULD YOU KINDLY HAND OVER THE DEER WOMAN SO THAT WE CAN TAKE CARE OF HER... *HUMANELY*.
THIS HAS **NOTHING** TO DO WITH MY PARENTS. THIS IS ABOUT A DEADLY ANIMAL. THE ONLY GOOD CRYPTID IS A DEAD CRYPTID!
THAT'S AN ORDER, MISS KANE.
SORRY, I'M NOT A *WAITRESS*!
I DON'T TAKE ORDERS!
LOP

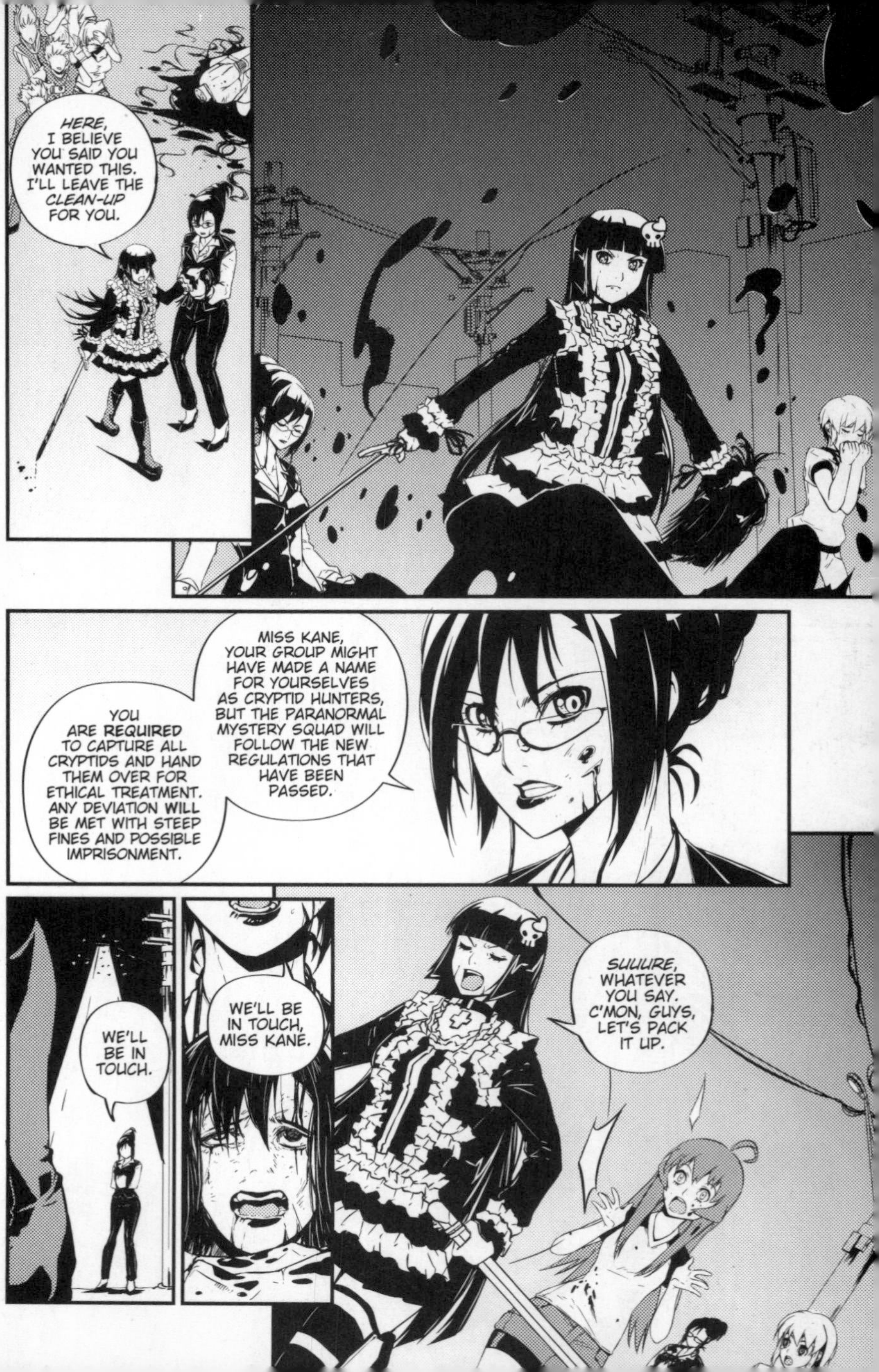
HERE, I BELIEVE YOU SAID YOU WANTED THIS. I'LL LEAVE THE CLEAN-UP FOR YOU.
MISS KANE, YOUR GROUP MIGHT HAVE MADE A NAME FOR YOURSELVES AS CRYPTID HUNTERS, BUT THE PARANORMAL MYSTERY SQUAD WILL FOLLOW THE NEW REGULATIONS THAT HAVE BEEN PASSED.
YOU ARE REQUIRED TO CAPTURE ALL CRYPTIDS AND HAND THEM OVER FOR ETHICAL TREATMENT. ANY DEVIATION WILL BE MET WITH STEEP FINES AND POSSIBLE IMPRISONMENT.
SUUURE, WHATEVER YOU SAY. C'MON, GUYS, LET'S PACK IT UP.
WE'LL BE IN TOUCH, MISS KANE.
WE'LL BE IN TOUCH.

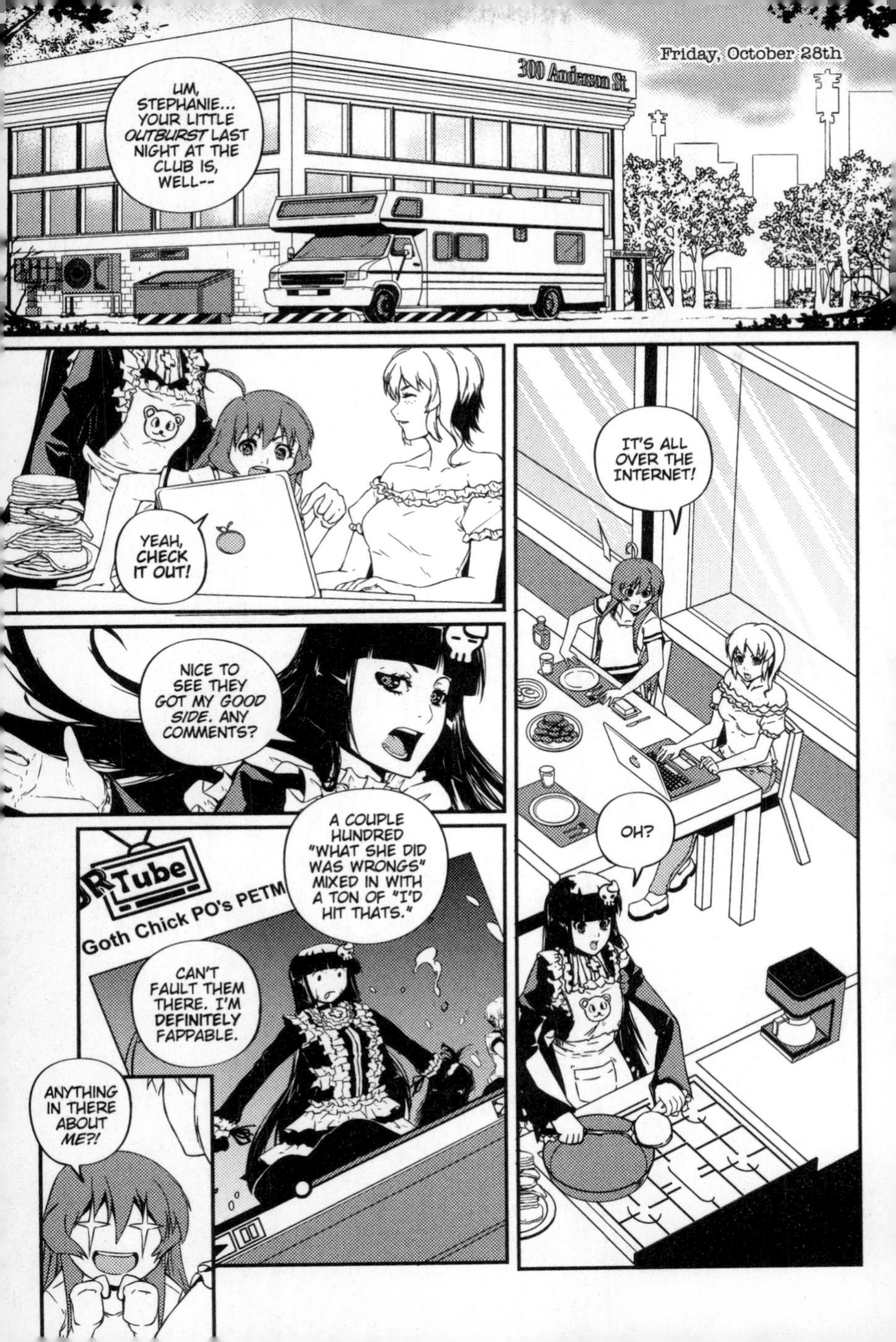
Friday, October 28th
300 Anderson St.
UM, STEPHANIE... YOUR LITTLE *OUTBURST* LAST NIGHT AT THE CLUB IS, WELL--
IT'S ALL OVER THE INTERNET!
OH?
YEAH, CHECK IT OUT!
NICE TO SEE THEY GOT MY *GOOD SIDE*. ANY COMMENTS?
RTube
Goth Chick PO's PETM
A COUPLE HUNDRED "WHAT SHE DID WAS WRONGS" MIXED IN WITH A TON OF "I'D HIT THATS."
CAN'T FAULT THEM THERE. I'M DEFINITELY FAPPABLE.
ANYTHING IN THERE ABOUT *ME*?!

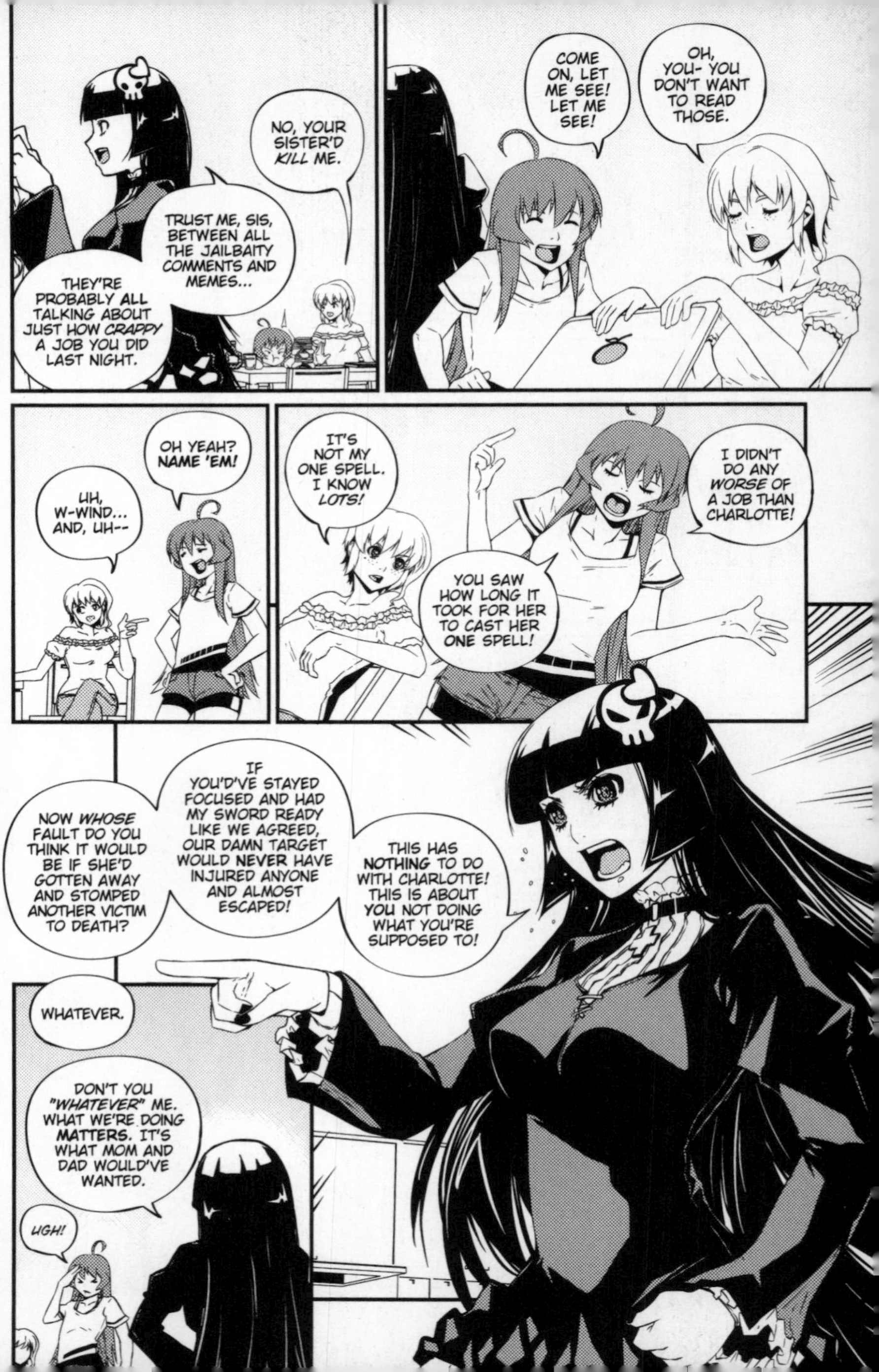

OH, YOU- YOU DON'T WANT TO READ THOSE.
COME ON, LET ME SEE! LET ME SEE!
NO, YOUR SISTER'D *KILL* ME.
TRUST ME, SIS, BETWEEN ALL THE JAILBAITY COMMENTS AND MEMES...
THEY'RE PROBABLY ALL TALKING ABOUT JUST HOW *CRAPPY* A JOB YOU DID LAST NIGHT.
I DIDN'T DO ANY *WORSE* OF A JOB THAN CHARLOTTE!
IT'S NOT MY ONE SPELL. I KNOW *LOTS!*
YOU SAW HOW LONG IT TOOK FOR HER TO CAST HER **ONE SPELL**!
OH YEAH? **NAME 'EM!**
UH, W-WIND... AND, UH--
THIS HAS **NOTHING** TO DO WITH CHARLOTTE! THIS IS ABOUT **YOU** NOT DOING WHAT YOU'RE SUPPOSED TO!
IF YOU'D'VE STAYED FOCUSED AND HAD MY SWORD READY LIKE WE AGREED, OUR DAMN TARGET WOULD **NEVER** HAVE INJURED ANYONE AND ALMOST ESCAPED!
NOW *WHOSE* FAULT DO YOU THINK IT WOULD BE IF SHE'D GOTTEN AWAY AND STOMPED ANOTHER VICTIM TO DEATH?
WHATEVER.
DON'T YOU *"WHATEVER"* ME. WHAT WE'RE DOING **MATTERS**. IT'S WHAT MOM AND DAD WOULD'VE WANTED.
UGH!

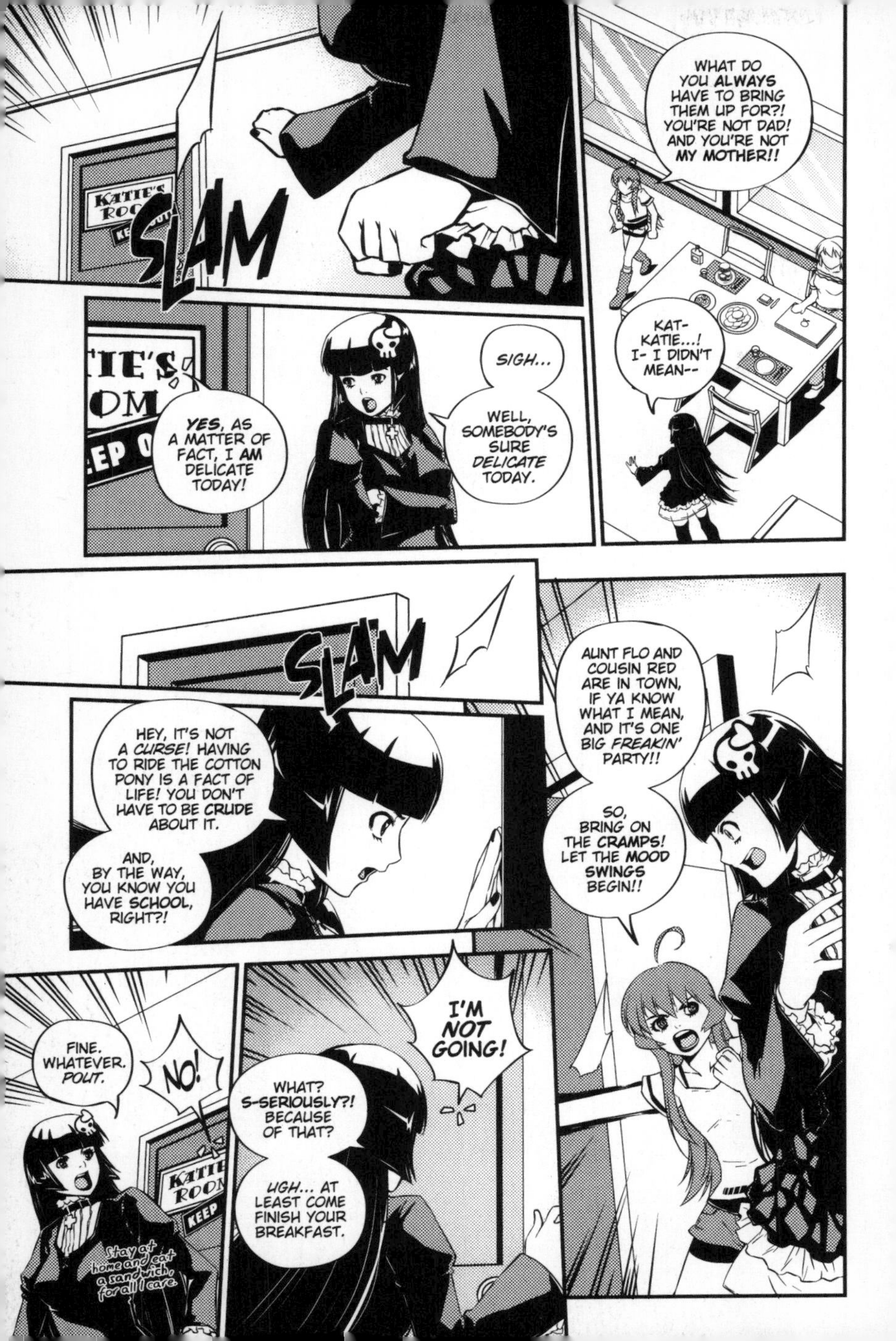
WHAT DO YOU ALWAYS HAVE TO BRING THEM UP FOR?! YOU'RE NOT DAD! AND YOU'RE NOT MY MOTHER!!
KAT-KATIE...! I- I DIDN'T MEAN--
KATIE'S ROOM KEEP OUT
SLAM
SIGH...
WELL, SOMEBODY'S SURE DELICATE TODAY.
YES, AS A MATTER OF FACT, I AM DELICATE TODAY!
AUNT FLO AND COUSIN RED ARE IN TOWN, IF YA KNOW WHAT I MEAN, AND IT'S ONE BIG FREAKIN' PARTY!!
SO, BRING ON THE CRAMPS! LET THE MOOD SWINGS BEGIN!!
SLAM
HEY, IT'S NOT A CURSE! HAVING TO RIDE THE COTTON PONY IS A FACT OF LIFE! YOU DON'T HAVE TO BE CRUDE ABOUT IT.
AND, BY THE WAY, YOU KNOW YOU HAVE SCHOOL, RIGHT?!
I'M NOT GOING!
WHAT? S-SERIOUSLY?! BECAUSE OF THAT?
UGH... AT LEAST COME FINISH YOUR BREAKFAST.
NO!
FINE. WHATEVER. POUT.
Stay at home and eat a sandwich, for all I care.

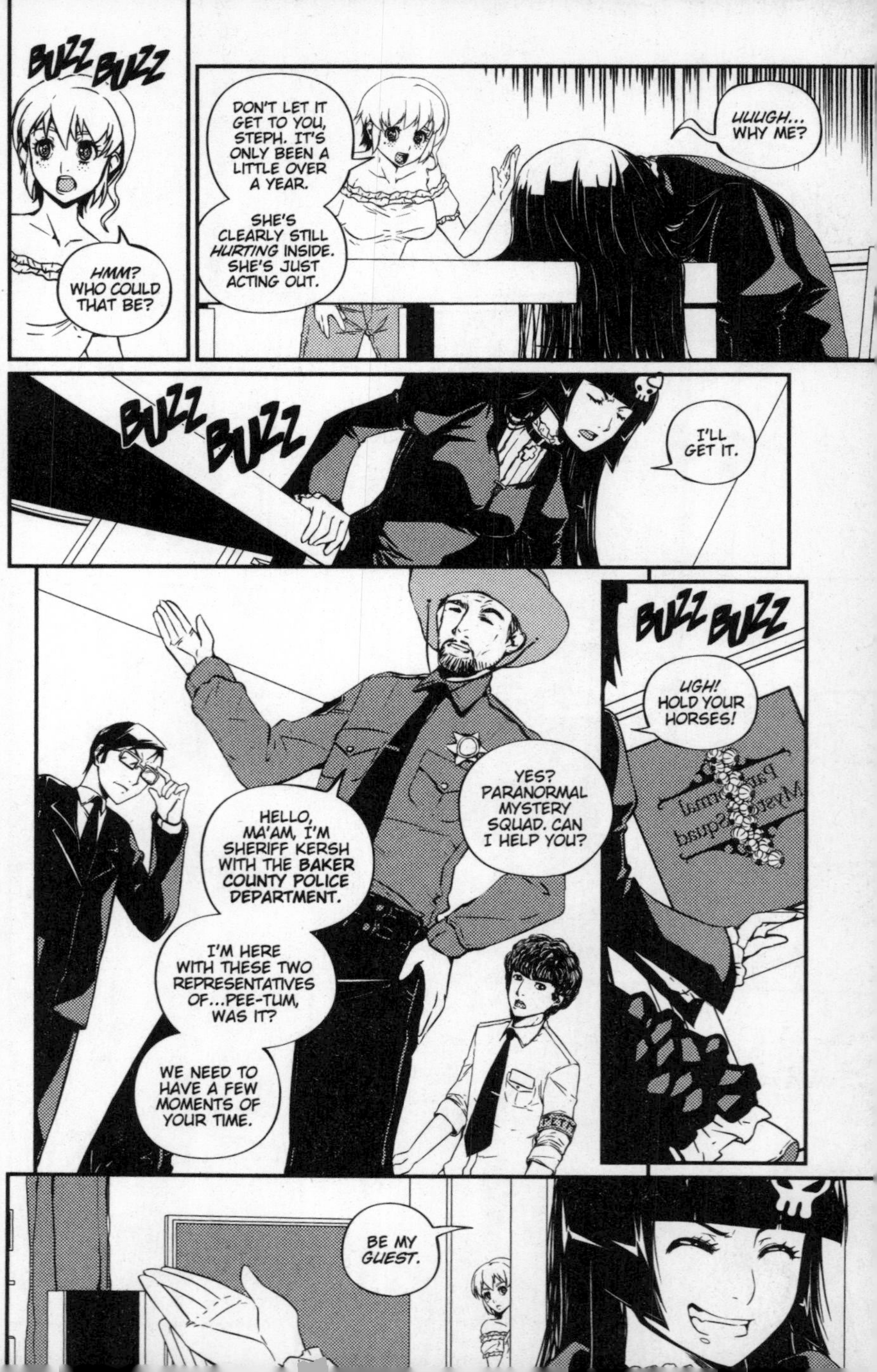
UUUGH... WHY ME?
DON'T LET IT GET TO YOU, STEPH. IT'S ONLY BEEN A LITTLE OVER A YEAR.
SHE'S CLEARLY STILL *HURTING* INSIDE. SHE'S JUST ACTING OUT.
BUZZ BUZZ
HMM? WHO COULD THAT BE?
I'LL GET IT.
BUZZ BUZZ
BUZZ BUZZ
UGH! HOLD YOUR HORSES!
YES? PARANORMAL MYSTERY SQUAD. CAN I HELP YOU?
HELLO, MA'AM, I'M SHERIFF KERSH WITH THE BAKER COUNTY POLICE DEPARTMENT.
I'M HERE WITH THESE TWO REPRESENTATIVES OF...PEE-TUM, WAS IT?
WE NEED TO HAVE A FEW MOMENTS OF YOUR TIME.
BE MY *GUEST*.

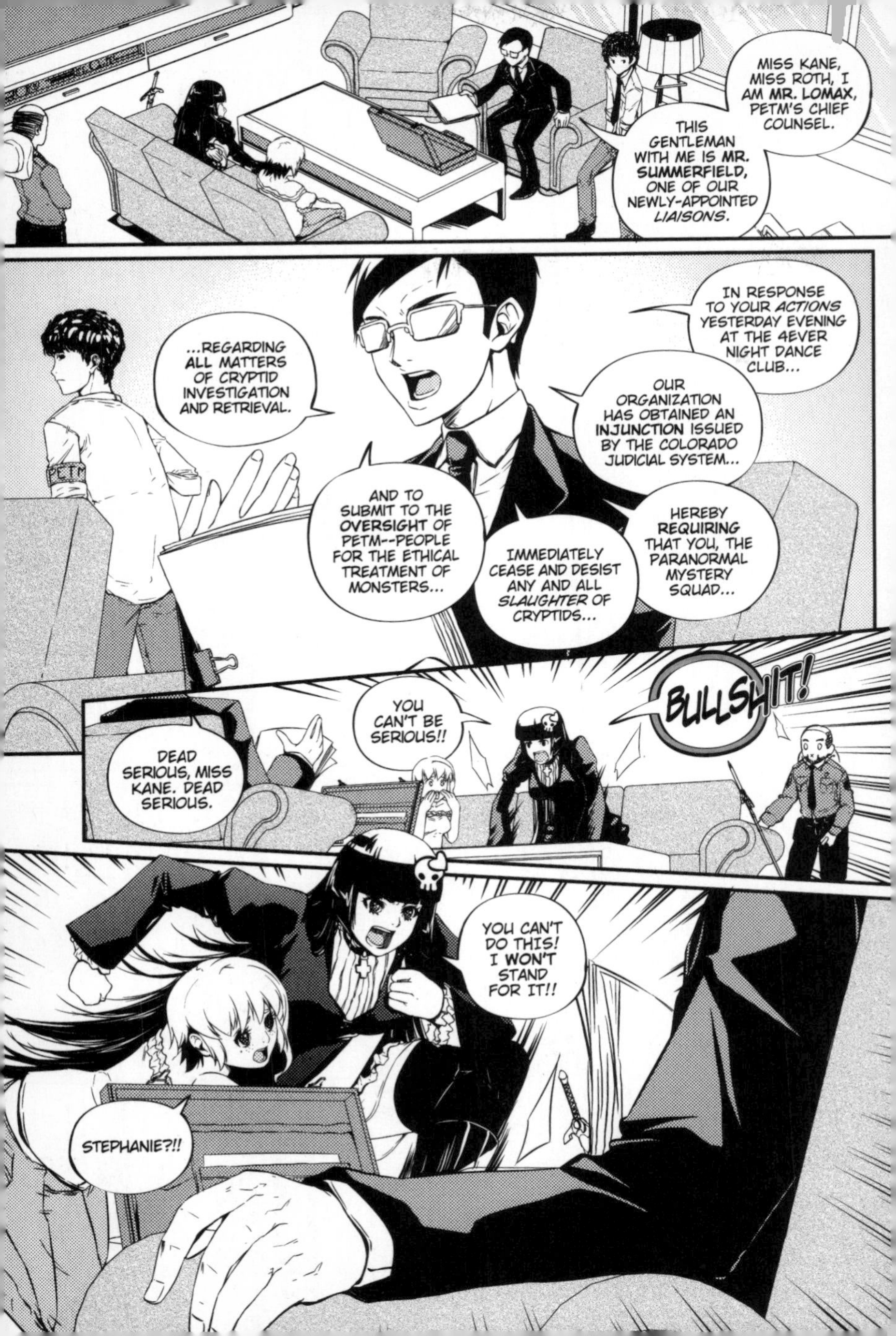
MISS KANE, MISS ROTH, I AM MR. LOMAX, PETM'S CHIEF COUNSEL.
THIS GENTLEMAN WITH ME IS MR. SUMMERFIELD, ONE OF OUR NEWLY-APPOINTED LIAISONS.
IN RESPONSE TO YOUR ACTIONS YESTERDAY EVENING AT THE 4EVER NIGHT DANCE CLUB...
OUR ORGANIZATION HAS OBTAINED AN INJUNCTION ISSUED BY THE COLORADO JUDICIAL SYSTEM...
HEREBY REQUIRING THAT YOU, THE PARANORMAL MYSTERY SQUAD...
IMMEDIATELY CEASE AND DESIST ANY AND ALL SLAUGHTER OF CRYPTIDS...
AND TO SUBMIT TO THE OVERSIGHT OF PETM--PEOPLE FOR THE ETHICAL TREATMENT OF MONSTERS...
...REGARDING ALL MATTERS OF CRYPTID INVESTIGATION AND RETRIEVAL.
BULLSHIT!
YOU CAN'T BE SERIOUS!!
DEAD SERIOUS, MISS KANE. DEAD SERIOUS.
YOU CAN'T DO THIS! I WON'T STAND FOR IT!!
STEPHANIE?!!

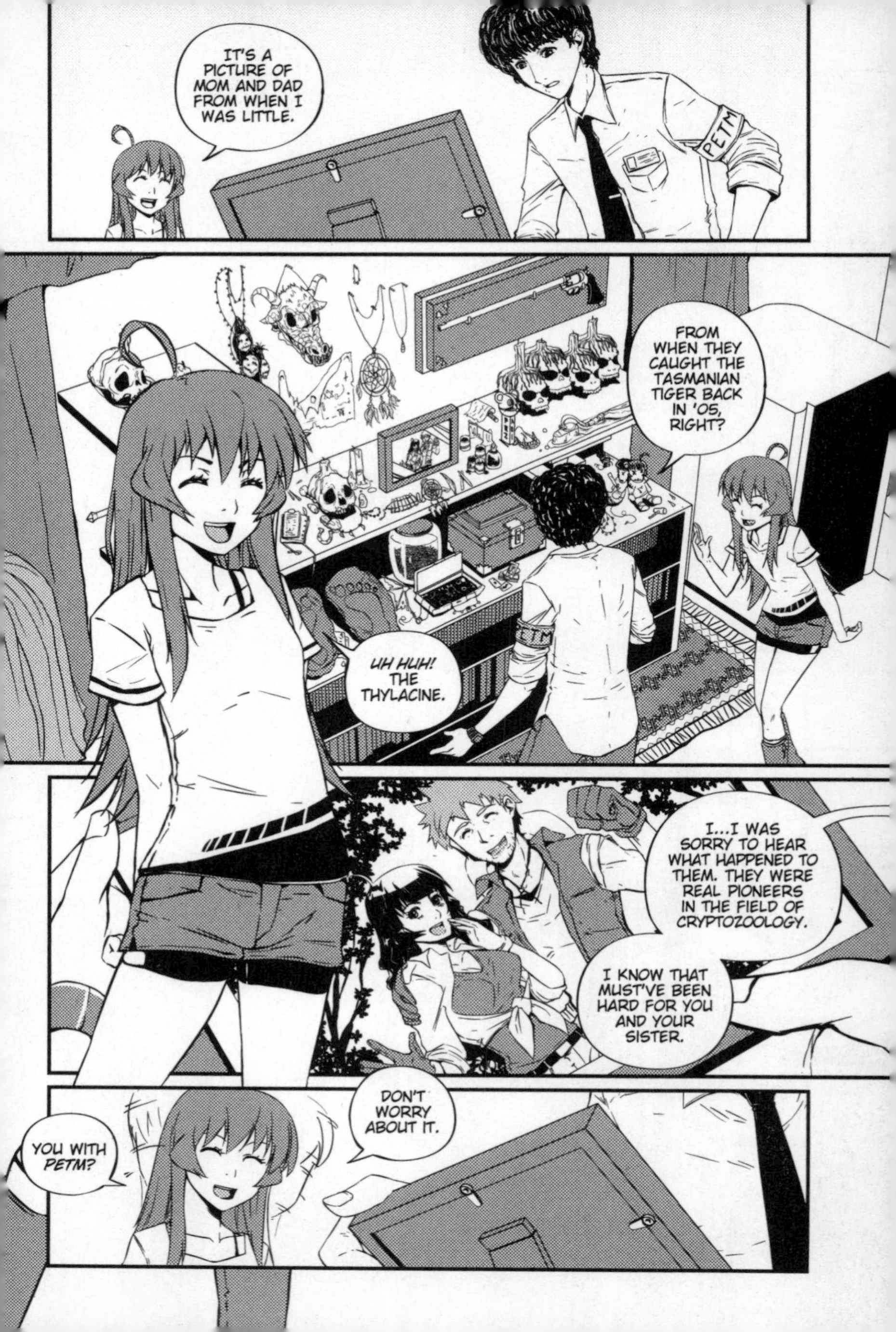
IT'S A PICTURE OF MOM AND DAD FROM WHEN I WAS LITTLE.
PETM
FROM WHEN THEY CAUGHT THE TASMANIAN TIGER BACK IN '05, RIGHT?
UH HUH! THE THYLACINE.
I...I WAS SORRY TO HEAR WHAT HAPPENED TO THEM. THEY WERE REAL PIONEERS IN THE FIELD OF CRYPTOZOOLOGY.
I KNOW THAT MUST'VE BEEN HARD FOR YOU AND YOUR SISTER.
DON'T WORRY ABOUT IT.
YOU WITH *PETM?*

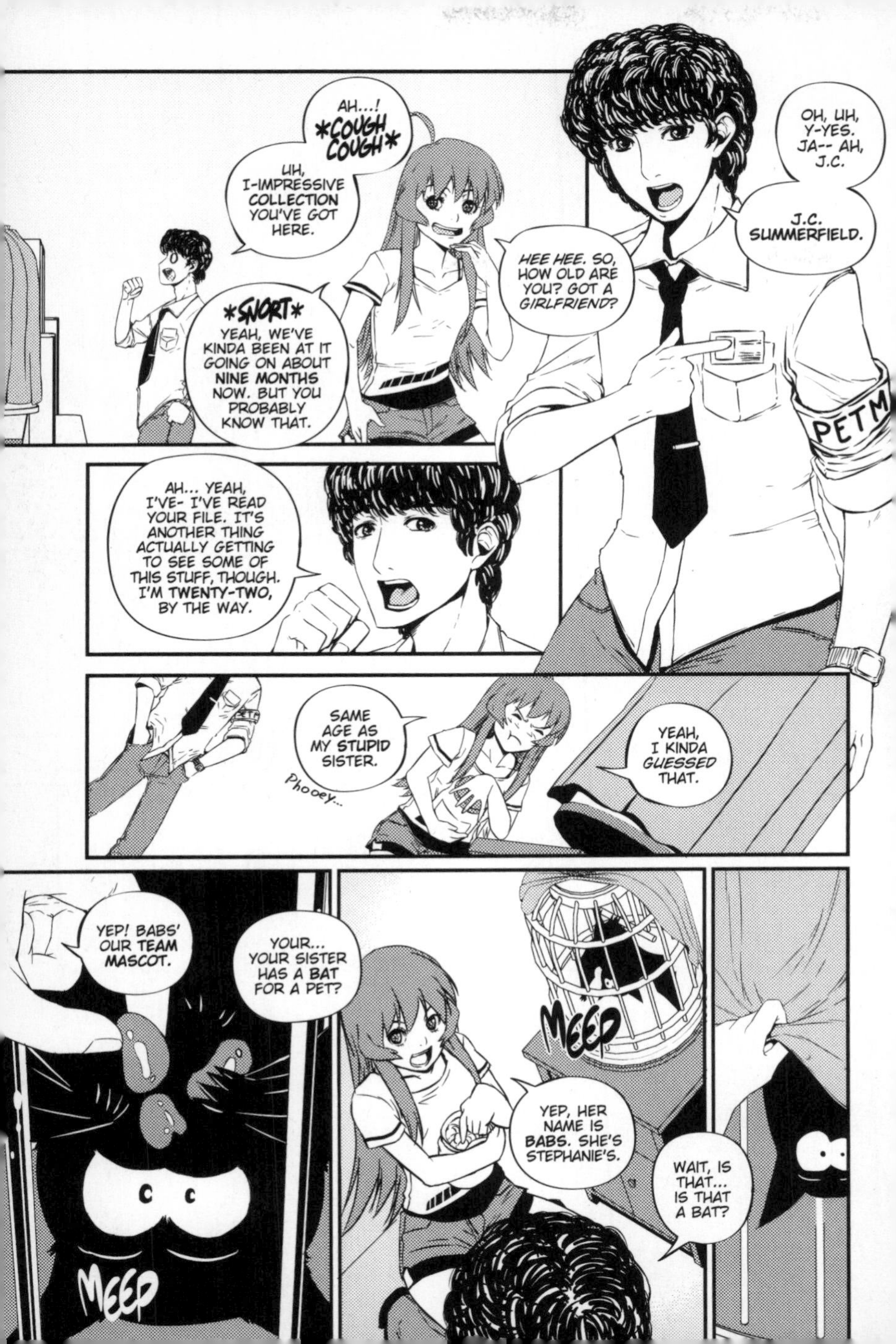
OH, UH, Y-YES. JA-- AH, J.C.
J.C. SUMMERFIELD.
PETM
AH...! *COUGH COUGH*
UH, I-IMPRESSIVE COLLECTION YOU'VE GOT HERE.
HEE HEE. SO, HOW OLD ARE YOU? GOT A GIRLFRIEND?
SNORT YEAH, WE'VE KINDA BEEN AT IT GOING ON ABOUT NINE MONTHS NOW. BUT YOU PROBABLY KNOW THAT.
AH... YEAH, I'VE- I'VE READ YOUR FILE. IT'S ANOTHER THING ACTUALLY GETTING TO SEE SOME OF THIS STUFF, THOUGH. I'M TWENTY-TWO, BY THE WAY.
YEAH, I KINDA GUESSED THAT.
SAME AGE AS MY STUPID SISTER.
Phooey...
WAIT, IS THAT... IS THAT A BAT?
YEP, HER NAME IS BABS. SHE'S STEPHANIE'S.
MEEP
YOUR... YOUR SISTER HAS A BAT FOR A PET?
YEP! BABS' OUR TEAM MASCOT.
MEEP

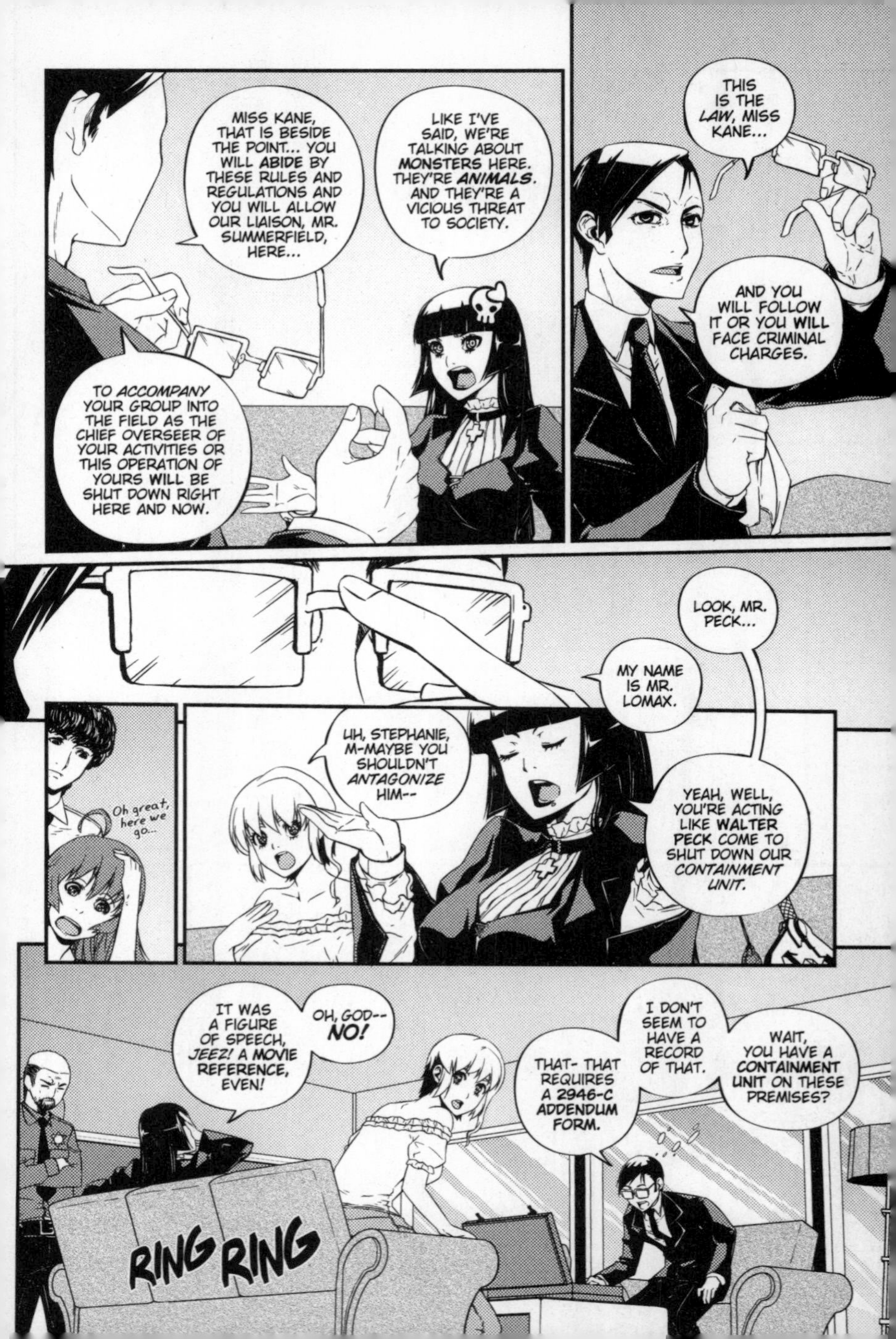
MISS KANE, THAT IS BESIDE THE POINT... YOU WILL **ABIDE** BY THESE RULES AND REGULATIONS AND YOU WILL ALLOW OUR LIAISON, MR. SUMMERFIELD, HERE...
LIKE I'VE SAID, WE'RE TALKING ABOUT **MONSTERS** HERE. THEY'RE ***ANIMALS***. AND THEY'RE A VICIOUS THREAT TO SOCIETY.
TO *ACCOMPANY* YOUR GROUP INTO THE FIELD AS THE CHIEF OVERSEER OF YOUR ACTIVITIES OR THIS OPERATION OF YOURS **WILL** BE SHUT DOWN RIGHT HERE AND NOW.
THIS IS THE *LAW*, MISS KANE...
AND YOU WILL FOLLOW IT OR YOU **WILL** FACE CRIMINAL CHARGES.
LOOK, MR. PECK...
MY NAME IS MR. LOMAX.
Oh great, here we go...
UH, STEPHANIE, M-MAYBE YOU SHOULDN'T *ANTAGONIZE* HIM--
YEAH, WELL, YOU'RE ACTING LIKE **WALTER PECK** COME TO SHUT DOWN OUR *CONTAINMENT UNIT*.
IT WAS A FIGURE OF SPEECH, *JEEZ!* A **MOVIE** REFERENCE, EVEN!
OH, GOD-- ***NO!***
I DON'T SEEM TO HAVE A RECORD OF THAT.
THAT- THAT REQUIRES **A 2946-C ADDENDUM FORM.**
WAIT, YOU HAVE A **CONTAINMENT UNIT** ON THESE PREMISES?
RING RING

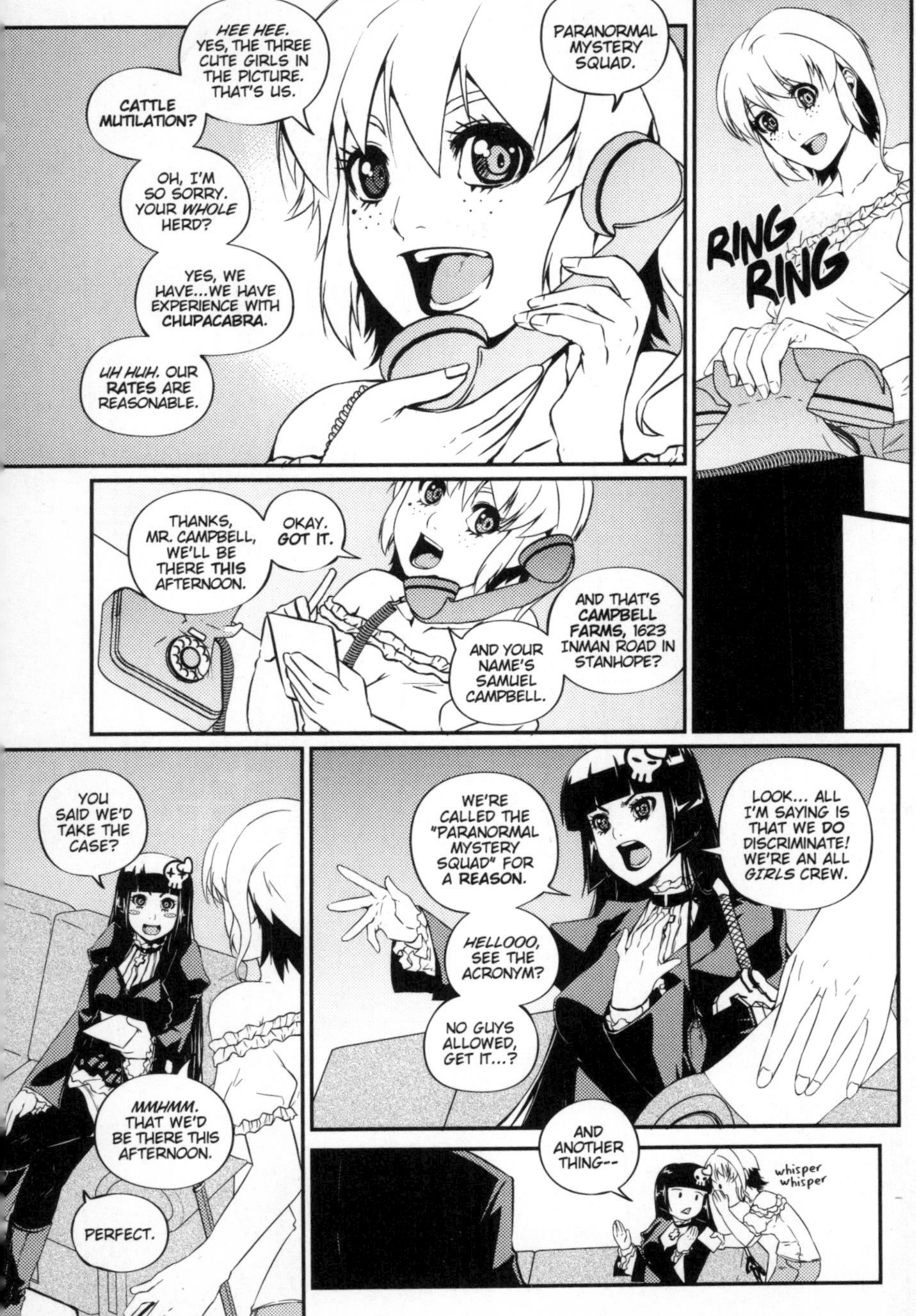
RING RING
PARANORMAL MYSTERY SQUAD.
HEE HEE. YES, THE THREE CUTE GIRLS IN THE PICTURE. THAT'S US.
CATTLE MUTILATION?
OH, I'M SO SORRY. YOUR WHOLE HERD?
YES, WE HAVE...WE HAVE EXPERIENCE WITH CHUPACABRA.
UH HUH. OUR RATES ARE REASONABLE.
OKAY. GOT IT.
THANKS, MR. CAMPBELL, WE'LL BE THERE THIS AFTERNOON.
AND THAT'S CAMPBELL FARMS, 1623 INMAN ROAD IN STANHOPE?
AND YOUR NAME'S SAMUEL CAMPBELL.
LOOK... ALL I'M SAYING IS THAT WE DO DISCRIMINATE! WE'RE AN ALL GIRLS CREW.
WE'RE CALLED THE "PARANORMAL MYSTERY SQUAD" FOR A REASON.
HELLOOO, SEE THE ACRONYM?
NO GUYS ALLOWED, GET IT...?
AND ANOTHER THING--
whisper whisper
YOU SAID WE'D TAKE THE CASE?
MMHMM. THAT WE'D BE THERE THIS AFTERNOON.
PERFECT.

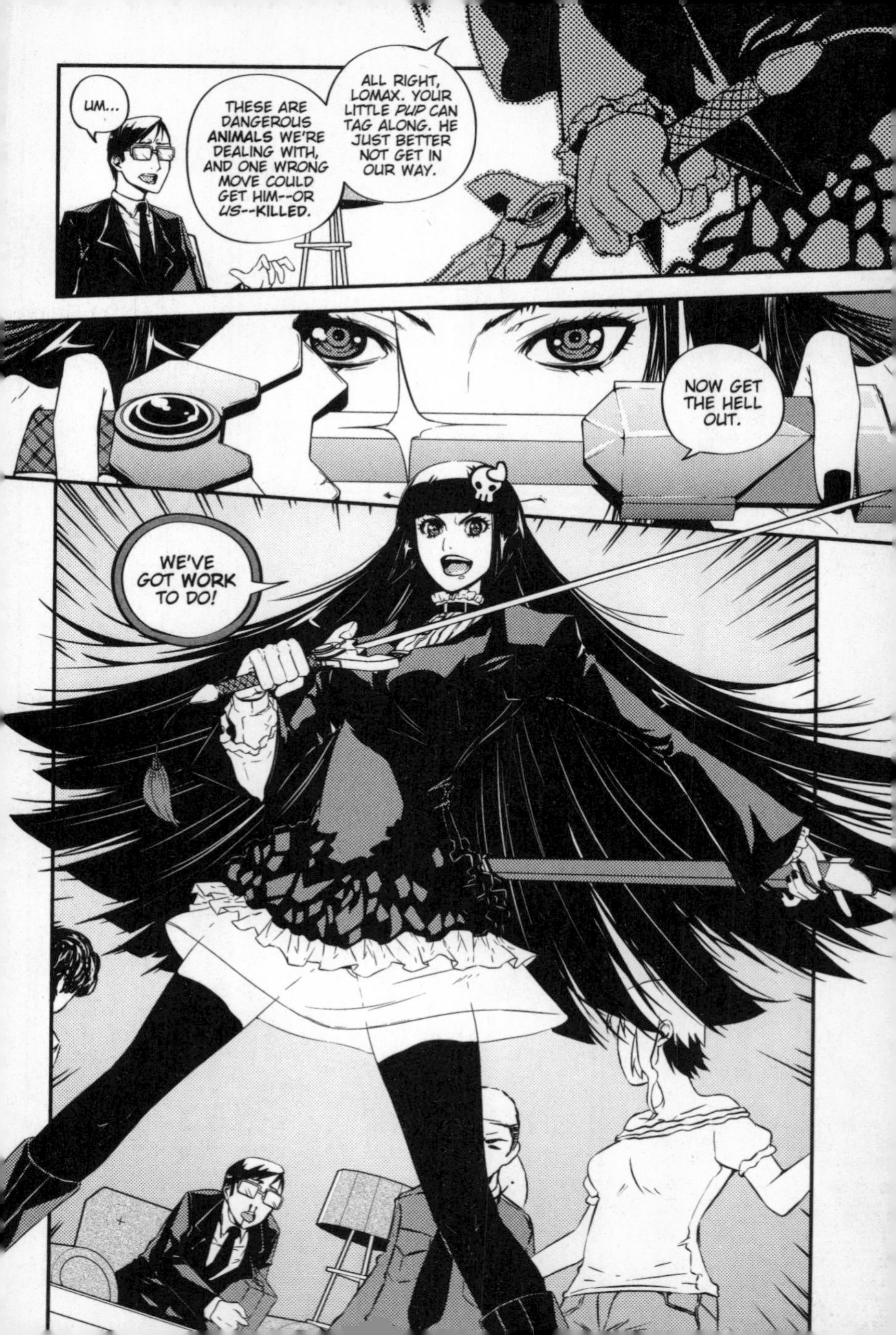
ALL RIGHT, LOMAX. YOUR LITTLE PUP CAN TAG ALONG. HE JUST BETTER NOT GET IN OUR WAY.
THESE ARE DANGEROUS ANIMALS WE'RE DEALING WITH, AND ONE WRONG MOVE COULD GET HIM--OR US--KILLED.
UM...
NOW GET THE HELL OUT.
WE'VE GOT WORK TO DO!

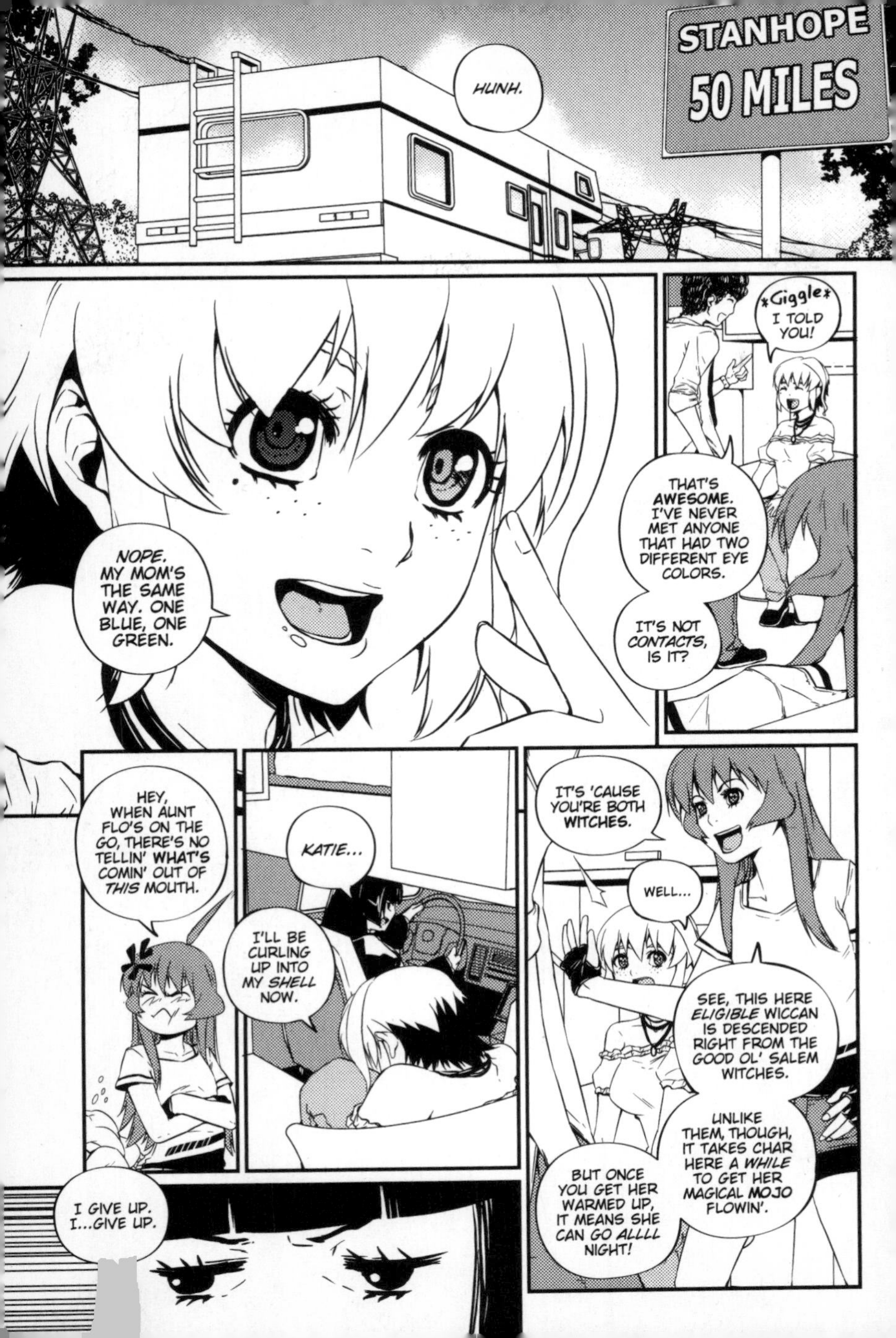
STANHOPE
50 MILES
HUNH.
Giggle I TOLD YOU!
THAT'S AWESOME. I'VE NEVER MET ANYONE THAT HAD TWO DIFFERENT EYE COLORS.
IT'S NOT CONTACTS, IS IT?
NOPE. MY MOM'S THE SAME WAY. ONE BLUE, ONE GREEN.
IT'S 'CAUSE YOU'RE BOTH WITCHES.
WELL...
SEE, THIS HERE ELIGIBLE WICCAN IS DESCENDED RIGHT FROM THE GOOD OL' SALEM WITCHES.
UNLIKE THEM, THOUGH, IT TAKES CHAR HERE A WHILE TO GET HER MAGICAL MOJO FLOWIN'.
BUT ONCE YOU GET HER WARMED UP, IT MEANS SHE CAN GO ALLLL NIGHT!
KATIE...
I'LL BE CURLING UP INTO MY SHELL NOW.
HEY, WHEN AUNT FLO'S ON THE GO, THERE'S NO TELLIN' WHAT'S COMIN' OUT OF THIS MOUTH.
I GIVE UP. I...GIVE UP.

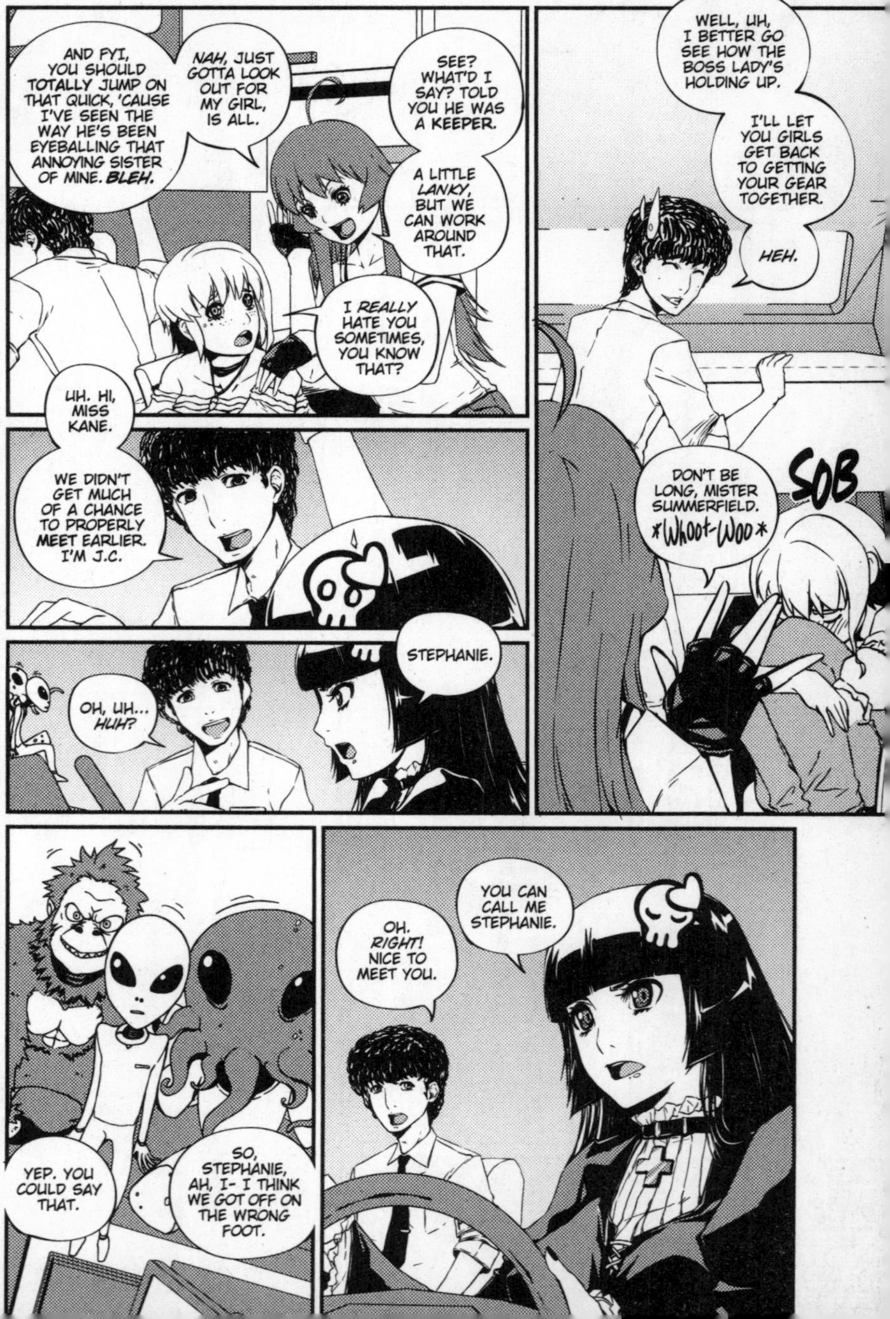
WELL, UH, I BETTER GO SEE HOW THE BOSS LADY'S HOLDING UP.
I'LL LET YOU GIRLS GET BACK TO GETTING YOUR GEAR TOGETHER.
HEH.
SOB
DON'T BE LONG, MISTER SUMMERFIELD.
Whoot-Woo
SEE? WHAT'D I SAY? TOLD YOU HE WAS A KEEPER.
A LITTLE *LANKY*, BUT WE CAN WORK AROUND THAT.
I *REALLY* HATE YOU SOMETIMES, YOU KNOW THAT?
NAH, JUST GOTTA LOOK OUT FOR MY GIRL, IS ALL.
AND FYI, YOU SHOULD TOTALLY JUMP ON THAT QUICK, 'CAUSE I'VE SEEN THE WAY HE'S BEEN EYEBALLING THAT ANNOYING SISTER OF MINE. ***BLEH.***
UH. HI, MISS KANE.
WE DIDN'T GET MUCH OF A CHANCE TO PROPERLY MEET EARLIER. I'M J.C.
STEPHANIE.
OH, UH... *HUH?*
YOU CAN CALL ME STEPHANIE.
OH. *RIGHT!* NICE TO MEET YOU.
SO, STEPHANIE, AH, I- I THINK WE GOT OFF ON THE WRONG FOOT.
YEP. YOU COULD SAY THAT.

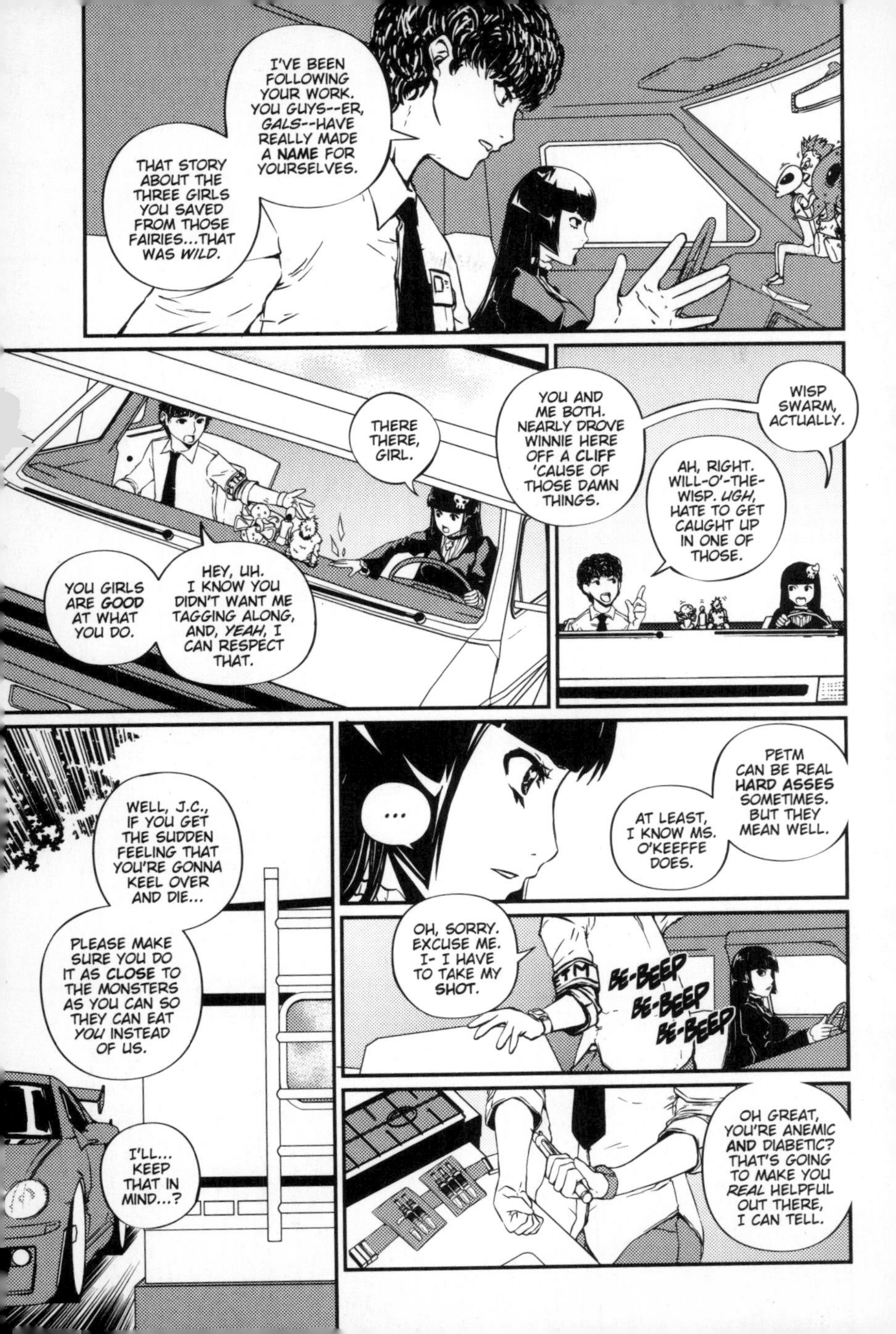
I'VE BEEN FOLLOWING YOUR WORK. YOU GUYS--ER, GALS--HAVE REALLY MADE A NAME FOR YOURSELVES.
THAT STORY ABOUT THE THREE GIRLS YOU SAVED FROM THOSE FAIRIES...THAT WAS WILD.
YOU AND ME BOTH. NEARLY DROVE WINNIE HERE OFF A CLIFF 'CAUSE OF THOSE DAMN THINGS.
WISP SWARM, ACTUALLY.
AH, RIGHT. WILL-O'-THE-WISP. UGH, HATE TO GET CAUGHT UP IN ONE OF THOSE.
THERE THERE, GIRL.
HEY, UH. I KNOW YOU DIDN'T WANT ME TAGGING ALONG, AND, YEAH, I CAN RESPECT THAT.
YOU GIRLS ARE GOOD AT WHAT YOU DO.
PETM CAN BE REAL HARD ASSES SOMETIMES. BUT THEY MEAN WELL.
AT LEAST, I KNOW MS. O'KEEFFE DOES.
...
OH, SORRY. EXCUSE ME. I- I HAVE TO TAKE MY SHOT.
BE-BEEP
BE-BEEP
BE-BEEP
OH GREAT, YOU'RE ANEMIC AND DIABETIC? THAT'S GOING TO MAKE YOU REAL HELPFUL OUT THERE, I CAN TELL.
WELL, J.C., IF YOU GET THE SUDDEN FEELING THAT YOU'RE GONNA KEEL OVER AND DIE...
PLEASE MAKE SURE YOU DO IT AS CLOSE TO THE MONSTERS AS YOU CAN SO THEY CAN EAT YOU INSTEAD OF US.
I'LL... KEEP THAT IN MIND...?

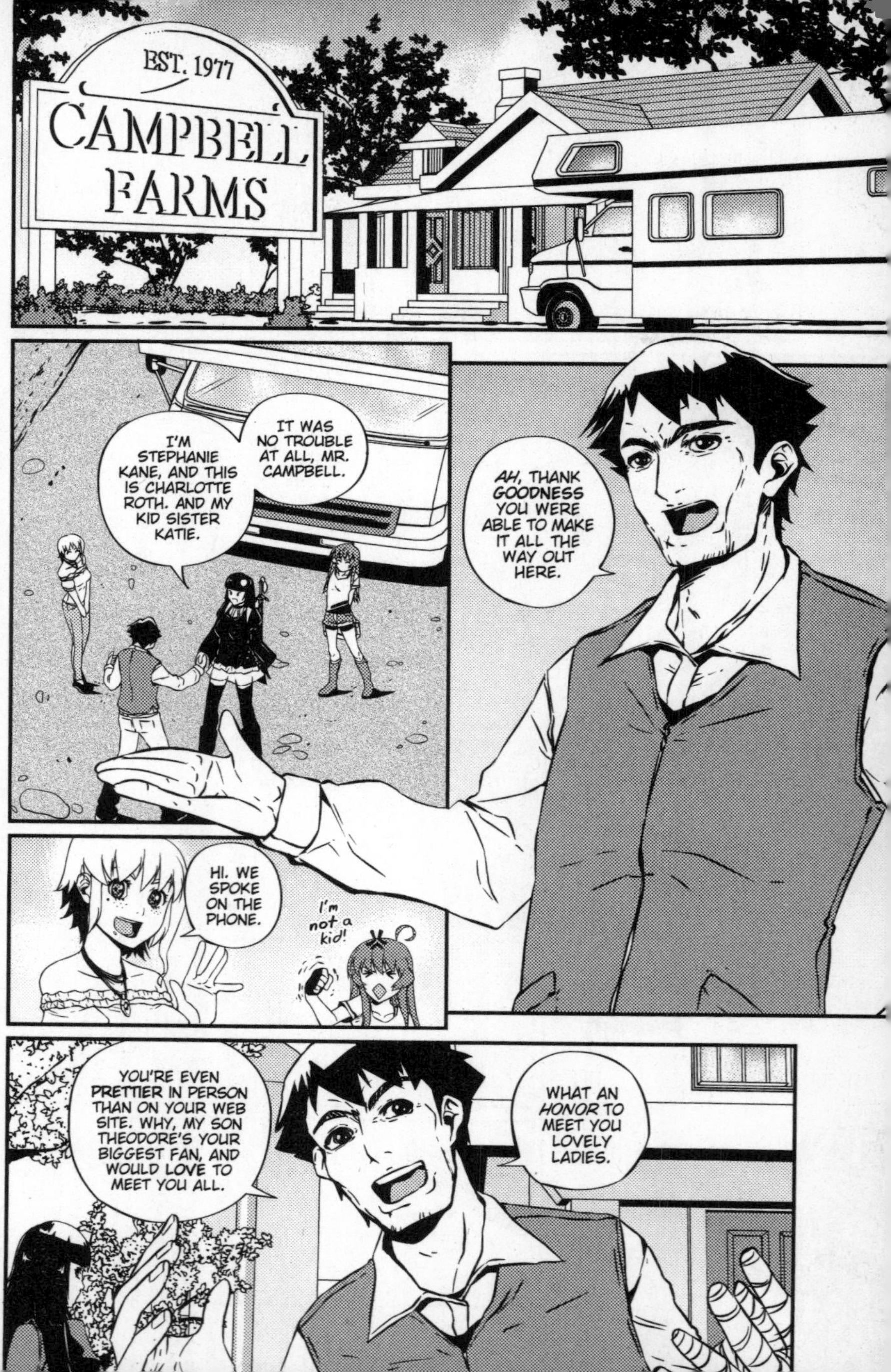
EST. 1977
CAMPBELL FARMS
AH, THANK GOODNESS YOU WERE ABLE TO MAKE IT ALL THE WAY OUT HERE.
IT WAS NO TROUBLE AT ALL, MR. CAMPBELL.
I'M STEPHANIE KANE, AND THIS IS CHARLOTTE ROTH. AND MY KID SISTER KATIE.
HI. WE SPOKE ON THE PHONE.
I'm not a kid!
WHAT AN HONOR TO MEET YOU LOVELY LADIES.
YOU'RE EVEN PRETTIER IN PERSON THAN ON YOUR WEB SITE. WHY, MY SON THEODORE'S YOUR BIGGEST FAN, AND WOULD LOVE TO MEET YOU ALL.

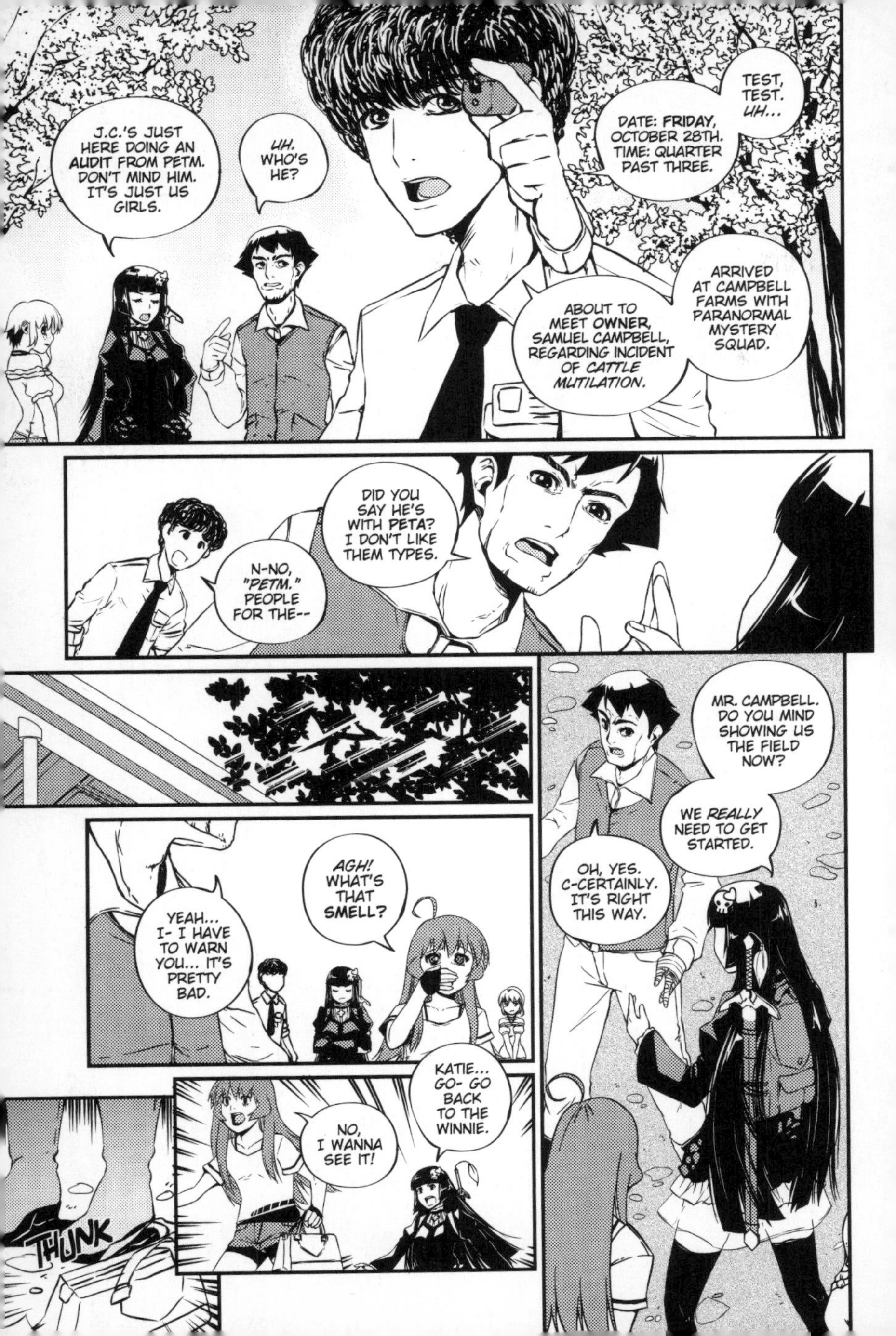
TEST, TEST. UH...
DATE: FRIDAY, OCTOBER 28TH. TIME: QUARTER PAST THREE.
ARRIVED AT CAMPBELL FARMS WITH PARANORMAL MYSTERY SQUAD.
ABOUT TO MEET OWNER, SAMUEL CAMPBELL, REGARDING INCIDENT OF CATTLE MUTILATION.
UH. WHO'S HE?
J.C.'S JUST HERE DOING AN AUDIT FROM PETM. DON'T MIND HIM. IT'S JUST US GIRLS.
DID YOU SAY HE'S WITH PETA? I DON'T LIKE THEM TYPES.
N-NO, "PETM." PEOPLE FOR THE--
MR. CAMPBELL. DO YOU MIND SHOWING US THE FIELD NOW?
WE REALLY NEED TO GET STARTED.
OH, YES. C-CERTAINLY. IT'S RIGHT THIS WAY.
AGH! WHAT'S THAT SMELL?
YEAH... I- I HAVE TO WARN YOU... IT'S PRETTY BAD.
KATIE... GO- GO BACK TO THE WINNIE.
NO, I WANNA SEE IT!
THUNK

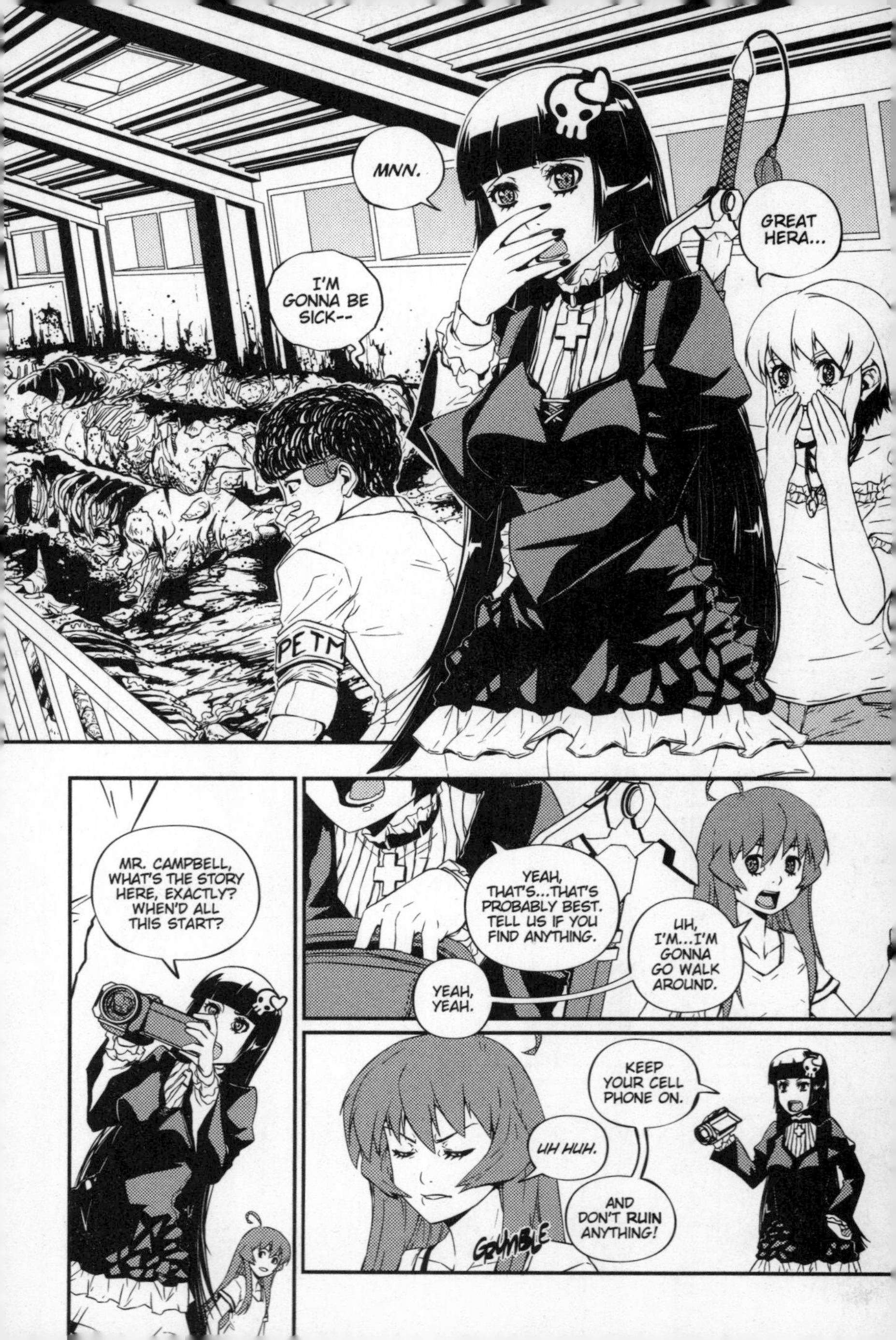
GREAT HERA...
MNN.
I'M GONNA BE SICK--
UH, I'M...I'M GONNA GO WALK AROUND.
YEAH, THAT'S...THAT'S PROBABLY BEST. TELL US IF YOU FIND ANYTHING.
YEAH, YEAH.
KEEP YOUR CELL PHONE ON.
UH HUH.
AND DON'T RUIN ANYTHING!
GRUMBLE
MR. CAMPBELL, WHAT'S THE STORY HERE, EXACTLY? WHEN'D ALL THIS START?

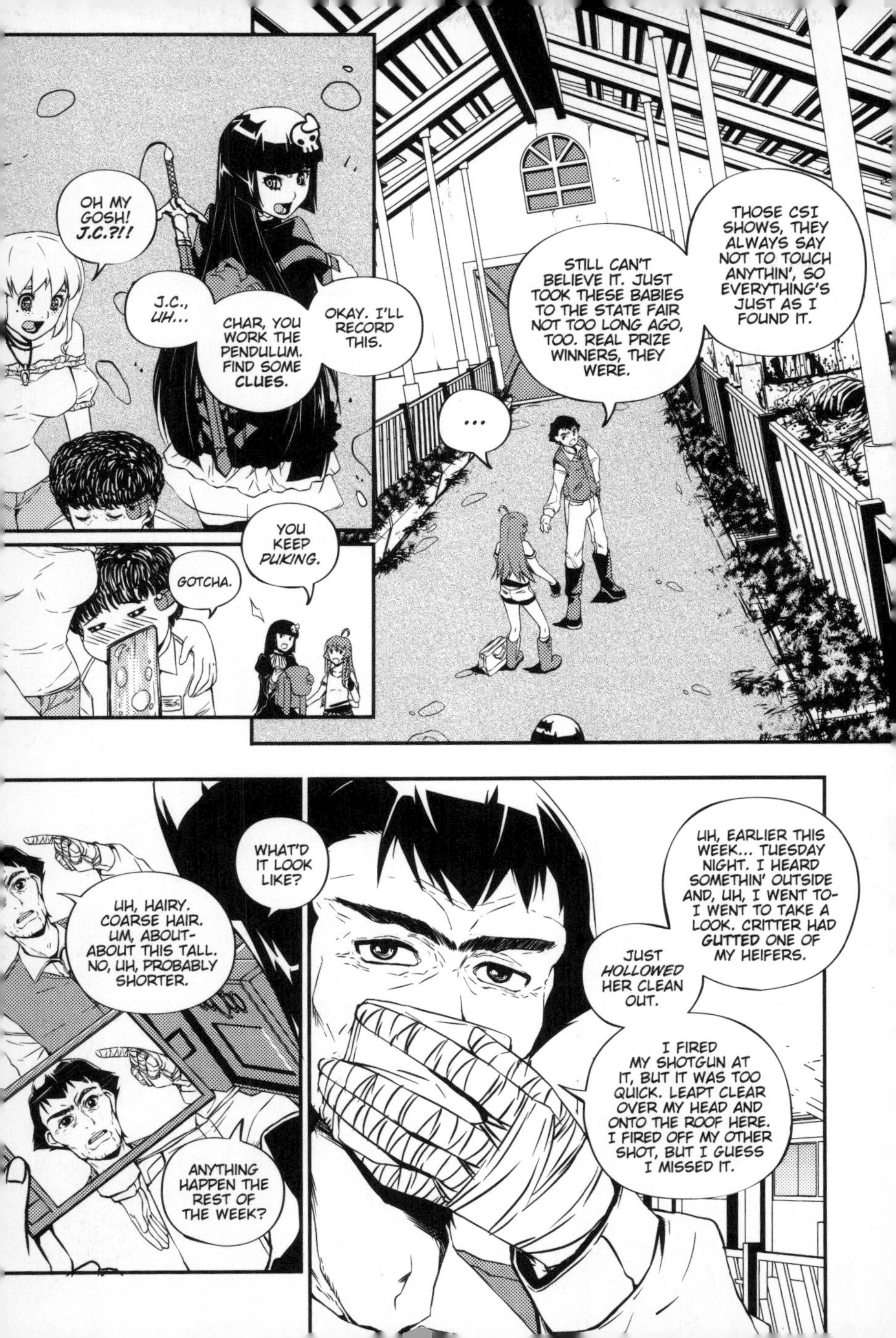
THOSE CSI SHOWS, THEY ALWAYS SAY NOT TO TOUCH ANYTHIN', SO EVERYTHING'S JUST AS I FOUND IT.
STILL CAN'T BELIEVE IT. JUST TOOK THESE BABIES TO THE STATE FAIR NOT TOO LONG AGO, TOO. REAL PRIZE WINNERS, THEY WERE.
...
OKAY. I'LL RECORD THIS.
CHAR, YOU WORK THE PENDULUM. FIND SOME CLUES.
J.C., UH...
OH MY GOSH! J.C.?!!
YOU KEEP PUKING.
GOTCHA.
UH, EARLIER THIS WEEK... TUESDAY NIGHT. I HEARD SOMETHIN' OUTSIDE AND, UH, I WENT TO- I WENT TO TAKE A LOOK. CRITTER HAD GUTTED ONE OF MY HEIFERS.
JUST HOLLOWED HER CLEAN OUT.
I FIRED MY SHOTGUN AT IT, BUT IT WAS TOO QUICK. LEAPT CLEAR OVER MY HEAD AND ONTO THE ROOF HERE. I FIRED OFF MY OTHER SHOT, BUT I GUESS I MISSED IT.
WHAT'D IT LOOK LIKE?
UH, HAIRY. COARSE HAIR. UM, ABOUT- ABOUT THIS TALL. NO, UH, PROBABLY SHORTER.
ANYTHING HAPPEN THE REST OF THE WEEK?

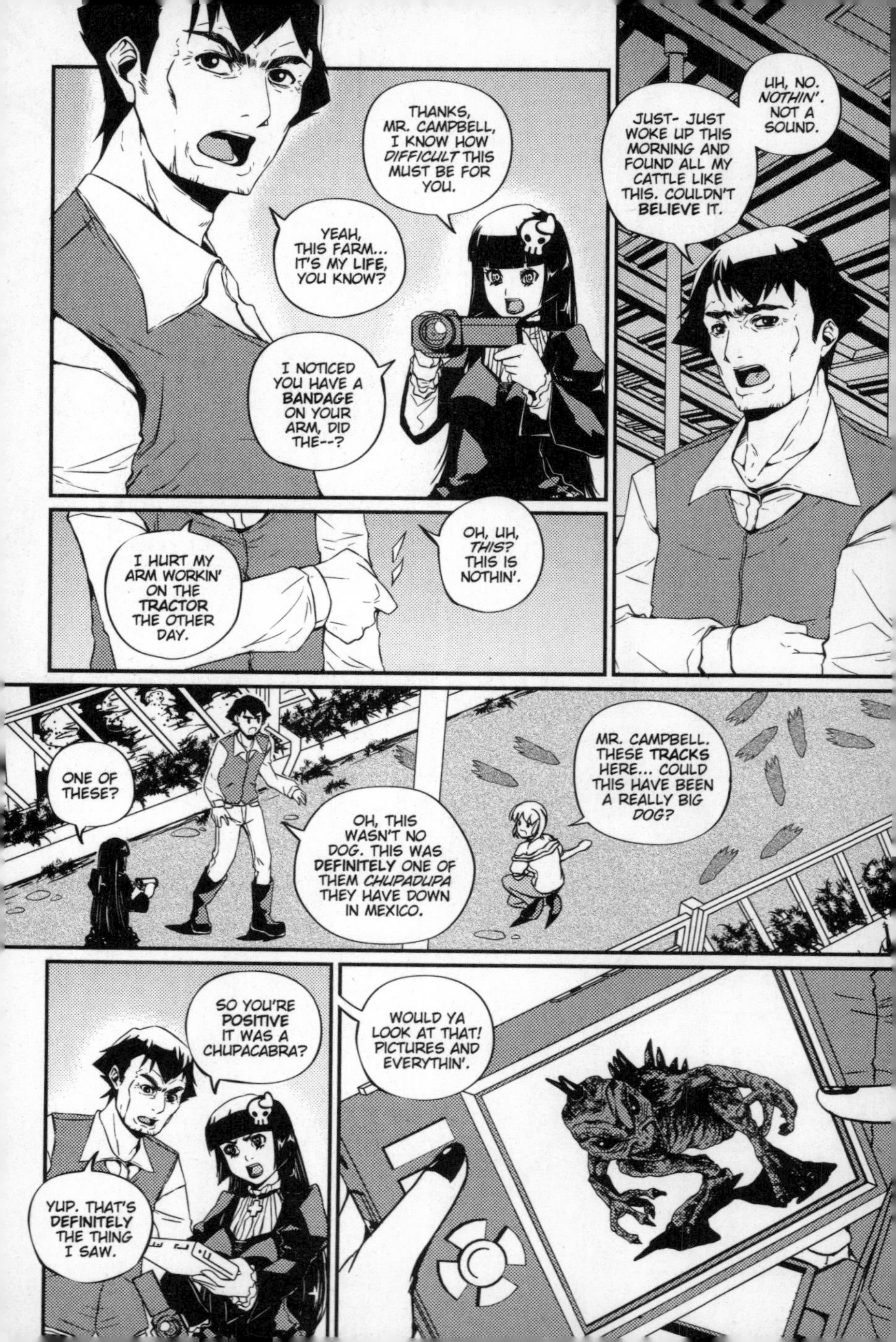
UH, NO. *NOTHIN'*. NOT A SOUND.
JUST- JUST WOKE UP THIS MORNING AND FOUND ALL MY CATTLE LIKE THIS. COULDN'T **BELIEVE** IT.
THANKS, MR. CAMPBELL, I KNOW HOW *DIFFICULT* THIS MUST BE FOR YOU.
YEAH, THIS FARM... IT'S MY LIFE, YOU KNOW?
I NOTICED YOU HAVE A **BANDAGE** ON YOUR ARM, DID THE--?
OH, UH, *THIS?* THIS IS NOTHIN'.
I HURT MY ARM WORKIN' ON THE **TRACTOR** THE OTHER DAY.
MR. CAMPBELL. THESE **TRACKS** HERE... COULD THIS HAVE BEEN A REALLY BIG *DOG?*
OH, THIS WASN'T NO DOG. THIS WAS **DEFINITELY** ONE OF THEM *CHUPADUPA* THEY HAVE DOWN IN MEXICO.
ONE OF THESE?
WOULD YA LOOK AT THAT! PICTURES AND EVERYTHIN'.
SO YOU'RE **POSITIVE** IT WAS A CHUPACABRA?
YUP. THAT'S **DEFINITELY** THE THING I SAW.

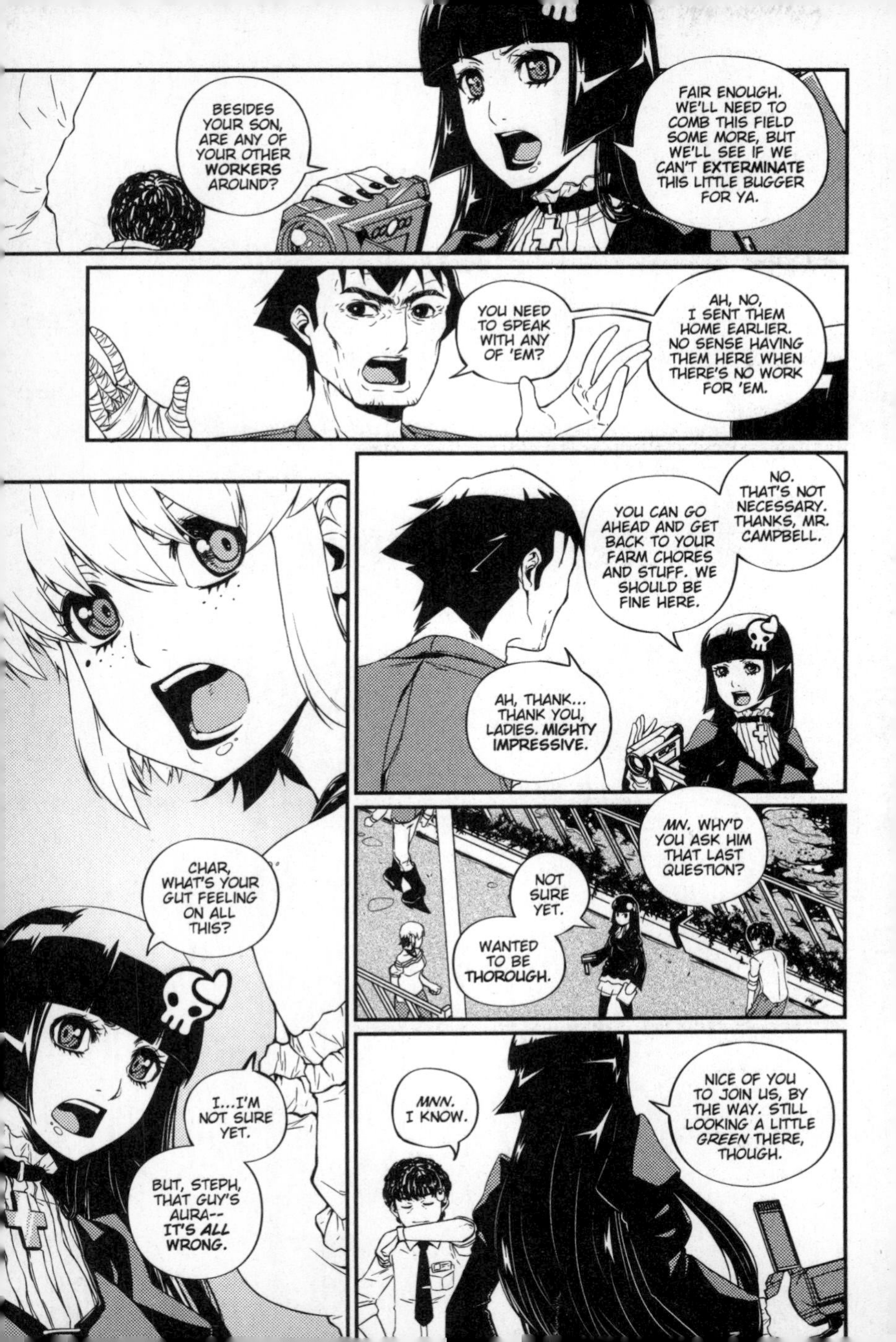
FAIR ENOUGH. WE'LL NEED TO COMB THIS FIELD SOME MORE, BUT WE'LL SEE IF WE CAN'T **EXTERMINATE** THIS LITTLE BUGGER FOR YA.
BESIDES YOUR SON, ARE ANY OF YOUR OTHER **WORKERS** AROUND?
AH, NO, I SENT THEM HOME EARLIER. NO SENSE HAVING THEM HERE WHEN THERE'S NO WORK FOR 'EM.
YOU NEED TO SPEAK WITH ANY OF 'EM?
NO. THAT'S NOT NECESSARY. THANKS, MR. CAMPBELL.
YOU CAN GO AHEAD AND GET BACK TO YOUR FARM CHORES AND STUFF. WE SHOULD BE FINE HERE.
AH, THANK... THANK YOU, LADIES. **MIGHTY IMPRESSIVE.**
MN. WHY'D YOU ASK HIM THAT LAST QUESTION?
NOT SURE YET.
WANTED TO BE **THOROUGH.**
NICE OF YOU TO JOIN US, BY THE WAY. STILL LOOKING A LITTLE *GREEN* THERE, THOUGH.
MNN. I KNOW.
CHAR, WHAT'S YOUR GUT FEELING ON ALL THIS?
I...I'M NOT SURE YET.
BUT, STEPH, THAT GUY'S AURA-- IT'S ***ALL*** **WRONG.**

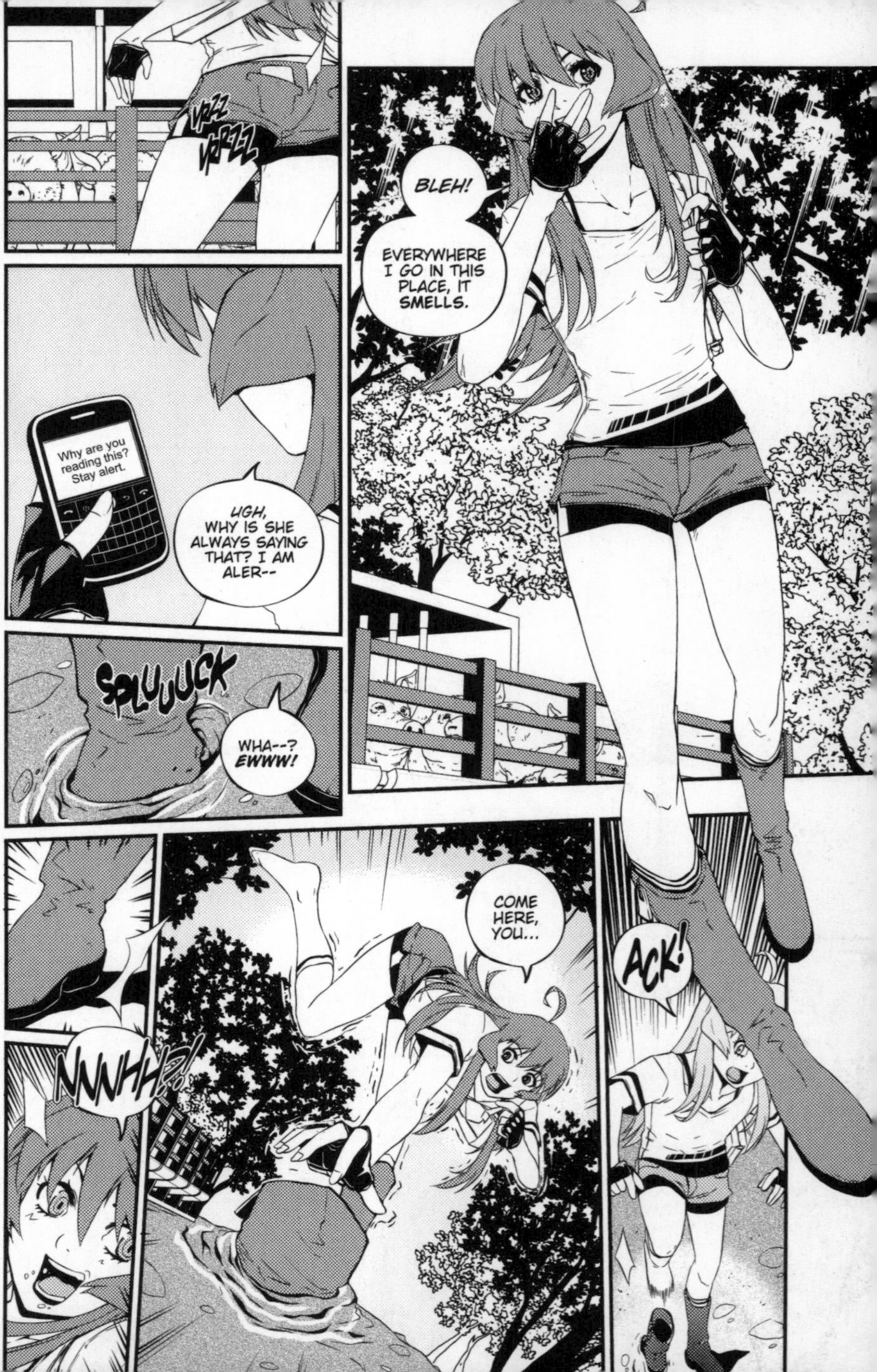

BLEH!
EVERYWHERE I GO IN THIS PLACE, IT SMELLS.
VRZZ
VRZZZ
Why are you reading this? Stay alert.
UGH, WHY IS SHE ALWAYS SAYING THAT? I AM ALER--
SPLUUUCK
WHA--? EWWW!
ACK!
COME HERE, YOU...
NNNH?!

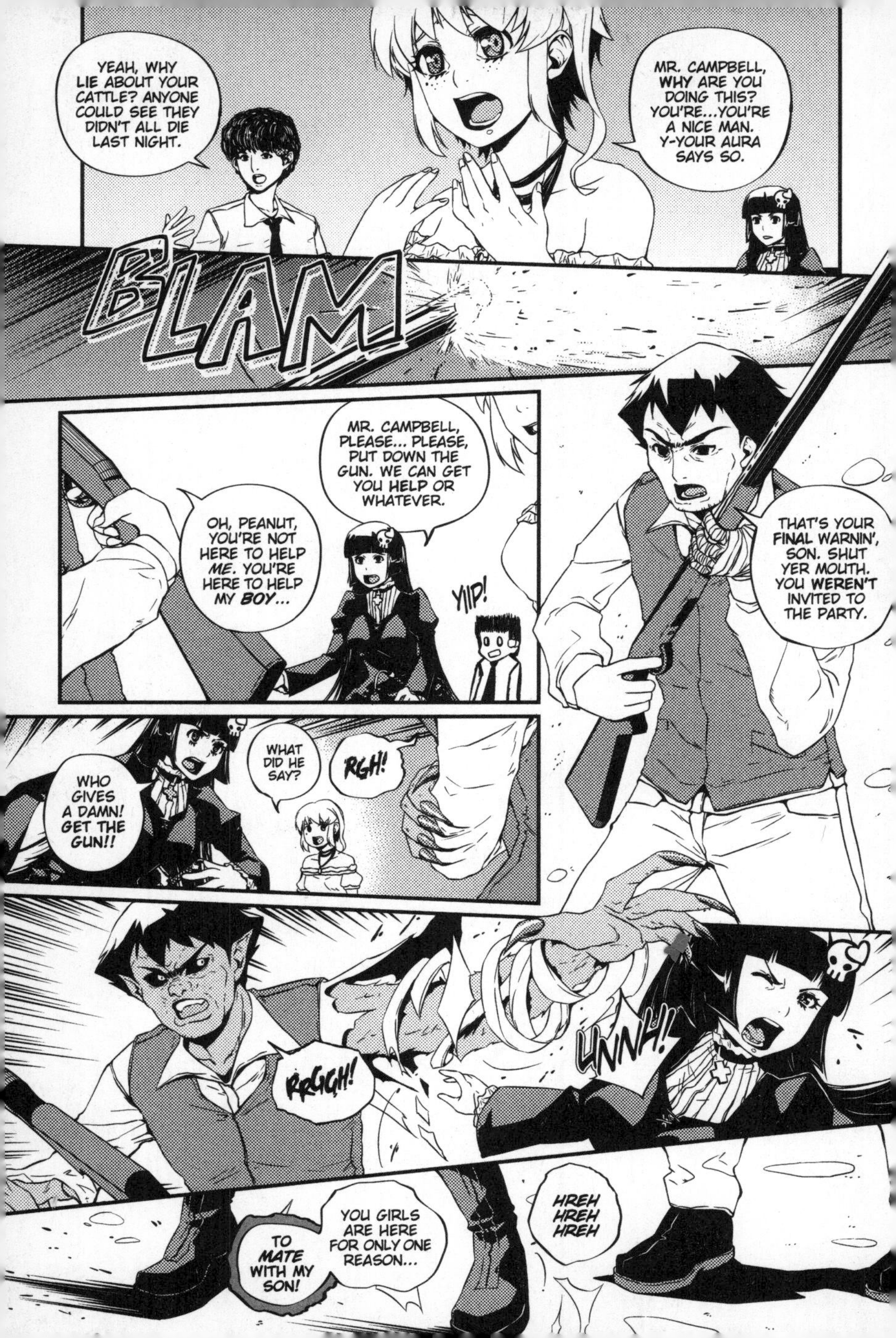
MR. CAMPBELL, WHY ARE YOU DOING THIS? YOU'RE...YOU'RE A NICE MAN. Y-YOUR AURA SAYS SO.
YEAH, WHY LIE ABOUT YOUR CATTLE? ANYONE COULD SEE THEY DIDN'T ALL DIE LAST NIGHT.
BLAM
THAT'S YOUR FINAL WARNIN', SON. SHUT YER MOUTH. YOU WEREN'T INVITED TO THE PARTY.
MR. CAMPBELL, PLEASE... PLEASE, PUT DOWN THE GUN. WE CAN GET YOU HELP OR WHATEVER.
YIIP!
OH, PEANUT, YOU'RE NOT HERE TO HELP ME. YOU'RE HERE TO HELP MY BOY...
RGH!
WHAT DID HE SAY?
WHO GIVES A DAMN! GET THE GUN!!
UNNH!
RRGGH!
HREH HREH HREH
YOU GIRLS ARE HERE FOR ONLY ONE REASON...
TO MATE WITH MY SON!

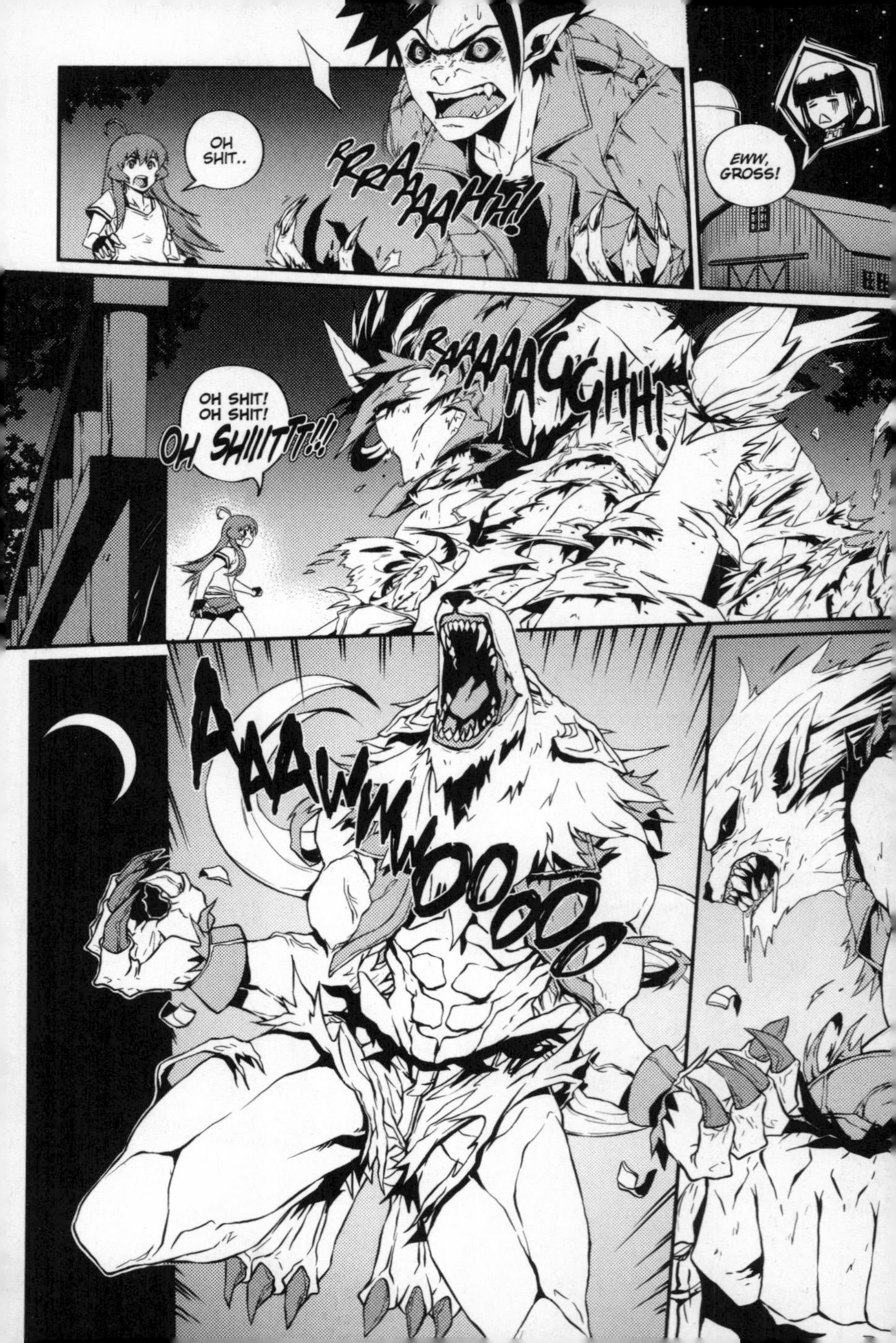
EWW, GROSS!
RRRAAAAAHHH!
OH SHIT..
RAAAAAAGHH!
OH SHIT! OH SHIT! OH SHIIITTT!!
AAAWWWOOOOOO

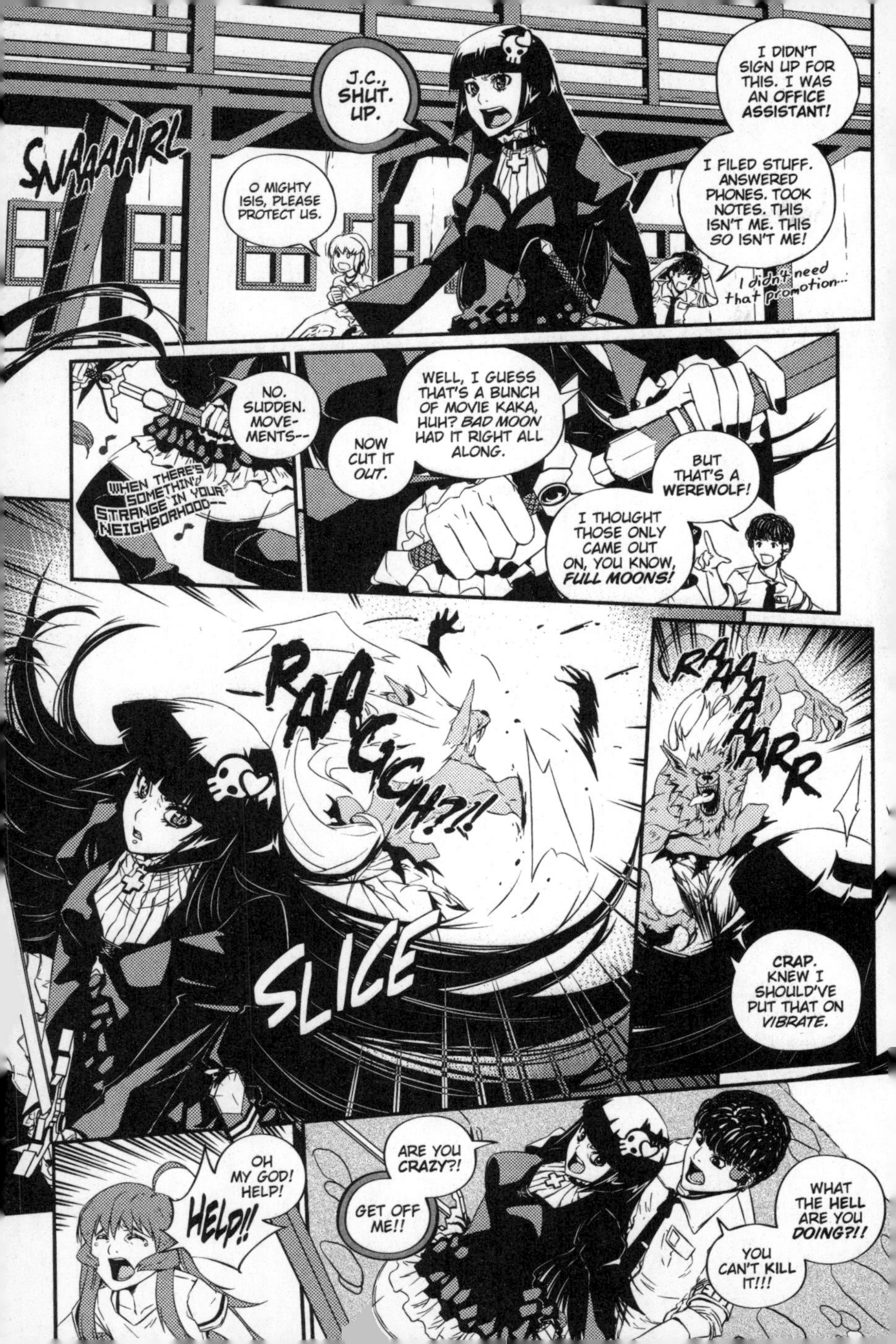
I DIDN'T SIGN UP FOR THIS. I WAS AN OFFICE ASSISTANT!
J.C., SHUT. UP.
I FILED STUFF. ANSWERED PHONES. TOOK NOTES. THIS ISN'T ME. THIS SO ISN'T ME!
I didn't need that promotion...
SNAAAARL
O MIGHTY ISIS, PLEASE PROTECT US.
WELL, I GUESS THAT'S A BUNCH OF MOVIE KAKA, HUH? BAD MOON HAD IT RIGHT ALL ALONG.
NOW CUT IT OUT.
BUT THAT'S A WEREWOLF!
I THOUGHT THOSE ONLY CAME OUT ON, YOU KNOW, FULL MOONS!
NO. SUDDEN. MOVE-MENTS--
WHEN THERE'S SOMETHIN' STRANGE IN YOUR NEIGHBORHOOD--
RAAAAAARRR
CRAP. KNEW I SHOULD'VE PUT THAT ON VIBRATE.
RAAGCH?!!
SLICE
WHAT THE HELL ARE YOU DOING?!!
YOU CAN'T KILL IT!!!
ARE YOU CRAZY?!
GET OFF ME!!
OH MY GOD! HELP!
HELP!!

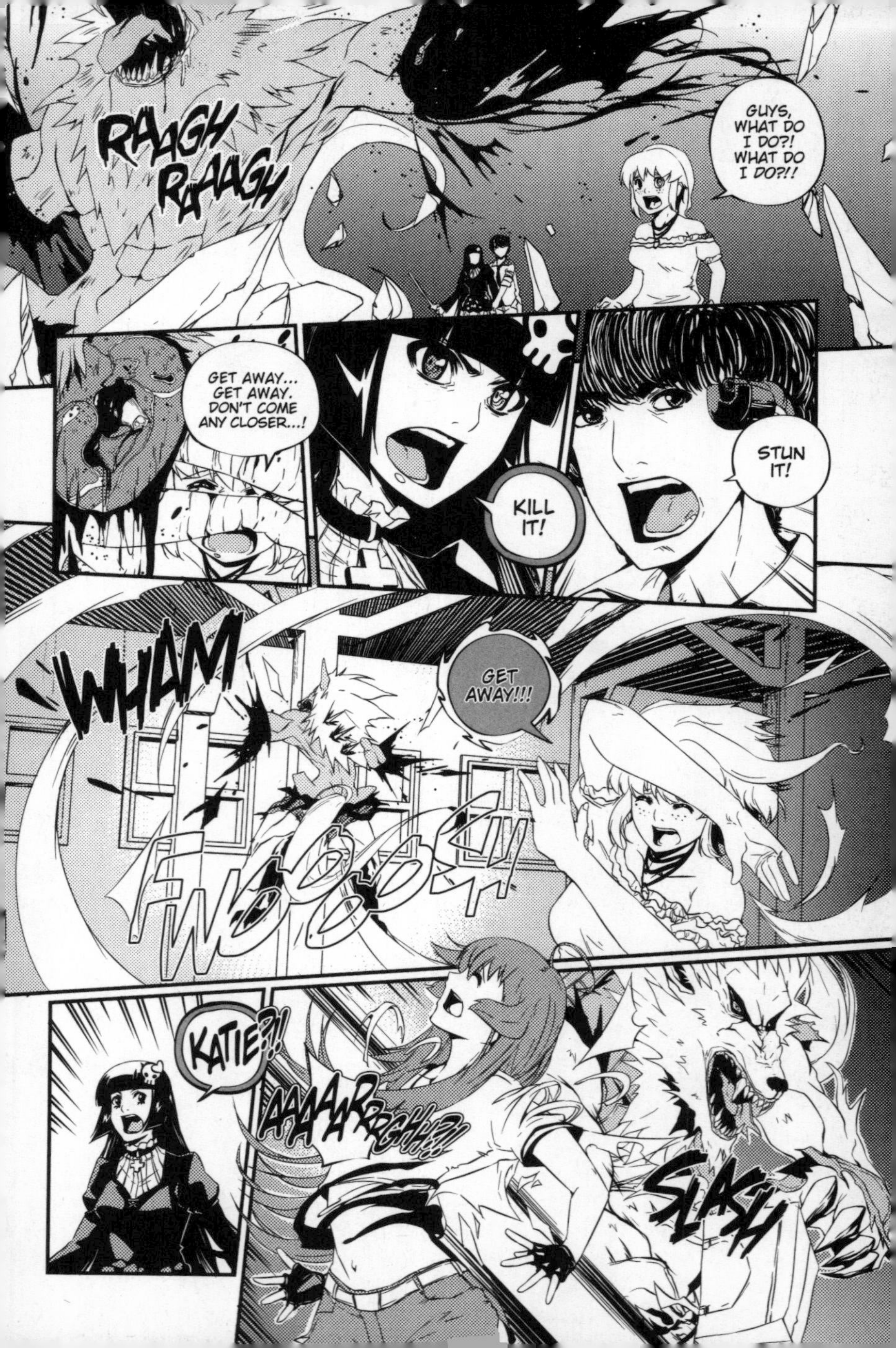
GUYS, WHAT DO I DO?! WHAT DO I DO?!!
RAAGH
RAAAGH
STUN IT!
KILL IT!
GET AWAY... GET AWAY. DON'T COME ANY CLOSER...!
GET AWAY!!!
WHAM
FWOOOSH
SLASH
AAAARRGHH!!?
KATIE?!!

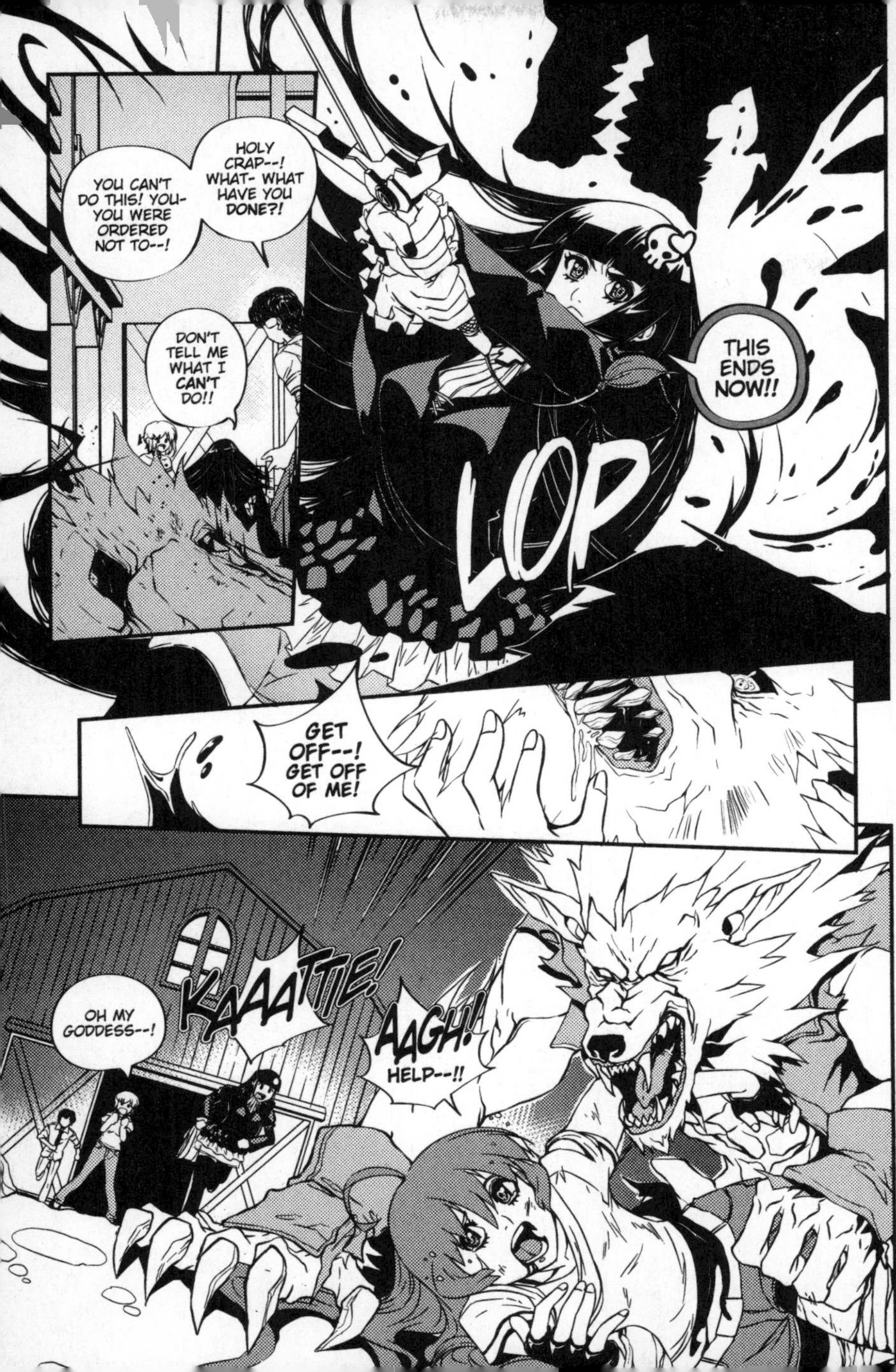
THIS ENDS NOW!!
LOP
HOLY CRAP--! WHAT- WHAT HAVE YOU DONE?!
YOU CAN'T DO THIS! YOU- YOU WERE ORDERED NOT TO--!
DON'T TELL ME WHAT I CAN'T DO!!
GET OFF--! GET OFF OF ME!
AAGH! HELP--!!
KAAATTIE!
OH MY GODDESS--!

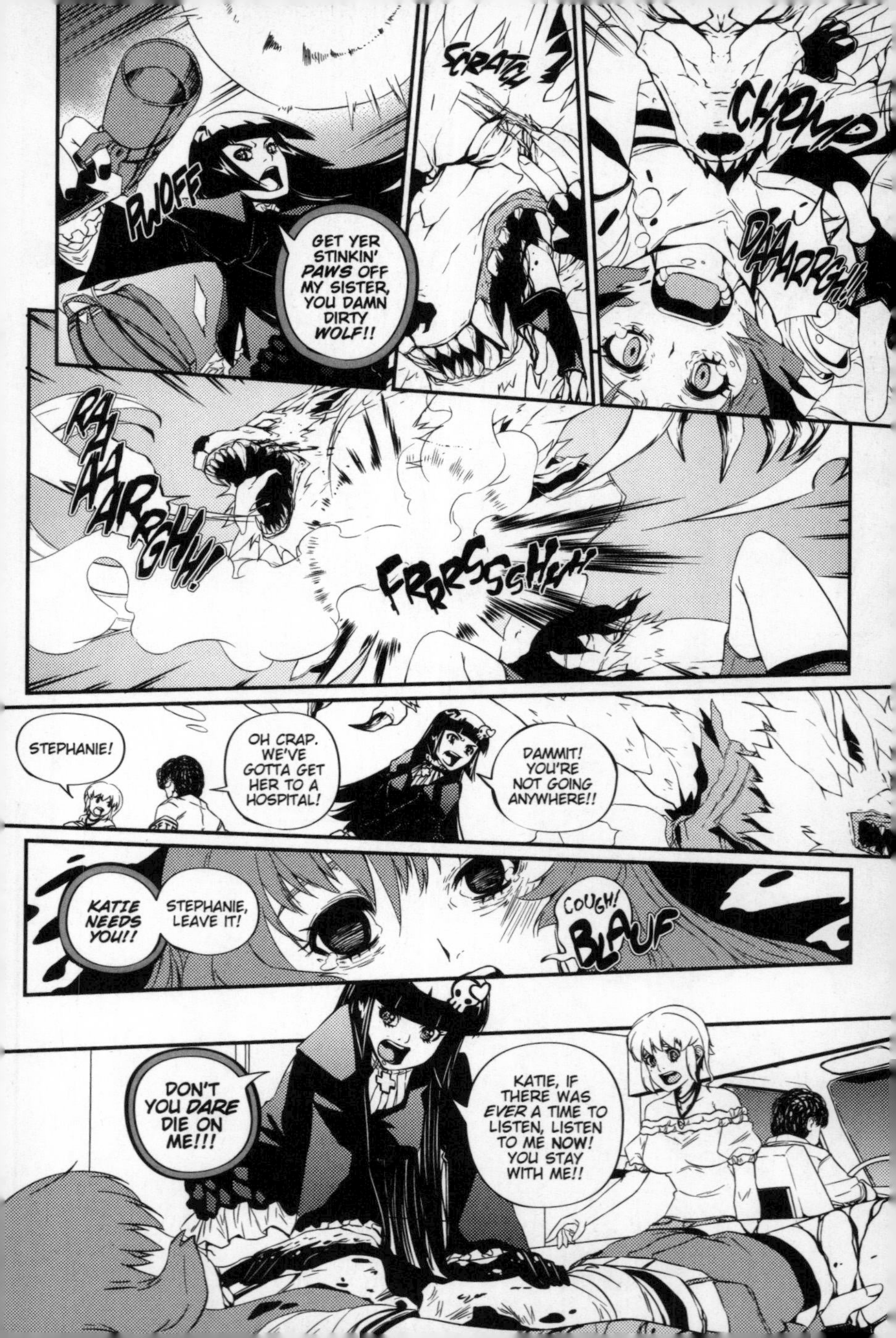
CHOMP
DAAARRGH!!
SCRATCH
PWOFF
GET YER STINKIN' *PAWS* OFF MY SISTER, YOU DAMN DIRTY *WOLF*!!
RAAAARRGHH!
FRRRSSSHHH
DAMMIT! YOU'RE NOT GOING ANYWHERE!!
OH CRAP. WE'VE GOTTA GET HER TO A HOSPITAL!
STEPHANIE!
COUGH! BLAUF
STEPHANIE, LEAVE IT!
KATIE NEEDS YOU!!
KATIE, IF THERE WAS *EVER* A TIME TO LISTEN, LISTEN TO ME NOW! YOU STAY WITH ME!!
DON'T YOU *DARE* DIE ON ME!!!

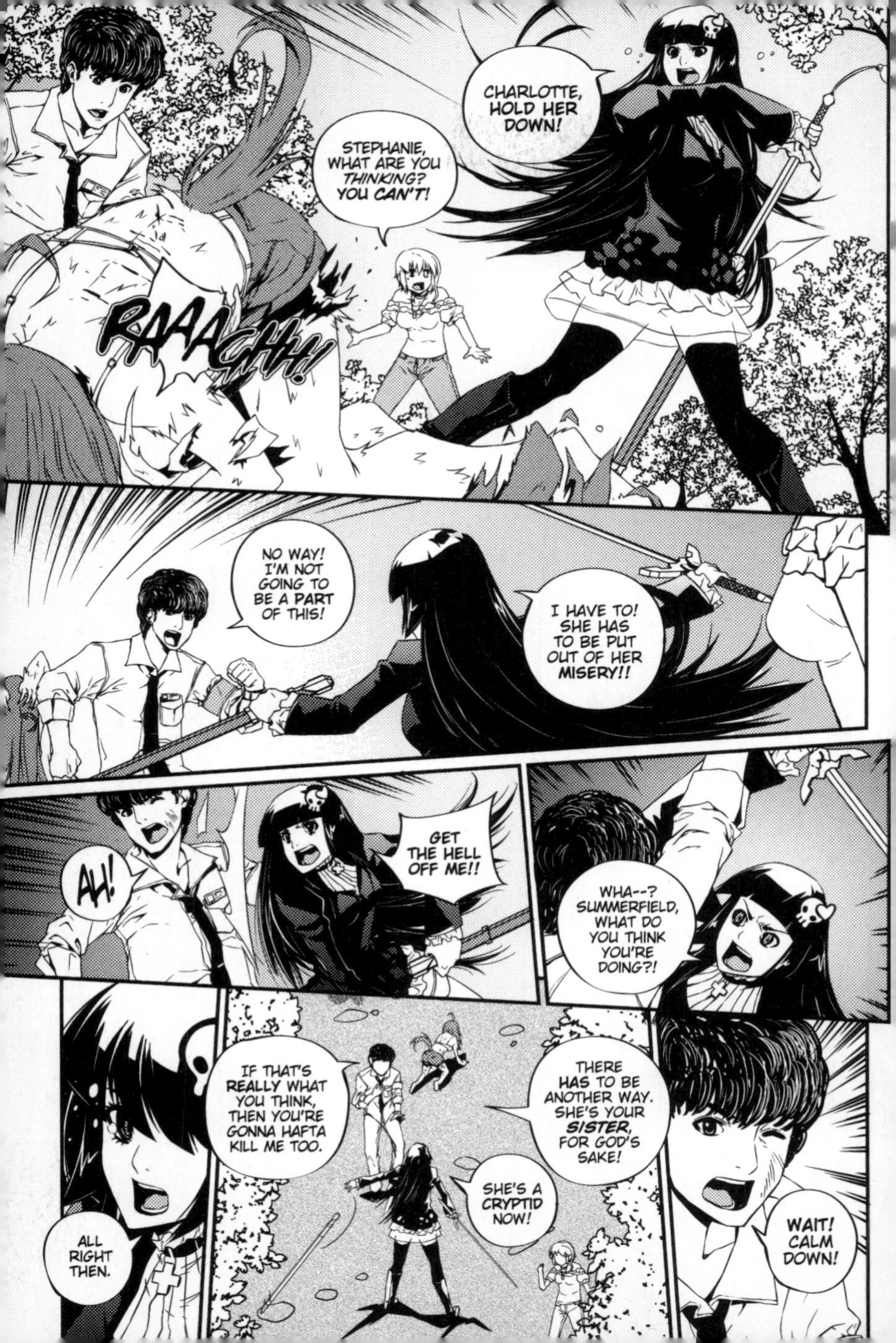
CHARLOTTE, HOLD HER DOWN!
STEPHANIE, WHAT ARE YOU *THINKING?* YOU **CAN'T!**
RAAACHH!
I HAVE TO! SHE HAS TO BE PUT OUT OF HER **MISERY!!**
NO WAY! I'M NOT GOING TO BE A **PART** OF THIS!
WHA--? SUMMERFIELD, WHAT DO YOU THINK YOU'RE DOING?!
GET THE HELL OFF ME!!
AH!
WAIT! CALM DOWN!
THERE **HAS** TO BE ANOTHER WAY. SHE'S YOUR ***SISTER***, FOR GOD'S SAKE!
SHE'S A CRYPTID NOW!
IF THAT'S **REALLY** WHAT YOU THINK, THEN YOU'RE GONNA HAFTA KILL ME TOO.
ALL RIGHT THEN.

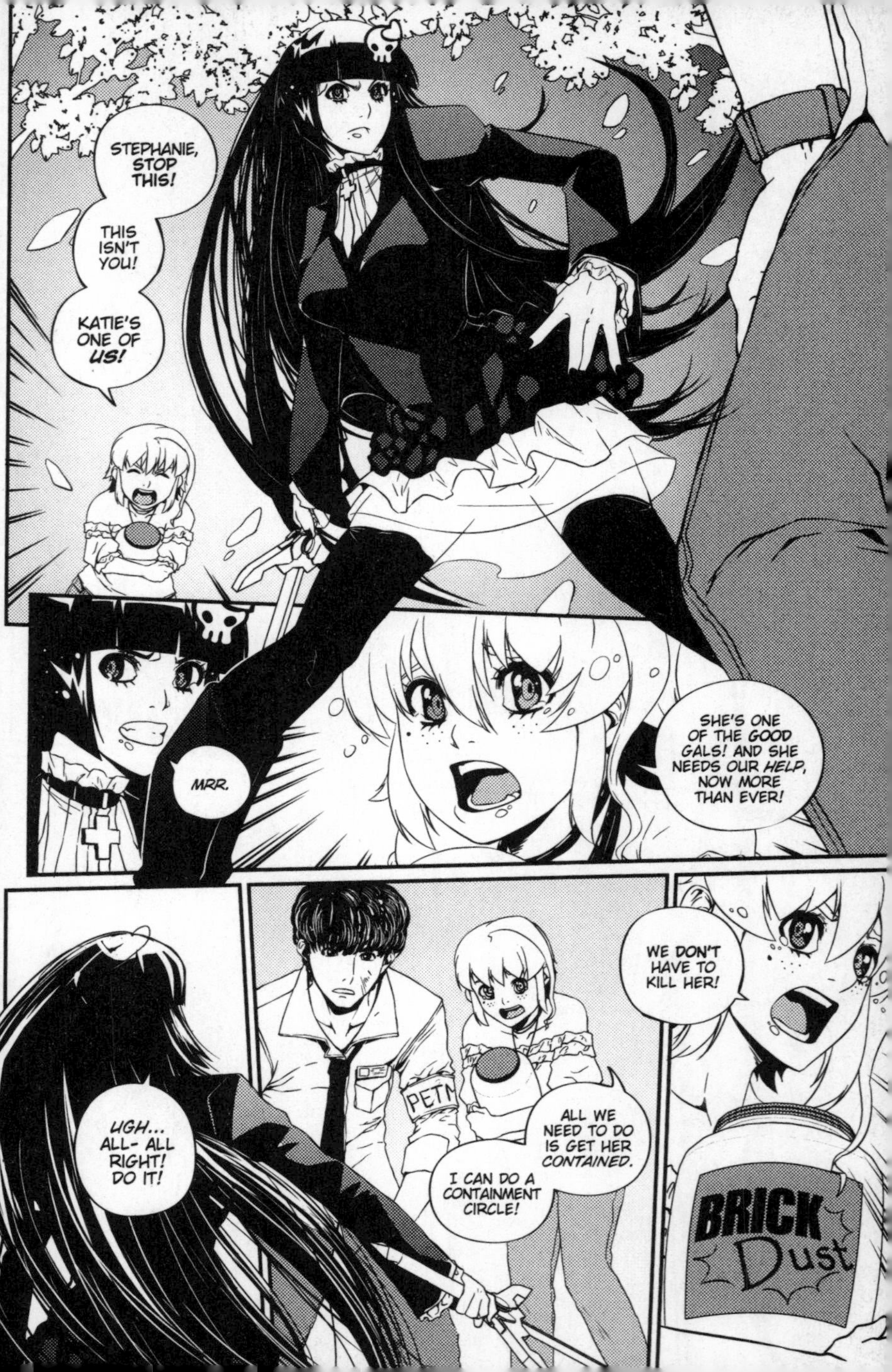
STEPHANIE, STOP THIS!
THIS ISN'T YOU!
KATIE'S ONE OF *US!*
SHE'S ONE OF THE *GOOD* GALS! AND SHE NEEDS OUR *HELP*, NOW MORE THAN EVER!
MRR.
WE DON'T HAVE TO KILL HER!
BRICK Dust
ALL WE NEED TO DO IS GET HER *CONTAINED*.
I CAN DO A CONTAINMENT CIRCLE!
UGH... ALL- ALL RIGHT! DO IT!

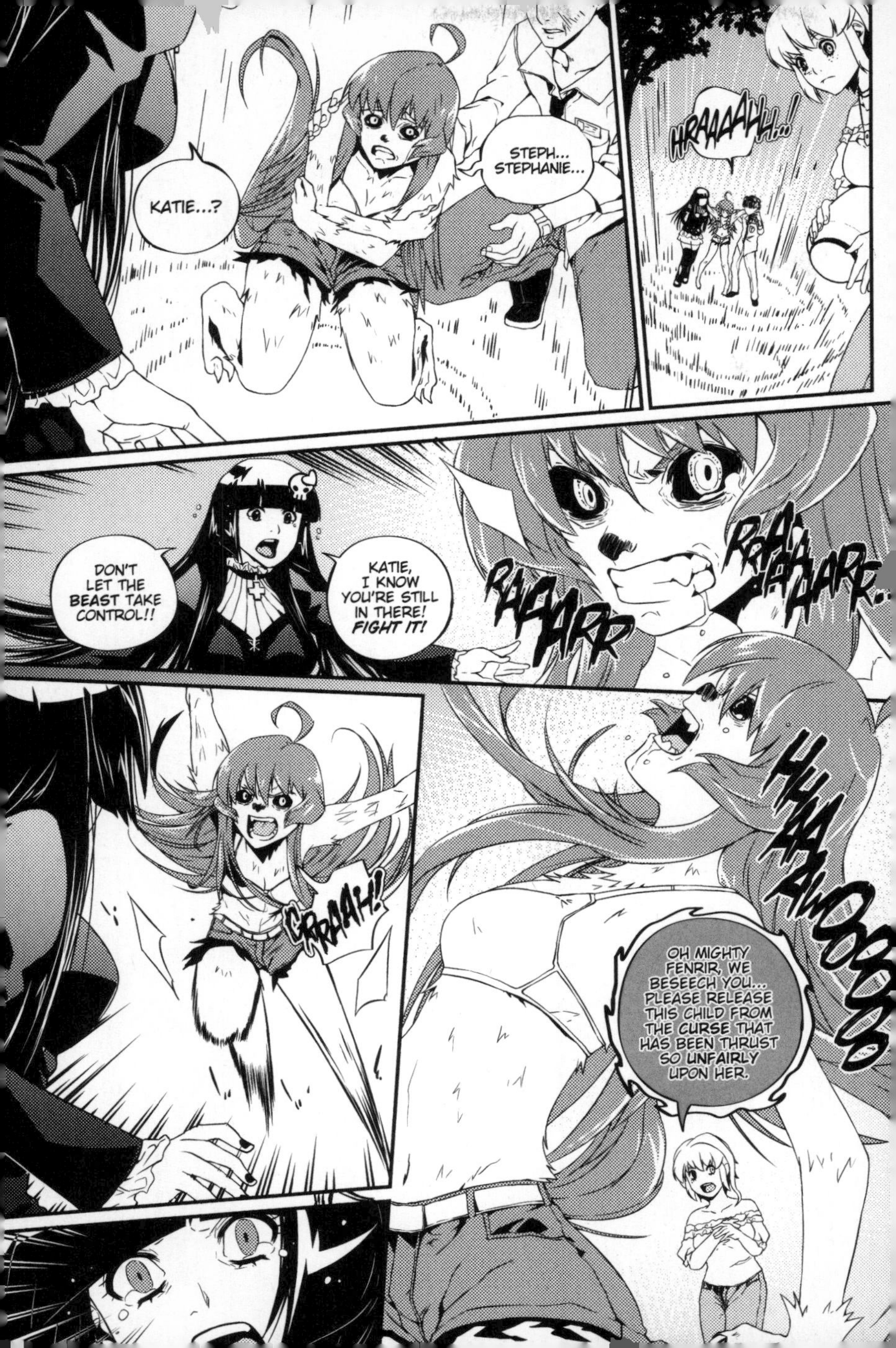
KATIE...?
STEPH... STEPHANIE...
HRAAAAHH..!
DON'T LET THE BEAST TAKE CONTROL!!
KATIE, I KNOW YOU'RE STILL IN THERE! FIGHT IT!
GRAAH!
OH MIGHTY FENRIR, WE BESEECH YOU... PLEASE RELEASE THIS CHILD FROM THE CURSE THAT HAS BEEN THRUST SO UNFAIRLY UPON HER.

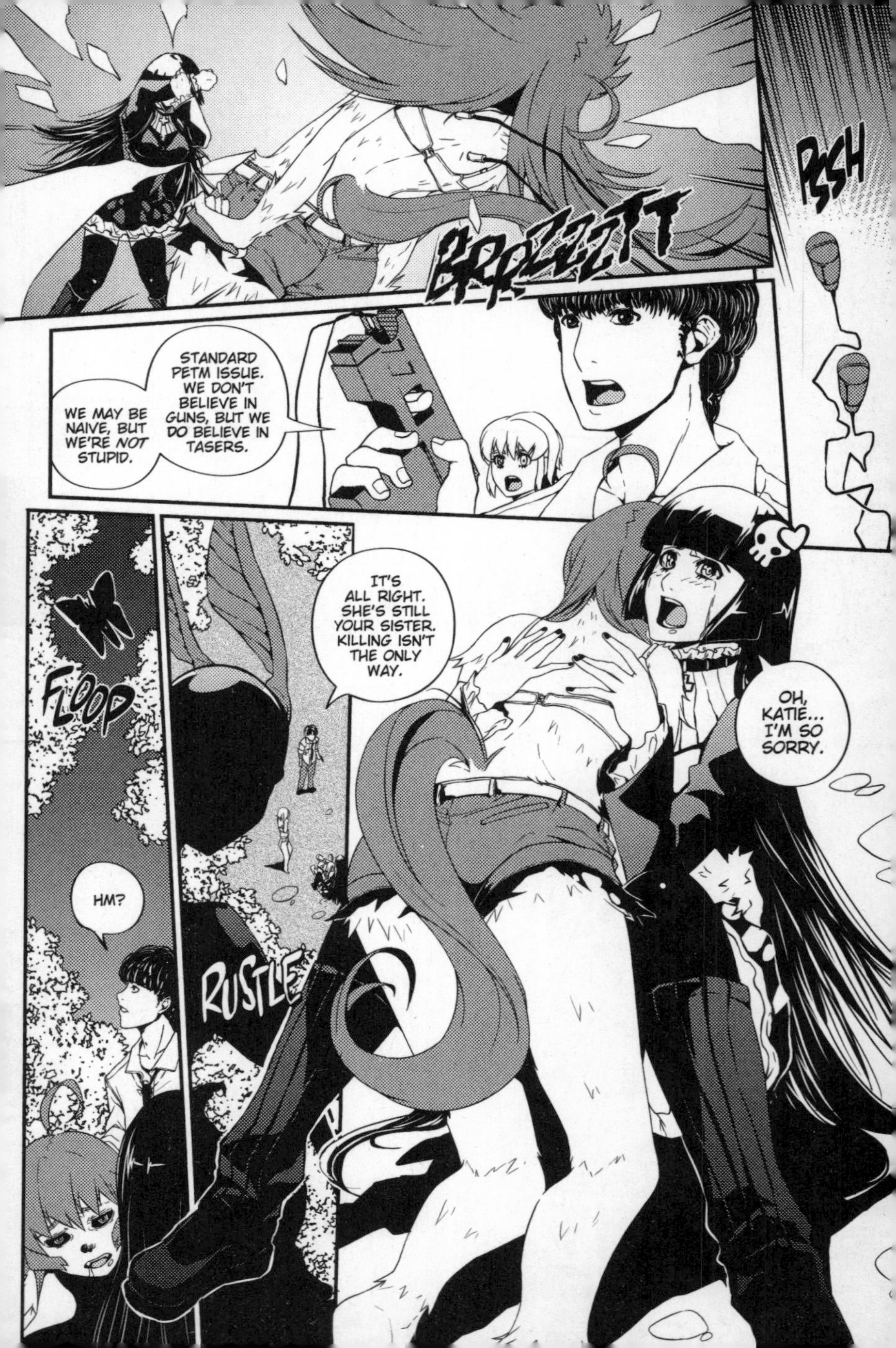
PSSH
BRZZZZTT
STANDARD PETM ISSUE. WE DON'T BELIEVE IN GUNS, BUT WE DO BELIEVE IN TASERS.
WE MAY BE NAIVE, BUT WE'RE *NOT* STUPID.
OH, KATIE... I'M SO SORRY.
IT'S ALL RIGHT. SHE'S STILL YOUR SISTER. KILLING ISN'T THE ONLY WAY.
RUSTLE
FLOOP
HM?

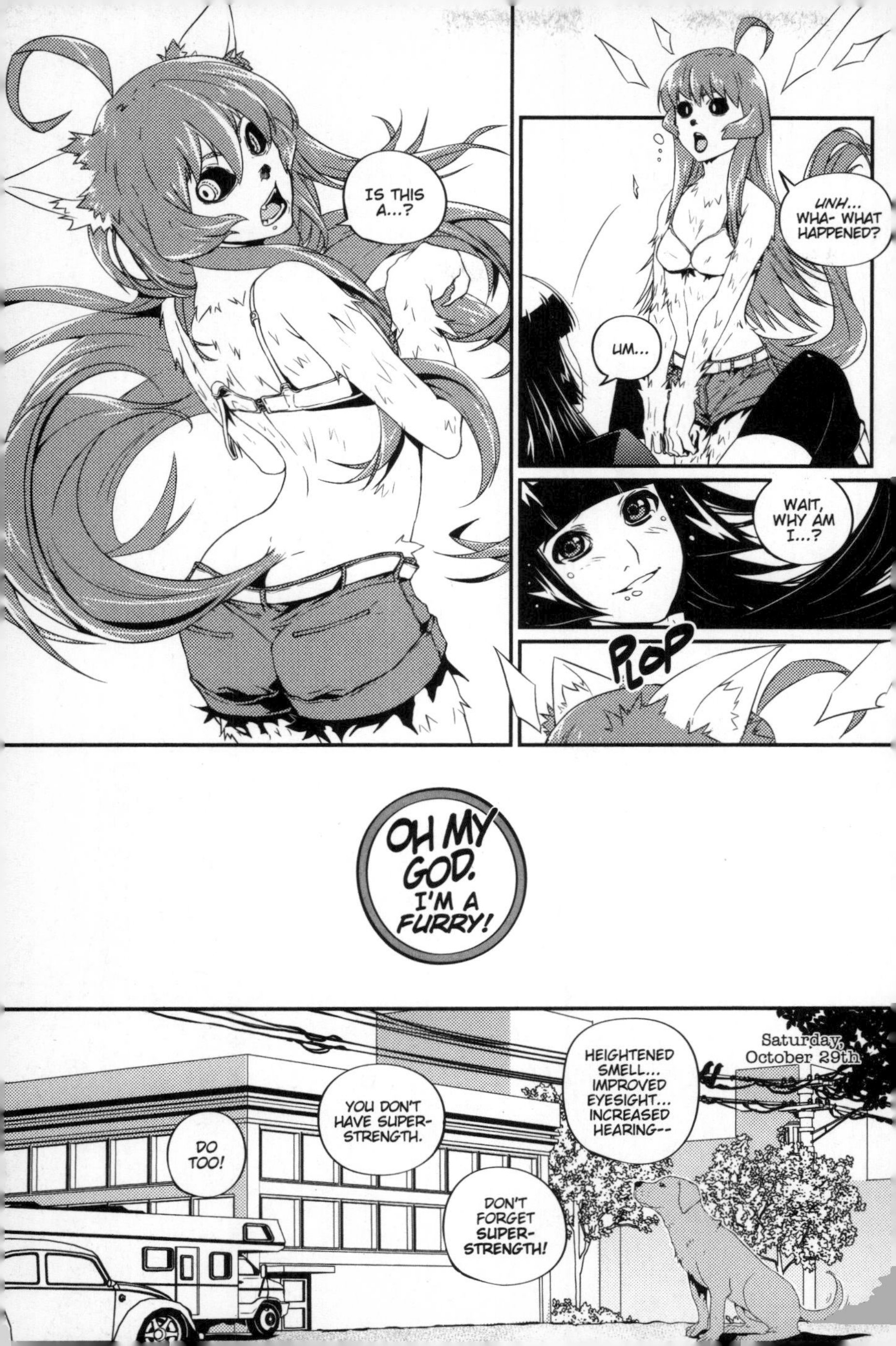
UNH... WHA- WHAT HAPPENED?
UM...
WAIT, WHY AM I...?
PLOP
IS THIS A...?
OH MY GOD. I'M A FURRY!
Saturday, October 29th
HEIGHTENED SMELL... IMPROVED EYESIGHT... INCREASED HEARING--
DON'T FORGET SUPER-STRENGTH!
YOU DON'T HAVE SUPER-STRENGTH.
DO TOO!

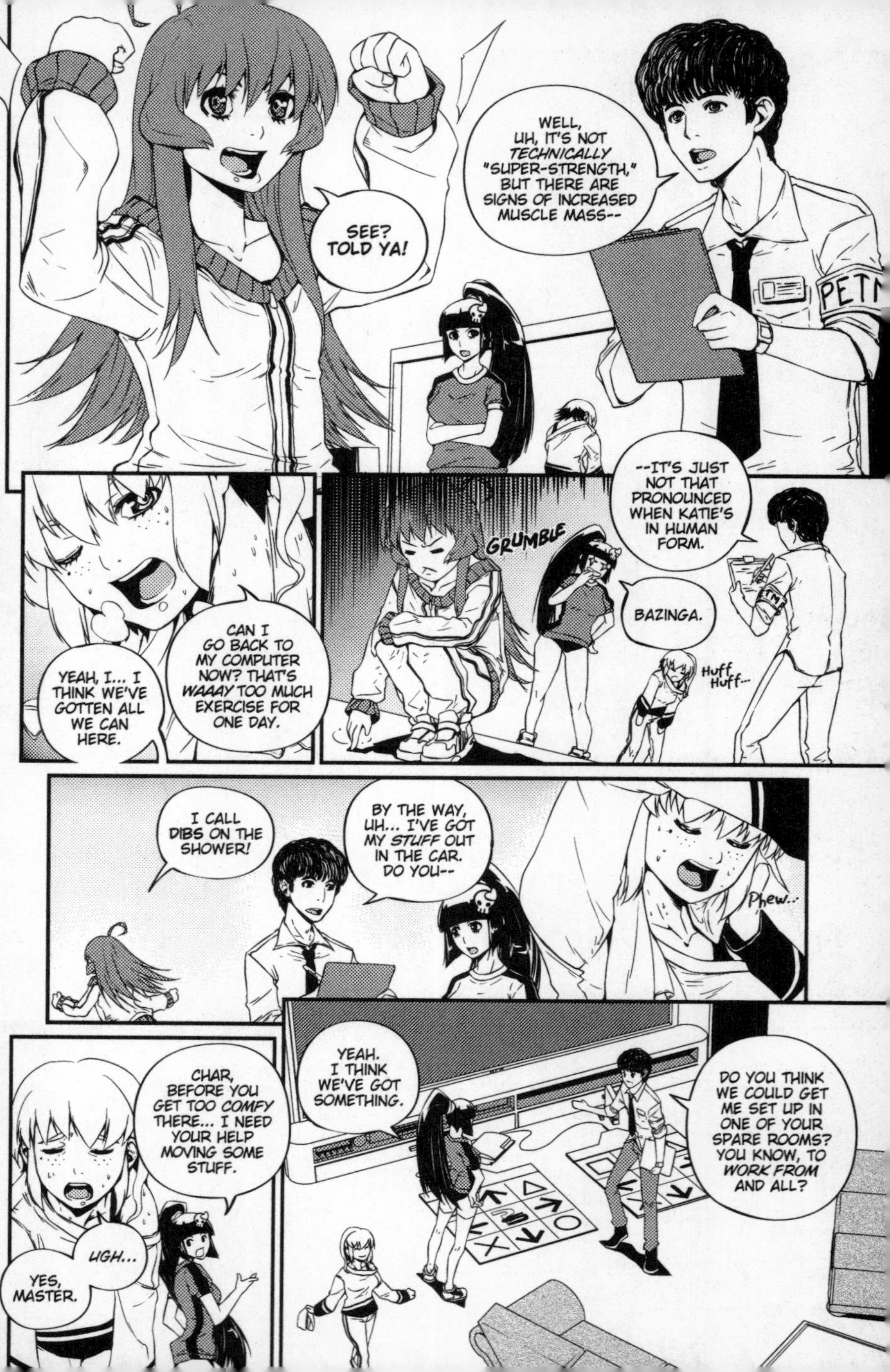
WELL, UH, IT'S NOT *TECHNICALLY* "SUPER-STRENGTH," BUT THERE ARE SIGNS OF INCREASED MUSCLE MASS--
SEE? TOLD YA!
--IT'S JUST NOT THAT PRONOUNCED WHEN KATIE'S IN HUMAN FORM.
GRUMBLE
BAZINGA.
Huff Huff...
CAN I GO BACK TO MY COMPUTER NOW? THAT'S *WAAAY* TOO MUCH EXERCISE FOR ONE DAY.
YEAH, I... I THINK WE'VE GOTTEN ALL WE CAN HERE.
Phew...
BY THE WAY, UH... I'VE GOT MY *STUFF* OUT IN THE CAR. DO YOU--
I CALL DIBS ON THE SHOWER!
DO YOU THINK WE COULD GET ME SET UP IN ONE OF YOUR SPARE ROOMS? YOU KNOW, TO *WORK FROM* AND ALL?
YEAH. I THINK WE'VE GOT SOMETHING.
CHAR, BEFORE YOU GET TOO *COMFY* THERE... I NEED YOUR HELP MOVING SOME STUFF.
UGH...
YES, MASTER.

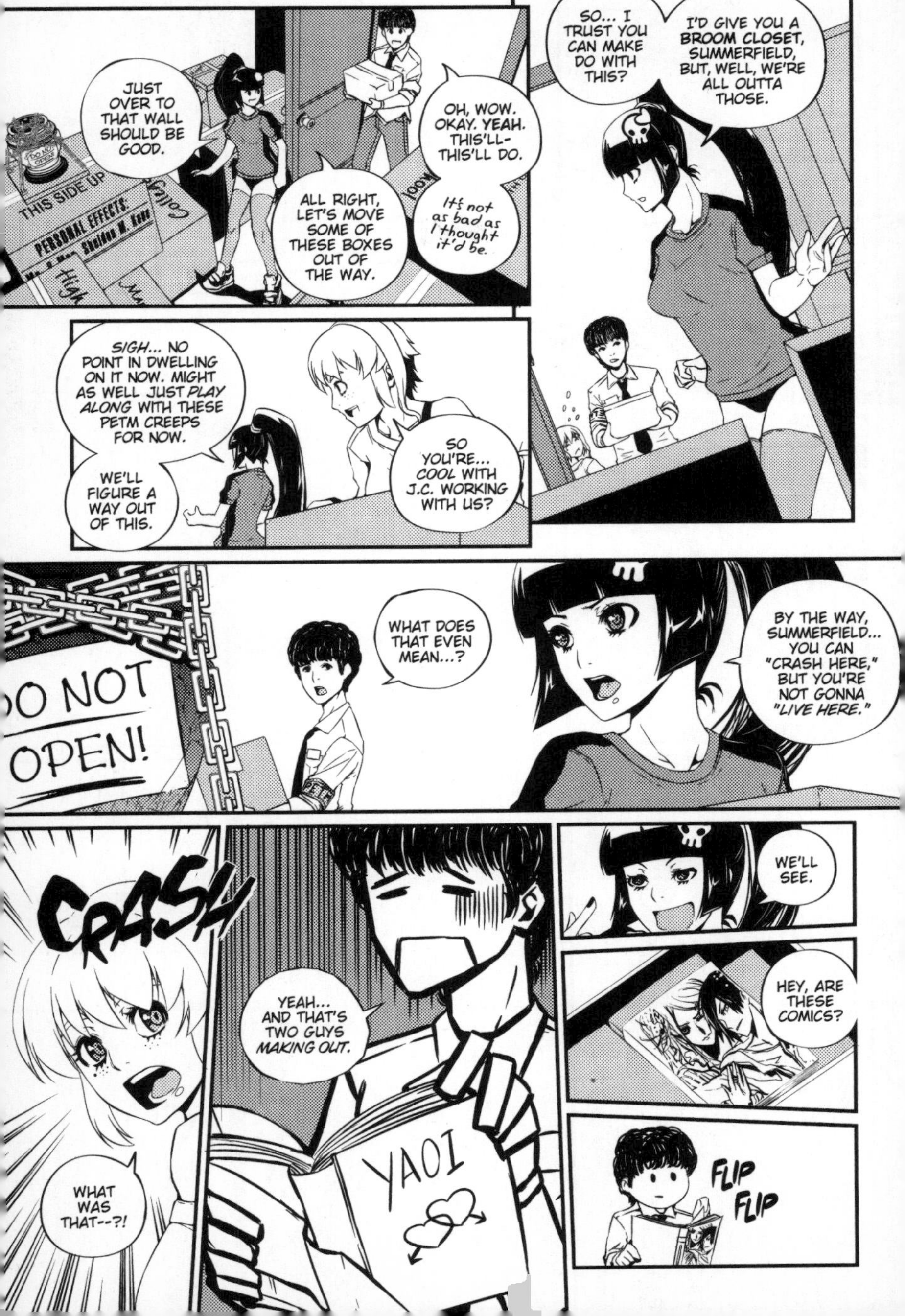
I'D GIVE YOU A **BROOM CLOSET**, SUMMERFIELD, BUT, WELL, WE'RE ALL OUTTA THOSE.
SO... I TRUST YOU CAN MAKE DO WITH THIS?
OH, WOW. OKAY. **YEAH.** THIS'LL-THIS'LL DO.
It's not as bad as I thought it'd be.
ALL RIGHT, LET'S MOVE SOME OF THESE BOXES OUT OF THE WAY.
JUST OVER TO THAT WALL SHOULD BE GOOD.
DO NOT OPEN
THIS SIDE UP
PERSONAL EFFECTS
SO YOU'RE... *COOL* WITH J.C. WORKING WITH US?
SIGH... NO POINT IN DWELLING ON IT NOW. MIGHT AS WELL JUST *PLAY ALONG* WITH THESE PETM CREEPS FOR NOW.
WE'LL FIGURE A WAY OUT OF THIS.
BY THE WAY, SUMMERFIELD... YOU CAN "CRASH HERE," BUT YOU'RE NOT GONNA *"LIVE HERE."*
WHAT DOES THAT EVEN MEAN...?
DO NOT OPEN!
WE'LL SEE.
HEY, ARE THESE COMICS?
FLIP FLIP
YEAH... AND THAT'S TWO GUYS *MAKING OUT.*
YAOI
CRASH
WHAT WAS THAT--?!

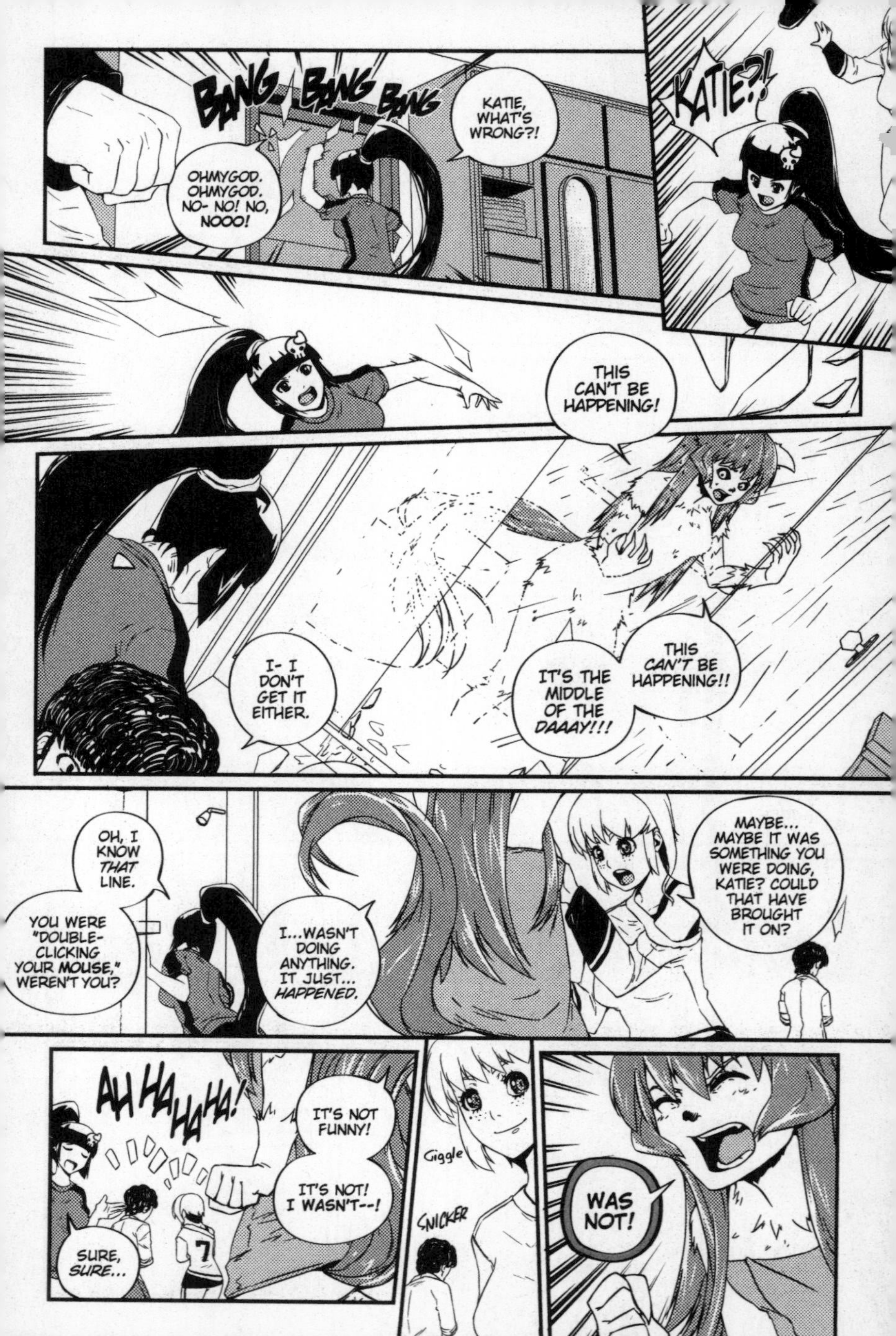
KATIE?!
KATIE, WHAT'S WRONG?!
BANG BANG BANG
OHMYGOD. OHMYGOD. NO- NO! NO, NOOO!
THIS CAN'T BE HAPPENING!
THIS *CAN'T* BE HAPPENING!!
IT'S THE MIDDLE OF THE *DAAAY!!!*
I- I DON'T GET IT EITHER.
MAYBE... MAYBE IT WAS SOMETHING YOU WERE DOING, KATIE? COULD THAT HAVE BROUGHT IT ON?
I...WASN'T DOING ANYTHING. IT JUST... *HAPPENED.*
OH, I KNOW *THAT* LINE.
YOU WERE "DOUBLE-CLICKING YOUR *MOUSE,*" WEREN'T YOU?
WAS NOT!
Giggle
SNICKER
IT'S NOT FUNNY!
AH HAHAHA!
IT'S NOT! I WASN'T--!
SURE, *SURE*...

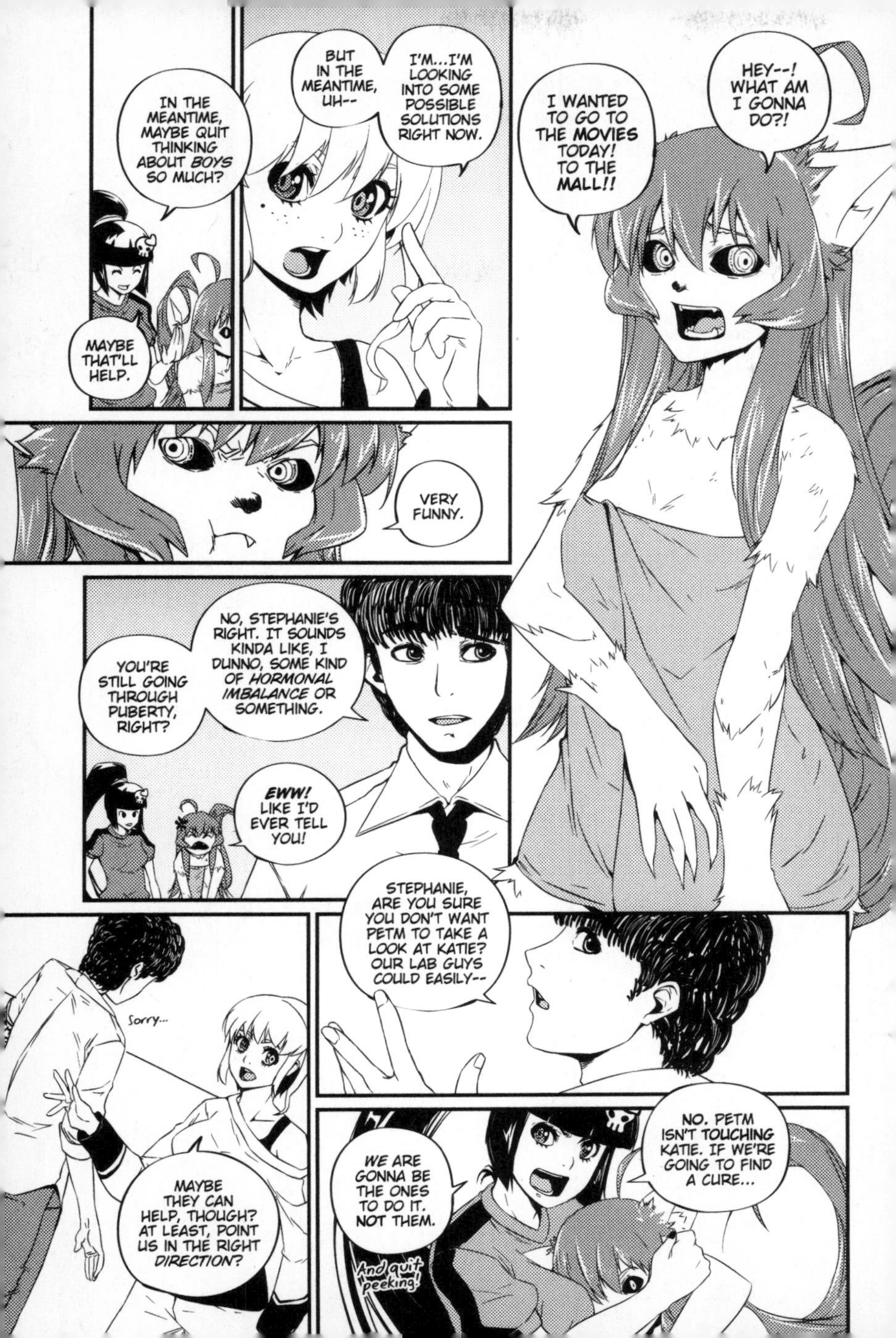
HEY--! WHAT AM I GONNA DO?!
I WANTED TO GO TO THE MOVIES TODAY! TO THE MALL!!
I'M...I'M LOOKING INTO SOME POSSIBLE SOLUTIONS RIGHT NOW.
BUT IN THE MEANTIME, UH--
IN THE MEANTIME, MAYBE QUIT THINKING ABOUT BOYS SO MUCH?
MAYBE THAT'LL HELP.
VERY FUNNY.
NO, STEPHANIE'S RIGHT. IT SOUNDS KINDA LIKE, I DUNNO, SOME KIND OF HORMONAL IMBALANCE OR SOMETHING.
YOU'RE STILL GOING THROUGH PUBERTY, RIGHT?
EWW! LIKE I'D EVER TELL YOU!
STEPHANIE, ARE YOU SURE YOU DON'T WANT PETM TO TAKE A LOOK AT KATIE? OUR LAB GUYS COULD EASILY--
NO. PETM ISN'T TOUCHING KATIE. IF WE'RE GOING TO FIND A CURE...
WE ARE GONNA BE THE ONES TO DO IT. NOT THEM.
And quit peeking!
Sorry...
MAYBE THEY CAN HELP, THOUGH? AT LEAST, POINT US IN THE RIGHT DIRECTION?

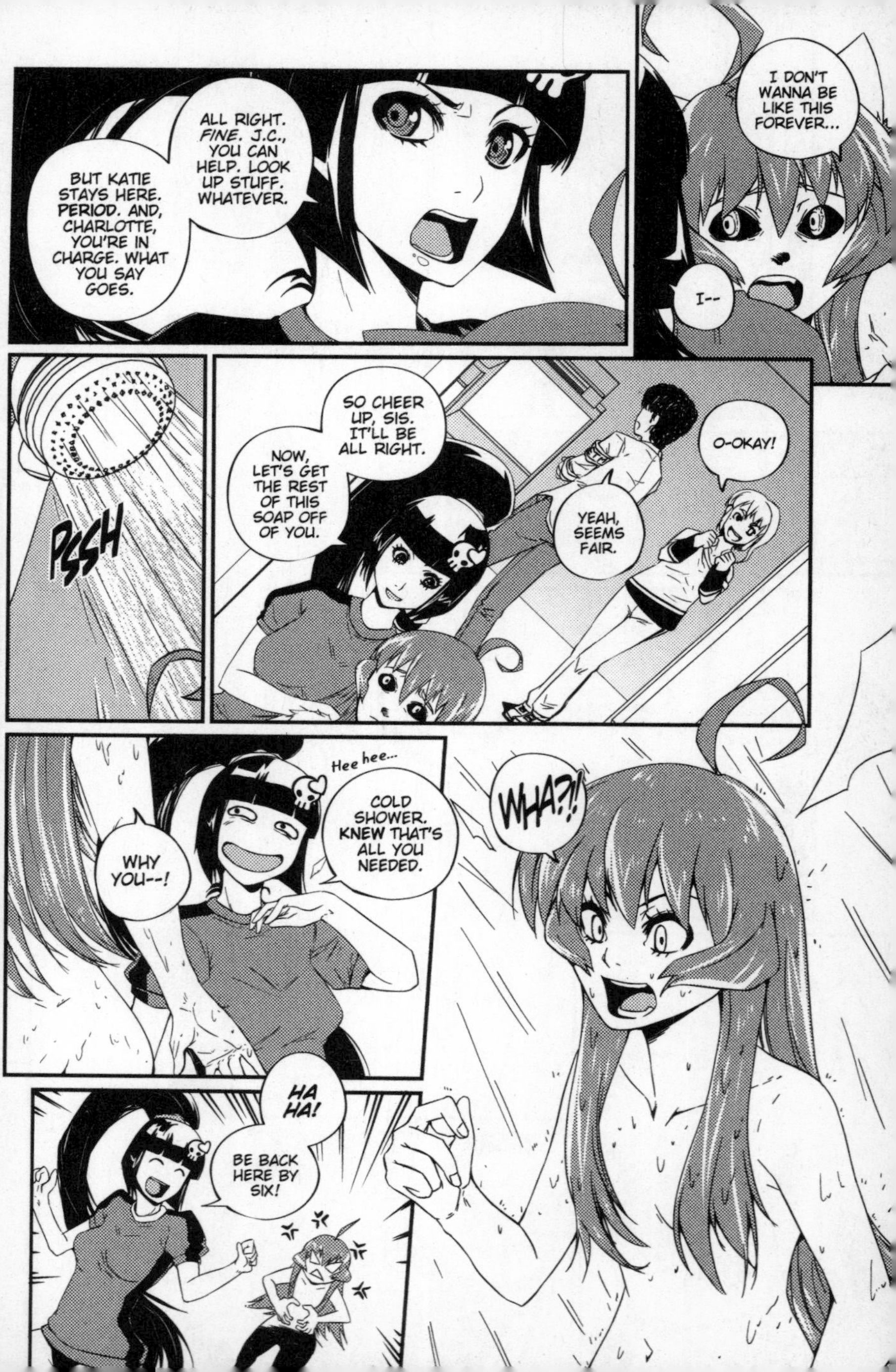
I DON'T WANNA BE LIKE THIS FOREVER...
I--
ALL RIGHT. *FINE.* J.C., YOU CAN HELP. LOOK UP STUFF. WHATEVER.
BUT KATIE STAYS HERE. PERIOD. AND, CHARLOTTE, YOU'RE IN CHARGE. WHAT YOU SAY GOES.
O-OKAY!
YEAH, SEEMS FAIR.
SO CHEER UP, SIS. IT'LL BE ALL RIGHT.
NOW, LET'S GET THE REST OF THIS SOAP OFF OF YOU.
PSSH
WHA?!!
Hee hee...
COLD SHOWER. KNEW THAT'S ALL YOU NEEDED.
WHY YOU--!
HA HA!
BE BACK HERE BY SIX!

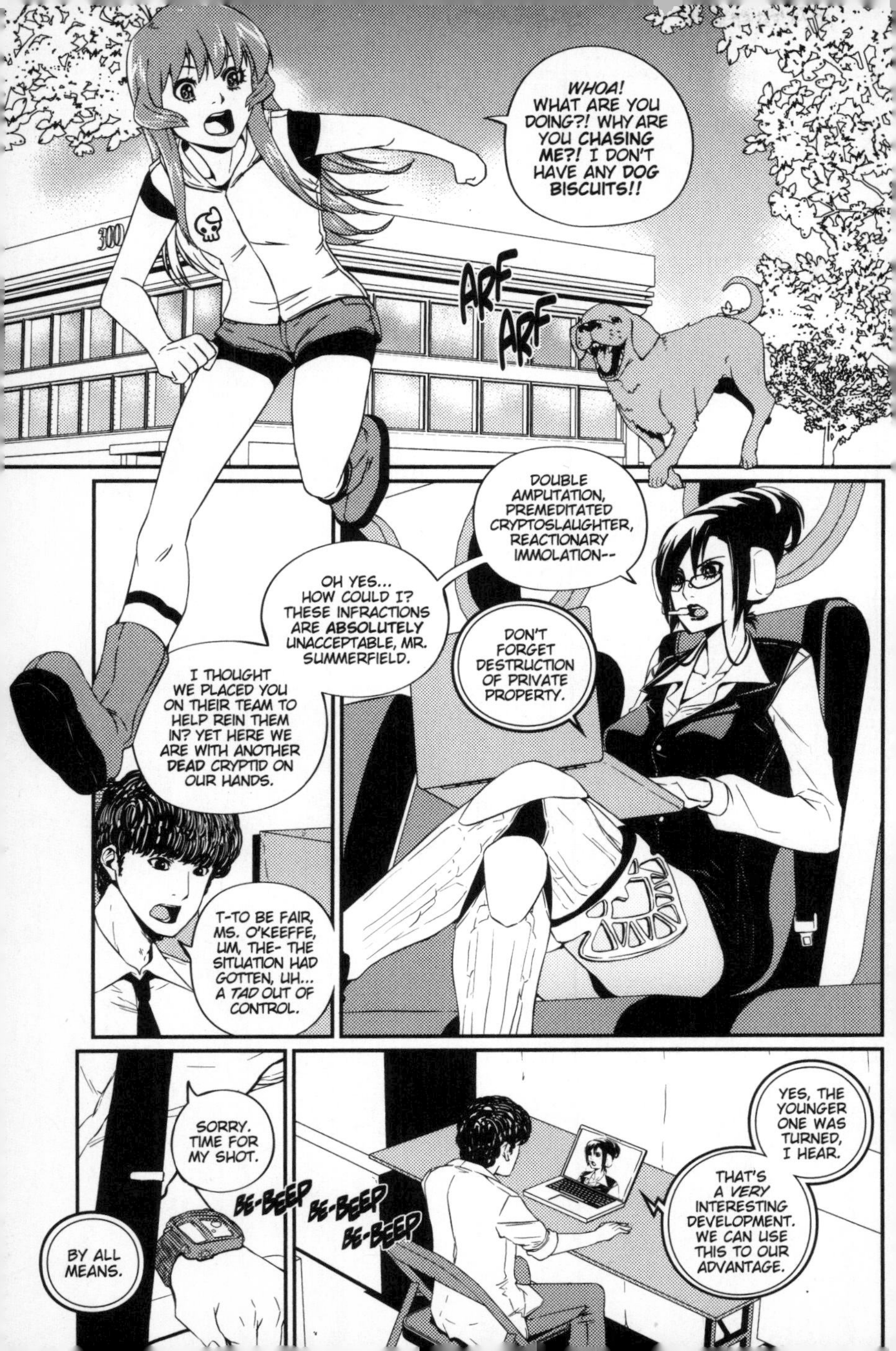

WHOA! WHAT ARE YOU DOING?! WHY ARE YOU **CHASING** ME?! I DON'T HAVE ANY DOG BISCUITS!!
ARF ARF
DOUBLE AMPUTATION, PREMEDITATED CRYPTOSLAUGHTER, REACTIONARY IMMOLATION--
OH YES... HOW COULD I? THESE INFRACTIONS ARE **ABSOLUTELY** UNACCEPTABLE, MR. SUMMERFIELD.
DON'T FORGET DESTRUCTION OF PRIVATE PROPERTY.
I THOUGHT WE PLACED YOU ON THEIR TEAM TO HELP REIN THEM IN? YET HERE WE ARE WITH ANOTHER DEAD CRYPTID ON OUR HANDS.
T-TO BE FAIR, MS. O'KEEFFE, UM, THE- THE SITUATION HAD GOTTEN, UH... A *TAD* OUT OF CONTROL.
YES, THE YOUNGER ONE WAS TURNED, I HEAR.
THAT'S A *VERY* INTERESTING DEVELOPMENT. WE CAN USE THIS TO OUR ADVANTAGE.
SORRY. TIME FOR MY SHOT.
BE-BEEP BE-BEEP BE-BEEP
BY ALL MEANS.

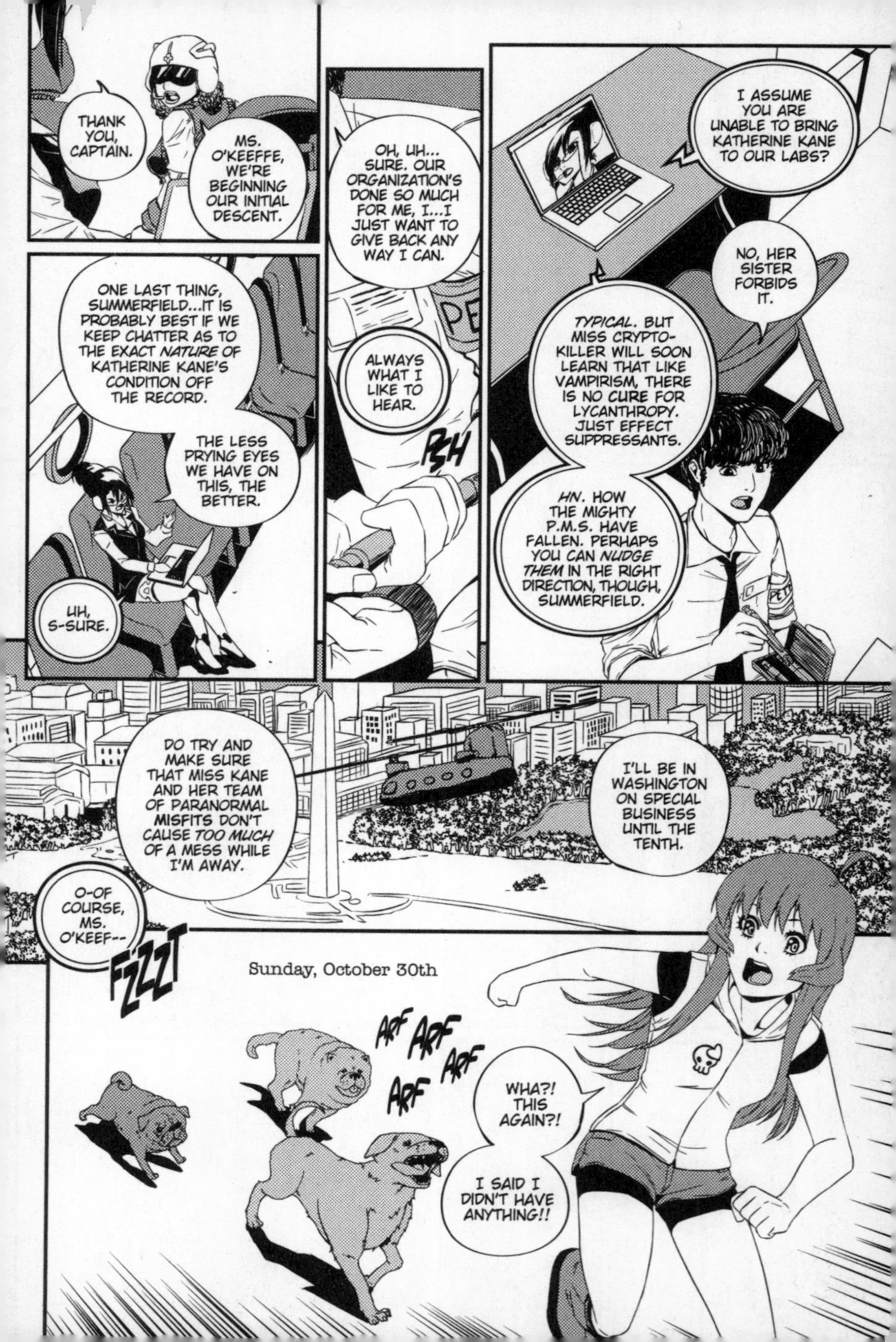
I ASSUME YOU ARE UNABLE TO BRING KATHERINE KANE TO OUR LABS?
NO, HER SISTER FORBIDS IT.
TYPICAL. BUT MISS CRYPTO-KILLER WILL SOON LEARN THAT LIKE VAMPIRISM, THERE IS NO **CURE** FOR LYCANTHROPY. JUST EFFECT SUPPRESSANTS.
HN. HOW THE MIGHTY P.M.S. HAVE FALLEN. PERHAPS YOU CAN *NUDGE THEM* IN THE RIGHT DIRECTION, THOUGH, SUMMERFIELD.
OH, UH... SURE. OUR ORGANIZATION'S DONE SO MUCH FOR ME, I...I JUST WANT TO GIVE BACK ANY WAY I CAN.
ALWAYS WHAT I LIKE TO HEAR.
PSH
MS. O'KEEFFE, WE'RE BEGINNING OUR INITIAL DESCENT.
THANK YOU, CAPTAIN.
ONE LAST THING, SUMMERFIELD...IT IS PROBABLY BEST IF WE KEEP CHATTER AS TO THE EXACT *NATURE* OF KATHERINE KANE'S CONDITION OFF THE RECORD.
THE LESS PRYING EYES WE HAVE ON THIS, THE BETTER.
UH, S-SURE.
I'LL BE IN WASHINGTON ON SPECIAL BUSINESS UNTIL THE TENTH.
DO TRY AND MAKE SURE THAT MISS KANE AND HER TEAM OF PARANORMAL MISFITS DON'T CAUSE *TOO MUCH* OF A MESS WHILE I'M AWAY.
O-OF COURSE, MS. O'KEEF--
FZZZT
Sunday, October 30th
WHA?! THIS AGAIN?!
I SAID I DIDN'T HAVE ANYTHING!!
ARF ARF ARF ARF

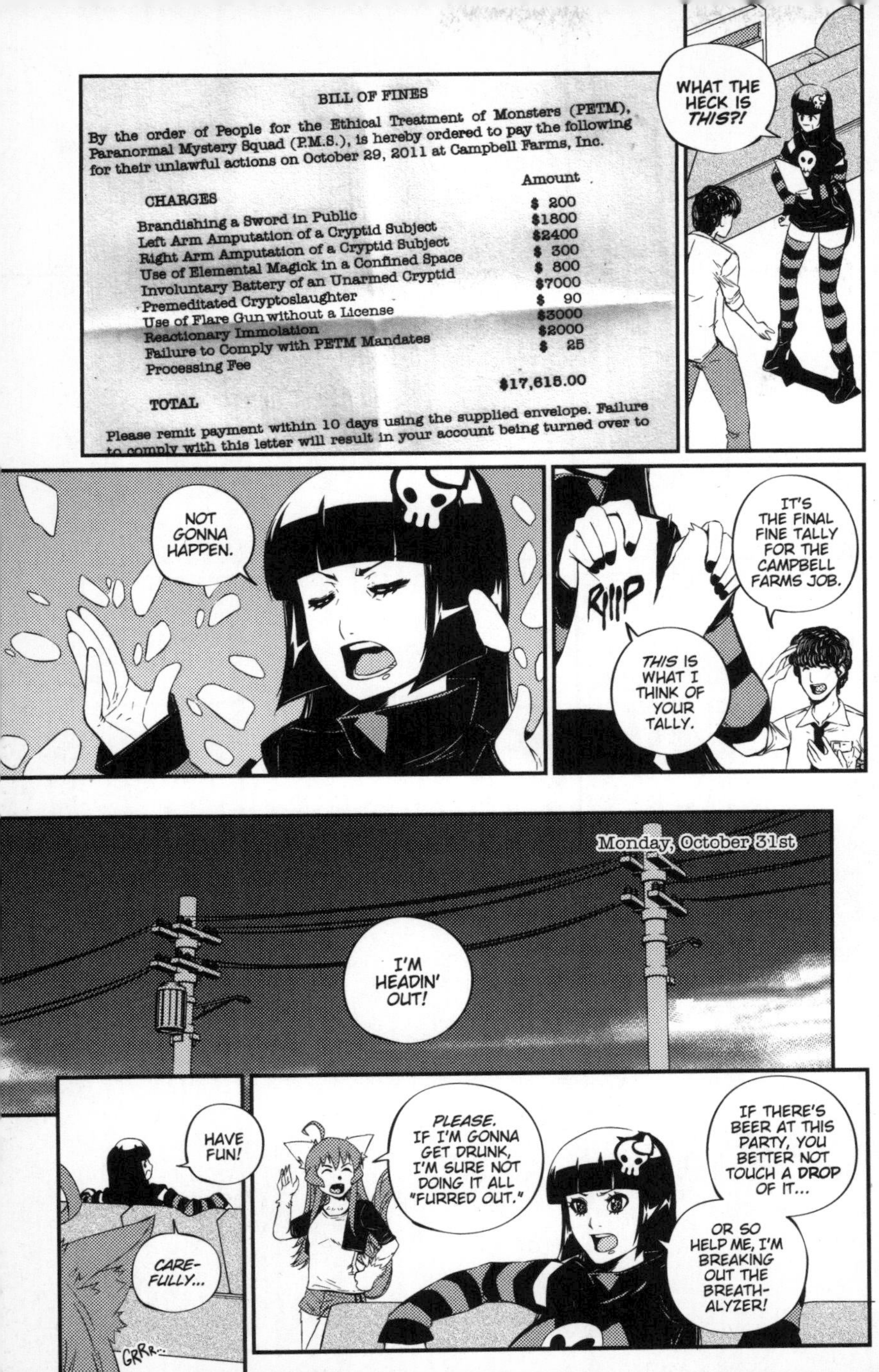
WHAT THE HECK IS *THIS?!*
BILL OF FINES
By the order of People for the Ethical Treatment of Monsters (PETM), Paranormal Mystery Squad (P.M.S.), is hereby ordered to pay the following for their unlawful actions on October 29, 2011 at Campbell Farms, Inc.
CHARGES | Amount
Brandishing a Sword in Public | $ 200
Left Arm Amputation of a Cryptid Subject | $1800
Right Arm Amputation of a Cryptid Subject | $2400
Use of Elemental Magick in a Confined Space | $ 300
Involuntary Battery of an Unarmed Cryptid | $ 800
Premeditated Cryptoslaughter | $7000
Use of Flare Gun without a License | $ 90
Reactionary Immolation | $3000
Failure to Comply with PETM Mandates | $2000
Processing Fee | $ 25
TOTAL | $17,615.00
Please remit payment within 10 days using the supplied envelope. Failure to comply with this letter will result in your account being turned over to
IT'S THE FINAL FINE TALLY FOR THE CAMPBELL FARMS JOB.
RIIIP
THIS IS WHAT I THINK OF YOUR TALLY.
NOT GONNA HAPPEN.
Monday, October 31st
I'M HEADIN' OUT!
IF THERE'S BEER AT THIS PARTY, YOU BETTER NOT TOUCH A **DROP** OF IT...
OR SO HELP ME, I'M BREAKING OUT THE BREATH-ALYZER!
PLEASE. IF I'M GONNA GET DRUNK, I'M SURE NOT DOING IT ALL "FURRED OUT."
HAVE FUN!
CARE-FULLY...
GRRR...

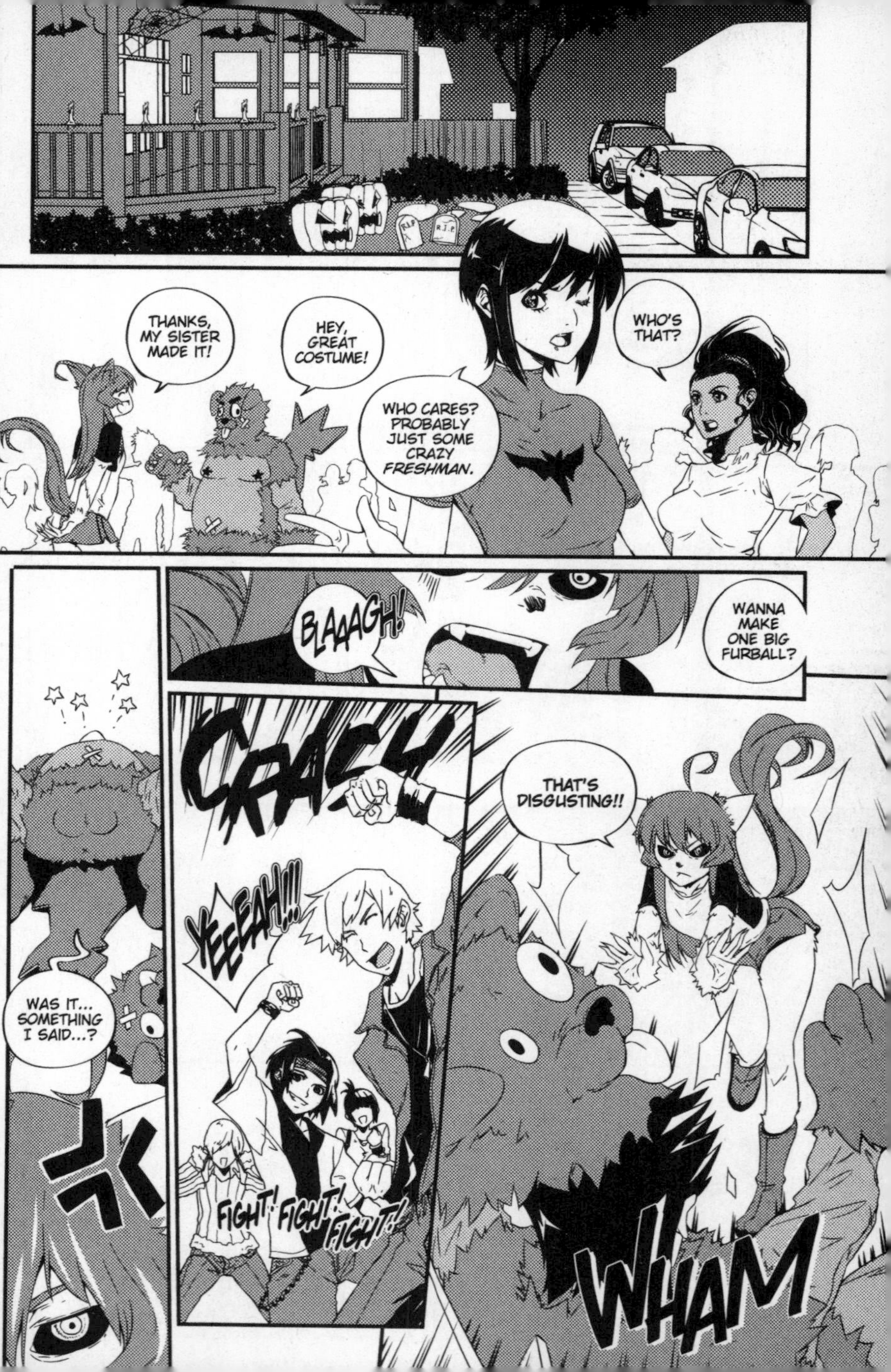

WHO'S THAT?
WHO CARES? PROBABLY JUST SOME CRAZY FRESHMAN.
HEY, GREAT COSTUME!
THANKS, MY SISTER MADE IT!
WANNA MAKE ONE BIG FURBALL?
BLAAAGH!
THAT'S DISGUSTING!!
CRACK
WHAM
YEEEAH!!!
FIGHT! FIGHT! FIGHT!
WAS IT... SOMETHING I SAID...?

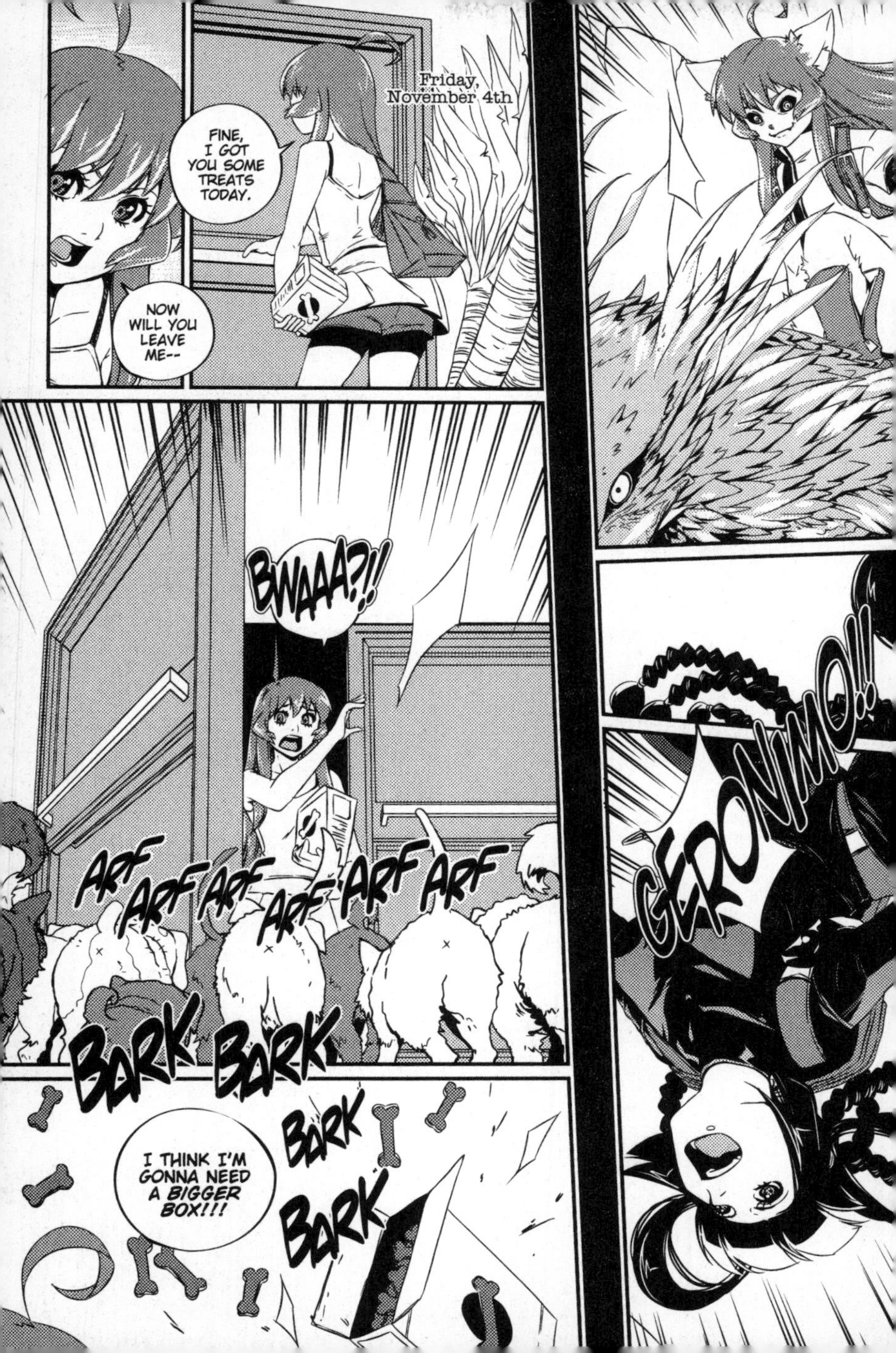
GERONIMO!!
Friday, November 4th
FINE, I GOT YOU SOME TREATS TODAY.
NOW WILL YOU LEAVE ME--
BWAAA?!!
ARF ARF ARF ARF ARF ARF
BARK BARK
BARK BARK
I THINK I'M GONNA NEED A BIGGER BOX!!!

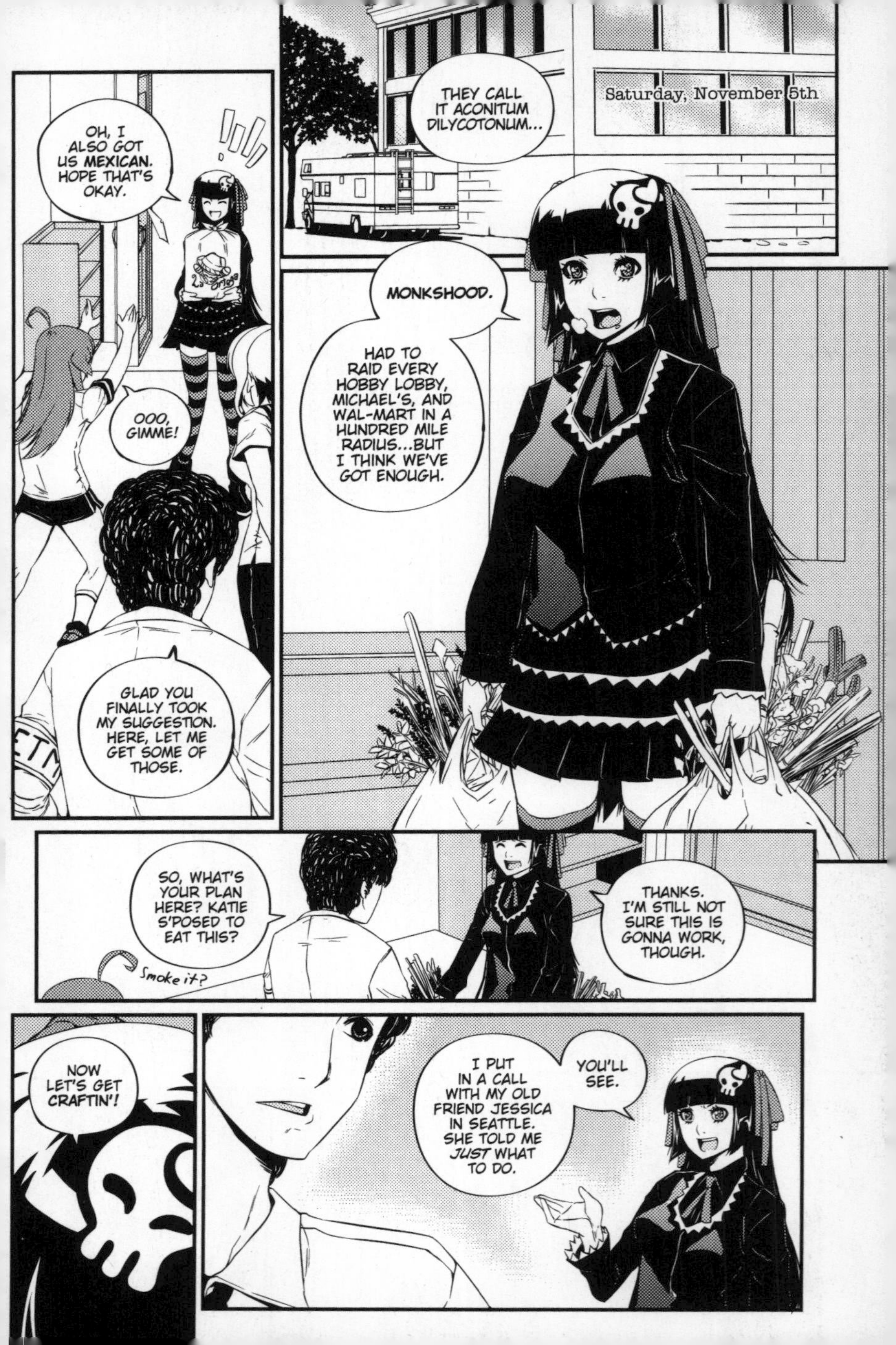
Saturday, November 5th
THEY CALL IT ACONITUM DILYCOTONUM...
MONKSHOOD.
HAD TO RAID EVERY HOBBY LOBBY, MICHAEL'S, AND WAL-MART IN A HUNDRED MILE RADIUS...BUT I THINK WE'VE GOT ENOUGH.
OH, I ALSO GOT US MEXICAN. HOPE THAT'S OKAY.
OOO, GIMME!
GLAD YOU FINALLY TOOK MY SUGGESTION. HERE, LET ME GET SOME OF THOSE.
THANKS. I'M STILL NOT SURE THIS IS GONNA WORK, THOUGH.
SO, WHAT'S YOUR PLAN HERE? KATIE S'POSED TO EAT THIS?
Smoke it?
YOU'LL SEE.
I PUT IN A CALL WITH MY OLD FRIEND JESSICA IN SEATTLE. SHE TOLD ME *JUST* WHAT TO DO.
NOW LET'S GET CRAFTIN'!

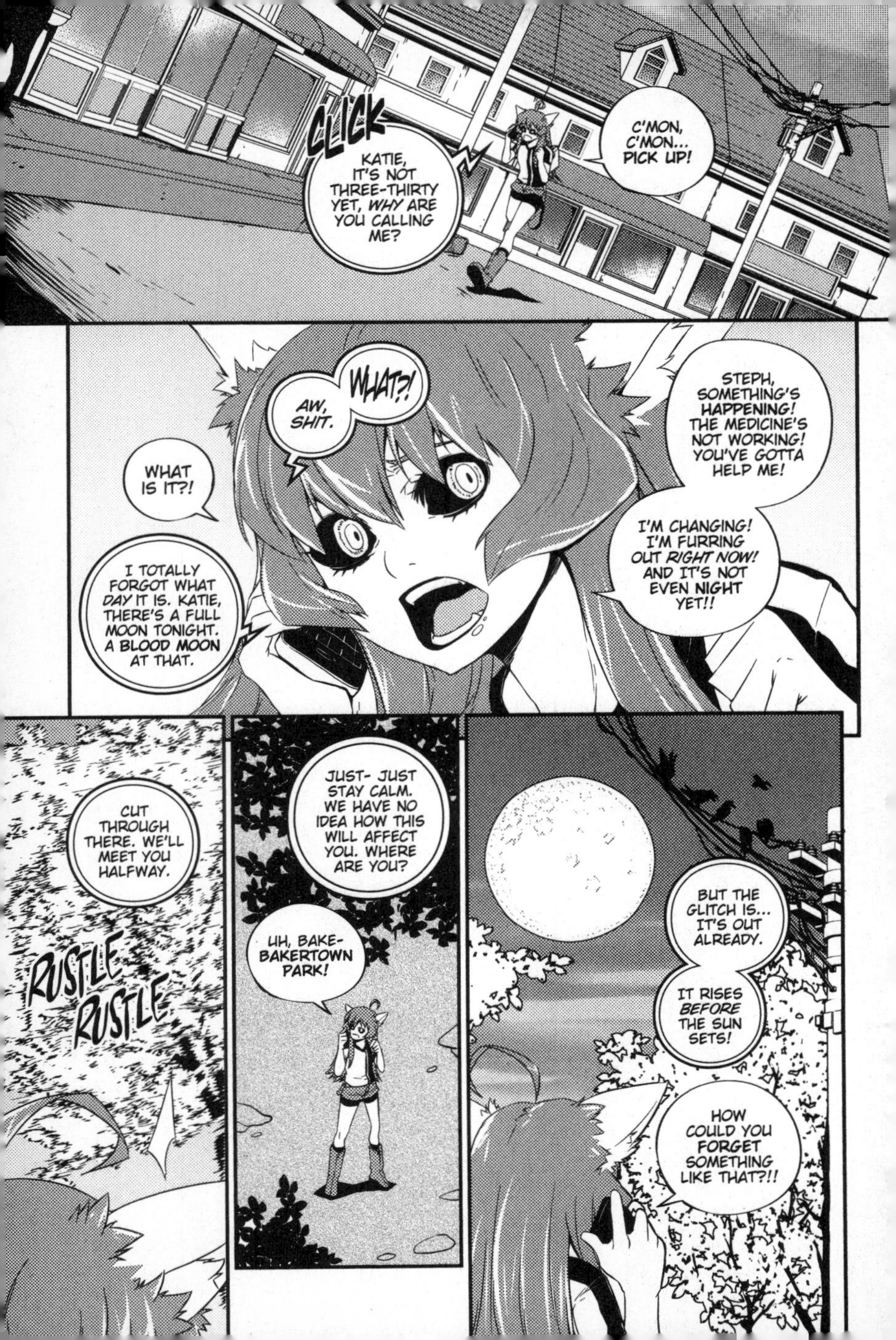
C'MON, C'MON... PICK UP!
CLICK
KATIE, IT'S NOT THREE-THIRTY YET, *WHY* ARE YOU CALLING ME?
STEPH, SOMETHING'S **HAPPENING**! THE MEDICINE'S NOT WORKING! YOU'VE GOTTA HELP ME!
WHAT?!
I'M CHANGING! I'M FURRING OUT *RIGHT NOW!* AND IT'S NOT EVEN **NIGHT** YET!!
AW, SHIT.
WHAT IS IT?!
I TOTALLY FORGOT WHAT *DAY* IT IS. KATIE, THERE'S A FULL MOON TONIGHT. A **BLOOD MOON** AT THAT.
BUT THE GLITCH IS... IT'S OUT ALREADY.
IT RISES *BEFORE* THE SUN SETS!
HOW COULD YOU **FORGET** SOMETHING LIKE THAT?!!
JUST- JUST STAY CALM. WE HAVE NO IDEA HOW THIS WILL AFFECT YOU. WHERE ARE YOU?
UH, BAKE- BAKERTOWN PARK!
CUT THROUGH THERE. WE'LL MEET YOU HALFWAY.
RUSTLE RUSTLE

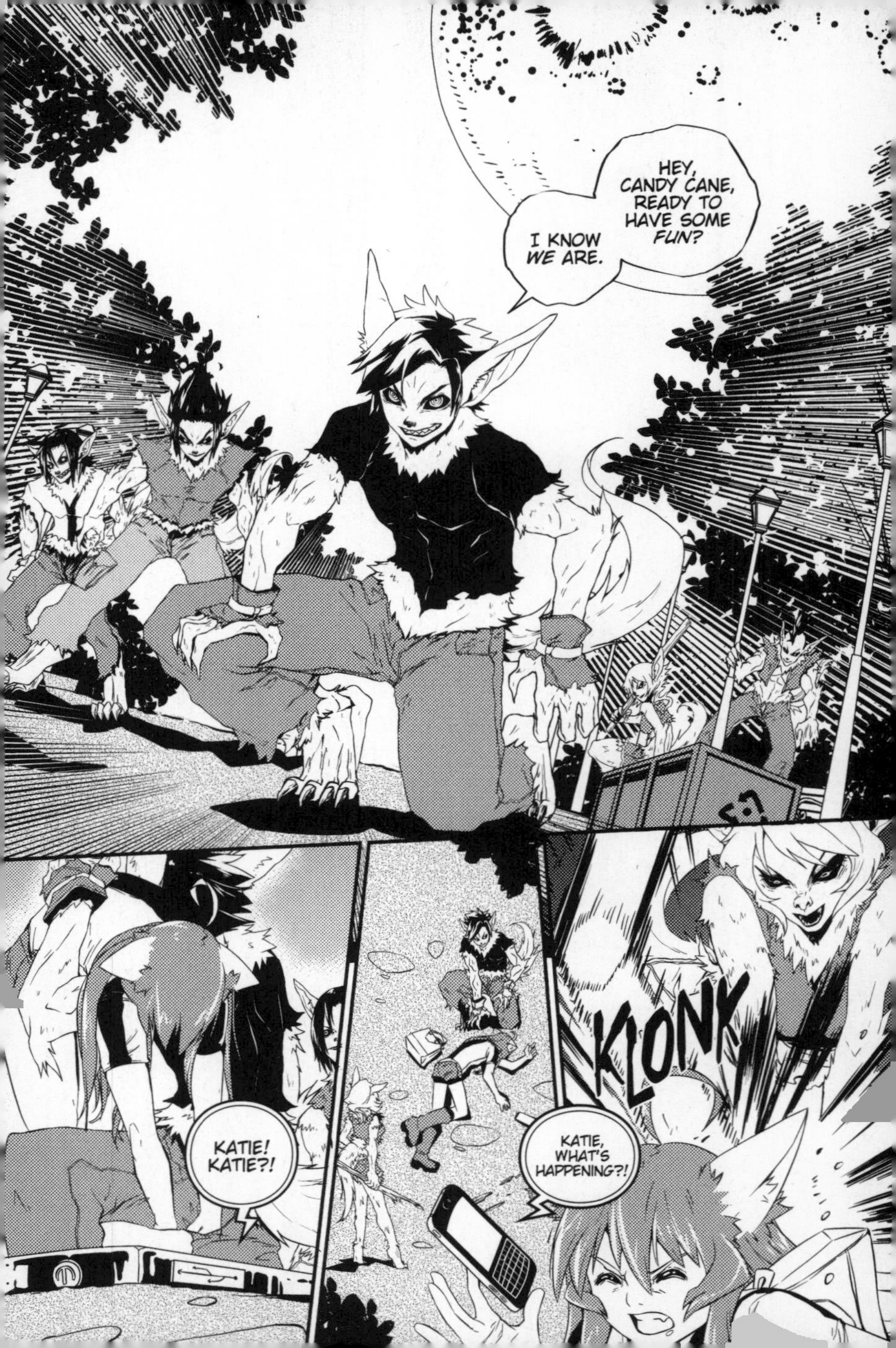
HEY, CANDY CANE, READY TO HAVE SOME FUN?
I KNOW WE ARE.
KLONK
KATIE, WHAT'S HAPPENING?!
KATIE! KATIE?!

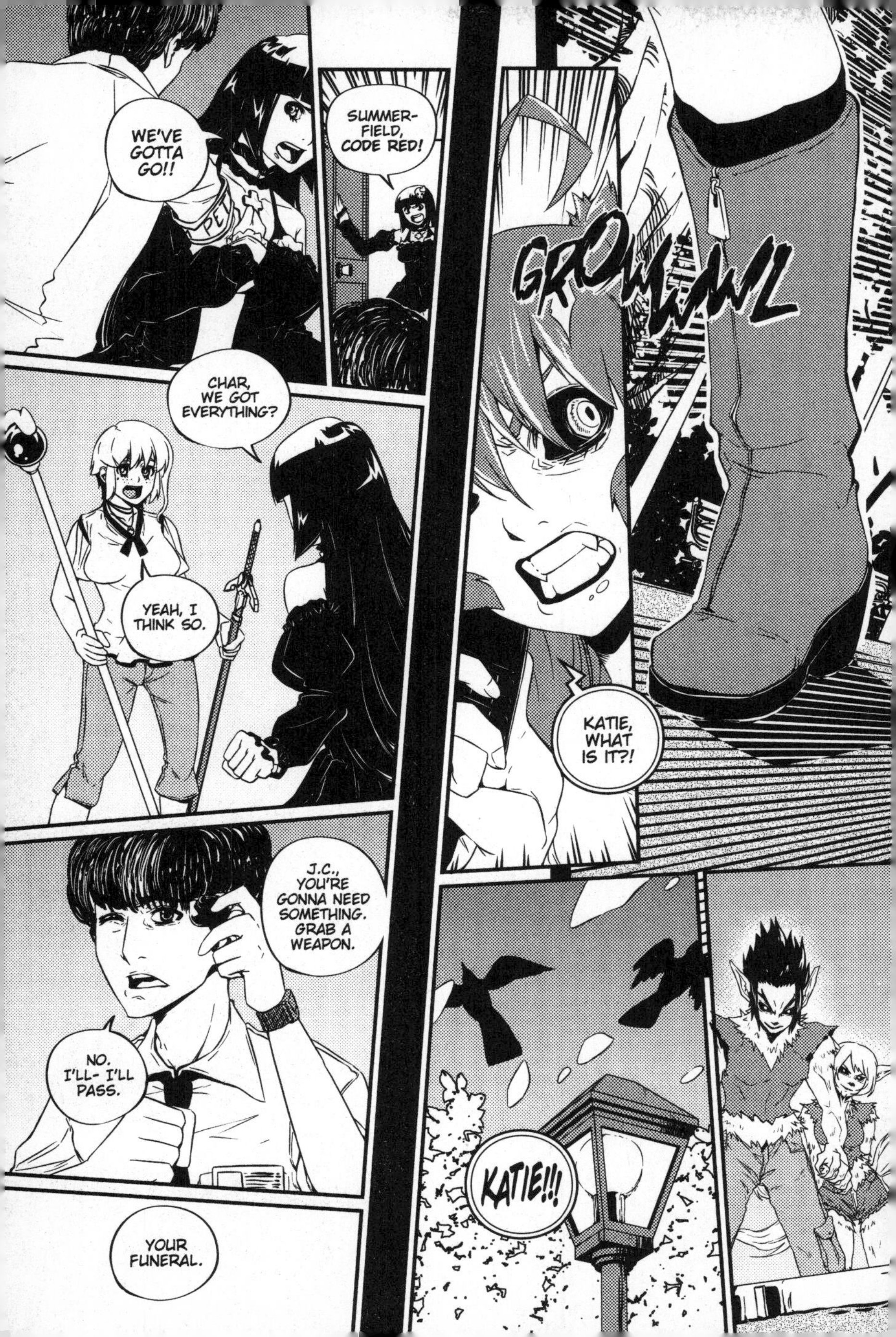
GROWWWL
KATIE, WHAT IS IT?!
KATIE!!!
SUMMER-FIELD, CODE RED!
WE'VE GOTTA GO!!
CHAR, WE GOT EVERYTHING?
YEAH, I THINK SO.
J.C., YOU'RE GONNA NEED SOMETHING. GRAB A WEAPON.
NO. I'LL- I'LL PASS.
YOUR FUNERAL.

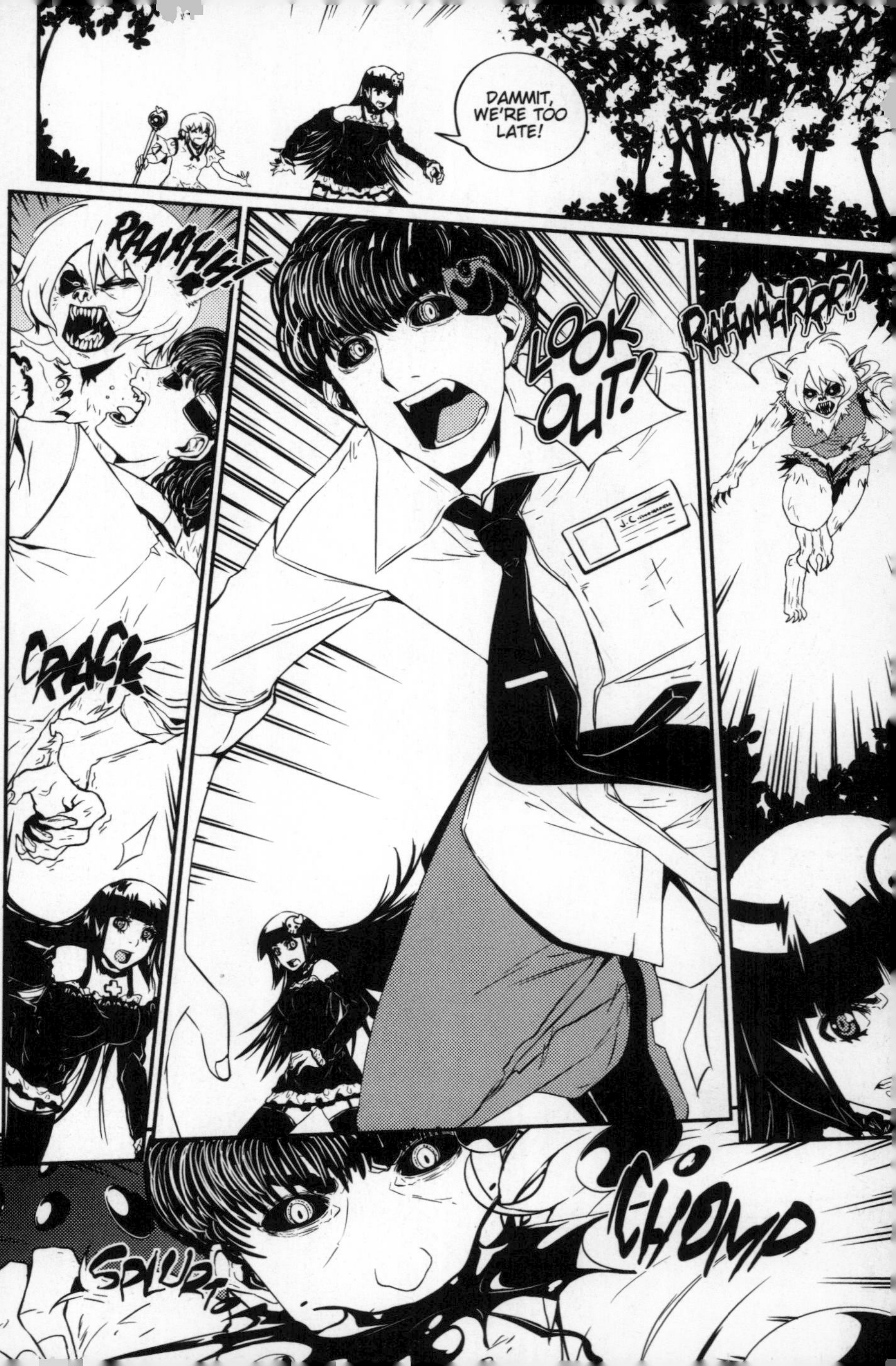
DAMMIT, WE'RE TOO LATE!
RAAAARRR!!
LOOK OUT!
RAAAHHS!!
CRACK
CHOMP
SPLURT

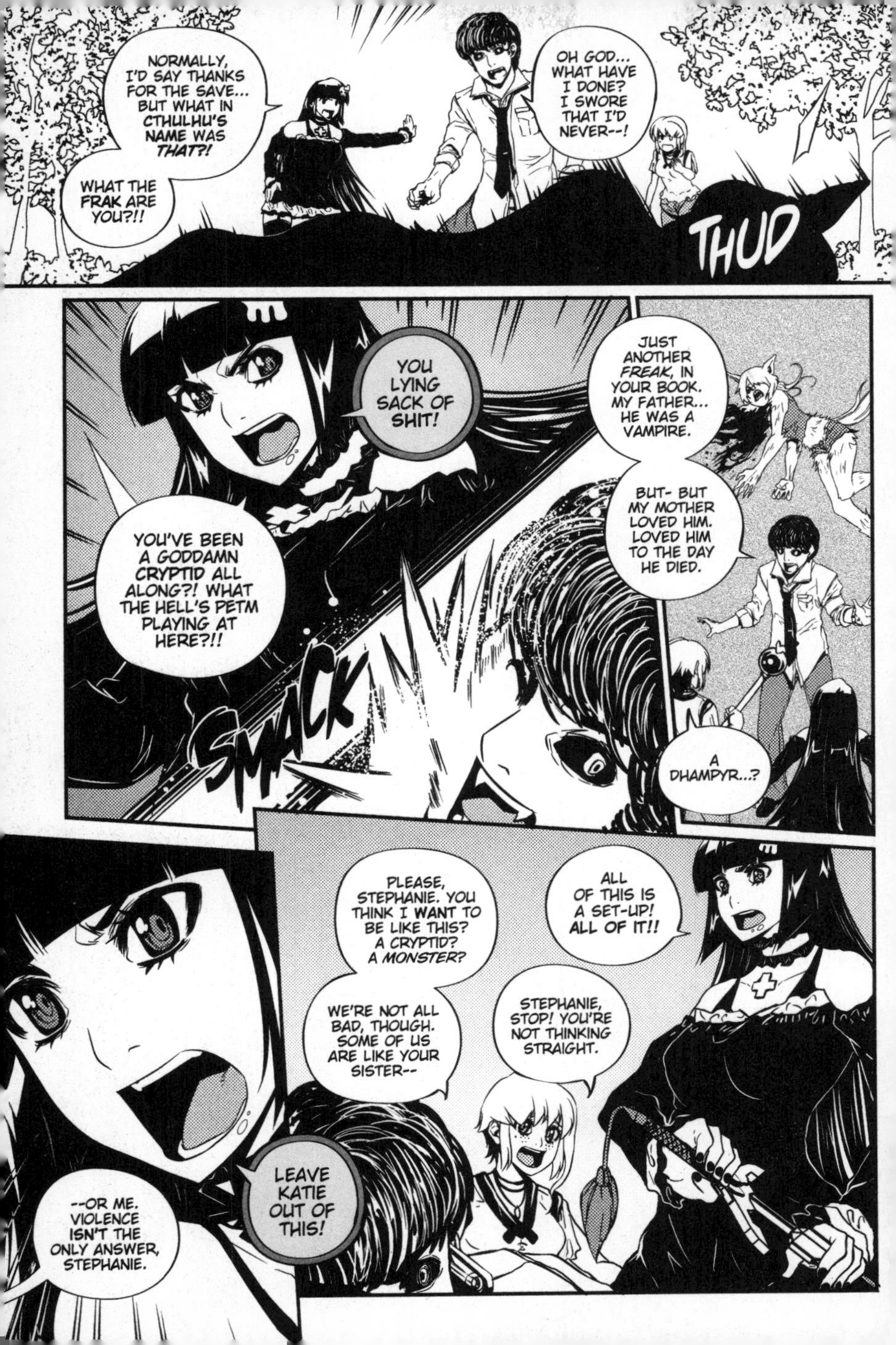

OH GOD... WHAT HAVE I DONE? I SWORE THAT I'D NEVER--!
NORMALLY, I'D SAY THANKS FOR THE SAVE... BUT WHAT IN CTHULHU'S NAME WAS *THAT*?!
THUD
WHAT THE FRAK ARE YOU?!!
JUST ANOTHER *FREAK*, IN YOUR BOOK. MY FATHER... HE WAS A VAMPIRE.
BUT- BUT MY MOTHER LOVED HIM. LOVED HIM TO THE DAY HE DIED.
A DHAMPYR...?
YOU LYING SACK OF SHIT!
YOU'VE BEEN A GODDAMN CRYPTID ALL ALONG?! WHAT THE HELL'S PETM PLAYING AT HERE?!!
SMACK
ALL OF THIS IS A SET-UP! ALL OF IT!!
PLEASE, STEPHANIE. YOU THINK I WANT TO BE LIKE THIS? A CRYPTID? A *MONSTER*?
STEPHANIE, STOP! YOU'RE NOT THINKING STRAIGHT.
WE'RE NOT ALL BAD, THOUGH. SOME OF US ARE LIKE YOUR SISTER--
LEAVE KATIE OUT OF THIS!
--OR ME. VIOLENCE ISN'T THE ONLY ANSWER, STEPHANIE.

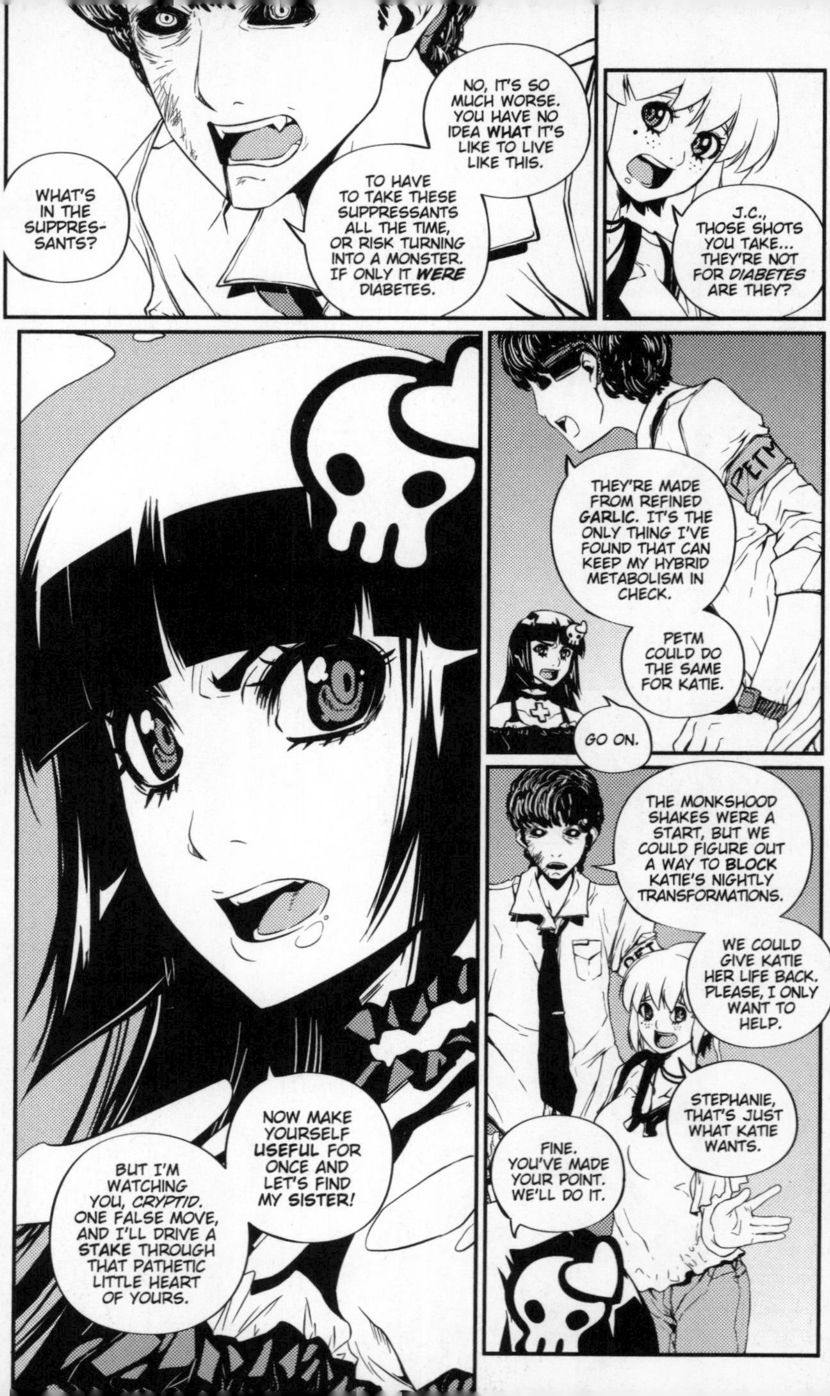
J.C., THOSE SHOTS YOU TAKE... THEY'RE NOT FOR *DIABETES* ARE THEY?
NO, IT'S SO MUCH WORSE. YOU HAVE NO IDEA **WHAT** IT'S LIKE TO LIVE LIKE THIS.
TO HAVE TO TAKE THESE SUPPRESSANTS ALL THE TIME, OR RISK TURNING INTO A MONSTER. IF ONLY IT ***WERE*** DIABETES.
WHAT'S IN THE SUPPRES- SANTS?
THEY'RE MADE FROM REFINED **GARLIC**. IT'S THE ONLY THING I'VE FOUND THAT CAN KEEP MY HYBRID METABOLISM IN CHECK.
PETM COULD DO THE SAME FOR KATIE.
GO ON.
THE MONKSHOOD SHAKES WERE A START, BUT WE COULD FIGURE OUT A WAY TO **BLOCK** KATIE'S NIGHTLY TRANSFORMATIONS.
WE COULD GIVE KATIE HER LIFE BACK. PLEASE, I ONLY WANT TO HELP.
STEPHANIE, THAT'S JUST WHAT KATIE WANTS.
FINE. YOU'VE MADE YOUR POINT. WE'LL DO IT.
NOW MAKE YOURSELF **USEFUL** FOR ONCE AND LET'S FIND MY **SISTER**!
BUT I'M WATCHING YOU, *CRYPTID*. ONE FALSE MOVE, AND I'LL DRIVE A **STAKE** THROUGH THAT PATHETIC LITTLE HEART OF YOURS.

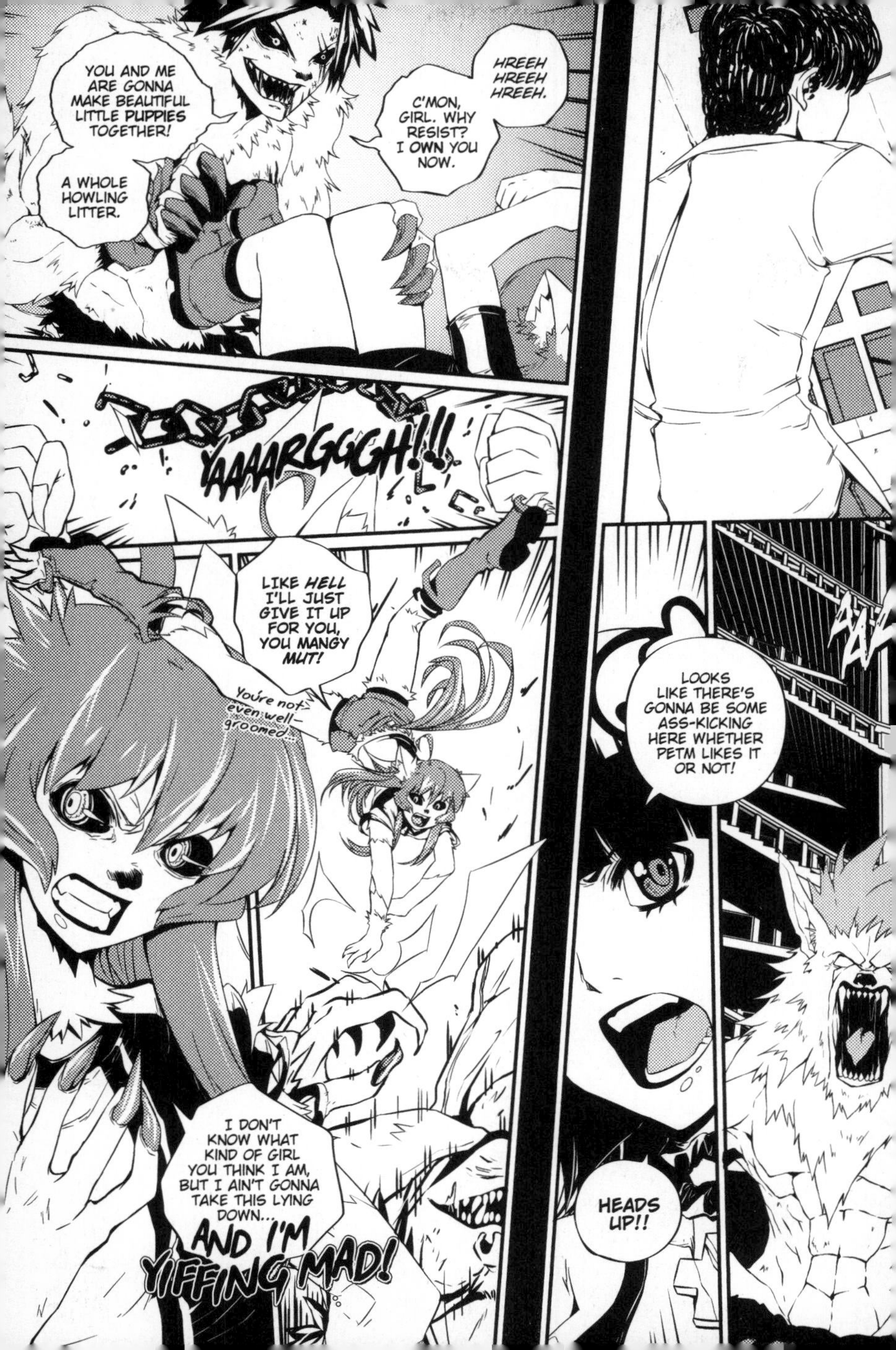
HREEH HREEH HREEH.
C'MON, GIRL. WHY RESIST? I OWN YOU NOW.
YOU AND ME ARE GONNA MAKE BEAUTIFUL LITTLE PUPPIES TOGETHER!
A WHOLE HOWLING LITTER.
YAAAARGGGH!!!
LOOKS LIKE THERE'S GONNA BE SOME ASS-KICKING HERE WHETHER PETM LIKES IT OR NOT!
HEADS UP!!
LIKE HELL I'LL JUST GIVE IT UP FOR YOU, YOU MANGY MUT!
You're not even well-groomed.
I DON'T KNOW WHAT KIND OF GIRL YOU THINK I AM, BUT I AIN'T GONNA TAKE THIS LYING DOWN...
AND I'M YIFFING MAD!

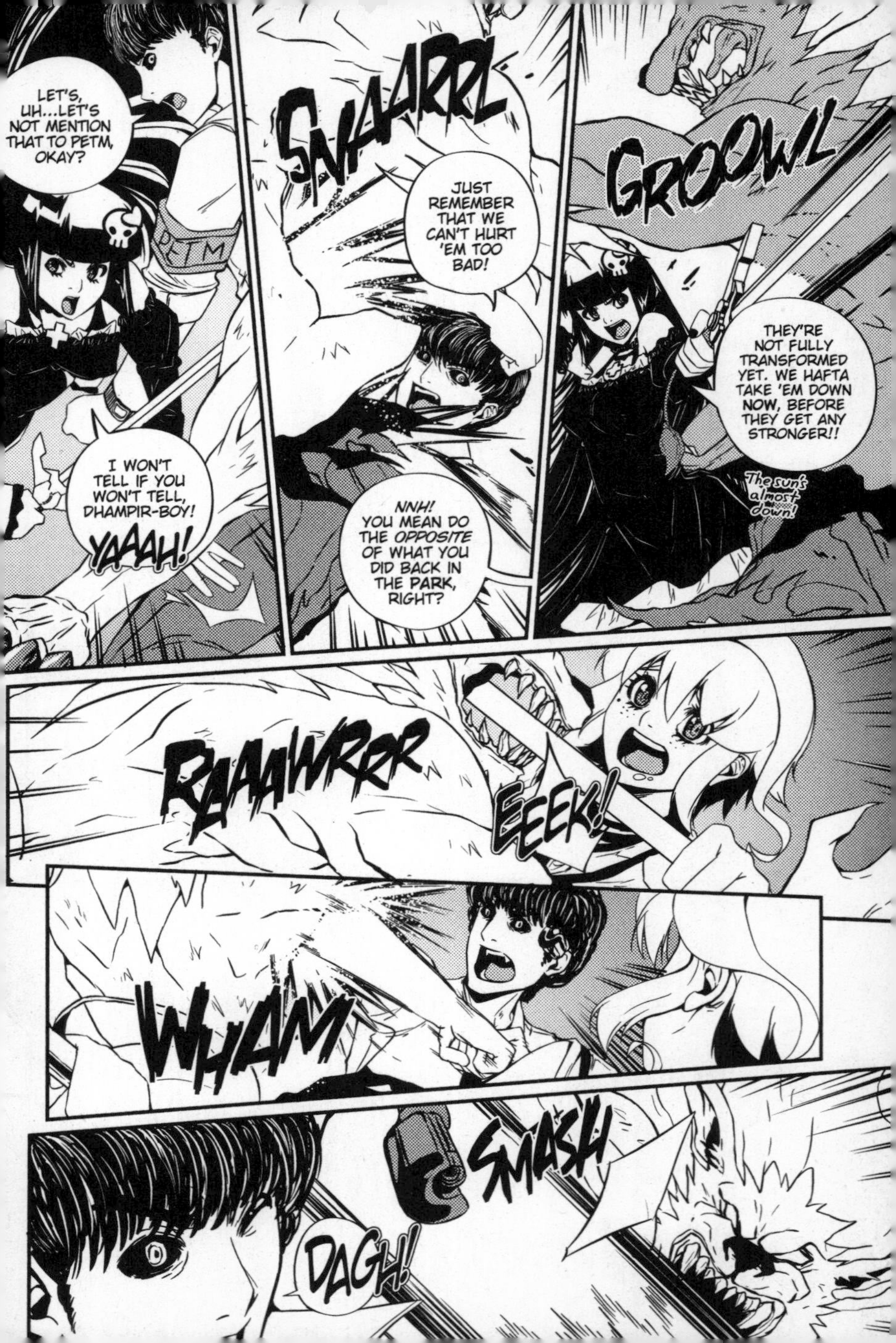
GROOWL
THEY'RE NOT FULLY TRANSFORMED YET. WE HAFTA TAKE 'EM DOWN NOW, BEFORE THEY GET ANY STRONGER!!
The sun's almost down!
SNAARRL
JUST REMEMBER THAT WE CAN'T HURT 'EM TOO BAD!
NNH! YOU MEAN DO THE *OPPOSITE* OF WHAT YOU DID BACK IN THE PARK, RIGHT?
LET'S, UH...LET'S NOT MENTION THAT TO PETM, OKAY?
I WON'T TELL IF YOU WON'T TELL, DHAMPIR-BOY!
YAAAH!
EEEK!
RAAAWRRR
WHAM
SMASH
DAGH!

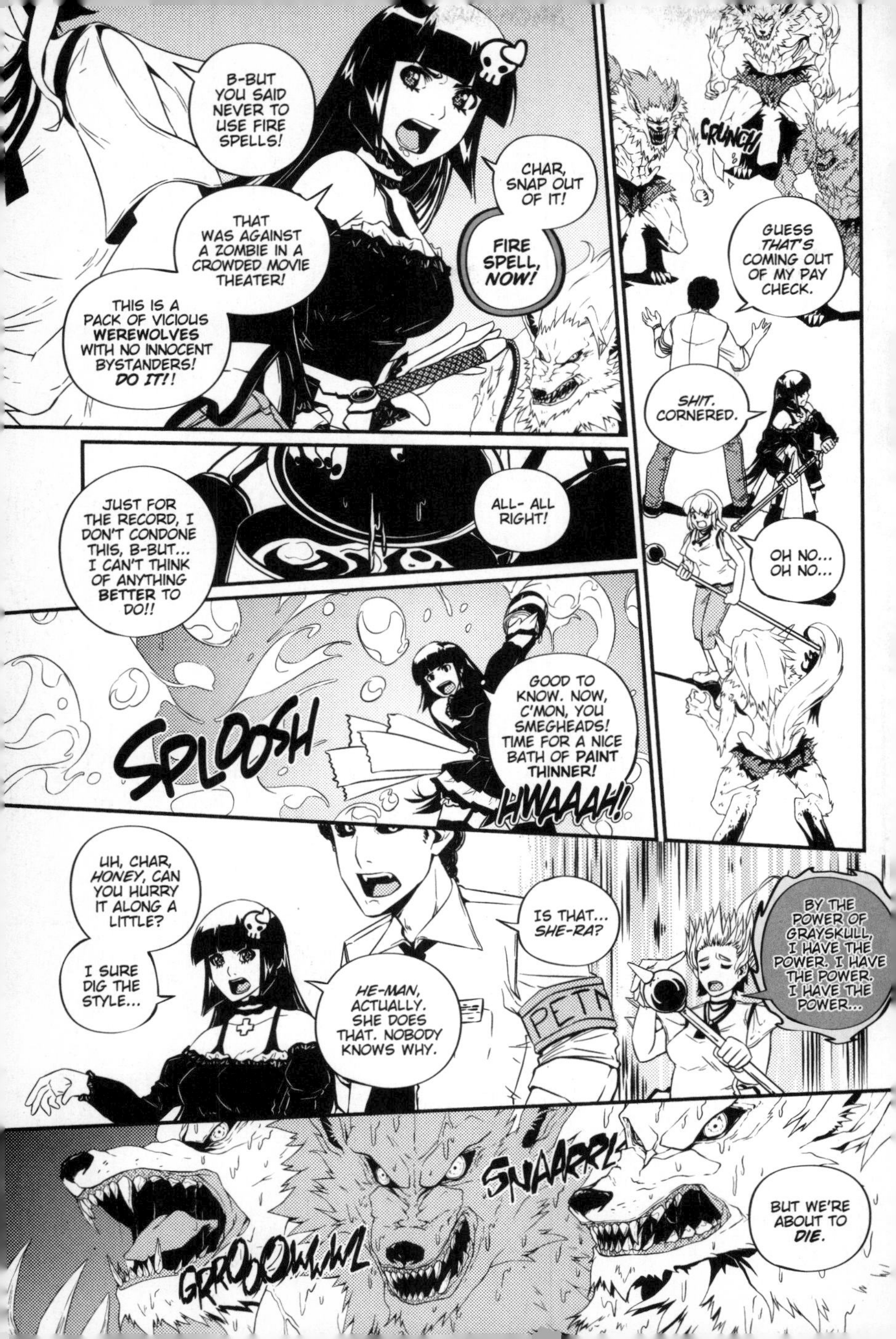
CRUNCH
GUESS *THAT'S* COMING OUT OF MY PAY CHECK.
CHAR, SNAP OUT OF IT!
FIRE SPELL, *NOW!*
B-BUT YOU SAID NEVER TO USE FIRE SPELLS!
THAT WAS AGAINST A ZOMBIE IN A CROWDED MOVIE THEATER!
THIS IS A PACK OF VICIOUS **WEREWOLVES** WITH NO INNOCENT BYSTANDERS! ***DO IT!!***
SHIT. CORNERED.
OH NO... OH NO...
ALL- ALL RIGHT!
JUST FOR THE RECORD, I DON'T CONDONE THIS, B-BUT... I CAN'T THINK OF ANYTHING **BETTER** TO DO!!
HWAAAH!
GOOD TO KNOW. NOW, C'MON, YOU SMEGHEADS! TIME FOR A NICE BATH OF PAINT THINNER!
SPLOOSH
BY THE POWER OF GRAYSKULL, I HAVE THE POWER. I HAVE THE POWER. I HAVE THE POWER...
PETA
IS THAT... *SHE-RA?*
HE-MAN, ACTUALLY. SHE DOES THAT. NOBODY KNOWS WHY.
UH, CHAR, *HONEY,* CAN YOU HURRY IT ALONG A LITTLE?
I SURE DIG THE STYLE...
BUT WE'RE ABOUT TO ***DIE.***
SNAARRL
GRROOWWL

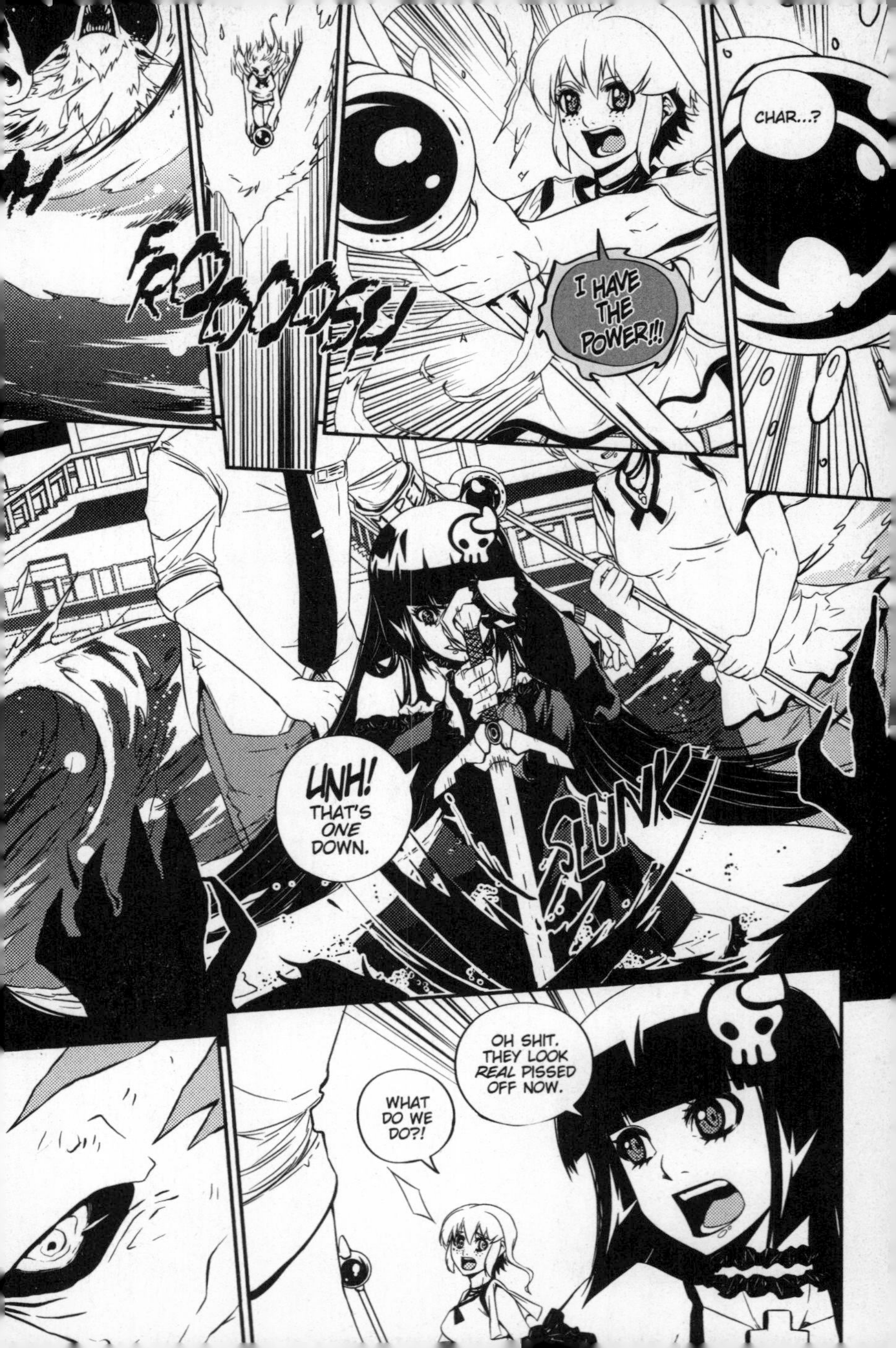
CHAR...?
I HAVE THE POWER!!!
FROOOOSH
UNH! THAT'S *ONE* DOWN.
SLUNK
OH SHIT. THEY LOOK *REAL* PISSED OFF NOW.
WHAT DO WE DO?!

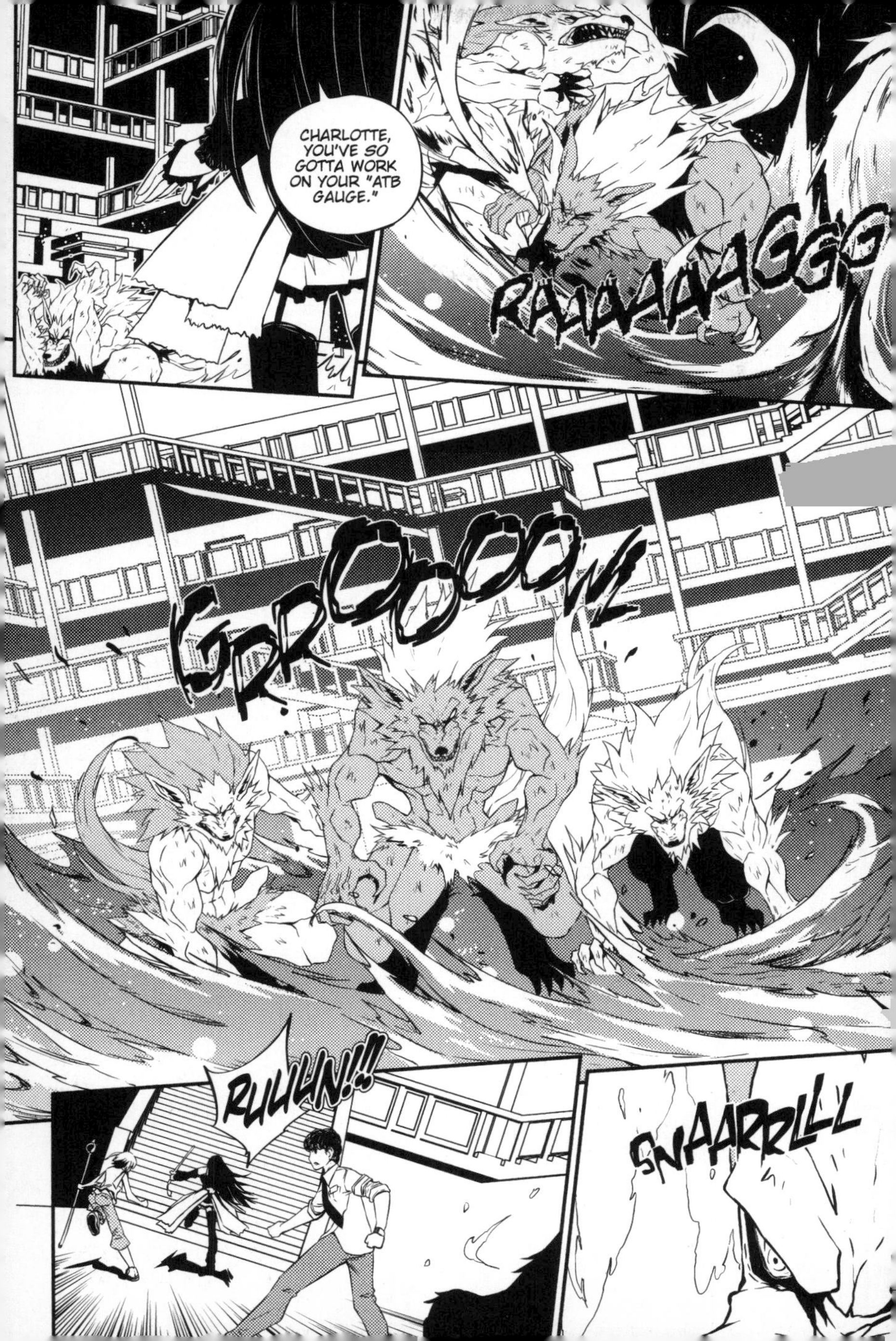
RAAAAAGGG
CHARLOTTE, YOU'VE SO GOTTA WORK ON YOUR "ATB GAUGE."
GRROOOOW
SNAARRLLL
RUUUN!!!

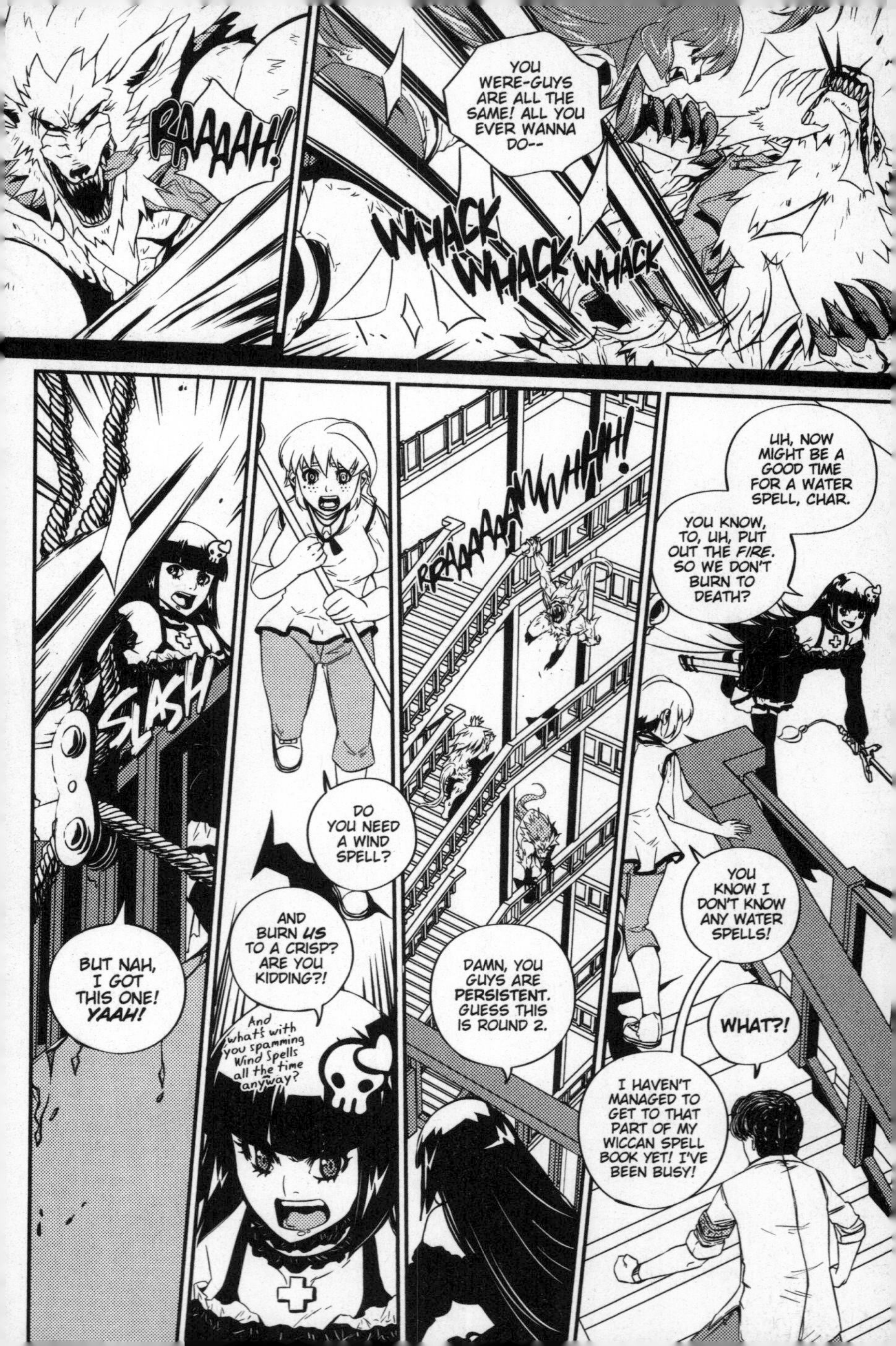

YOU WERE-GUYS ARE ALL THE SAME! ALL YOU EVER WANNA DO--
WHACK WHACK WHACK
RAAAAH!
UH, NOW MIGHT BE A GOOD TIME FOR A WATER SPELL, CHAR.
YOU KNOW, TO, UH, PUT OUT THE *FIRE*. SO WE DON'T BURN TO DEATH?
YOU KNOW I DON'T KNOW ANY WATER SPELLS!
WHAT?!
I HAVEN'T MANAGED TO GET TO THAT PART OF MY WICCAN SPELL BOOK YET! I'VE BEEN BUSY!
RRAAAAAAAWWHHH!
DAMN, YOU GUYS ARE PERSISTENT. GUESS THIS IS ROUND 2.
DO YOU NEED A WIND SPELL?
AND BURN *US* TO A CRISP? ARE YOU KIDDING?!
And what's with you spamming Wind Spells all the time anyway?
SLASH
BUT NAH, I GOT THIS ONE! ***YAAH!***

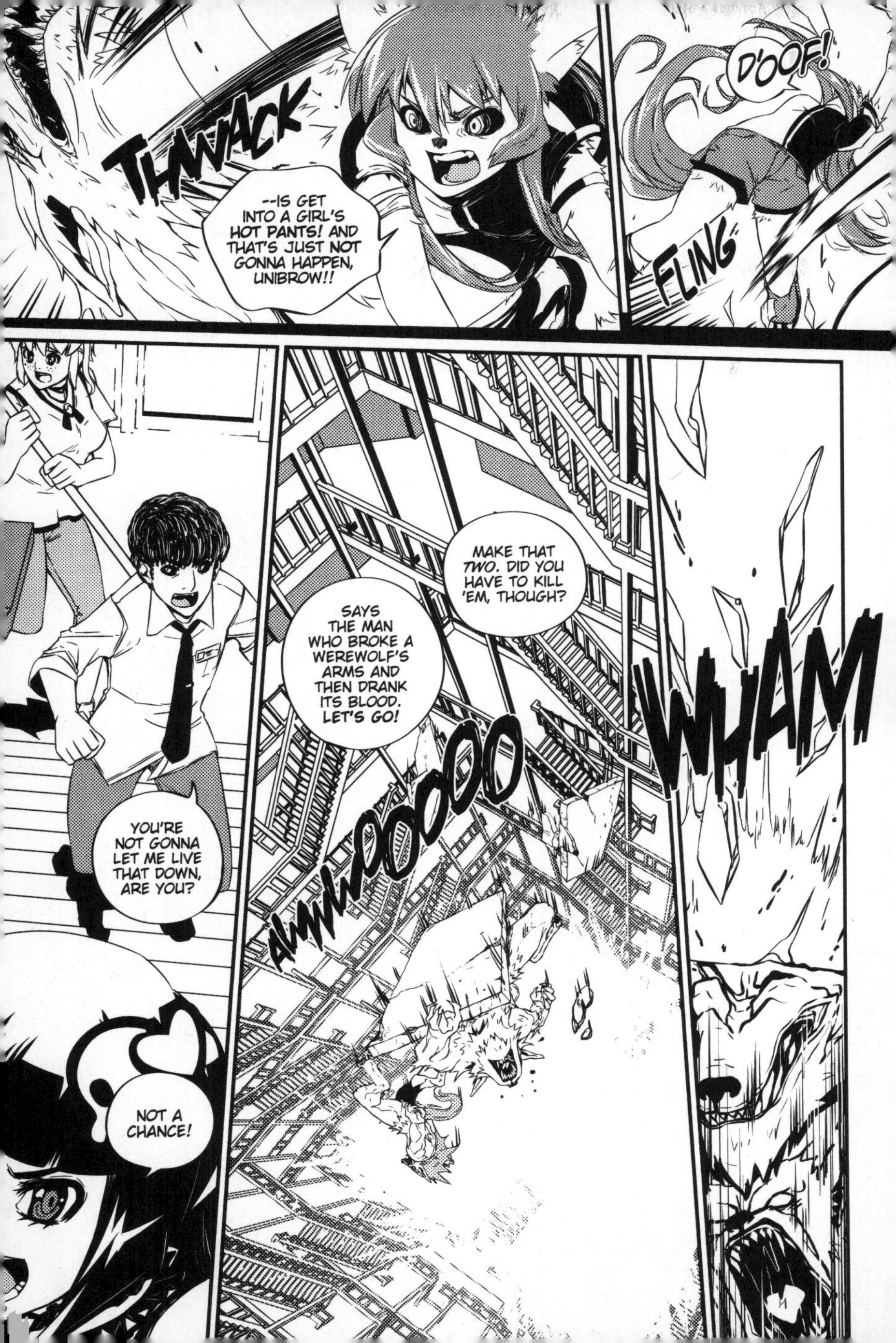
D'OOF!
FLING
THWACK
--IS GET INTO A GIRL'S HOT PANTS! AND THAT'S JUST NOT GONNA HAPPEN, UNIBROW!!
WHAM
AWWWOOOOOO
MAKE THAT *TWO*. DID YOU HAVE TO KILL 'EM, THOUGH?
SAYS THE MAN WHO BROKE A WEREWOLF'S ARMS AND THEN DRANK ITS BLOOD. LET'S GO!
YOU'RE NOT GONNA LET ME LIVE THAT DOWN, ARE YOU?
NOT A CHANCE!

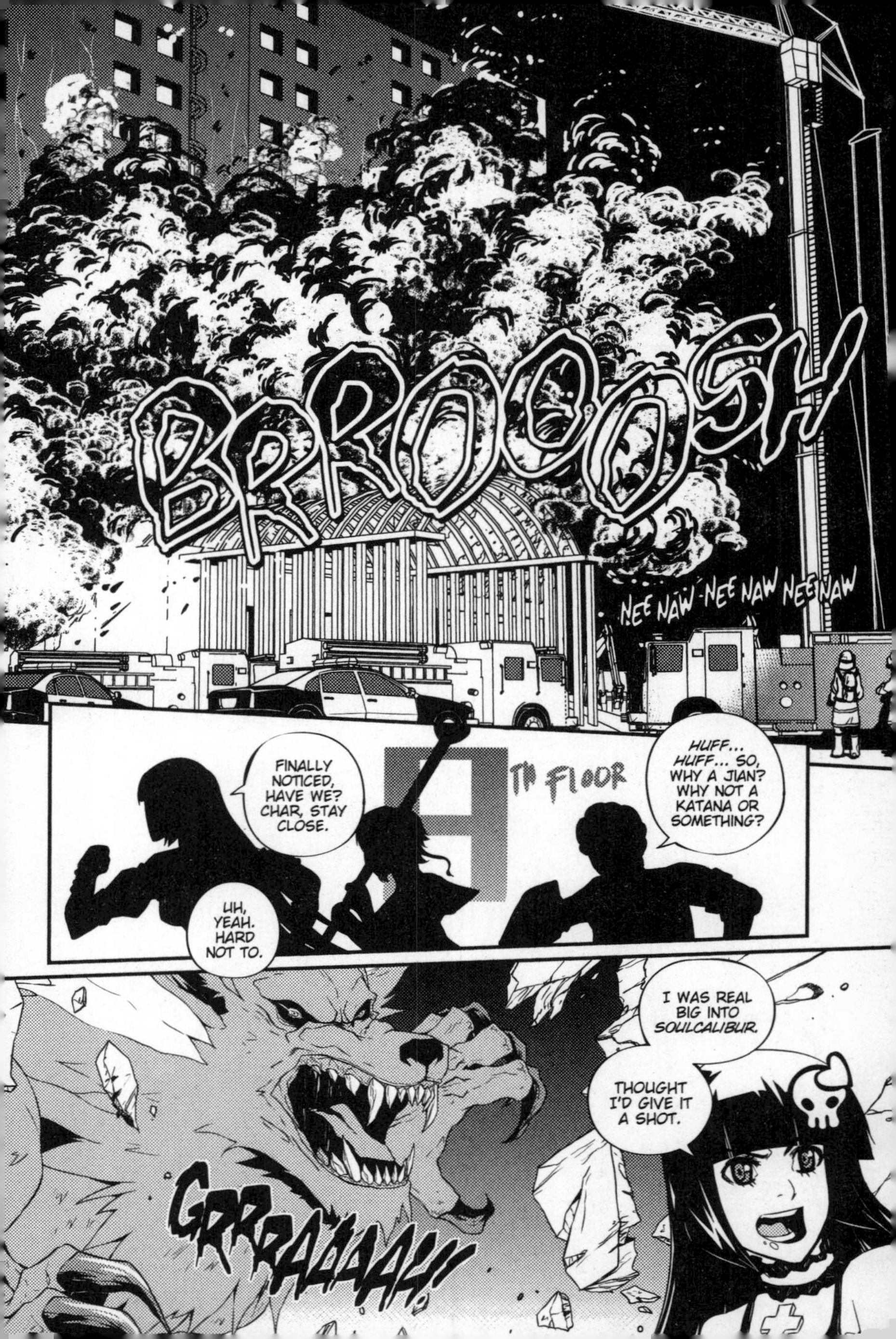
BRROOOSH
NEE NAW NEE NAW NEE NAW
HUFF... HUFF... SO, WHY A JIAN? WHY NOT A KATANA OR SOMETHING?
9TH FLOOR
FINALLY NOTICED, HAVE WE? CHAR, STAY CLOSE.
UH, YEAH. HARD NOT TO.
I WAS REAL BIG INTO *SOULCALIBUR*.
THOUGHT I'D GIVE IT A SHOT.
GRRAAAAAH!!

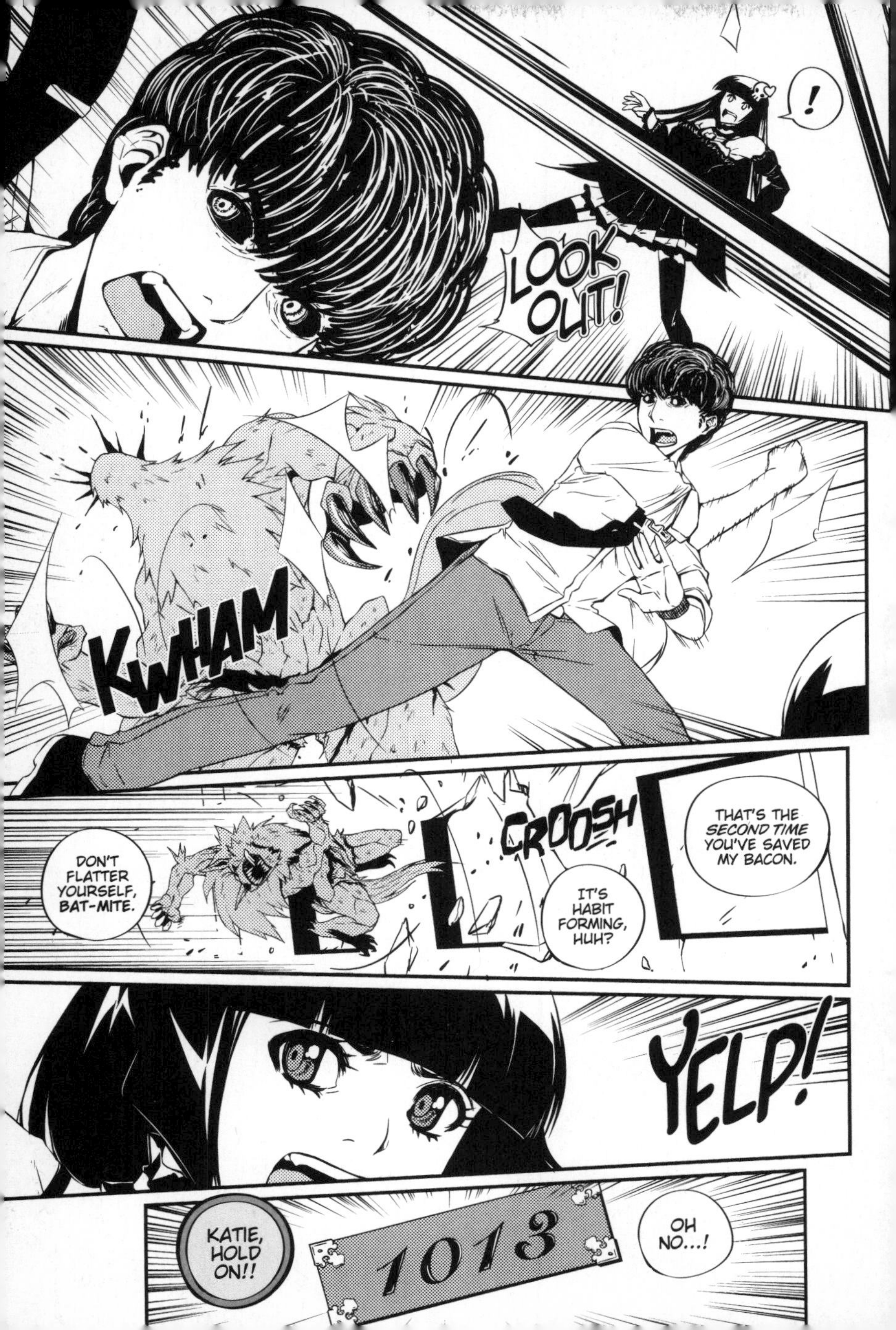
!
LOOK OUT!
KWHAM
THAT'S THE *SECOND TIME* YOU'VE SAVED MY BACON.
CROOSH
IT'S HABIT FORMING, HUH?
DON'T FLATTER YOURSELF, BAT-MITE.
YELP!
OH NO...!
1013
KATIE, HOLD ON!!

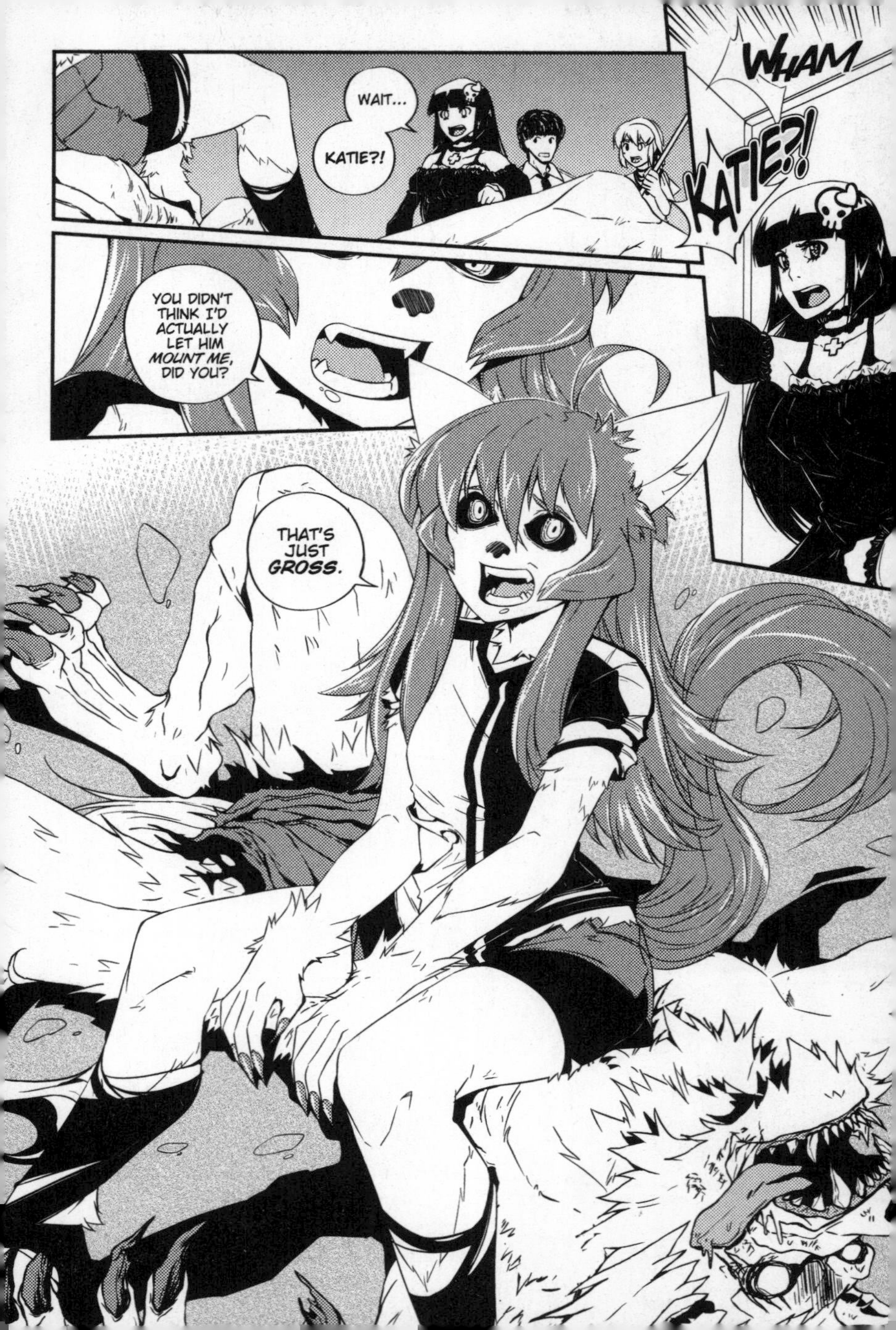
WHAM
KATIE?!
WAIT...
KATIE?!
YOU DIDN'T THINK I'D ACTUALLY LET HIM *MOUNT ME*, DID YOU?
THAT'S JUST **GROSS.**

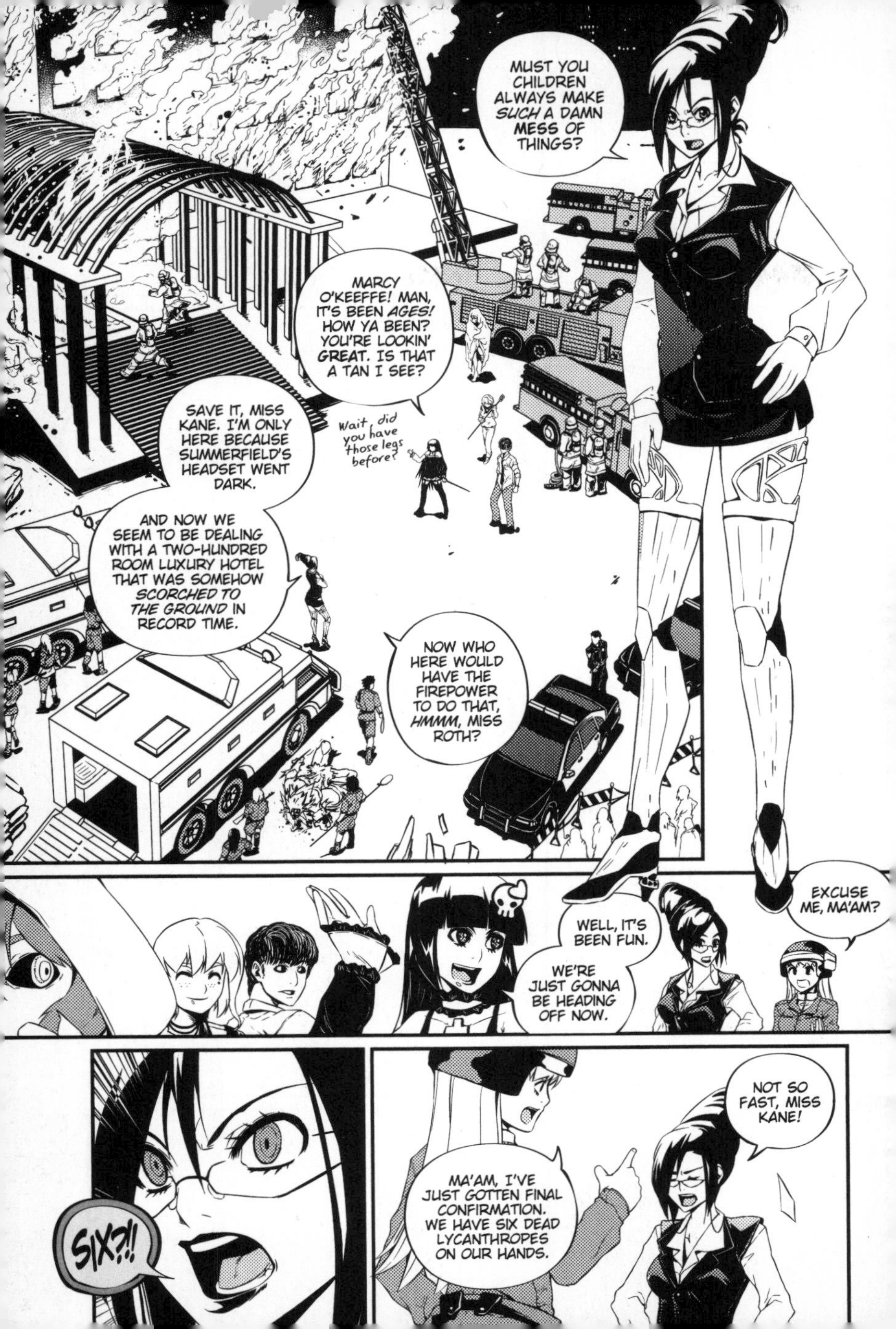
MUST YOU CHILDREN ALWAYS MAKE *SUCH* A DAMN MESS OF THINGS?
MARCY O'KEEFFE! MAN, IT'S BEEN *AGES!* HOW YA BEEN? YOU'RE LOOKIN' GREAT. IS THAT A TAN I SEE?
Wait, did you have those legs before?
SAVE IT, MISS KANE. I'M ONLY HERE BECAUSE SUMMERFIELD'S HEADSET WENT DARK.
AND NOW WE SEEM TO BE DEALING WITH A TWO-HUNDRED ROOM LUXURY HOTEL THAT WAS SOMEHOW *SCORCHED TO THE GROUND* IN RECORD TIME.
NOW WHO HERE WOULD HAVE THE FIREPOWER TO DO THAT, *HMMM,* MISS ROTH?
EXCUSE ME, MA'AM?
WELL, IT'S BEEN FUN.
WE'RE JUST GONNA BE HEADING OFF NOW.
NOT SO FAST, MISS KANE!
MA'AM, I'VE JUST GOTTEN FINAL CONFIRMATION. WE HAVE SIX DEAD LYCANTHROPES ON OUR HANDS.
SIX?!!

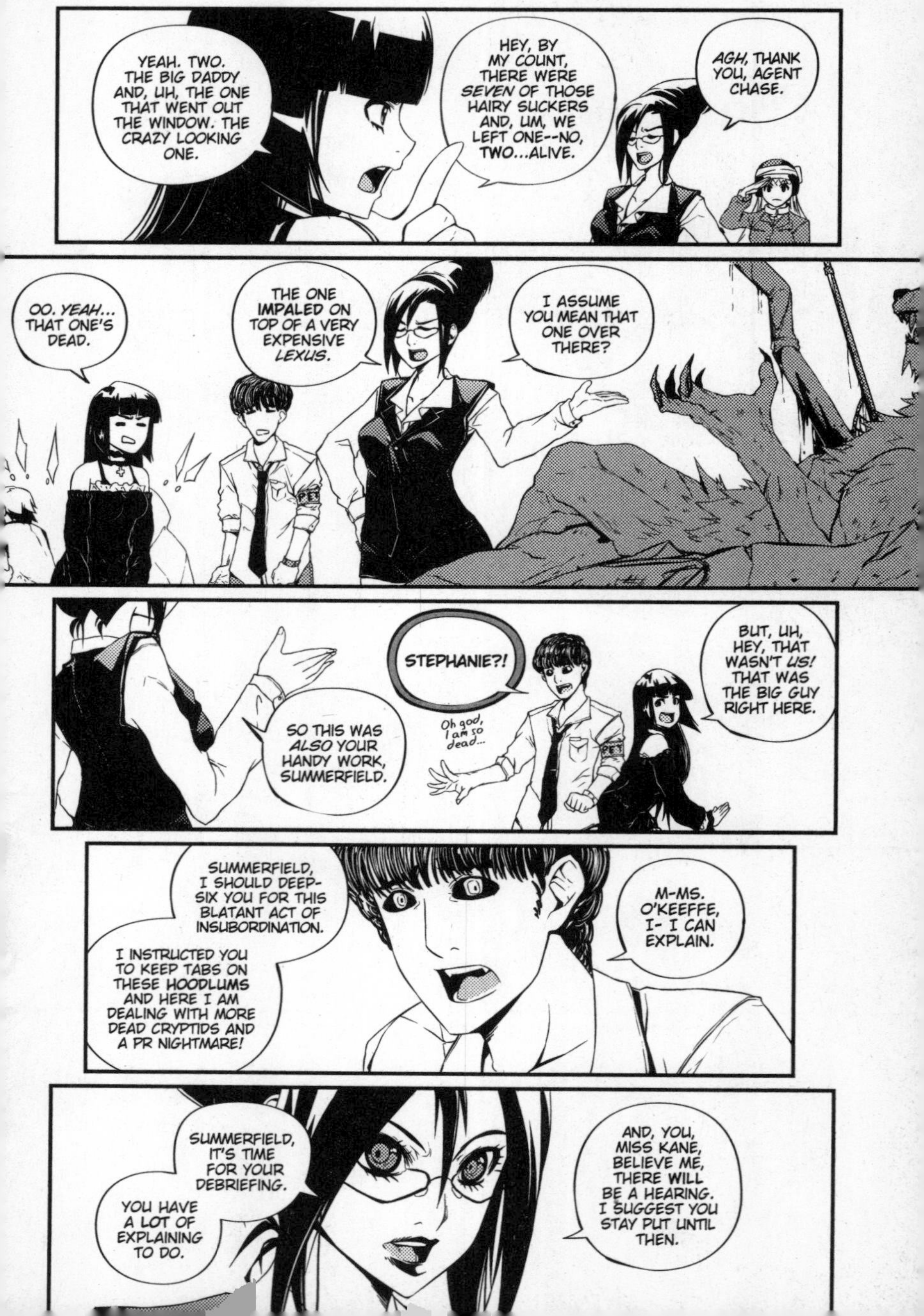
AGH, THANK YOU, AGENT CHASE.
HEY, BY MY COUNT, THERE WERE SEVEN OF THOSE HAIRY SUCKERS AND, UM, WE LEFT ONE--NO, TWO...ALIVE.
YEAH. TWO. THE BIG DADDY AND, UH, THE ONE THAT WENT OUT THE WINDOW. THE CRAZY LOOKING ONE.
I ASSUME YOU MEAN THAT ONE OVER THERE?
THE ONE IMPALED ON TOP OF A VERY EXPENSIVE LEXUS.
OO. YEAH... THAT ONE'S DEAD.
BUT, UH, HEY, THAT WASN'T US! THAT WAS THE BIG GUY RIGHT HERE.
STEPHANIE?!
Oh god, I am so dead...
SO THIS WAS ALSO YOUR HANDY WORK, SUMMERFIELD.
M-MS. O'KEEFFE, I- I CAN EXPLAIN.
SUMMERFIELD, I SHOULD DEEP-SIX YOU FOR THIS BLATANT ACT OF INSUBORDINATION.
I INSTRUCTED YOU TO KEEP TABS ON THESE HOODLUMS AND HERE I AM DEALING WITH MORE DEAD CRYPTIDS AND A PR NIGHTMARE!
AND, YOU, MISS KANE, BELIEVE ME, THERE WILL BE A HEARING. I SUGGEST YOU STAY PUT UNTIL THEN.
SUMMERFIELD, IT'S TIME FOR YOUR DEBRIEFING.
YOU HAVE A LOT OF EXPLAINING TO DO.

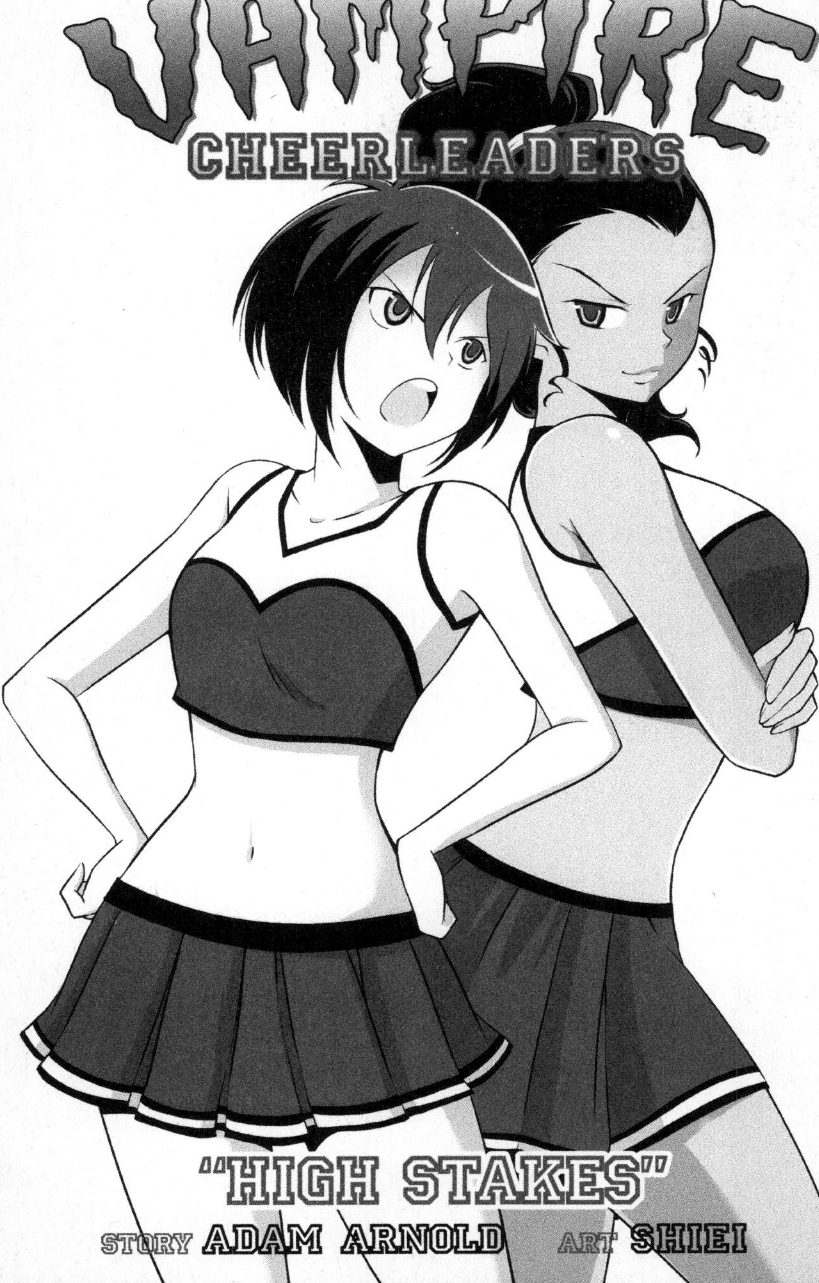
VAMPIRE
CHEERLEADERS
"HIGH STAKES"
STORY ADAM ARNOLD ART SHIEI

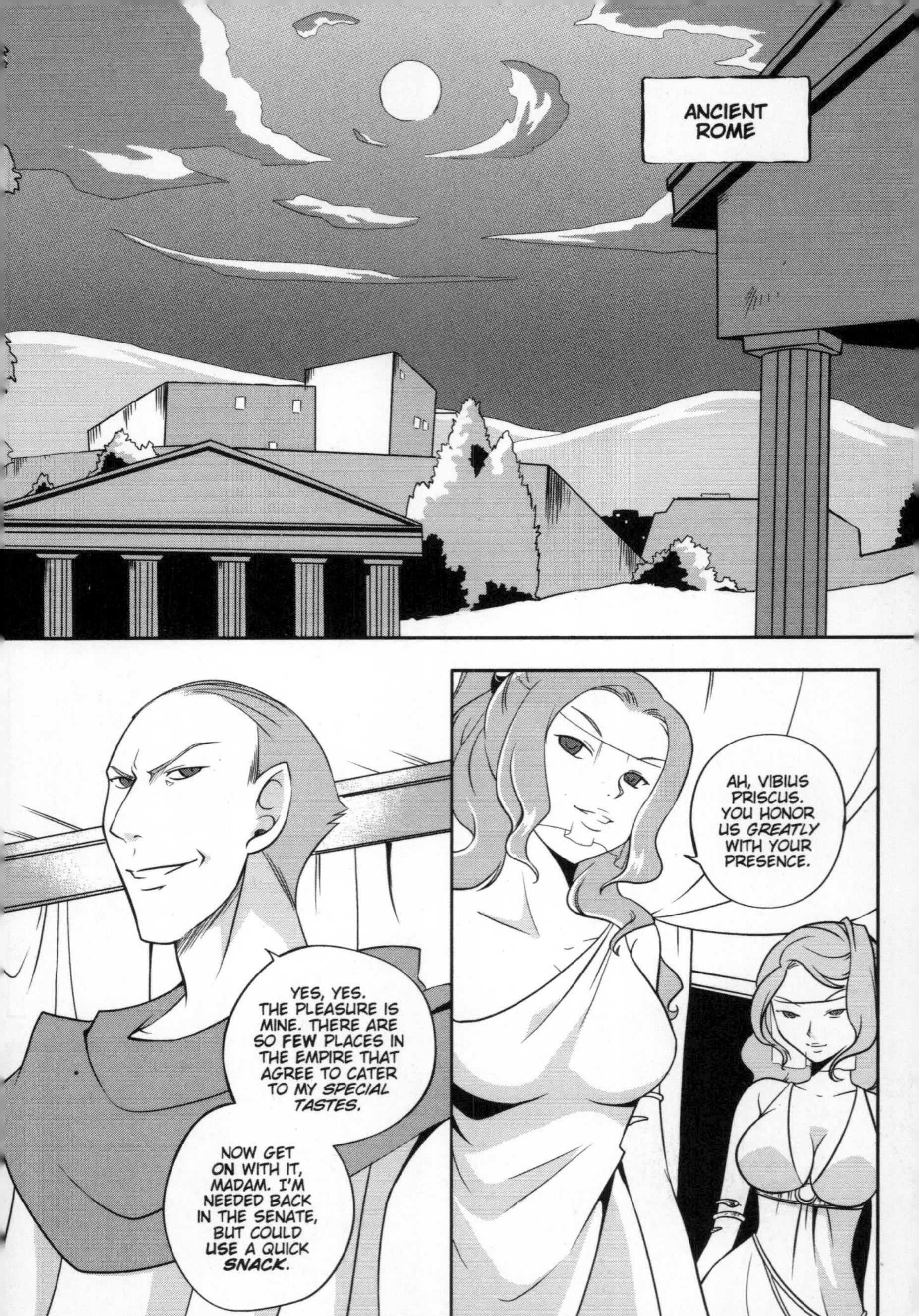
ANCIENT ROME
AH, VIBIUS PRISCUS. YOU HONOR US GREATLY WITH YOUR PRESENCE.
YES, YES. THE PLEASURE IS MINE. THERE ARE SO FEW PLACES IN THE EMPIRE THAT AGREE TO CATER TO MY SPECIAL TASTES.
NOW GET ON WITH IT, MADAM. I'M NEEDED BACK IN THE SENATE, BUT COULD USE A QUICK SNACK.

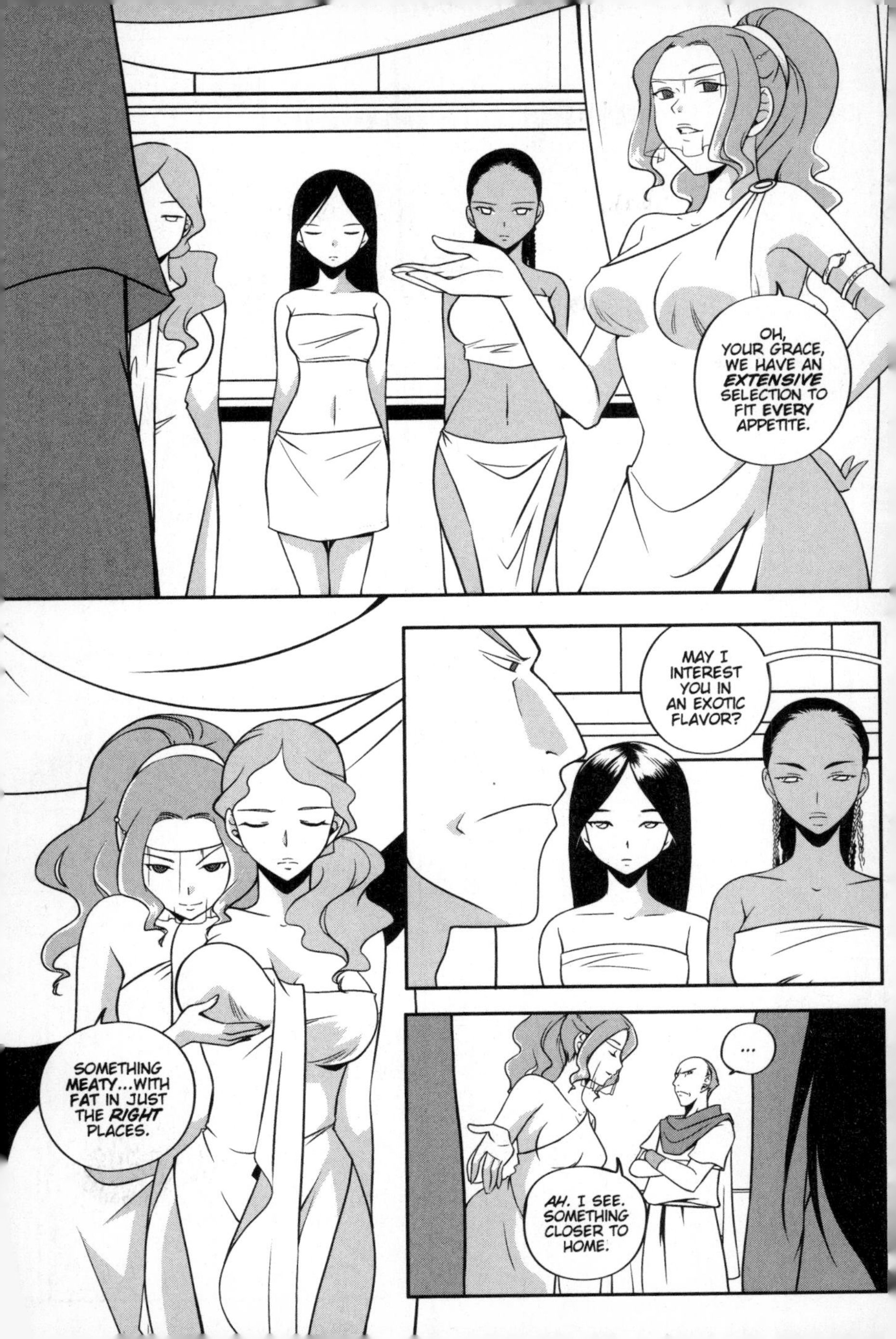
OH, YOUR GRACE, WE HAVE AN ***EXTENSIVE*** SELECTION TO FIT EVERY APPETITE.
MAY I INTEREST YOU IN AN EXOTIC FLAVOR?
...
AH. I SEE. SOMETHING CLOSER TO HOME.
SOMETHING ***MEATY***...WITH FAT IN JUST THE ***RIGHT*** PLACES.

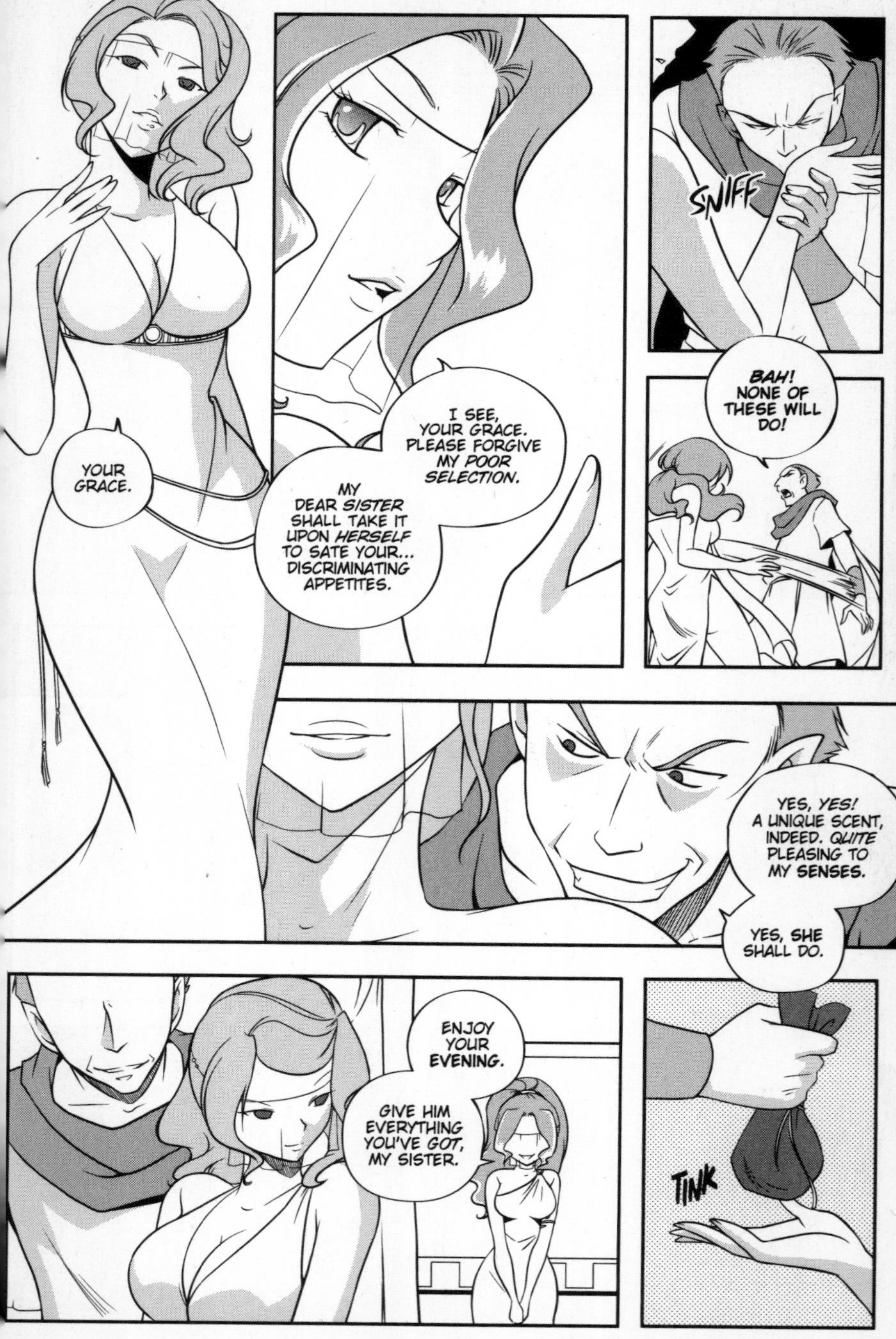
SNIFF
BAH! NONE OF THESE WILL DO!
I SEE, YOUR GRACE. PLEASE FORGIVE MY POOR SELECTION.
MY DEAR SISTER SHALL TAKE IT UPON HERSELF TO SATE YOUR... DISCRIMINATING APPETITES.
YOUR GRACE.
YES, YES! A UNIQUE SCENT, INDEED. QUITE PLEASING TO MY SENSES.
YES, SHE SHALL DO.
TINK
ENJOY YOUR EVENING.
GIVE HIM EVERYTHING YOU'VE GOT, MY SISTER.

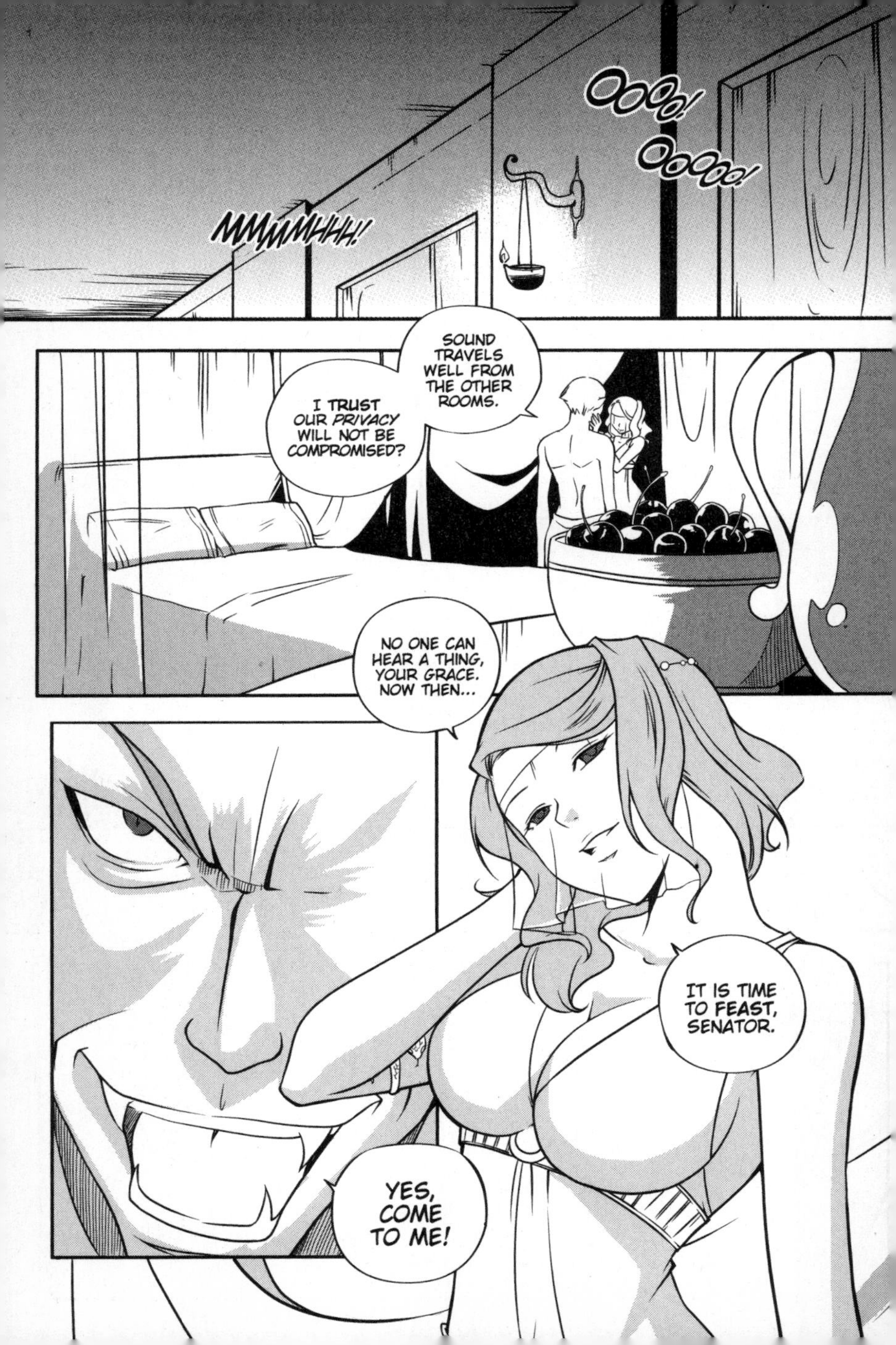

OOOo!
OOOoo!
MMMMHHH!
SOUND TRAVELS WELL FROM THE OTHER ROOMS.
I TRUST OUR *PRIVACY* WILL NOT BE COMPROMISED?
NO ONE CAN HEAR A THING, YOUR GRACE. NOW THEN...
IT IS TIME TO FEAST, SENATOR.
YES, COME TO ME!

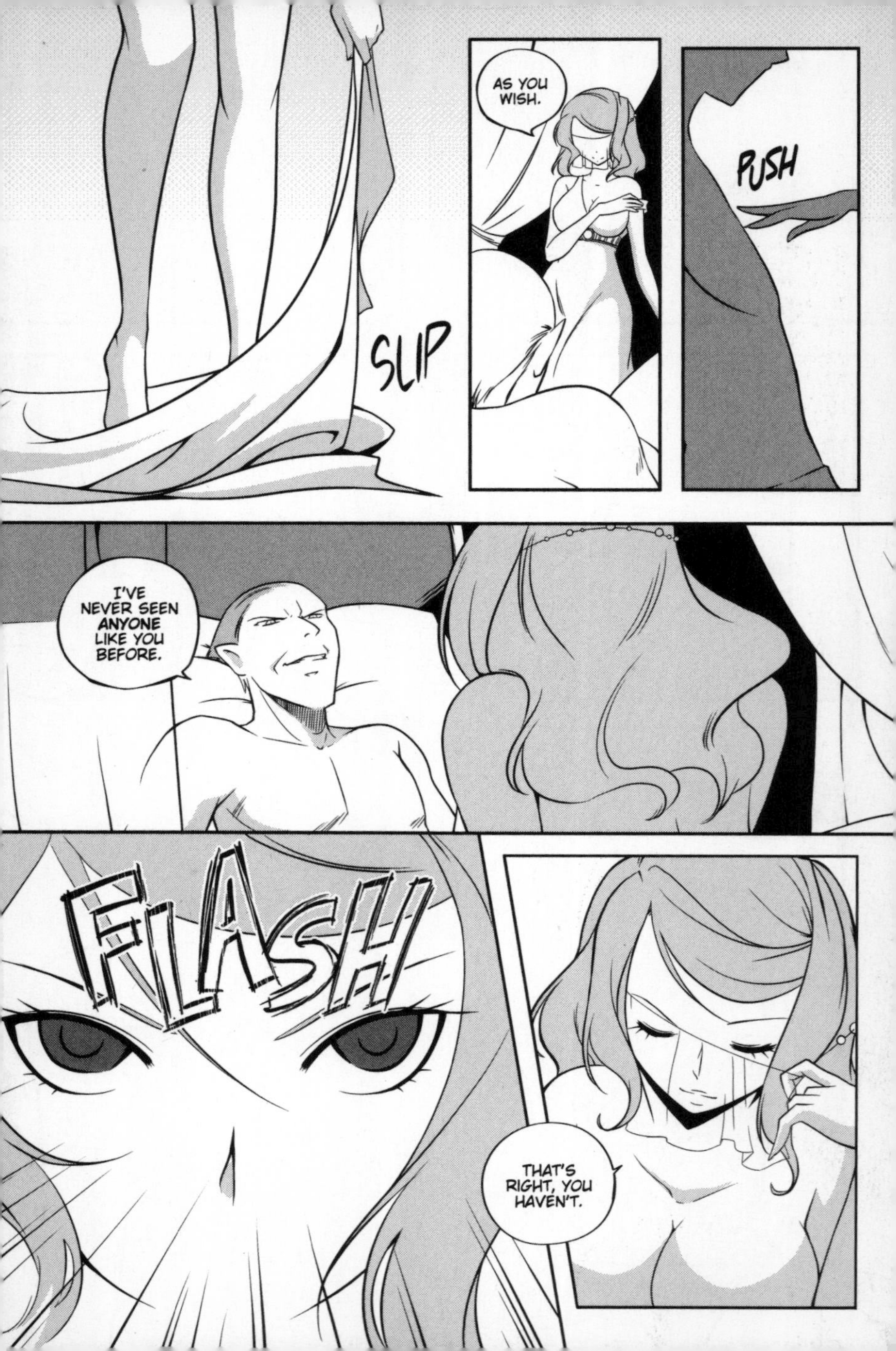
PUSH
AS YOU WISH.
SLIP
I'VE NEVER SEEN ANYONE LIKE YOU BEFORE.
THAT'S RIGHT, YOU HAVEN'T.
FLASH

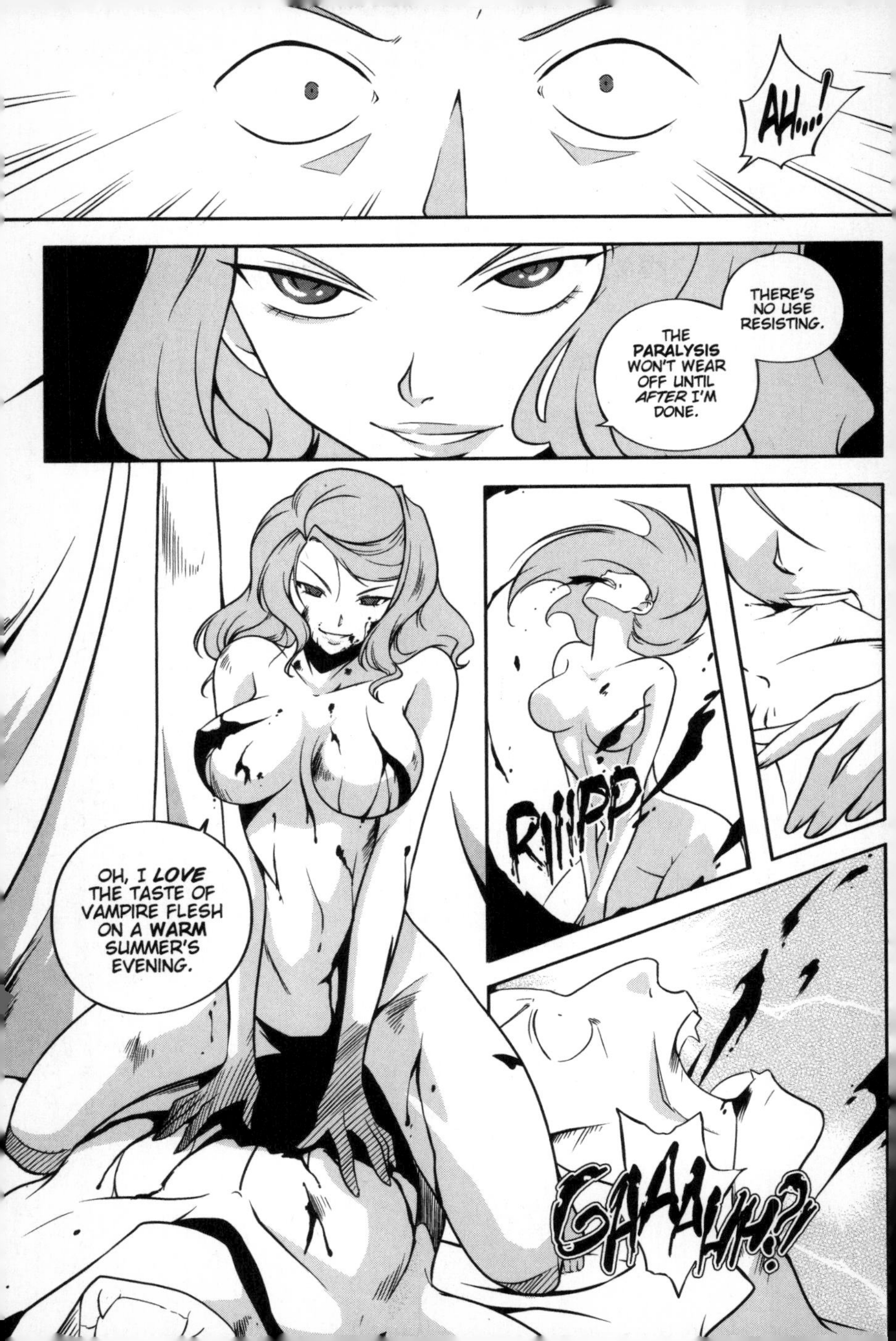
AH...!
THERE'S NO USE RESISTING.
THE PARALYSIS WON'T WEAR OFF UNTIL AFTER I'M DONE.
RIIIPP
GAAUH?!
OH, I LOVE THE TASTE OF VAMPIRE FLESH ON A WARM SUMMER'S EVENING.

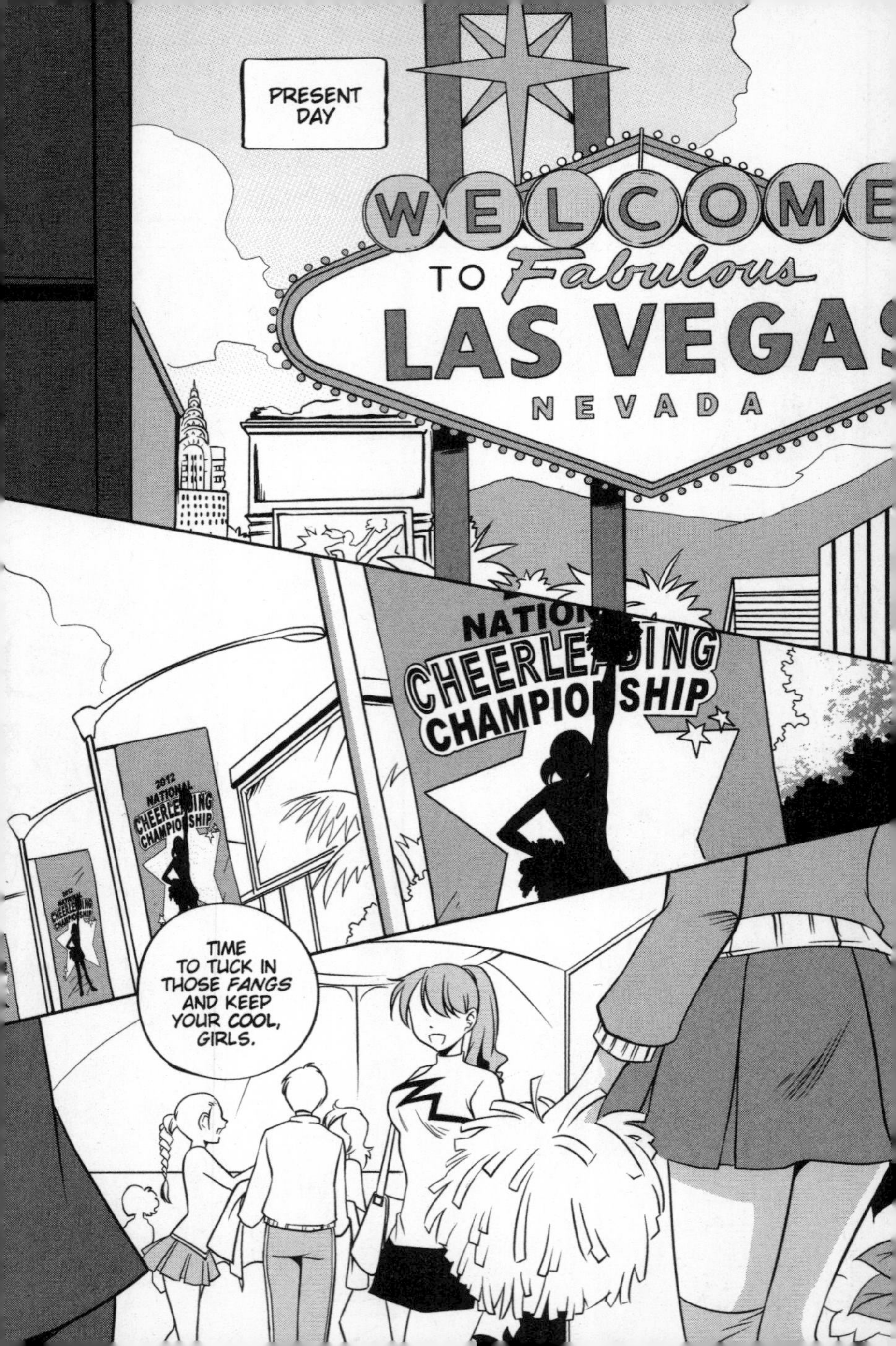
PRESENT DAY
WELCOME TO Fabulous LAS VEGAS NEVADA
NATIONAL CHEERLEADING CHAMPIONSHIP
2012 NATIONAL CHEERLEADING CHAMPIONSHIP
TIME TO TUCK IN THOSE *FANGS* AND KEEP YOUR COOL, GIRLS.

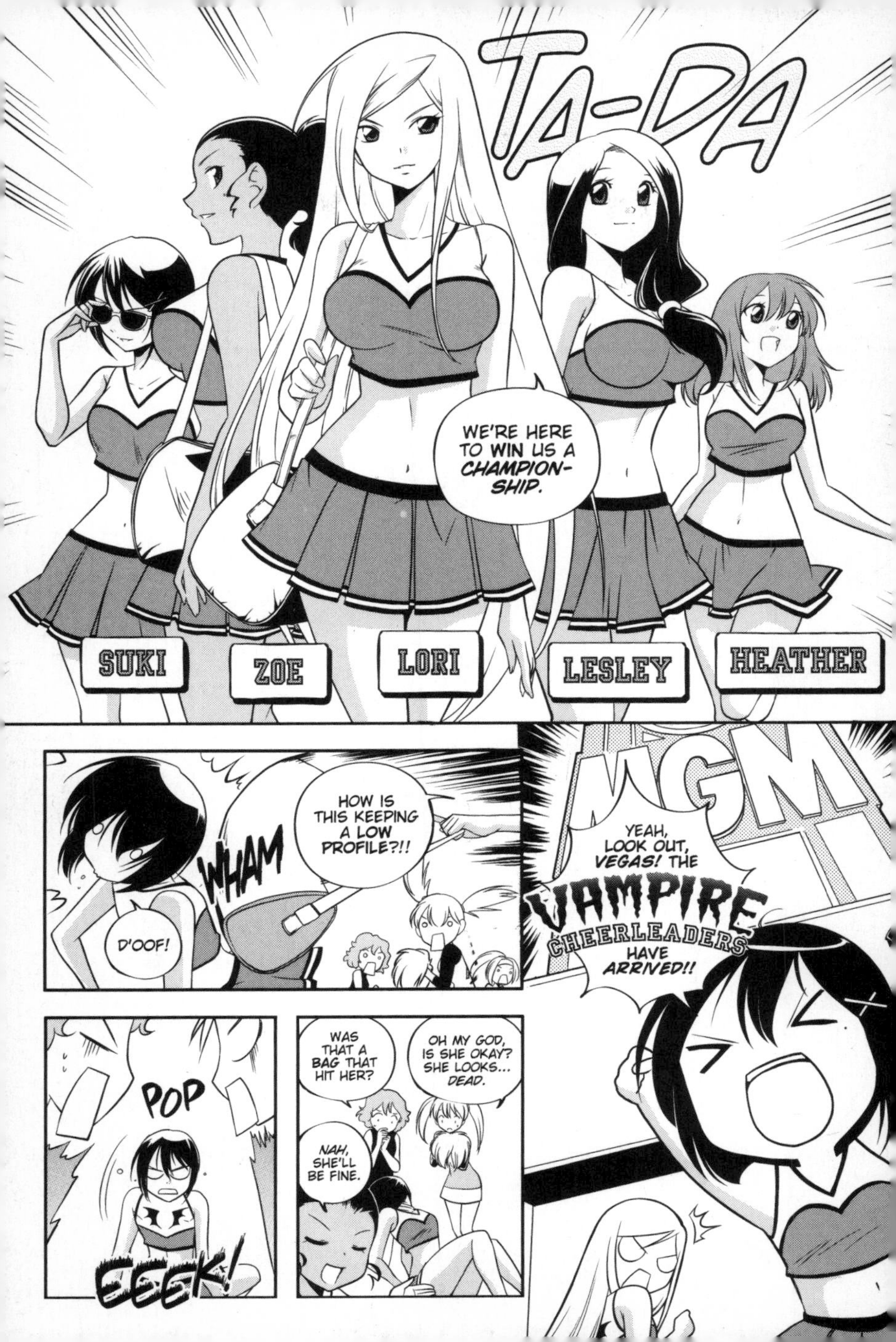
TA-DA
WE'RE HERE TO WIN US A CHAMPION-SHIP.
HEATHER
LESLEY
LORI
ZOE
SUKI
MGM
YEAH, LOOK OUT, VEGAS! THE VAMPIRE CHEERLEADERS HAVE ARRIVED!!
HOW IS THIS KEEPING A LOW PROFILE?!!
WHAM
D'OOF!
OH MY GOD, IS SHE OKAY? SHE LOOKS... DEAD.
WAS THAT A BAG THAT HIT HER?
NAH, SHE'LL BE FINE.
POP
EEEK!

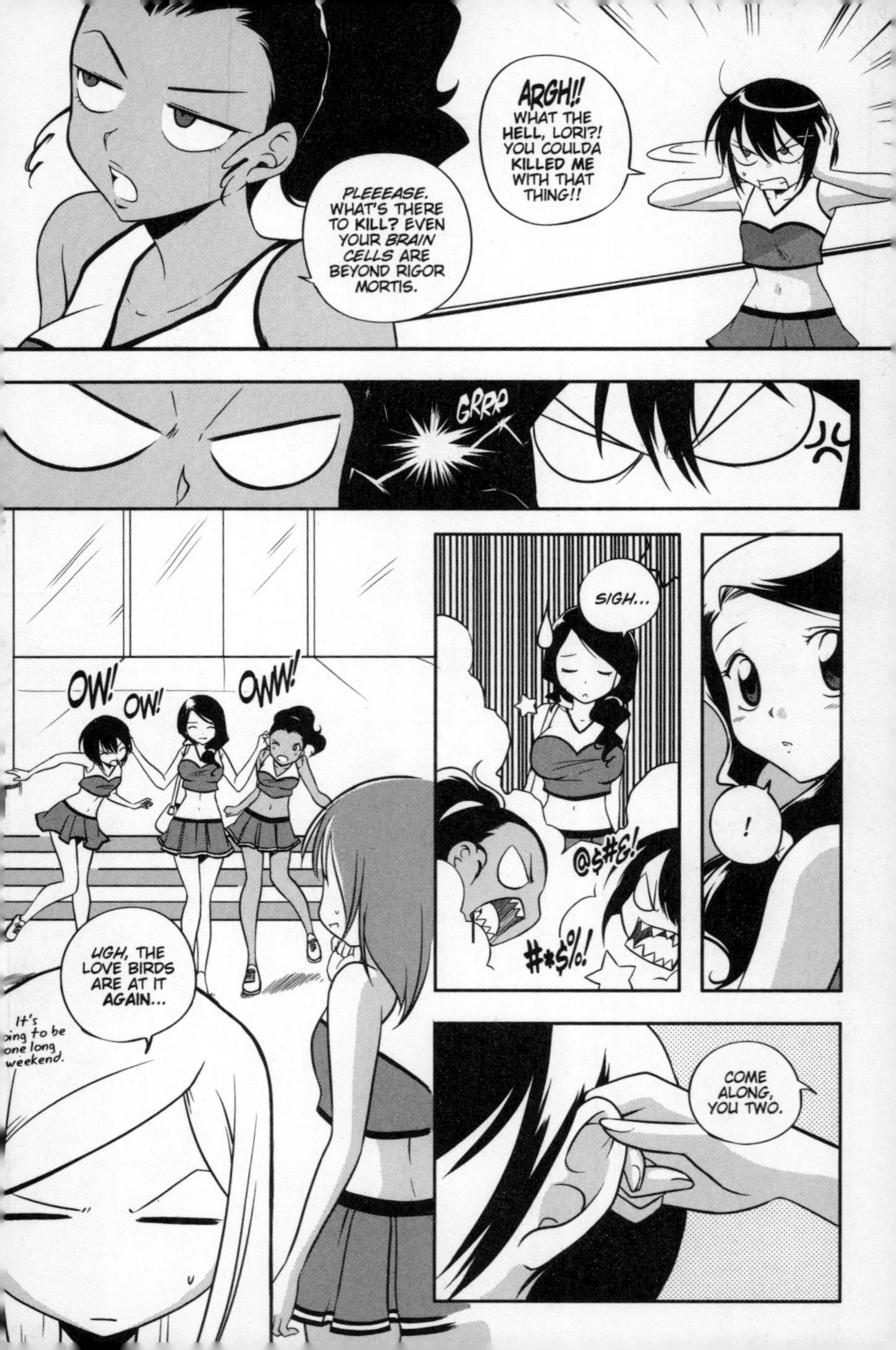
ARGH!! WHAT THE HELL, LORI?! YOU COULDA KILLED ME WITH THAT THING!!
PLEEEASE. WHAT'S THERE TO KILL? EVEN YOUR BRAIN CELLS ARE BEYOND RIGOR MORTIS.
GRRR
!
SIGH...
@$#&!
#*$%!
COME ALONG, YOU TWO.
OWW!
OW!
OW!
UGH, THE LOVE BIRDS ARE AT IT AGAIN...
It's oing to be one long weekend.

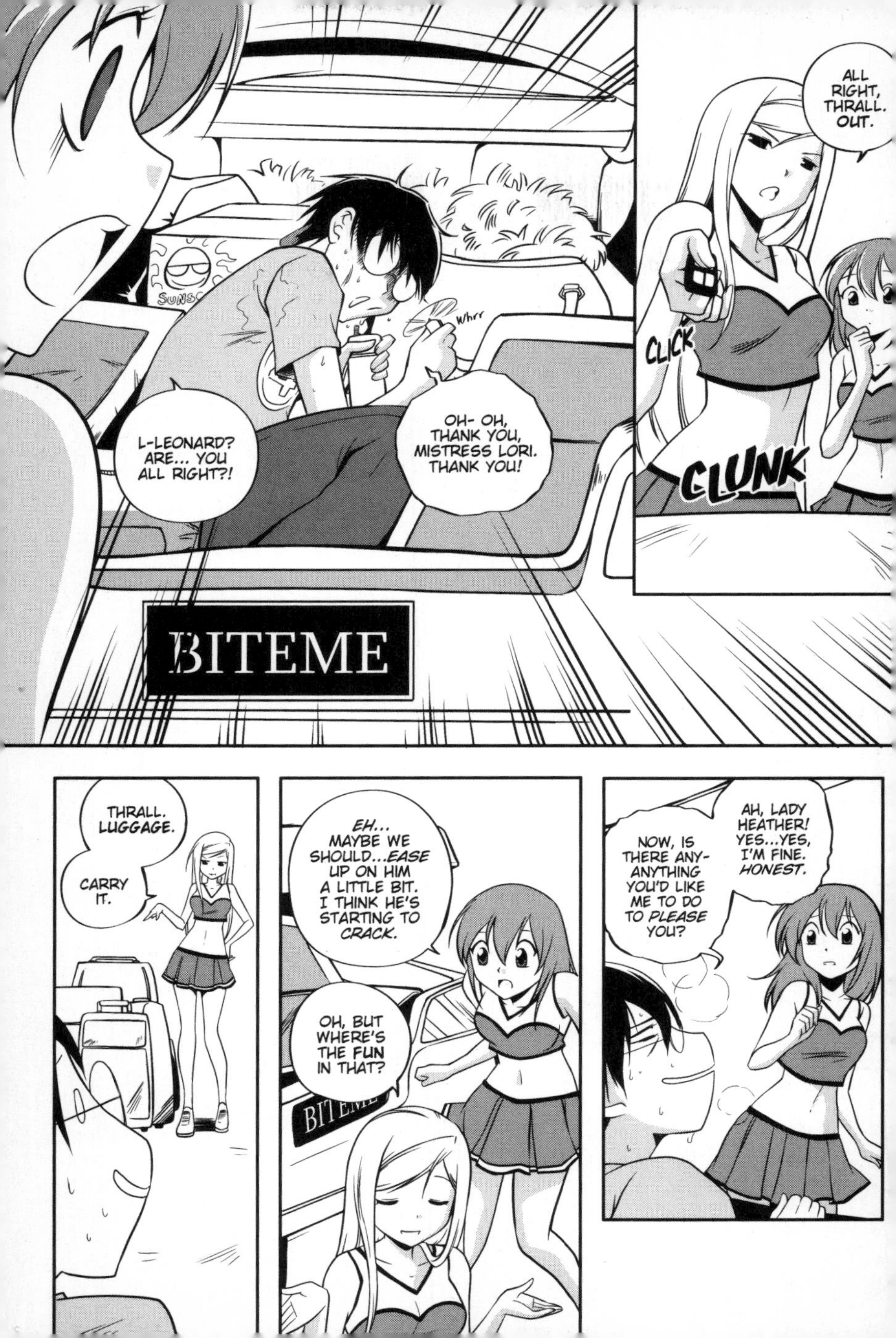
ALL RIGHT, THRALL. OUT.
CLICK
CLUNK
Whrr
L-LEONARD? ARE... YOU ALL RIGHT?!
OH- OH, THANK YOU, MISTRESS LORI. THANK YOU!
BITEME
AH, LADY HEATHER! YES...YES, I'M FINE. *HONEST*.
NOW, IS THERE ANY- ANYTHING YOU'D LIKE ME TO DO TO *PLEASE* YOU?
EH... MAYBE WE SHOULD...*EASE* UP ON HIM A LITTLE BIT. I THINK HE'S STARTING TO *CRACK*.
OH, BUT WHERE'S THE FUN IN THAT?
BITEME
THRALL. LUGGAGE.
CARRY IT.

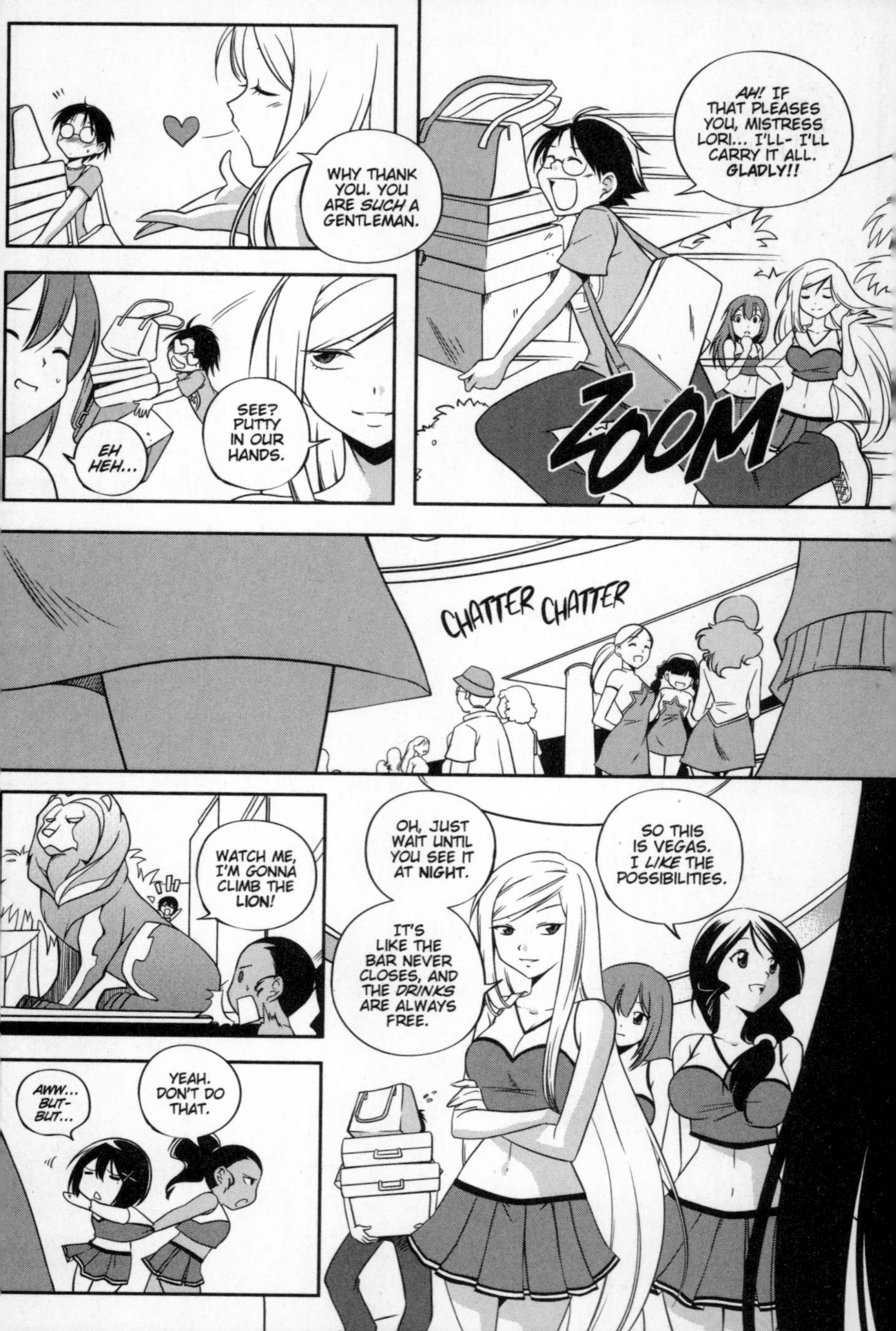
AH! IF THAT PLEASES YOU, MISTRESS LORI... I'LL- I'LL CARRY IT ALL. GLADLY!!
ZOOM
WHY THANK YOU. YOU ARE SUCH A GENTLEMAN.
SEE? PUTTY IN OUR HANDS.
EH HEH...
CHATTER CHATTER
SO THIS IS VEGAS. I LIKE THE POSSIBILITIES.
OH, JUST WAIT UNTIL YOU SEE IT AT NIGHT.
IT'S LIKE THE BAR NEVER CLOSES, AND THE DRINKS ARE ALWAYS FREE.
WATCH ME, I'M GONNA CLIMB THE LION!
YEAH. DON'T DO THAT.
AWW... BUT-BUT...

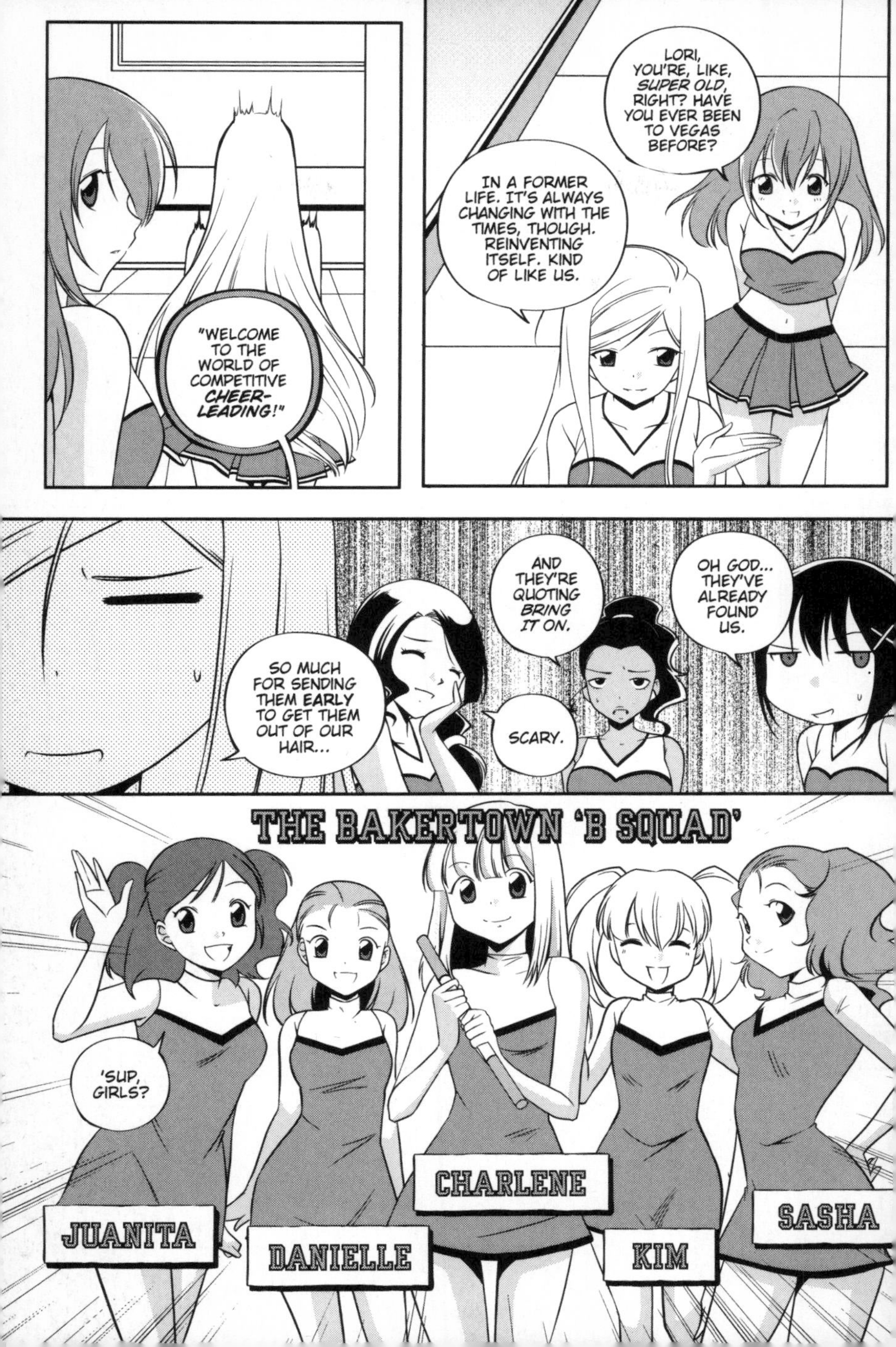
LORI, YOU'RE, LIKE, *SUPER OLD*, RIGHT? HAVE YOU EVER BEEN TO VEGAS BEFORE?
IN A FORMER LIFE. IT'S ALWAYS CHANGING WITH THE TIMES, THOUGH. REINVENTING ITSELF. KIND OF LIKE US.
"WELCOME TO THE WORLD OF COMPETITIVE ***CHEER-LEADING!***"
OH GOD... THEY'VE ALREADY FOUND US.
AND THEY'RE QUOTING *BRING IT ON.*
SCARY.
SO MUCH FOR SENDING THEM **EARLY** TO GET THEM OUT OF OUR HAIR...
THE BAKERTOWN 'B SQUAD'
'SUP, GIRLS?
CHARLENE
SASHA
JUANITA
KIM
DANIELLE

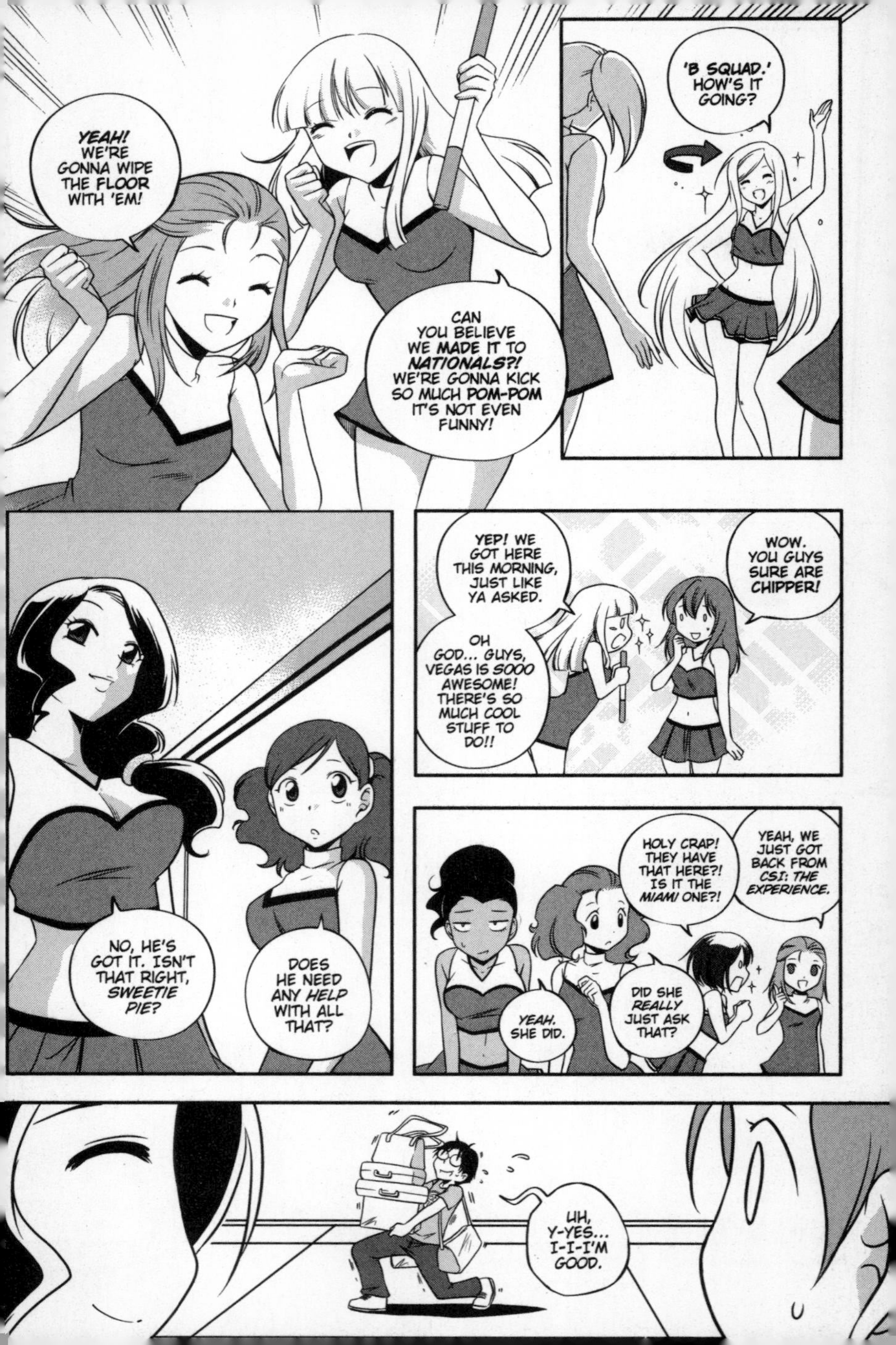
'B SQUAD.' HOW'S IT GOING?
CAN YOU BELIEVE WE MADE IT TO NATIONALS?! WE'RE GONNA KICK SO MUCH POM-POM IT'S NOT EVEN FUNNY!
YEAH! WE'RE GONNA WIPE THE FLOOR WITH 'EM!
WOW. YOU GUYS SURE ARE CHIPPER!
YEP! WE GOT HERE THIS MORNING, JUST LIKE YA ASKED.
OH GOD... GUYS, VEGAS IS SOOO AWESOME! THERE'S SO MUCH COOL STUFF TO DO!!
YEAH, WE JUST GOT BACK FROM CSI: THE EXPERIENCE.
HOLY CRAP! THEY HAVE THAT HERE?! IS IT THE MIAMI ONE?!
DID SHE REALLY JUST ASK THAT?
YEAH. SHE DID.
DOES HE NEED ANY HELP WITH ALL THAT?
NO, HE'S GOT IT. ISN'T THAT RIGHT, SWEETIE PIE?
UH, Y-YES... I-I-I'M GOOD.

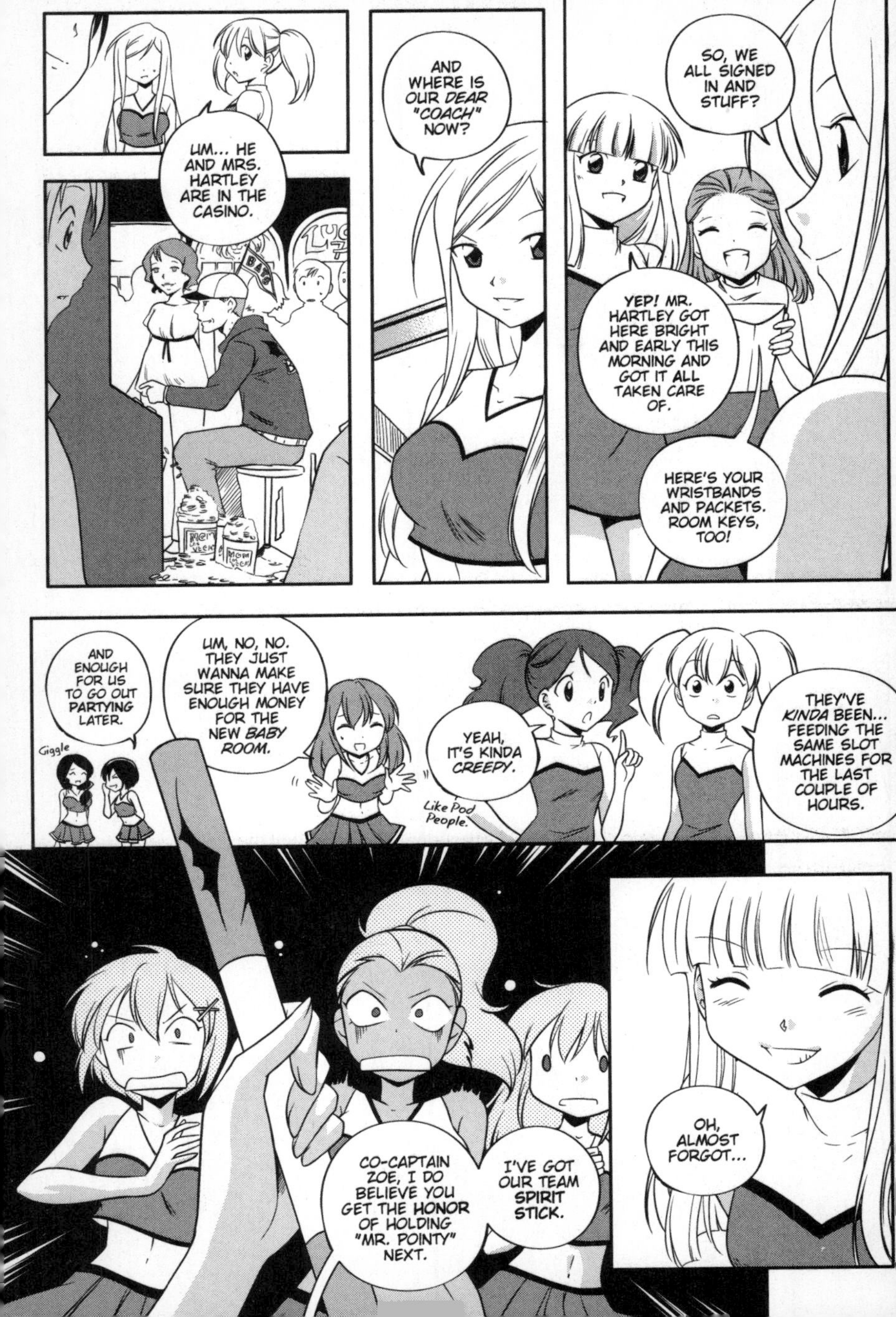
SO, WE ALL SIGNED IN AND STUFF?
YEP! MR. HARTLEY GOT HERE BRIGHT AND EARLY THIS MORNING AND GOT IT ALL TAKEN CARE OF.
HERE'S YOUR WRISTBANDS AND PACKETS. ROOM KEYS, TOO!
AND WHERE IS OUR *DEAR* "*COACH*" NOW?
UM... HE AND MRS. HARTLEY ARE IN THE CASINO.
THEY'VE *KINDA* BEEN... FEEDING THE SAME SLOT MACHINES FOR THE LAST COUPLE OF HOURS.
YEAH, IT'S KINDA *CREEPY*.
Like Pod People.
UM, NO, NO. THEY JUST WANNA MAKE SURE THEY HAVE ENOUGH MONEY FOR THE NEW *BABY ROOM*.
AND ENOUGH FOR US TO GO OUT PARTYING LATER.
Giggle
OH, ALMOST FORGOT...
I'VE GOT OUR TEAM **SPIRIT STICK**.
CO-CAPTAIN ZOE, I DO BELIEVE YOU GET THE **HONOR** OF HOLDING "MR. POINTY" NEXT.

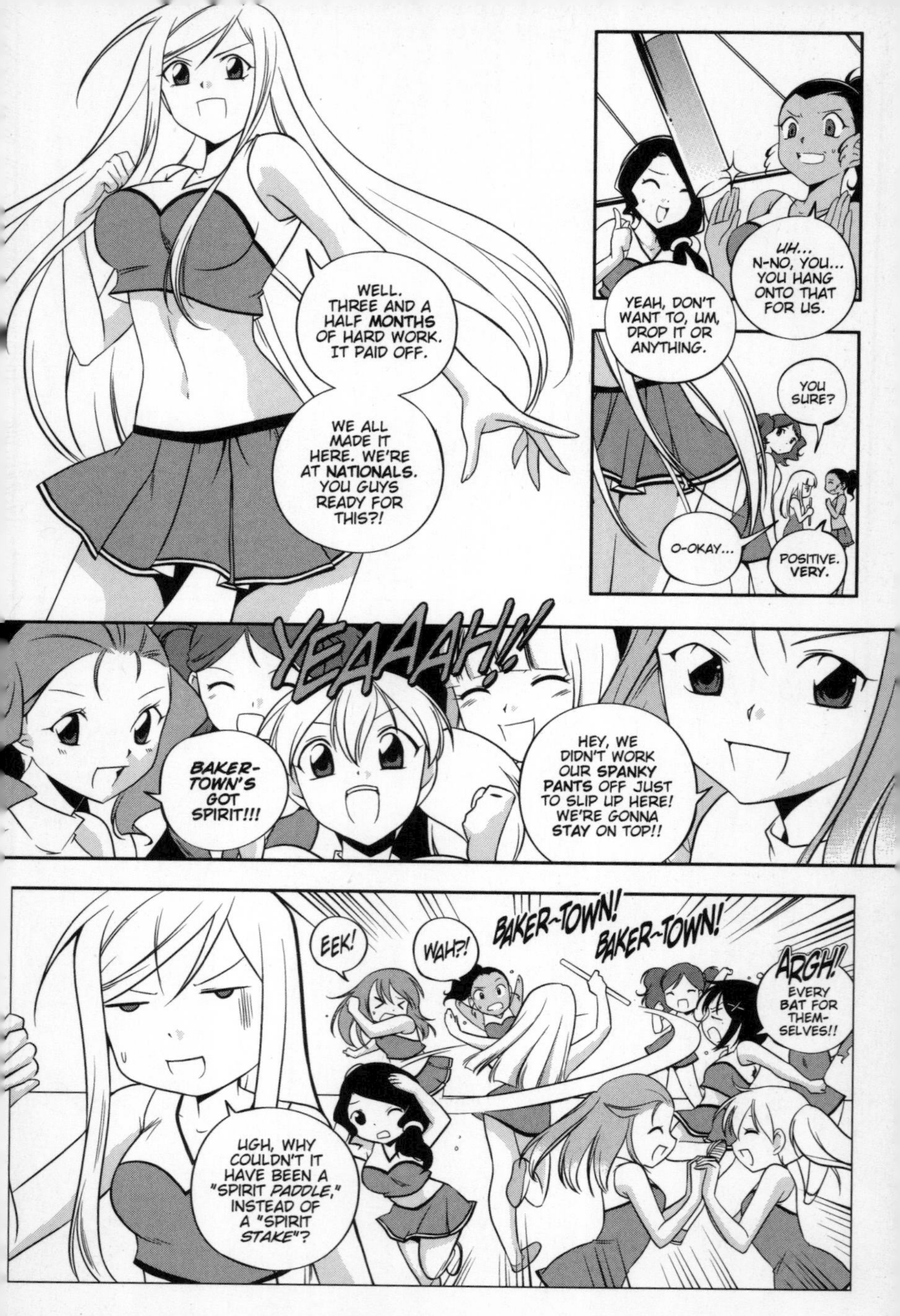
UH... N-NO, YOU... YOU HANG ONTO THAT FOR US.
YEAH, DON'T WANT TO, UM, DROP IT OR ANYTHING.
YOU SURE?
POSITIVE. VERY.
O-OKAY...
WELL. THREE AND A HALF MONTHS OF HARD WORK. IT PAID OFF.
WE ALL MADE IT HERE. WE'RE AT NATIONALS. YOU GUYS READY FOR THIS?!
YEAAAH!!
HEY, WE DIDN'T WORK OUR SPANKY PANTS OFF JUST TO SLIP UP HERE! WE'RE GONNA STAY ON TOP!!
BAKER-TOWN'S GOT SPIRIT!!!
ARGH! EVERY BAT FOR THEM-SELVES!!
BAKER~TOWN! BAKER~TOWN!
WAH?!
EEK!
UGH, WHY COULDN'T IT HAVE BEEN A "SPIRIT PADDLE," INSTEAD OF A "SPIRIT STAKE"?

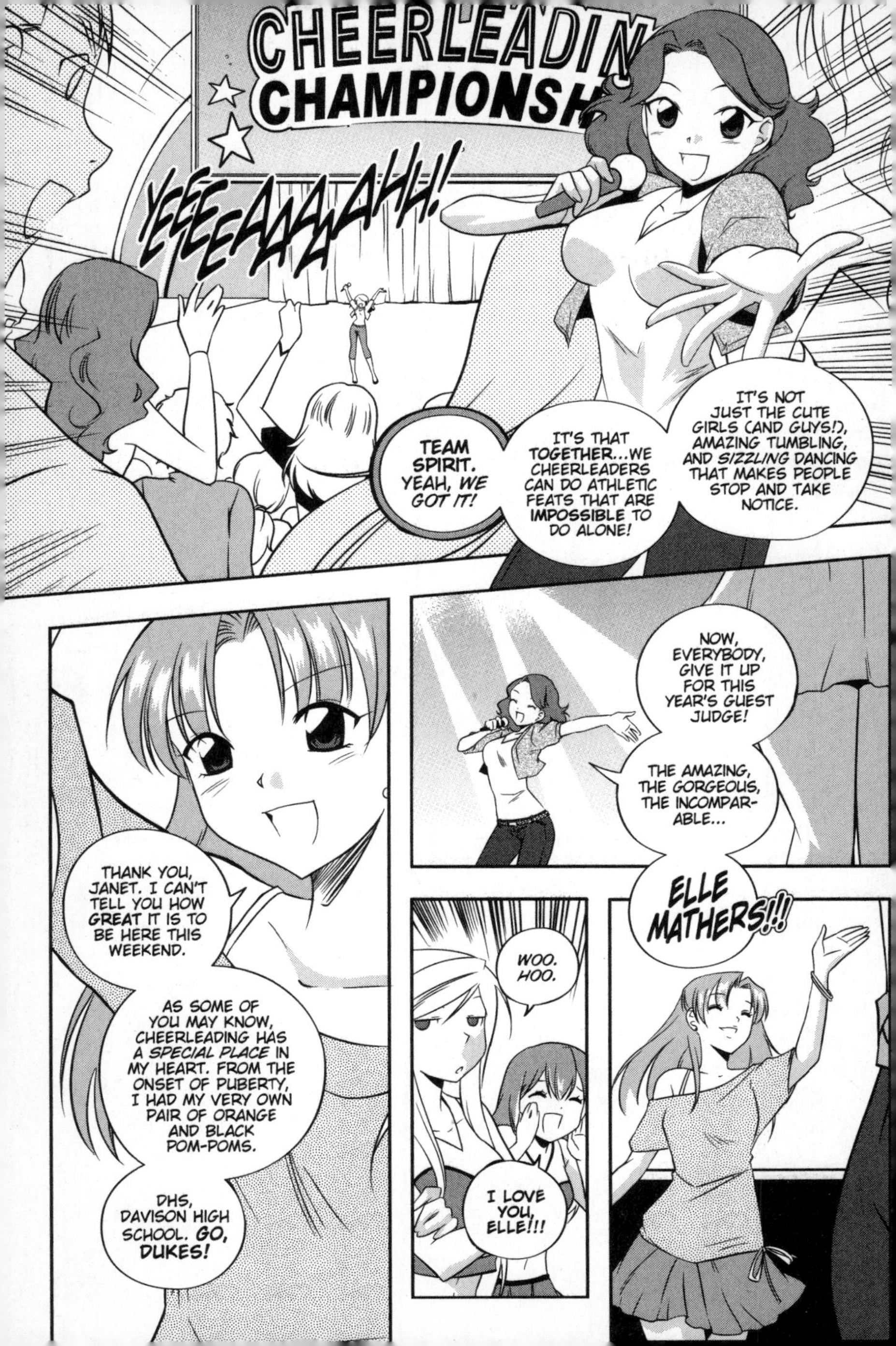
CHEERLEADIN
CHAMPIONSH
YEEEEAAAAAHH!
IT'S NOT JUST THE CUTE GIRLS (AND GUYS!), AMAZING TUMBLING, AND *SIZZLING* DANCING THAT MAKES PEOPLE STOP AND TAKE NOTICE.
IT'S THAT TOGETHER...WE CHEERLEADERS CAN DO ATHLETIC FEATS THAT ARE **IMPOSSIBLE** TO DO ALONE!
TEAM SPIRIT. YEAH, *WE GOT IT!*
NOW, EVERYBODY, GIVE IT UP FOR THIS YEAR'S GUEST JUDGE!
THE AMAZING, THE GORGEOUS, THE INCOMPAR-ABLE...
ELLE MATHERS!!!
WOO. HOO.
I LOVE YOU, ELLE!!!
THANK YOU, JANET. I CAN'T TELL YOU HOW **GREAT** IT IS TO BE HERE THIS WEEKEND.
AS SOME OF YOU MAY KNOW, CHEERLEADING HAS A *SPECIAL PLACE* IN MY HEART. FROM THE ONSET OF PUBERTY, I HAD MY VERY OWN PAIR OF ORANGE AND BLACK POM-POMS.
DHS, DAVISON HIGH SCHOOL. **GO, DUKES!**

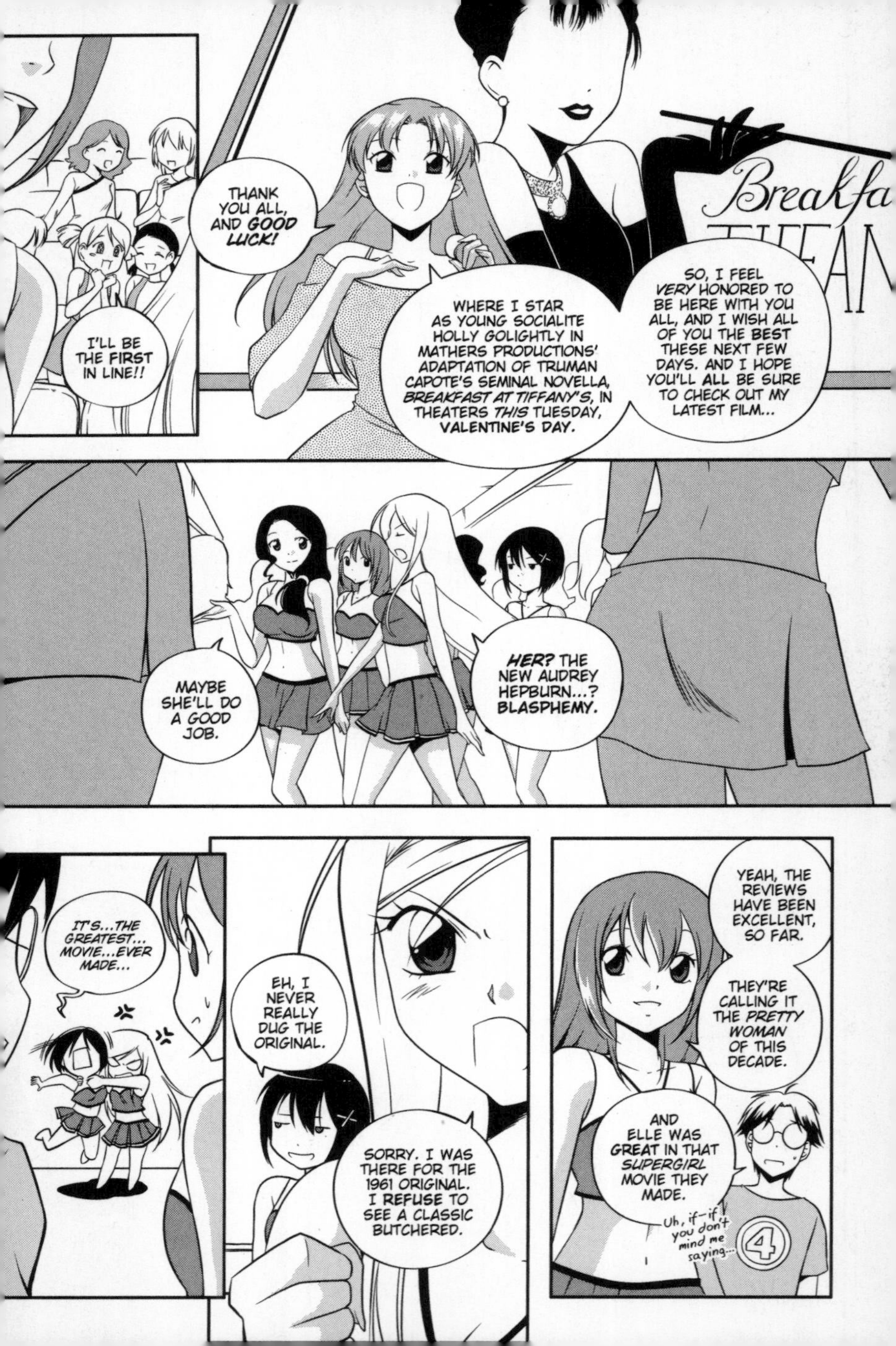
SO, I FEEL *VERY* HONORED TO BE HERE WITH YOU ALL, AND I WISH ALL OF YOU THE **BEST** THESE NEXT FEW DAYS. AND I HOPE YOU'LL **ALL** BE SURE TO CHECK OUT MY LATEST FILM...
WHERE I STAR AS YOUNG SOCIALITE HOLLY GOLIGHTLY IN MATHERS PRODUCTIONS' ADAPTATION OF TRUMAN CAPOTE'S SEMINAL NOVELLA, *BREAKFAST AT TIFFANY'S*, IN THEATERS *THIS* TUESDAY, **VALENTINE'S DAY.**
THANK YOU ALL, AND **GOOD LUCK!**
I'LL BE THE **FIRST** IN LINE!!
HER? THE NEW AUDREY HEPBURN...? **BLASPHEMY.**
MAYBE SHE'LL DO A GOOD JOB.
YEAH, THE REVIEWS HAVE BEEN EXCELLENT, SO FAR.
THEY'RE CALLING IT THE *PRETTY WOMAN* OF THIS DECADE.
Uh, if—if you don't mind me saying...
AND ELLE WAS **GREAT** IN THAT *SUPERGIRL* MOVIE THEY MADE.
EH, I NEVER REALLY DUG THE ORIGINAL.
SORRY. I WAS THERE FOR THE 1961 ORIGINAL. I **REFUSE** TO SEE A CLASSIC BUTCHERED.
IT'S...THE GREATEST... MOVIE...EVER MADE...

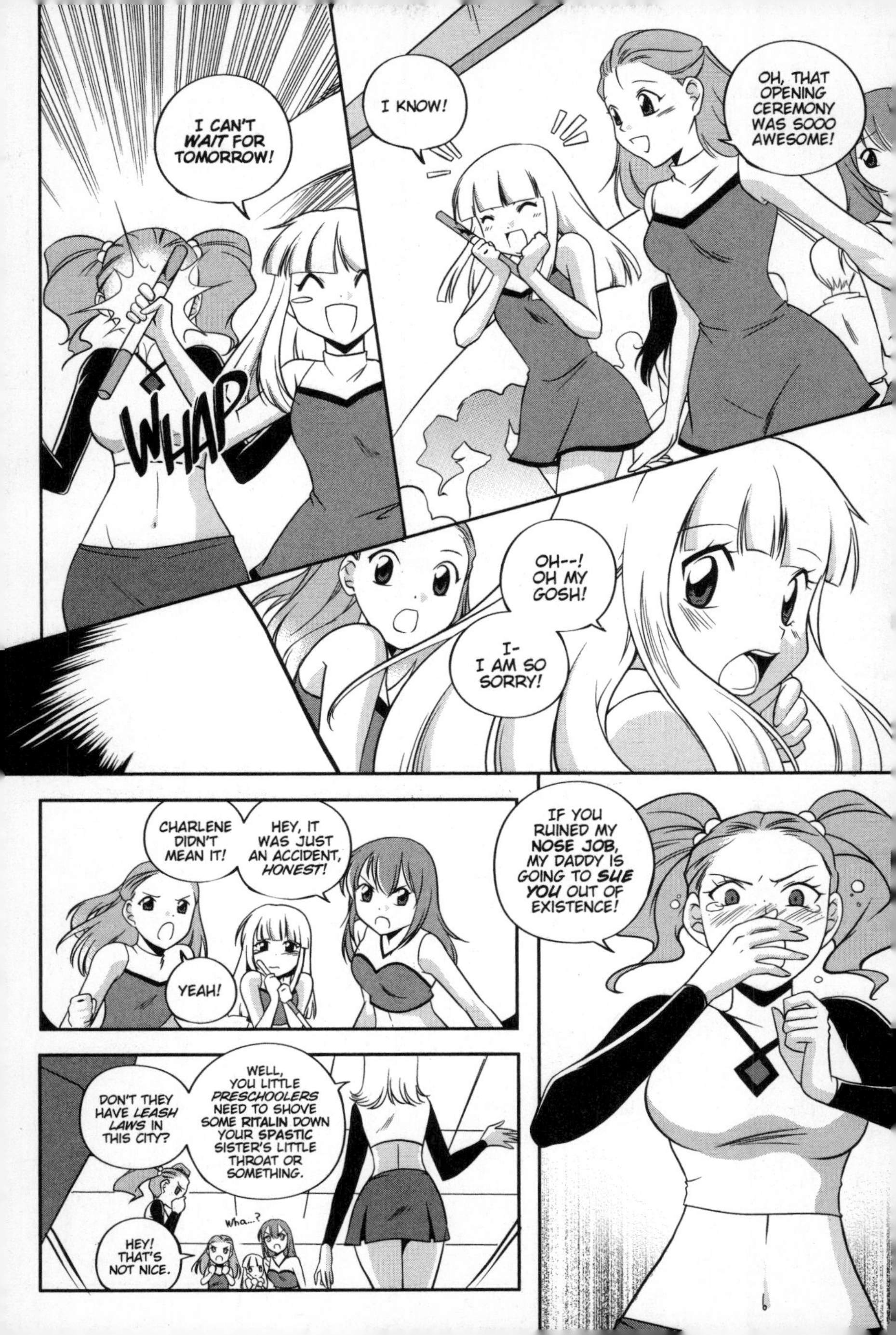
OH, THAT OPENING CEREMONY WAS SOOO AWESOME!
I KNOW!
I CAN'T *WAIT* FOR TOMORROW!
WHAP
OH--! OH MY GOSH!
I- I AM SO SORRY!
IF YOU RUINED MY **NOSE JOB**, MY DADDY IS GOING TO ***SUE YOU*** OUT OF EXISTENCE!
HEY, IT WAS JUST AN ACCIDENT, *HONEST*!
CHARLENE DIDN'T MEAN IT!
YEAH!
WELL, YOU LITTLE *PRESCHOOLERS* NEED TO SHOVE SOME **RITALIN** DOWN YOUR **SPASTIC** SISTER'S LITTLE THROAT OR SOMETHING.
DON'T THEY HAVE *LEASH LAWS* IN THIS CITY?
wha...?
HEY! THAT'S NOT NICE.

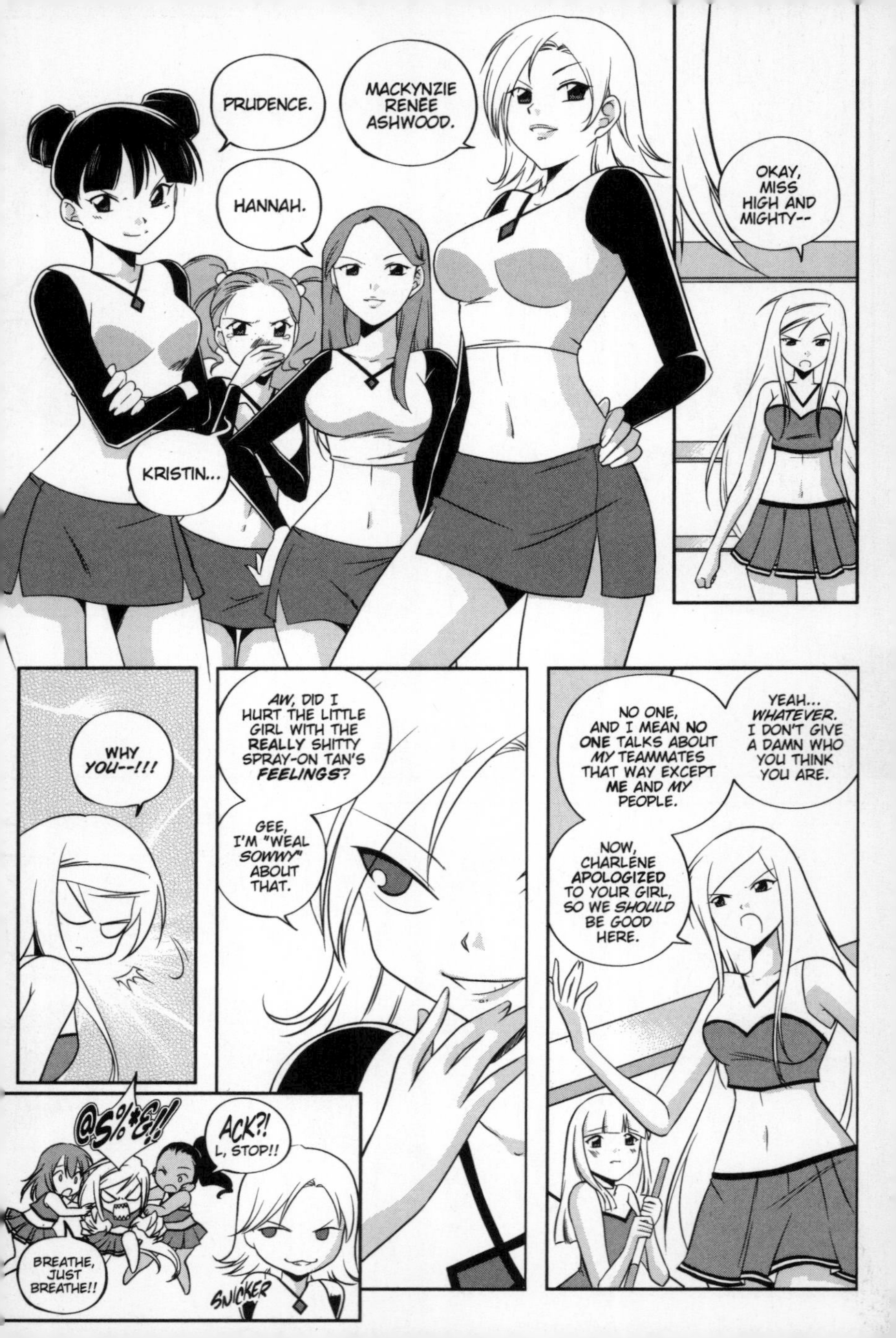
OKAY, MISS HIGH AND MIGHTY--
MACKYNZIE RENÉE ASHWOOD.
PRUDENCE.
HANNAH.
KRISTIN...
YEAH... WHATEVER. I DON'T GIVE A DAMN WHO YOU THINK YOU ARE.
NO ONE, AND I MEAN NO ONE TALKS ABOUT MY TEAMMATES THAT WAY EXCEPT ME AND MY PEOPLE.
NOW, CHARLENE APOLOGIZED TO YOUR GIRL, SO WE SHOULD BE GOOD HERE.
AW, DID I HURT THE LITTLE GIRL WITH THE REALLY SHITTY SPRAY-ON TAN'S FEELINGS?
GEE, I'M "WEAL SOWWY" ABOUT THAT.
WHY YOU--!!!
ACK?! L, STOP!!
@$%*&!!
BREATHE, JUST BREATHE!!
SNICKER

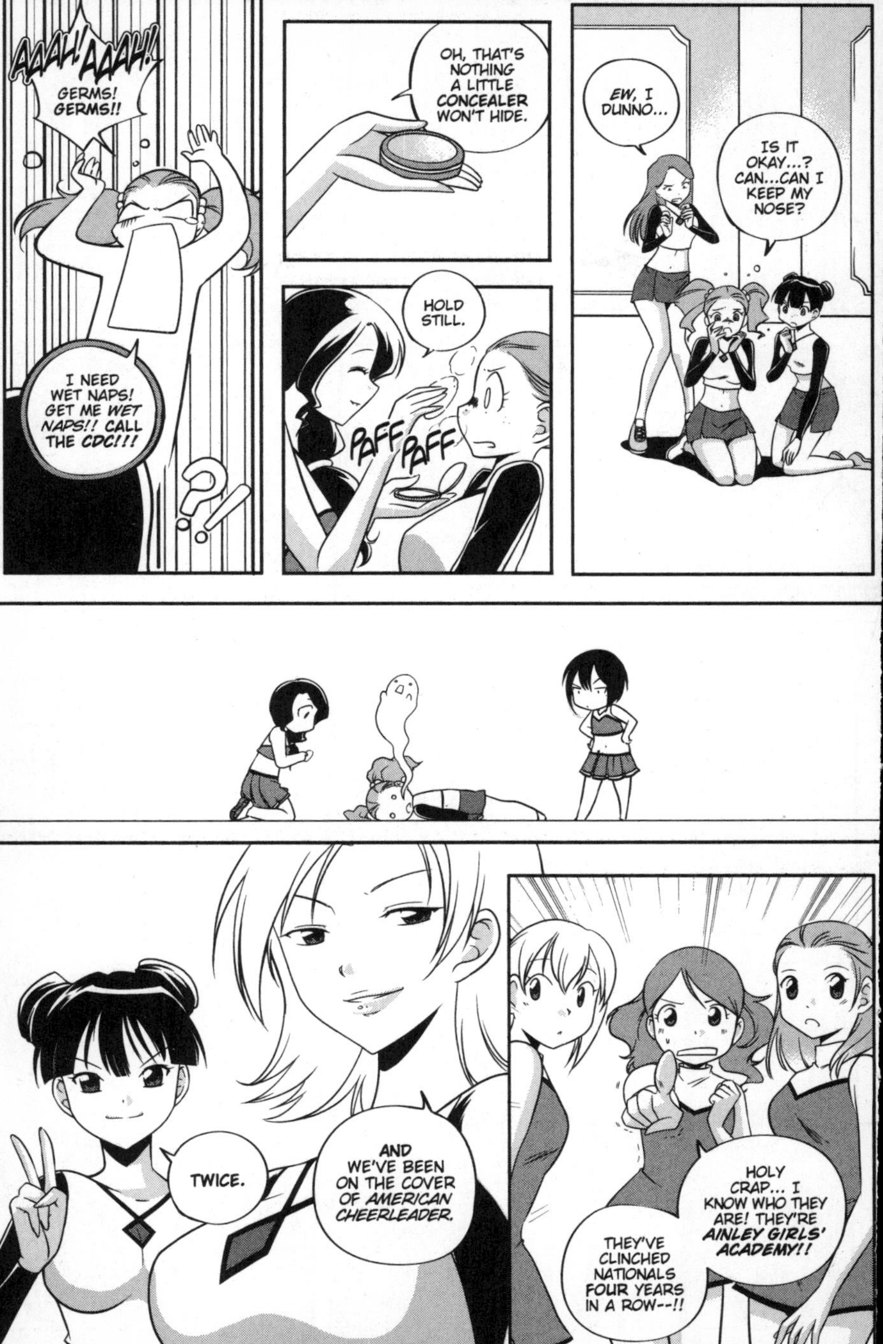
IS IT OKAY...? CAN...CAN I KEEP MY NOSE?
EW, I DUNNO...
OH, THAT'S NOTHING A LITTLE CONCEALER WON'T HIDE.
HOLD STILL.
PAFF PAFF
AAAH! AAAH!
GERMS! GERMS!!
I NEED WET NAPS! GET ME WET NAPS!! CALL THE CDC!!!
?!
HOLY CRAP... I KNOW WHO THEY ARE! THEY'RE AINLEY GIRLS' ACADEMY!!
THEY'VE CLINCHED NATIONALS FOUR YEARS IN A ROW--!!
AND WE'VE BEEN ON THE COVER OF AMERICAN CHEERLEADER.
TWICE.

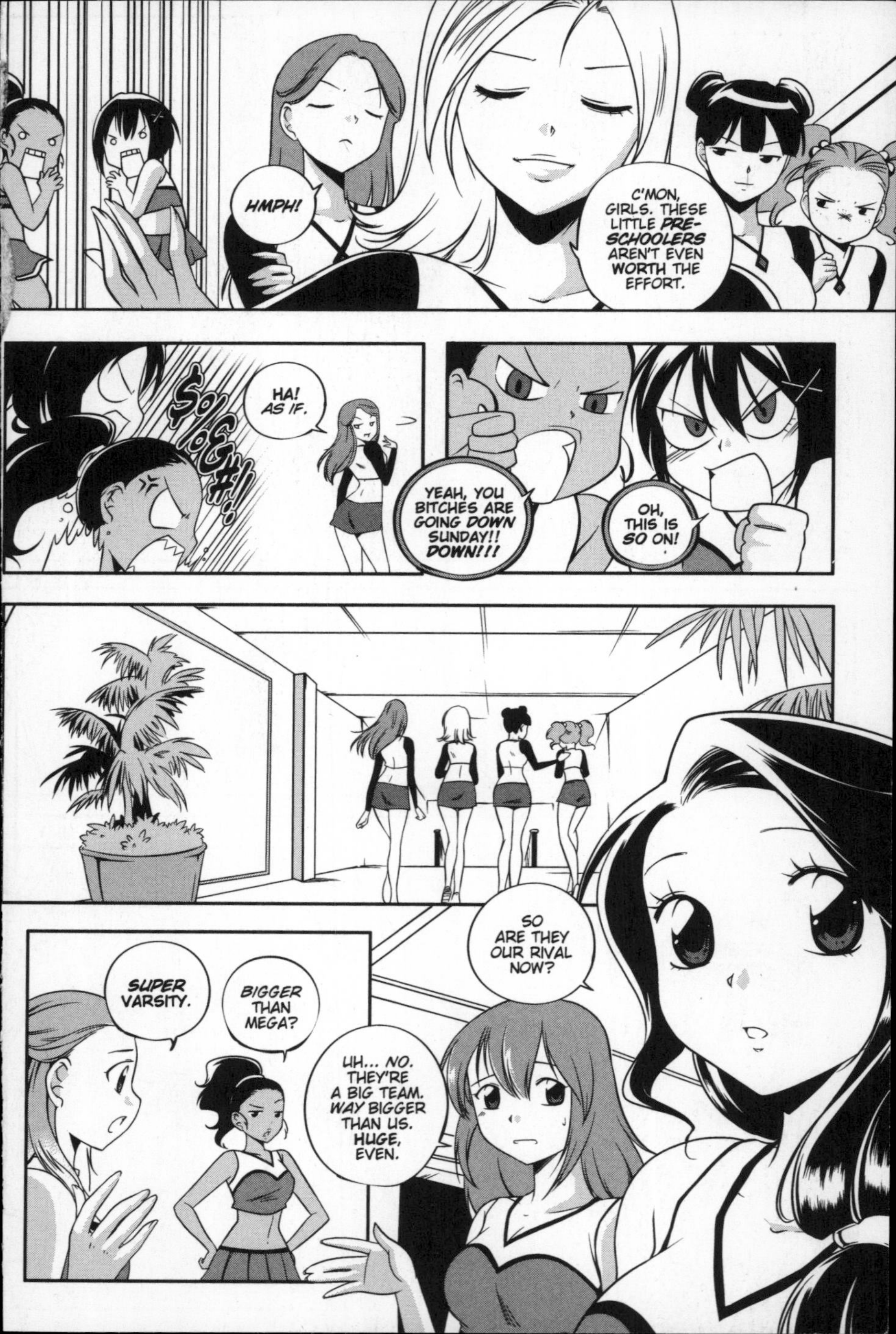
C'MON, GIRLS. THESE LITTLE PRE-SCHOOLERS AREN'T EVEN WORTH THE EFFORT.
HMPH!
OH, THIS IS SO ON!
YEAH, YOU BITCHES ARE GOING DOWN SUNDAY!! DOWN!!!
HA! AS IF.
$%@#!!
SO ARE THEY OUR RIVAL NOW?
UH... NO. THEY'RE A BIG TEAM. WAY BIGGER THAN US. HUGE, EVEN.
BIGGER THAN MEGA?
SUPER VARSITY.

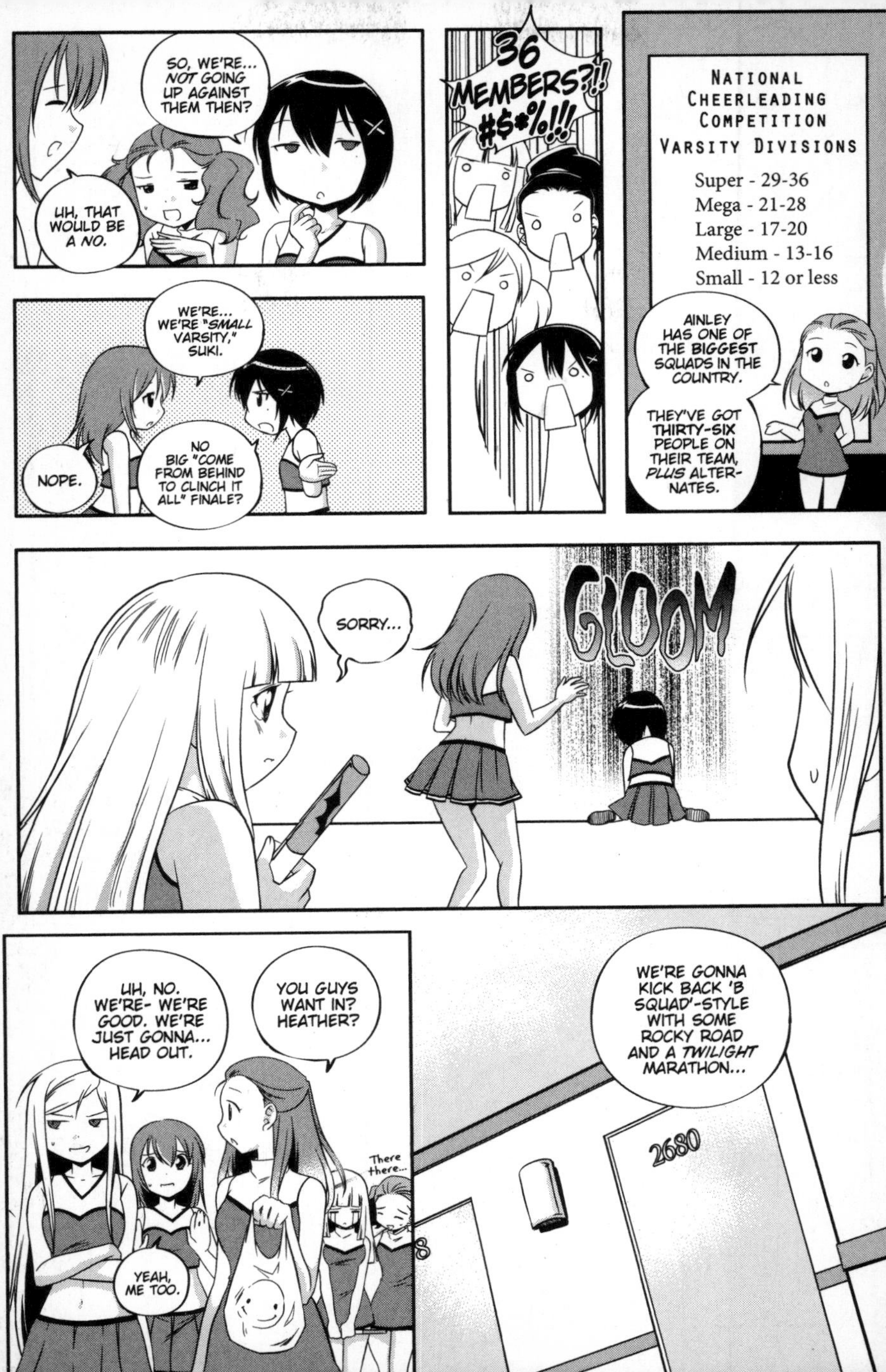
NATIONAL CHEERLEADING COMPETITION
VARSITY DIVISIONS
Super - 29-36
Mega - 21-28
Large - 17-20
Medium - 13-16
Small - 12 or less
AINLEY HAS ONE OF THE BIGGEST SQUADS IN THE COUNTRY.
THEY'VE GOT THIRTY-SIX PEOPLE ON THEIR TEAM, PLUS ALTER-NATES.
36 MEMBERS?!! #$*%!!!
SO, WE'RE... NOT GOING UP AGAINST THEM THEN?
UH, THAT WOULD BE A NO.
WE'RE... WE'RE "SMALL VARSITY," SUKI.
NO BIG "COME FROM BEHIND TO CLINCH IT ALL" FINALE?
NOPE.
GLOOM
SORRY...
WE'RE GONNA KICK BACK 'B SQUAD'-STYLE WITH SOME ROCKY ROAD AND A TWILIGHT MARATHON...
2680
YOU GUYS WANT IN? HEATHER?
UH, NO. WE'RE- WE'RE GOOD. WE'RE JUST GONNA... HEAD OUT.
There there...
YEAH, ME TOO.

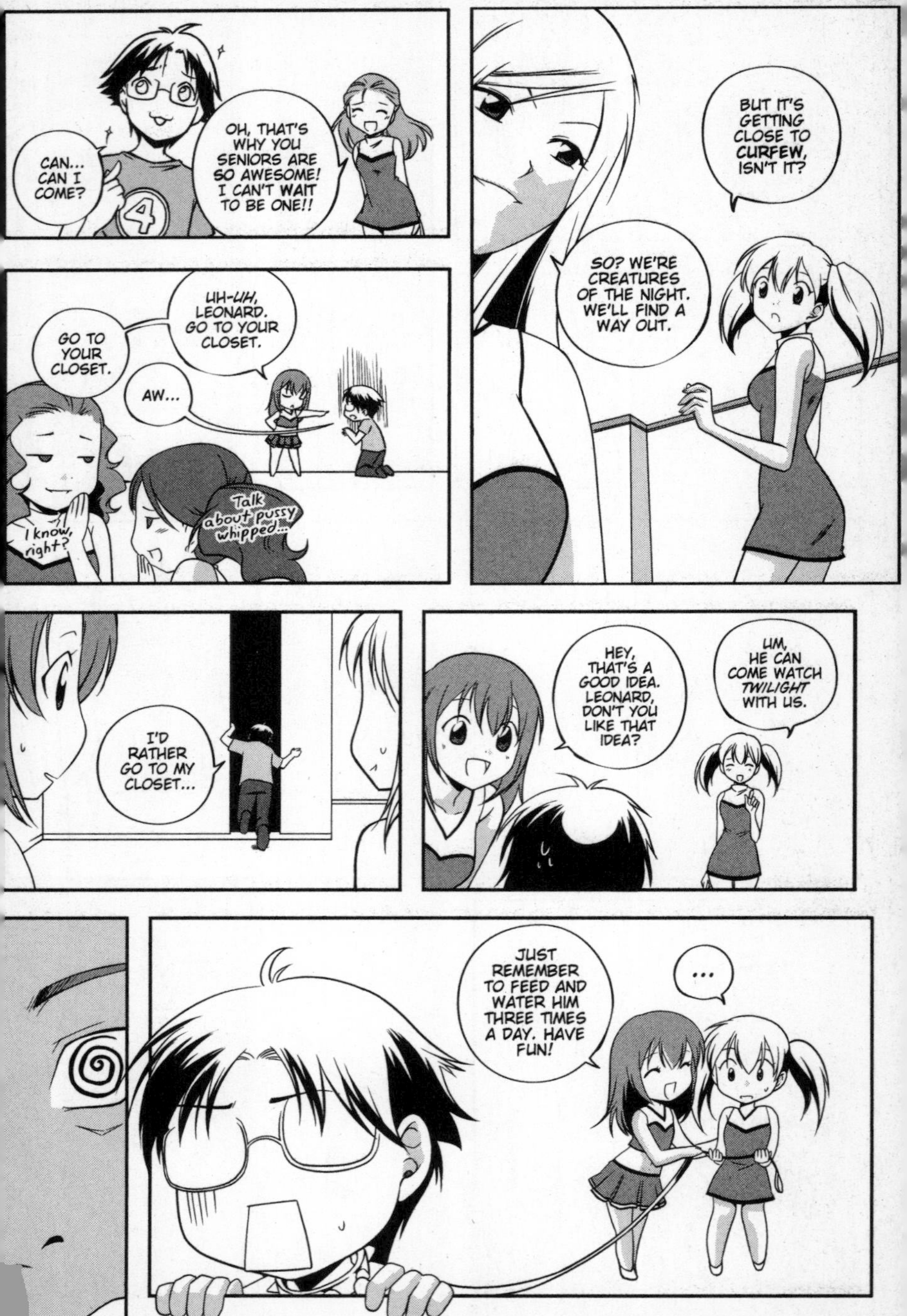
BUT IT'S GETTING CLOSE TO CURFEW, ISN'T IT?
SO? WE'RE CREATURES OF THE NIGHT. WE'LL FIND A WAY OUT.
OH, THAT'S WHY YOU SENIORS ARE SO AWESOME! I CAN'T WAIT TO BE ONE!!
CAN... CAN I COME?
UH-UH, LEONARD. GO TO YOUR CLOSET.
GO TO YOUR CLOSET.
AW...
Talk about pussy whipped...
I know, right?
UM, HE CAN COME WATCH TWILIGHT WITH US.
HEY, THAT'S A GOOD IDEA. LEONARD, DON'T YOU LIKE THAT IDEA?
I'D RATHER GO TO MY CLOSET...
...
JUST REMEMBER TO FEED AND WATER HIM THREE TIMES A DAY. HAVE FUN!

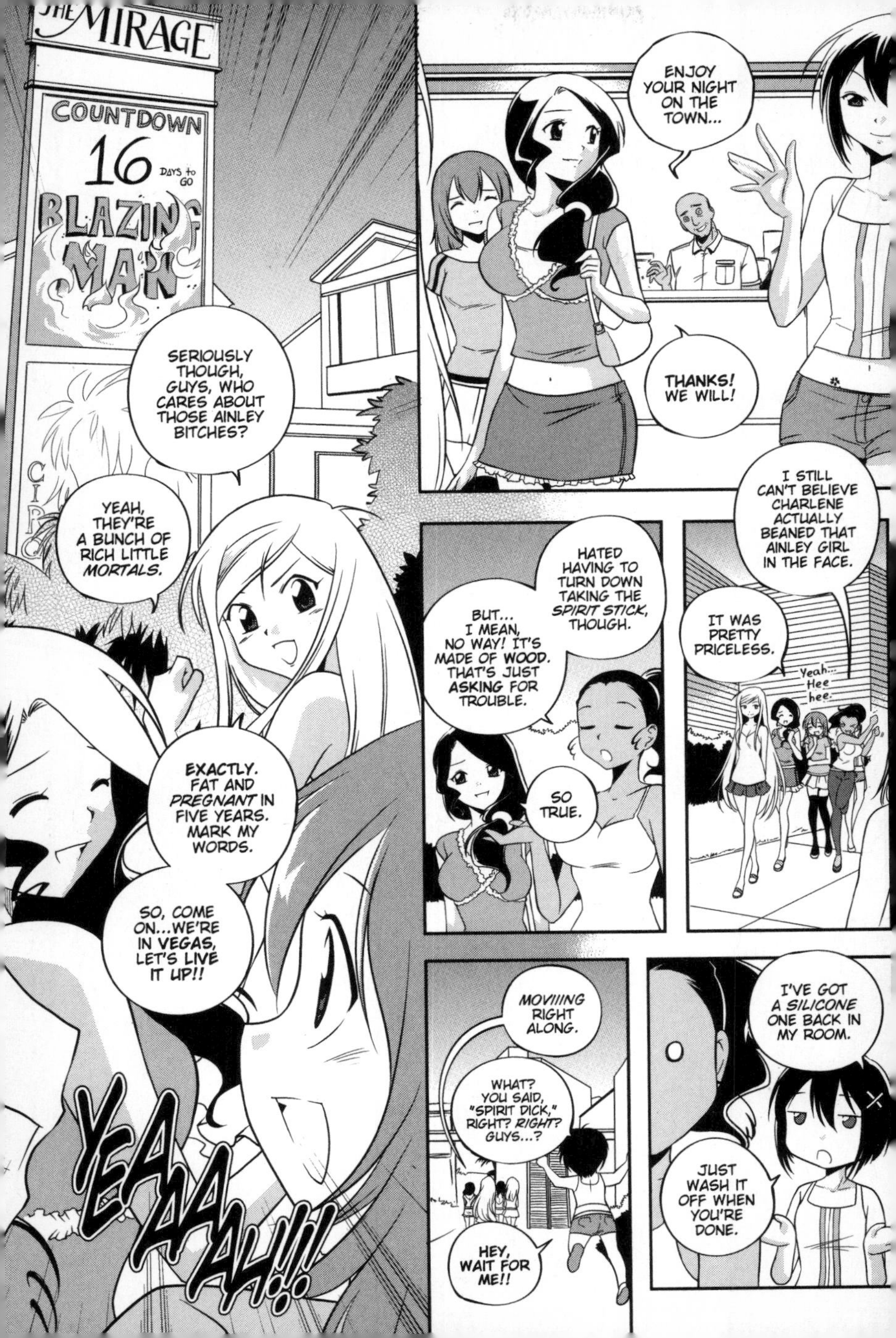
ENJOY YOUR NIGHT ON THE TOWN...
THANKS! WE WILL!
I STILL CAN'T BELIEVE CHARLENE ACTUALLY BEANED THAT AINLEY GIRL IN THE FACE.
IT WAS PRETTY PRICELESS.
Yeah... Hee hee.
HATED HAVING TO TURN DOWN TAKING THE *SPIRIT STICK*, THOUGH.
BUT... I MEAN, NO WAY! IT'S MADE OF WOOD. THAT'S JUST ASKING FOR TROUBLE.
SO TRUE.
I'VE GOT A *SILICONE* ONE BACK IN MY ROOM.
JUST WASH IT OFF WHEN YOU'RE DONE.
MOVIIING RIGHT ALONG.
WHAT? YOU SAID, "SPIRIT DICK," RIGHT? *RIGHT?* GUYS...?
HEY, WAIT FOR ME!!
THE MIRAGE
COUNTDOWN
16 DAYS to GO
BLAZING MAN
SERIOUSLY THOUGH, GUYS, WHO CARES ABOUT THOSE AINLEY BITCHES?
YEAH, THEY'RE A BUNCH OF RICH LITTLE *MORTALS*.
EXACTLY. FAT AND *PREGNANT* IN FIVE YEARS. MARK MY WORDS.
SO, COME ON...WE'RE IN VEGAS, LET'S LIVE IT UP!!
YEAAAAH!!!

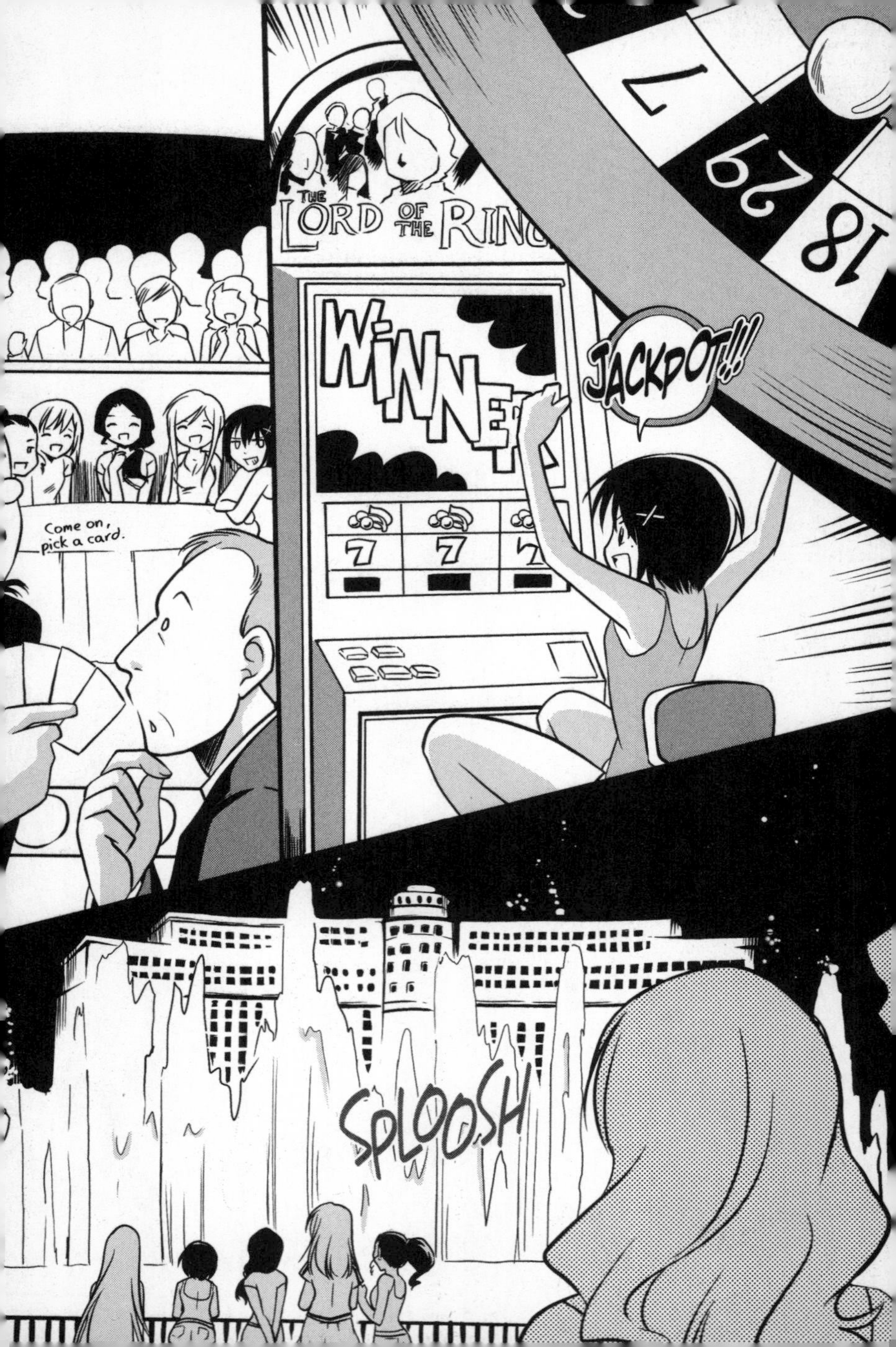
THE LORD OF THE RIN
JACKPOT!!
Come on, pick a card.
SPLOOSH

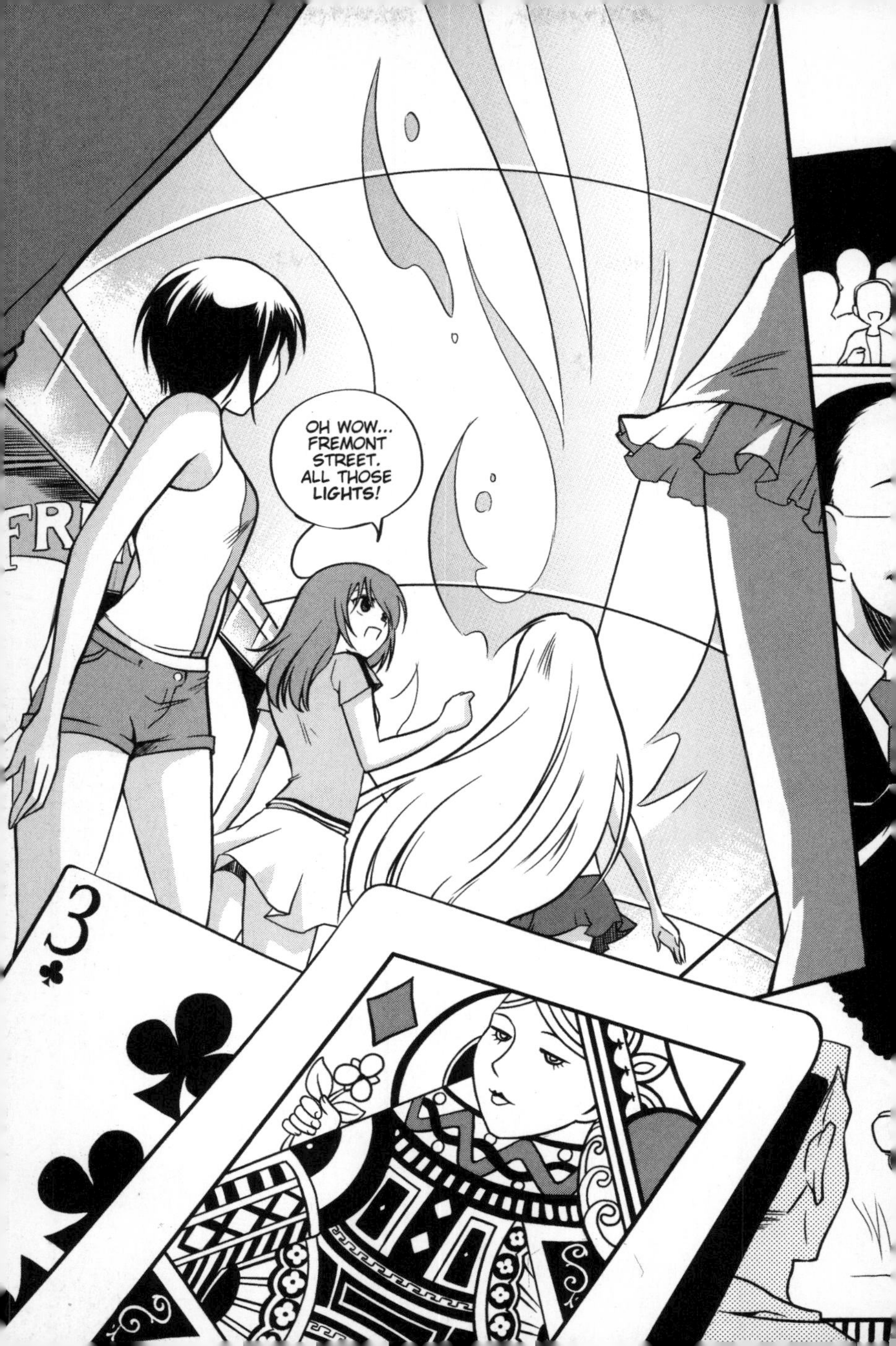
OH WOW... FREMONT STREET. ALL THOSE LIGHTS!

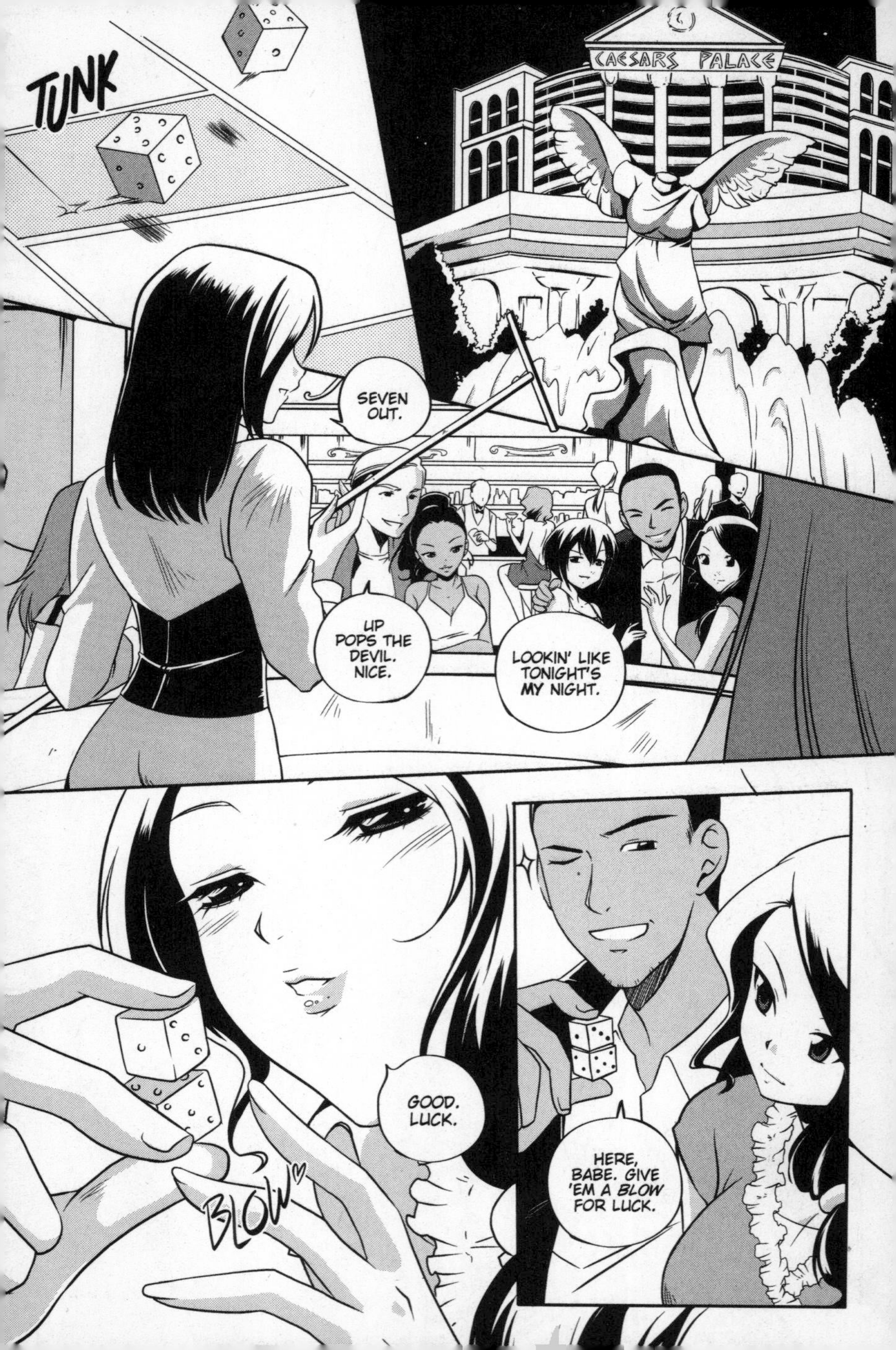
CAESARS PALACE
TUNK
SEVEN OUT.
UP POPS THE DEVIL. NICE.
LOOKIN' LIKE TONIGHT'S MY NIGHT.
HERE, BABE. GIVE 'EM A *BLOW* FOR LUCK.
GOOD. LUCK.
BLOW♥

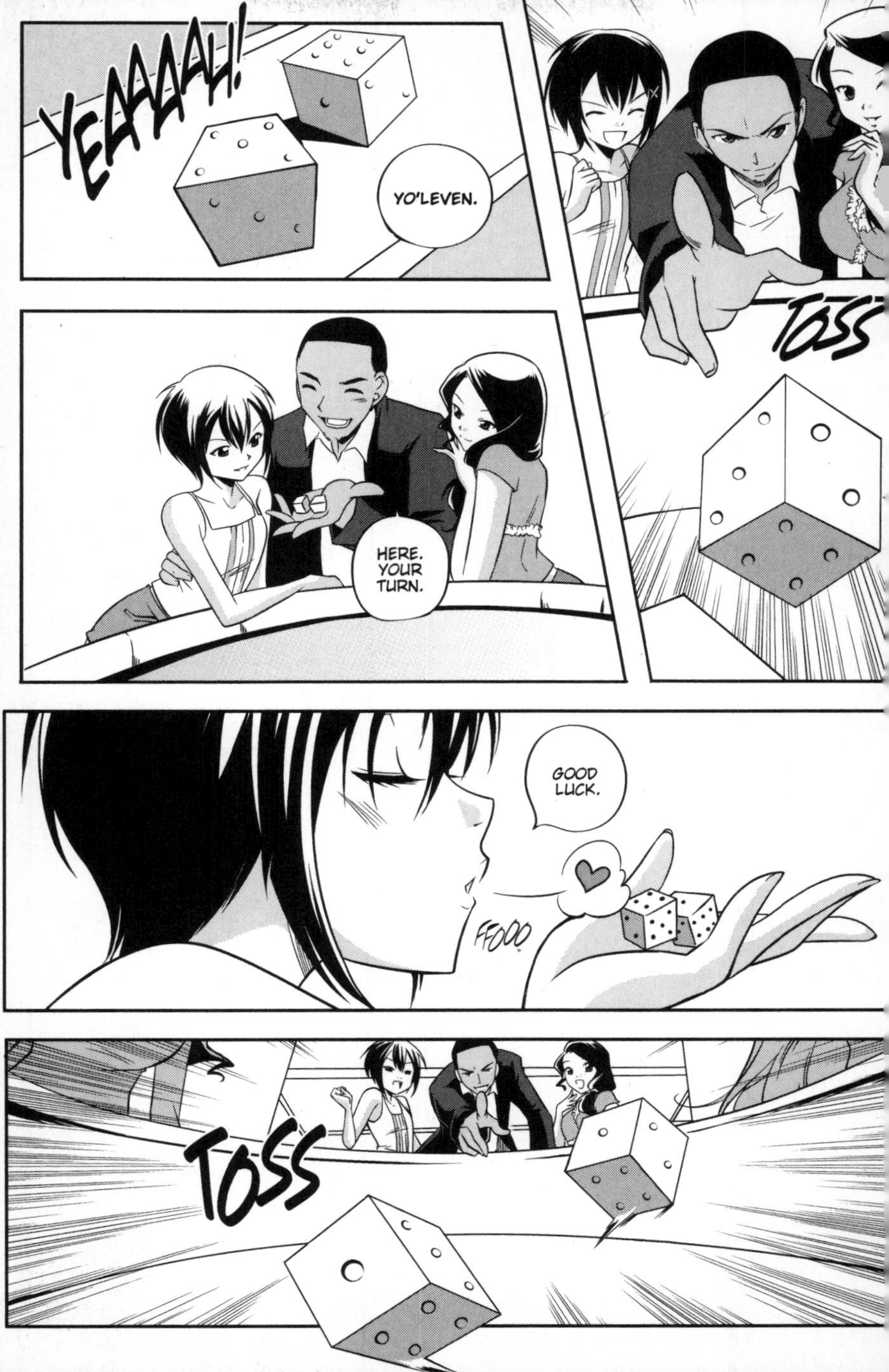
TOSS
YEAAAAH!
YO'LEVEN.
HERE. YOUR TURN.
GOOD LUCK.
FFOOO
TOSS

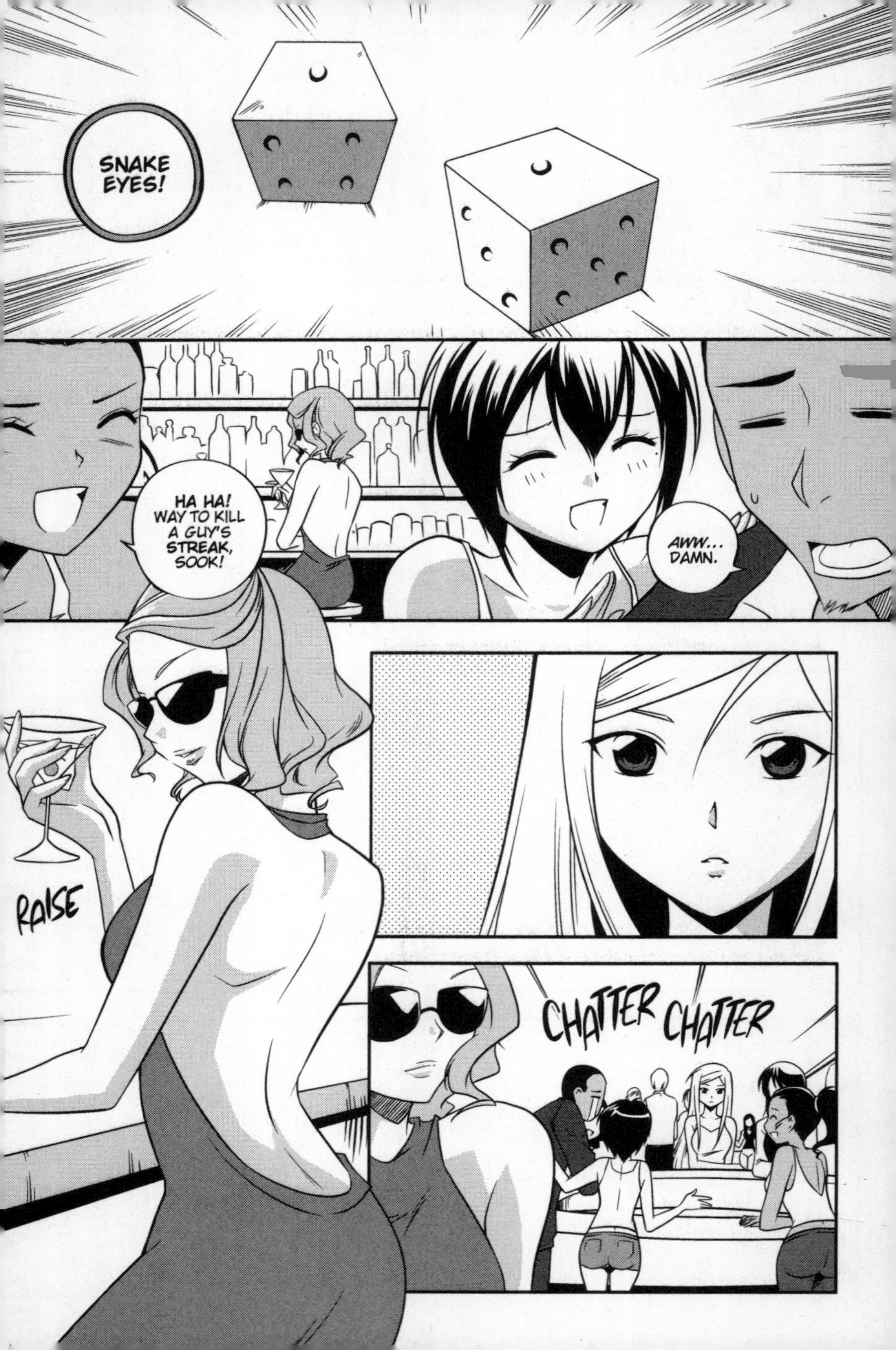
SNAKE EYES!
AWW... DAMN.
HA HA! WAY TO KILL A GUY'S STREAK, SOOK!
CHATTER CHATTER
RAISE

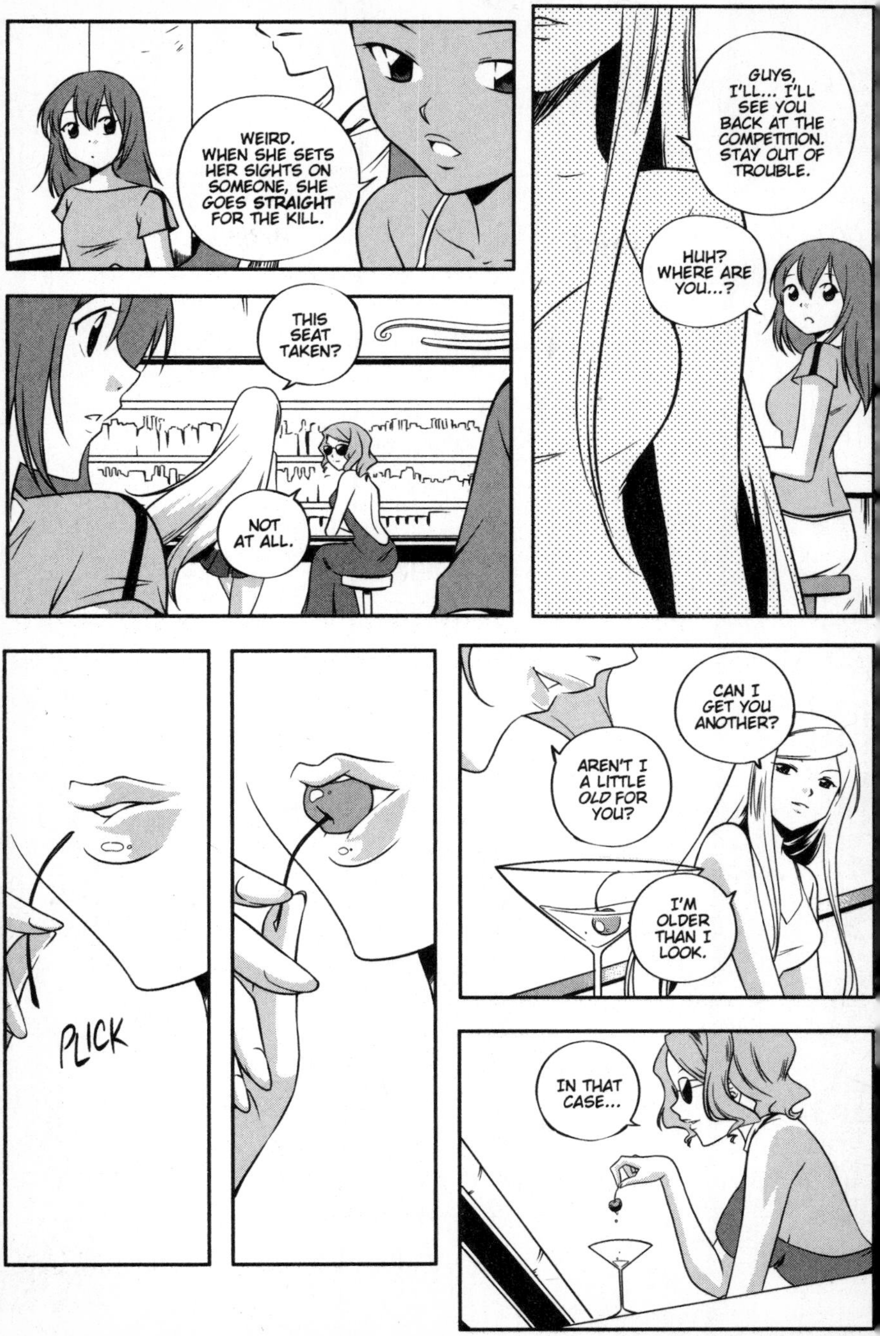
GUYS, I'LL... I'LL SEE YOU BACK AT THE COMPETITION. STAY OUT OF TROUBLE.
HUH? WHERE ARE YOU...?
WEIRD. WHEN SHE SETS HER SIGHTS ON SOMEONE, SHE GOES STRAIGHT FOR THE KILL.
THIS SEAT TAKEN?
NOT AT ALL.
CAN I GET YOU ANOTHER?
AREN'T I A LITTLE OLD FOR YOU?
I'M OLDER THAN I LOOK.
IN THAT CASE...
PLICK

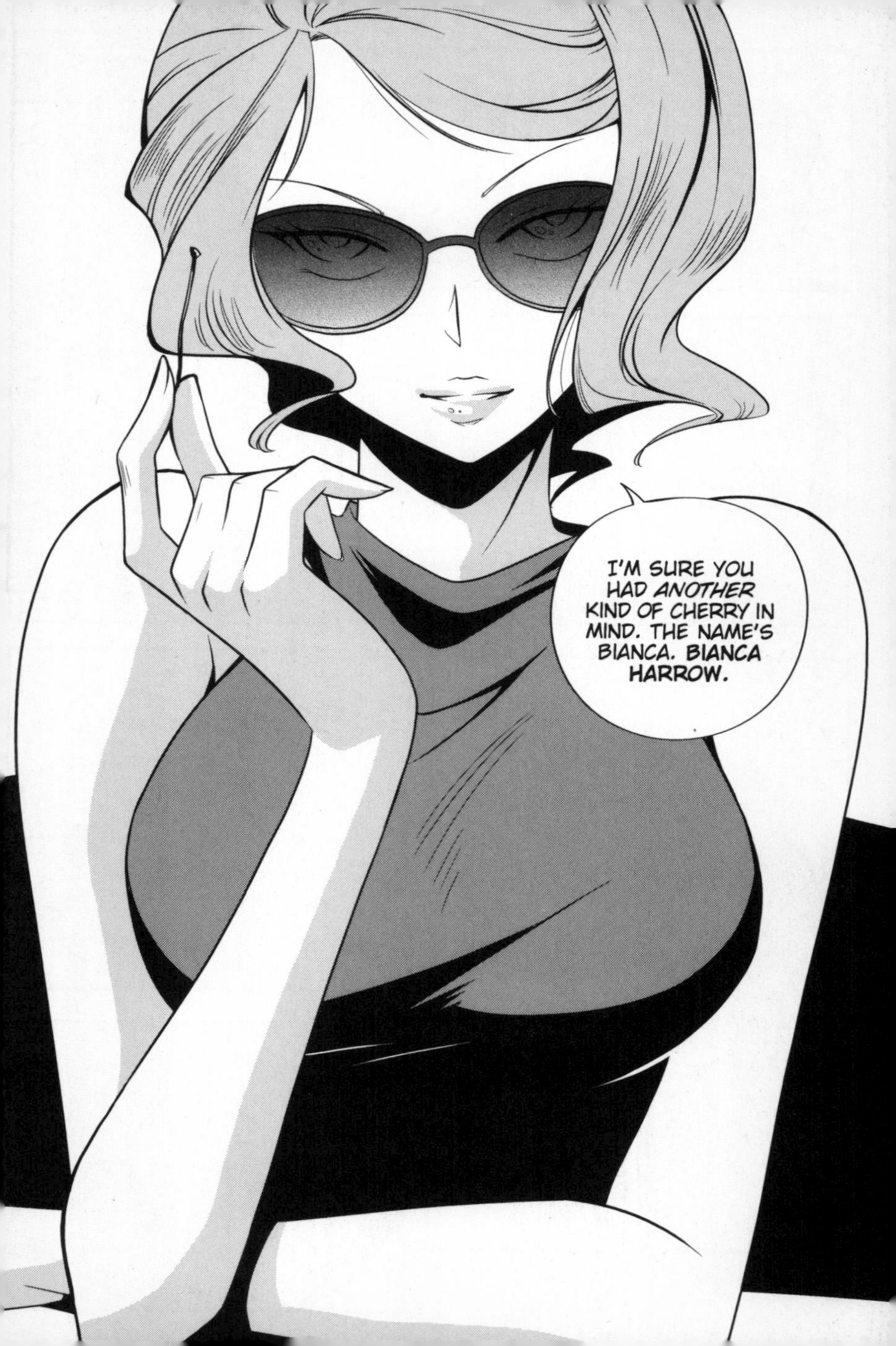
I'M SURE YOU HAD *ANOTHER* KIND OF CHERRY IN MIND. THE NAME'S BIANCA. BIANCA HARROW.

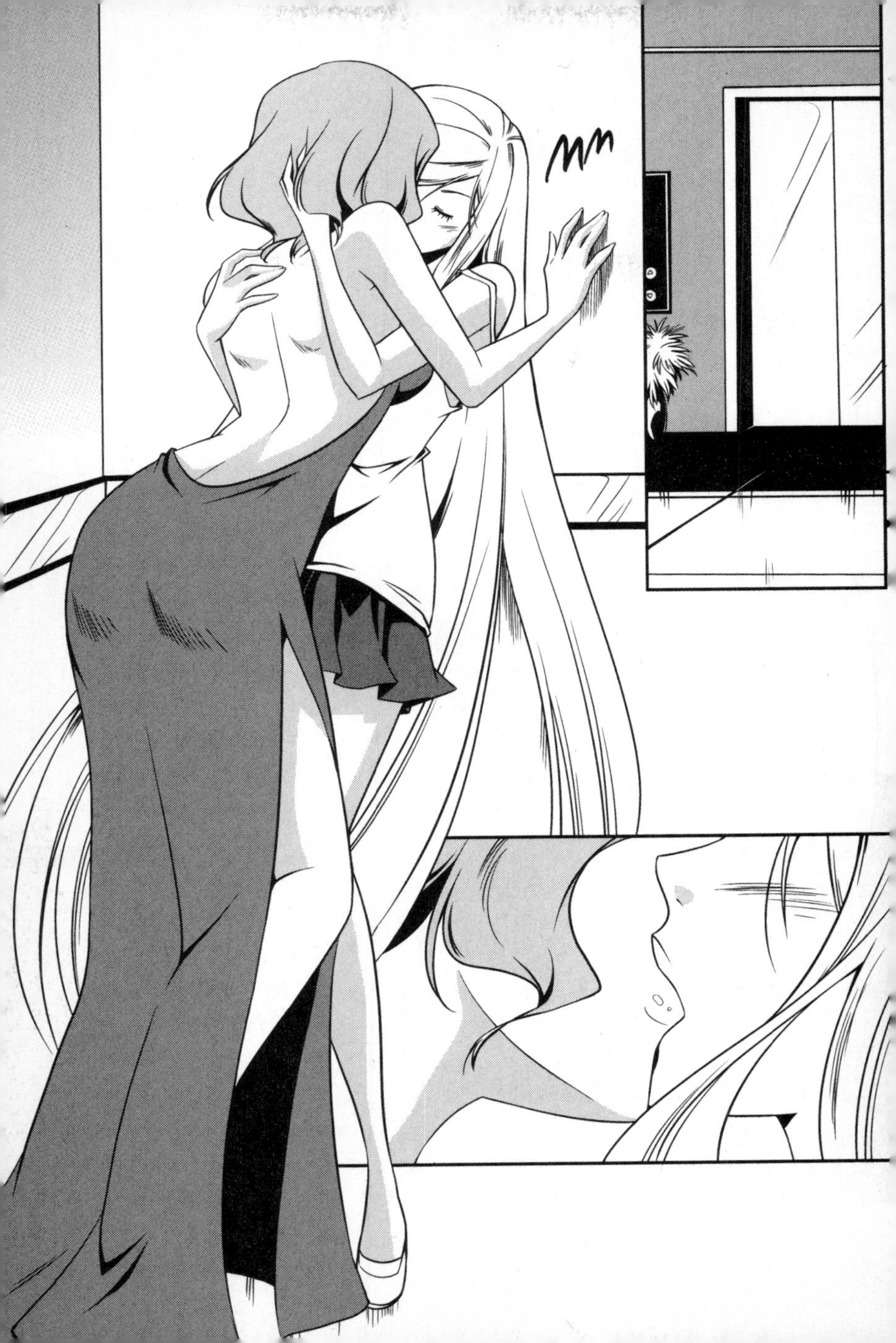
MM

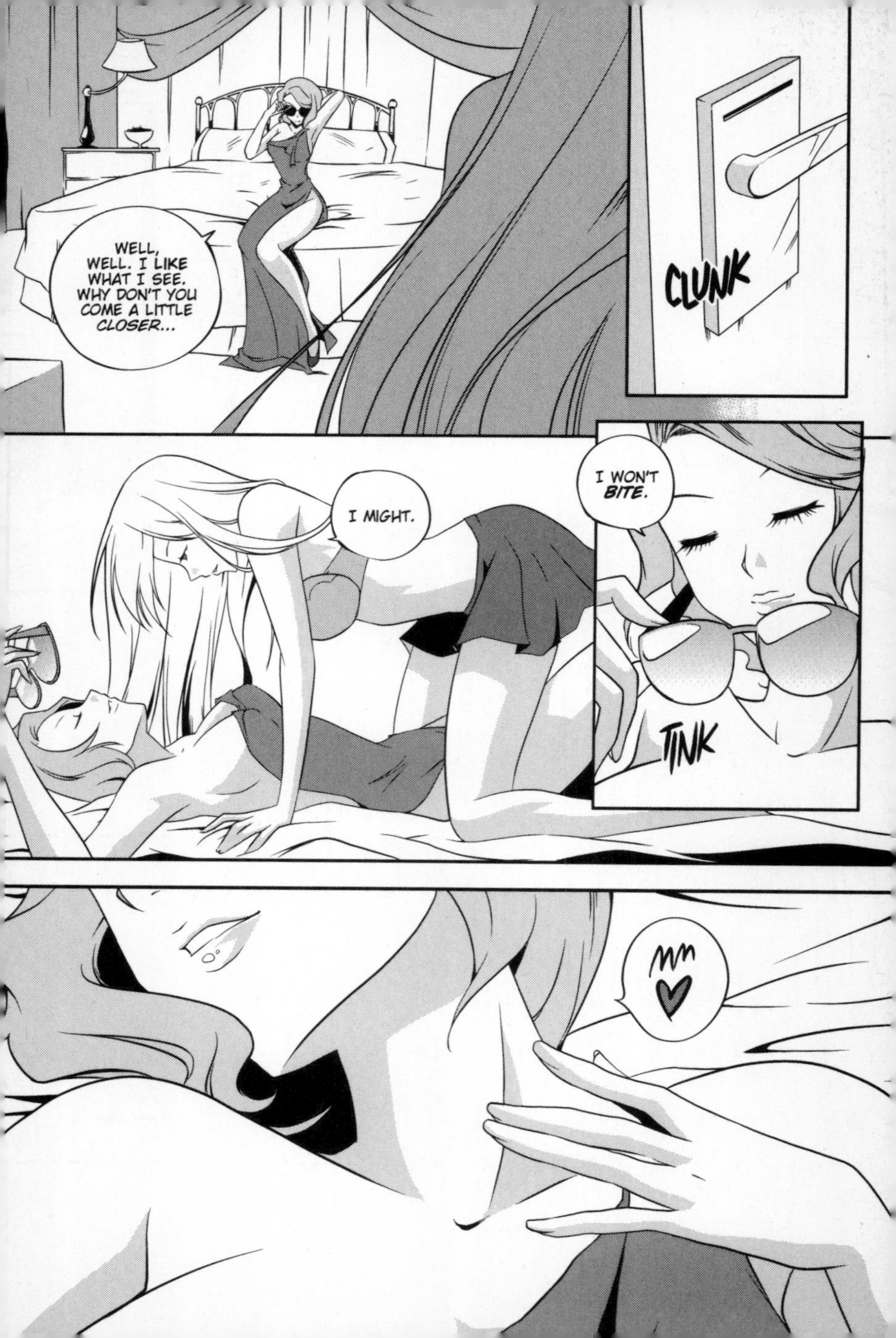
CLUNK
WELL, WELL. I LIKE WHAT I SEE. WHY DON'T YOU COME A LITTLE CLOSER...
I WON'T BITE.
TINK
I MIGHT.
mm ♥

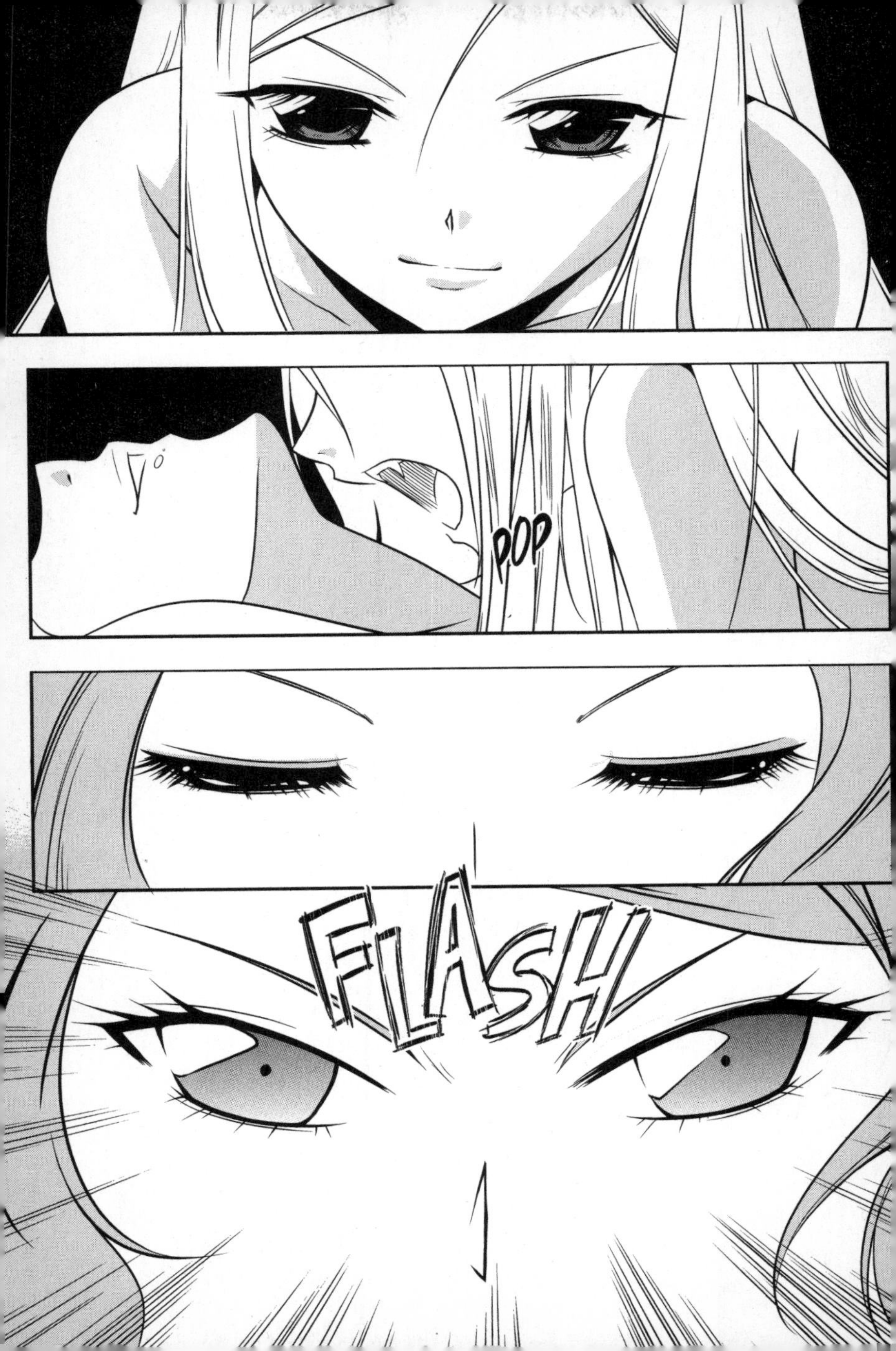

POP
FLASH

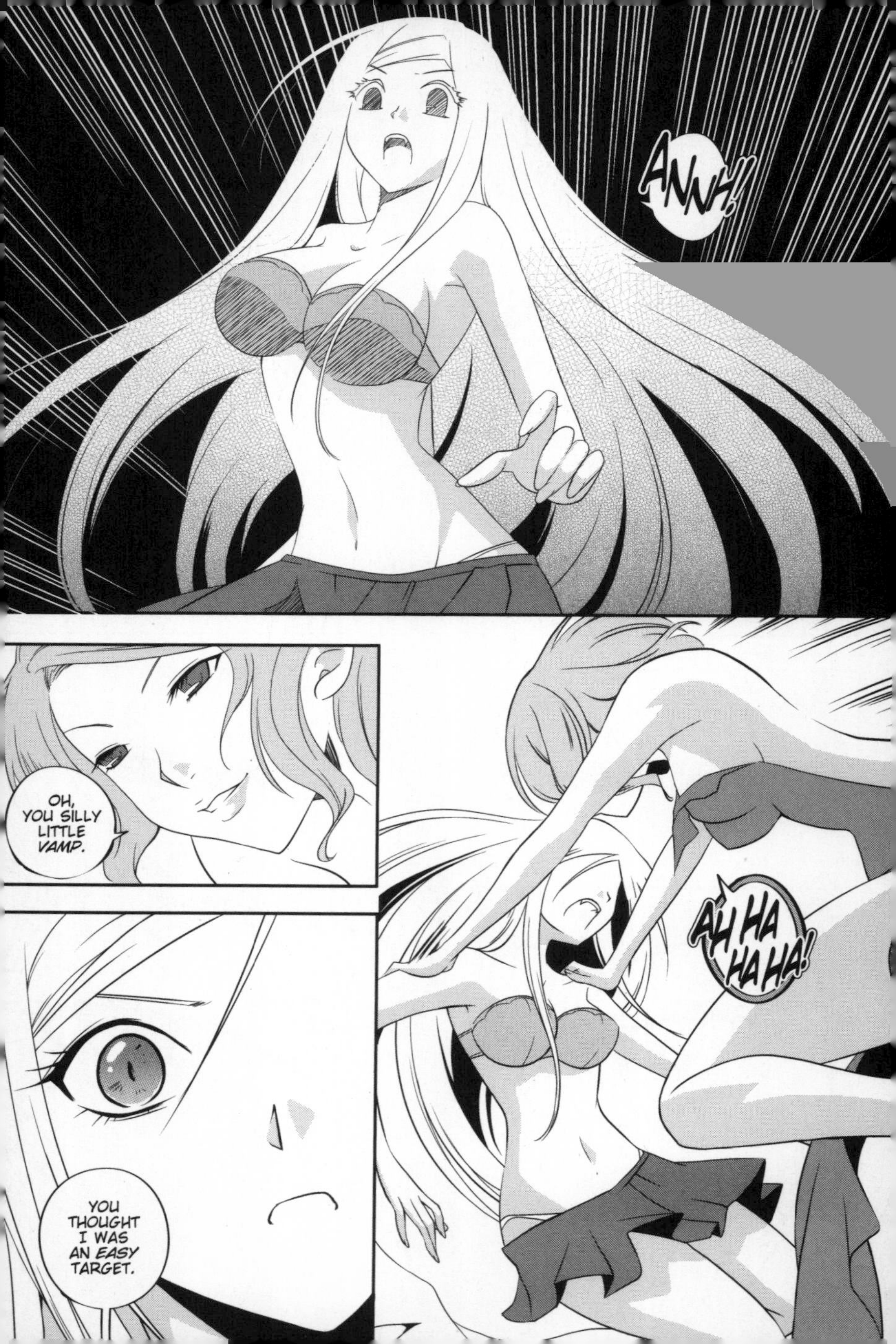
ANNH!
AH HA HA HA!
OH, YOU SILLY LITTLE VAMP.
YOU THOUGHT I WAS AN EASY TARGET.

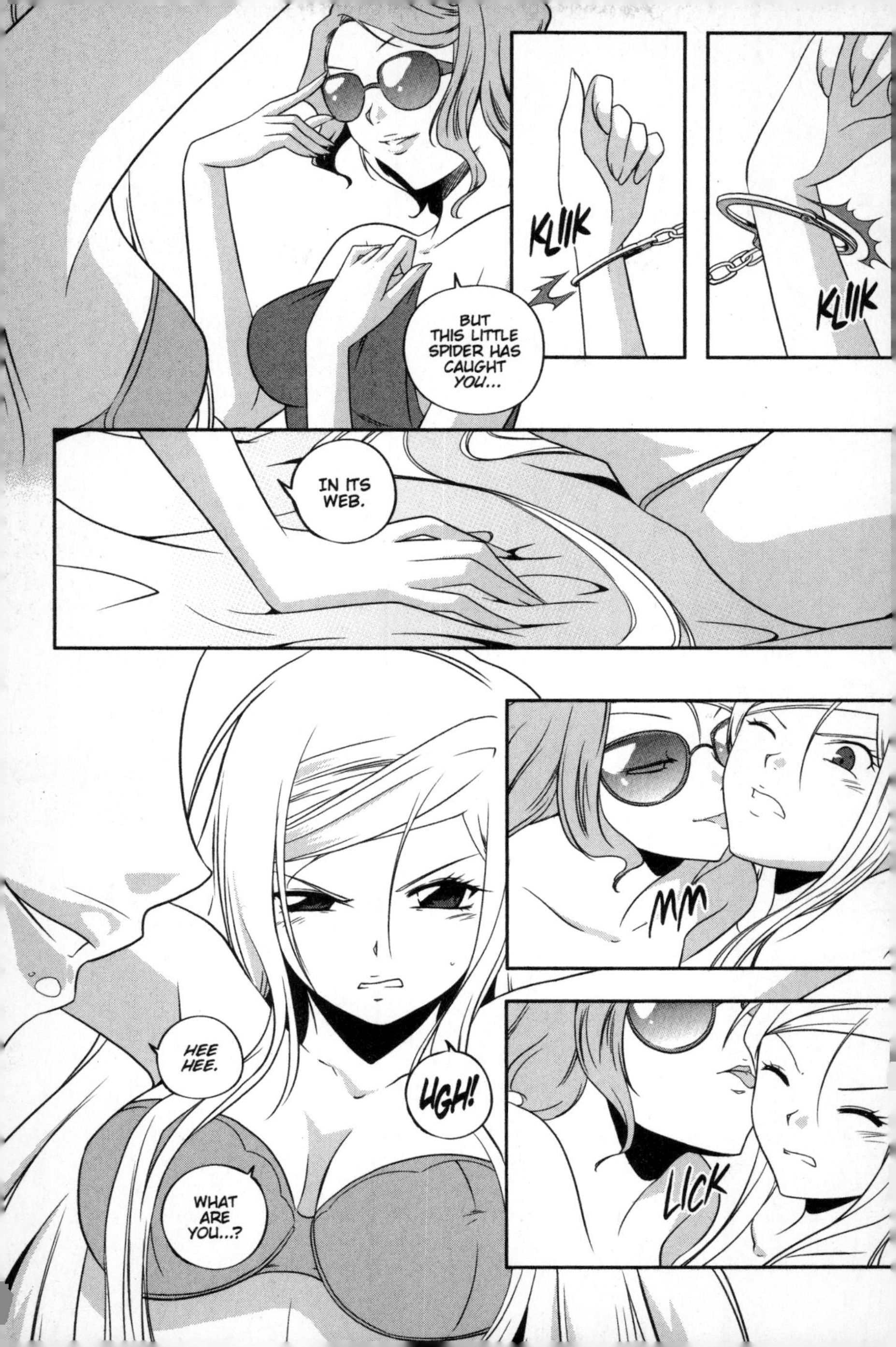
KLIIK
KLIIK
BUT THIS LITTLE SPIDER HAS CAUGHT YOU...
IN ITS WEB.
MM
LICK
HEE HEE.
UGH!
WHAT ARE YOU...?

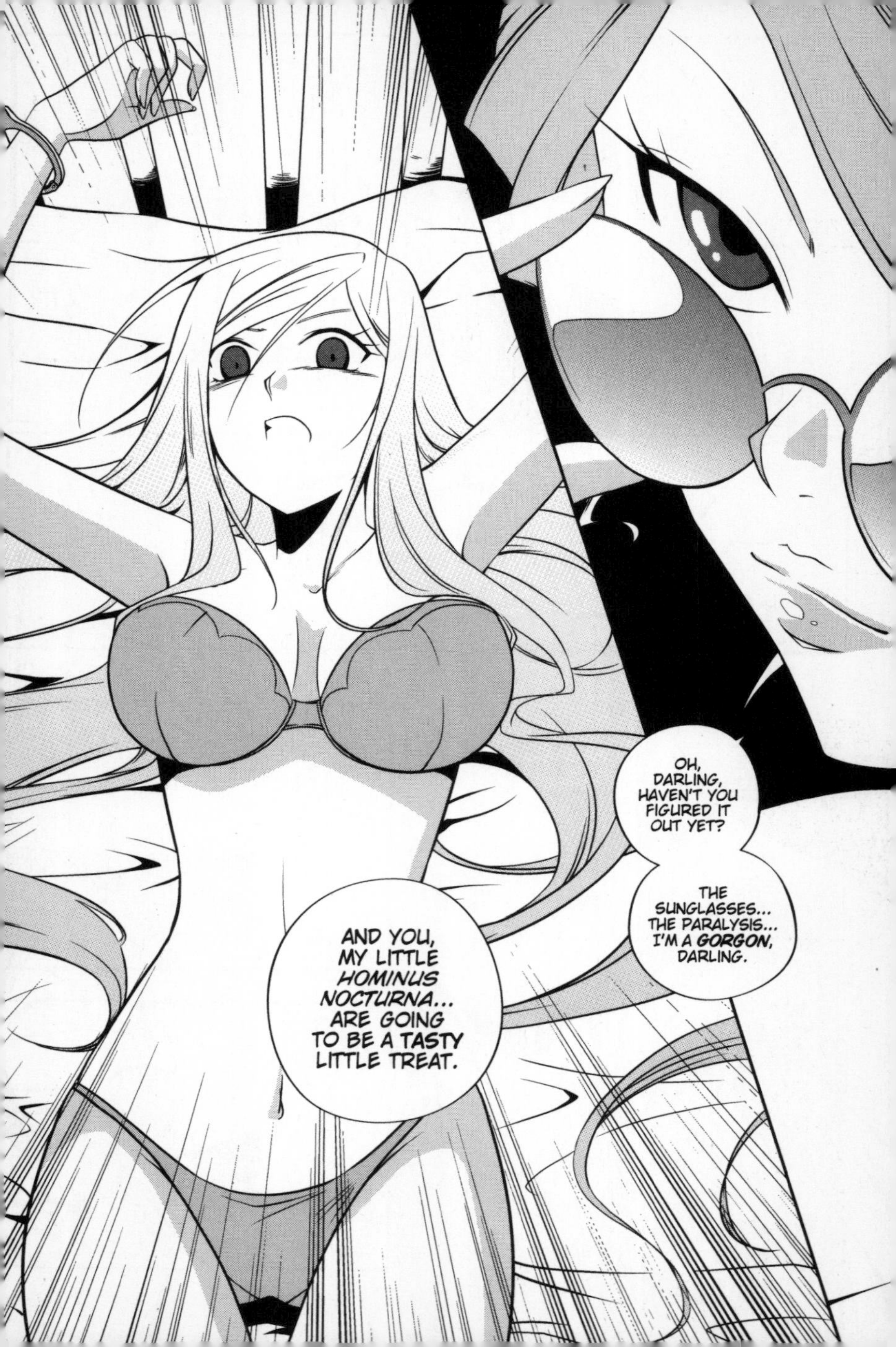
OH, DARLING, HAVEN'T YOU FIGURED IT OUT YET?
THE SUNGLASSES... THE PARALYSIS... I'M A *GORGON*, DARLING.
AND YOU, MY LITTLE *HOMINUS NOCTURNA*... ARE GOING TO BE A TASTY LITTLE TREAT.

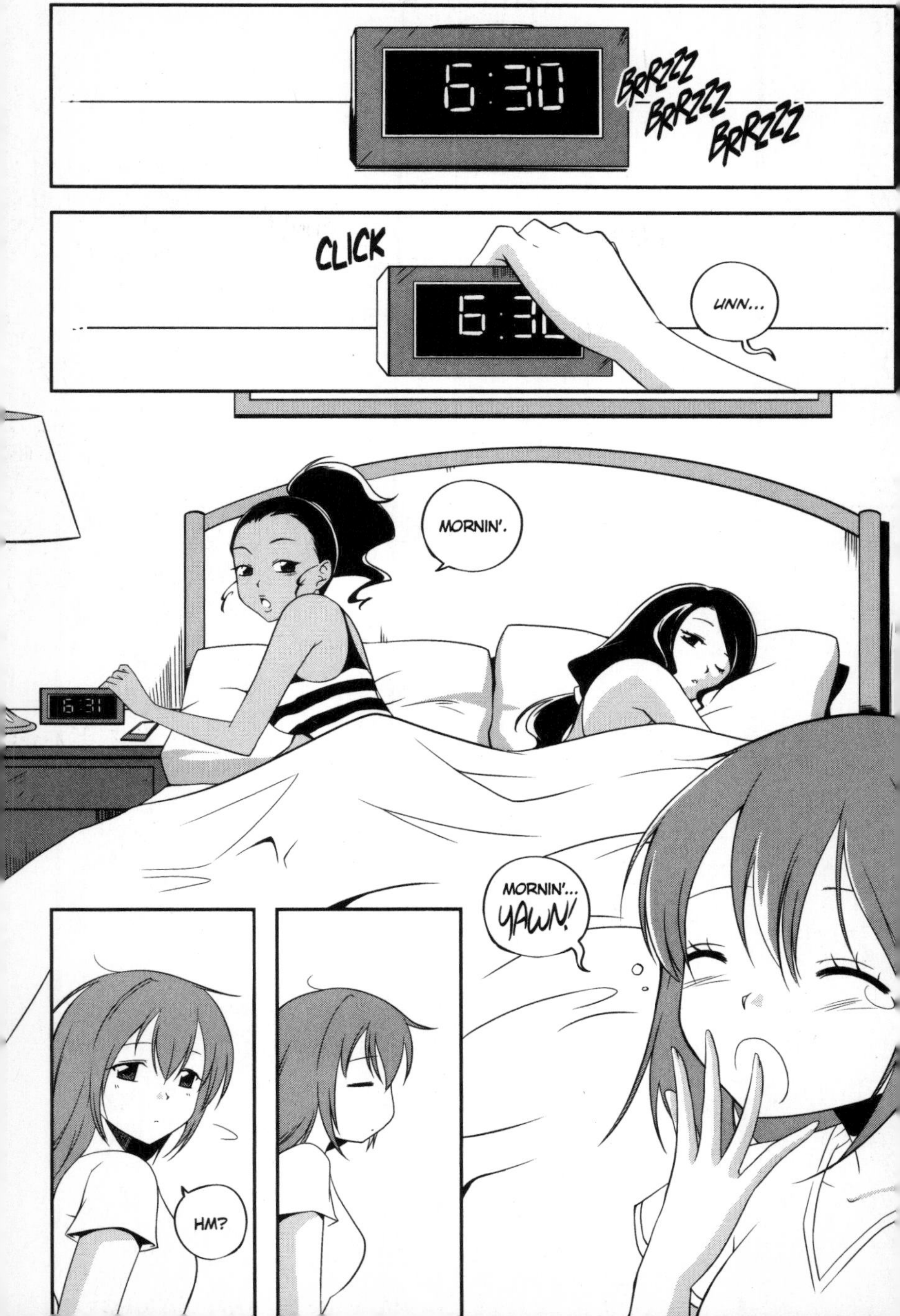
6:30
BRRZZZ
BRRZZZ
BRRZZZ
CLICK
UNN...
MORNIN'.
MORNIN'... YAWN!
HM?

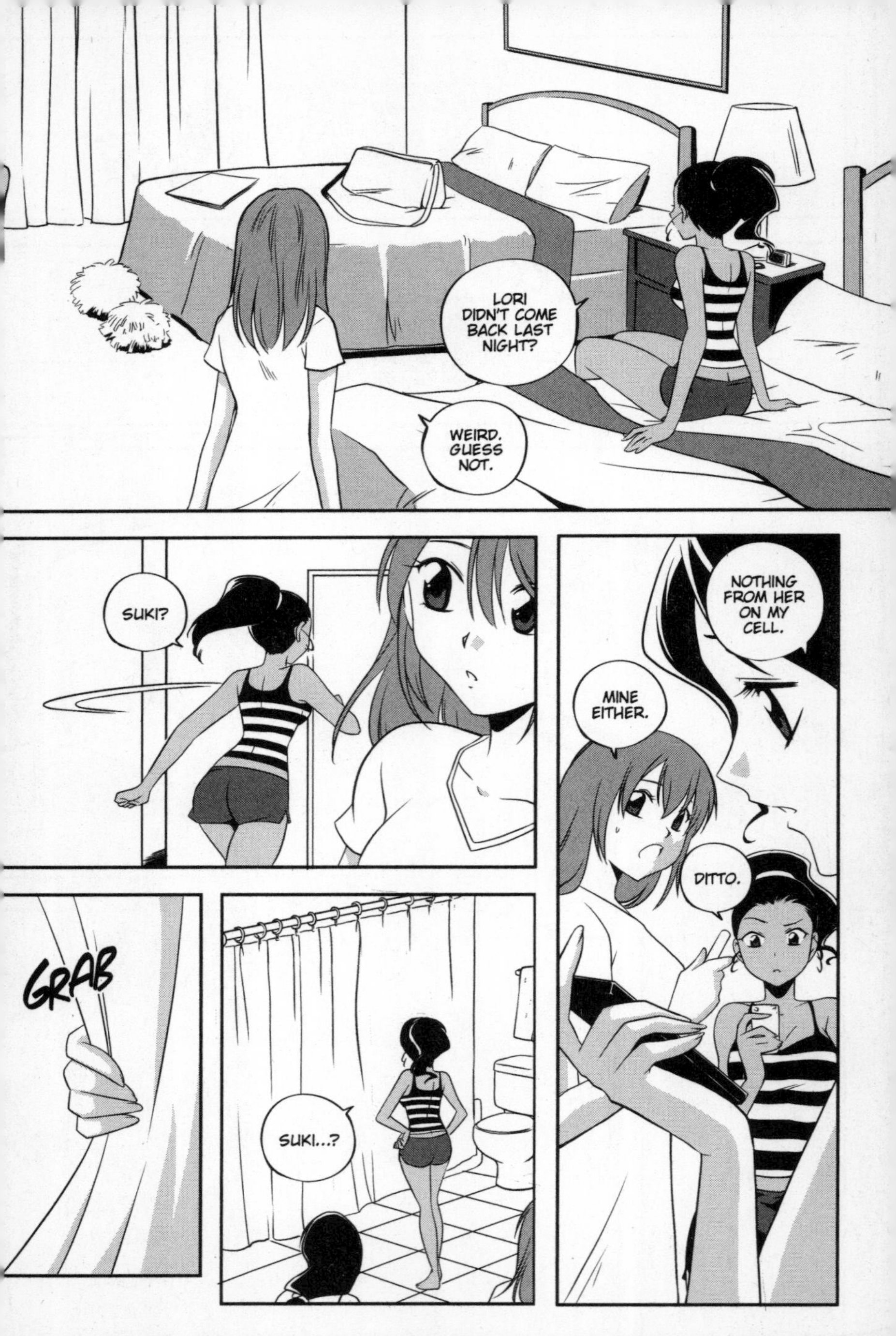
LORI DIDN'T COME BACK LAST NIGHT?
WEIRD. GUESS NOT.
NOTHING FROM HER ON MY CELL.
MINE EITHER.
DITTO.
SUKI?
SUKI...?
GRAB

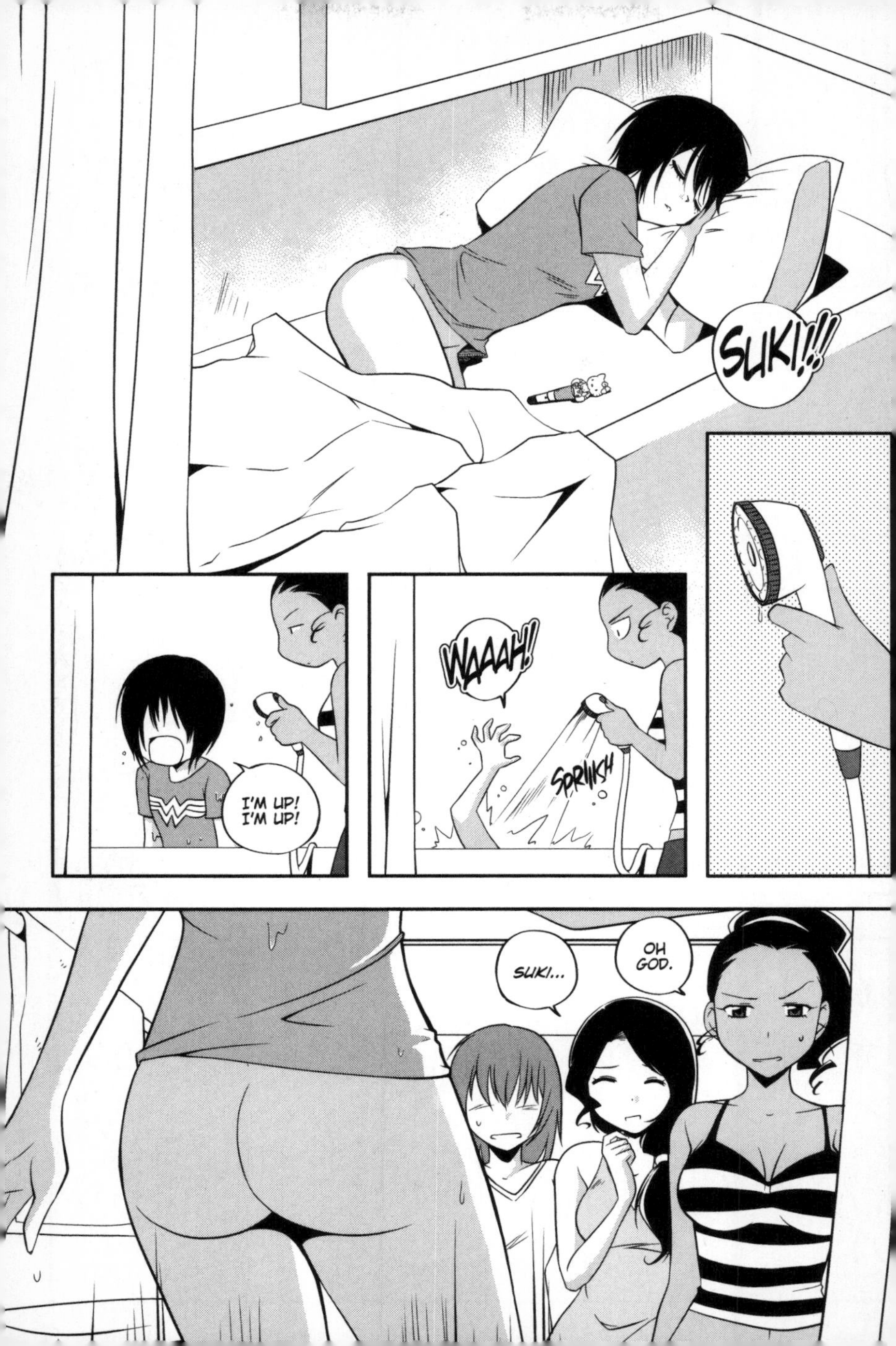
SUKI!!!
WAAAH!
SPRIIISH
I'M UP! I'M UP!
OH GOD.
SUKI...

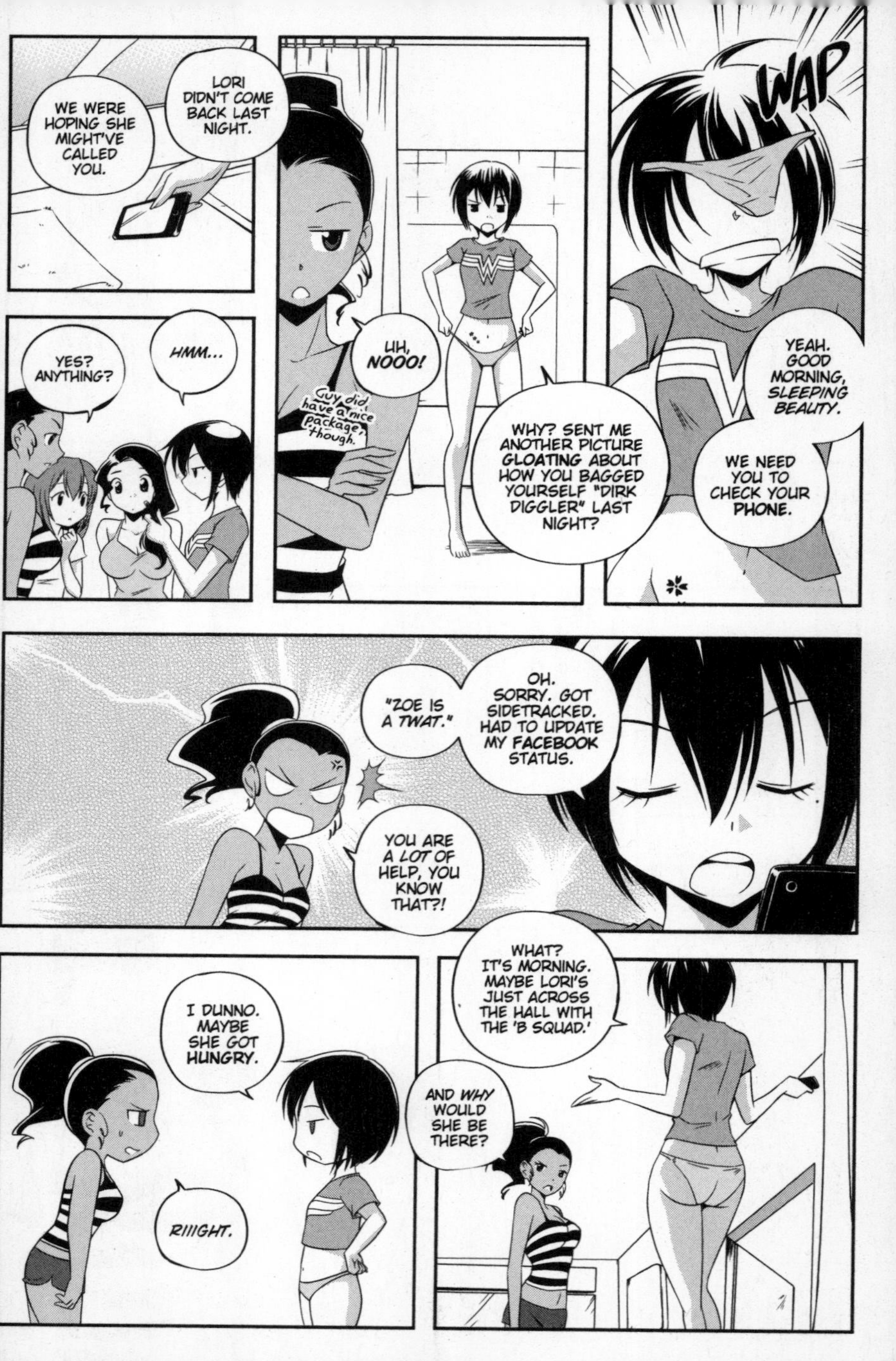
WAP
YEAH. GOOD MORNING, SLEEPING BEAUTY.
WE NEED YOU TO CHECK YOUR PHONE.
WHY? SENT ME ANOTHER PICTURE GLOATING ABOUT HOW YOU BAGGED YOURSELF "DIRK DIGGLER" LAST NIGHT?
UH, NOOO!
Guy did have a nice package, though.
LORI DIDN'T COME BACK LAST NIGHT.
WE WERE HOPING SHE MIGHT'VE CALLED YOU.
HMM...
YES? ANYTHING?
OH. SORRY. GOT SIDETRACKED. HAD TO UPDATE MY FACEBOOK STATUS.
"ZOE IS A TWAT."
YOU ARE A LOT OF HELP, YOU KNOW THAT?!
WHAT? IT'S MORNING. MAYBE LORI'S JUST ACROSS THE HALL WITH THE 'B SQUAD.'
AND WHY WOULD SHE BE THERE?
I DUNNO. MAYBE SHE GOT HUNGRY.
RIIIGHT.

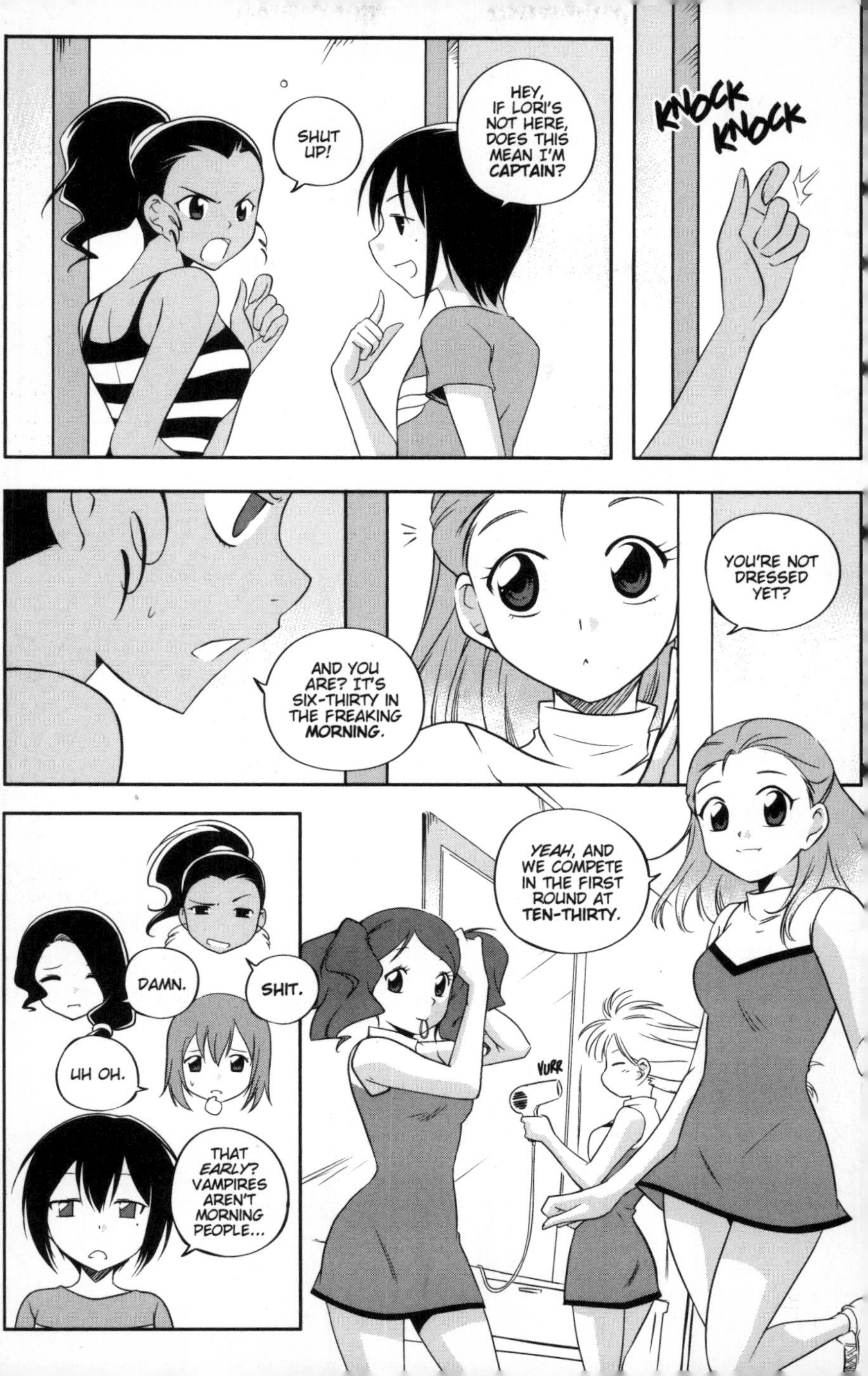
KNOCK KNOCK
HEY, IF LORI'S NOT HERE, DOES THIS MEAN I'M CAPTAIN?
SHUT UP!
YOU'RE NOT DRESSED YET?
AND YOU ARE? IT'S SIX-THIRTY IN THE FREAKING MORNING.
YEAH, AND WE COMPETE IN THE FIRST ROUND AT TEN-THIRTY.
VURR
SHIT.
DAMN.
UH OH.
THAT *EARLY*? VAMPIRES AREN'T MORNING PEOPLE...

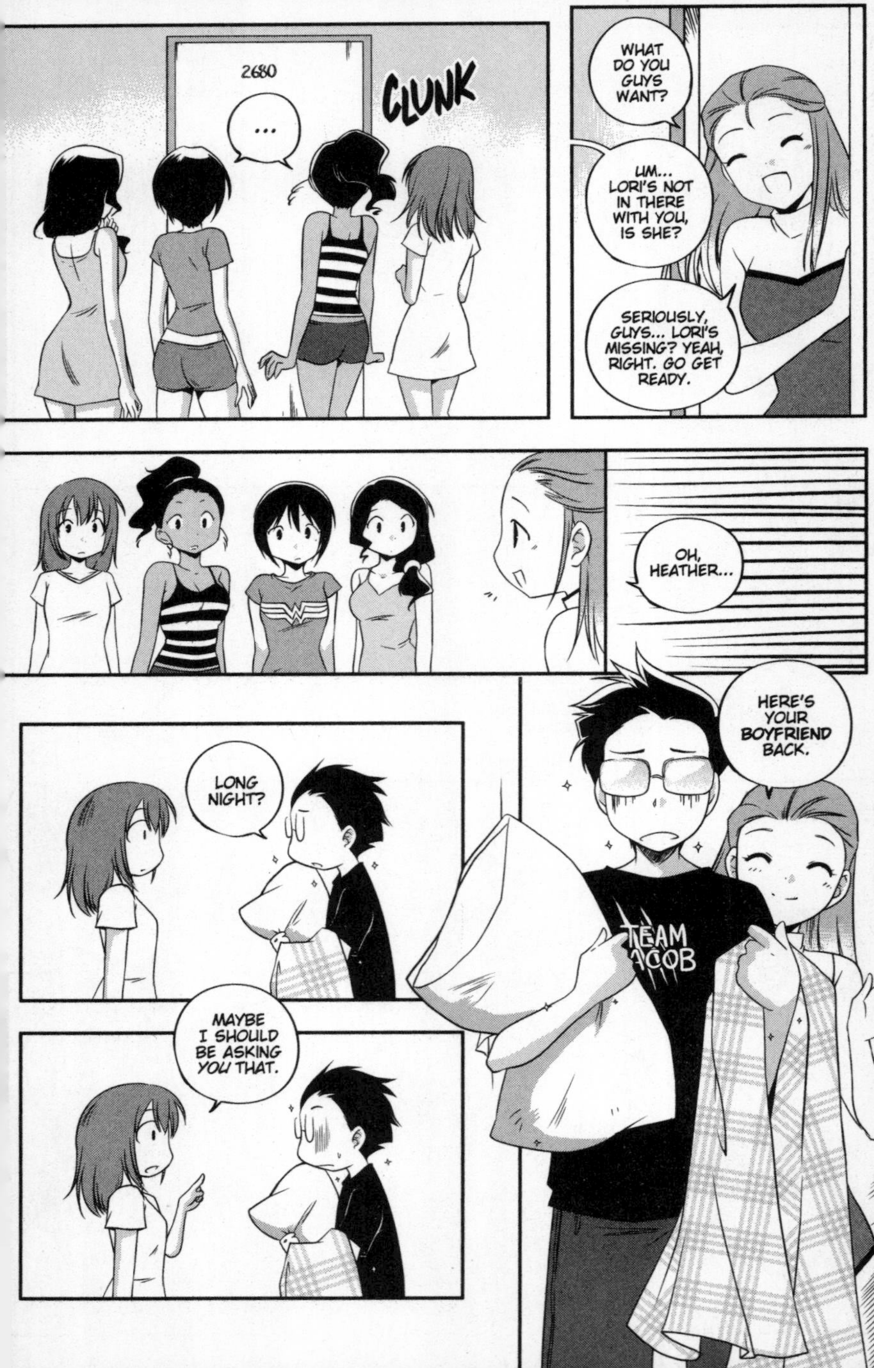
WHAT DO YOU GUYS WANT?
UM... LORI'S NOT IN THERE WITH YOU, IS SHE?
SERIOUSLY, GUYS... LORI'S MISSING? YEAH, RIGHT. GO GET READY.
2680
CLUNK
...
OH, HEATHER...
HERE'S YOUR BOYFRIEND BACK.
TEAM
ACOB
LONG NIGHT?
MAYBE I SHOULD BE ASKING *YOU* THAT.

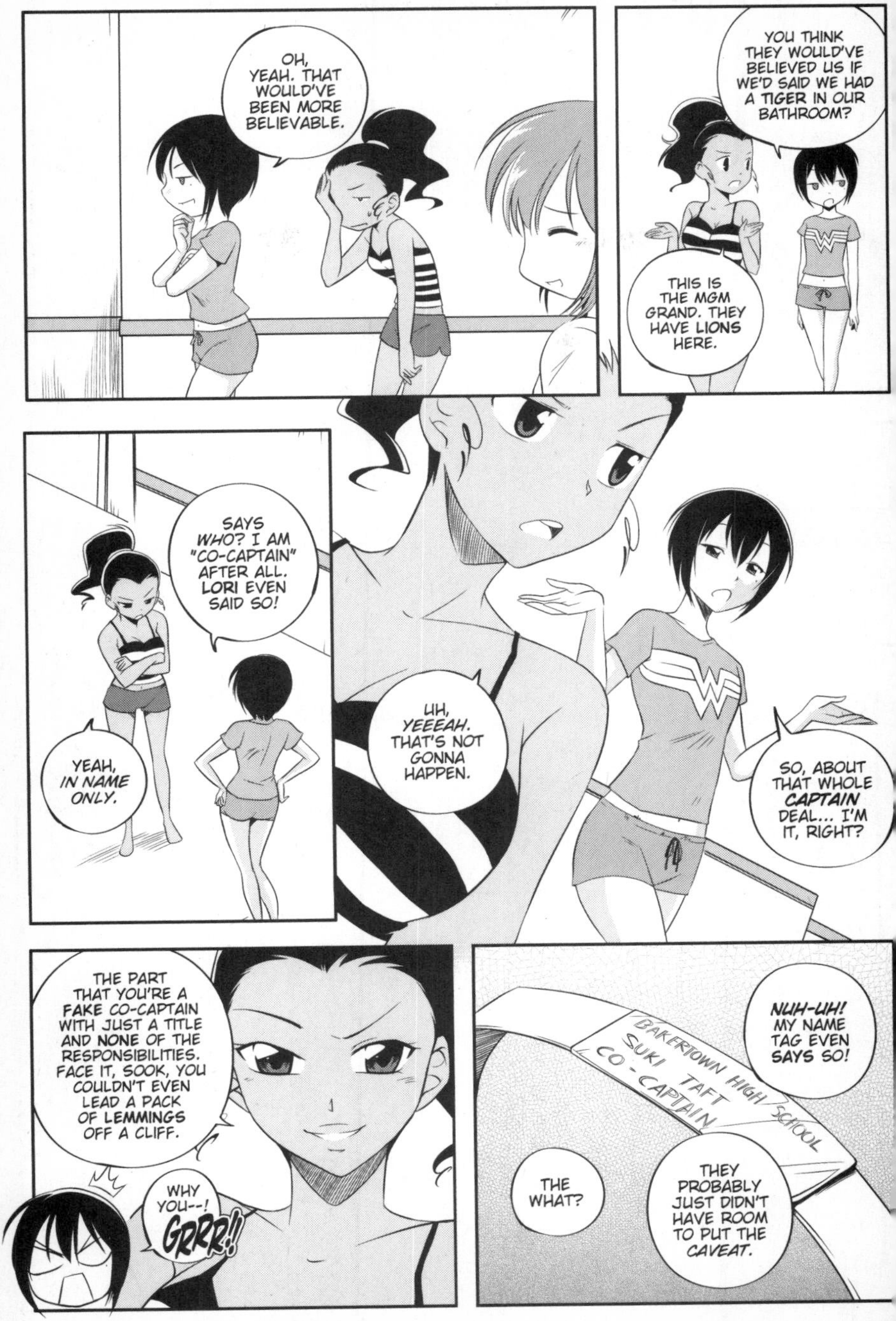
YOU THINK THEY WOULD'VE BELIEVED US IF WE'D SAID WE HAD A **TIGER** IN OUR BATHROOM?
THIS IS THE MGM GRAND. THEY HAVE **LIONS** HERE.
OH, YEAH. THAT WOULD'VE BEEN MORE BELIEVABLE.
SO, ABOUT THAT WHOLE ***CAPTAIN*** DEAL... I'M IT, RIGHT?
UH, *YEEEAH.* THAT'S NOT GONNA HAPPEN.
SAYS *WHO?* I AM "CO-CAPTAIN" AFTER ALL. **LORI** EVEN SAID SO!
YEAH, *IN NAME ONLY.*
NUH-UH! MY NAME TAG EVEN **SAYS** SO!
BAKERTOWN HIGH SCHOOL
SUKI TAFT
CO-CAPTAIN
THEY PROBABLY JUST DIDN'T HAVE ROOM TO PUT THE *CAVEAT.*
THE WHAT?
THE PART THAT YOU'RE A **FAKE** CO-CAPTAIN WITH JUST A TITLE AND **NONE** OF THE RESPONSIBILITIES. FACE IT, SOOK, YOU COULDN'T EVEN LEAD A PACK OF **LEMMINGS** OFF A CLIFF.
WHY YOU--!
GRRR!!

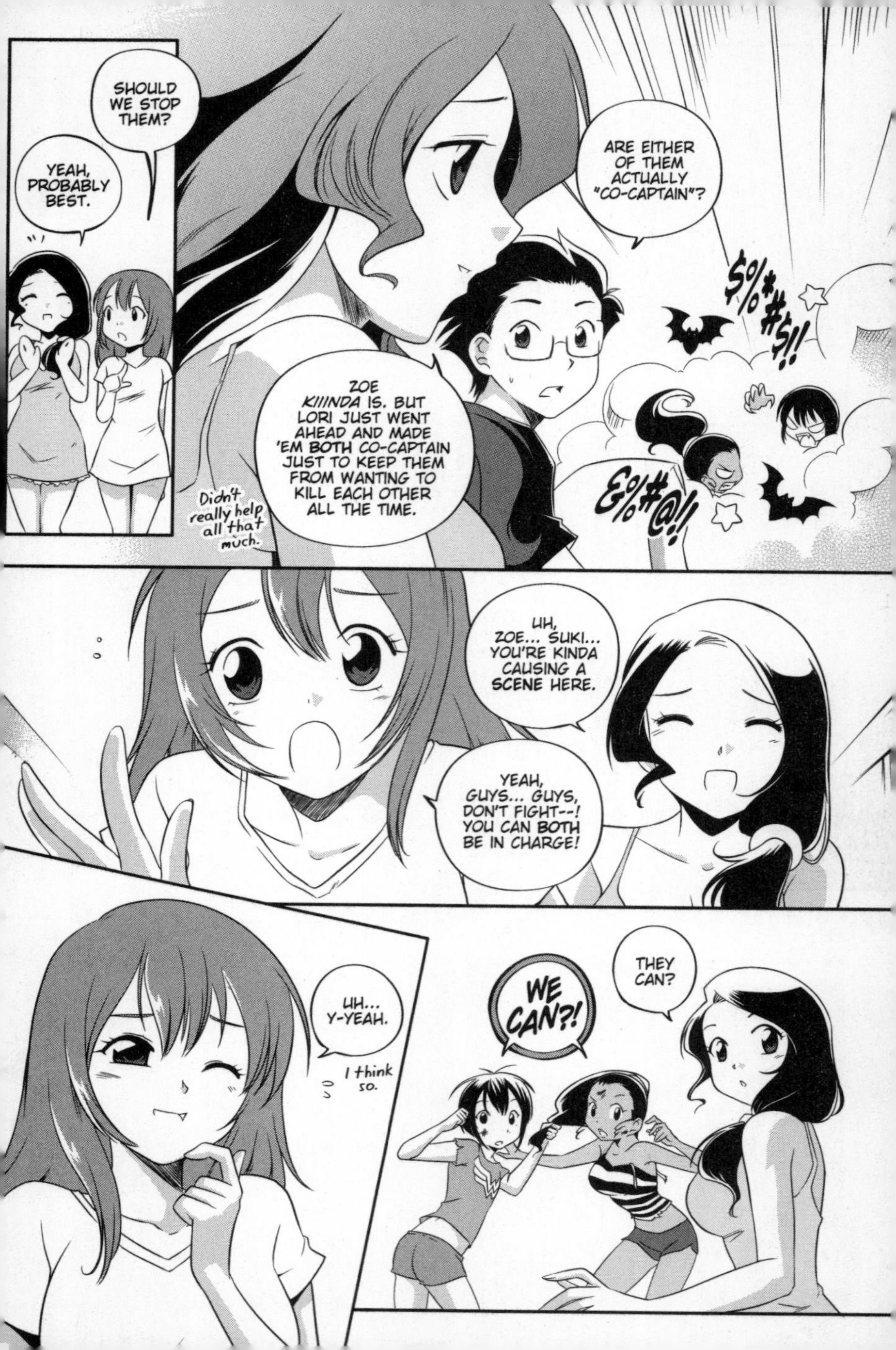
ARE EITHER OF THEM ACTUALLY "CO-CAPTAIN"?
$%*#$!!
ZOE *KIIINDA* IS. BUT LORI JUST WENT AHEAD AND MADE 'EM BOTH CO-CAPTAIN JUST TO KEEP THEM FROM WANTING TO KILL EACH OTHER ALL THE TIME.
&%#@!!
Didn't really help all that much.
SHOULD WE STOP THEM?
YEAH, PROBABLY BEST.
UH, ZOE... SUKI... YOU'RE KINDA CAUSING A SCENE HERE.
YEAH, GUYS... GUYS, DON'T FIGHT--! YOU CAN BOTH BE IN CHARGE!
THEY CAN?
WE CAN?!
UH... Y-YEAH.
I think so.

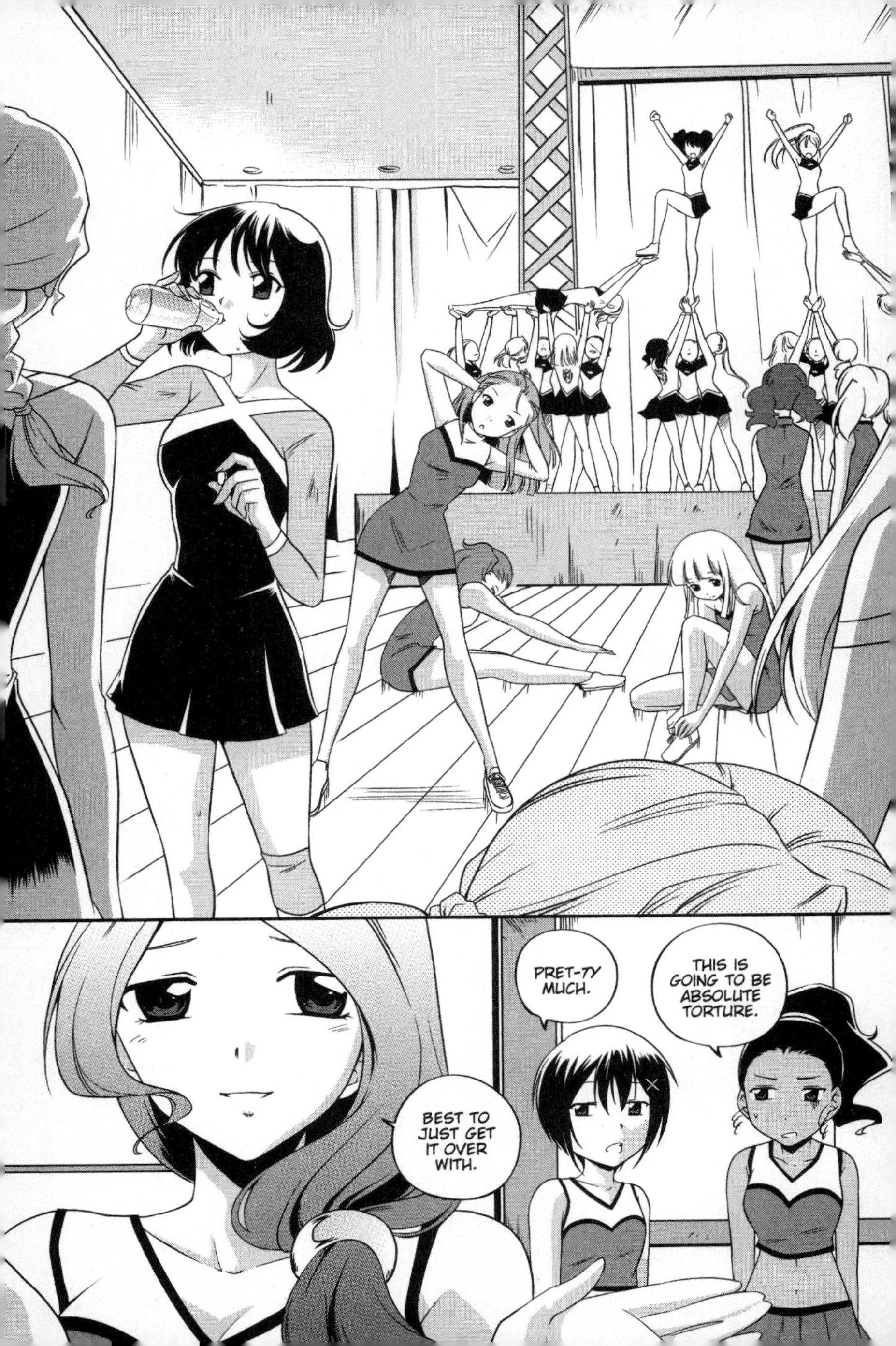
THIS IS GOING TO BE ABSOLUTE TORTURE.
PRET-TY MUCH.
BEST TO JUST GET IT OVER WITH.

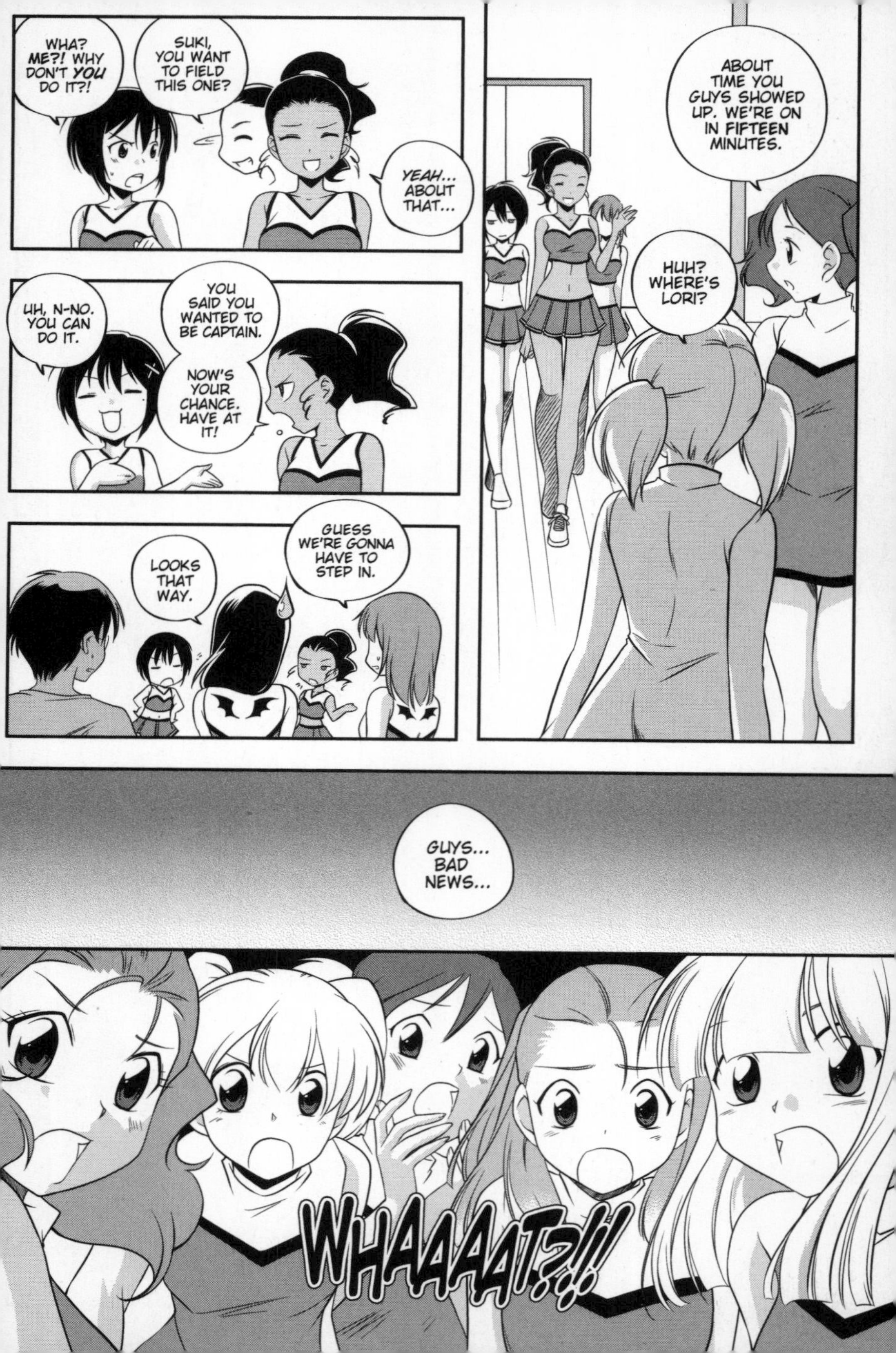
ABOUT TIME YOU GUYS SHOWED UP. WE'RE ON IN FIFTEEN MINUTES.
HUH? WHERE'S LORI?
SUKI, YOU WANT TO FIELD THIS ONE?
YEAH... ABOUT THAT...
WHA? ME?! WHY DON'T *YOU* DO IT?!
YOU SAID YOU WANTED TO BE CAPTAIN.
NOW'S YOUR CHANCE. HAVE AT IT!
UH, N-NO. YOU CAN DO IT.
GUESS WE'RE GONNA HAVE TO STEP IN.
LOOKS THAT WAY.
GUYS... BAD NEWS...
WHAAAAAT?!!

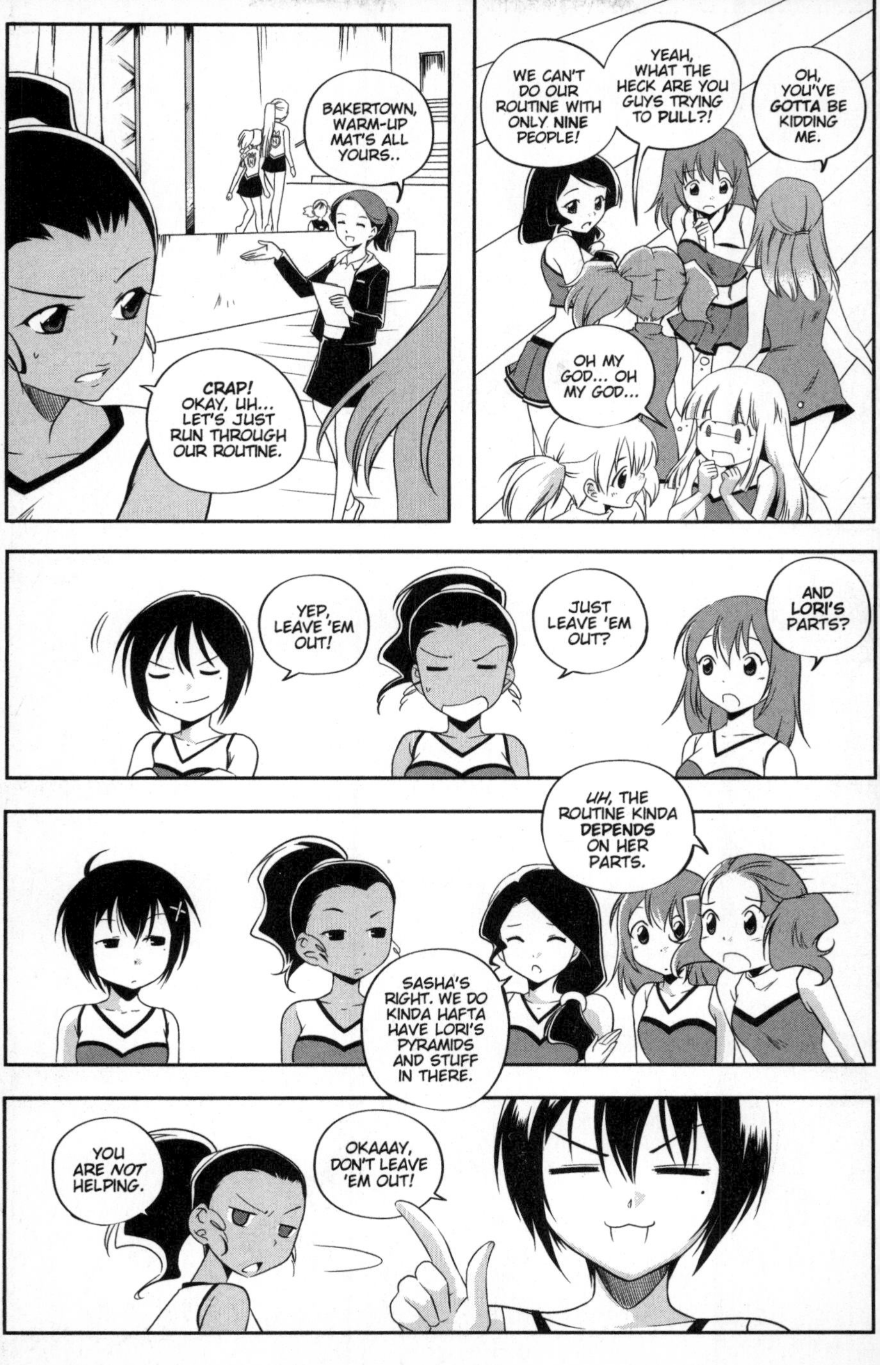
OH, YOU'VE GOTTA BE KIDDING ME.
YEAH, WHAT THE HECK ARE YOU GUYS TRYING TO **PULL**?!
WE CAN'T DO OUR ROUTINE WITH ONLY **NINE** PEOPLE!
OH MY GOD... OH MY GOD...
BAKERTOWN, WARM-UP MAT'S ALL YOURS..
CRAP! OKAY, UH... LET'S JUST RUN THROUGH OUR ROUTINE.
AND **LORI'S** PARTS?
JUST LEAVE 'EM OUT?
YEP, LEAVE 'EM OUT!
UH, THE ROUTINE KINDA **DEPENDS** ON HER PARTS.
SASHA'S RIGHT. WE DO KINDA HAFTA HAVE LORI'S PYRAMIDS AND STUFF IN THERE.
OKAAAY, DON'T LEAVE 'EM OUT!
YOU ARE *NOT* HELPING.

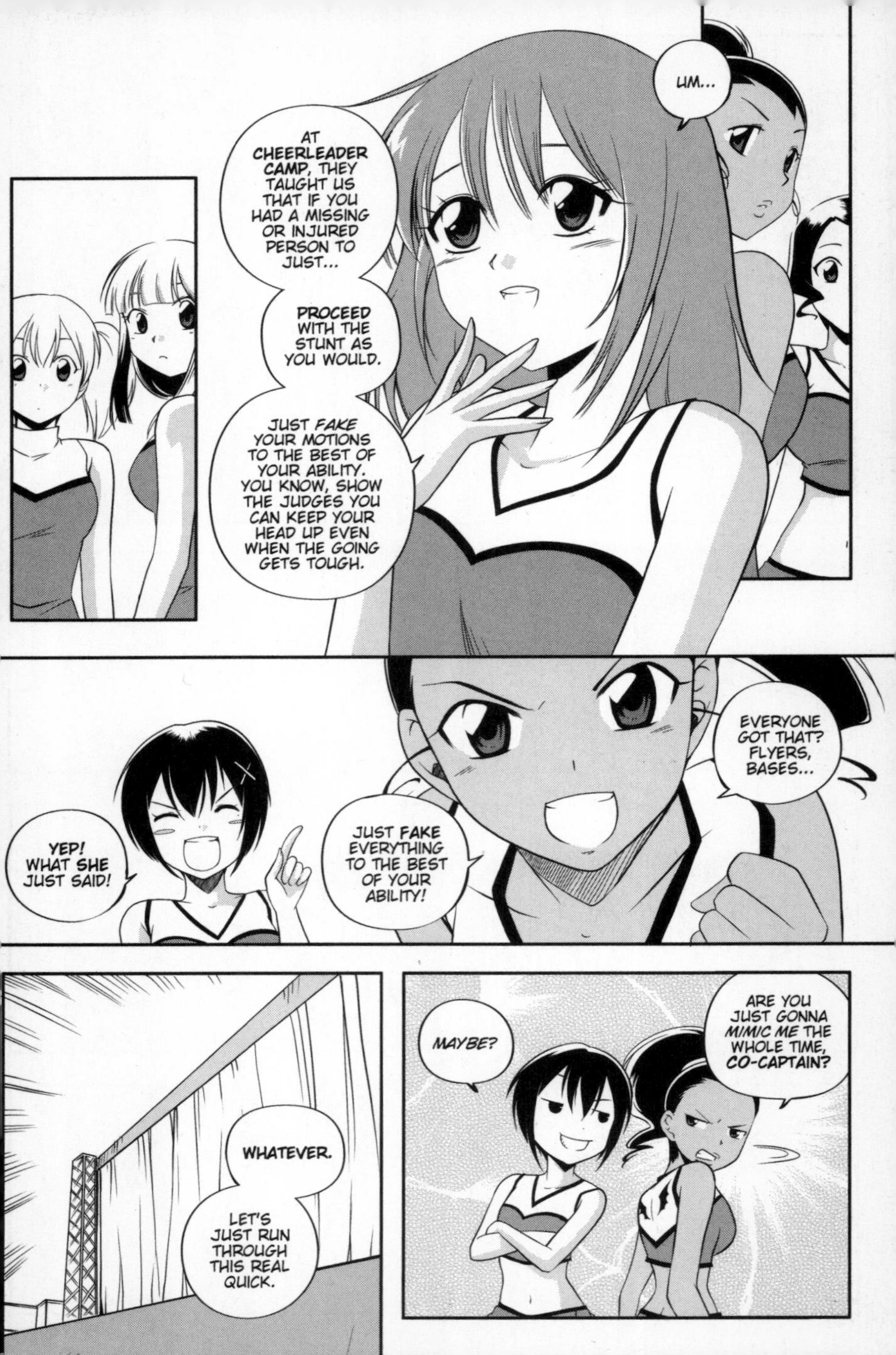
UM...
AT CHEERLEADER CAMP, THEY TAUGHT US THAT IF YOU HAD A MISSING OR INJURED PERSON TO JUST...
PROCEED WITH THE STUNT AS YOU WOULD.
JUST *FAKE* YOUR MOTIONS TO THE BEST OF YOUR ABILITY. YOU KNOW, SHOW THE JUDGES YOU CAN KEEP YOUR HEAD UP EVEN WHEN THE GOING GETS TOUGH.
EVERYONE GOT THAT? FLYERS, BASES...
JUST FAKE EVERYTHING TO THE BEST OF YOUR ABILITY!
YEP! WHAT SHE JUST SAID!
ARE YOU JUST GONNA *MIMIC ME* THE WHOLE TIME, CO-CAPTAIN?
MAYBE?
WHATEVER.
LET'S JUST RUN THROUGH THIS REAL QUICK.

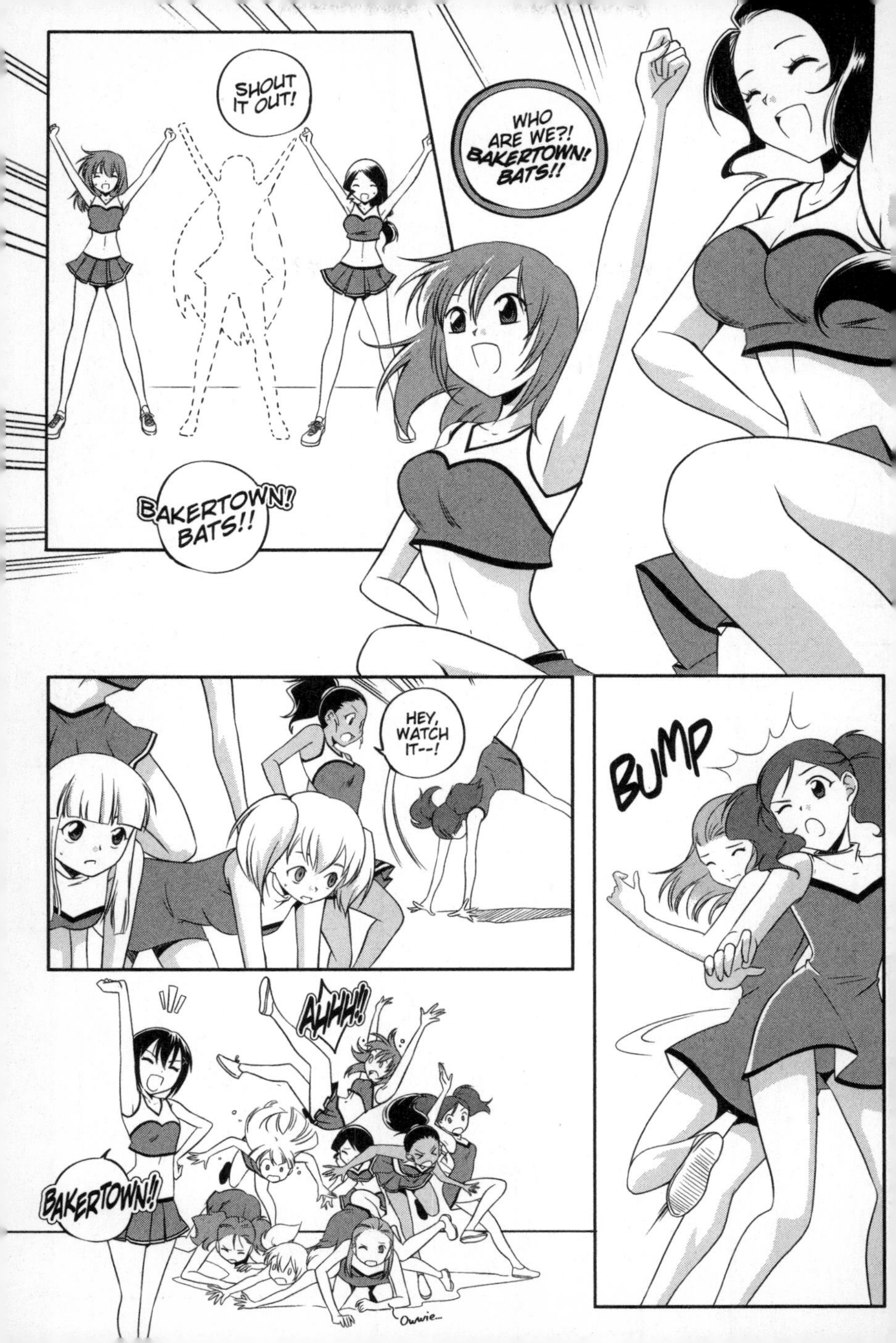
WHO ARE WE?! BAKERTOWN! BATS!!
SHOUT IT OUT!
BAKERTOWN! BATS!!
BUMP
HEY, WATCH IT--!
AHHH!!
BAKERTOWN!!
Owwie...

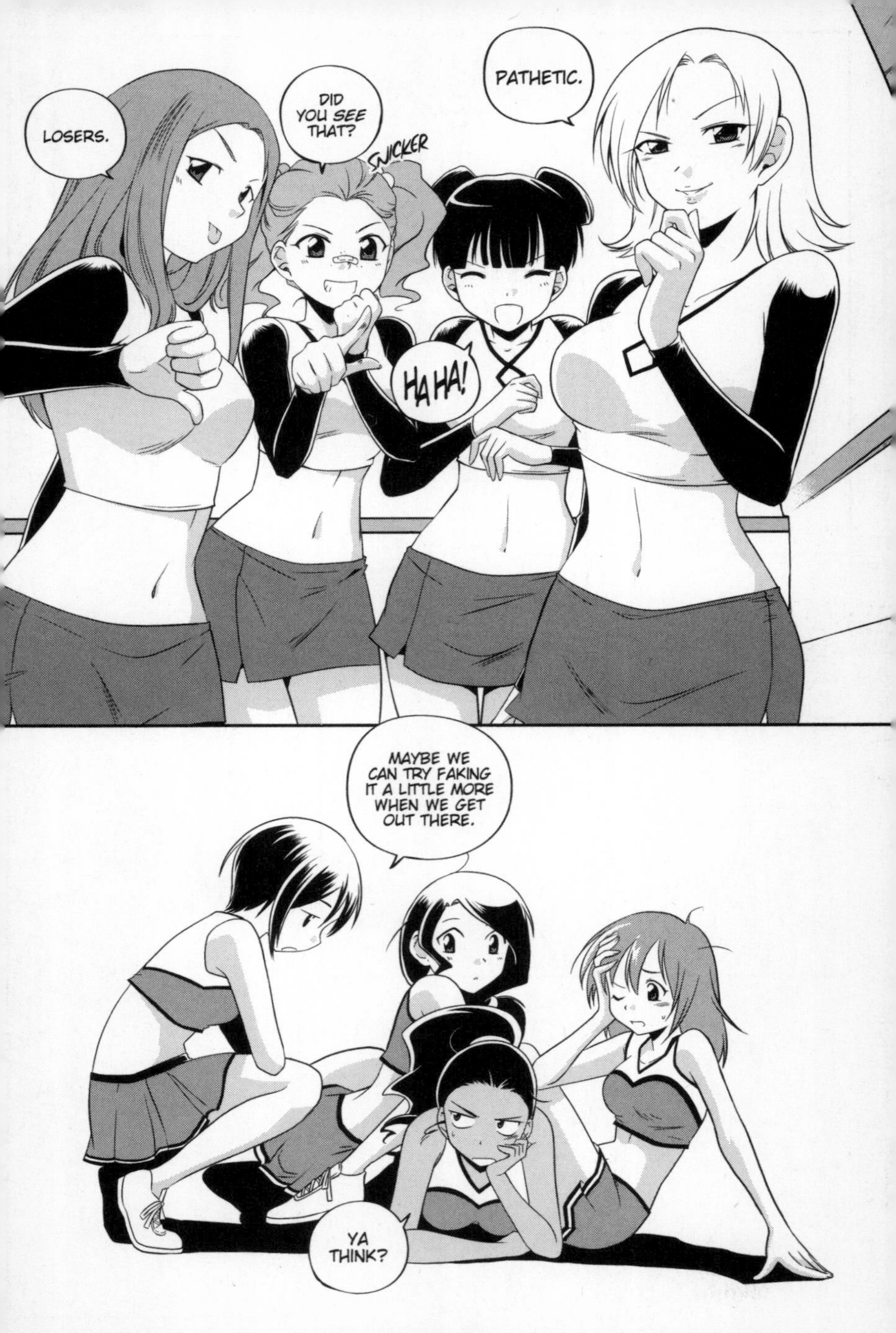
PATHETIC.
DID YOU SEE THAT?
LOSERS.
SNICKER
HA HA!
MAYBE WE CAN TRY FAKING IT A LITTLE MORE WHEN WE GET OUT THERE.
YA THINK?

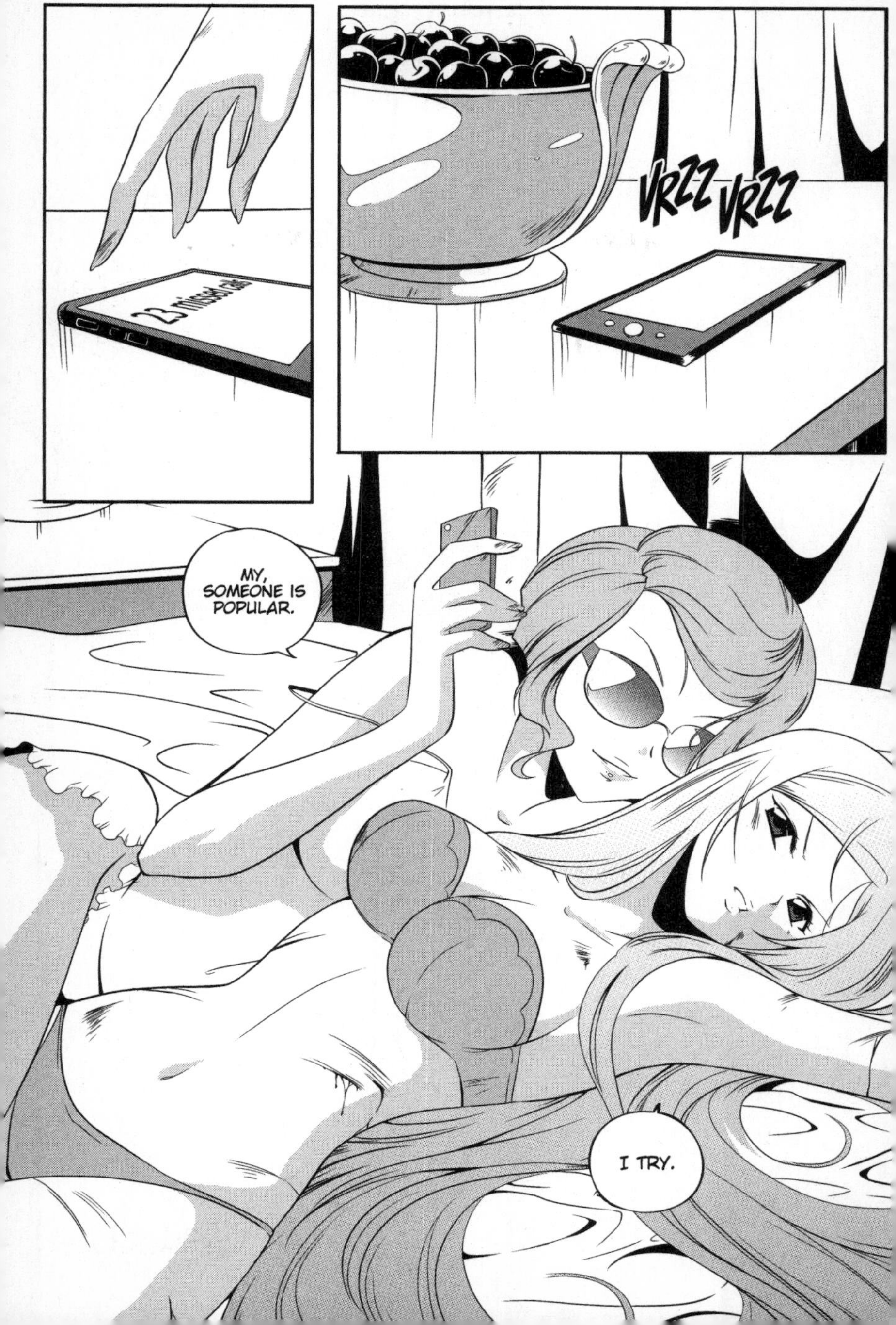
VRZZ VRZZ
23 missed calls
MY, SOMEONE IS POPULAR.
I TRY.

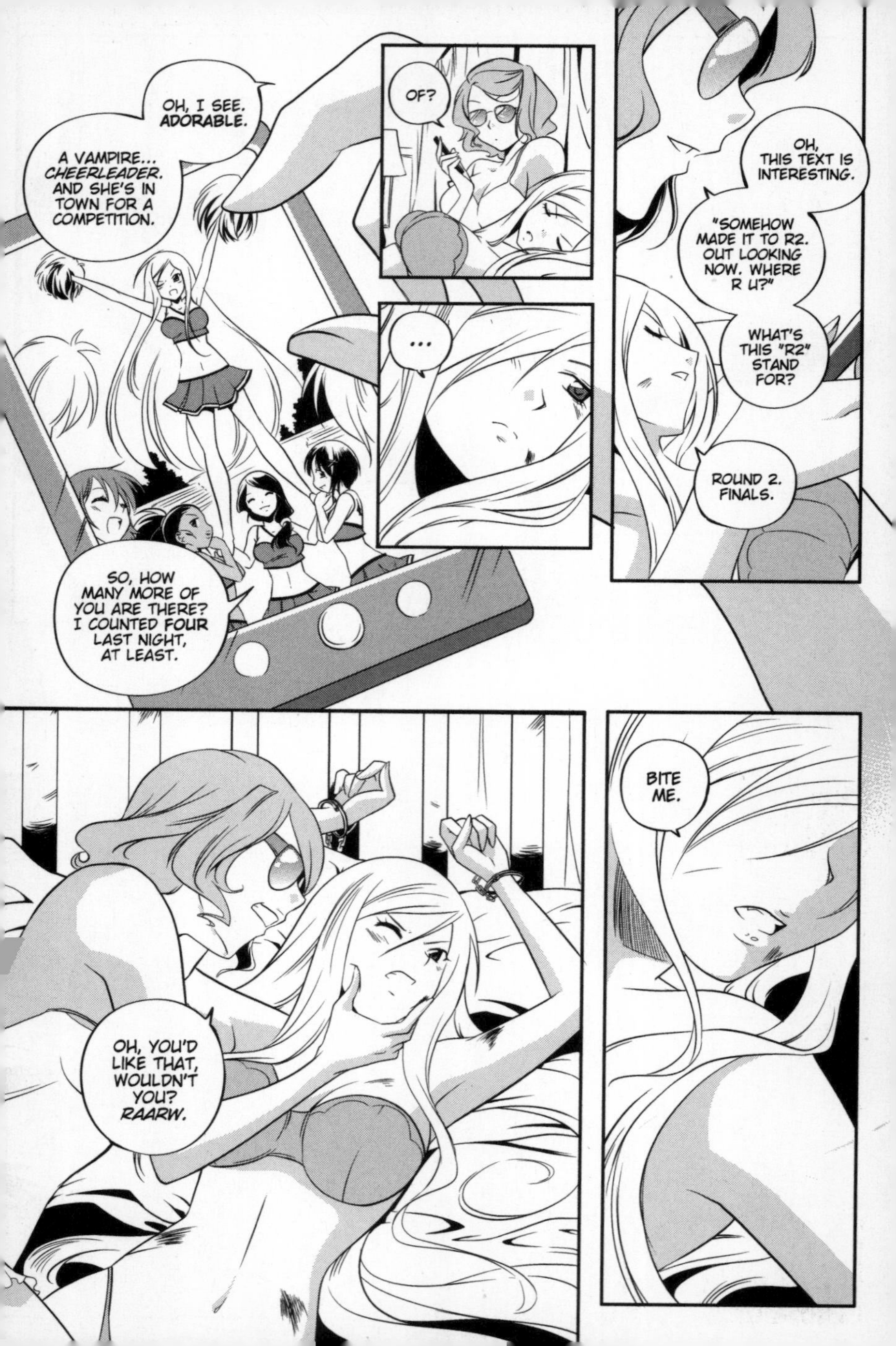

OH, THIS TEXT IS INTERESTING.
"SOMEHOW MADE IT TO R2. OUT LOOKING NOW. WHERE R U?"
WHAT'S THIS "R2" STAND FOR?
ROUND 2. FINALS.
OF?
...
OH, I SEE. ADORABLE.
A VAMPIRE... CHEERLEADER. AND SHE'S IN TOWN FOR A COMPETITION.
SO, HOW MANY MORE OF YOU ARE THERE? I COUNTED FOUR LAST NIGHT, AT LEAST.
BITE ME.
OH, YOU'D LIKE THAT, WOULDN'T YOU? RAARW.

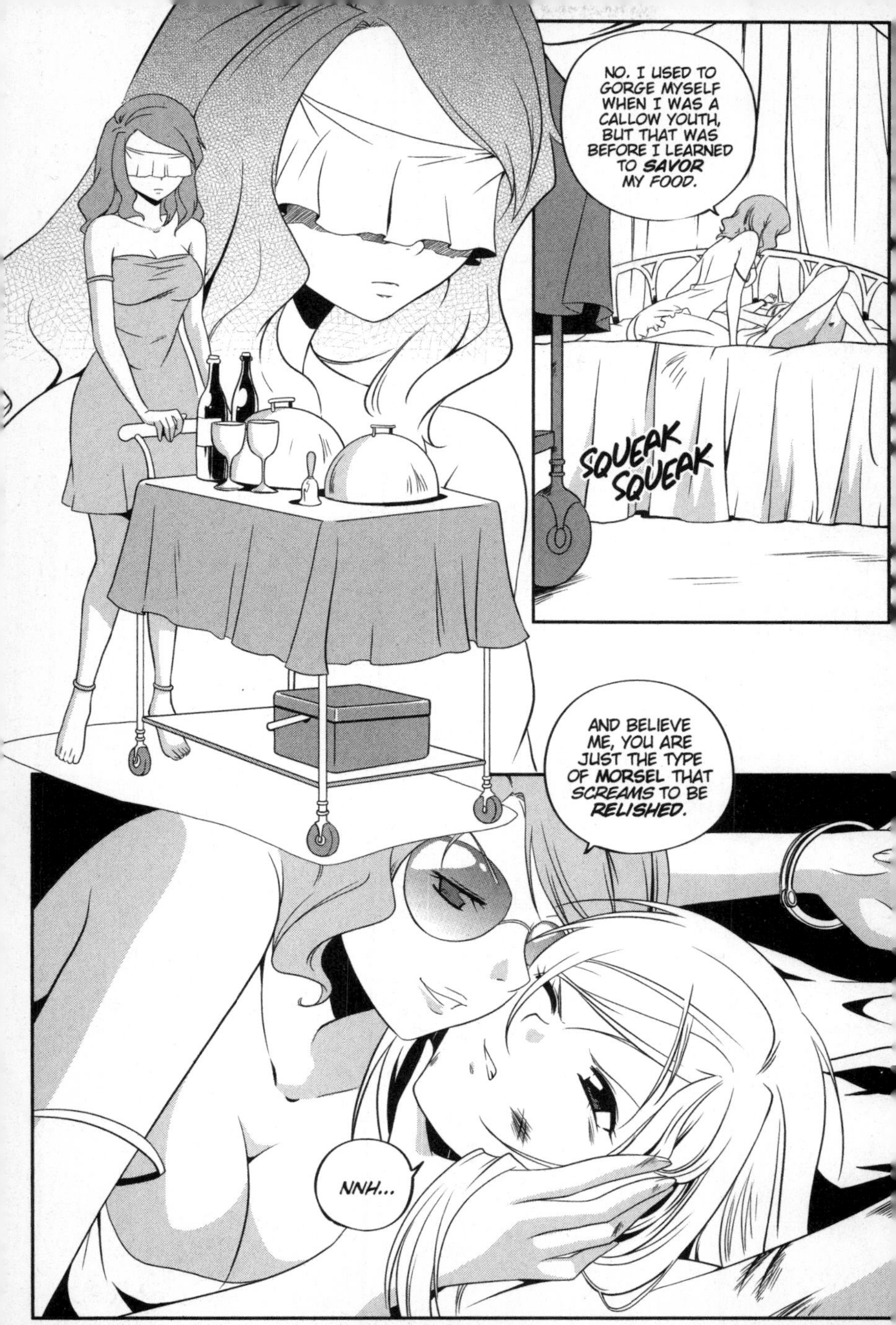
NO. I USED TO GORGE MYSELF WHEN I WAS A CALLOW YOUTH, BUT THAT WAS BEFORE I LEARNED TO **SAVOR** MY *FOOD*.
SQUEAK SQUEAK
AND BELIEVE ME, YOU ARE JUST THE TYPE OF **MORSEL** THAT *SCREAMS* TO BE ***RELISHED***.
NNH...

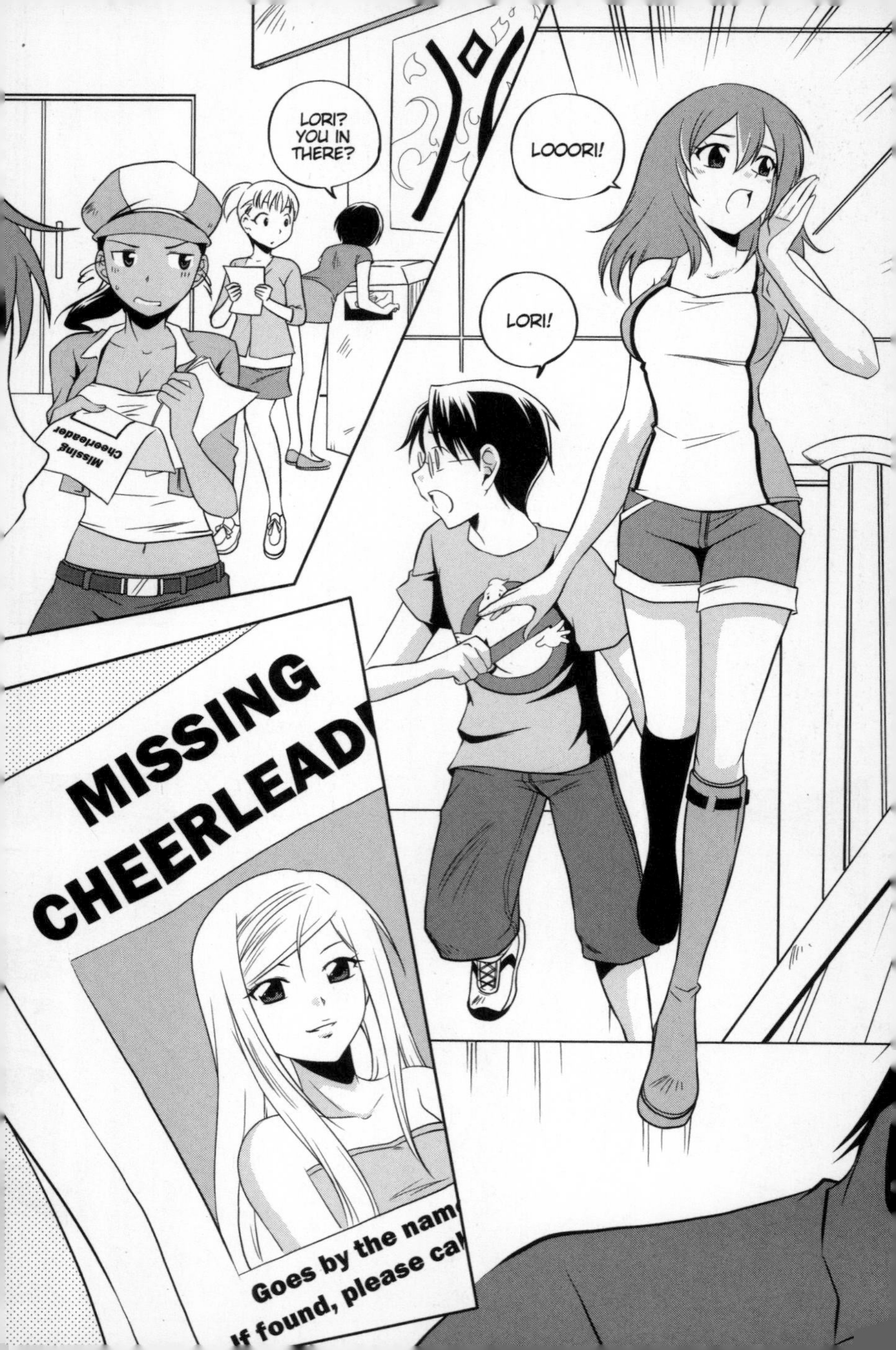

LOOORI!
LORI!
LORI? YOU IN THERE?
Missing Cheerleader
MISSING
CHEERLEAD
Goes by the nam
If found, please ca

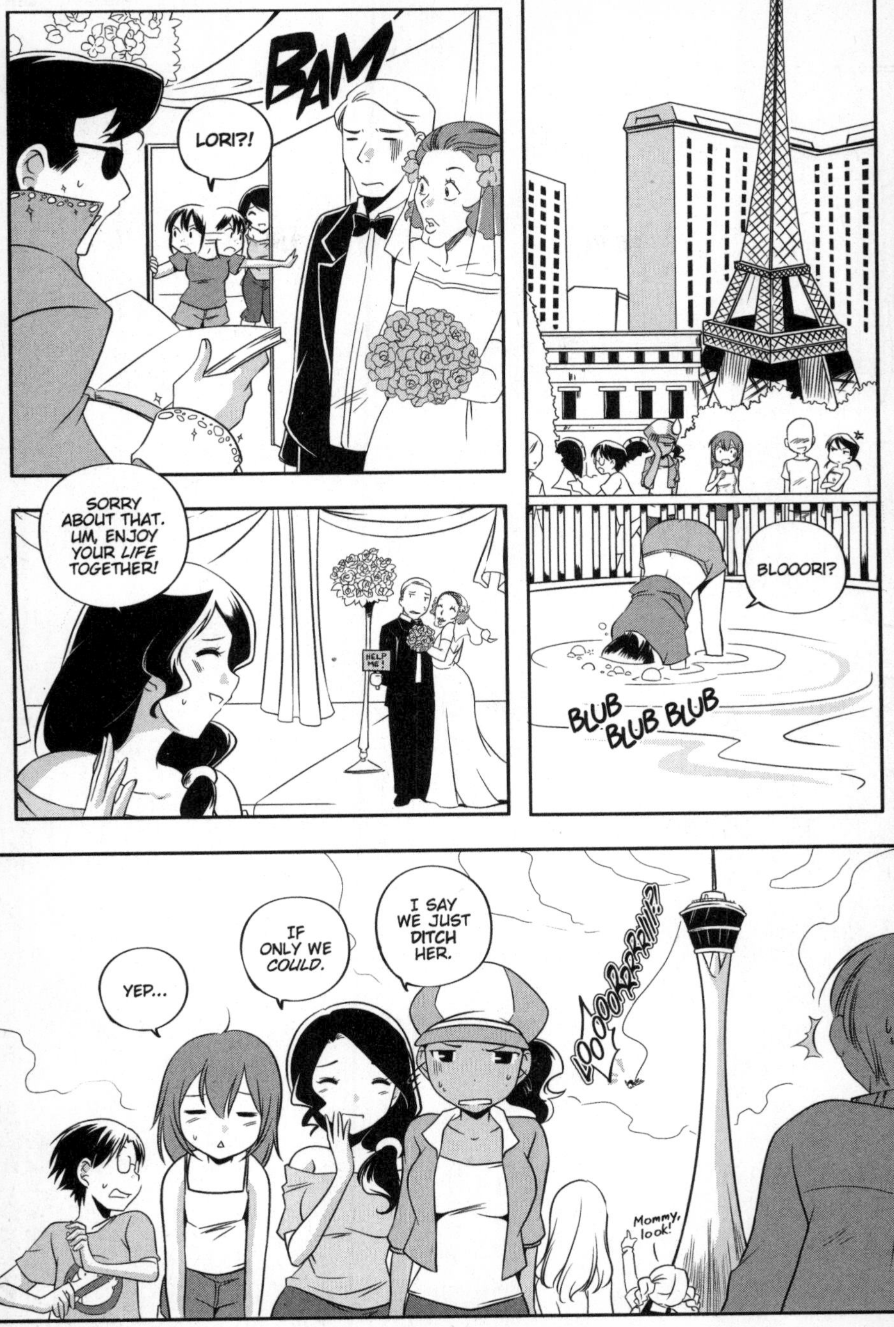
BAM
LORI?!
BLOOORI?
BLUB BLUB BLUB
SORRY ABOUT THAT. UM, ENJOY YOUR *LIFE* TOGETHER!
HELP ME!
LOOOORRRIII?!
Mommy, look!
I SAY WE JUST DITCH HER.
IF ONLY WE COULD.
YEP...

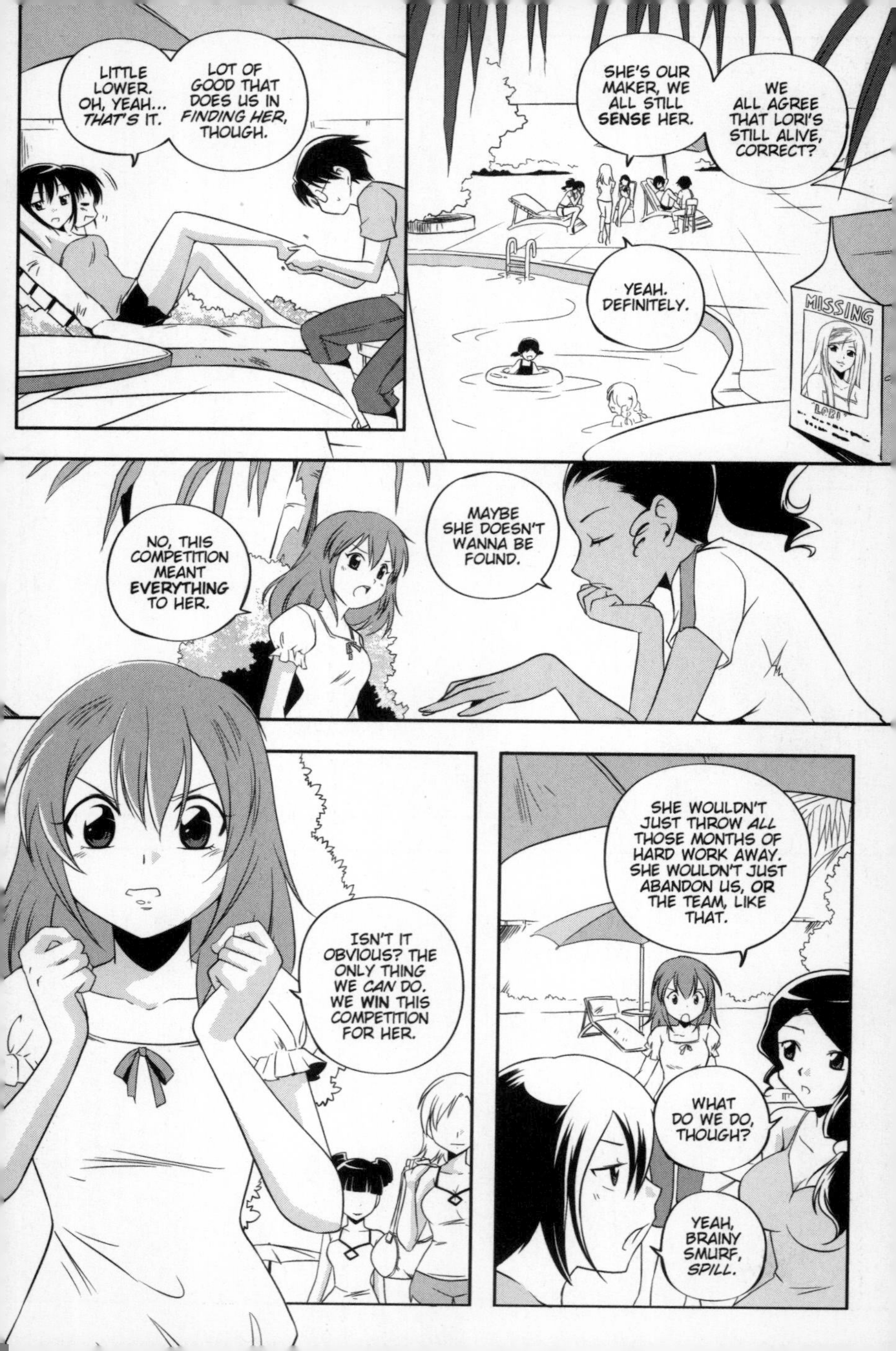

WE ALL AGREE THAT LORI'S STILL ALIVE, CORRECT?
SHE'S OUR MAKER, WE ALL STILL SENSE HER.
YEAH. DEFINITELY.
MISSING
LORI
LOT OF GOOD THAT DOES US IN *FINDING HER*, THOUGH.
LITTLE LOWER. OH, YEAH... *THAT'S* IT.
MAYBE SHE DOESN'T WANNA BE FOUND.
NO, THIS COMPETITION MEANT **EVERYTHING** TO HER.
SHE WOULDN'T JUST THROW *ALL* THOSE MONTHS OF HARD WORK AWAY. SHE WOULDN'T JUST ABANDON US, OR THE TEAM, LIKE THAT.
WHAT DO WE DO, THOUGH?
YEAH, BRAINY SMURF, *SPILL*.
ISN'T IT OBVIOUS? THE ONLY THING WE *CAN* DO. WE **WIN** THIS COMPETITION FOR HER.

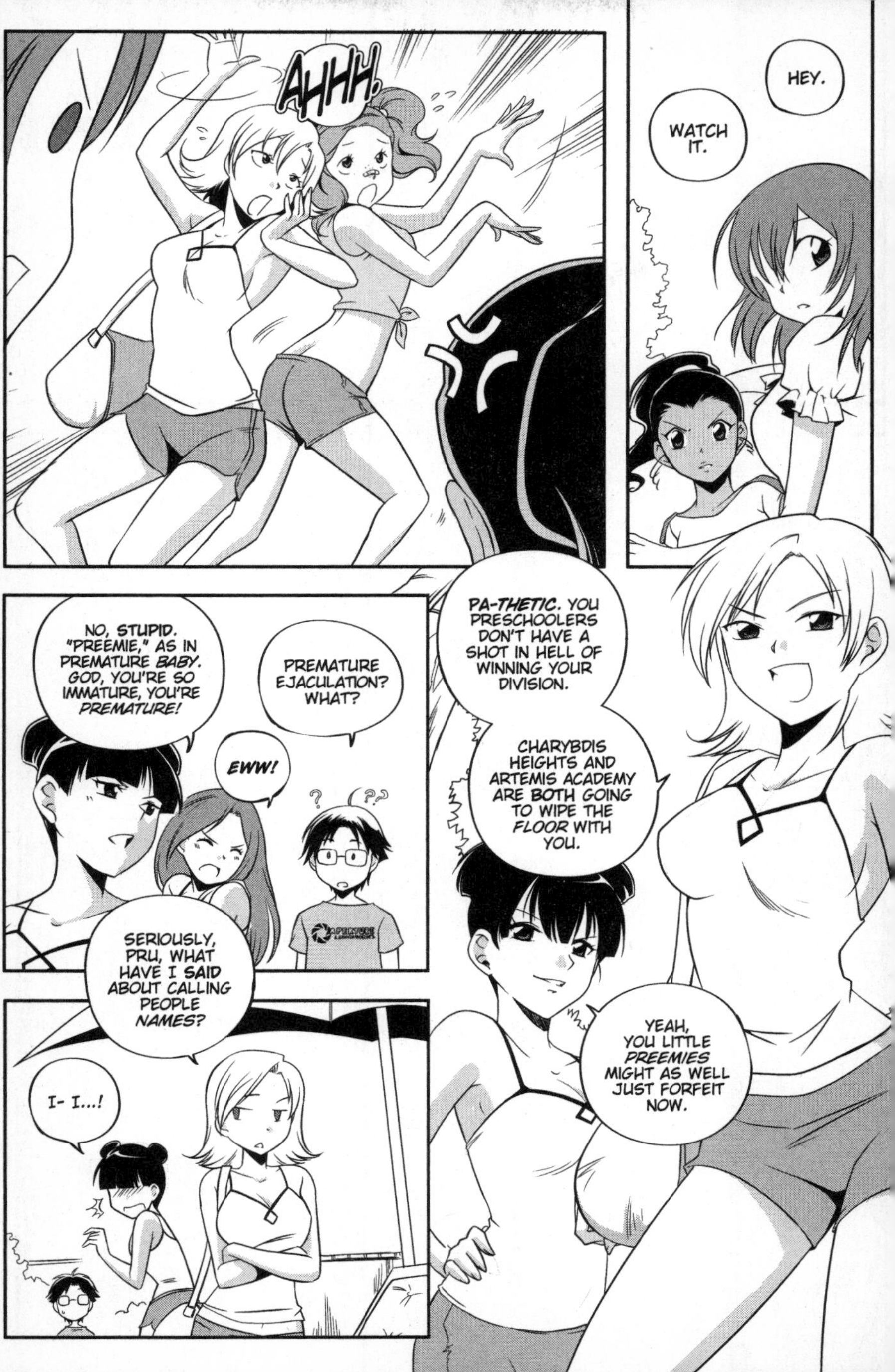
HEY.
WATCH IT.
AHHH
PA-THETIC. YOU PRESCHOOLERS DON'T HAVE A SHOT IN HELL OF WINNING YOUR DIVISION.
CHARYBDIS HEIGHTS AND ARTEMIS ACADEMY ARE BOTH GOING TO WIPE THE FLOOR WITH YOU.
YEAH, YOU LITTLE PREEMIES MIGHT AS WELL JUST FORFEIT NOW.
PREMATURE EJACULATION? WHAT?
NO, STUPID. "PREEMIE," AS IN PREMATURE BABY. GOD, YOU'RE SO IMMATURE, YOU'RE PREMATURE!
EWW!
SERIOUSLY, PRU, WHAT HAVE I SAID ABOUT CALLING PEOPLE NAMES?
I- I...!

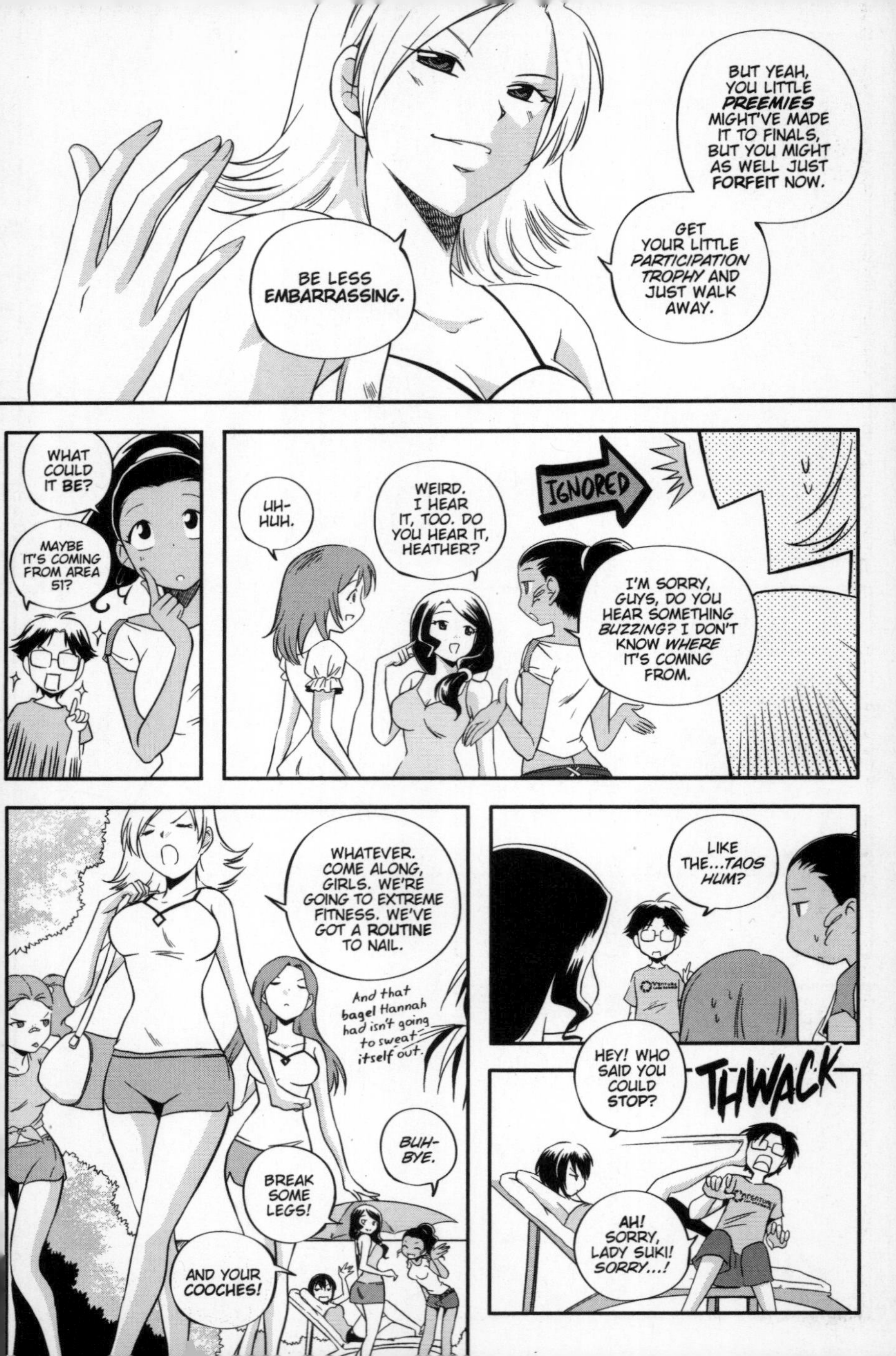
BUT YEAH, YOU LITTLE **PREEMIES** MIGHT'VE MADE IT TO FINALS, BUT YOU MIGHT AS WELL JUST **FORFEIT** NOW.
GET YOUR LITTLE *PARTICIPATION TROPHY* AND JUST WALK AWAY.
BE LESS **EMBARRASSING.**
IGNORED
I'M SORRY, GUYS, DO YOU HEAR SOMETHING *BUZZING*? I DON'T KNOW *WHERE* IT'S COMING FROM.
WEIRD. I HEAR IT, TOO. DO YOU HEAR IT, HEATHER?
UH-HUH.
WHAT COULD IT BE?
MAYBE IT'S COMING FROM AREA 51?
LIKE THE...*TAOS HUM*?
HEY! WHO SAID YOU COULD STOP?
THWACK
AH! SORRY, LADY SUKI! *SORRY...!*
WHATEVER. COME ALONG, GIRLS. WE'RE GOING TO EXTREME FITNESS. WE'VE GOT A **ROUTINE** TO NAIL.
And that bagel Hannah had isn't going to sweat itself out.
BUH-BYE.
BREAK SOME LEGS!
AND YOUR **COOCHES!**

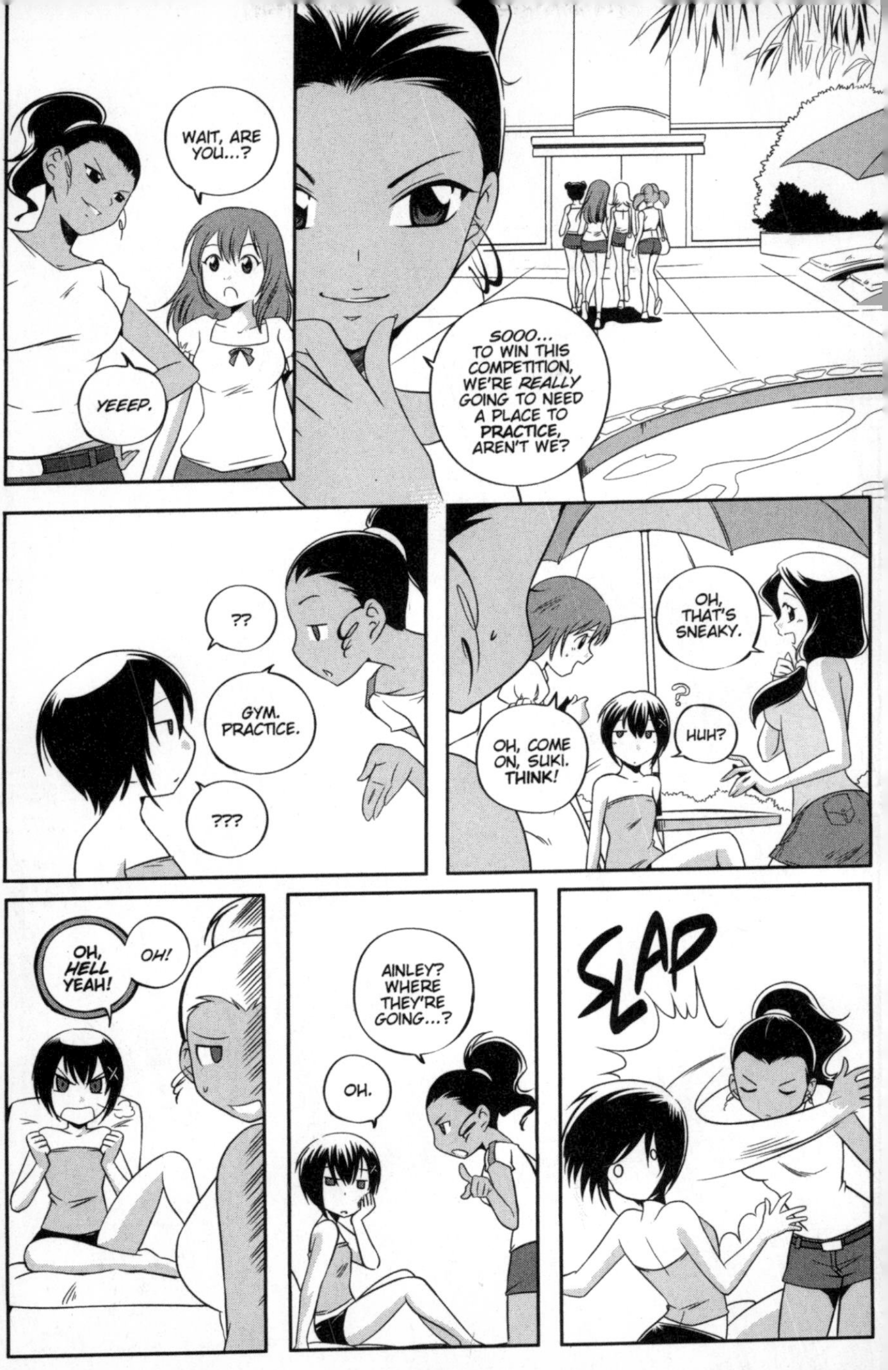
SOOO... TO WIN THIS COMPETITION, WE'RE *REALLY* GOING TO NEED A PLACE TO **PRACTICE**, AREN'T WE?
WAIT, ARE YOU...?
YEEEP.
OH, THAT'S SNEAKY.
HUH?
OH, COME ON, SUKI. **THINK!**
??
GYM. PRACTICE.
???
SLAP
AINLEY? WHERE THEY'RE GOING...?
OH.
OH!
OH, *HELL* YEAH!

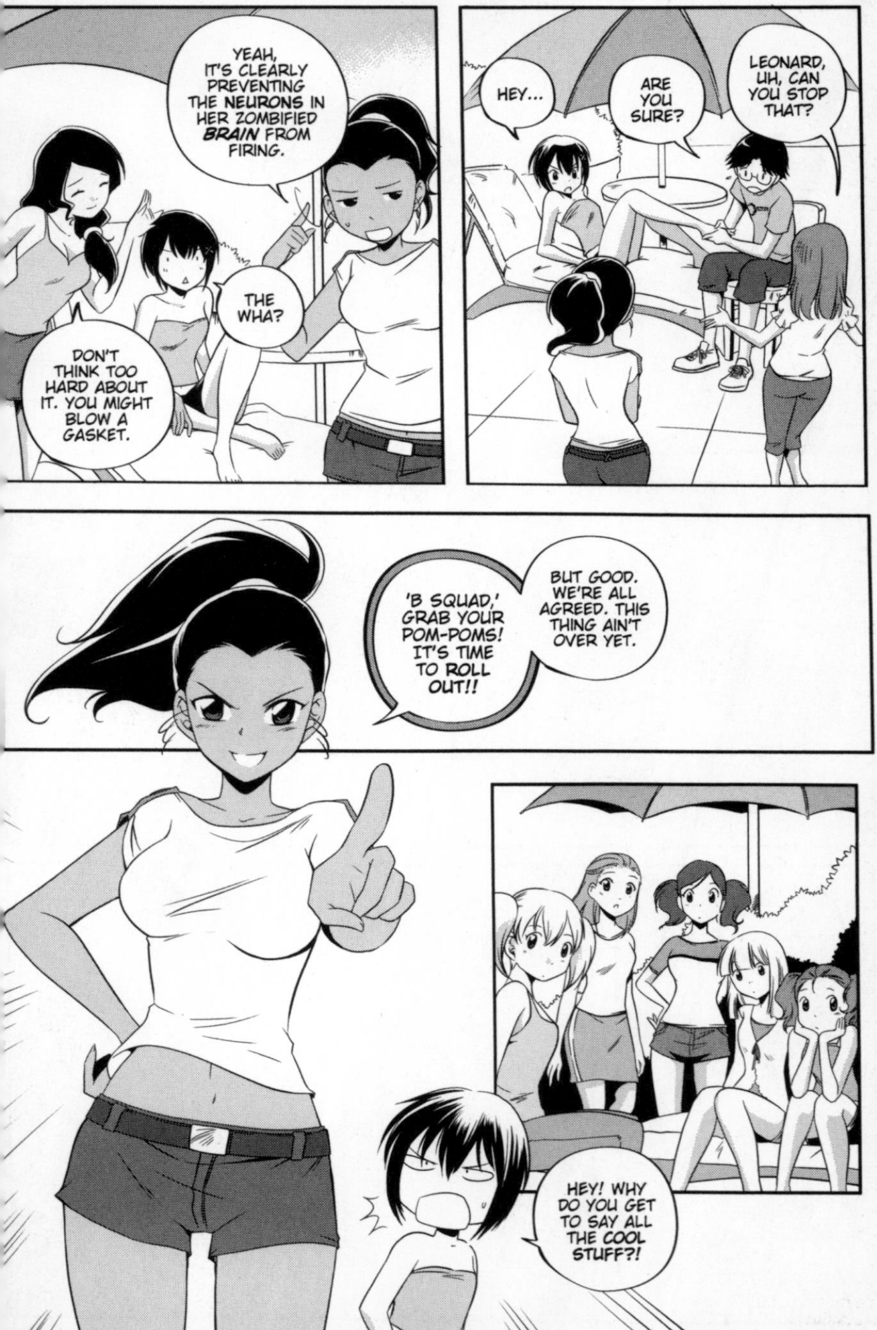
LEONARD, UH, CAN YOU STOP THAT?
ARE YOU SURE?
HEY...
YEAH, IT'S CLEARLY PREVENTING THE NEURONS IN HER ZOMBIFIED BRAIN FROM FIRING.
THE WHA?
DON'T THINK TOO HARD ABOUT IT. YOU MIGHT BLOW A GASKET.
BUT GOOD. WE'RE ALL AGREED. THIS THING AIN'T OVER YET.
'B SQUAD,' GRAB YOUR POM-POMS! IT'S TIME TO ROLL OUT!!
HEY! WHY DO YOU GET TO SAY ALL THE COOL STUFF?!

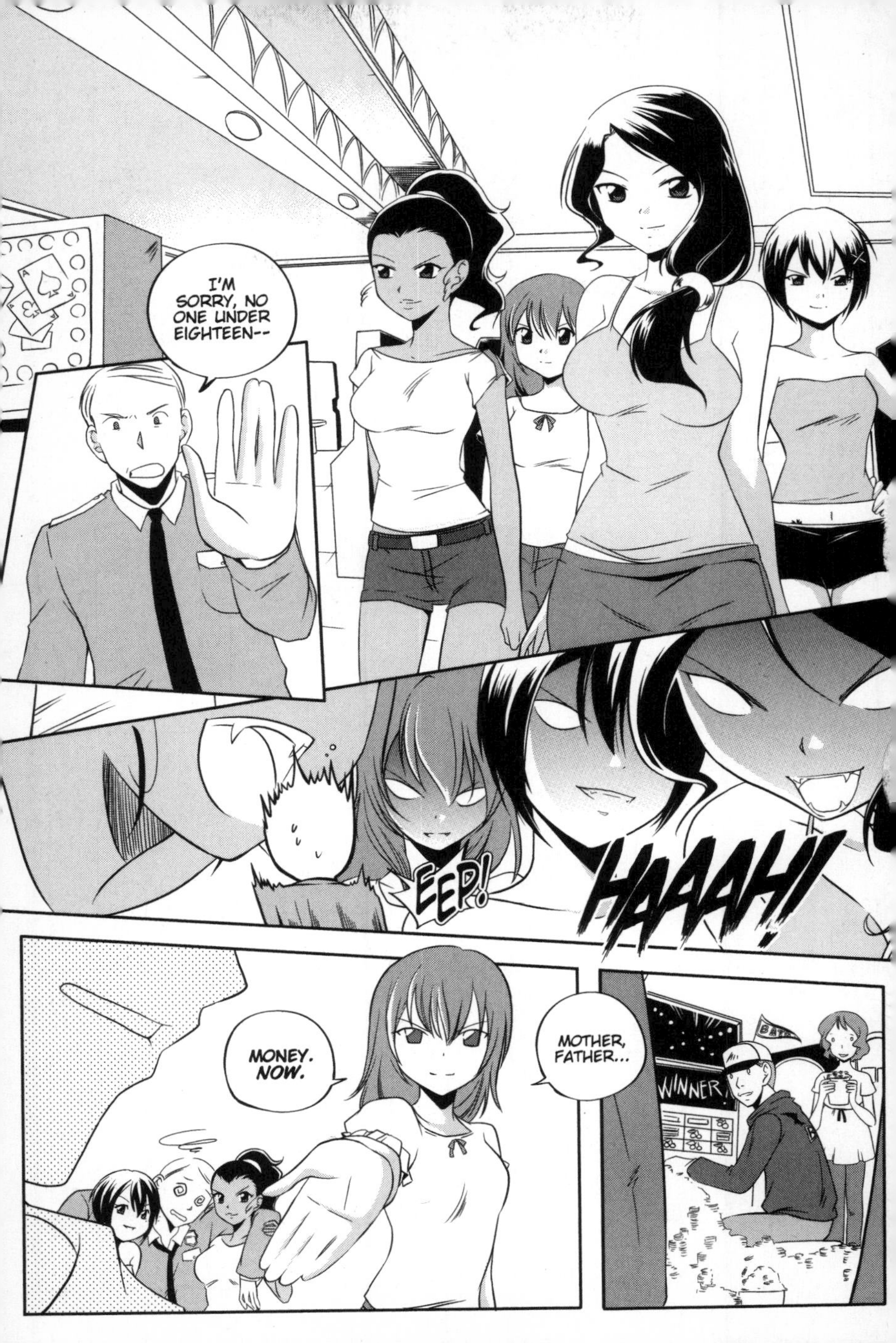

I'M SORRY, NO ONE UNDER EIGHTEEN--
HAAAH!
EEP!
WINNER
MOTHER, FATHER...
MONEY. NOW.

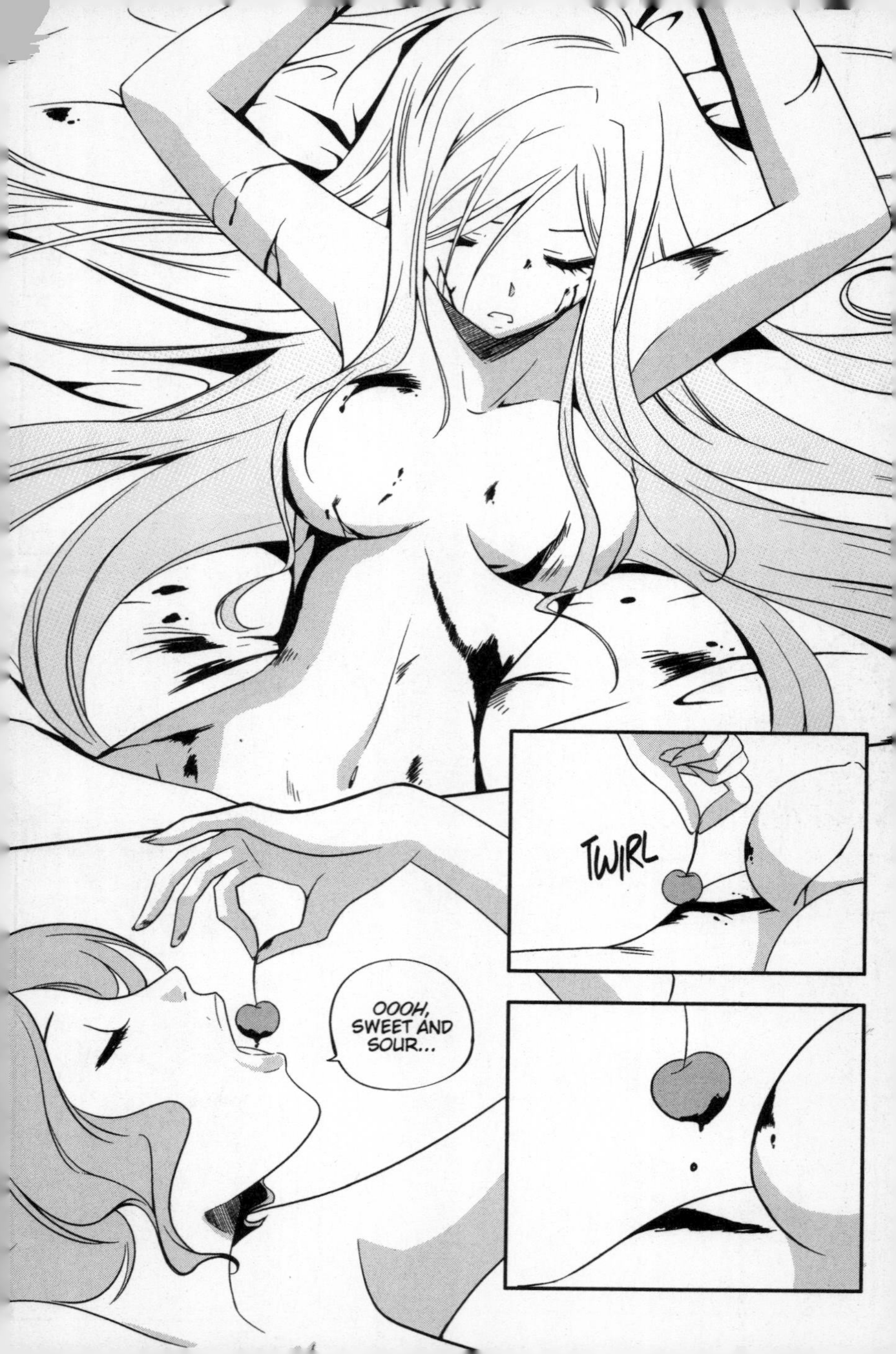
TWIRL
OOOH, SWEET AND SOUR...

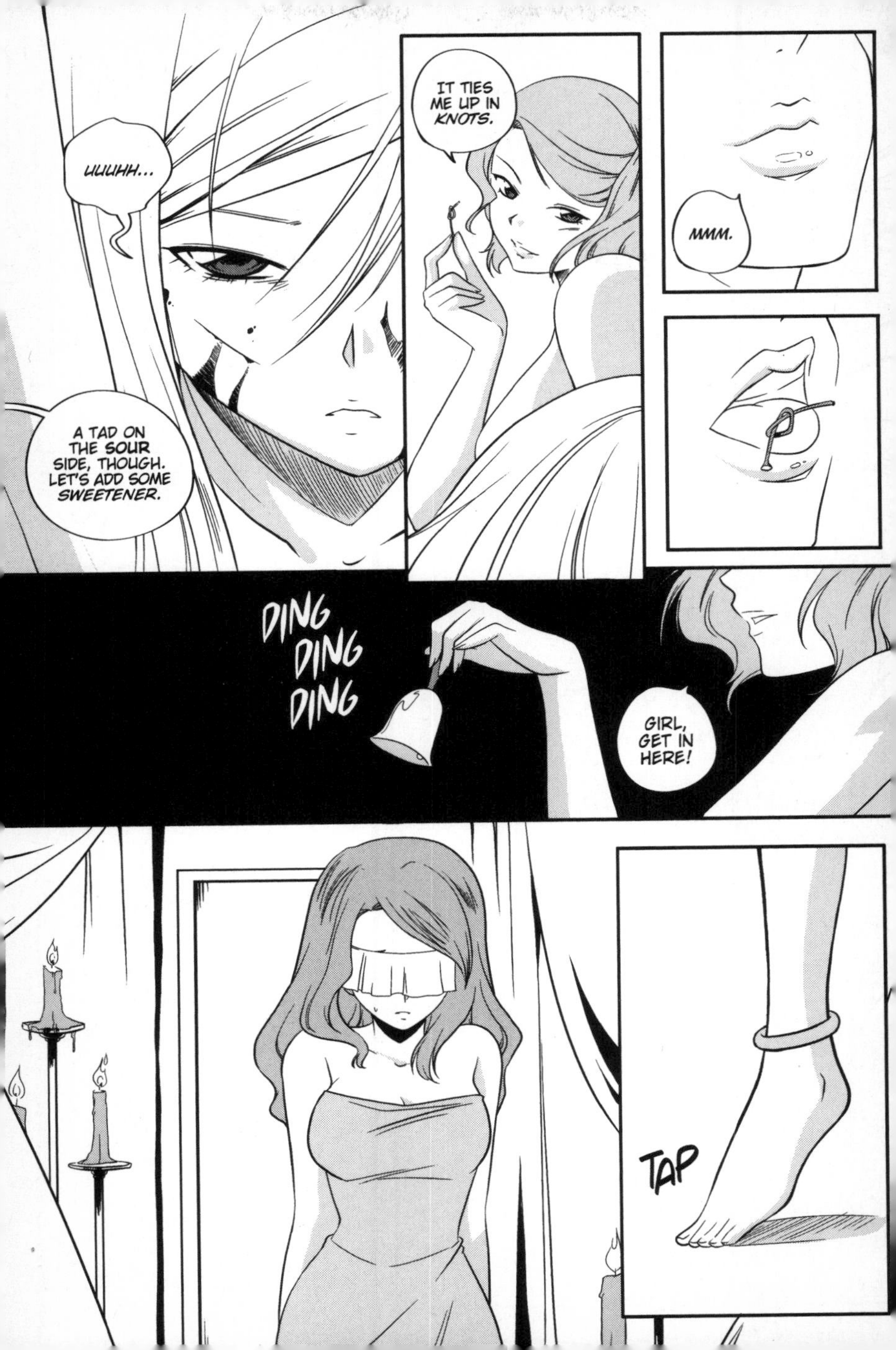
MMM.
IT TIES ME UP IN KNOTS.
UUUHH...
A TAD ON THE SOUR SIDE, THOUGH. LET'S ADD SOME SWEETENER.
GIRL, GET IN HERE!
DING DING DING
TAP

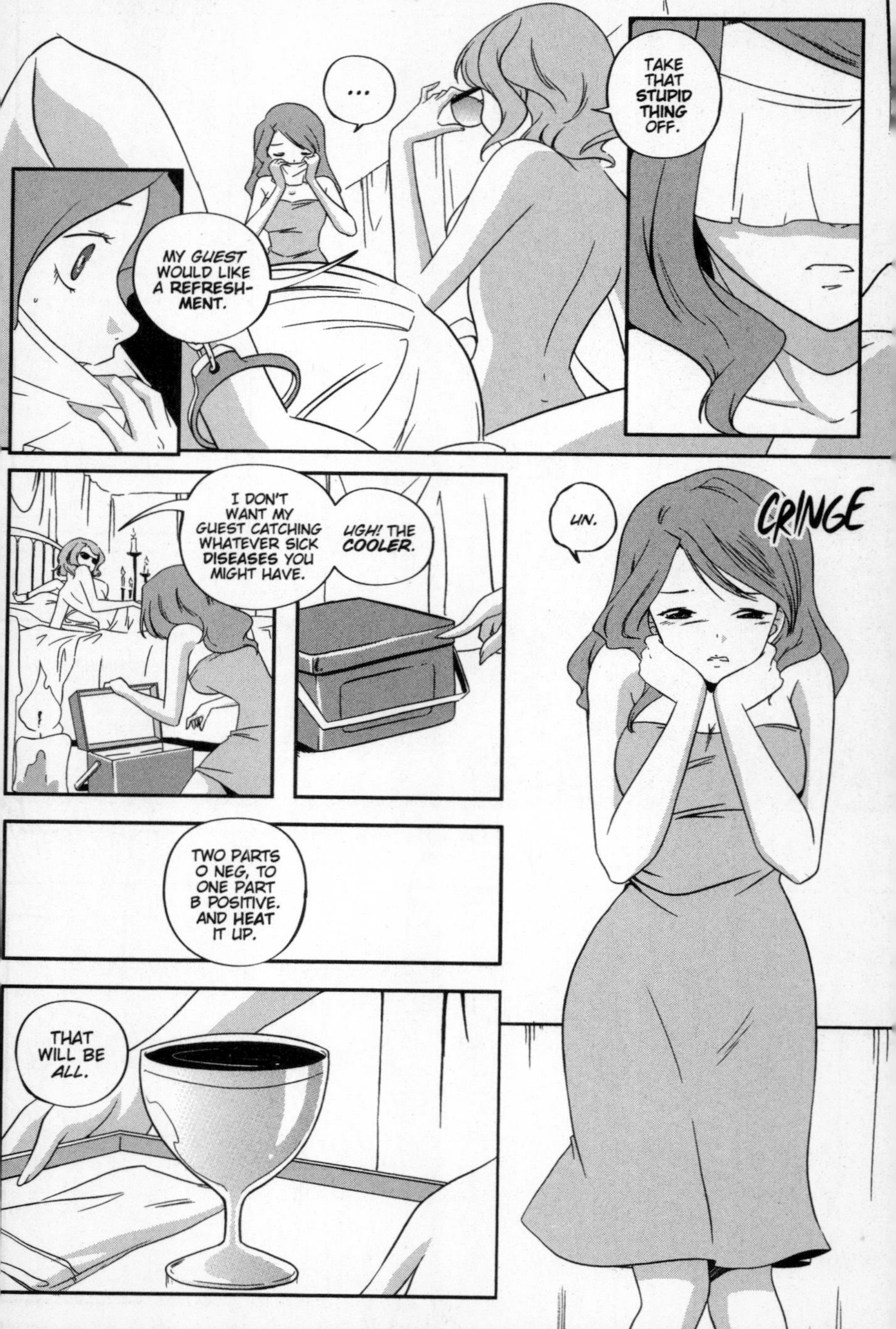
TAKE THAT STUPID THING OFF.
...
MY *GUEST* WOULD LIKE A REFRESHMENT.
UN.
CRINGE
UGH! THE **COOLER**.
I DON'T WANT MY GUEST CATCHING WHATEVER SICK DISEASES YOU MIGHT HAVE.
TWO PARTS O NEG, TO ONE PART B POSITIVE. AND HEAT IT UP.
THAT WILL BE *ALL*.

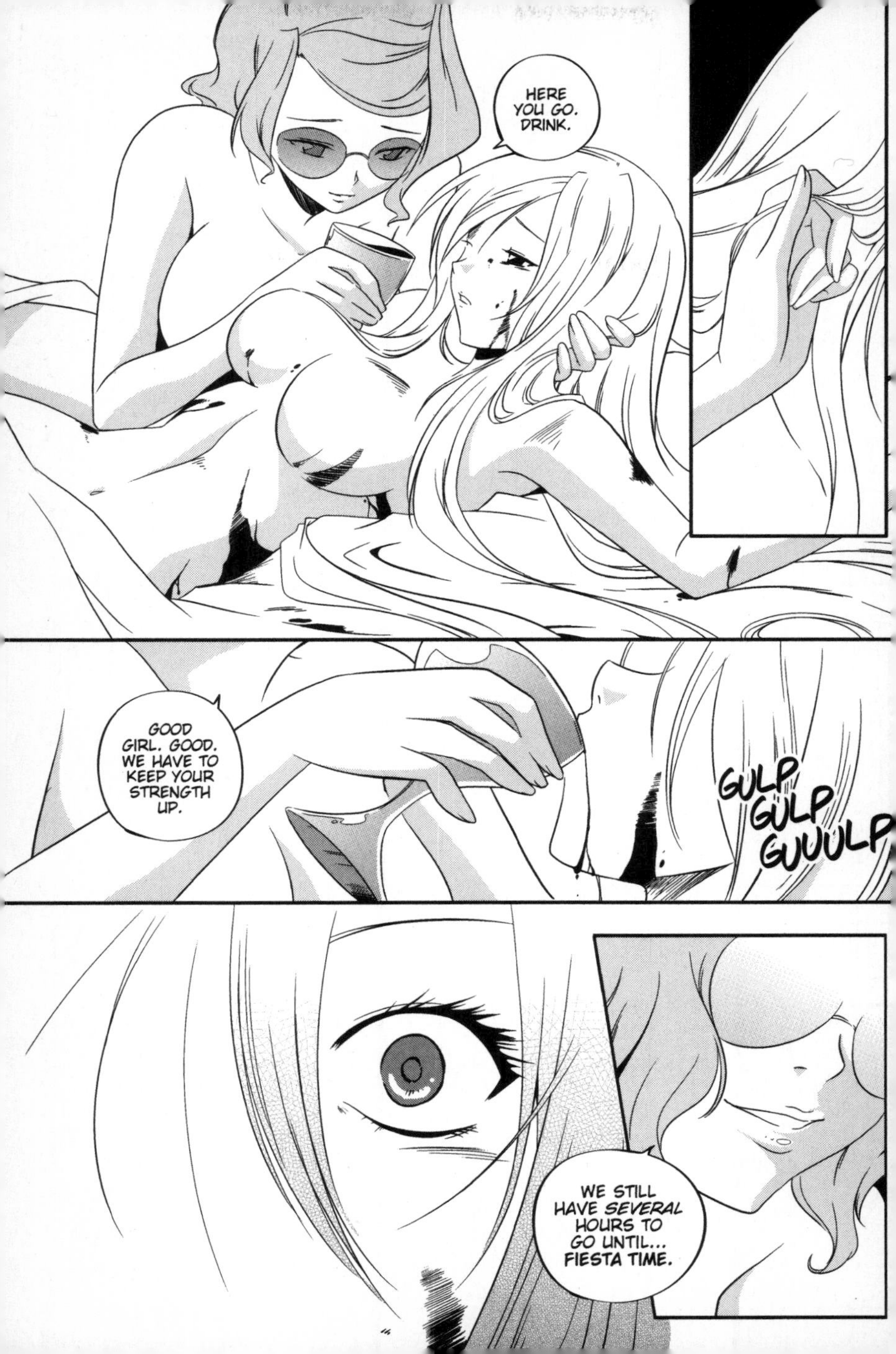
HERE YOU GO. DRINK.
GULP GULP GUUULP
GOOD GIRL. GOOD. WE HAVE TO KEEP YOUR STRENGTH UP.
WE STILL HAVE *SEVERAL* HOURS TO GO UNTIL... FIESTA TIME.

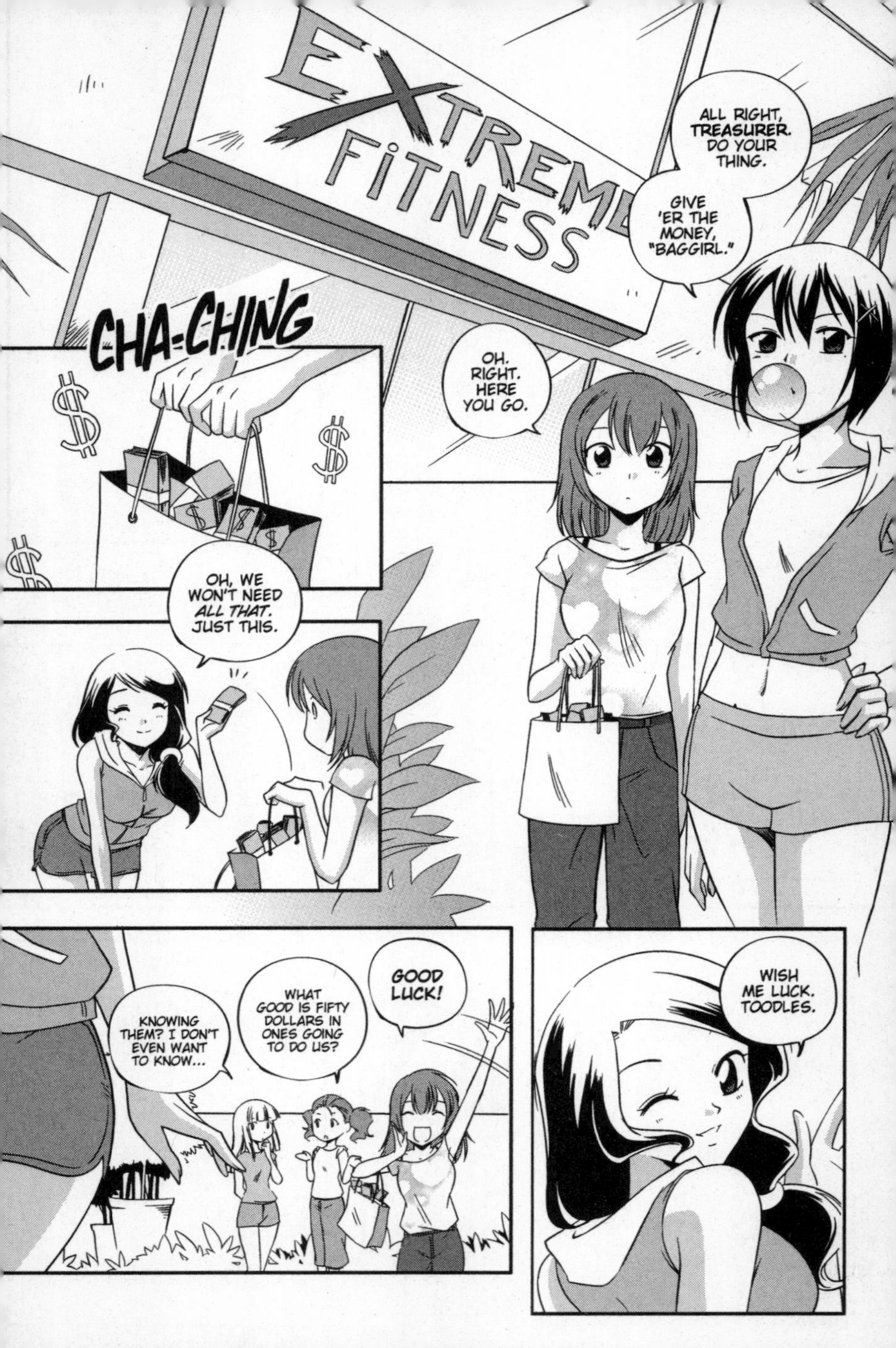
EXTREM
FITNESS
ALL RIGHT, TREASURER. DO YOUR THING.
GIVE 'ER THE MONEY, "BAGGIRL."
OH. RIGHT. HERE YOU GO.
CHA-CHING
OH, WE WON'T NEED *ALL THAT*. JUST THIS.
WISH ME LUCK. TOODLES.
GOOD LUCK!
WHAT GOOD IS FIFTY DOLLARS IN ONES GOING TO DO US?
KNOWING THEM? I DON'T EVEN WANT TO KNOW...

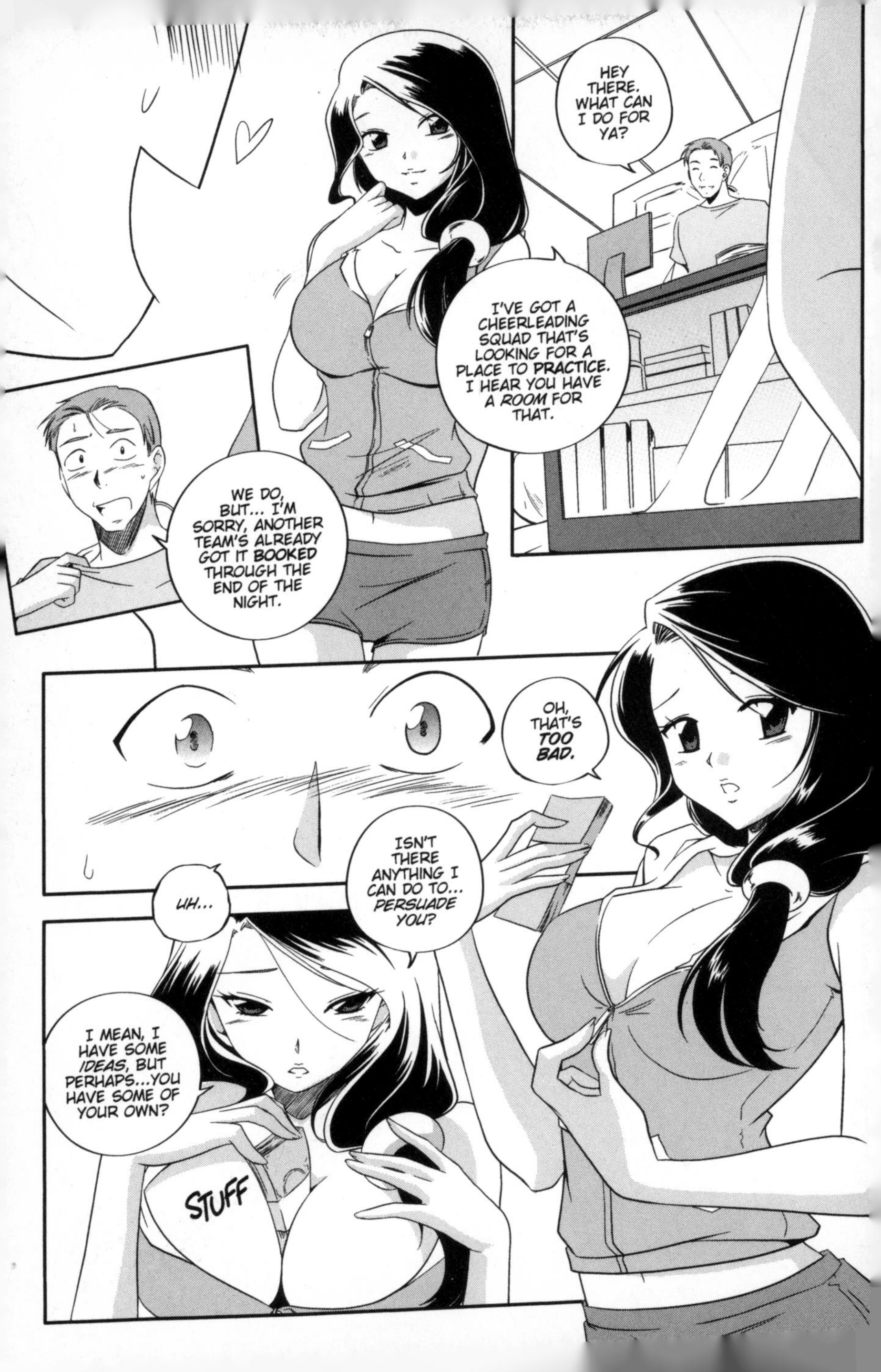
HEY THERE. WHAT CAN I DO FOR YA?
I'VE GOT A CHEERLEADING SQUAD THAT'S LOOKING FOR A PLACE TO **PRACTICE**. I HEAR YOU HAVE A *ROOM* FOR THAT.
WE DO, BUT... I'M SORRY, ANOTHER TEAM'S ALREADY GOT IT **BOOKED** THROUGH THE END OF THE NIGHT.
OH, THAT'S ***TOO BAD.***
ISN'T THERE ANYTHING I CAN DO TO... *PERSUADE* YOU?
UH...
I MEAN, I HAVE SOME *IDEAS*, BUT PERHAPS...YOU HAVE SOME OF YOUR OWN?
STUFF

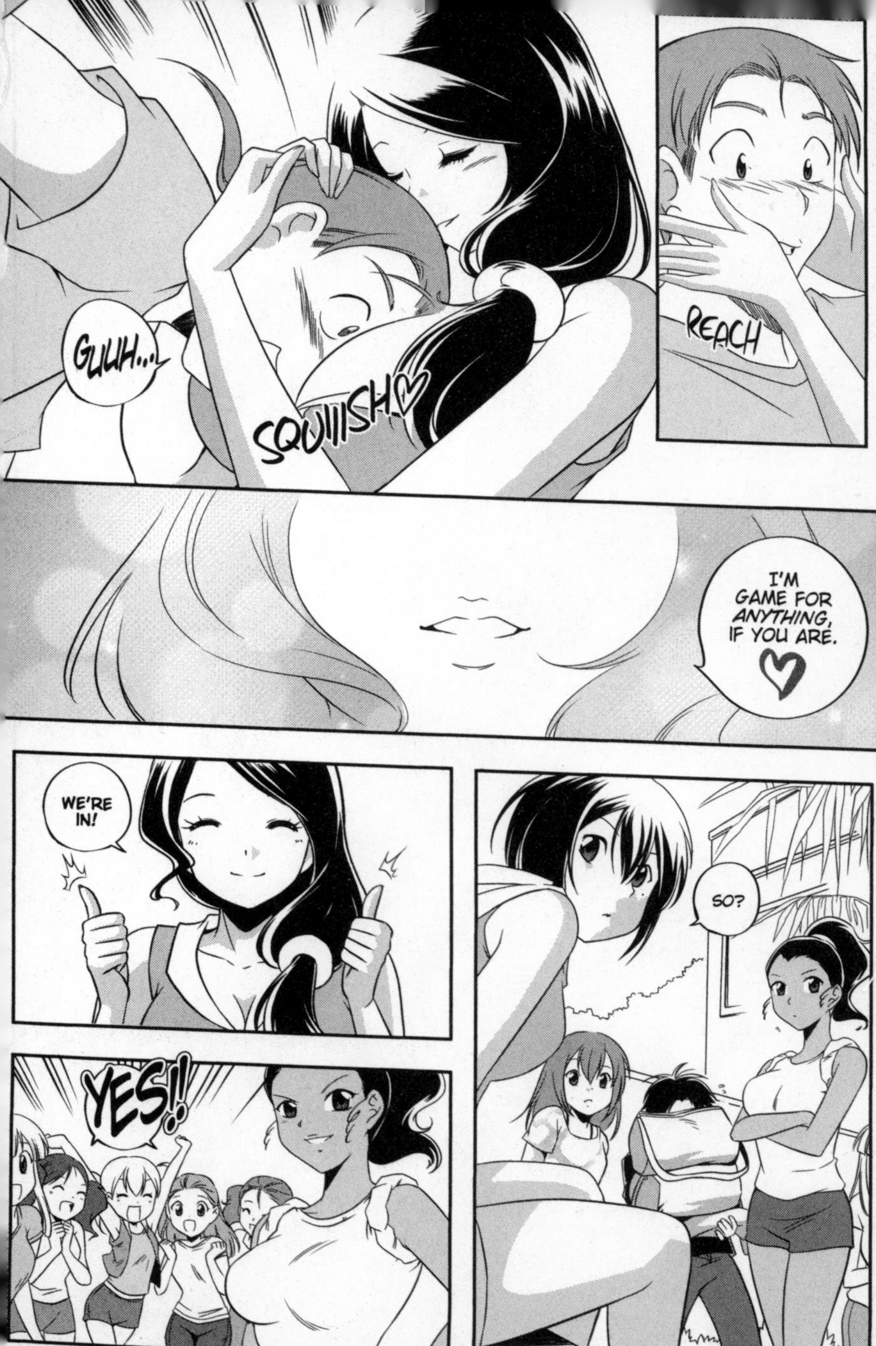
REACH
GUUH...
SQUIIISH♡
I'M GAME FOR ANYTHING, IF YOU ARE. ♥
SO?
WE'RE IN!
YES!!

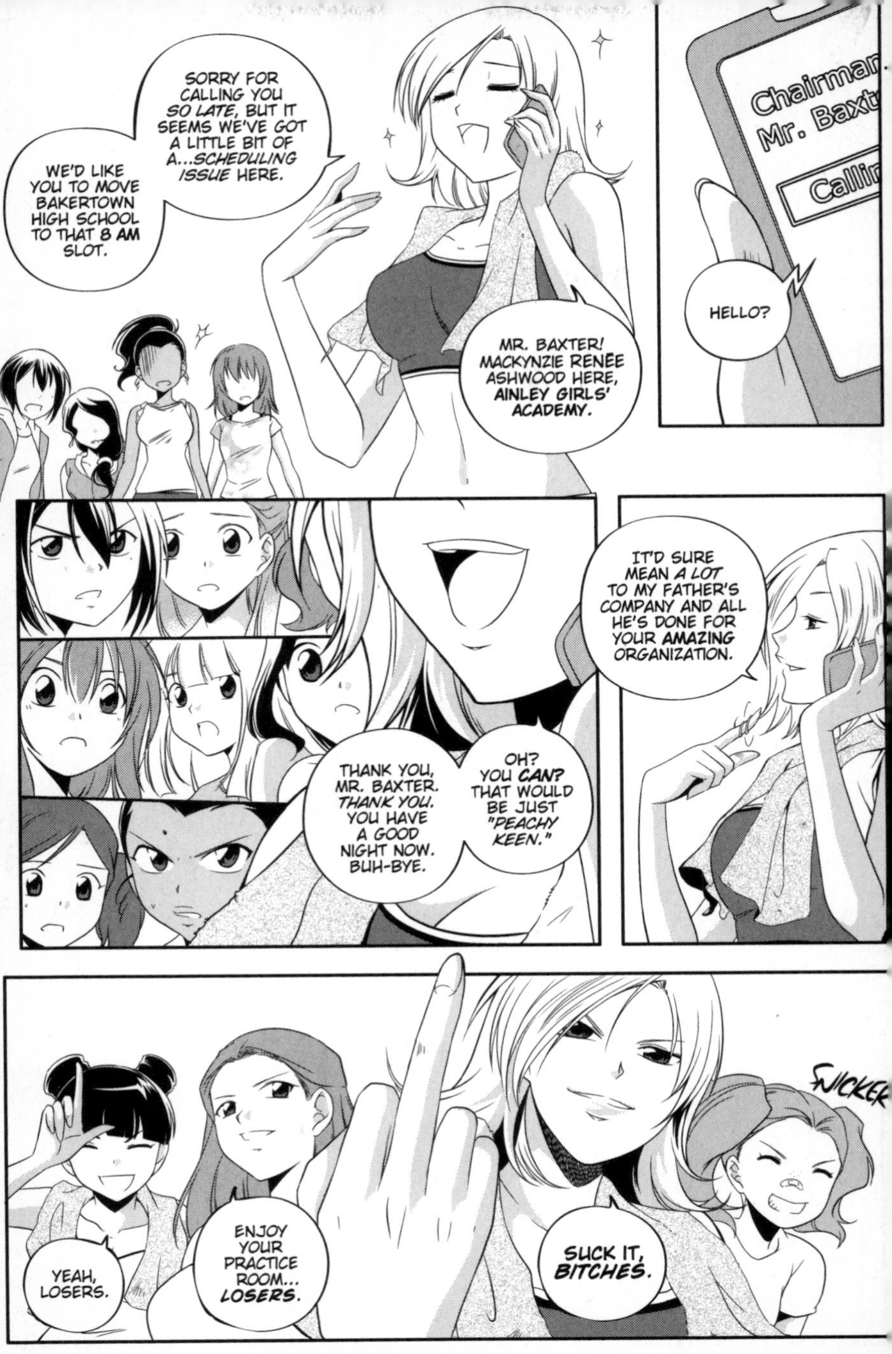
HELLO?
MR. BAXTER! MACKYNZIE RENÉE ASHWOOD HERE, AINLEY GIRLS' ACADEMY.
SORRY FOR CALLING YOU SO LATE, BUT IT SEEMS WE'VE GOT A LITTLE BIT OF A...SCHEDULING ISSUE HERE.
WE'D LIKE YOU TO MOVE BAKERTOWN HIGH SCHOOL TO THAT 8 AM SLOT.
IT'D SURE MEAN A LOT TO MY FATHER'S COMPANY AND ALL HE'S DONE FOR YOUR AMAZING ORGANIZATION.
OH? YOU CAN? THAT WOULD BE JUST "PEACHY KEEN."
THANK YOU, MR. BAXTER. THANK YOU. YOU HAVE A GOOD NIGHT NOW. BUH-BYE.
SNICKER
SUCK IT, BITCHES.
ENJOY YOUR PRACTICE ROOM... LOSERS.
YEAH, LOSERS.

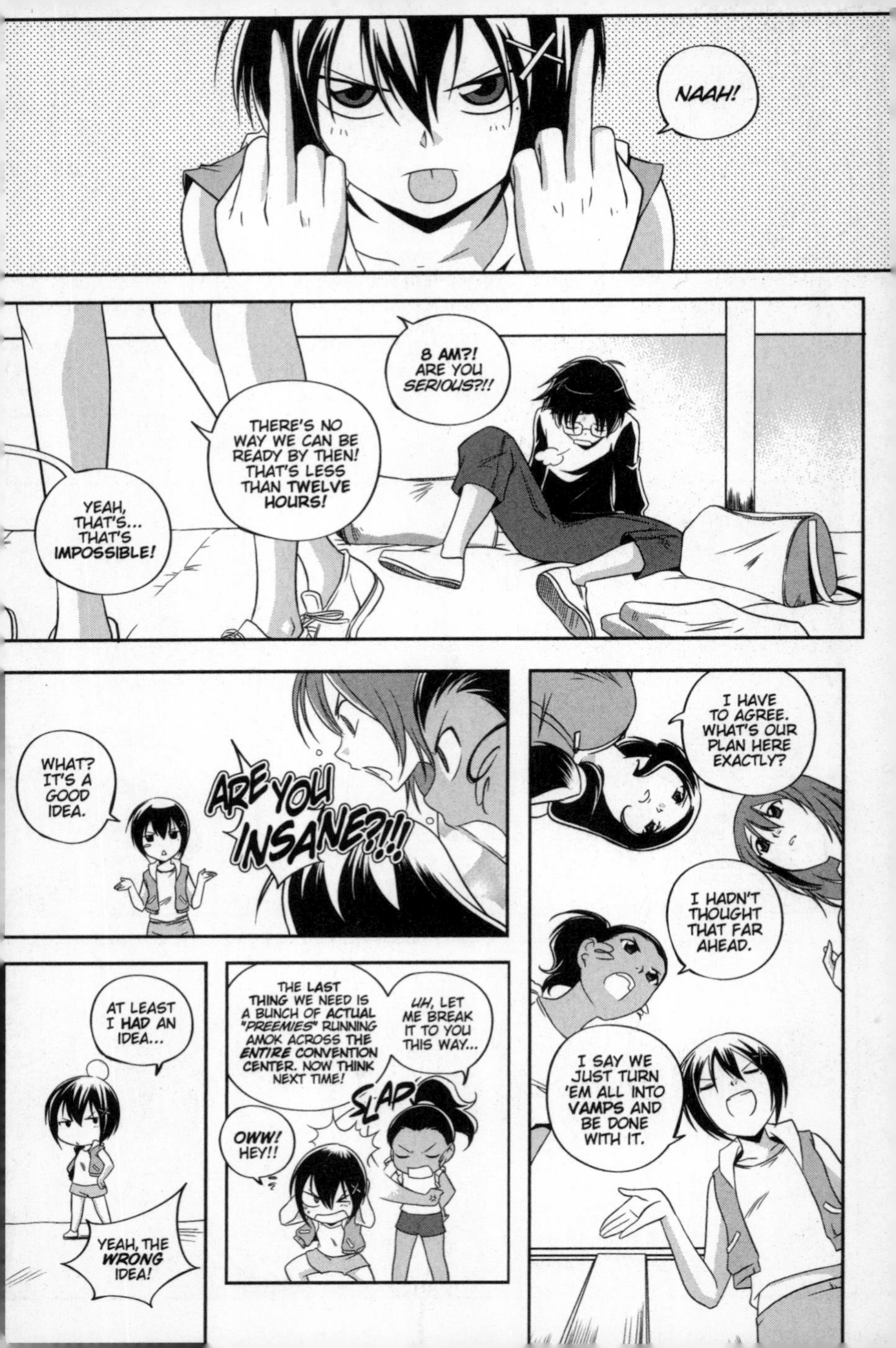
NAAH!
8 AM?! ARE YOU *SERIOUS*?!!
THERE'S NO WAY WE CAN BE READY BY THEN! THAT'S LESS THAN **TWELVE** HOURS!
YEAH, THAT'S... THAT'S **IMPOSSIBLE!**
I HAVE TO AGREE. WHAT'S OUR PLAN HERE EXACTLY?
I HADN'T THOUGHT THAT FAR AHEAD.
I SAY WE JUST TURN 'EM ALL INTO **VAMPS** AND BE DONE WITH IT.
ARE YOU INSANE?!!
WHAT? IT'S A GOOD IDEA.
UH, LET ME BREAK IT TO YOU THIS WAY...
THE LAST THING WE NEED IS A BUNCH OF ACTUAL *"PREEMIES"* RUNNING AMOK ACROSS THE *ENTIRE* CONVENTION CENTER. NOW THINK NEXT TIME!
SLAP
OWW! HEY!!
AT LEAST I **HAD** AN IDEA...
YEAH, THE *WRONG* IDEA!

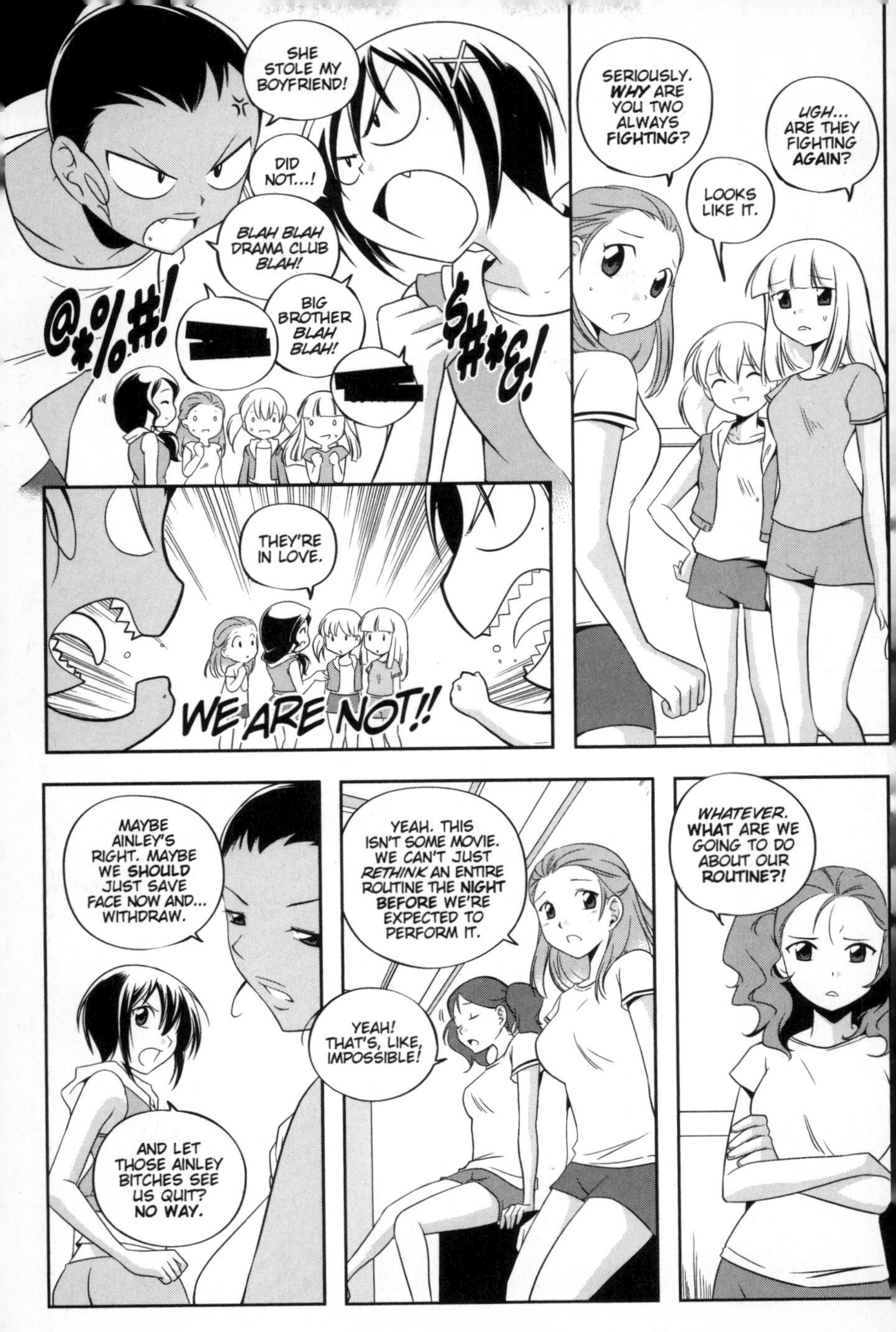

UGH... ARE THEY FIGHTING AGAIN?
LOOKS LIKE IT.
SERIOUSLY. WHY ARE YOU TWO ALWAYS FIGHTING?
SHE STOLE MY BOYFRIEND!
DID NOT...!
BLAH BLAH DRAMA CLUB BLAH!
$#*&!
BIG BROTHER BLAH BLAH!
[redacted]
[redacted]
@*%#!
THEY'RE IN LOVE.
WE ARE NOT!!
WHATEVER. WHAT ARE WE GOING TO DO ABOUT OUR ROUTINE?!
YEAH. THIS ISN'T SOME MOVIE. WE CAN'T JUST RETHINK AN ENTIRE ROUTINE THE NIGHT BEFORE WE'RE EXPECTED TO PERFORM IT.
YEAH! THAT'S, LIKE, IMPOSSIBLE!
MAYBE AINLEY'S RIGHT. MAYBE WE SHOULD JUST SAVE FACE NOW AND... WITHDRAW.
AND LET THOSE AINLEY BITCHES SEE US QUIT? NO WAY.

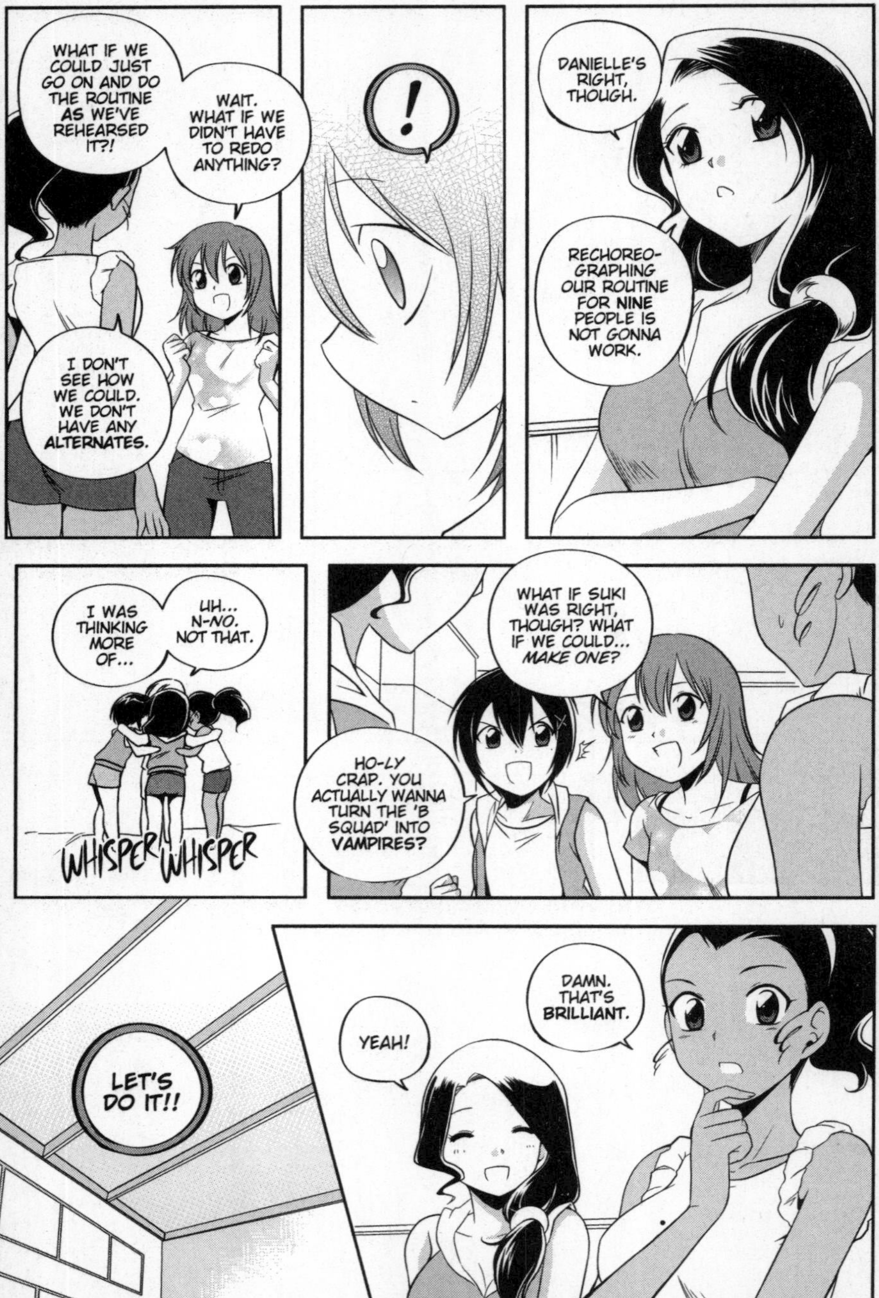
DANIELLE'S RIGHT, THOUGH.
RECHOREO-GRAPHING OUR ROUTINE FOR NINE PEOPLE IS NOT GONNA WORK.
!
WAIT. WHAT IF WE DIDN'T HAVE TO REDO ANYTHING?
WHAT IF WE COULD JUST GO ON AND DO THE ROUTINE AS WE'VE REHEARSED IT?!
I DON'T SEE HOW WE COULD. WE DON'T HAVE ANY ALTERNATES.
WHAT IF SUKI WAS RIGHT, THOUGH? WHAT IF WE COULD... MAKE ONE?
HO-LY CRAP. YOU ACTUALLY WANNA TURN THE 'B SQUAD' INTO VAMPIRES?
UH... N-NO. NOT THAT.
I WAS THINKING MORE OF...
WHISPER WHISPER
DAMN. THAT'S BRILLIANT.
YEAH!
LET'S DO IT!!

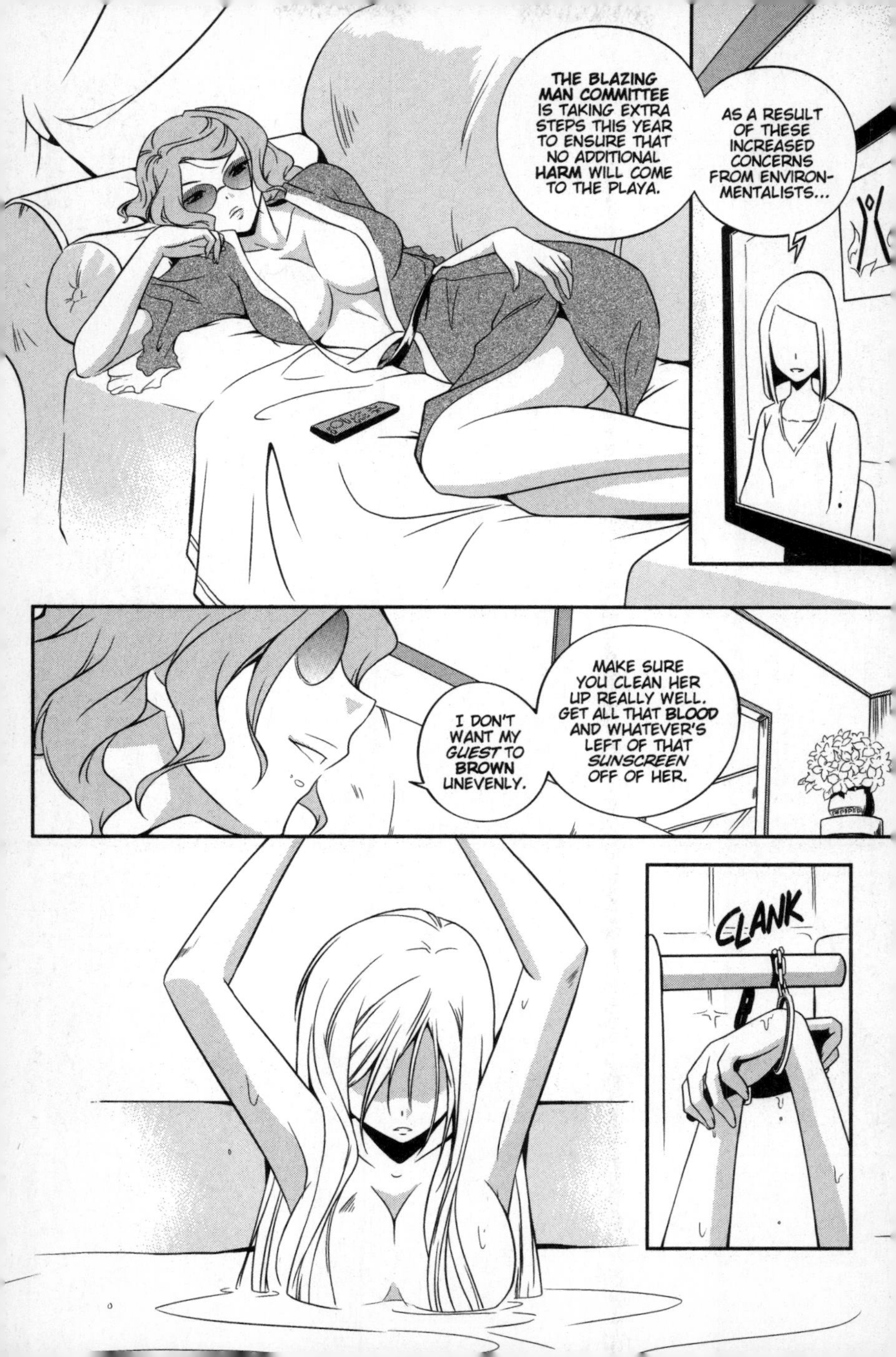
AS A RESULT OF THESE INCREASED CONCERNS FROM ENVIRONMENTALISTS...
THE BLAZING MAN COMMITTEE IS TAKING EXTRA STEPS THIS YEAR TO ENSURE THAT NO ADDITIONAL HARM WILL COME TO THE PLAYA.
MAKE SURE YOU CLEAN HER UP REALLY WELL. GET ALL THAT BLOOD AND WHATEVER'S LEFT OF THAT SUNSCREEN OFF OF HER.
I DON'T WANT MY GUEST TO BROWN UNEVENLY.
CLANK

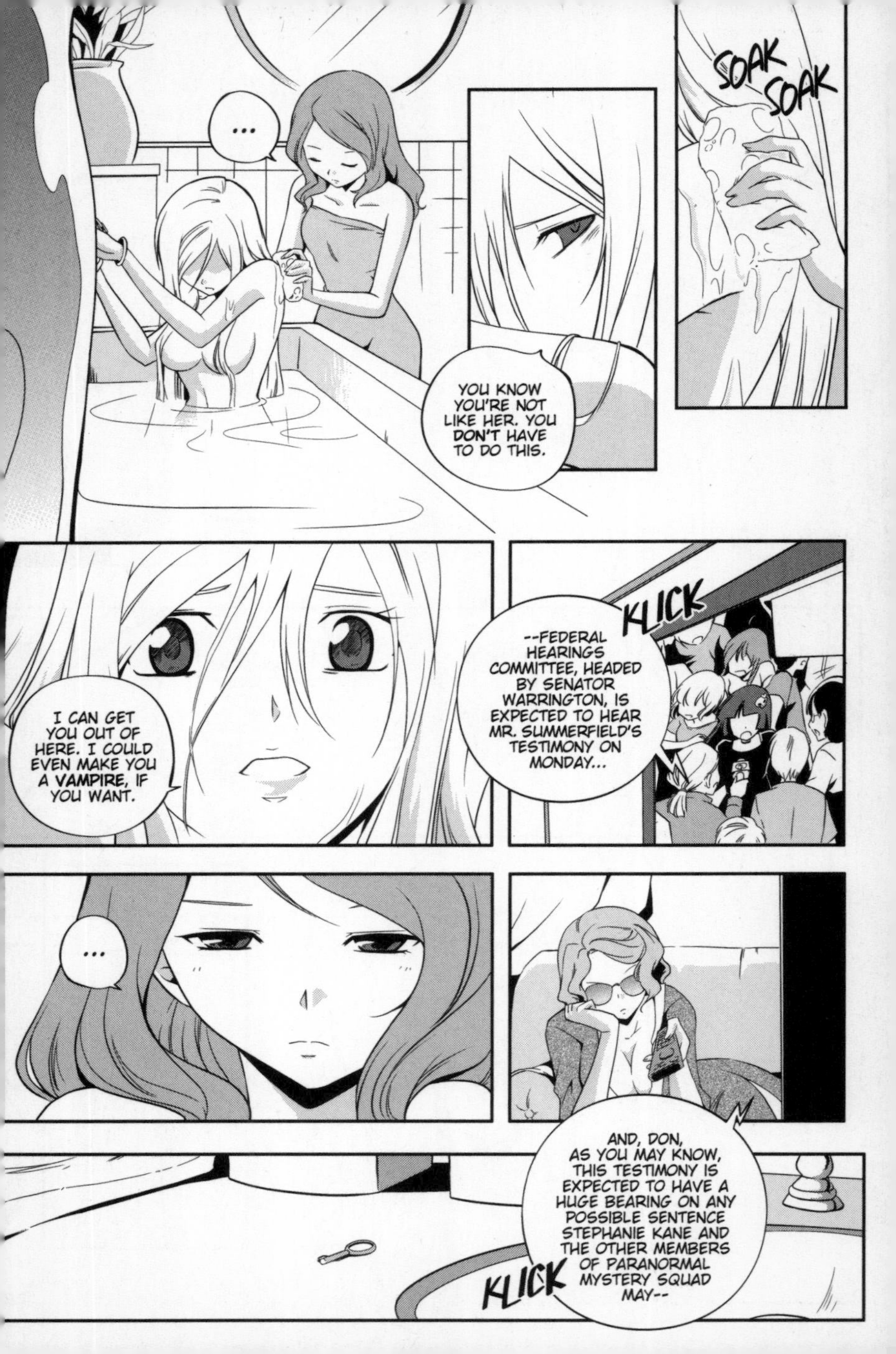
SOAK SOAK
YOU KNOW YOU'RE NOT LIKE HER. YOU DON'T HAVE TO DO THIS.
...
KLICK
--FEDERAL HEARINGS COMMITTEE, HEADED BY SENATOR WARRINGTON, IS EXPECTED TO HEAR MR. SUMMERFIELD'S TESTIMONY ON MONDAY...
I CAN GET YOU OUT OF HERE. I COULD EVEN MAKE YOU A VAMPIRE, IF YOU WANT.
...
AND, DON, AS YOU MAY KNOW, THIS TESTIMONY IS EXPECTED TO HAVE A HUGE BEARING ON ANY POSSIBLE SENTENCE STEPHANIE KANE AND THE OTHER MEMBERS OF PARANORMAL MYSTERY SQUAD MAY--
KLICK

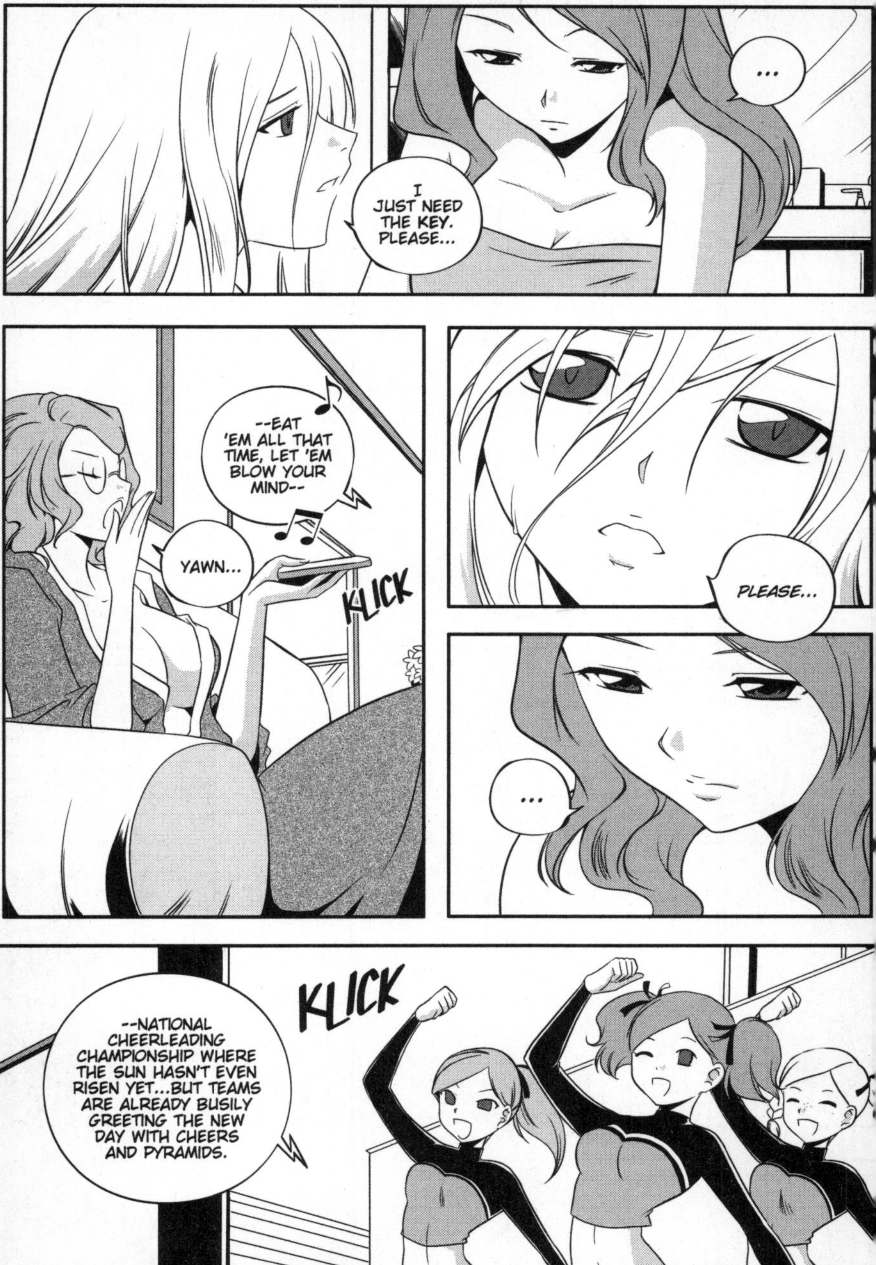
...
I JUST NEED THE KEY. PLEASE...
PLEASE...
...
--EAT 'EM ALL THAT TIME, LET 'EM BLOW YOUR MIND--
YAWN...
KLICK
KLICK
--NATIONAL CHEERLEADING CHAMPIONSHIP WHERE THE SUN HASN'T EVEN RISEN YET...BUT TEAMS ARE ALREADY BUSILY GREETING THE NEW DAY WITH CHEERS AND PYRAMIDS.

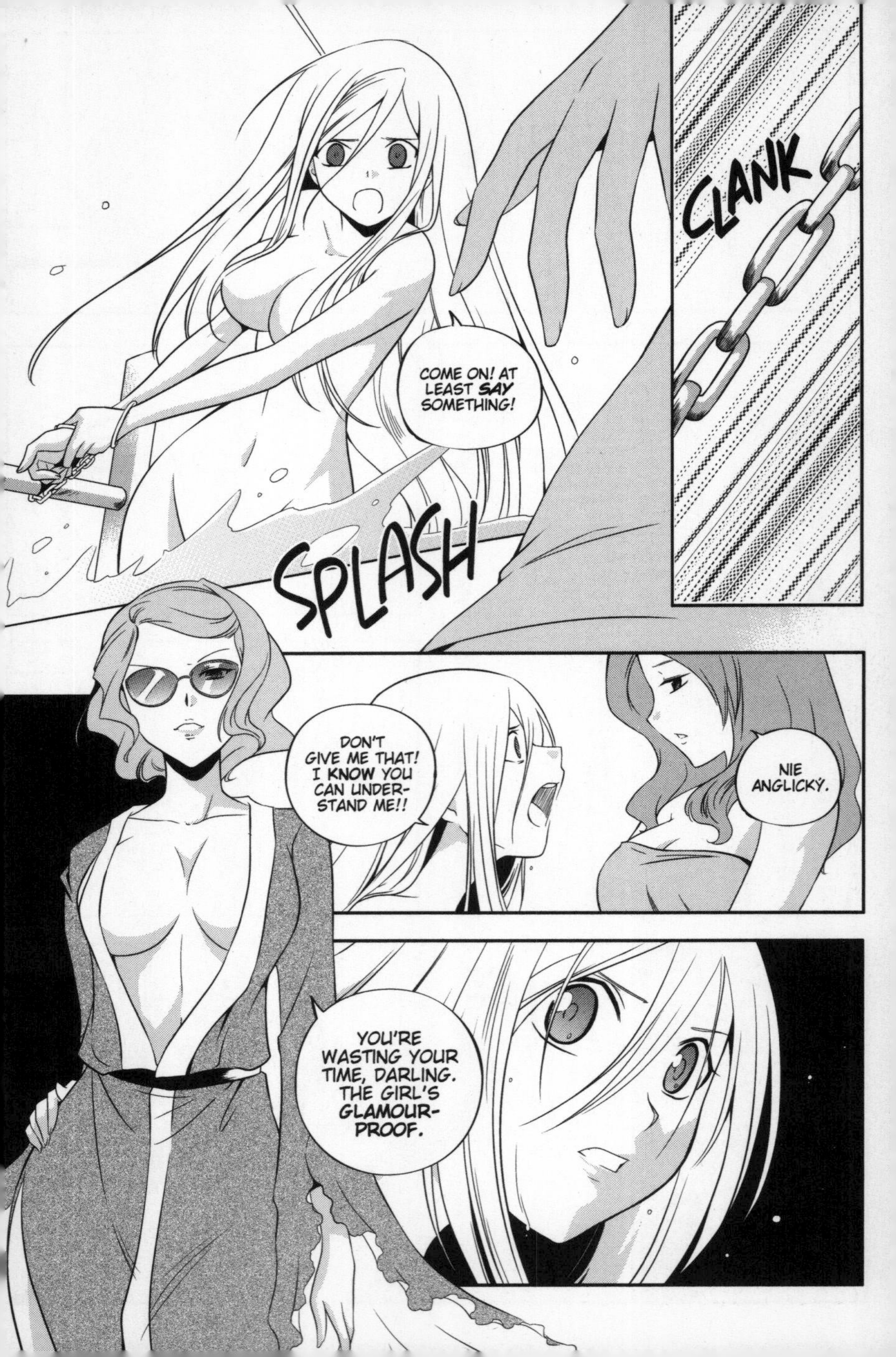
CLANK
COME ON! AT LEAST SAY SOMETHING!
SPLASH
NIE ANGLICKÝ.
DON'T GIVE ME THAT! I KNOW YOU CAN UNDERSTAND ME!!
YOU'RE WASTING YOUR TIME, DARLING. THE GIRL'S GLAMOUR-PROOF.

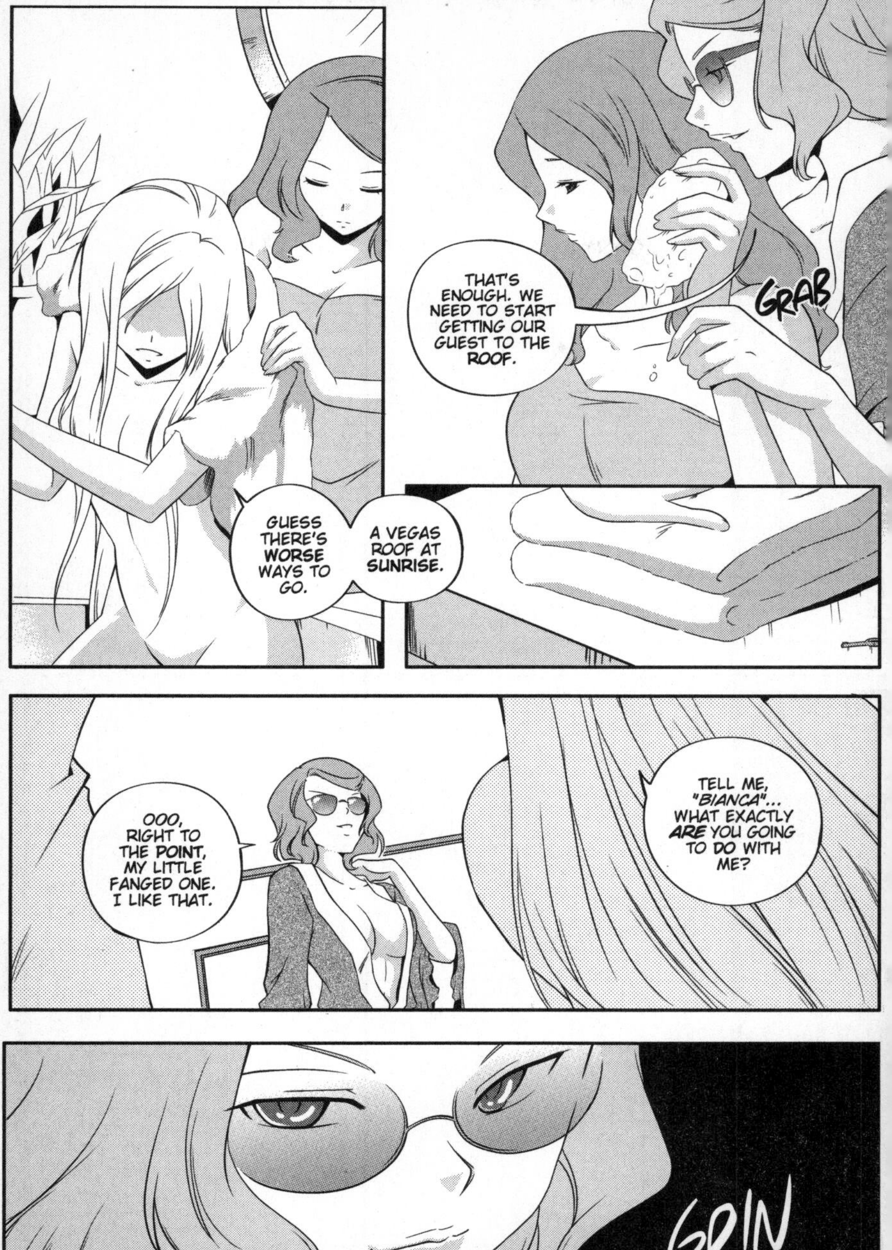
THAT'S ENOUGH. WE NEED TO START GETTING OUR GUEST TO THE ROOF.
GRAB
A VEGAS ROOF AT SUNRISE.
GUESS THERE'S WORSE WAYS TO GO.
TELL ME, "BIANCA"... WHAT EXACTLY ARE YOU GOING TO DO WITH ME?
OOO, RIGHT TO THE POINT, MY LITTLE FANGED ONE. I LIKE THAT.
GRIN

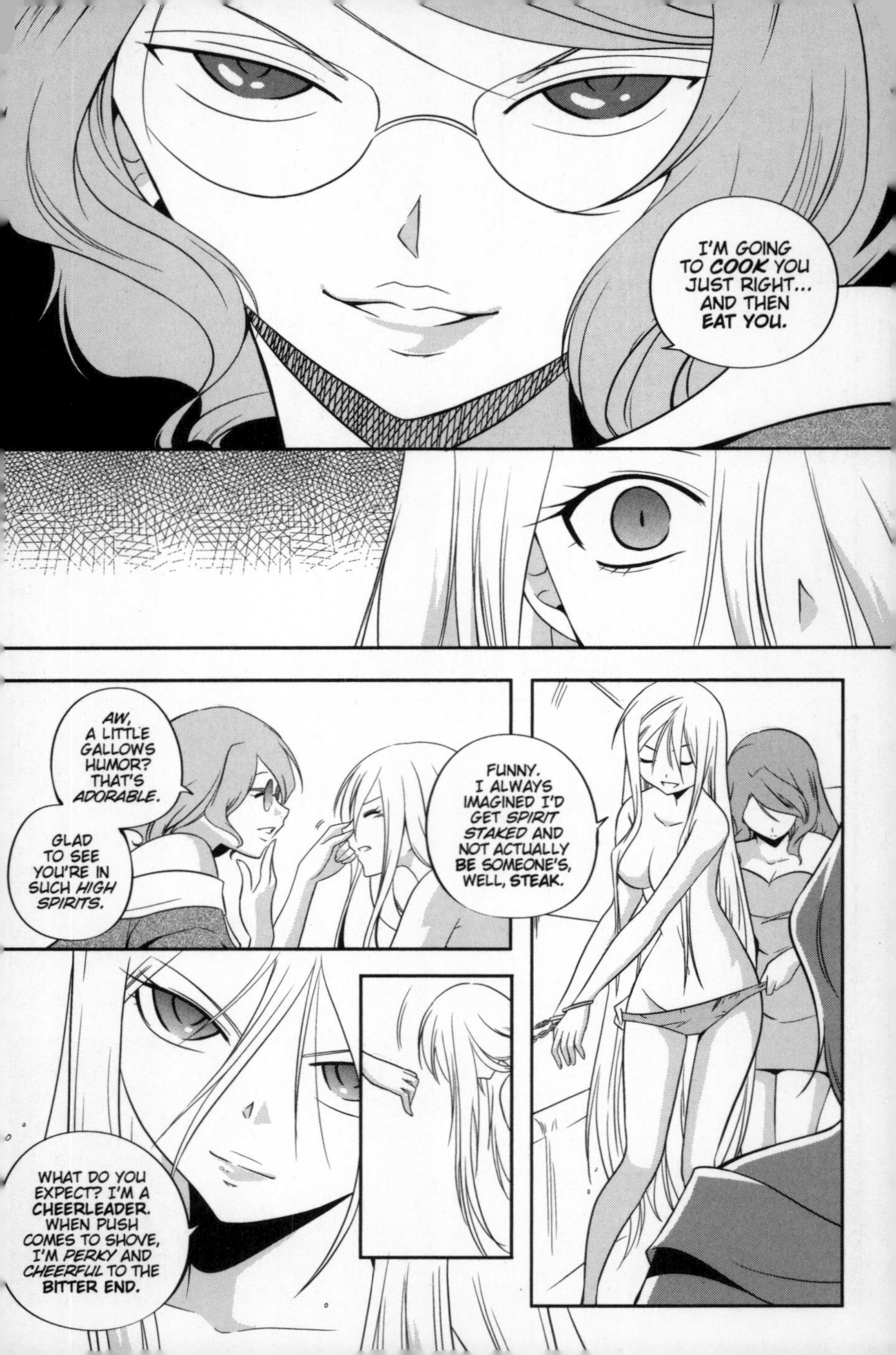
I'M GOING TO **COOK** YOU JUST RIGHT... AND THEN **EAT YOU.**
FUNNY. I ALWAYS IMAGINED I'D GET *SPIRIT STAKED* AND NOT ACTUALLY BE SOMEONE'S, WELL, **STEAK.**
AW, A LITTLE GALLOWS HUMOR? THAT'S *ADORABLE*.
GLAD TO SEE YOU'RE IN SUCH *HIGH SPIRITS*.
WHAT DO YOU EXPECT? I'M A **CHEERLEADER.** WHEN PUSH COMES TO SHOVE, I'M *PERKY* AND *CHEERFUL* TO THE **BITTER END.**

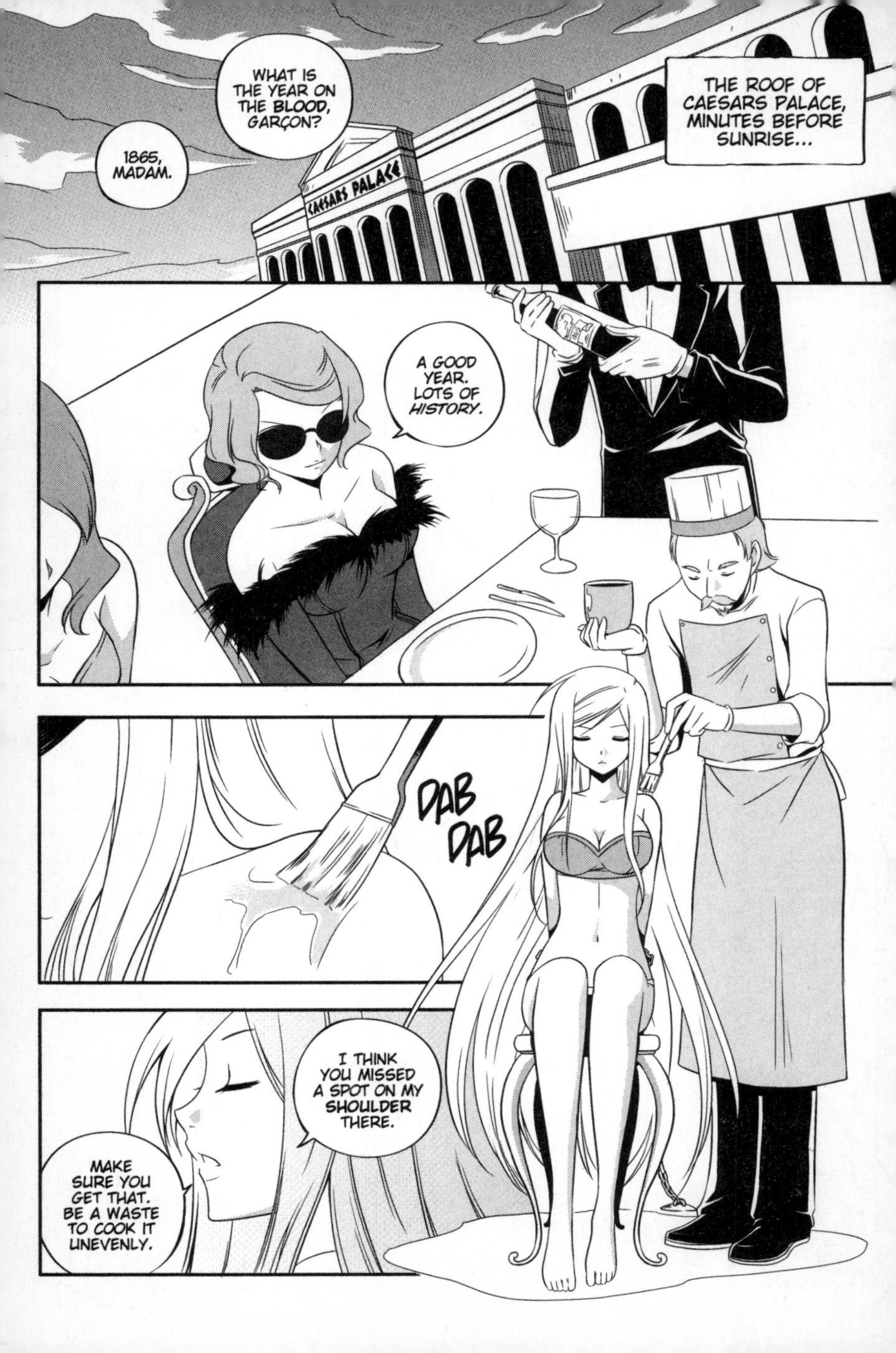
THE ROOF OF CAESARS PALACE, MINUTES BEFORE SUNRISE...
CAESARS PALACE
WHAT IS THE YEAR ON THE BLOOD, GARÇON?
1865, MADAM.
A GOOD YEAR. LOTS OF *HISTORY*.
DAB DAB
I THINK YOU MISSED A SPOT ON MY SHOULDER THERE.
MAKE SURE YOU GET THAT. BE A WASTE TO COOK IT UNEVENLY.

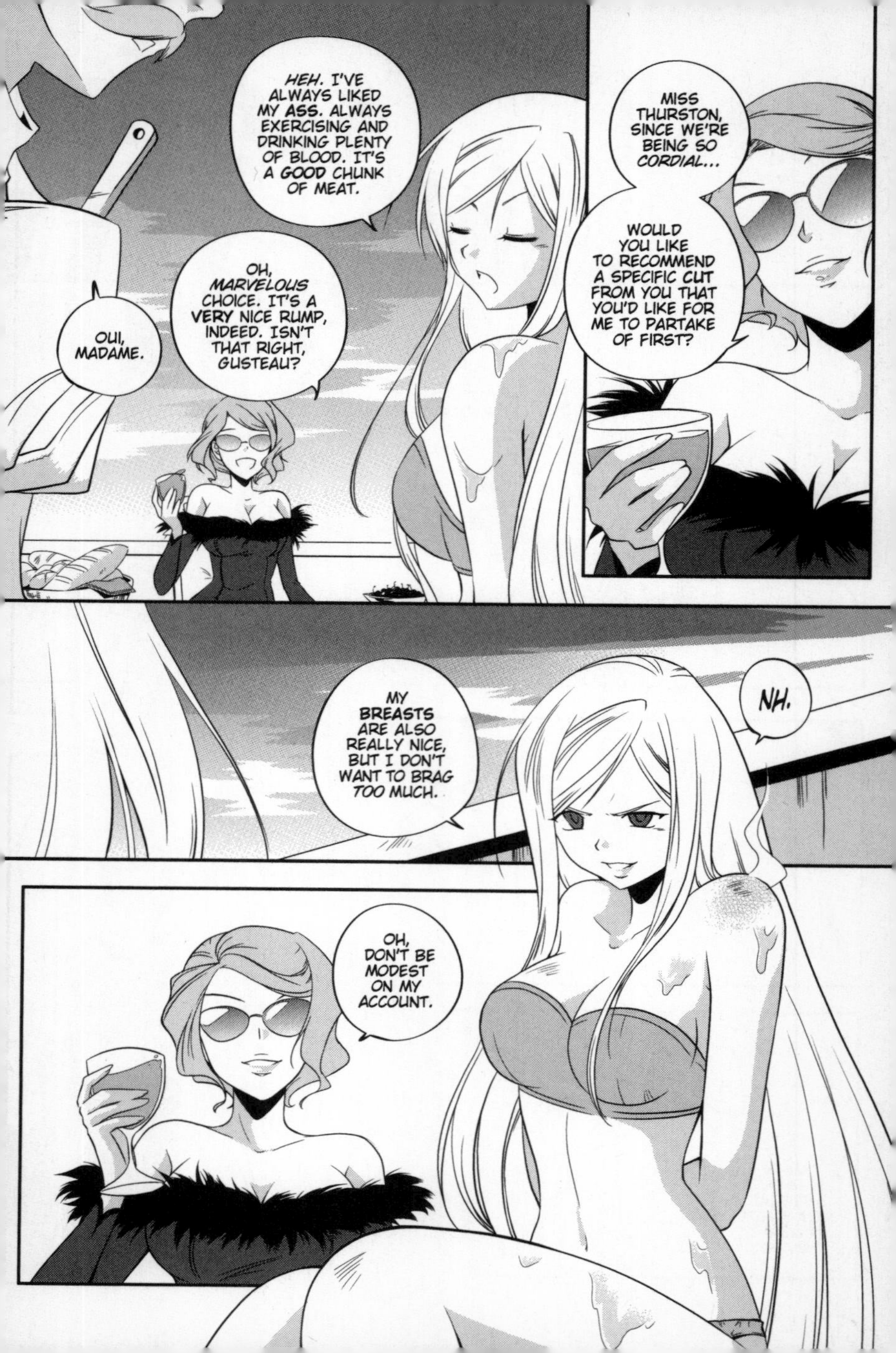
MISS THURSTON, SINCE WE'RE BEING SO CORDIAL...
WOULD YOU LIKE TO RECOMMEND A SPECIFIC CUT FROM YOU THAT YOU'D LIKE FOR ME TO PARTAKE OF FIRST?
HEH. I'VE ALWAYS LIKED MY ASS. ALWAYS EXERCISING AND DRINKING PLENTY OF BLOOD. IT'S A GOOD CHUNK OF MEAT.
OH, MARVELOUS CHOICE. IT'S A VERY NICE RUMP, INDEED. ISN'T THAT RIGHT, GUSTEAU?
OUI, MADAME.
NH.
MY BREASTS ARE ALSO REALLY NICE, BUT I DON'T WANT TO BRAG TOO MUCH.
OH, DON'T BE MODEST ON MY ACCOUNT.

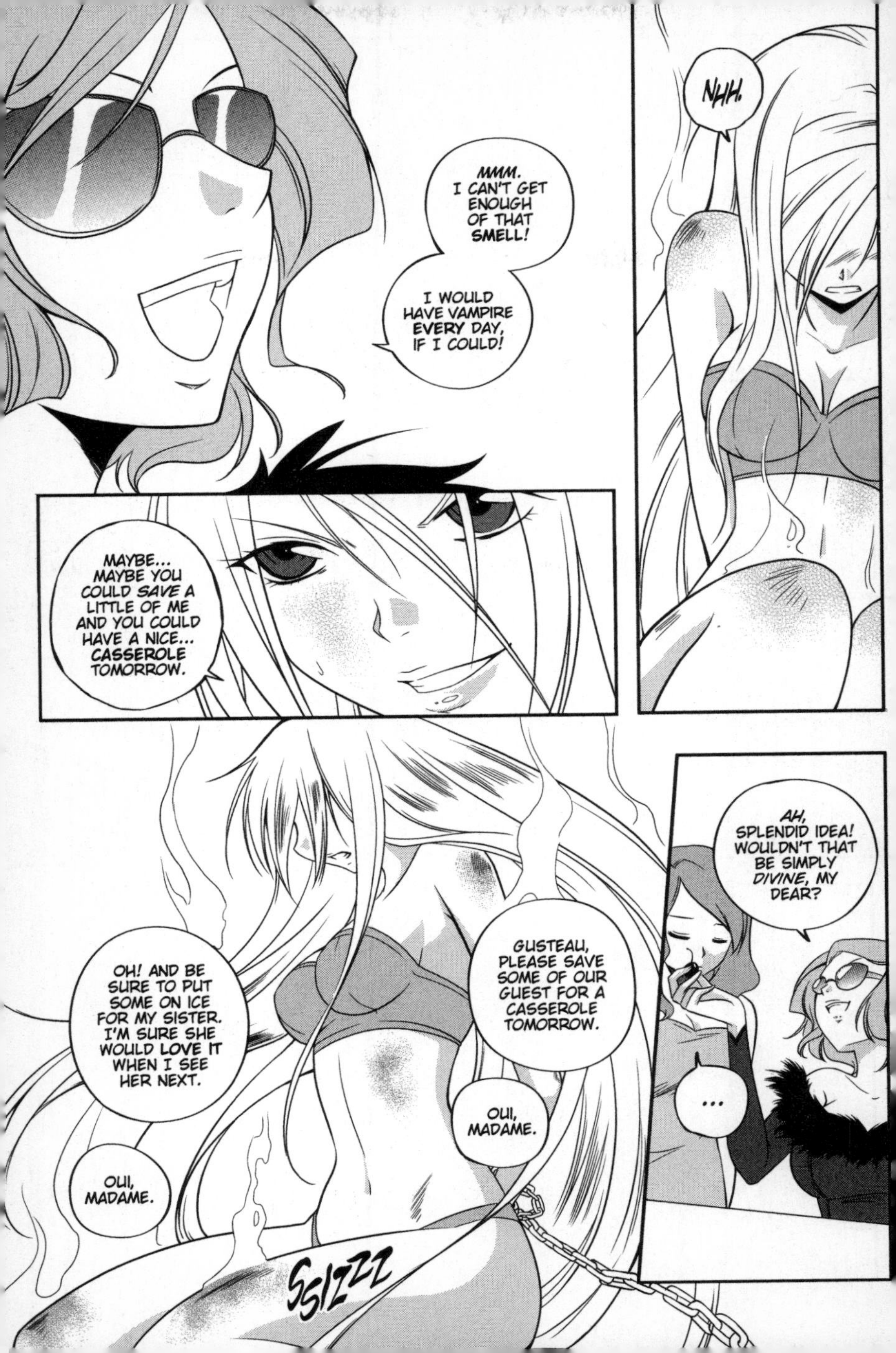
NHH.
MMM. I CAN'T GET ENOUGH OF THAT SMELL!
I WOULD HAVE VAMPIRE EVERY DAY, IF I COULD!
MAYBE... MAYBE YOU COULD SAVE A LITTLE OF ME AND YOU COULD HAVE A NICE... CASSEROLE TOMORROW.
AH, SPLENDID IDEA! WOULDN'T THAT BE SIMPLY DIVINE, MY DEAR?
...
GUSTEAU, PLEASE SAVE SOME OF OUR GUEST FOR A CASSEROLE TOMORROW.
OH! AND BE SURE TO PUT SOME ON ICE FOR MY SISTER. I'M SURE SHE WOULD LOVE IT WHEN I SEE HER NEXT.
OUI, MADAME.
OUI, MADAME.
SSIZZZ

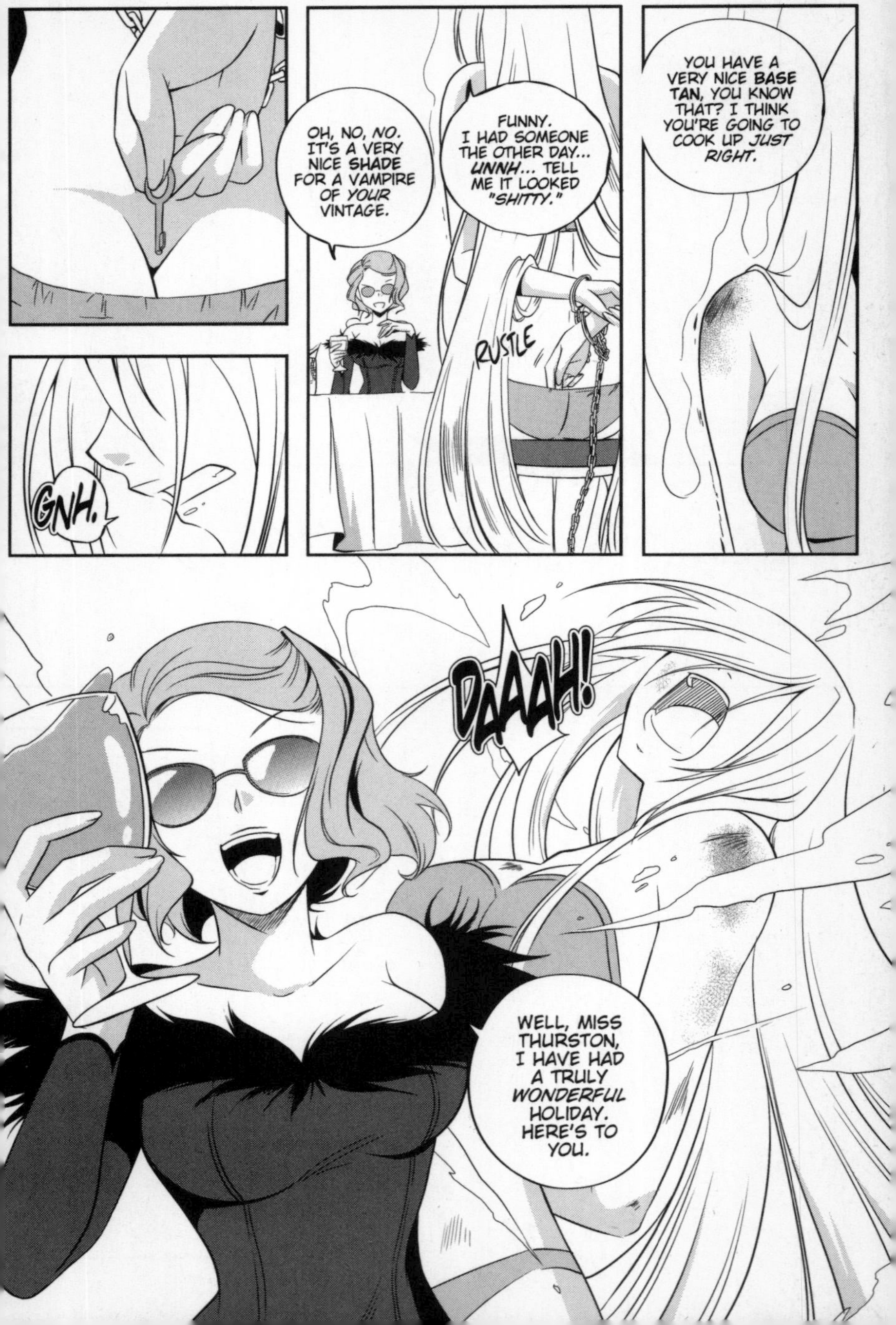
YOU HAVE A VERY NICE BASE TAN, YOU KNOW THAT? I THINK YOU'RE GOING TO COOK UP JUST RIGHT.
FUNNY. I HAD SOMEONE THE OTHER DAY... UNNH... TELL ME IT LOOKED "SHITTY."
OH, NO, NO. IT'S A VERY NICE SHADE FOR A VAMPIRE OF YOUR VINTAGE.
RUSTLE
GNH.
DAAAH!
WELL, MISS THURSTON, I HAVE HAD A TRULY WONDERFUL HOLIDAY. HERE'S TO YOU.

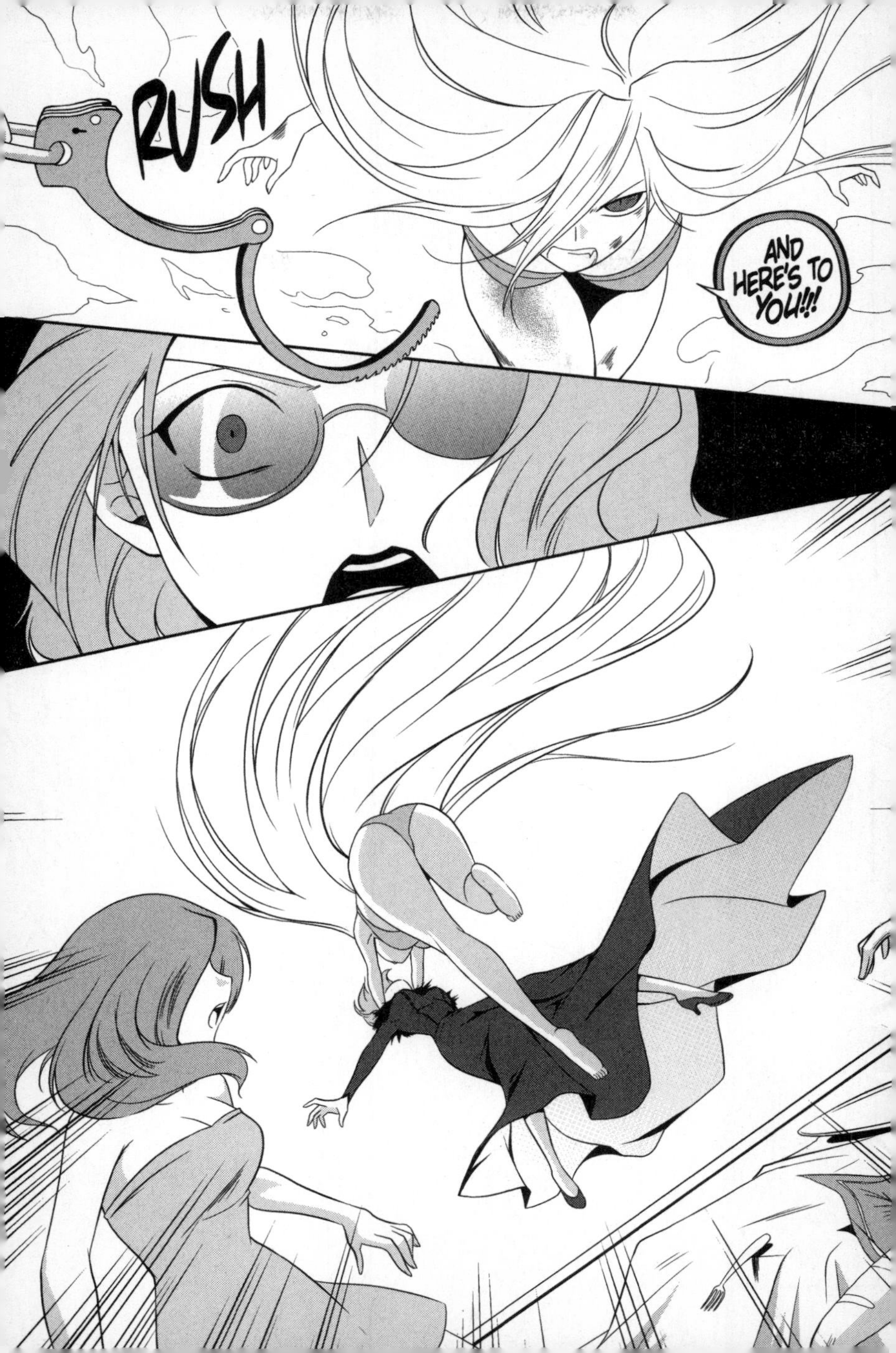
AND HERE'S TO YOU!!!
RUSH

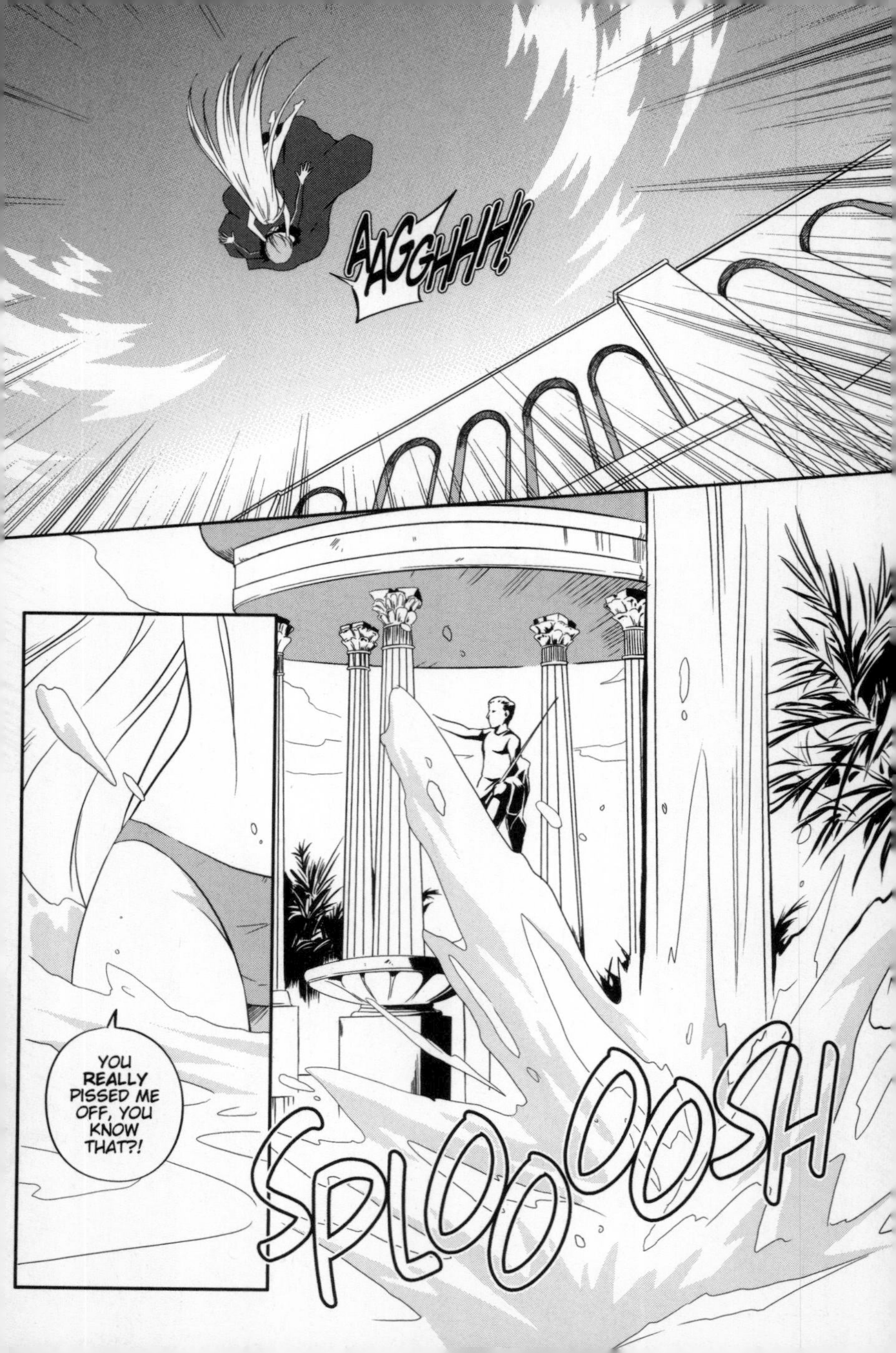
AAGGHHH!
SPLOOOOSH
YOU REALLY PISSED ME OFF, YOU KNOW THAT?!

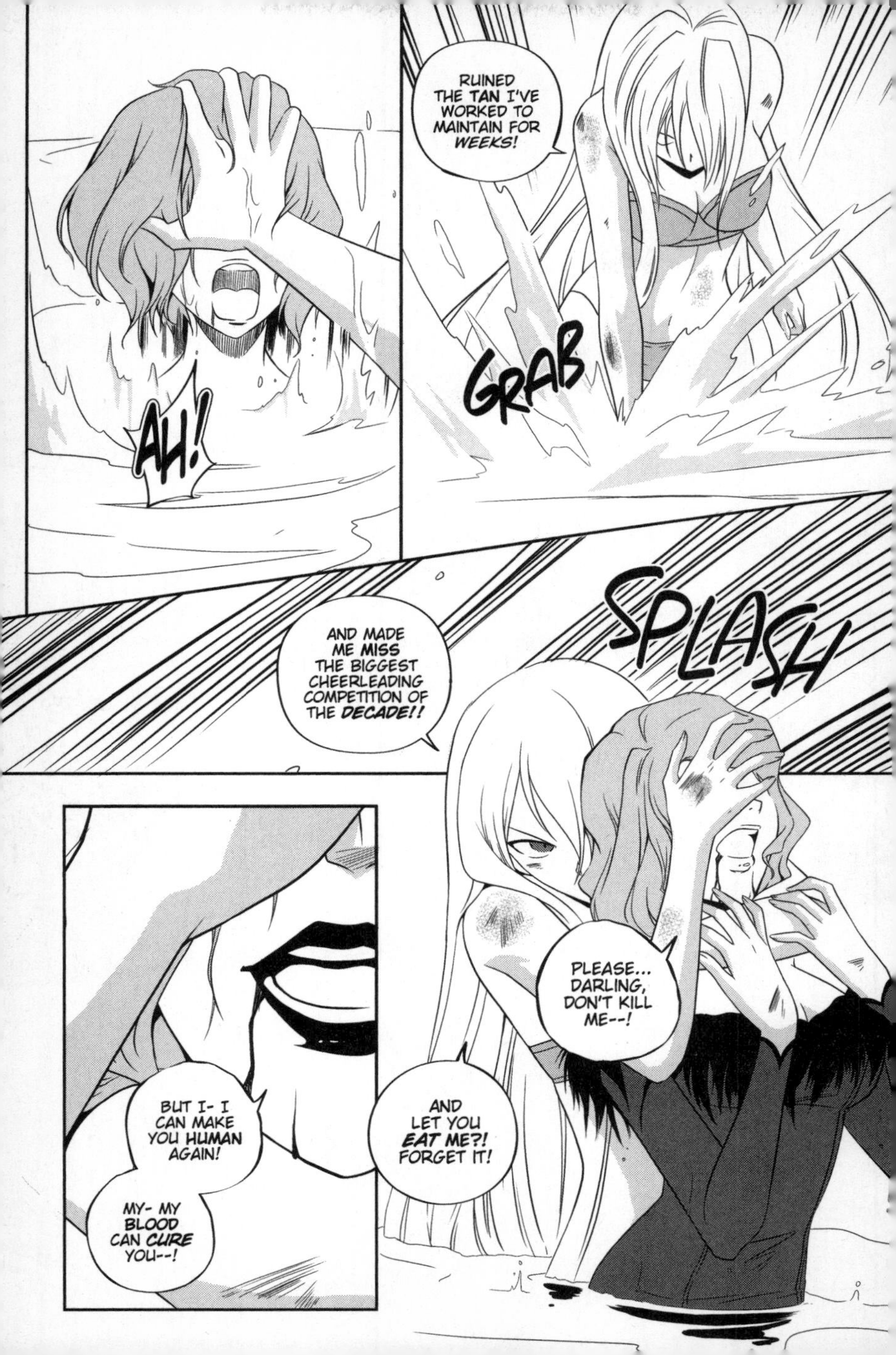
RUINED THE TAN I'VE WORKED TO MAINTAIN FOR WEEKS!
GRAB
AH!
SPLASH
AND MADE ME MISS THE BIGGEST CHEERLEADING COMPETITION OF THE DECADE!!
PLEASE... DARLING, DON'T KILL ME--!
BUT I- I CAN MAKE YOU HUMAN AGAIN!
MY- MY BLOOD CAN CURE YOU--!
AND LET YOU EAT ME?! FORGET IT!

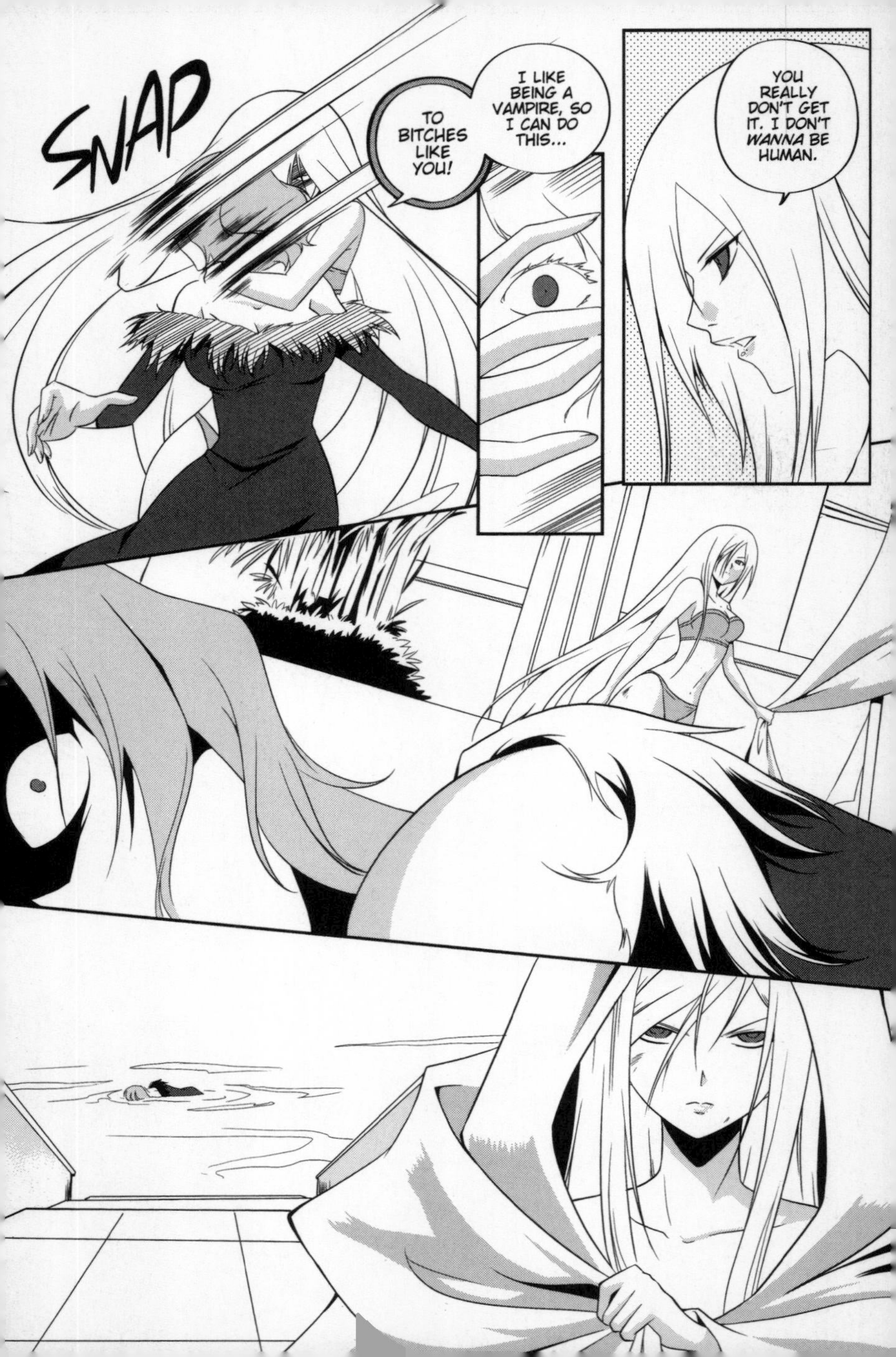
YOU REALLY DON'T GET IT. I DON'T *WANNA* BE HUMAN.
I LIKE BEING A VAMPIRE, SO I CAN DO THIS...
TO BITCHES LIKE YOU!
SNAP

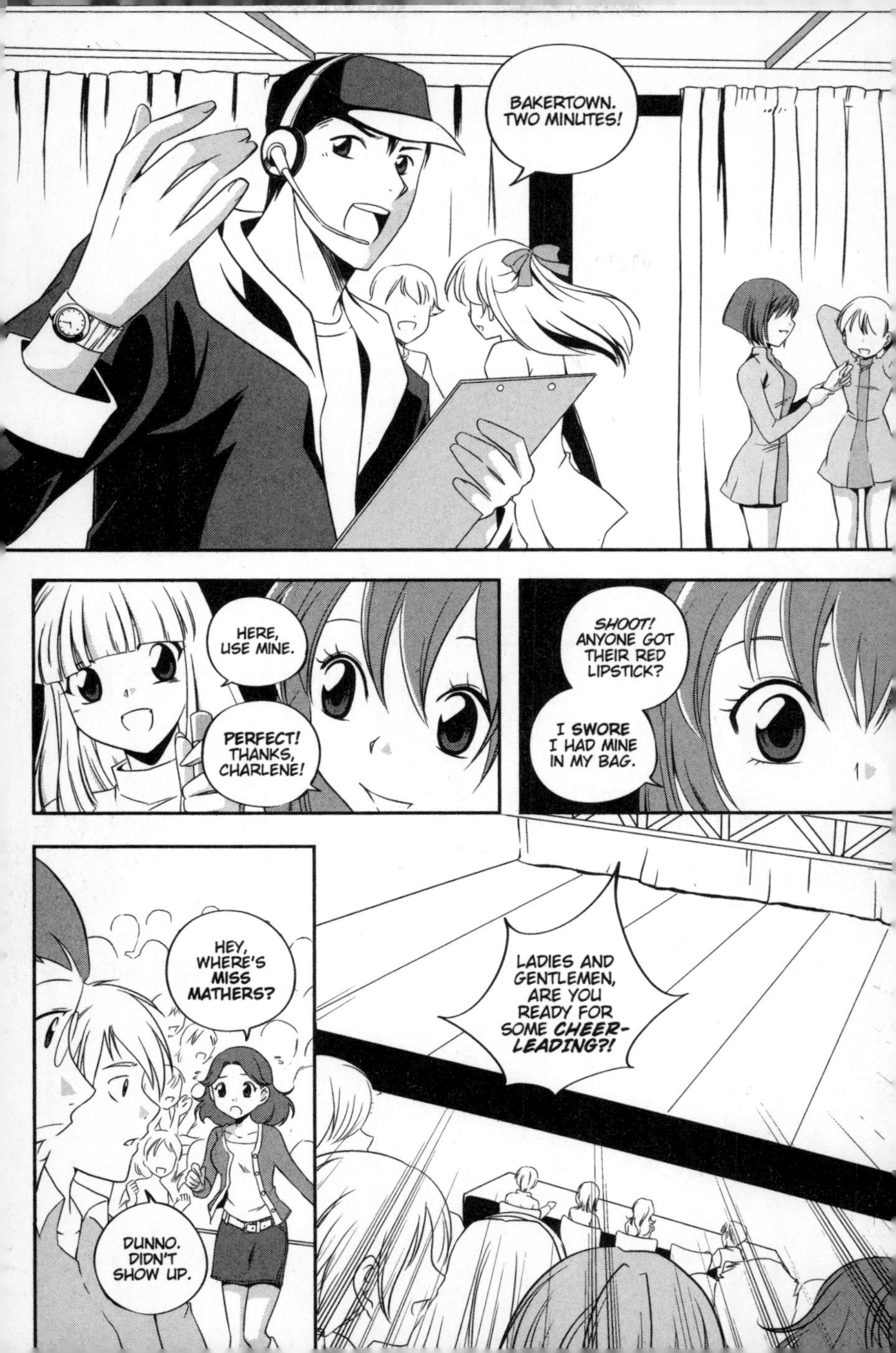
BAKERTOWN. TWO MINUTES!
SHOOT! ANYONE GOT THEIR RED LIPSTICK?
I SWORE I HAD MINE IN MY BAG.
HERE, USE MINE.
PERFECT! THANKS, CHARLENE!
LADIES AND GENTLEMEN, ARE YOU READY FOR SOME *CHEER-LEADING?!*
HEY, WHERE'S MISS MATHERS?
DUNNO. DIDN'T SHOW UP.

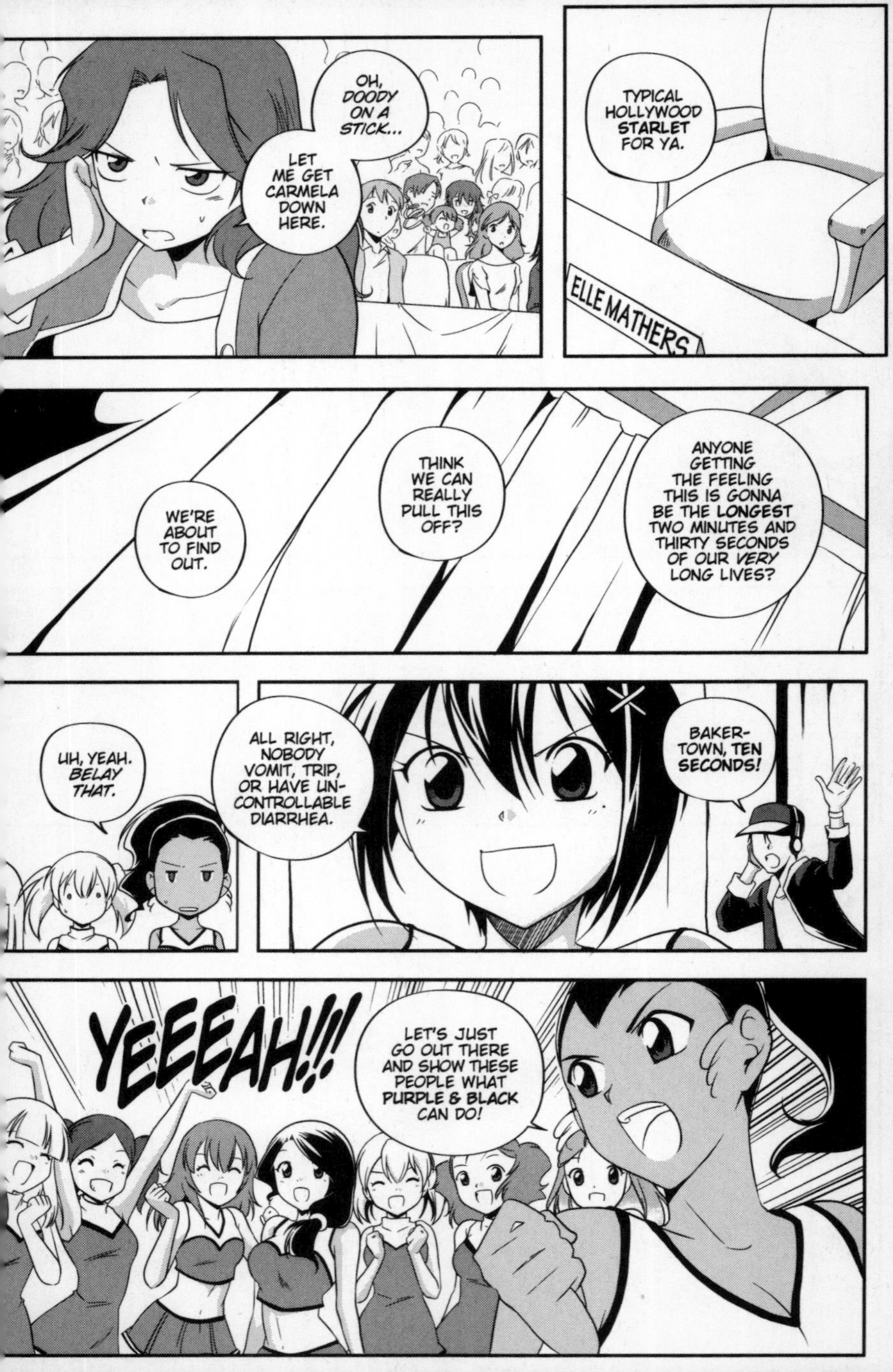
TYPICAL HOLLYWOOD STARLET FOR YA.
ELLE MATHERS
OH, DOODY ON A STICK...
LET ME GET CARMELA DOWN HERE.
ANYONE GETTING THE FEELING THIS IS GONNA BE THE **LONGEST** TWO MINUTES AND THIRTY SECONDS OF OUR *VERY* LONG LIVES?
THINK WE CAN REALLY PULL THIS OFF?
WE'RE ABOUT TO FIND OUT.
BAKER-TOWN, TEN SECONDS!
ALL RIGHT, NOBODY VOMIT, TRIP, OR HAVE UN-CONTROLLABLE DIARRHEA.
UH, YEAH. *BELAY* THAT.
LET'S JUST GO OUT THERE AND SHOW THESE PEOPLE WHAT **PURPLE & BLACK** CAN DO!
YEEEAH!!!

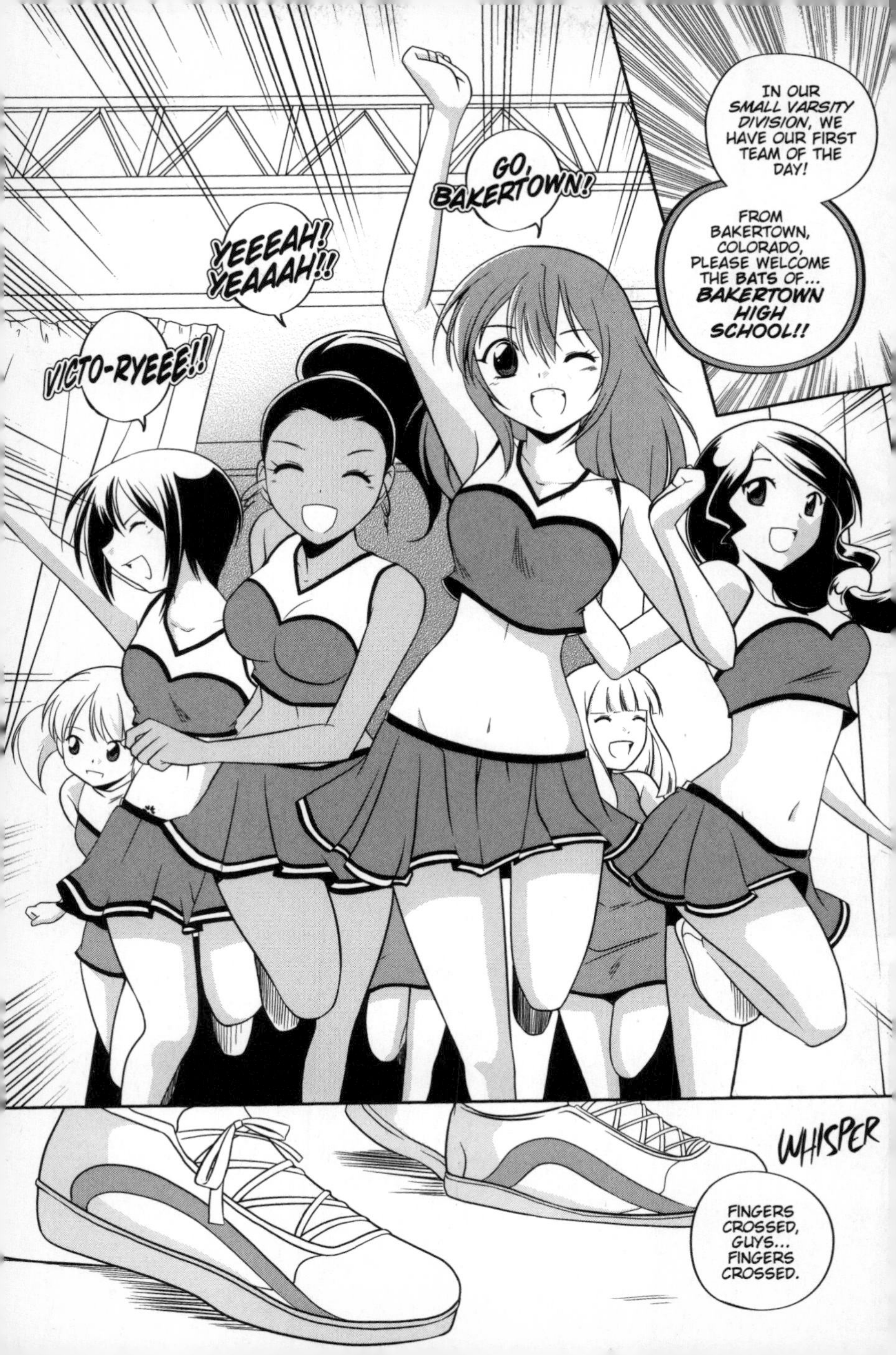
IN OUR SMALL VARSITY DIVISION, WE HAVE OUR FIRST TEAM OF THE DAY!
FROM BAKERTOWN, COLORADO, PLEASE WELCOME THE BATS OF... BAKERTOWN HIGH SCHOOL!!
GO, BAKERTOWN!
YEEEAH! YEAAAH!!
VICTO-RYEEE!!
WHISPER
FINGERS CROSSED, GUYS... FINGERS CROSSED.

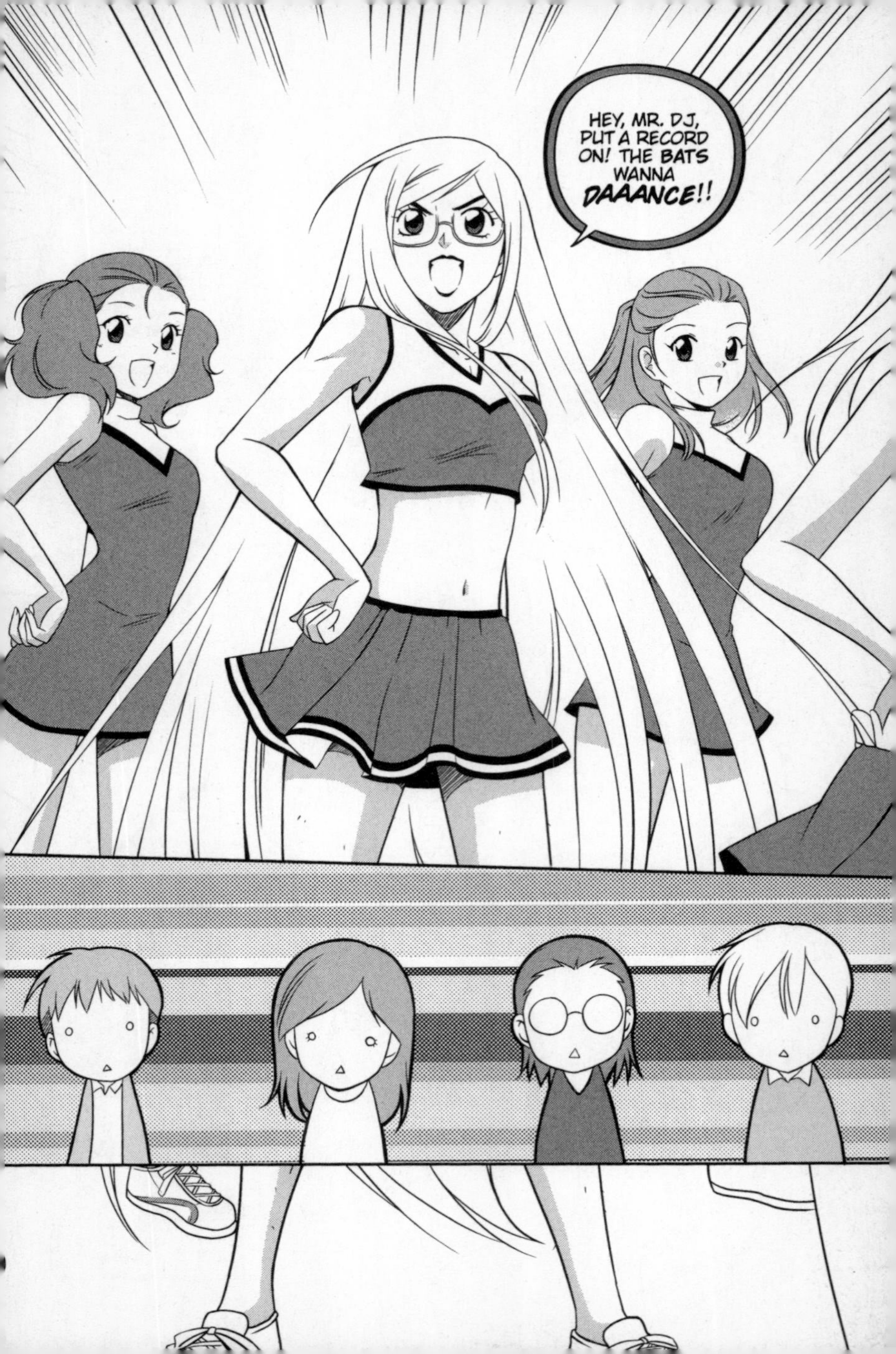
HEY, MR. DJ, PUT A RECORD ON! THE BATS WANNA DAAANCE!!

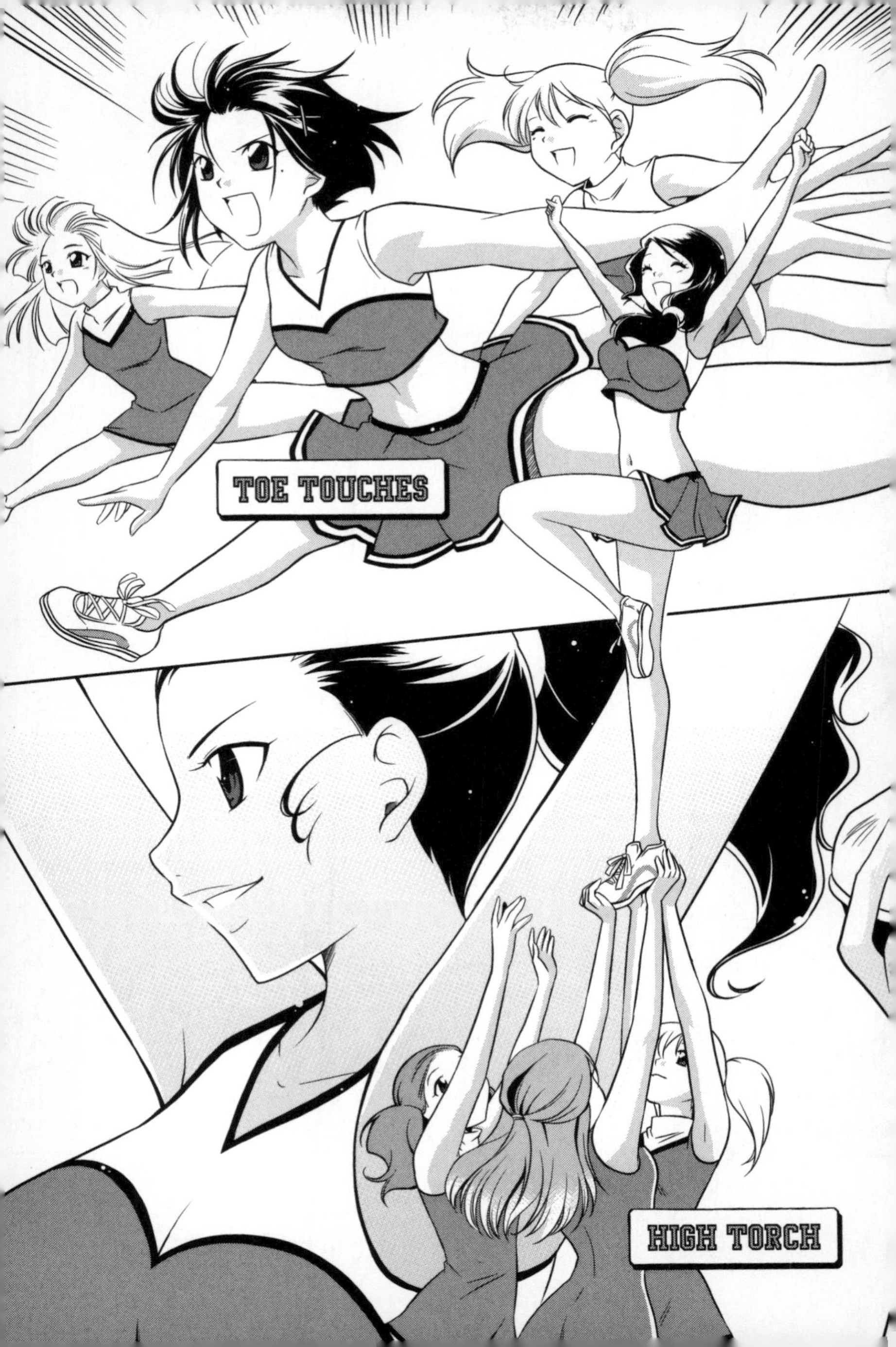
TOE TOUCHES
HIGH TORCH

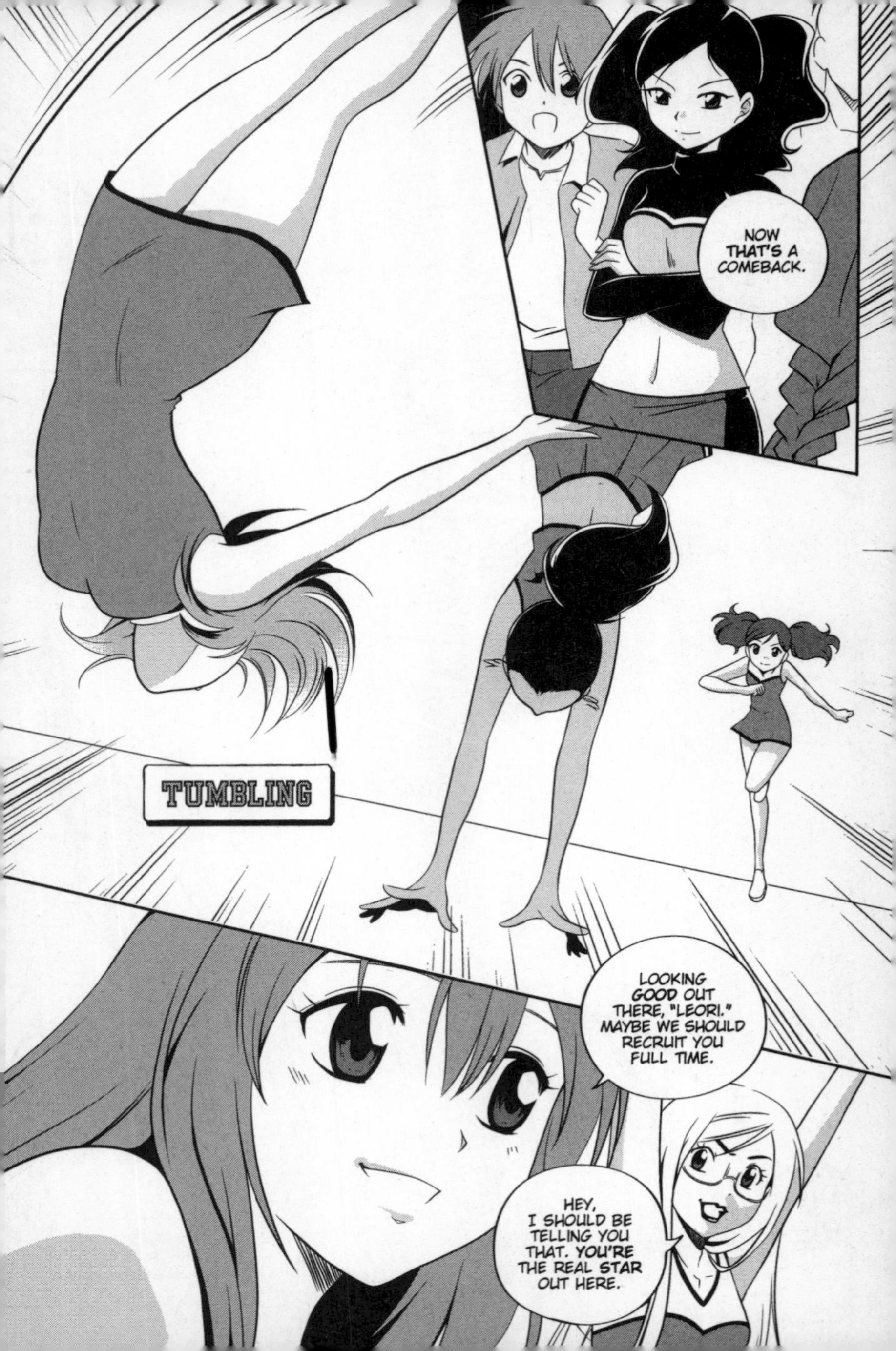
NOW THAT'S A COMEBACK.
TUMBLING
LOOKING GOOD OUT THERE, "LEORI." MAYBE WE SHOULD RECRUIT YOU FULL TIME.
HEY, I SHOULD BE TELLING YOU THAT. YOU'RE THE REAL STAR OUT HERE.

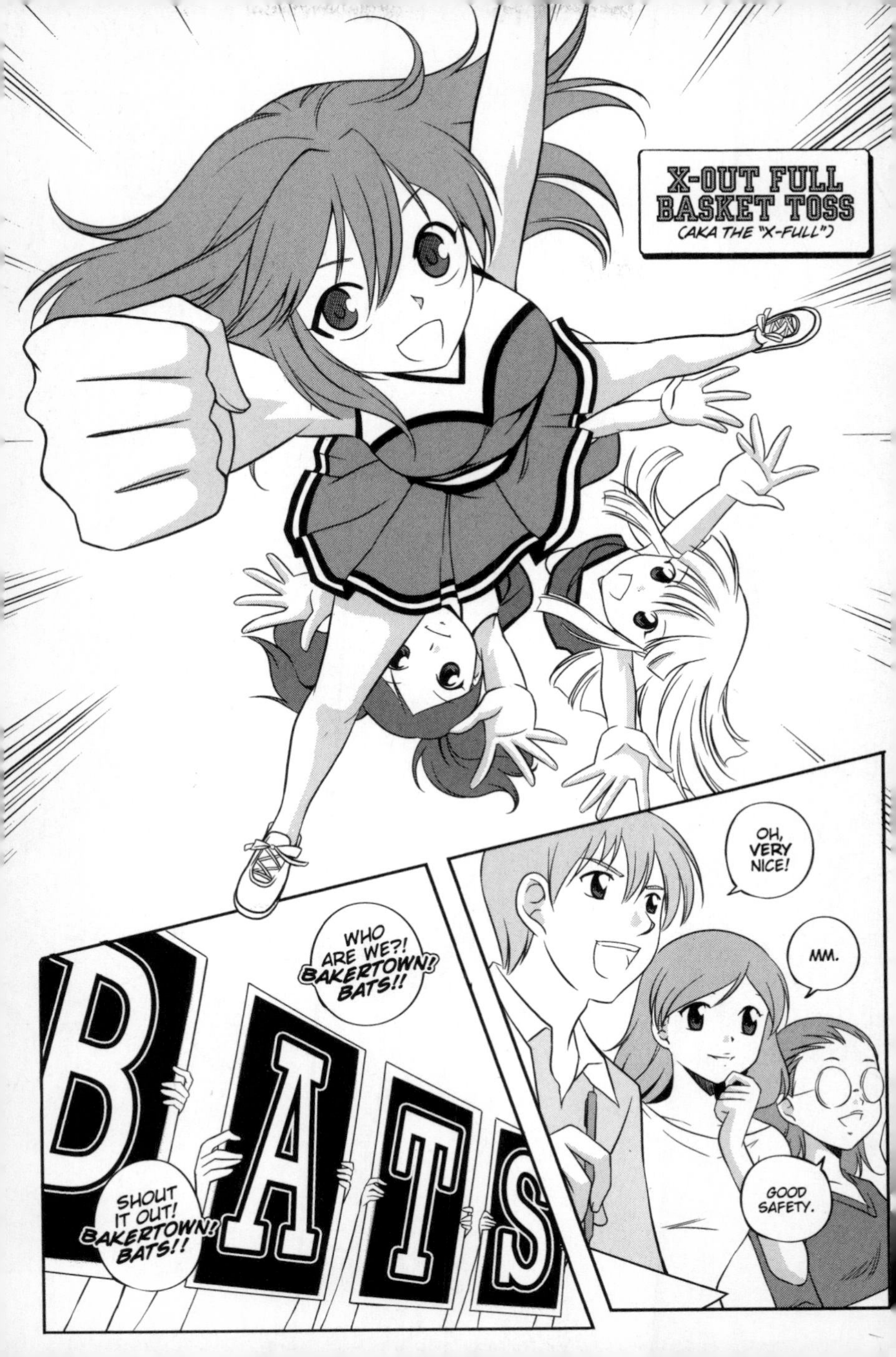
X-OUT FULL BASKET TOSS
(AKA THE "X-FULL")
OH, VERY NICE!
MM.
GOOD SAFETY.
WHO ARE WE?! BAKERTOWN! BATS!!
SHOUT IT OUT! BAKERTOWN! BATS!!
BATS

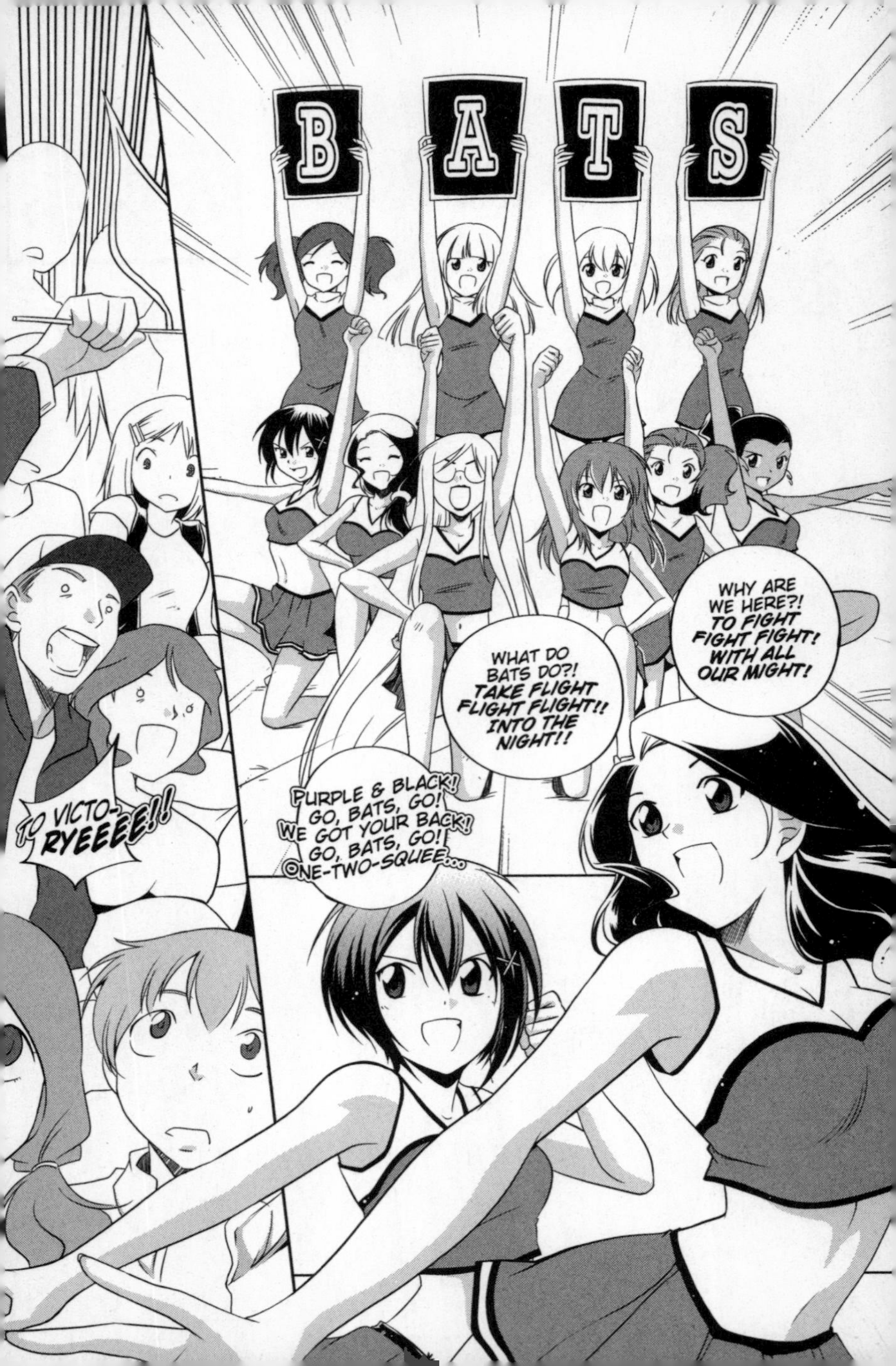
B A T S
WHY ARE WE HERE?! TO FIGHT FIGHT FIGHT! WITH ALL OUR MIGHT!
WHAT DO BATS DO?! TAKE FLIGHT FLIGHT FLIGHT!! INTO THE NIGHT!!
PURPLE & BLACK! GO, BATS, GO! WE GOT YOUR BACK! GO, BATS, GO! ONE-TWO-SQUEE...
TO VICTO-RYEEEEE!!

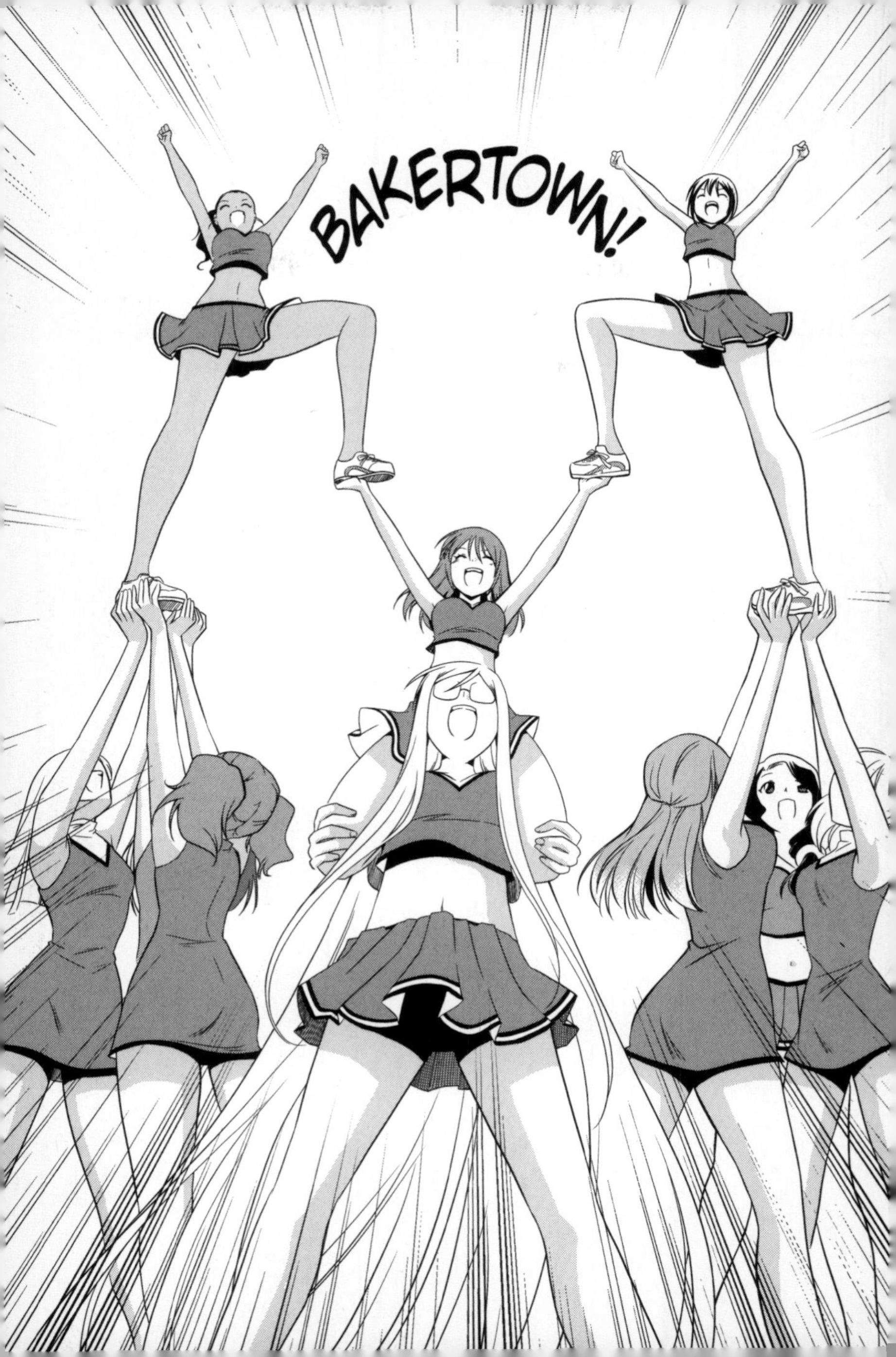
BAKERTOWN!

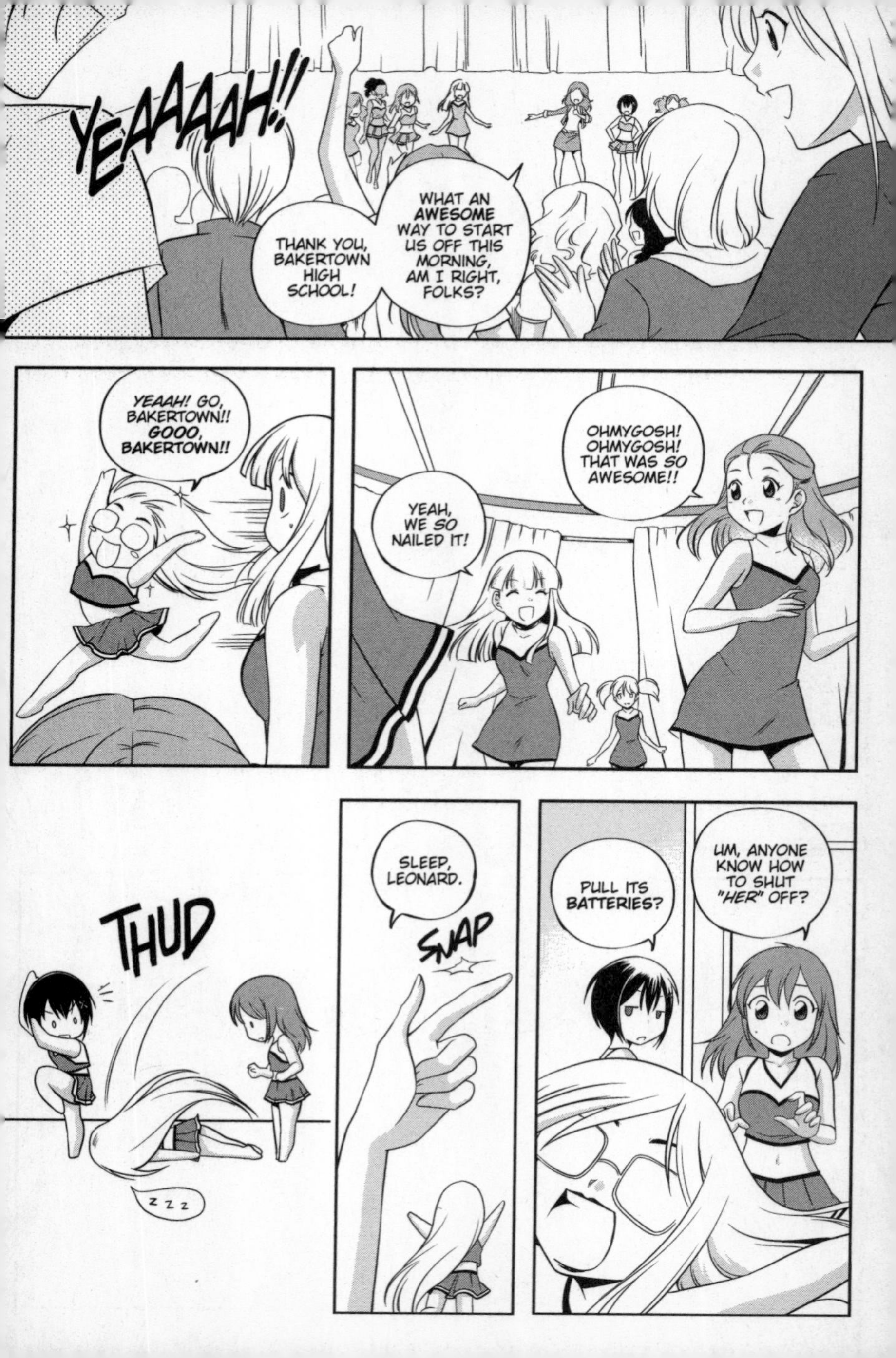
YEAAAAH!!
WHAT AN AWESOME WAY TO START US OFF THIS MORNING, AM I RIGHT, FOLKS?
THANK YOU, BAKERTOWN HIGH SCHOOL!
OHMYGOSH! OHMYGOSH! THAT WAS SO AWESOME!!
YEAH, WE SO NAILED IT!
YEAAH! GO, BAKERTOWN!! GOOO, BAKERTOWN!!
UM, ANYONE KNOW HOW TO SHUT "HER" OFF?
PULL ITS BATTERIES?
SLEEP, LEONARD.
SNAP
THUD
Z Z Z

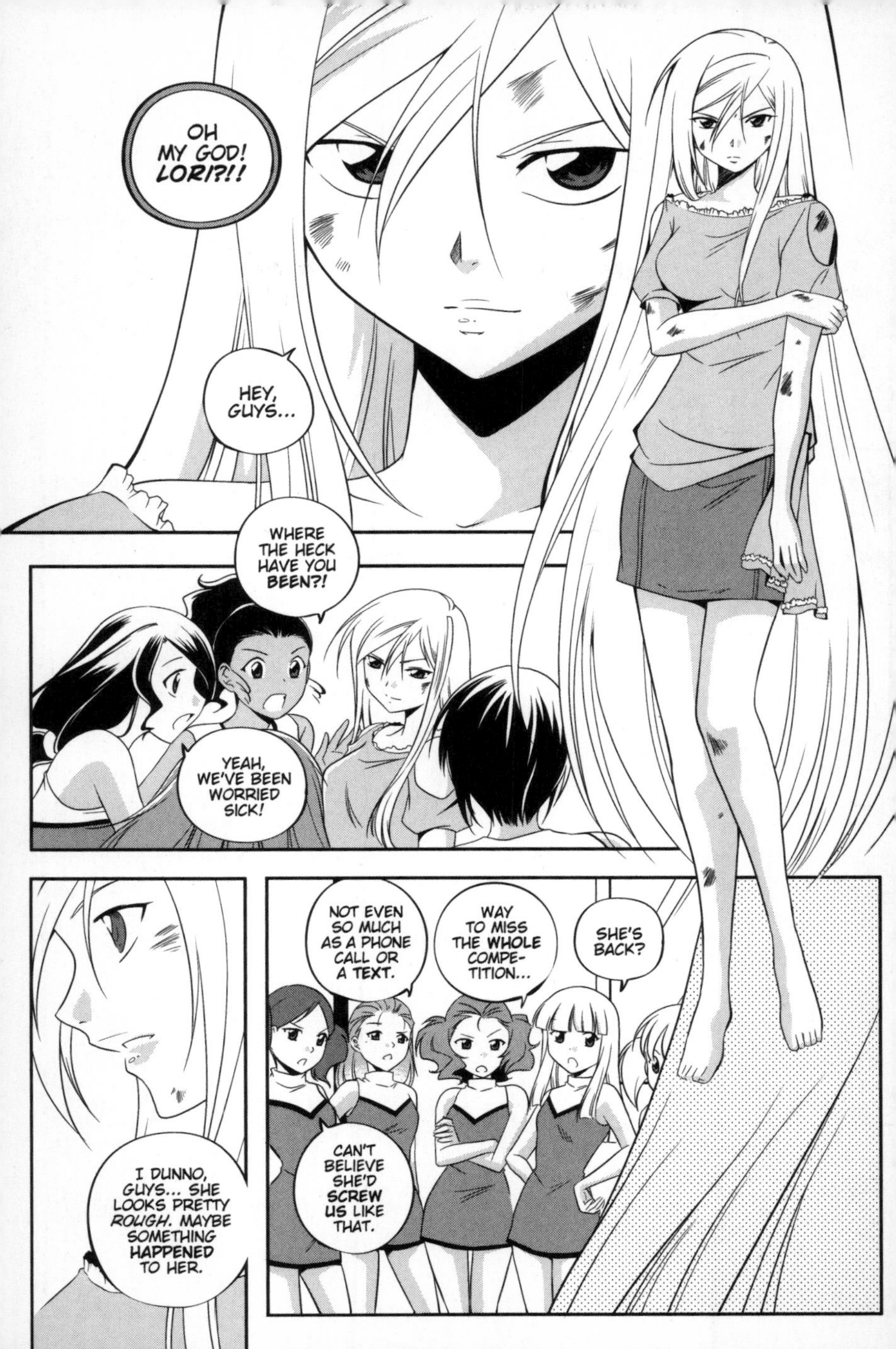
OH MY GOD! LORI?!!
HEY, GUYS...
WHERE THE HECK HAVE YOU BEEN?!
YEAH, WE'VE BEEN WORRIED SICK!
SHE'S BACK?
WAY TO MISS THE WHOLE COMPETITION...
NOT EVEN SO MUCH AS A PHONE CALL OR A TEXT.
CAN'T BELIEVE SHE'D SCREW US LIKE THAT.
I DUNNO, GUYS... SHE LOOKS PRETTY ROUGH. MAYBE SOMETHING HAPPENED TO HER.

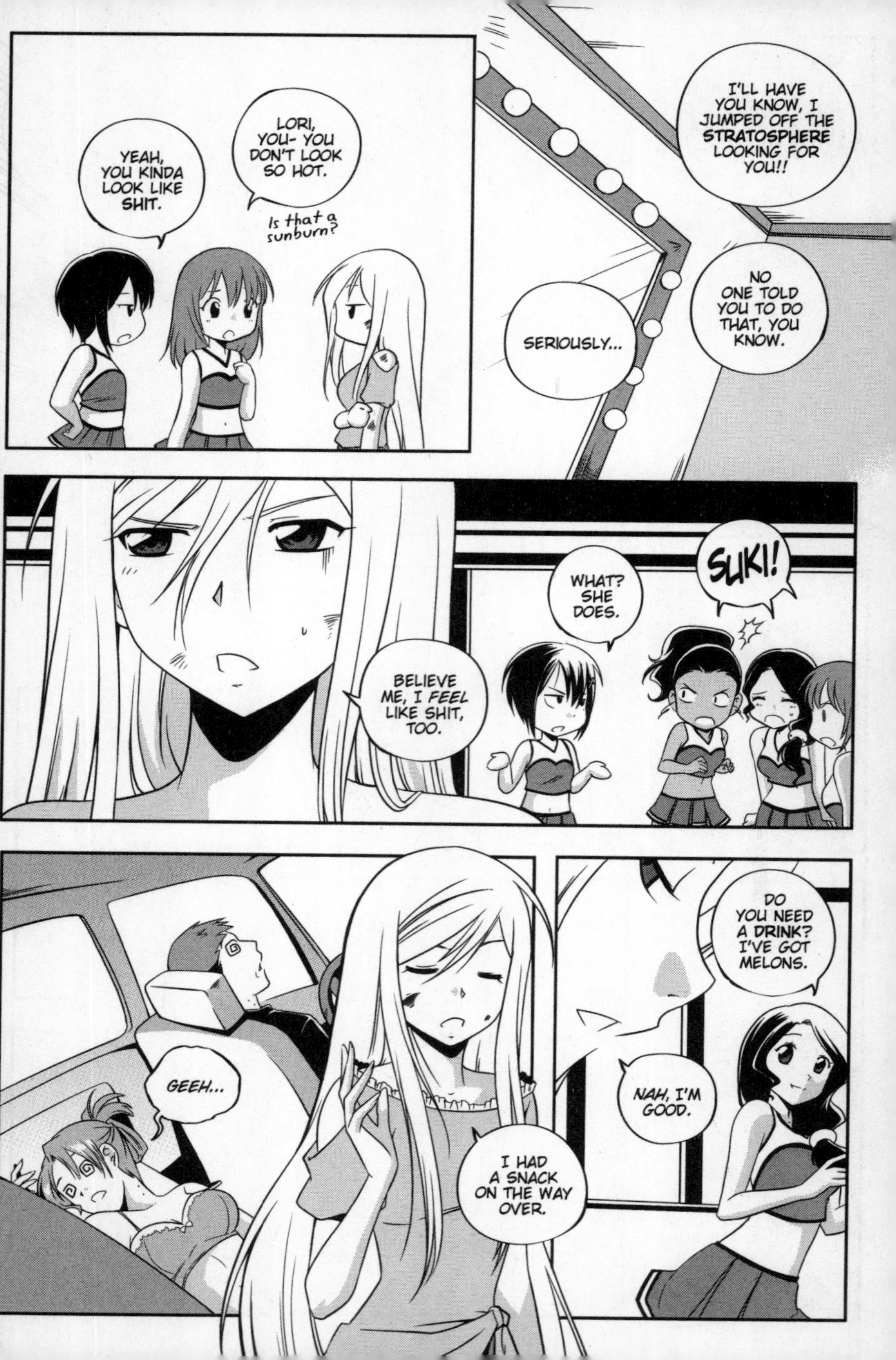
I'LL HAVE YOU KNOW, I JUMPED OFF THE STRATOSPHERE LOOKING FOR YOU!!
NO ONE TOLD YOU TO DO THAT, YOU KNOW.
SERIOUSLY...
LORI, YOU- YOU DON'T LOOK SO HOT.
Is that a sunburn?
YEAH, YOU KINDA LOOK LIKE SHIT.
SUKI!
WHAT? SHE DOES.
BELIEVE ME, I *FEEL* LIKE SHIT, TOO.
DO YOU NEED A DRINK? I'VE GOT MELONS.
NAH, I'M GOOD.
I HAD A SNACK ON THE WAY OVER.
GEEH...

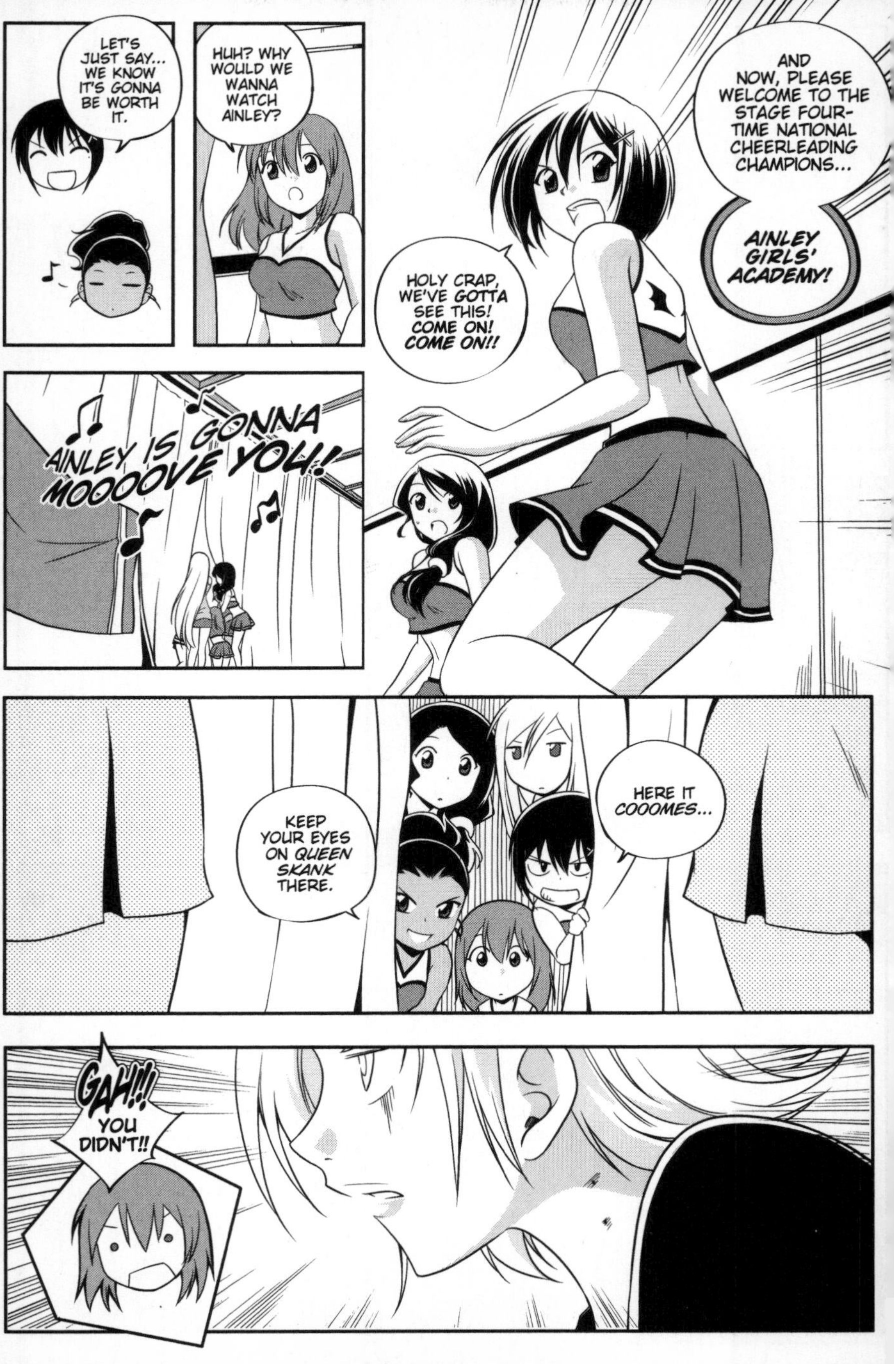
AND NOW, PLEASE WELCOME TO THE STAGE FOUR-TIME NATIONAL CHEERLEADING CHAMPIONS...
AINLEY GIRLS' ACADEMY!
HOLY CRAP, WE'VE GOTTA SEE THIS! COME ON! COME ON!!
HUH? WHY WOULD WE WANNA WATCH AINLEY?
LET'S JUST SAY... WE KNOW IT'S GONNA BE WORTH IT.
AINLEY IS GONNA MOOOOVE YOU!
HERE IT COOOMES...
KEEP YOUR EYES ON QUEEN SKANK THERE.
GAH!!!
YOU DIDN'T!!

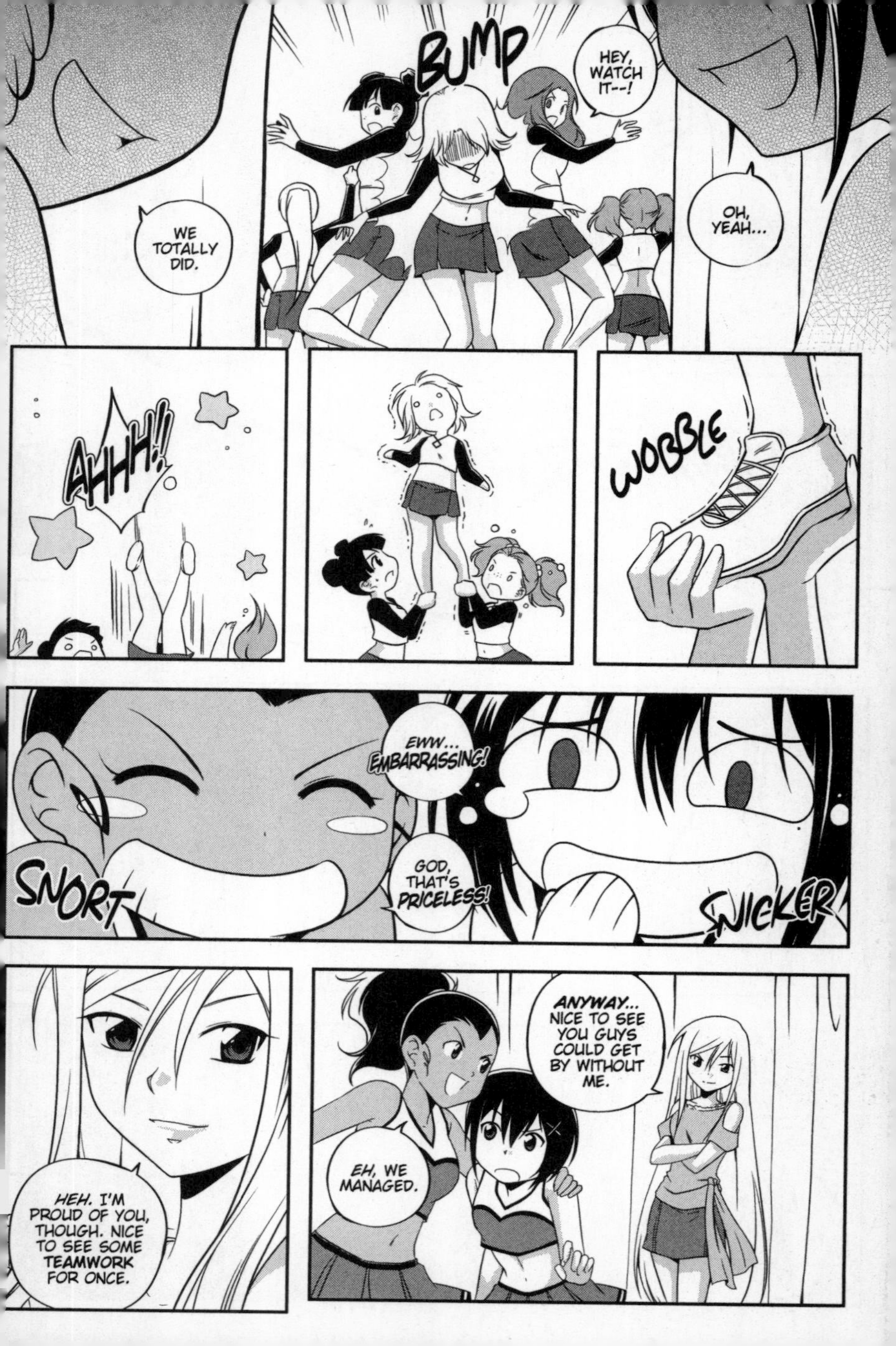
OH, YEAH...
BUMP
HEY, WATCH IT--!
WE TOTALLY DID.
WOBBLE
AHHH!!
EWW... EMBARRASSING!
GOD, THAT'S PRICELESS!
SNICKER
SNORT
ANYWAY... NICE TO SEE YOU GUYS COULD GET BY WITHOUT ME.
EH, WE MANAGED.
HEH. I'M PROUD OF YOU, THOUGH. NICE TO SEE SOME TEAMWORK FOR ONCE.

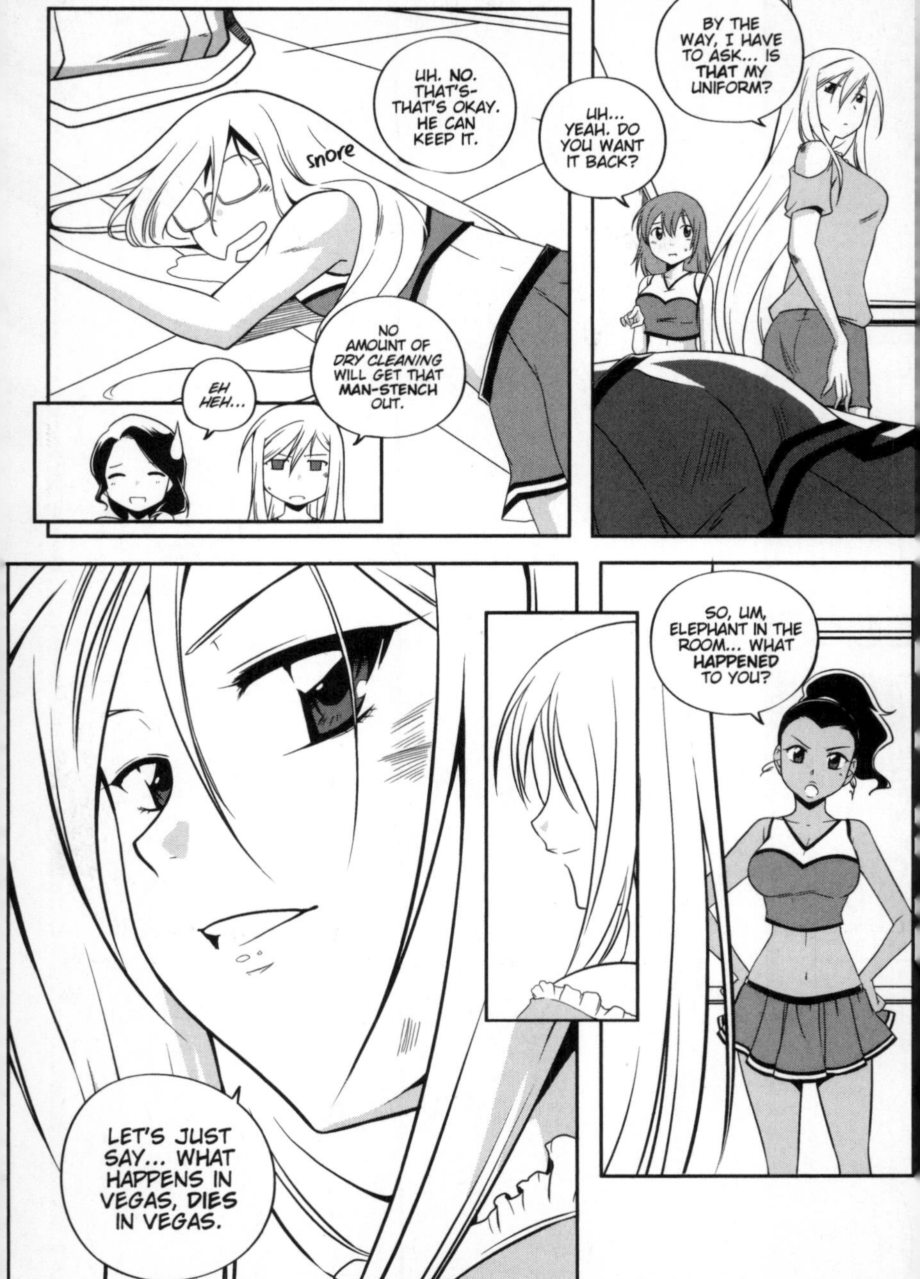
BY THE WAY, I HAVE TO ASK... IS THAT MY UNIFORM?
UH... YEAH. DO YOU WANT IT BACK?
UH. NO. THAT'S- THAT'S OKAY. HE CAN KEEP IT.
snore
NO AMOUNT OF DRY CLEANING WILL GET THAT MAN-STENCH OUT.
EH HEH...
SO, UM, ELEPHANT IN THE ROOM... WHAT HAPPENED TO YOU?
LET'S JUST SAY... WHAT HAPPENS IN VEGAS, DIES IN VEGAS.

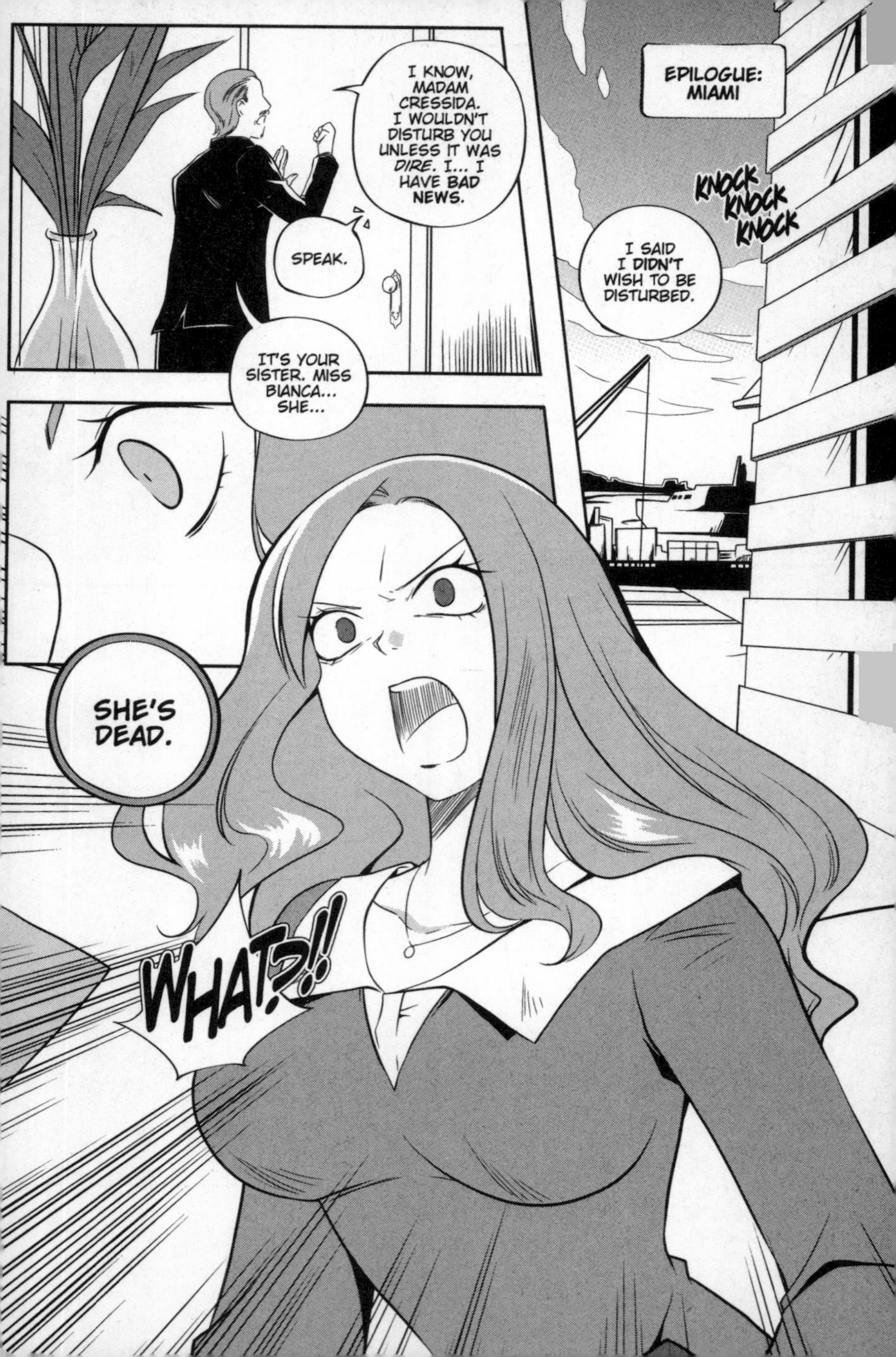
EPILOGUE: MIAMI
KNOCK KNOCK KNOCK
I SAID I DIDN'T WISH TO BE DISTURBED.
I KNOW, MADAM CRESSIDA. I WOULDN'T DISTURB YOU UNLESS IT WAS *DIRE*. I... I HAVE BAD NEWS.
SPEAK.
IT'S YOUR SISTER. MISS BIANCA... SHE...
SHE'S DEAD.
WHAT?!!

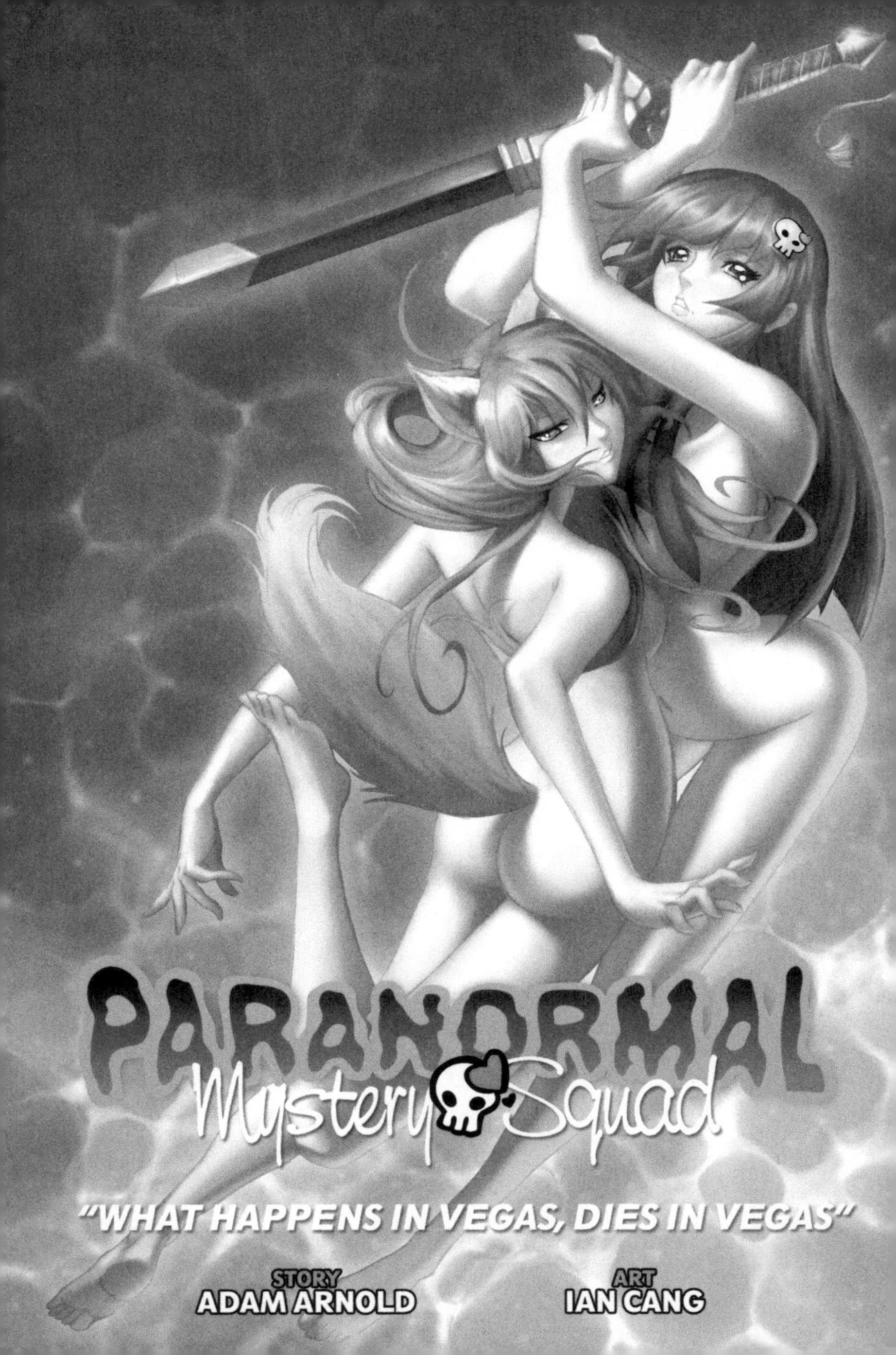
PARANORMAL
Mystery Squad
"WHAT HAPPENS IN VEGAS, DIES IN VEGAS"
STORY
ADAM ARNOLD
ART
IAN CANG

PARANORMAL Mystery Squad

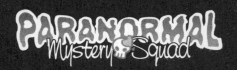

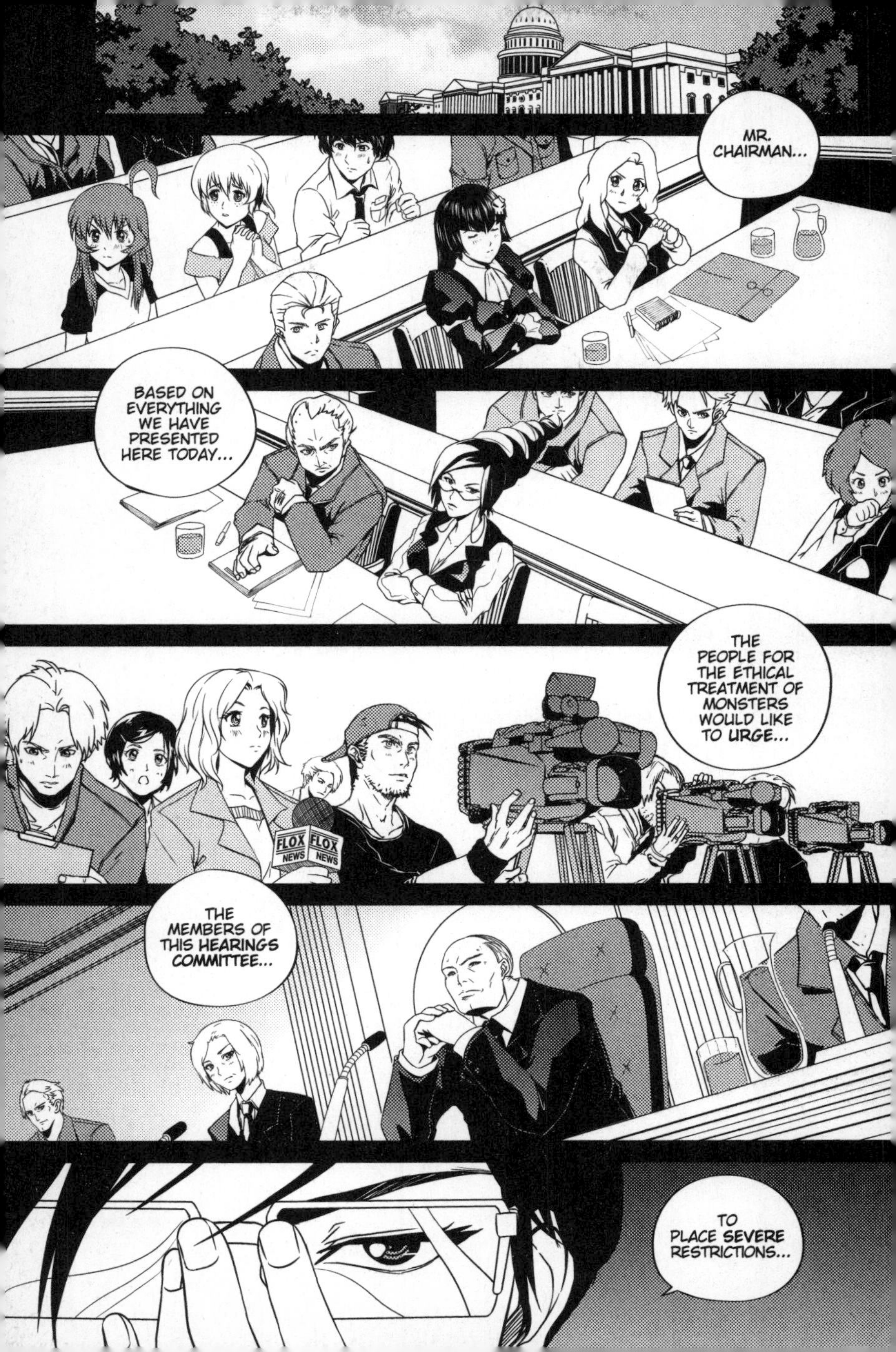
MR. CHAIRMAN...
BASED ON EVERYTHING WE HAVE PRESENTED HERE TODAY...
THE PEOPLE FOR THE ETHICAL TREATMENT OF MONSTERS WOULD LIKE TO URGE...
FLOX NEWS
FLOX NEWS
THE MEMBERS OF THIS HEARINGS COMMITTEE...
TO PLACE SEVERE RESTRICTIONS...

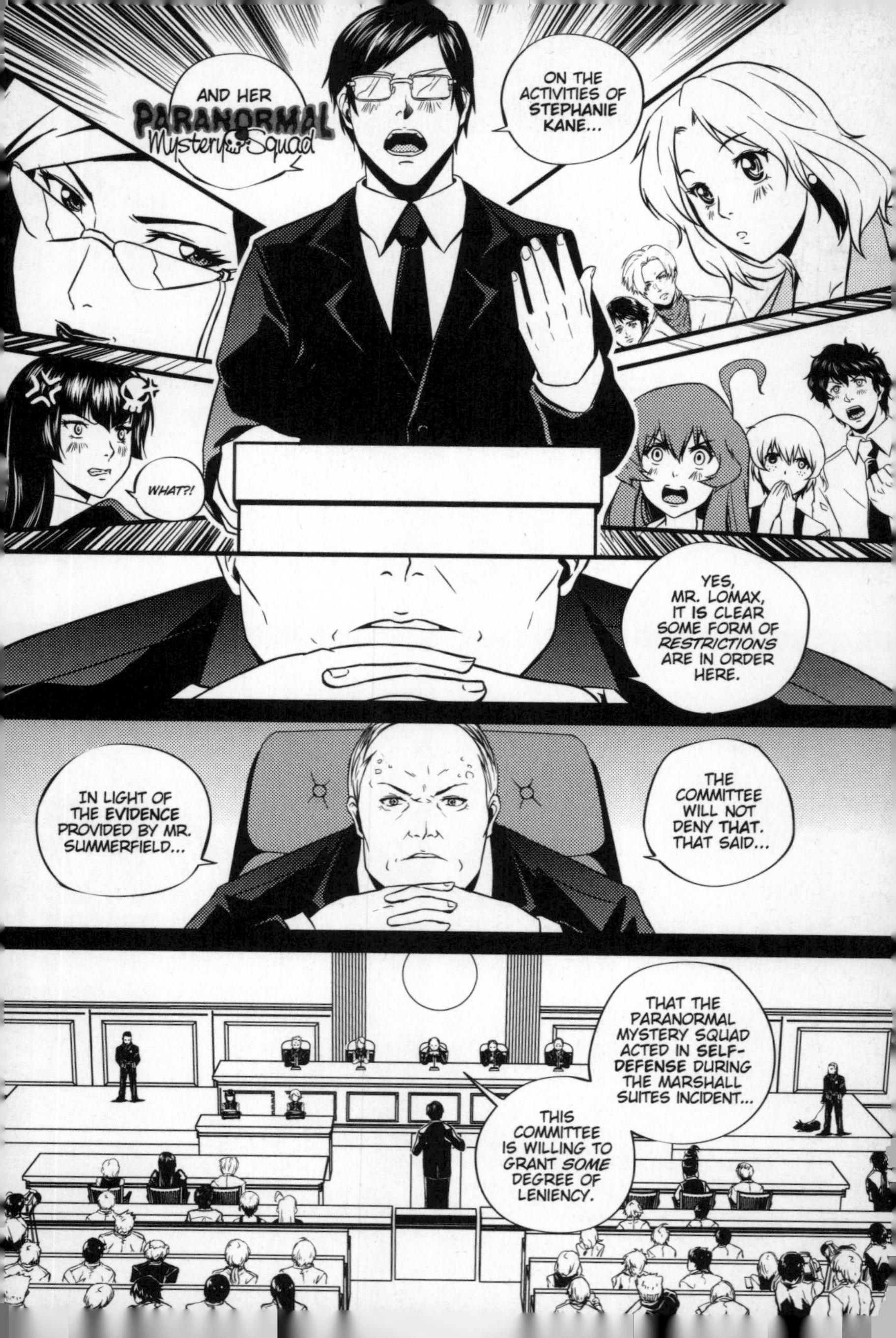

ON THE ACTIVITIES OF STEPHANIE KANE...
AND HER PARANORMAL Mystery Squad
WHAT?!
YES, MR. LOMAX, IT IS CLEAR SOME FORM OF *RESTRICTIONS* ARE IN ORDER HERE.
THE COMMITTEE WILL NOT DENY THAT. THAT SAID...
IN LIGHT OF THE EVIDENCE PROVIDED BY MR. SUMMERFIELD...
THAT THE PARANORMAL MYSTERY SQUAD ACTED IN SELF-DEFENSE DURING THE MARSHALL SUITES INCIDENT...
THIS COMMITTEE IS WILLING TO GRANT *SOME* DEGREE OF LENIENCY.

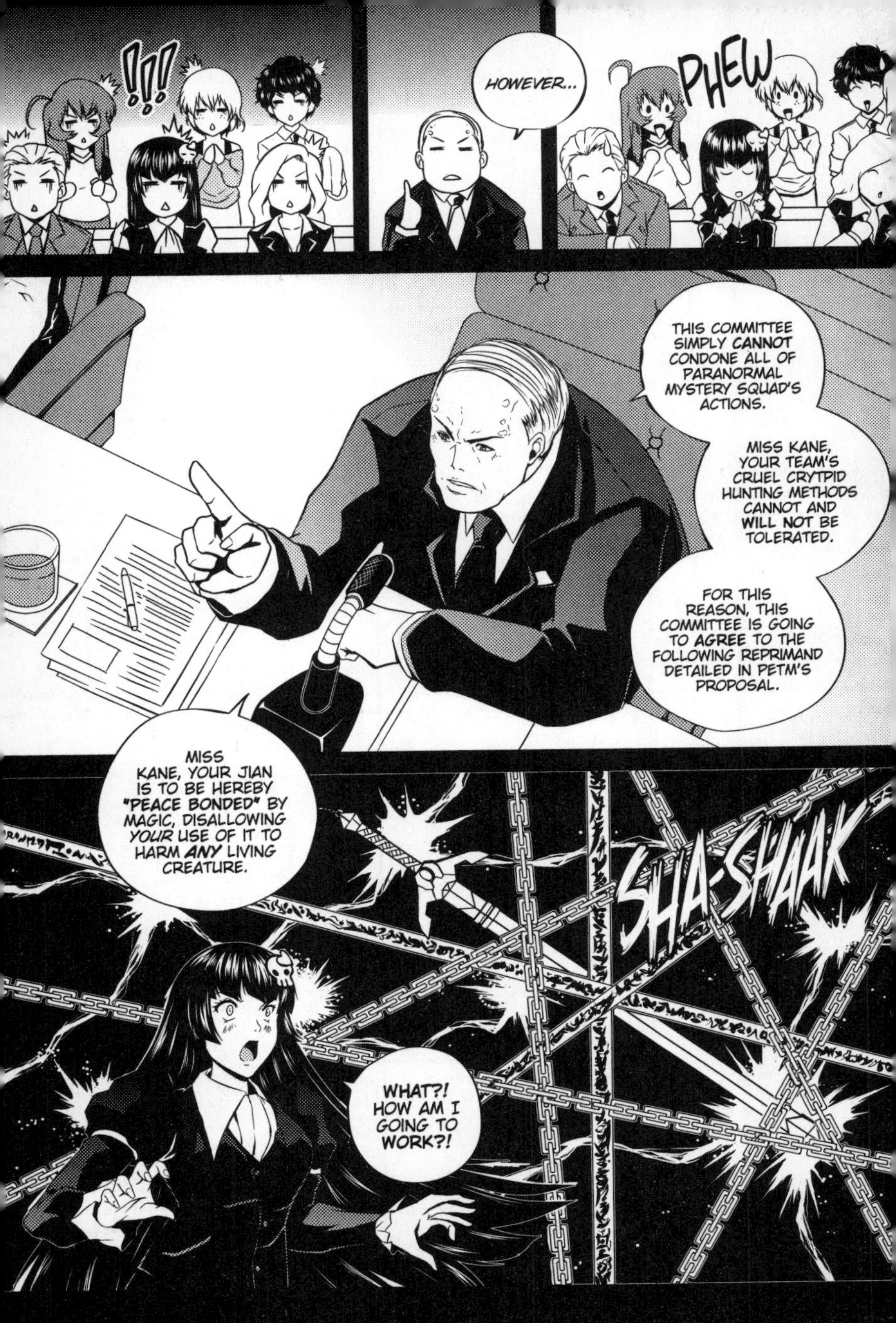
PHEW
HOWEVER...
!?!!
THIS COMMITTEE SIMPLY CANNOT CONDONE ALL OF PARANORMAL MYSTERY SQUAD'S ACTIONS.
MISS KANE, YOUR TEAM'S CRUEL CRYTPID HUNTING METHODS CANNOT AND WILL NOT BE TOLERATED.
FOR THIS REASON, THIS COMMITTEE IS GOING TO AGREE TO THE FOLLOWING REPRIMAND DETAILED IN PETM'S PROPOSAL.
SHA-SHAAK
MISS KANE, YOUR JIAN IS TO BE HEREBY "PEACE BONDED" BY MAGIC, DISALLOWING YOUR USE OF IT TO HARM ANY LIVING CREATURE.
WHAT?! HOW AM I GOING TO WORK?!

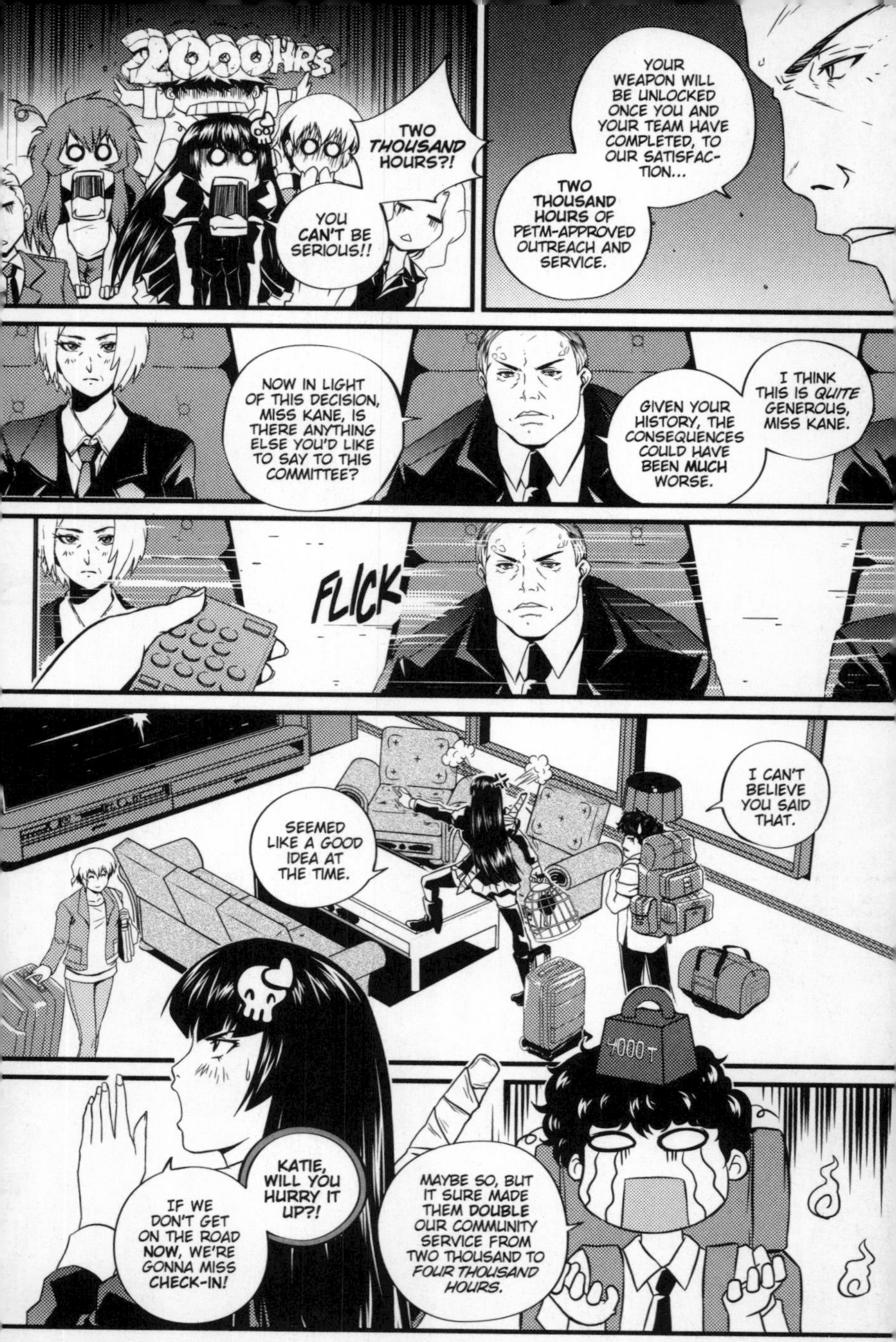
YOUR WEAPON WILL BE UNLOCKED ONCE YOU AND YOUR TEAM HAVE COMPLETED, TO OUR SATISFACTION...
TWO THOUSAND HOURS OF PETM-APPROVED OUTREACH AND SERVICE.
2000HRS
TWO *THOUSAND* HOURS?!
YOU CAN'T BE SERIOUS!!
I THINK THIS IS *QUITE* GENEROUS, MISS KANE.
GIVEN YOUR HISTORY, THE CONSEQUENCES COULD HAVE BEEN **MUCH** WORSE.
NOW IN LIGHT OF THIS DECISION, MISS KANE, IS THERE ANYTHING ELSE YOU'D LIKE TO SAY TO THIS COMMITTEE?
FLICK
I CAN'T BELIEVE YOU SAID THAT.
SEEMED LIKE A GOOD IDEA AT THE TIME.
4000T
MAYBE SO, BUT IT SURE MADE THEM **DOUBLE** OUR COMMUNITY SERVICE FROM TWO THOUSAND TO *FOUR THOUSAND HOURS.*
KATIE, WILL YOU HURRY IT UP?!
IF WE DON'T GET ON THE ROAD NOW, WE'RE GONNA MISS CHECK-IN!

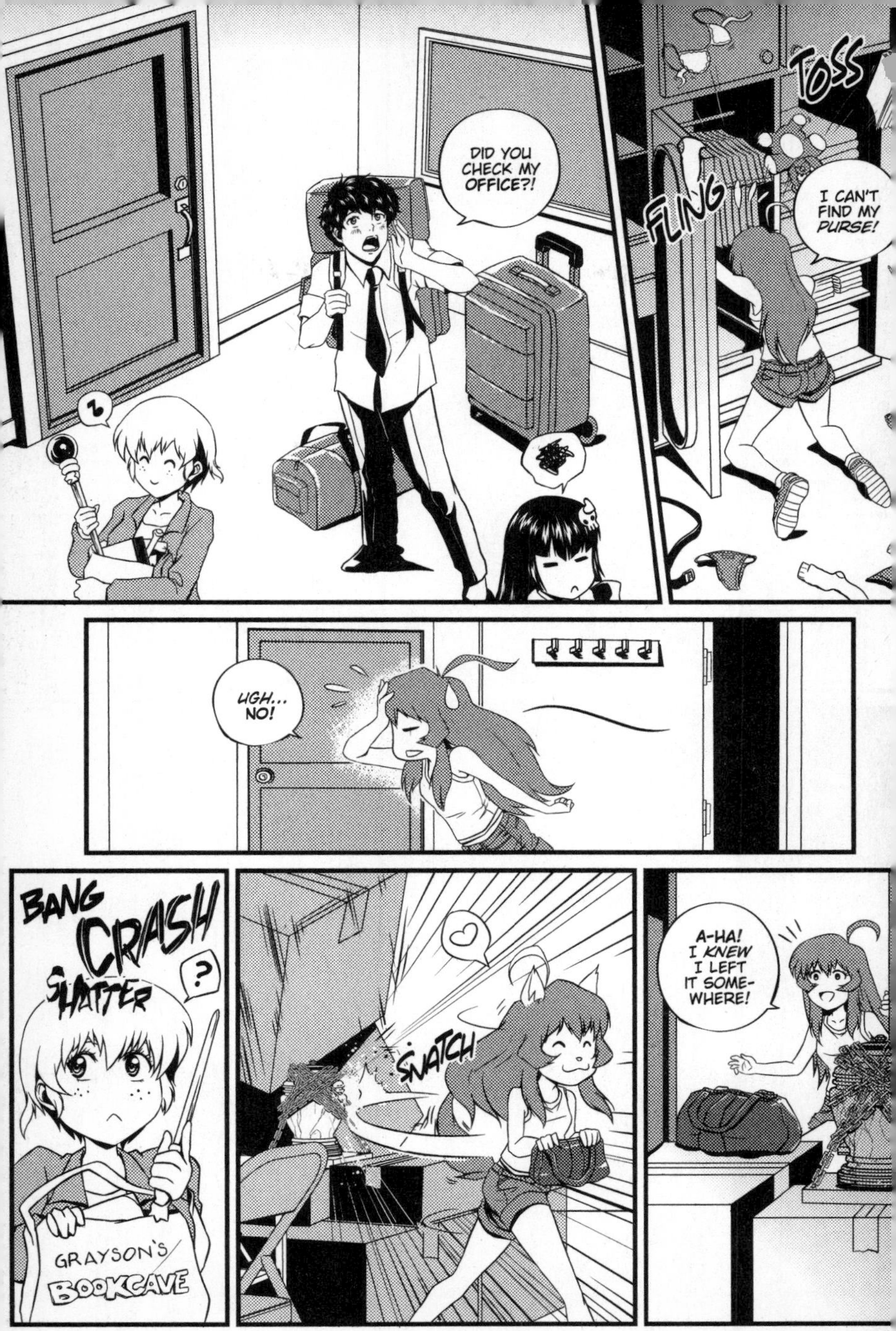
TOSS
FLING
I CAN'T FIND MY *PURSE!*
DID YOU CHECK MY OFFICE?!
UGH... NO!
A-HA! I *KNEW* I LEFT IT SOME-WHERE!
SNATCH
BANG
CRASH
SHATTER
?
GRAYSON'S BOOKCAVE

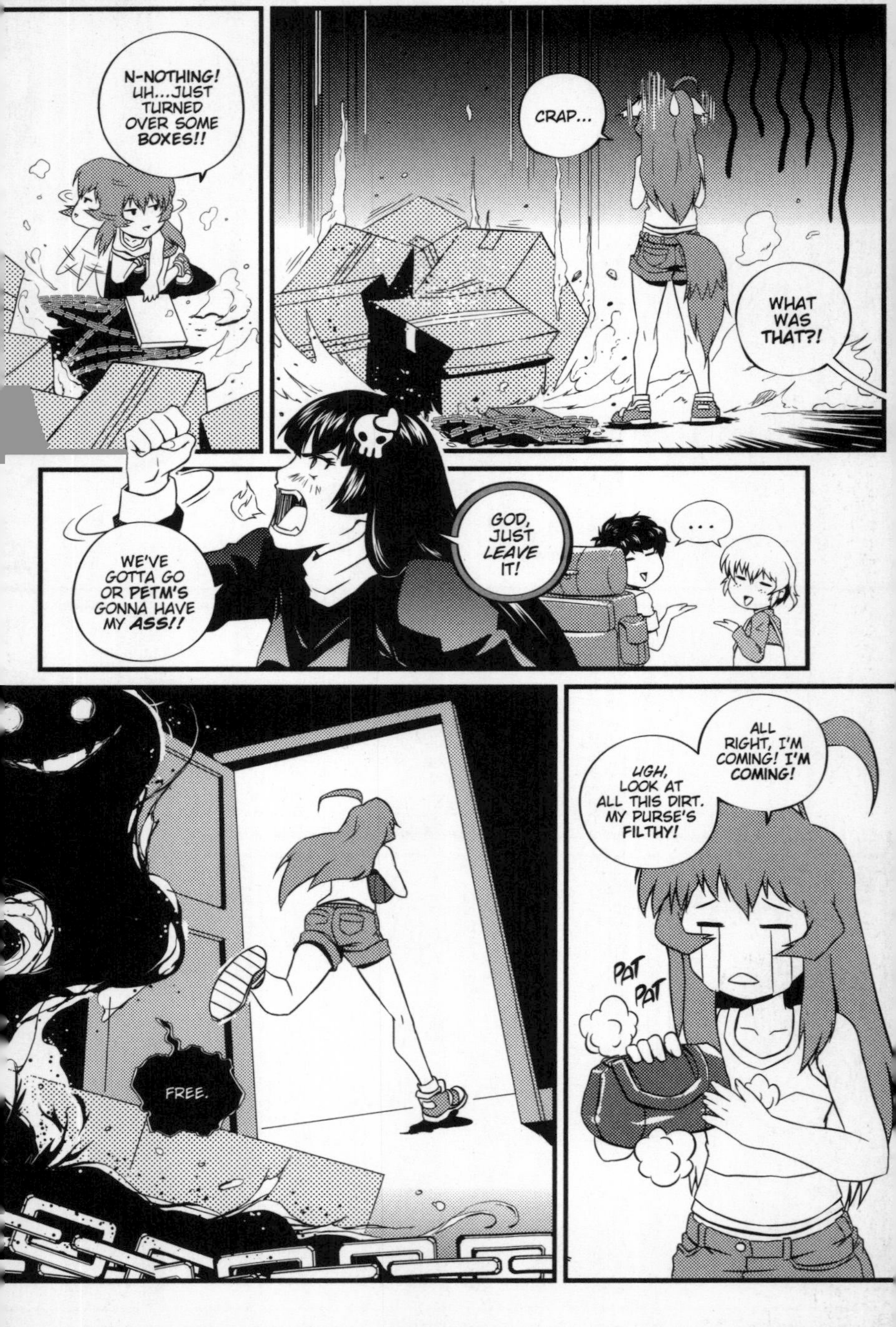
CRAP...
WHAT WAS THAT?!
N-NOTHING! UH...JUST TURNED OVER SOME BOXES!!
...
GOD, JUST LEAVE IT!
WE'VE GOTTA GO OR PETM'S GONNA HAVE MY ASS!!
ALL RIGHT, I'M COMING! I'M COMING!
UGH, LOOK AT ALL THIS DIRT. MY PURSE'S FILTHY!
PAT PAT
FREE.

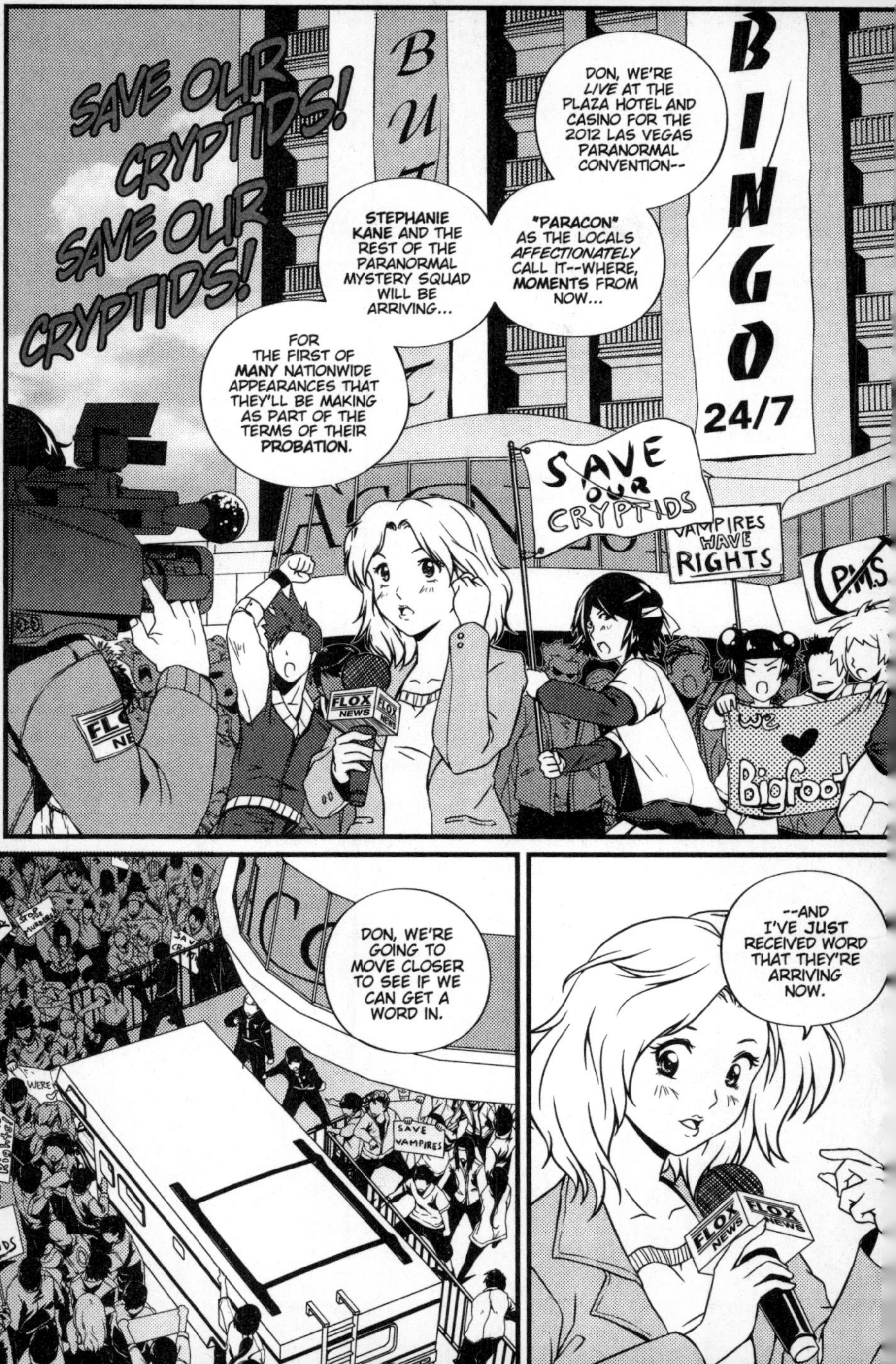
DON, WE'RE *LIVE* AT THE PLAZA HOTEL AND CASINO FOR THE 2012 LAS VEGAS PARANORMAL CONVENTION--
"PARACON" AS THE LOCALS *AFFECTIONATELY* CALL IT--WHERE, **MOMENTS FROM** NOW...
STEPHANIE KANE AND THE REST OF THE PARANORMAL MYSTERY SQUAD WILL BE ARRIVING...
FOR THE FIRST OF MANY NATIONWIDE APPEARANCES THAT THEY'LL BE MAKING AS PART OF THE TERMS OF THEIR PROBATION.
SAVE OUR CRYPTIDS! SAVE OUR CRYPTIDS!
BINGO 24/7
SAVE OUR CRYPTIDS
VAMPIRES HAVE RIGHTS
P.M.S
We ♥ Bigfoot
FLOX NEWS
--AND I'VE **JUST** RECEIVED WORD THAT THEY'RE ARRIVING NOW.
DON, WE'RE GOING TO MOVE CLOSER TO SEE IF WE CAN GET A WORD IN.
SAVE VAMPIRES
CRYPTID
FLOX NEWS

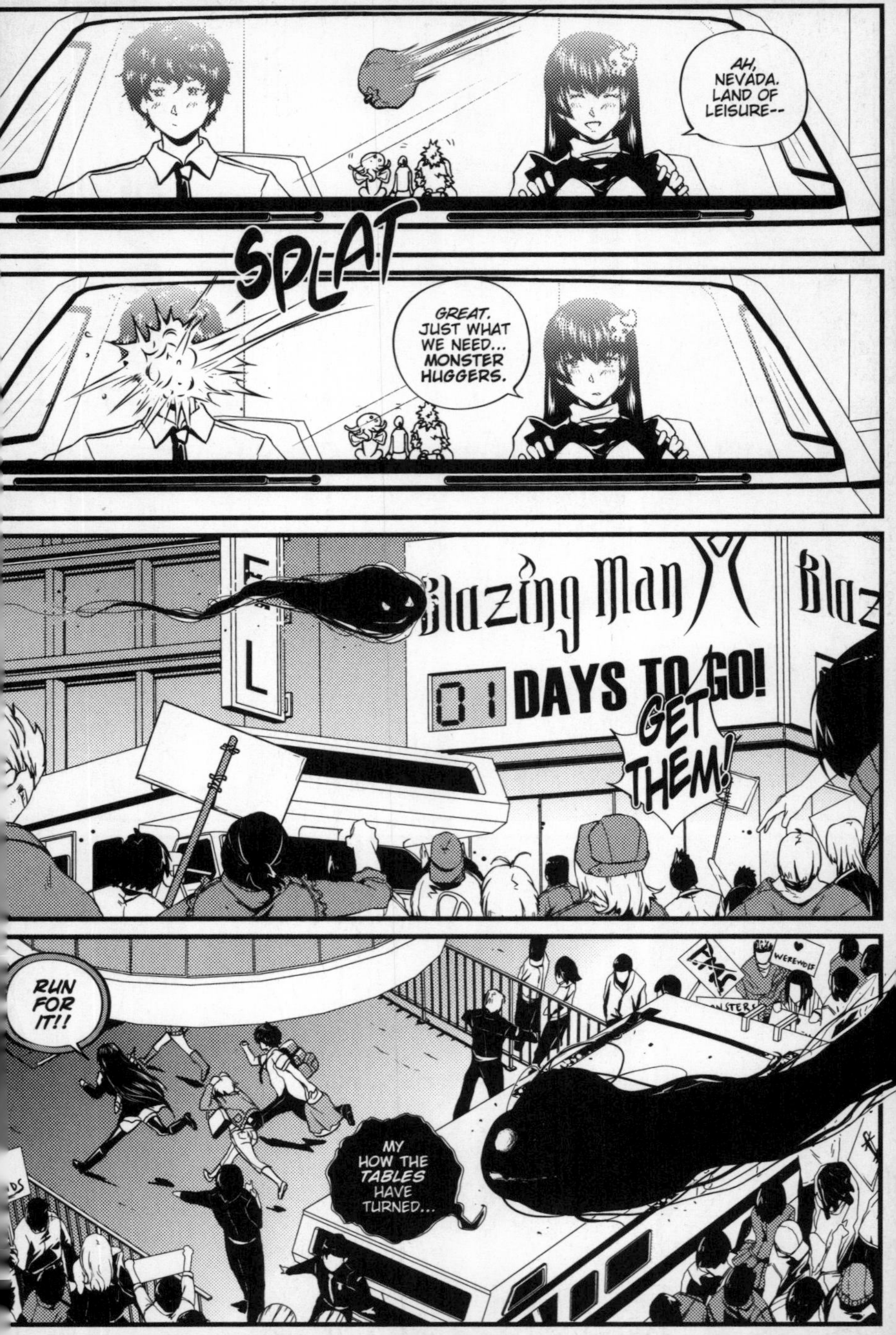
AH, NEVADA. LAND OF LEISURE--
SPLAT
GREAT. JUST WHAT WE NEED... MONSTER HUGGERS.
Blazing Man
Blaz
01 DAYS TO GO!
GET THEM!
WEREWOLF
RUN FOR IT!!
MY HOW THE TABLES HAVE TURNED...

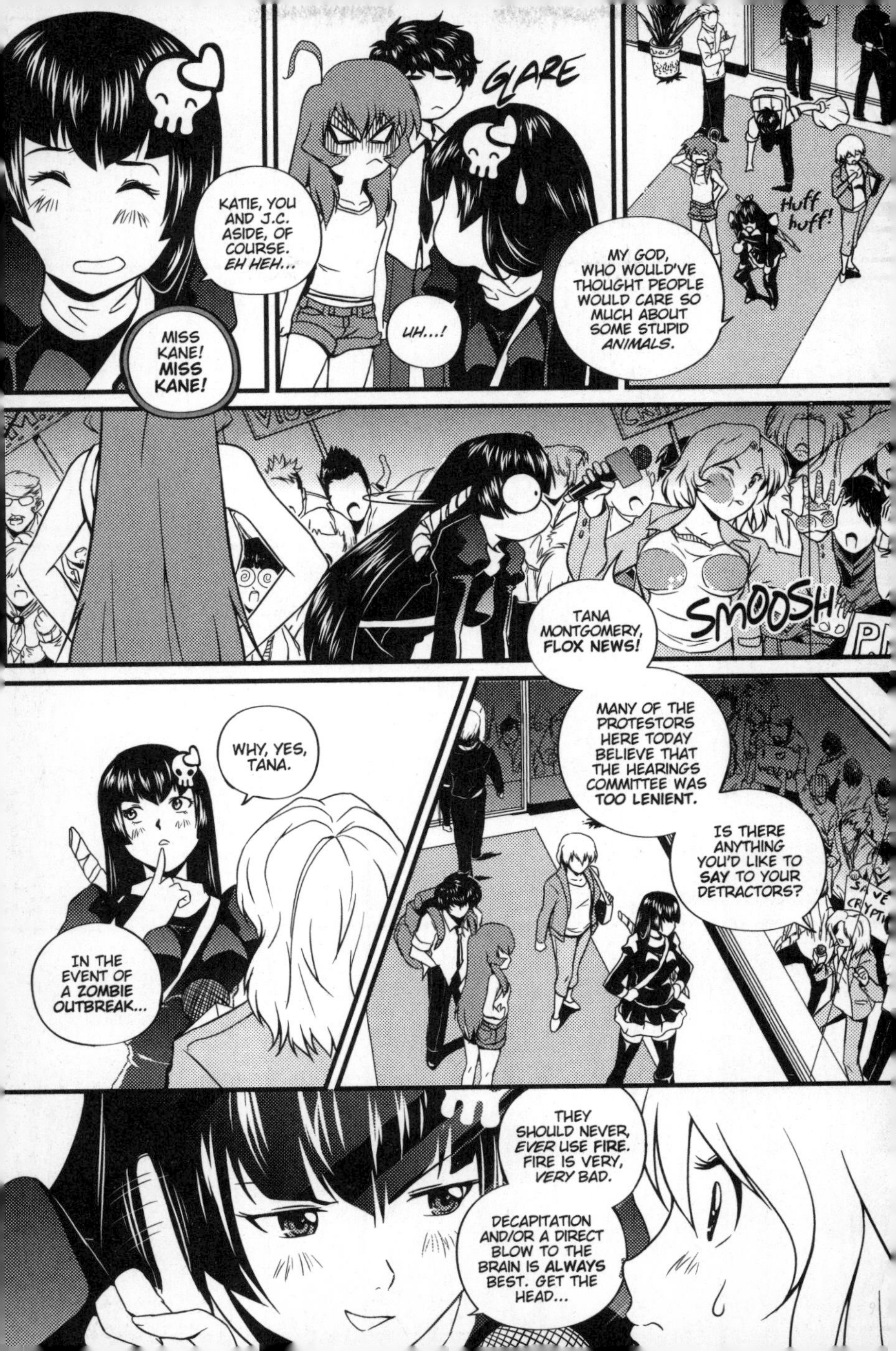
Huff huff!
MY GOD, WHO WOULD'VE THOUGHT PEOPLE WOULD CARE SO MUCH ABOUT SOME STUPID *ANIMALS*.
GLARE
KATIE, YOU AND J.C. ASIDE, OF COURSE. *EH HEH...*
UH...!
MISS KANE! **MISS KANE!**
SMOOSH
TANA MONTGOMERY, **FLOX NEWS!**
MANY OF THE PROTESTORS HERE TODAY BELIEVE THAT THE HEARINGS COMMITTEE WAS **TOO LENIENT.**
IS THERE ANYTHING YOU'D LIKE TO SAY TO YOUR DETRACTORS?
WHY, YES, TANA.
IN THE EVENT OF A ZOMBIE OUTBREAK...
THEY SHOULD NEVER, *EVER* USE **FIRE**. FIRE IS VERY, *VERY* BAD.
DECAPITATION AND/OR A DIRECT BLOW TO THE BRAIN IS **ALWAYS** BEST. GET THE HEAD...

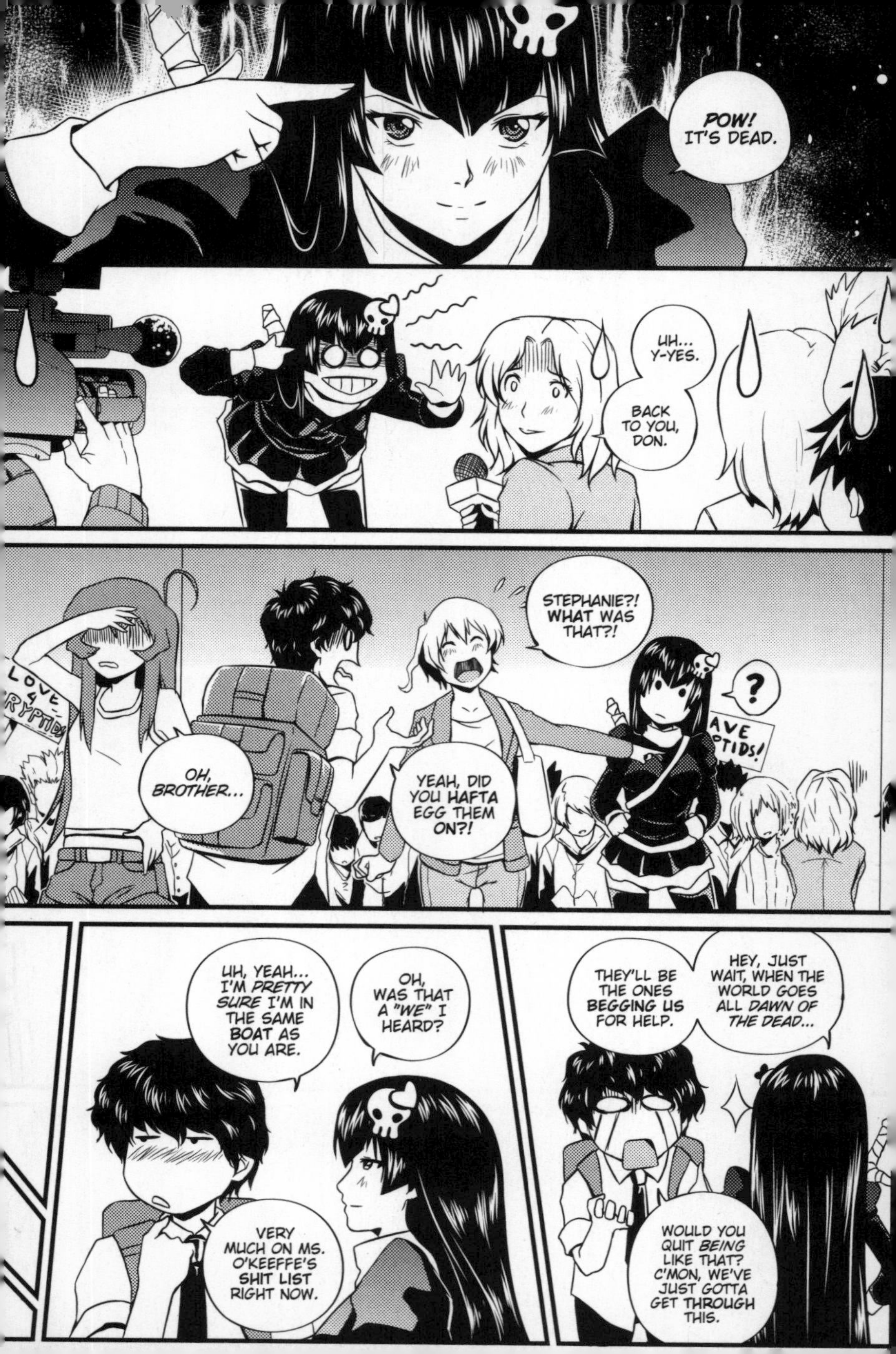
POW! IT'S DEAD.
UH... Y-YES.
BACK TO YOU, DON.
?
STEPHANIE?! WHAT WAS THAT?!
YEAH, DID YOU HAFTA EGG THEM ON?!
OH, BROTHER...
HEY, JUST WAIT, WHEN THE WORLD GOES ALL *DAWN OF THE DEAD...*
THEY'LL BE THE ONES BEGGING US FOR HELP.
WOULD YOU QUIT *BEING* LIKE THAT? C'MON, WE'VE JUST GOTTA GET THROUGH THIS.
OH, WAS THAT A *"WE"* I HEARD?
UH, YEAH... I'M *PRETTY SURE* I'M IN THE SAME BOAT AS YOU ARE.
VERY MUCH ON MS. O'KEEFFE'S SHIT LIST RIGHT NOW.

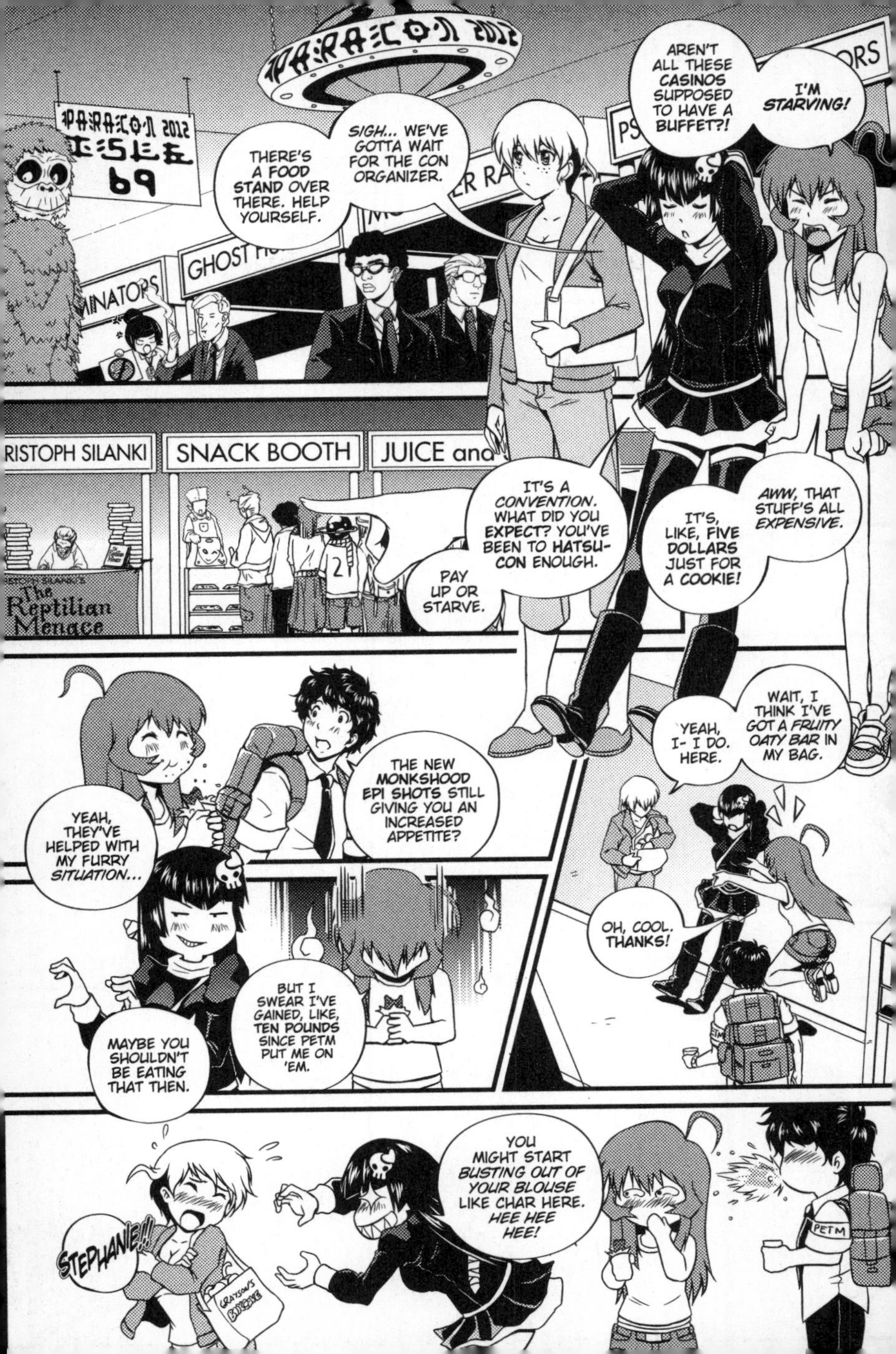
I'M *STARVING!*
AREN'T ALL THESE CASINOS SUPPOSED TO HAVE A BUFFET?!
SIGH... WE'VE GOTTA WAIT FOR THE CON ORGANIZER.
THERE'S A **FOOD STAND** OVER THERE. HELP YOURSELF.
SNACK BOOTH
The Reptilian Menace
AWW, THAT STUFF'S ALL *EXPENSIVE.*
IT'S, LIKE, FIVE DOLLARS JUST FOR A **COOKIE!**
IT'S A *CONVENTION.* WHAT DID YOU **EXPECT?** YOU'VE BEEN TO **HATSU-CON** ENOUGH.
PAY UP OR STARVE.
WAIT, I THINK I'VE GOT A *FRUITY OATY BAR* IN MY BAG.
YEAH, I- I DO. HERE.
OH, COOL. THANKS!
THE NEW **MONKSHOOD EPI SHOTS** STILL GIVING YOU AN INCREASED APPETITE?
YEAH, THEY'VE HELPED WITH MY FURRY *SITUATION...*
BUT I SWEAR I'VE GAINED, LIKE, TEN POUNDS SINCE PETM PUT ME ON 'EM.
MAYBE YOU SHOULDN'T BE EATING THAT THEN.
PETM
YOU MIGHT START *BUSTING OUT OF* YOUR BLOUSE LIKE CHAR HERE. *HEE HEE HEE!*
STEPHANIE!!

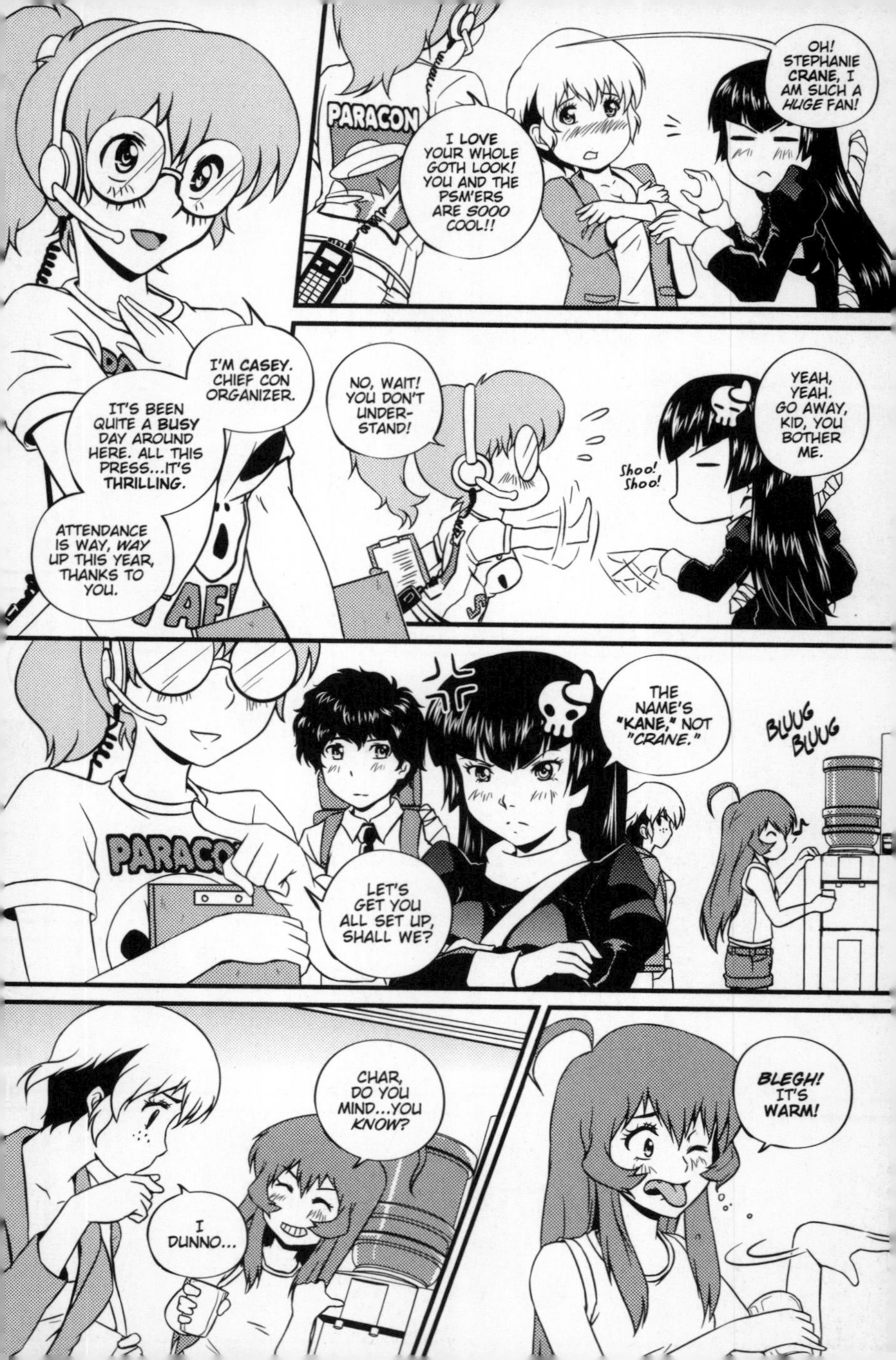
OH! STEPHANIE CRANE, I AM SUCH A *HUGE* FAN!
PARACON
I LOVE YOUR WHOLE GOTH LOOK! YOU AND THE PSM'ERS ARE *SOOO* COOL!!
YEAH, YEAH. GO AWAY, KID, YOU BOTHER ME.
Shoo! Shoo!
NO, WAIT! YOU DON'T UNDER-STAND!
I'M **CASEY**. CHIEF CON ORGANIZER.
IT'S BEEN QUITE A **BUSY** DAY AROUND HERE. ALL THIS PRESS...IT'S **THRILLING**.
ATTENDANCE IS WAY, *WAY* UP THIS YEAR, THANKS TO YOU.
BLUUG BLUUG
THE NAME'S "KANE," NOT "CRANE."
PARACO
LET'S GET YOU ALL SET UP, SHALL WE?
BLEGH! IT'S WARM!
CHAR, DO YOU MIND...YOU *KNOW?*
I DUNNO...

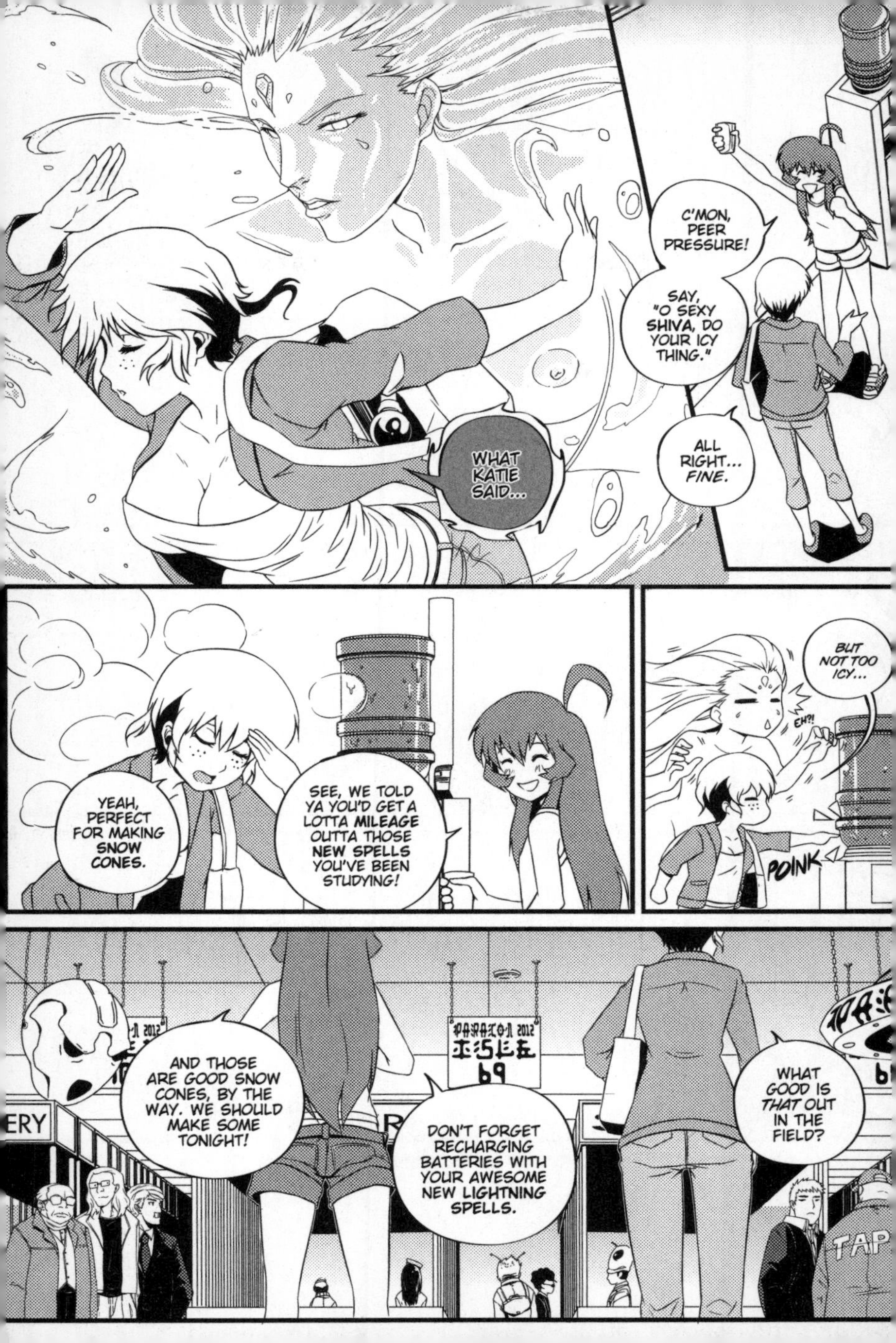
C'MON, PEER PRESSURE!
SAY, "O SEXY SHIVA, DO YOUR ICY THING."
ALL RIGHT... FINE.
WHAT KATIE SAID...
BUT NOT TOO ICY...
EH?!
POINK
SEE, WE TOLD YA YOU'D GET A LOTTA MILEAGE OUTTA THOSE NEW SPELLS YOU'VE BEEN STUDYING!
YEAH, PERFECT FOR MAKING SNOW CONES.
WHAT GOOD IS THAT OUT IN THE FIELD?
TAP
AND THOSE ARE GOOD SNOW CONES, BY THE WAY. WE SHOULD MAKE SOME TONIGHT!
DON'T FORGET RECHARGING BATTERIES WITH YOUR AWESOME NEW LIGHTNING SPELLS.

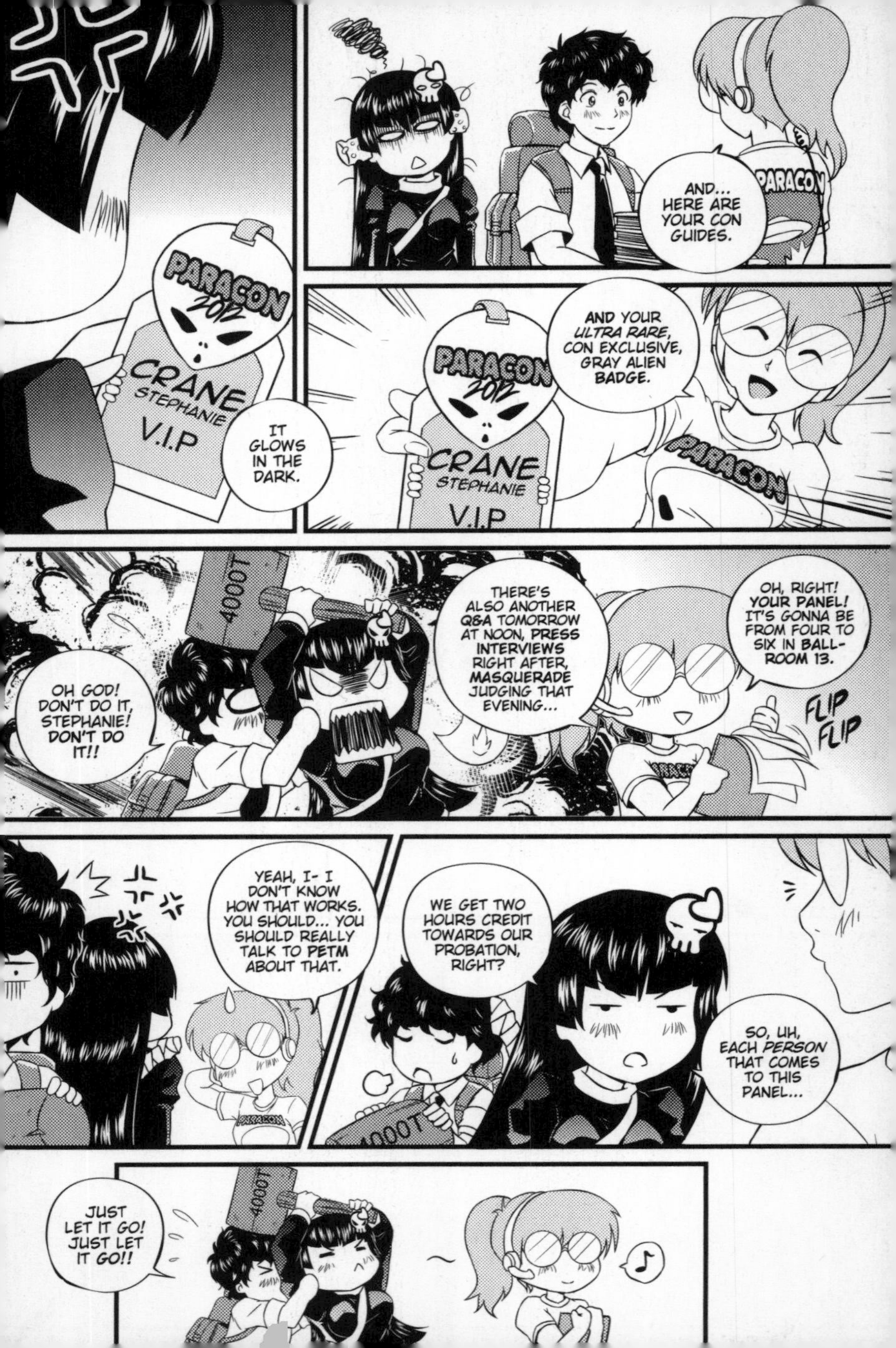
AND... HERE ARE YOUR CON GUIDES.
PARACON
AND YOUR ULTRA RARE, CON EXCLUSIVE, GRAY ALIEN BADGE.
PARACON 2012 CRANE STEPHANIE V.I.P
PARACON
PARACON 2012 CRANE STEPHANIE V.I.P
IT GLOWS IN THE DARK.
OH, RIGHT! YOUR PANEL! IT'S GONNA BE FROM FOUR TO SIX IN BALL-ROOM 13.
FLIP FLIP
THERE'S ALSO ANOTHER Q&A TOMORROW AT NOON, PRESS INTERVIEWS RIGHT AFTER, MASQUERADE JUDGING THAT EVENING...
4000T
OH GOD! DON'T DO IT, STEPHANIE! DON'T DO IT!!
SO, UH, EACH PERSON THAT COMES TO THIS PANEL...
WE GET TWO HOURS CREDIT TOWARDS OUR PROBATION, RIGHT?
4000T
YEAH, I- I DON'T KNOW HOW THAT WORKS. YOU SHOULD... YOU SHOULD REALLY TALK TO PETM ABOUT THAT.
PARACON
4000T
JUST LET IT GO! JUST LET IT GO!!

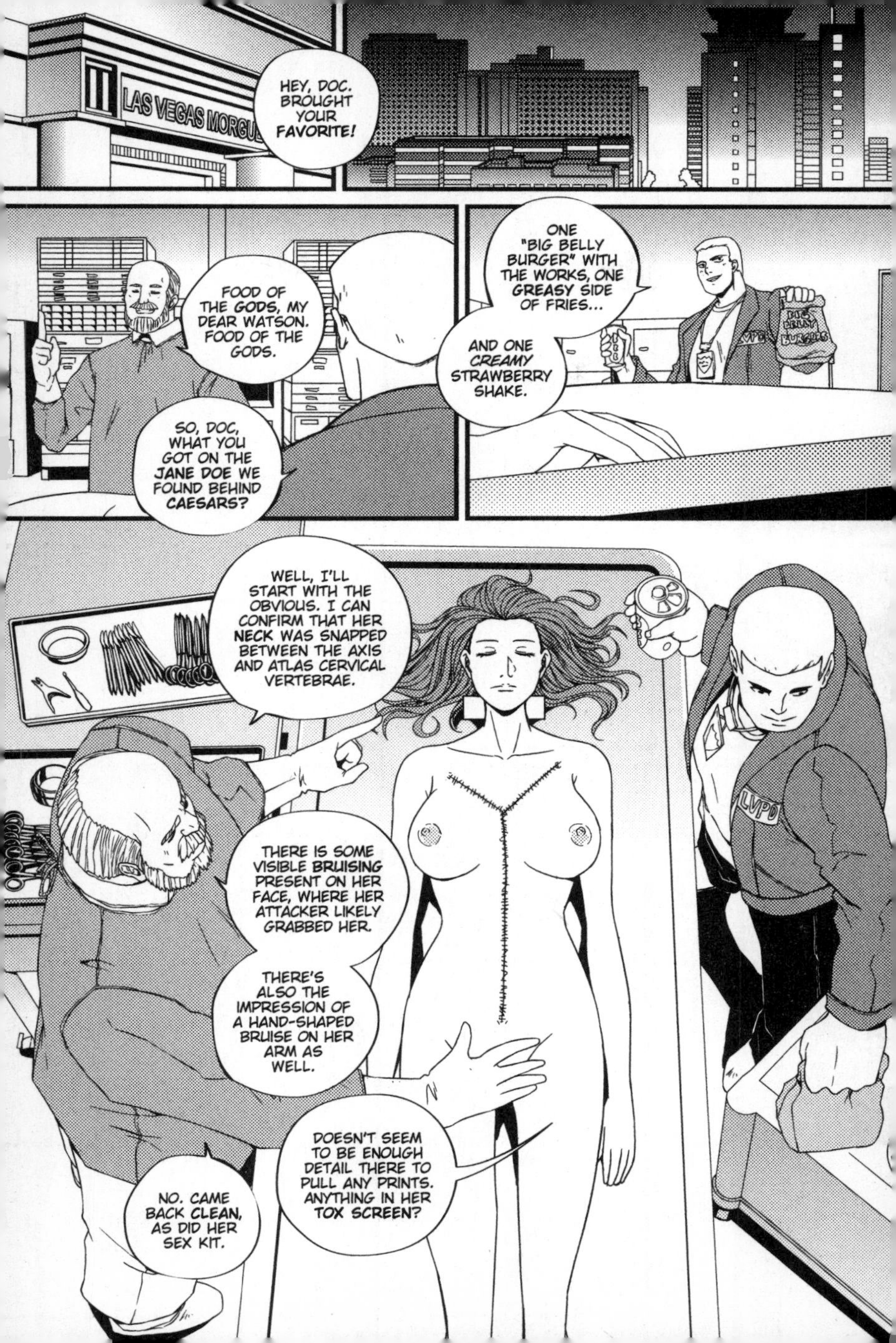
LAS VEGAS MORGU
HEY, DOC. BROUGHT YOUR **FAVORITE!**
ONE "BIG BELLY BURGER" WITH THE WORKS, ONE **GREASY** SIDE OF FRIES...
AND ONE *CREAMY* STRAWBERRY SHAKE.
LVPD
FOOD OF THE **GODS**, MY DEAR WATSON. FOOD OF THE GODS.
SO, DOC, WHAT YOU GOT ON THE **JANE DOE** WE FOUND BEHIND **CAESARS?**
WELL, I'LL START WITH THE OBVIOUS. I CAN CONFIRM THAT HER **NECK** WAS SNAPPED BETWEEN THE AXIS AND ATLAS CERVICAL VERTEBRAE.
LVPD
THERE IS SOME VISIBLE **BRUISING** PRESENT ON HER FACE, WHERE HER ATTACKER LIKELY GRABBED HER.
THERE'S ALSO THE IMPRESSION OF A HAND-SHAPED BRUISE ON HER ARM AS WELL.
DOESN'T SEEM TO BE ENOUGH DETAIL THERE TO PULL ANY PRINTS. ANYTHING IN HER **TOX SCREEN?**
NO. CAME BACK **CLEAN**, AS DID HER SEX KIT.

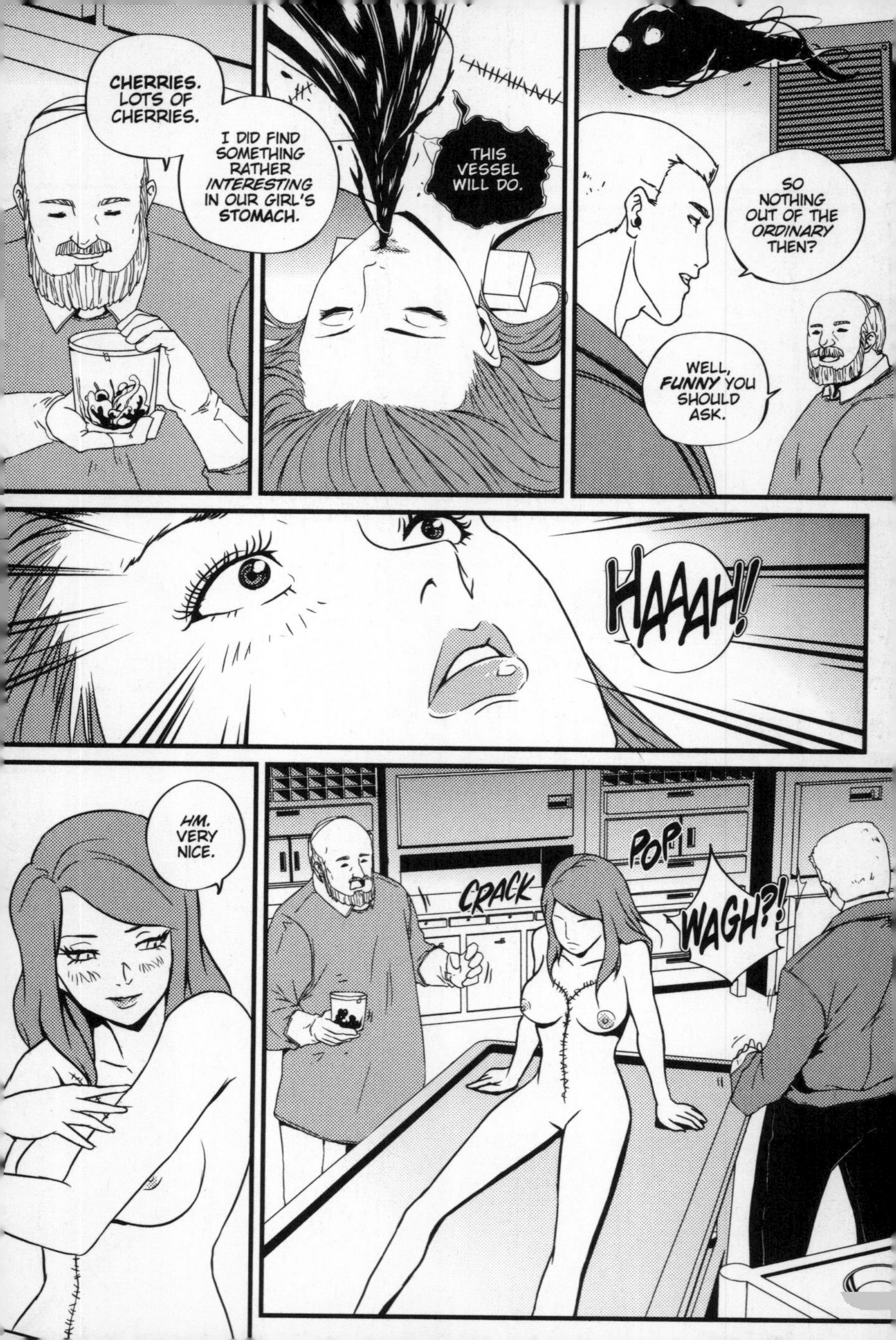
SO NOTHING OUT OF THE *ORDINARY* THEN?
WELL, ***FUNNY*** YOU SHOULD ASK.
THIS VESSEL WILL DO.
CHERRIES. LOTS OF CHERRIES.
I DID FIND SOMETHING RATHER *INTERESTING* IN OUR GIRL'S STOMACH.
HAAAH!
POP
WAGH?!
CRACK
HM. VERY NICE.

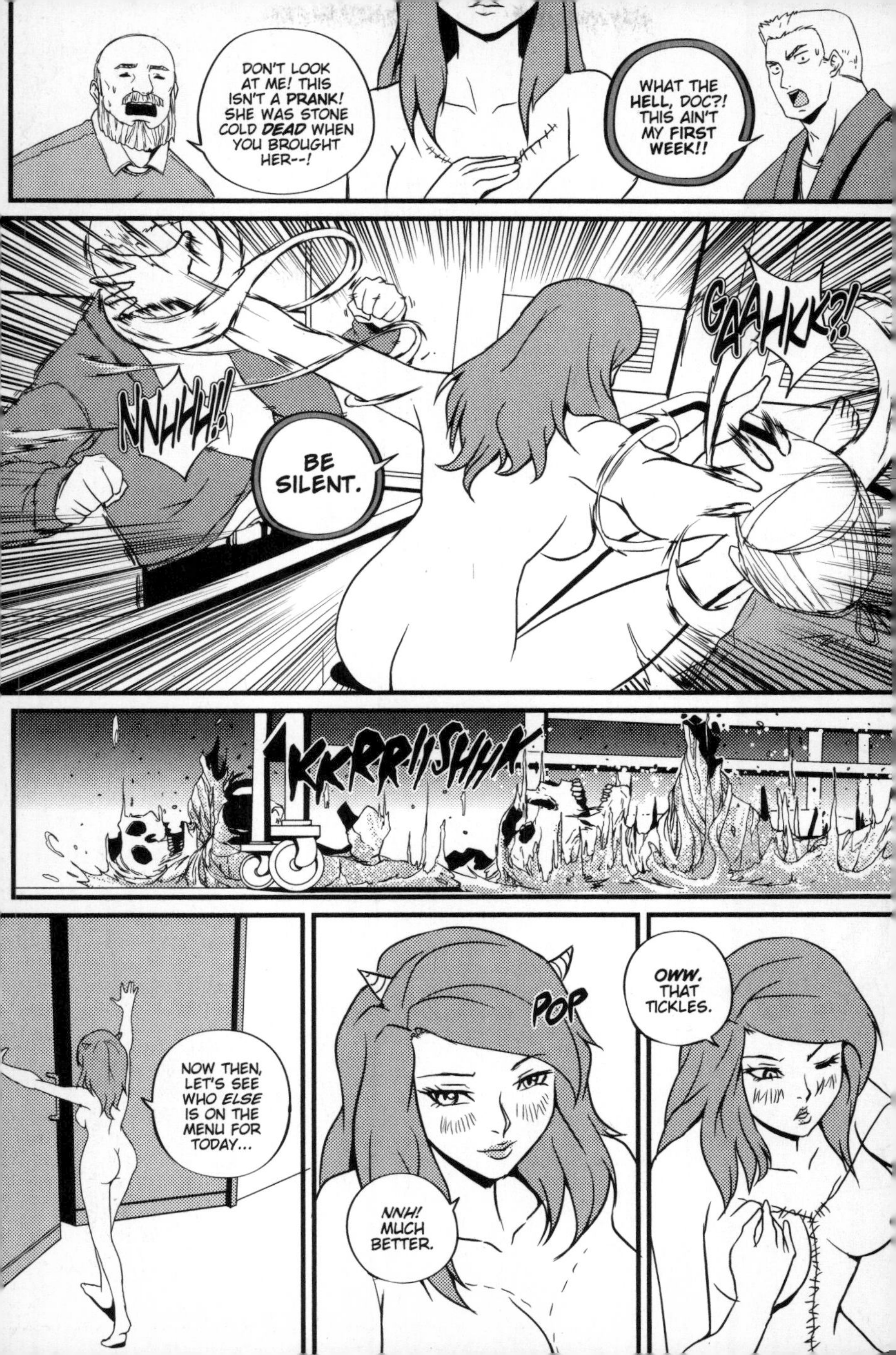
WHAT THE HELL, DOC?! THIS AIN'T MY FIRST WEEK!!
DON'T LOOK AT ME! THIS ISN'T A PRANK! SHE WAS STONE COLD DEAD WHEN YOU BROUGHT HER--!
GAAHKK?!
BE SILENT.
NNHHH!!
KKRRIISHHH
OWW. THAT TICKLES.
POP
NNH! MUCH BETTER.
NOW THEN, LET'S SEE WHO ELSE IS ON THE MENU FOR TODAY...

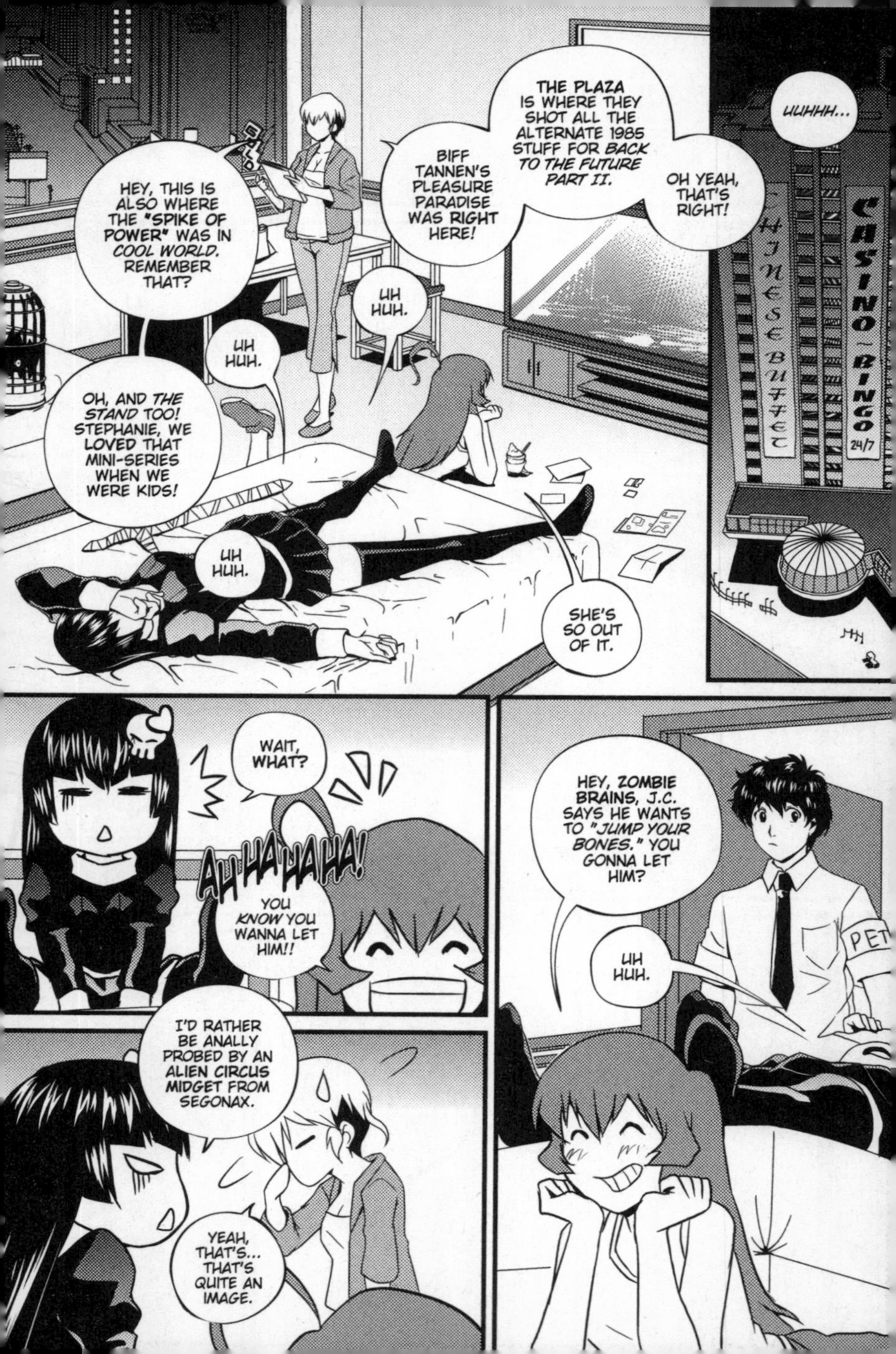
UUHHH...
CASINO – BINGO 24/7
CHINESE BUFFET
THE PLAZA IS WHERE THEY SHOT ALL THE ALTERNATE 1985 STUFF FOR *BACK TO THE FUTURE PART II.*
OH YEAH, THAT'S RIGHT!
BIFF TANNEN'S PLEASURE PARADISE WAS RIGHT HERE!
HEY, THIS IS ALSO WHERE THE "SPIKE OF POWER" WAS IN *COOL WORLD.* REMEMBER THAT?
UH HUH.
UH HUH.
OH, AND *THE STAND* TOO! STEPHANIE, WE LOVED THAT MINI-SERIES WHEN WE WERE KIDS!
UH HUH.
SHE'S SO OUT OF IT.
HEY, ZOMBIE BRAINS, J.C. SAYS HE WANTS TO *"JUMP YOUR BONES."* YOU GONNA LET HIM?
UH HUH.
PET
WAIT, WHAT?
AH HA HA HA HA!
YOU *KNOW* YOU WANNA LET HIM!!
I'D RATHER BE ANALLY PROBED BY AN ALIEN CIRCUS MIDGET FROM SEGONAX.
YEAH, THAT'S... THAT'S QUITE AN IMAGE.

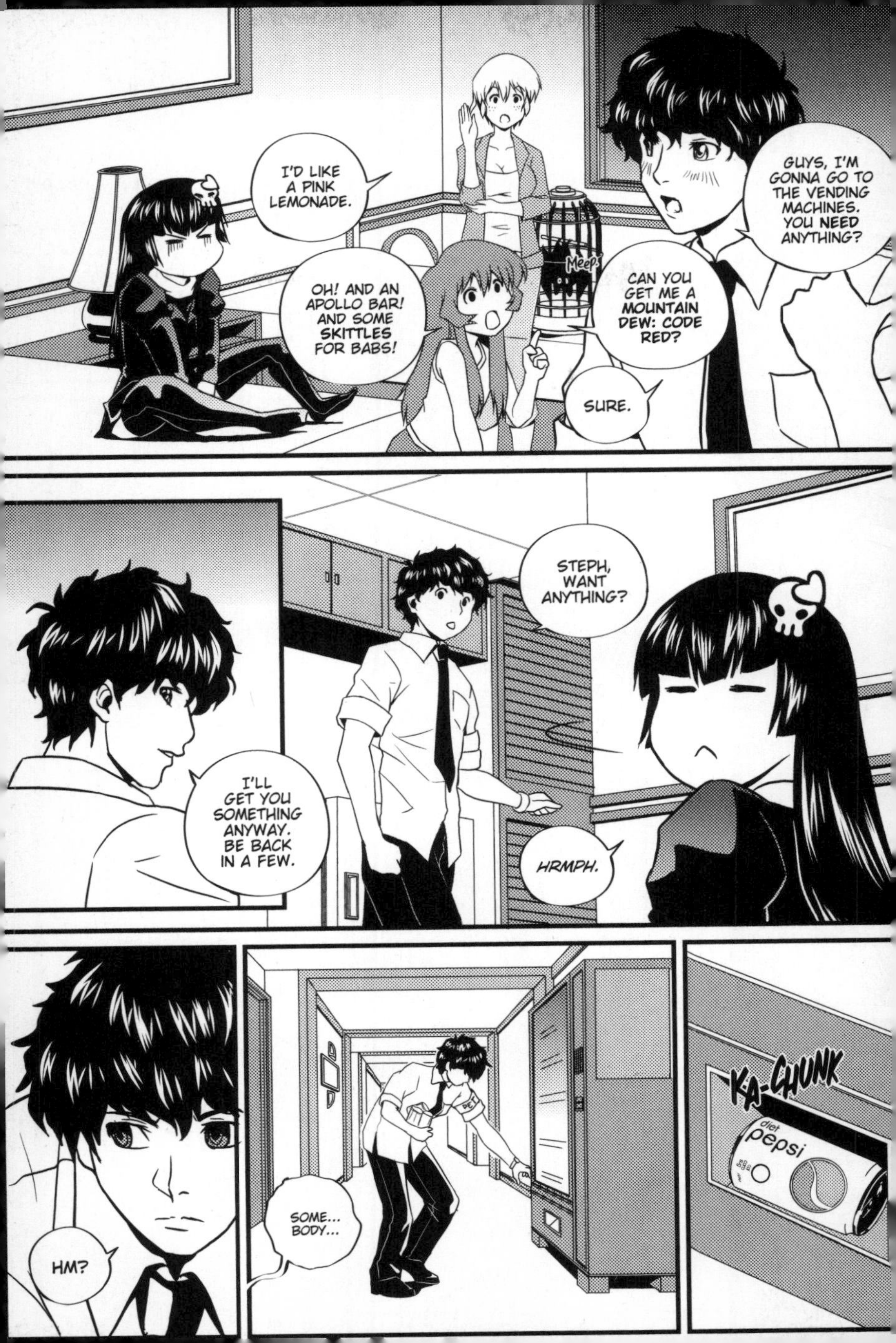
GUYS, I'M GONNA GO TO THE VENDING MACHINES. YOU NEED ANYTHING?
I'D LIKE A PINK LEMONADE.
Meep!
CAN YOU GET ME A MOUNTAIN DEW: CODE RED?
OH! AND AN APOLLO BAR! AND SOME SKITTLES FOR BABS!
SURE.
STEPH, WANT ANYTHING?
HRMPH.
I'LL GET YOU SOMETHING ANYWAY. BE BACK IN A FEW.
KA-CHUNK
diet pepsi
SOME... BODY...
HM?

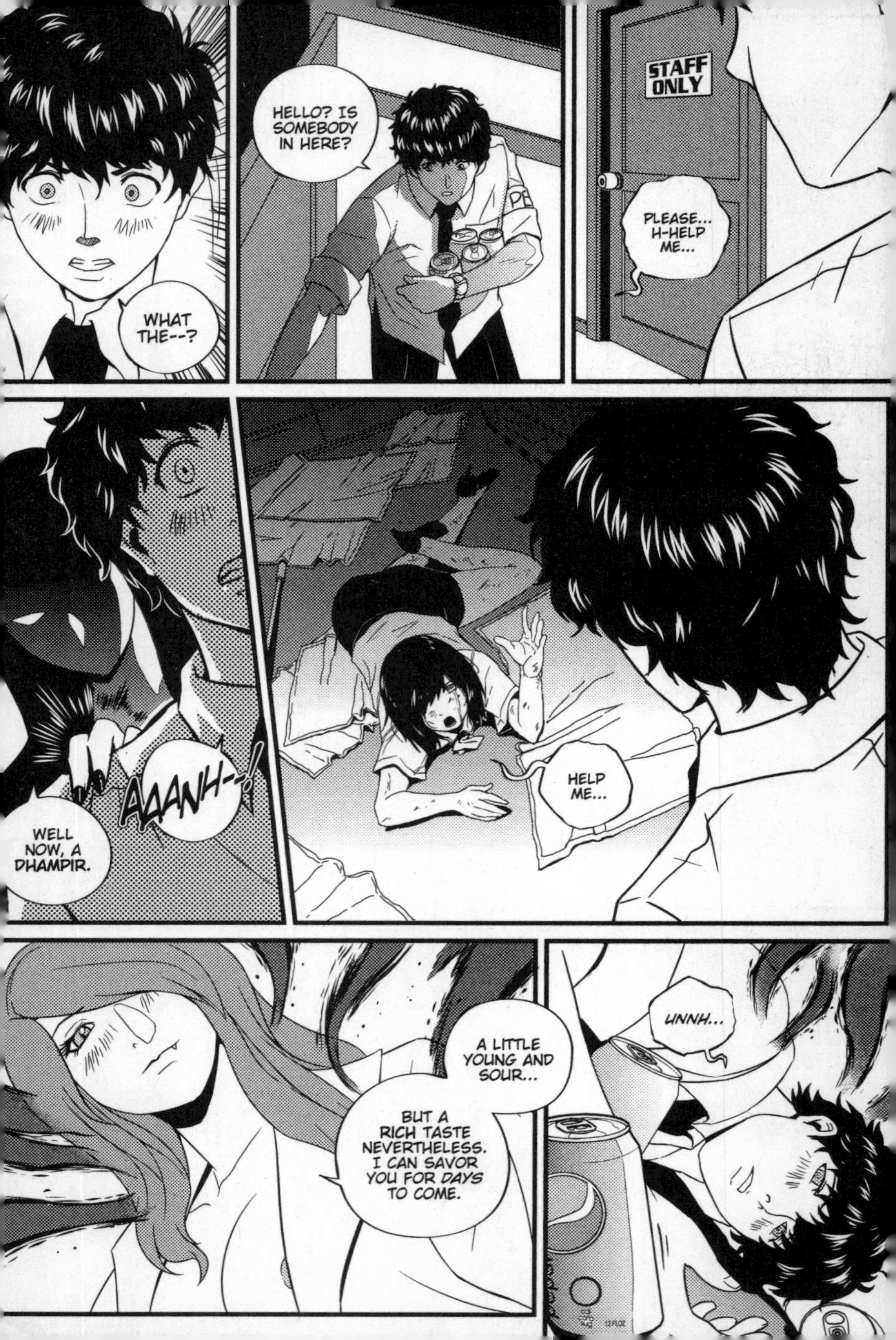
STAFF ONLY
PLEASE... H-HELP ME...
HELLO? IS SOMEBODY IN HERE?
WHAT THE--?
HELP ME...
AAANH--!
WELL NOW, A DHAMPIR.
UNNH...
A LITTLE YOUNG AND SOUR...
BUT A RICH TASTE NEVERTHELESS. I CAN SAVOR YOU FOR DAYS TO COME.
12 FL OZ

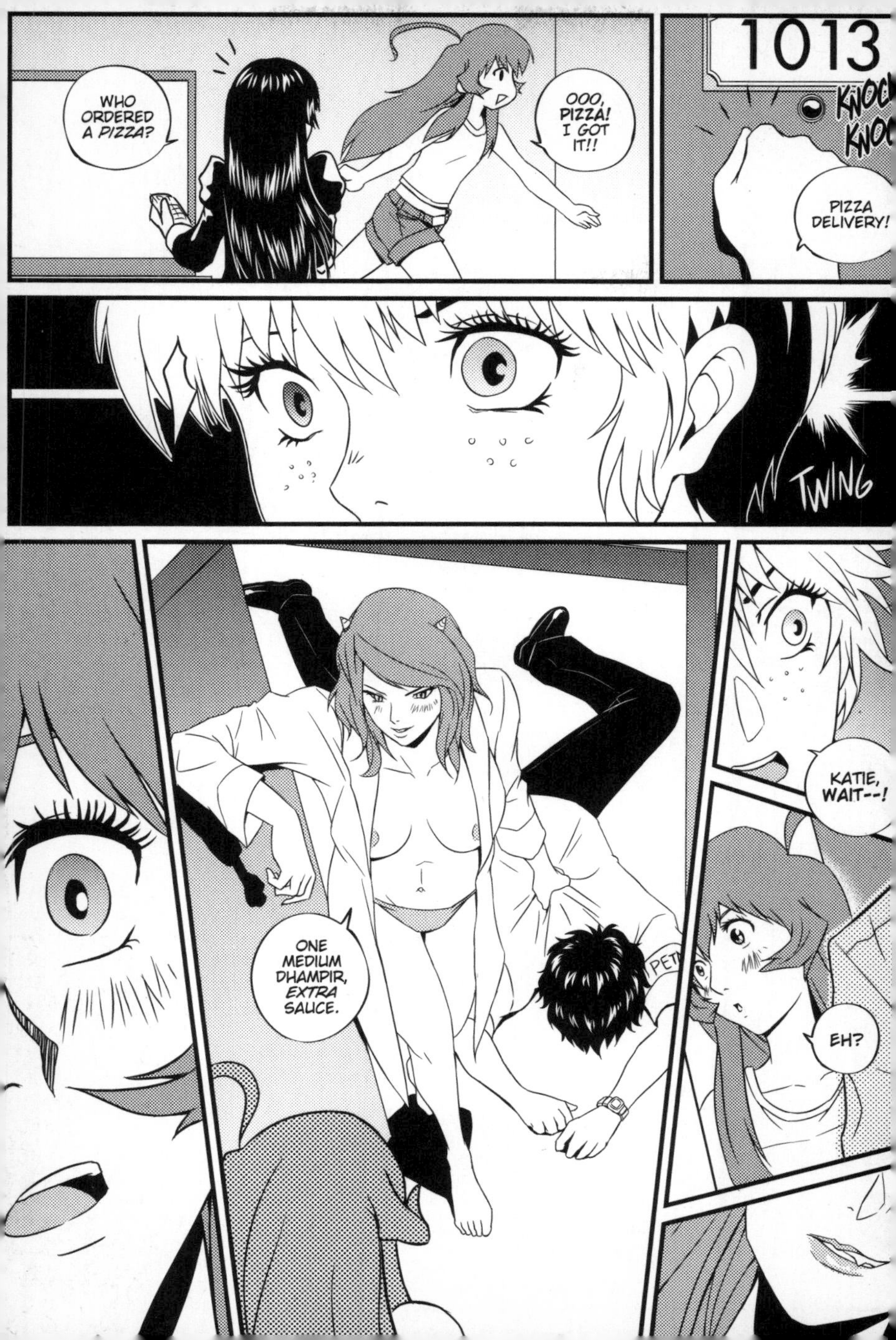
1013
PIZZA DELIVERY!
OOO, PIZZA! I GOT IT!!
WHO ORDERED A *PIZZA*?
TWING
KATIE, WAIT--!
EH?
ONE MEDIUM DHAMPIR, *EXTRA* SAUCE.

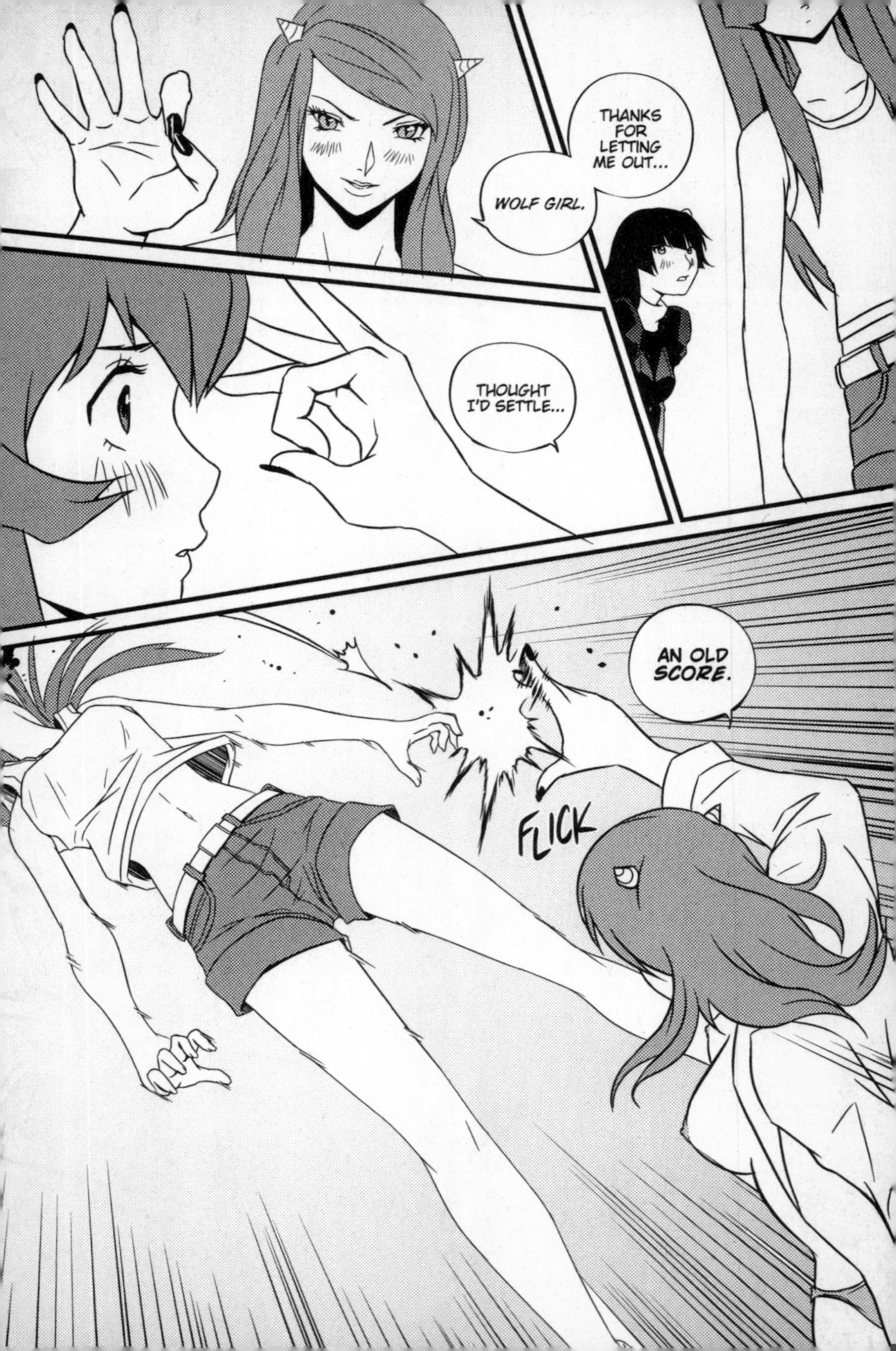
THANKS FOR LETTING ME OUT...
WOLF GIRL.
THOUGHT I'D SETTLE...
AN OLD SCORE.
FLICK

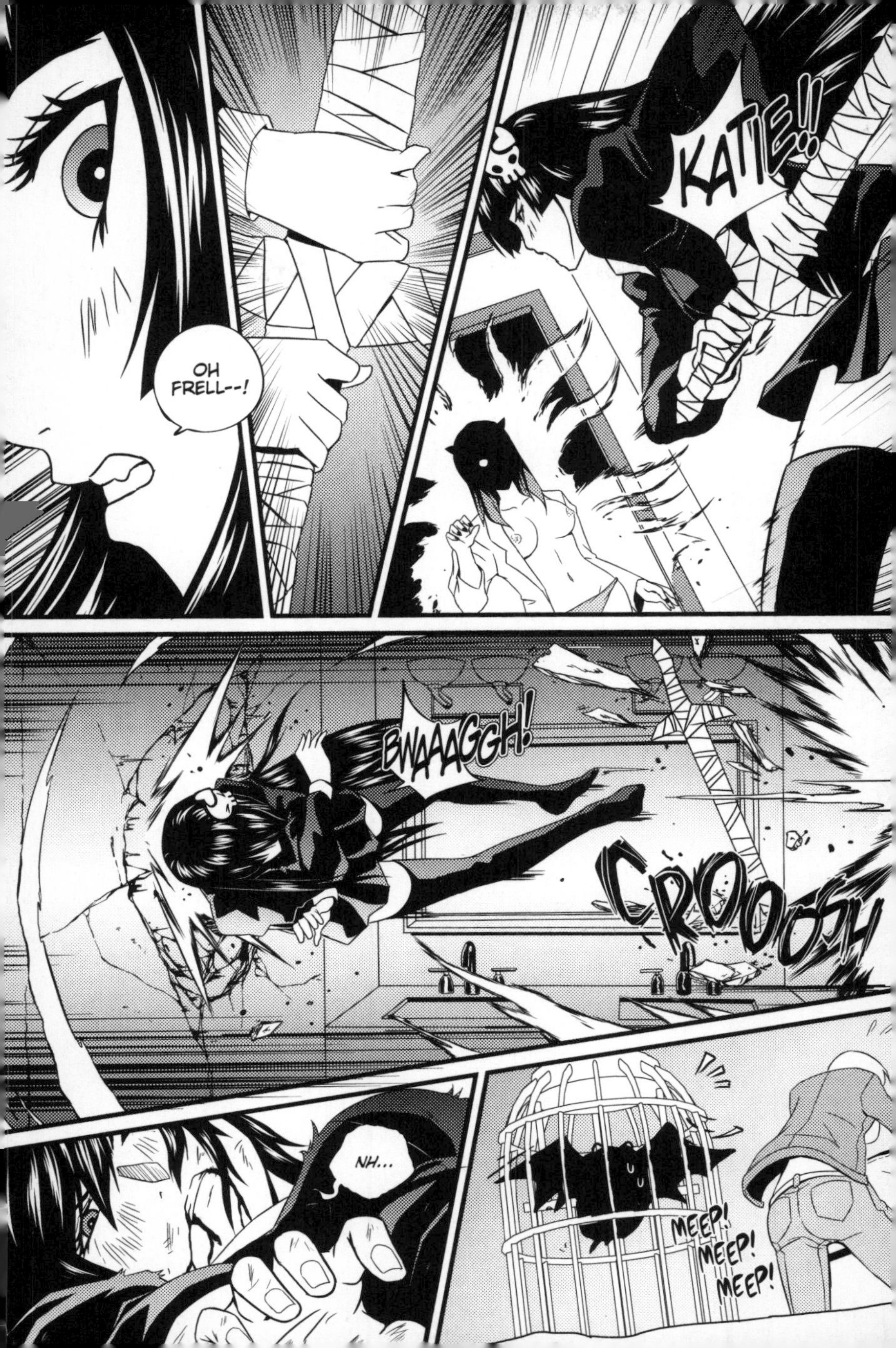
KATIE!!
OH FRELL--!
BWAAAGGH!
CROOOSH
MEEP! MEEP! MEEP!
NH...

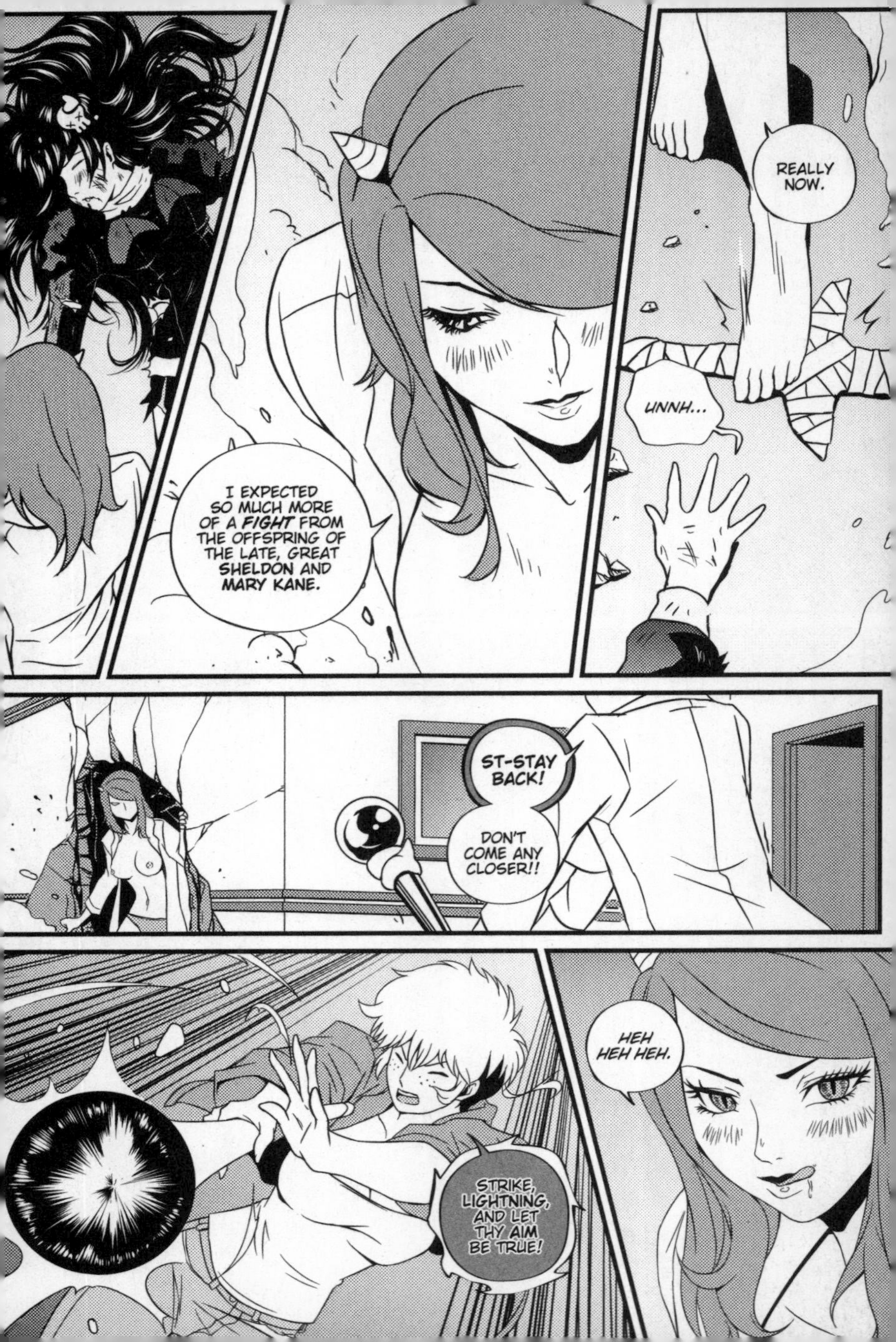

REALLY NOW.
UNNH...
I EXPECTED SO MUCH MORE OF A *FIGHT* FROM THE OFFSPRING OF THE LATE, GREAT SHELDON AND MARY KANE.
ST-STAY BACK!
DON'T COME ANY CLOSER!!
HEH HEH HEH.
STRIKE, LIGHTNING, AND LET THY AIM BE TRUE!

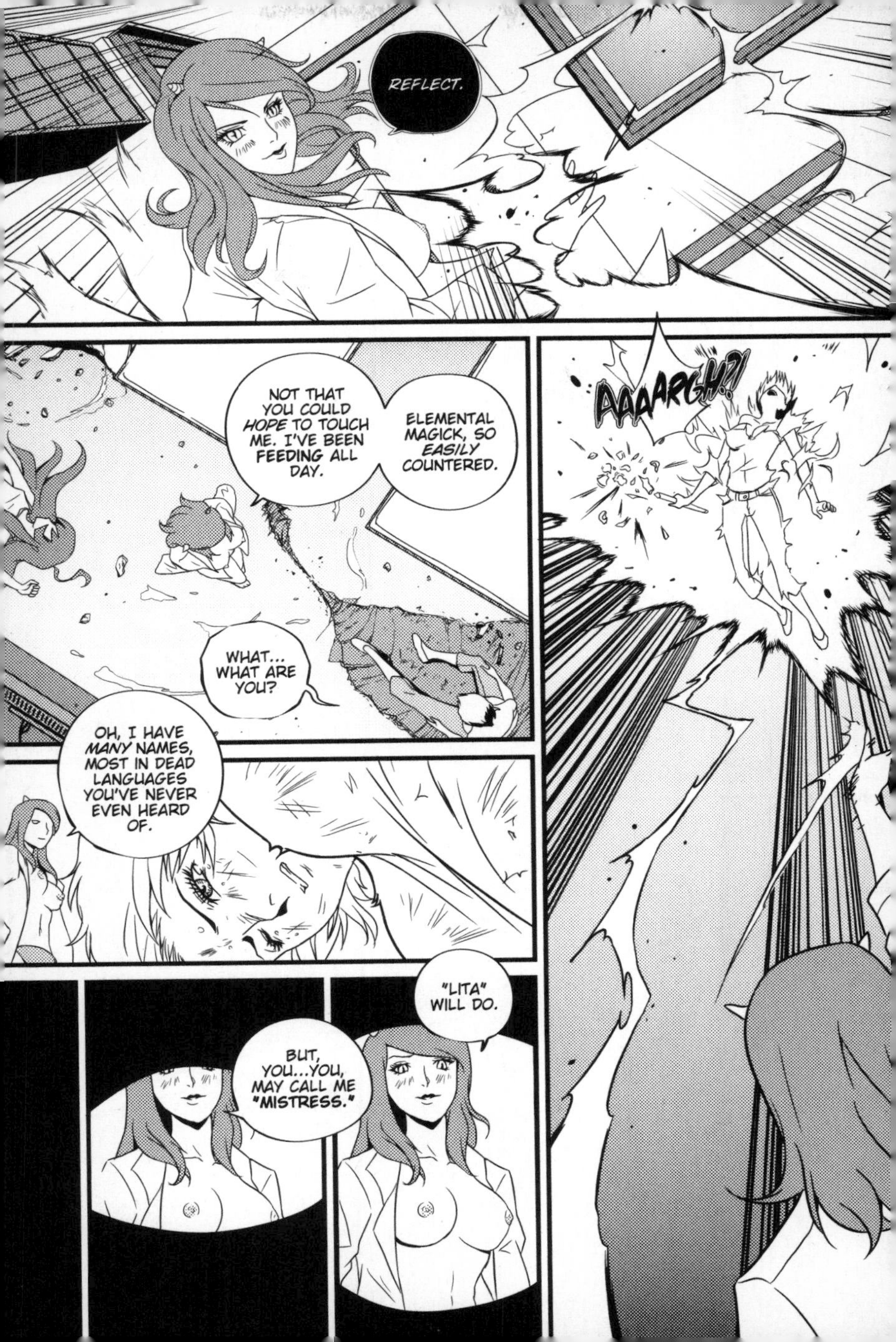
REFLECT.
AAAARGH!?
ELEMENTAL MAGICK, SO *EASILY* COUNTERED.
NOT THAT YOU COULD *HOPE* TO TOUCH ME. I'VE BEEN FEEDING ALL DAY.
WHAT... WHAT ARE YOU?
OH, I HAVE *MANY* NAMES, MOST IN DEAD LANGUAGES YOU'VE NEVER EVEN HEARD OF.
"LITA" WILL DO.
BUT, YOU...YOU, MAY CALL ME **"MISTRESS."**

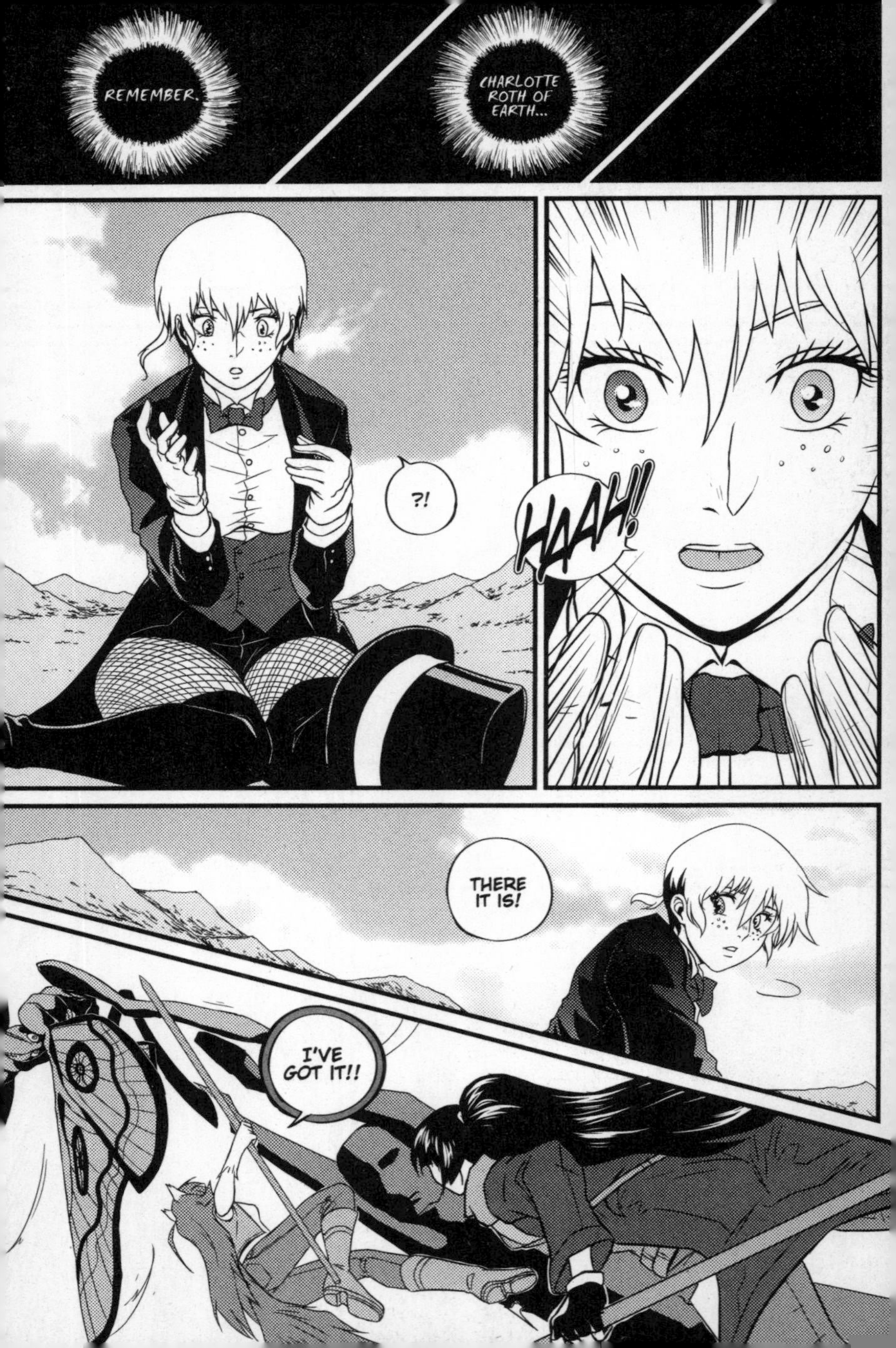
CHARLOTTE ROTH OF EARTH...
REMEMBER.
HAAH!
?!
THERE IT IS!
I'VE GOT IT!!

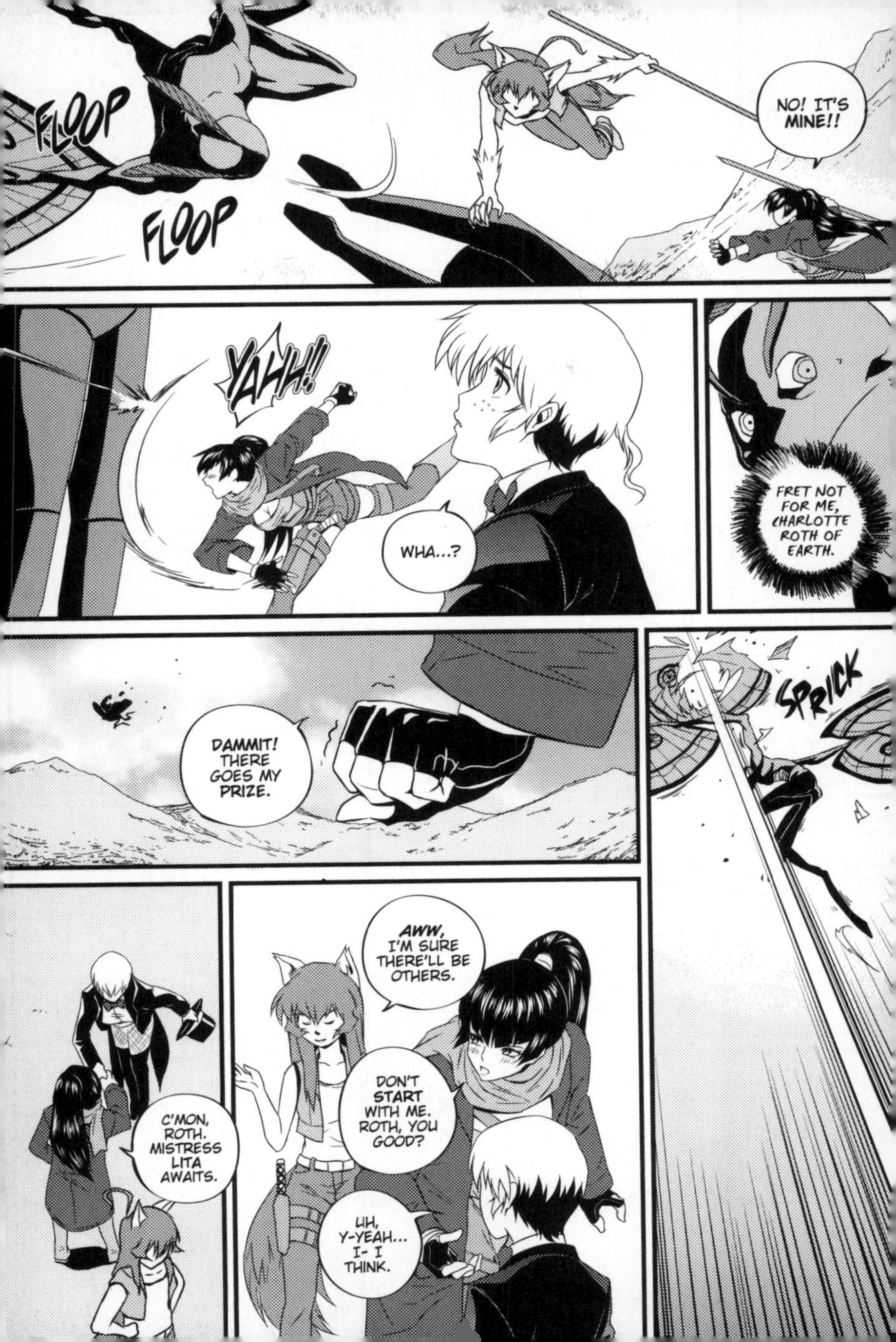
NO! IT'S MINE!!
FLOOP
FLOOP
FRET NOT FOR ME, CHARLOTTE ROTH OF EARTH.
YAHH!!
WHA...?
SPRICK
DAMMIT! THERE GOES MY PRIZE.
AWW, I'M SURE THERE'LL BE OTHERS.
DON'T START WITH ME. ROTH, YOU GOOD?
UH, Y-YEAH... I- I THINK.
C'MON, ROTH. MISTRESS LITA AWAITS.

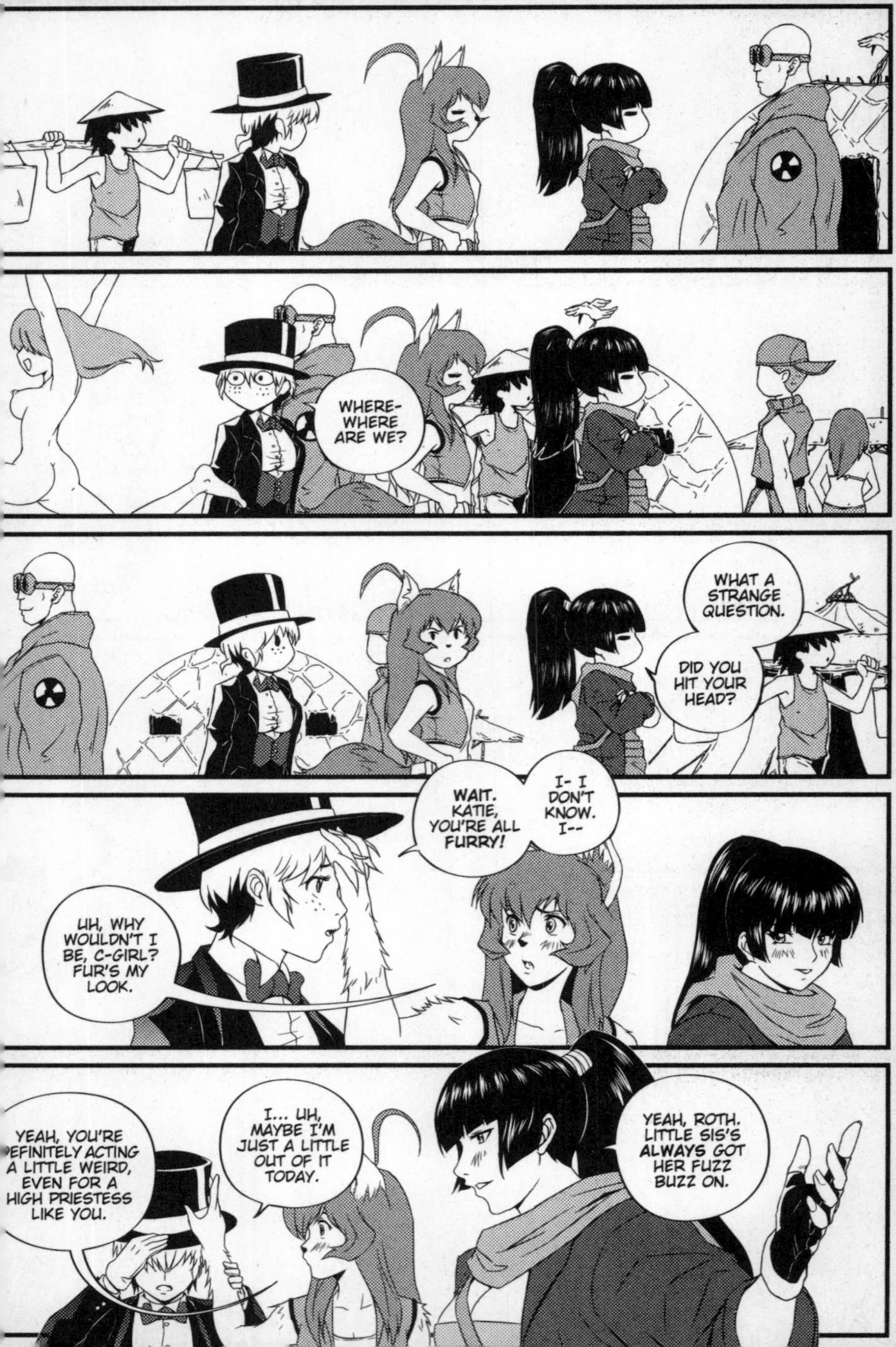
WHERE- WHERE ARE WE?
WHAT A STRANGE QUESTION.
DID YOU HIT YOUR HEAD?
I- I DON'T KNOW. I--
WAIT. KATIE, YOU'RE ALL FURRY!
UH, WHY WOULDN'T I BE, C-GIRL? FUR'S MY LOOK.
YEAH, ROTH. LITTLE SIS'S ALWAYS GOT HER FUZZ BUZZ ON.
I... UH, MAYBE I'M JUST A LITTLE OUT OF IT TODAY.
YEAH, YOU'RE DEFINITELY ACTING A LITTLE WEIRD, EVEN FOR A HIGH PRIESTESS LIKE YOU.

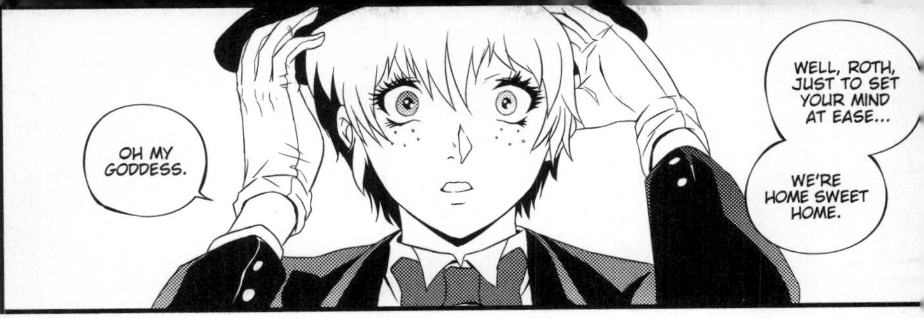
WELL, ROTH, JUST TO SET YOUR MIND AT EASE...
WE'RE HOME SWEET HOME.
OH MY GODDESS.

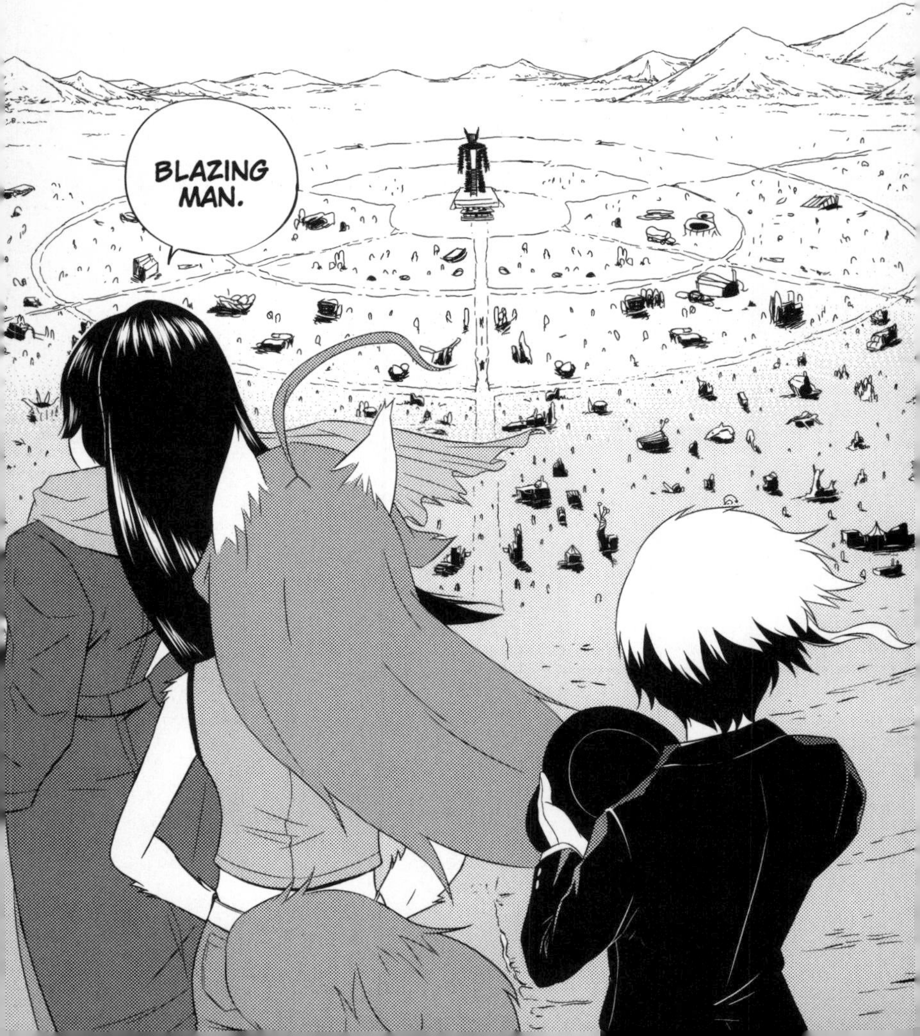
BLAZING MAN.

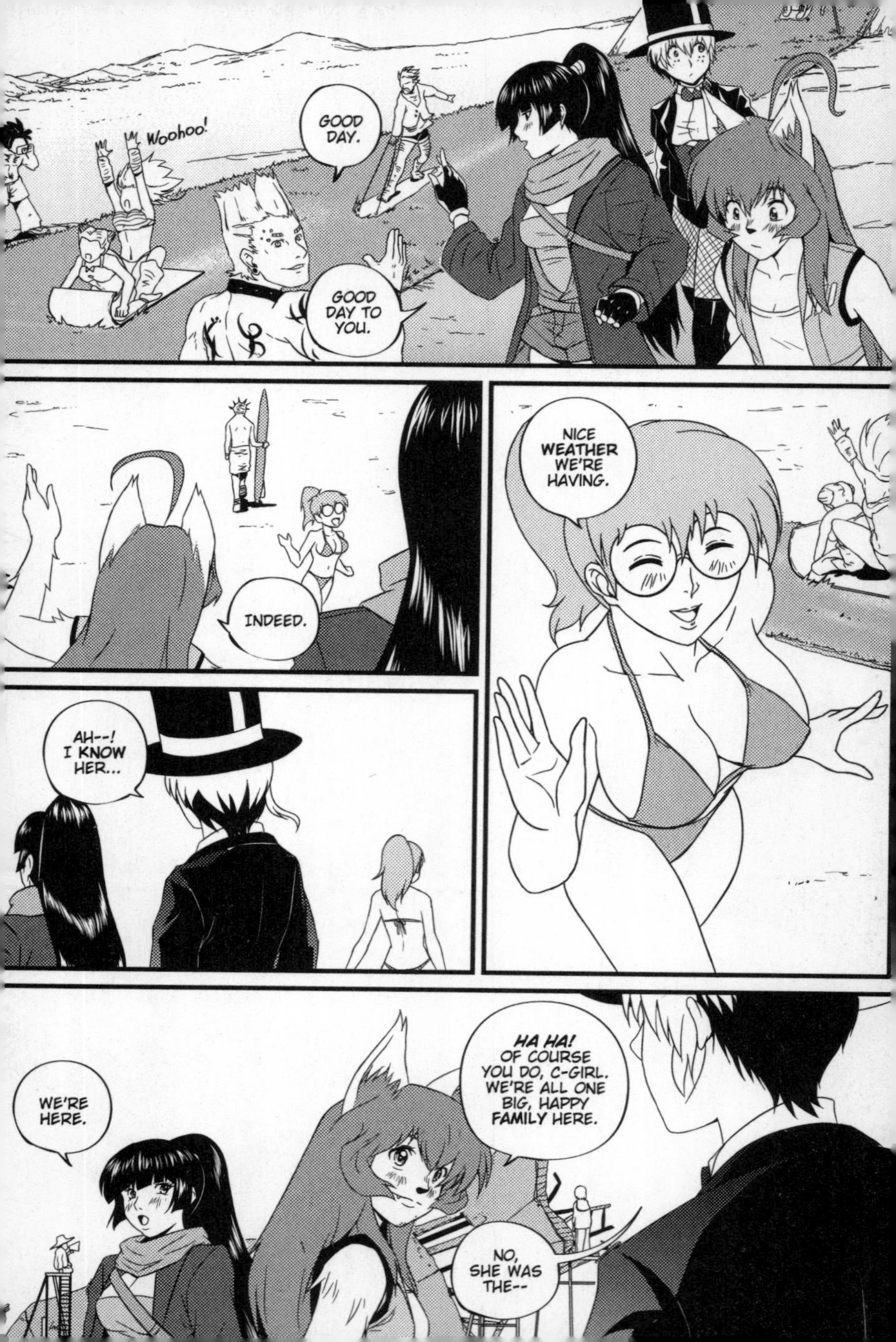
GOOD DAY.
Woohoo!
GOOD DAY TO YOU.
NICE WEATHER WE'RE HAVING.
INDEED.
AH--! I KNOW HER...
HA HA! OF COURSE YOU DO, C-GIRL. WE'RE ALL ONE BIG, HAPPY FAMILY HERE.
NO, SHE WAS THE--
WE'RE HERE.

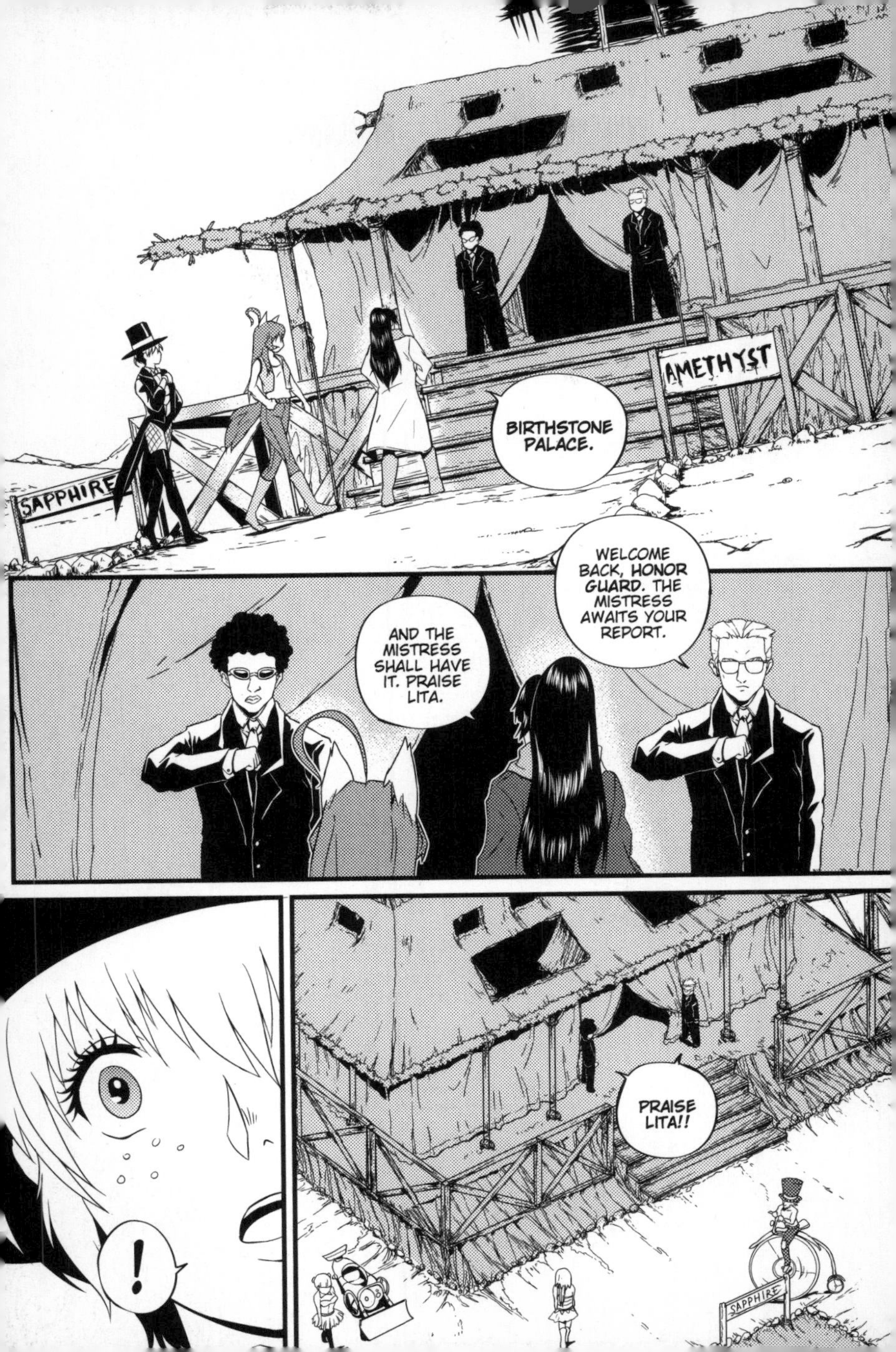
AMETHYST
BIRTHSTONE PALACE.
SAPPHIRE
WELCOME BACK, HONOR GUARD. THE MISTRESS AWAITS YOUR REPORT.
AND THE MISTRESS SHALL HAVE IT. PRAISE LITA.
PRAISE LITA!!
SAPPHIRE
!

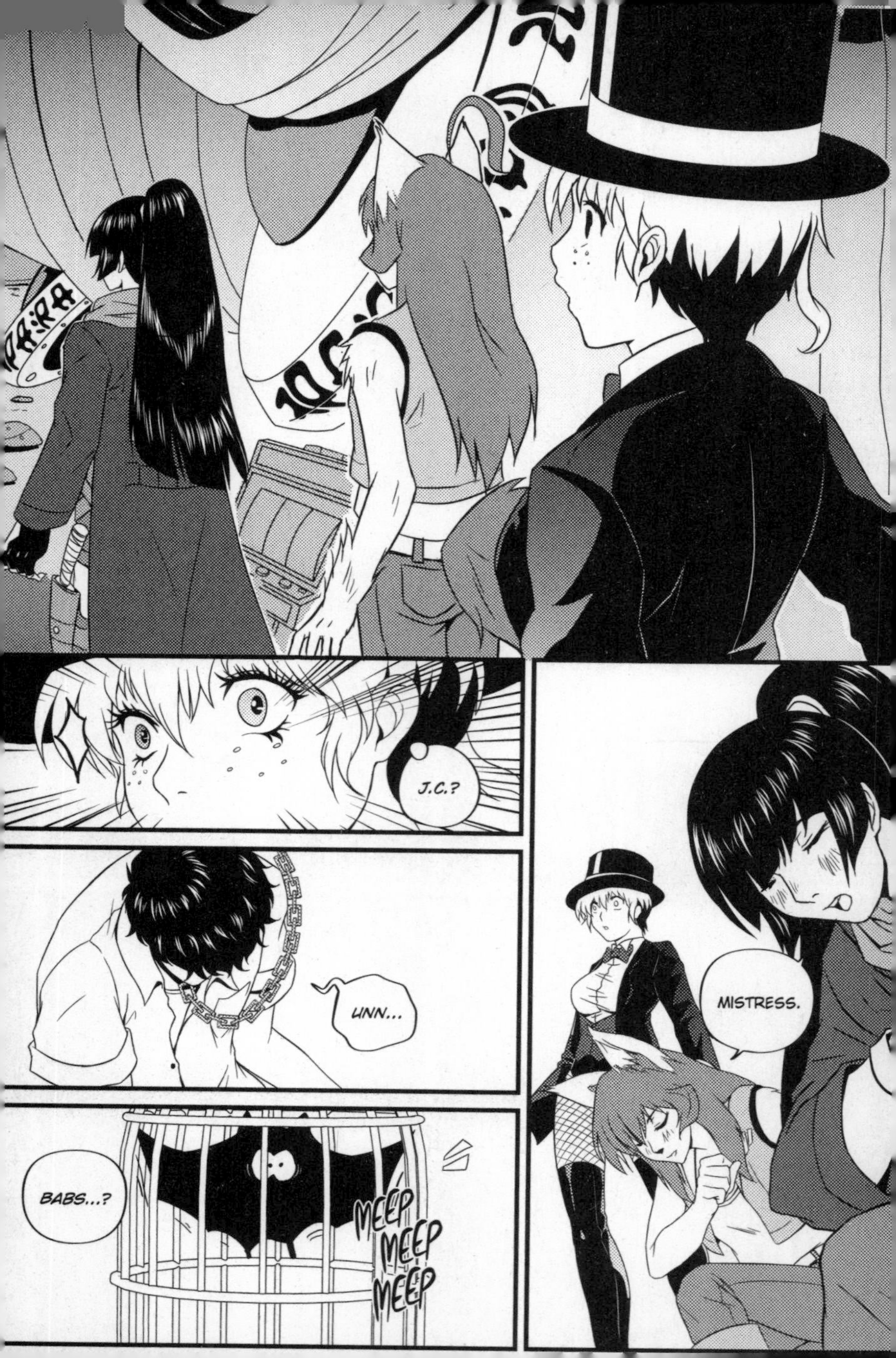
MISTRESS.
J.C.?
UNN...
BABS...?
MEEP
MEEP
MEEP

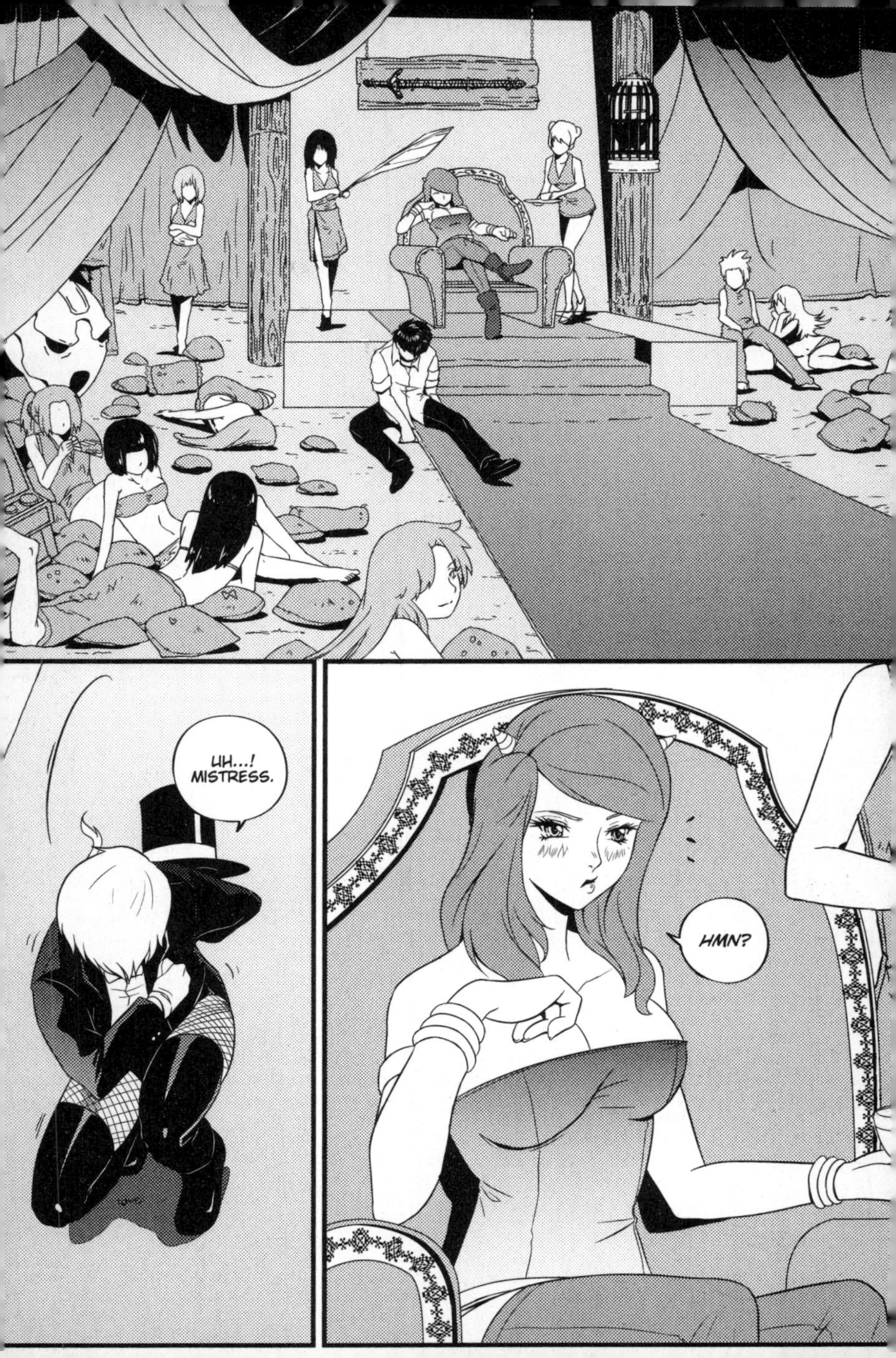
HMN?
UH...! MISTRESS.

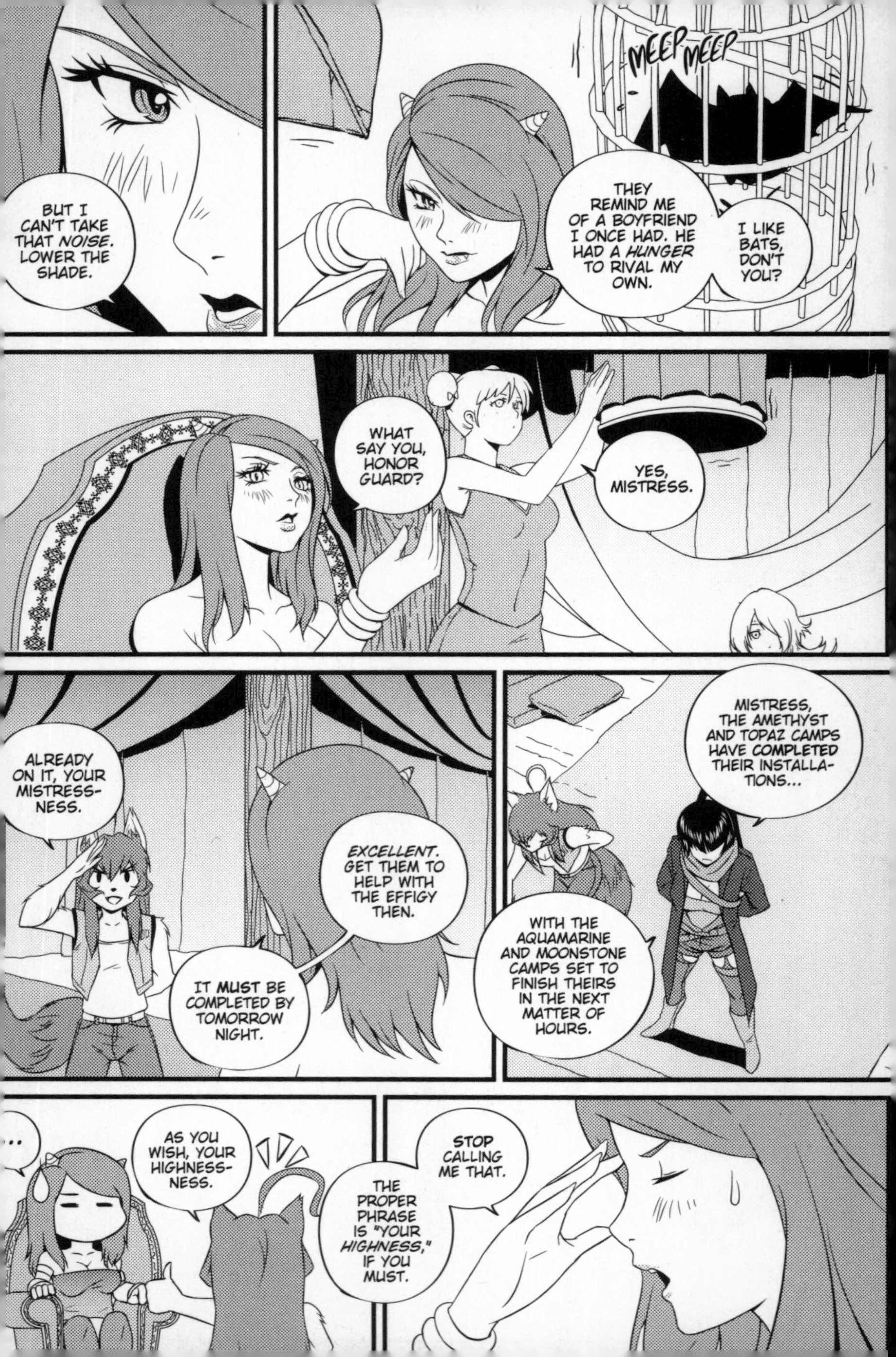
MEEP MEEP
I LIKE BATS, DON'T YOU?
THEY REMIND ME OF A BOYFRIEND I ONCE HAD. HE HAD A *HUNGER* TO RIVAL MY OWN.
BUT I CAN'T TAKE THAT *NOISE*. LOWER THE SHADE.
YES, MISTRESS.
WHAT SAY YOU, HONOR GUARD?
MISTRESS, THE AMETHYST AND TOPAZ CAMPS HAVE COMPLETED THEIR INSTALLA-TIONS...
WITH THE AQUAMARINE AND MOONSTONE CAMPS SET TO FINISH THEIRS IN THE NEXT MATTER OF HOURS.
EXCELLENT. GET THEM TO HELP WITH THE EFFIGY THEN.
IT MUST BE COMPLETED BY TOMORROW NIGHT.
ALREADY ON IT, YOUR MISTRESS-NESS.
STOP CALLING ME THAT.
THE PROPER PHRASE IS "YOUR *HIGHNESS*," IF YOU MUST.
AS YOU WISH, YOUR HIGHNESS-NESS.
...

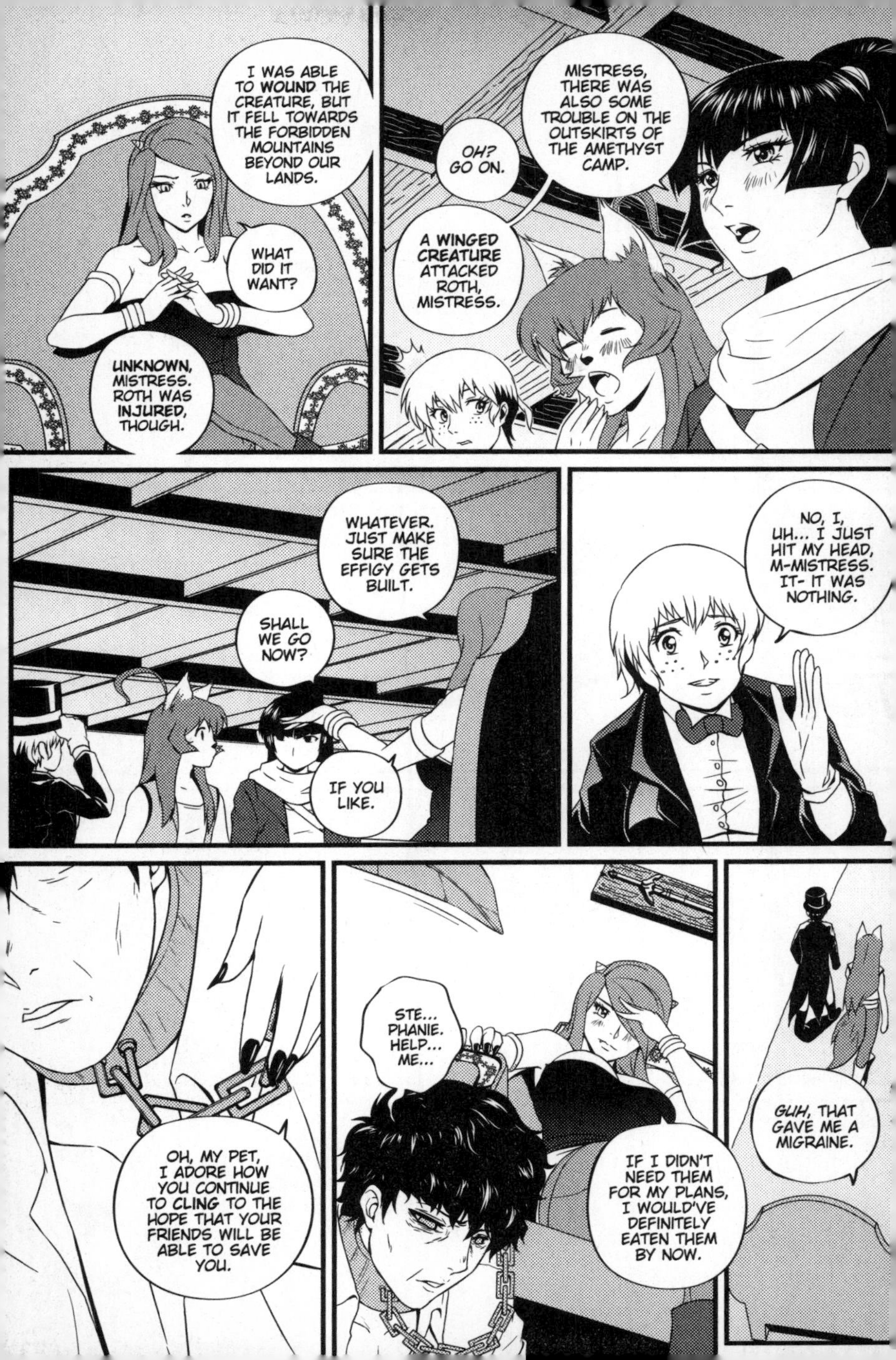

MISTRESS, THERE WAS ALSO SOME TROUBLE ON THE OUTSKIRTS OF THE AMETHYST CAMP.
OH? GO ON.
A WINGED CREATURE ATTACKED ROTH, MISTRESS.
I WAS ABLE TO WOUND THE CREATURE, BUT IT FELL TOWARDS THE FORBIDDEN MOUNTAINS BEYOND OUR LANDS.
WHAT DID IT WANT?
UNKNOWN, MISTRESS. ROTH WAS INJURED, THOUGH.
NO, I, UH... I JUST HIT MY HEAD, M-MISTRESS. IT- IT WAS NOTHING.
WHATEVER. JUST MAKE SURE THE EFFIGY GETS BUILT.
SHALL WE GO NOW?
IF YOU LIKE.
GUH, THAT GAVE ME A MIGRAINE.
STE... PHANIE. HELP... ME...
IF I DIDN'T NEED THEM FOR MY PLANS, I WOULD'VE DEFINITELY EATEN THEM BY NOW.
OH, MY PET, I ADORE HOW YOU CONTINUE TO CLING TO THE HOPE THAT YOUR FRIENDS WILL BE ABLE TO SAVE YOU.

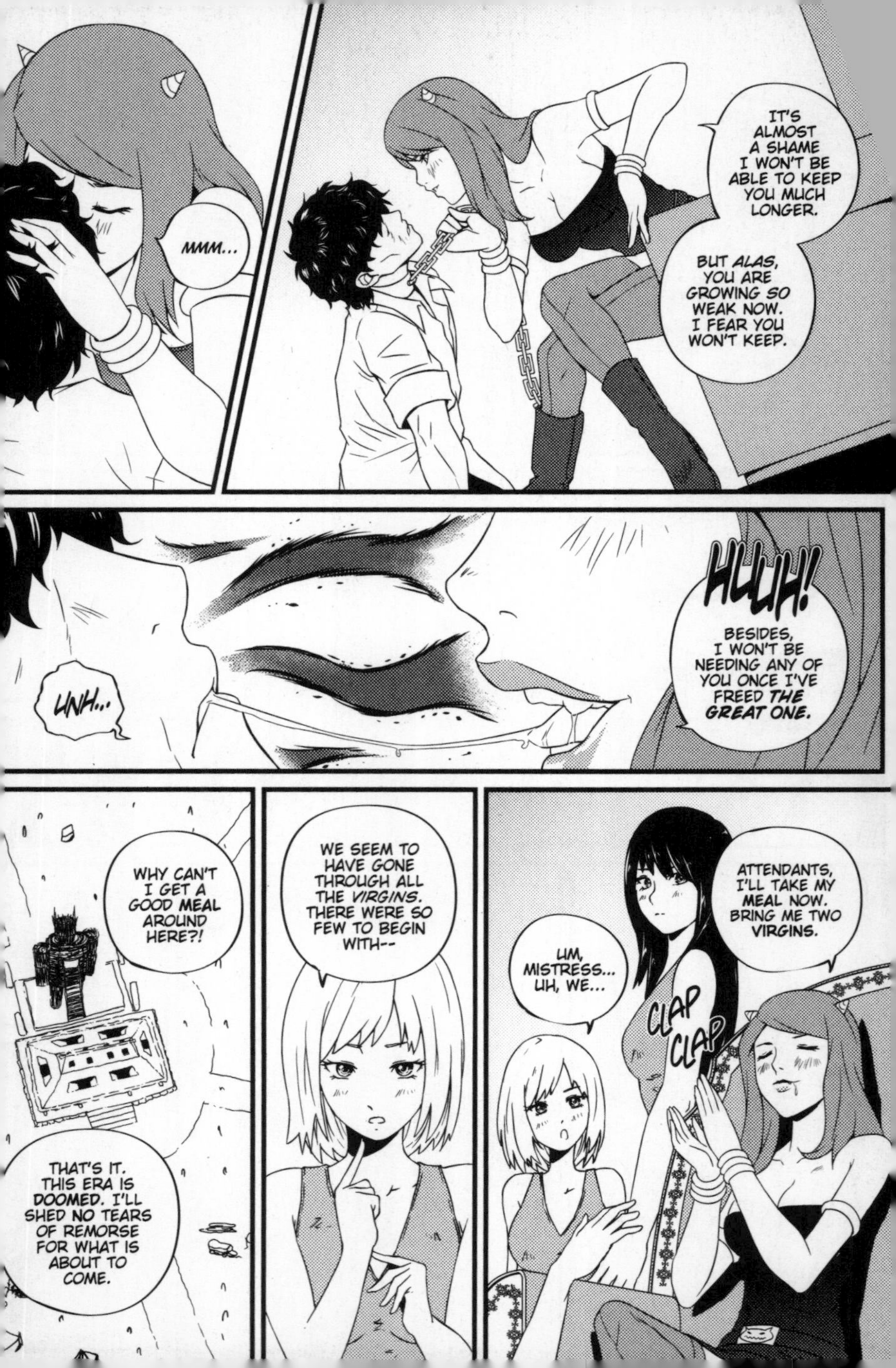
IT'S ALMOST A SHAME I WON'T BE ABLE TO KEEP YOU MUCH LONGER.
BUT *ALAS*, YOU ARE GROWING *SO* WEAK NOW. I FEAR YOU WON'T KEEP.
MMM...
HUUH!
BESIDES, I WON'T BE NEEDING ANY OF YOU ONCE I'VE FREED ***THE GREAT ONE.***
UNH...
ATTENDANTS, I'LL TAKE MY **MEAL** NOW. BRING ME TWO **VIRGINS.**
CLAP CLAP
UM, MISTRESS... UH, WE...
WE SEEM TO HAVE GONE THROUGH ALL THE *VIRGINS*. THERE WERE SO FEW TO BEGIN WITH--
WHY CAN'T I GET A GOOD **MEAL** AROUND HERE?!
THAT'S IT. THIS ERA IS **DOOMED**. I'LL SHED NO TEARS OF REMORSE FOR WHAT IS ABOUT TO COME.

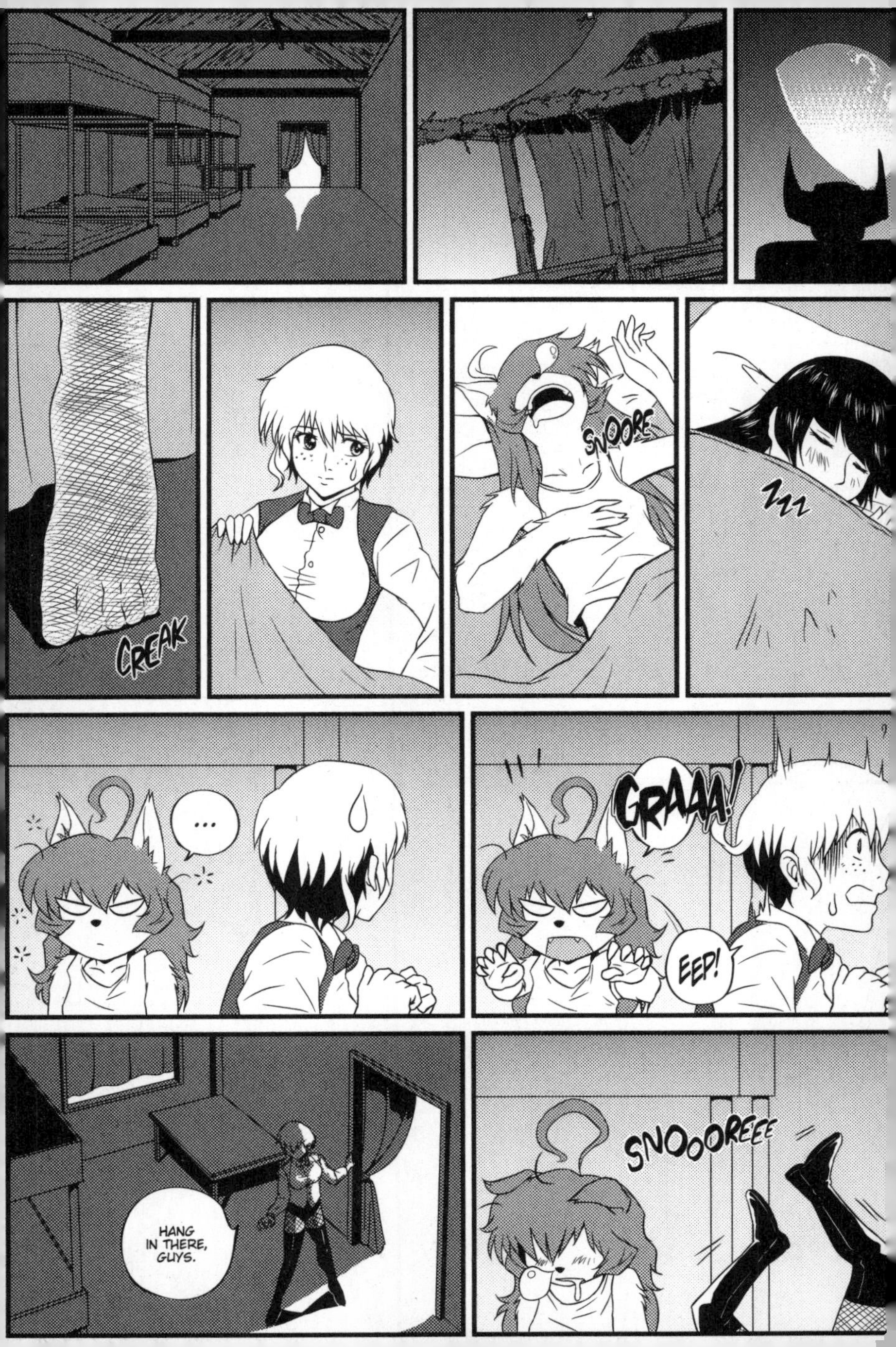
ZZZ
SNOORE
CREAK
GRAAA!
EEP!
...
SNOOOREEE
HANG IN THERE, GUYS.

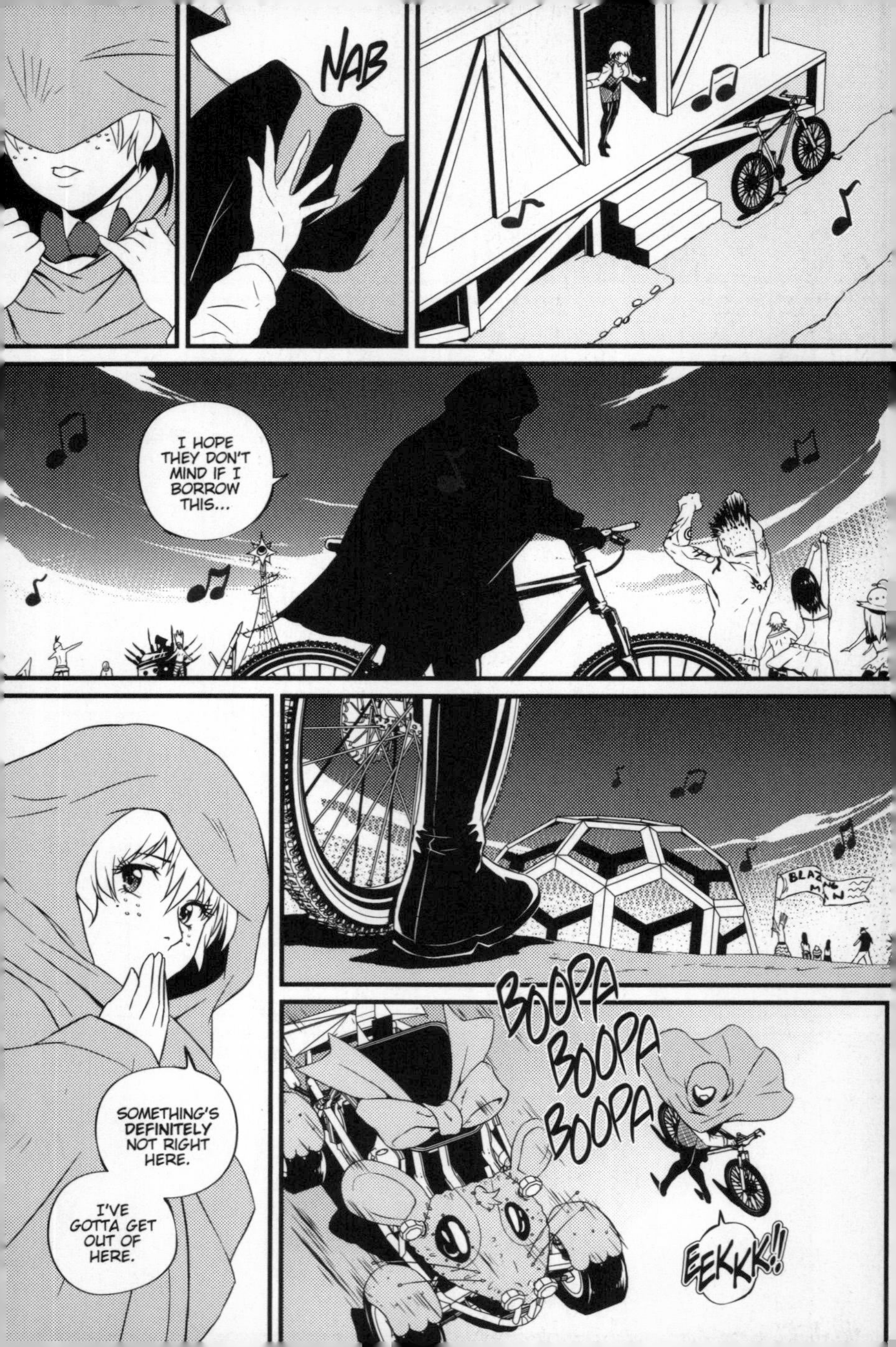
NAB
I HOPE THEY DON'T MIND IF I BORROW THIS...
BOOPA BOOPA BOOPA
EEKKK!!
SOMETHING'S DEFINITELY NOT RIGHT HERE.
I'VE GOTTA GET OUT OF HERE.

BE SEEING YOU.

RAISE

GOTTA ESCAPE--!

HALT!!

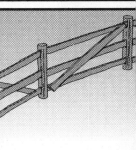

DON'T MOVE!!

HOLD IT RIGHT THERE!

CLAN

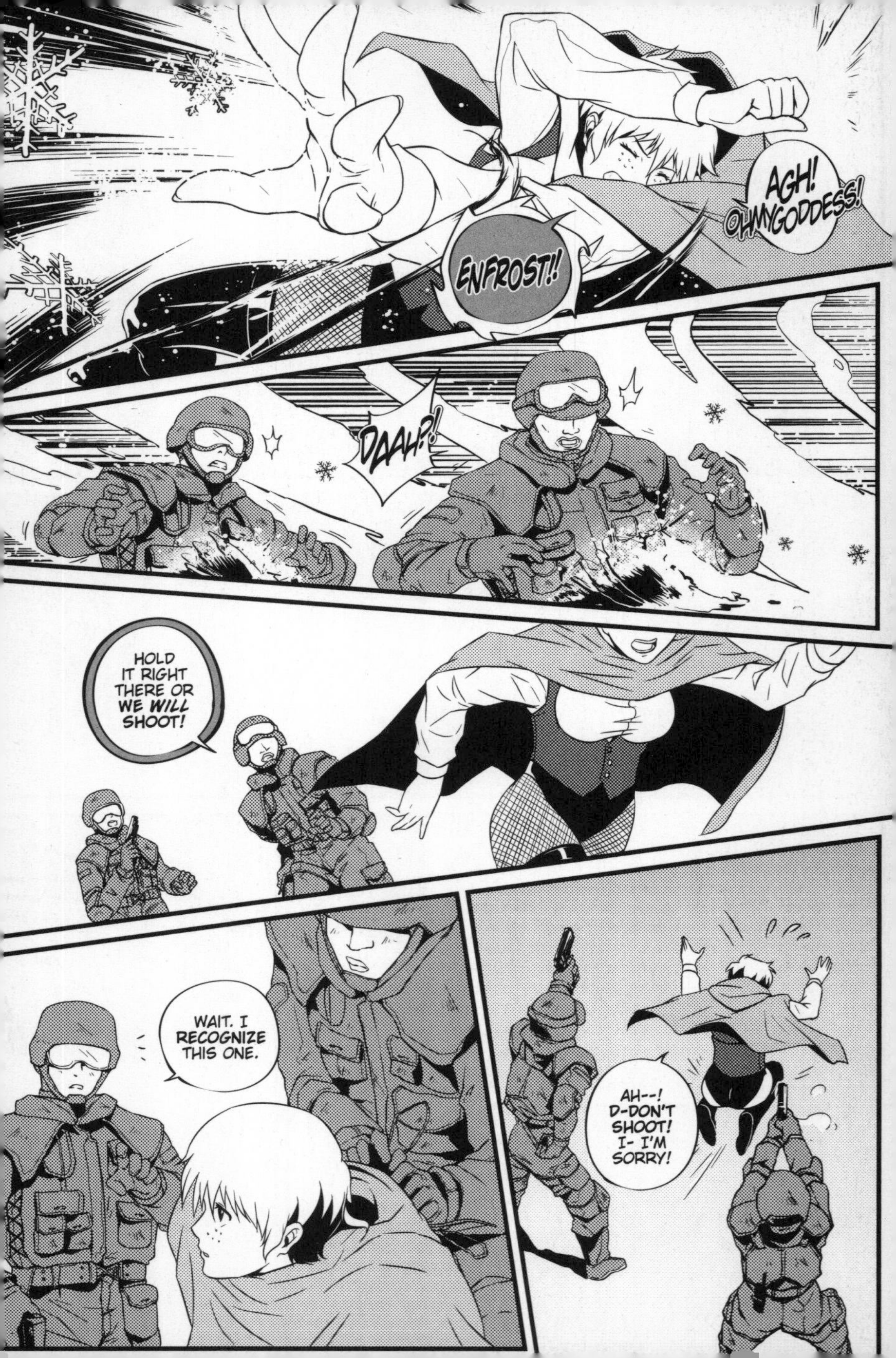
AGH! OHMYGODDESS!
ENFROST!!
DAAH?!
HOLD IT RIGHT THERE OR WE WILL SHOOT!
AH--! D-DON'T SHOOT! I- I'M SORRY!
WAIT. I RECOGNIZE THIS ONE.

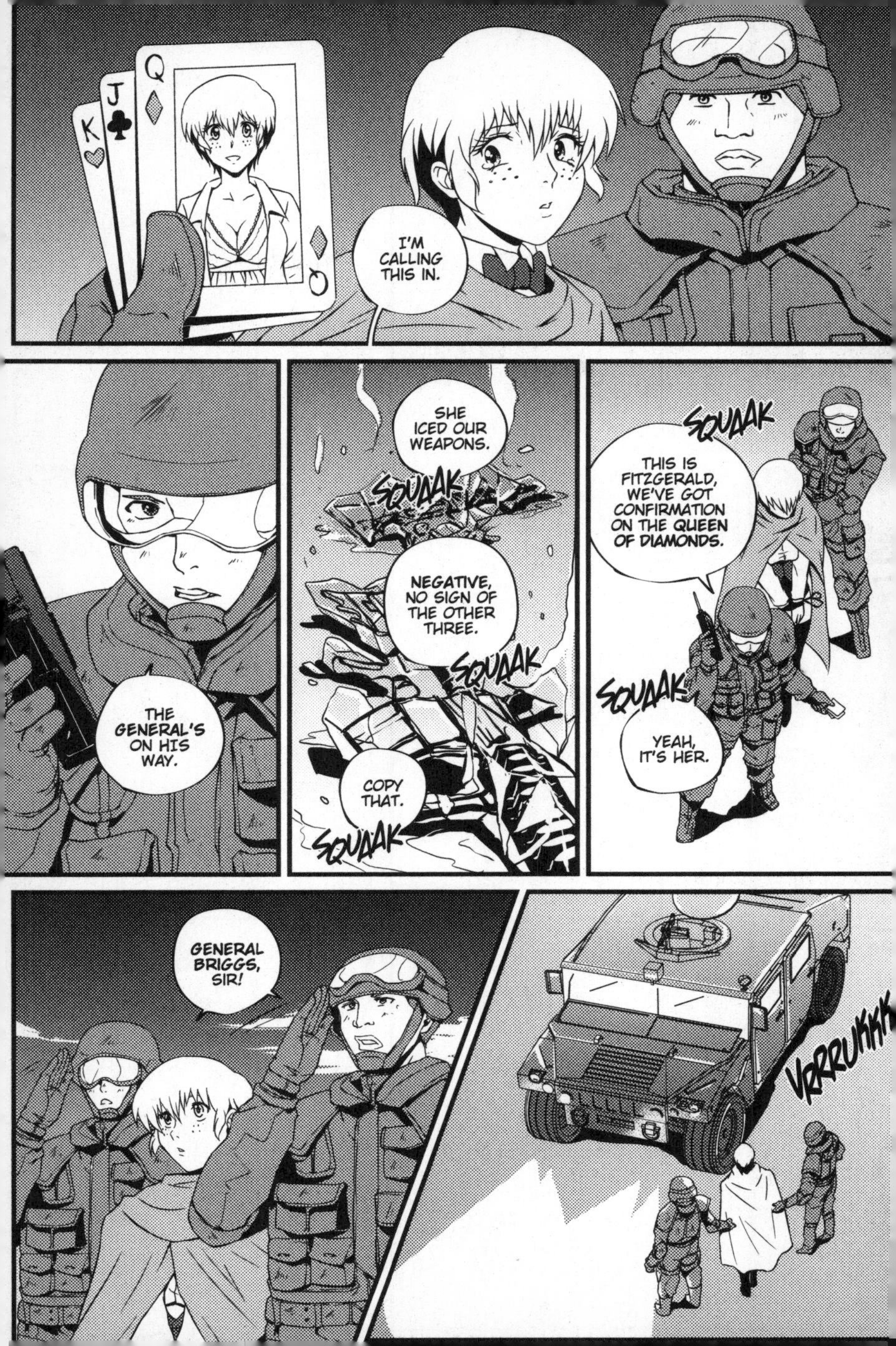
I'M CALLING THIS IN.
SQUAAK
THIS IS FITZGERALD, WE'VE GOT CONFIRMATION ON THE QUEEN OF DIAMONDS.
SQUAAK
YEAH, IT'S HER.
SHE ICED OUR WEAPONS.
SQUAAK
NEGATIVE, NO SIGN OF THE OTHER THREE.
SQUAAK
COPY THAT.
SQUAAK
THE GENERAL'S ON HIS WAY.
VRRRUKKK
GENERAL BRIGGS, SIR!

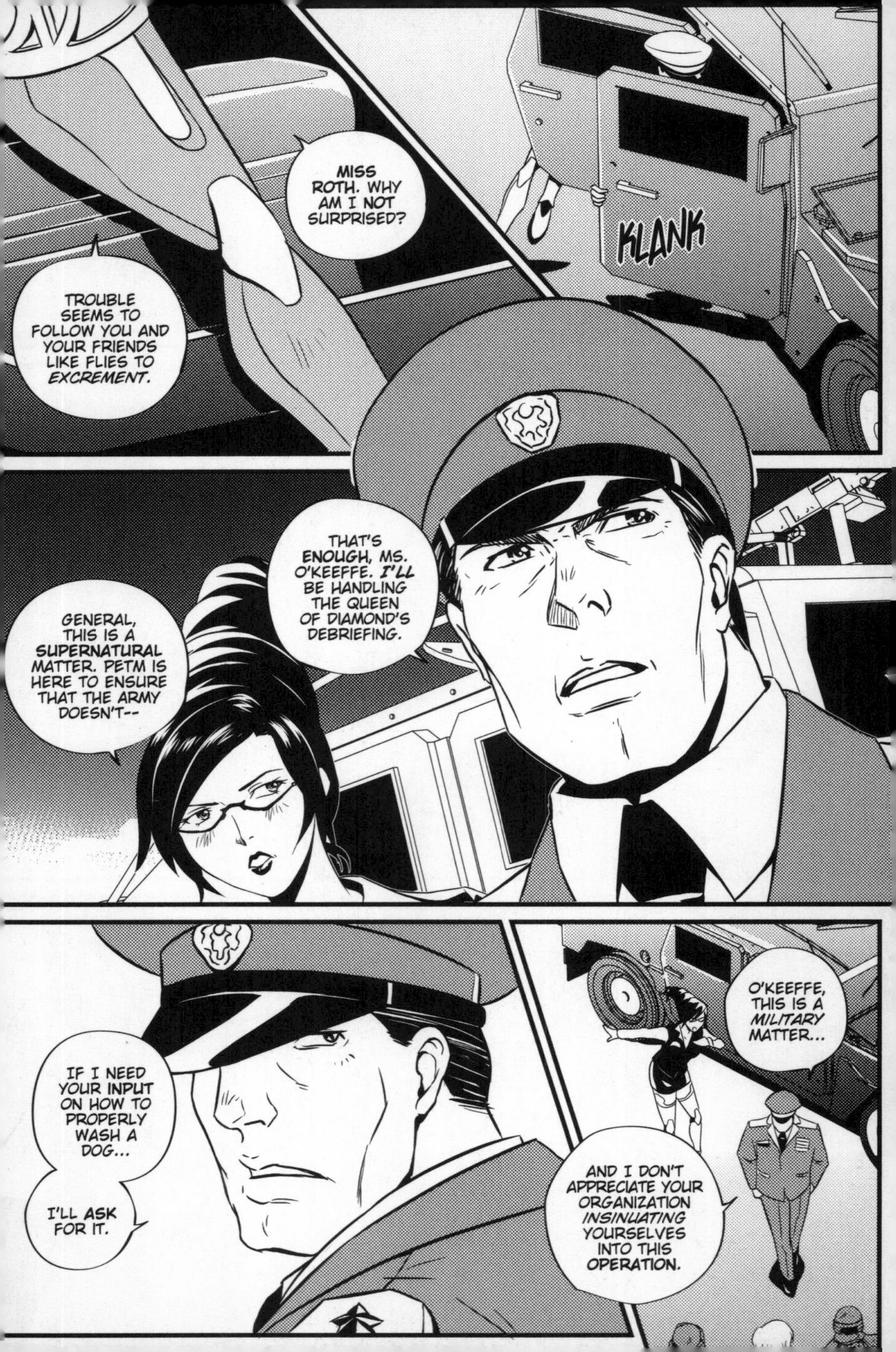
KLANK
MISS ROTH. WHY AM I NOT SURPRISED?
TROUBLE SEEMS TO FOLLOW YOU AND YOUR FRIENDS LIKE FLIES TO *EXCREMENT*.
THAT'S ENOUGH, MS. O'KEEFFE. *I'LL* BE HANDLING THE QUEEN OF DIAMOND'S DEBRIEFING.
GENERAL, THIS IS A **SUPERNATURAL** MATTER. PETM IS HERE TO ENSURE THAT THE ARMY DOESN'T--
O'KEEFFE, THIS IS A *MILITARY* MATTER...
AND I DON'T APPRECIATE YOUR ORGANIZATION *INSINUATING* YOURSELVES INTO THIS OPERATION.
IF I NEED YOUR **INPUT** ON HOW TO PROPERLY WASH A DOG...
I'LL **ASK** FOR IT.

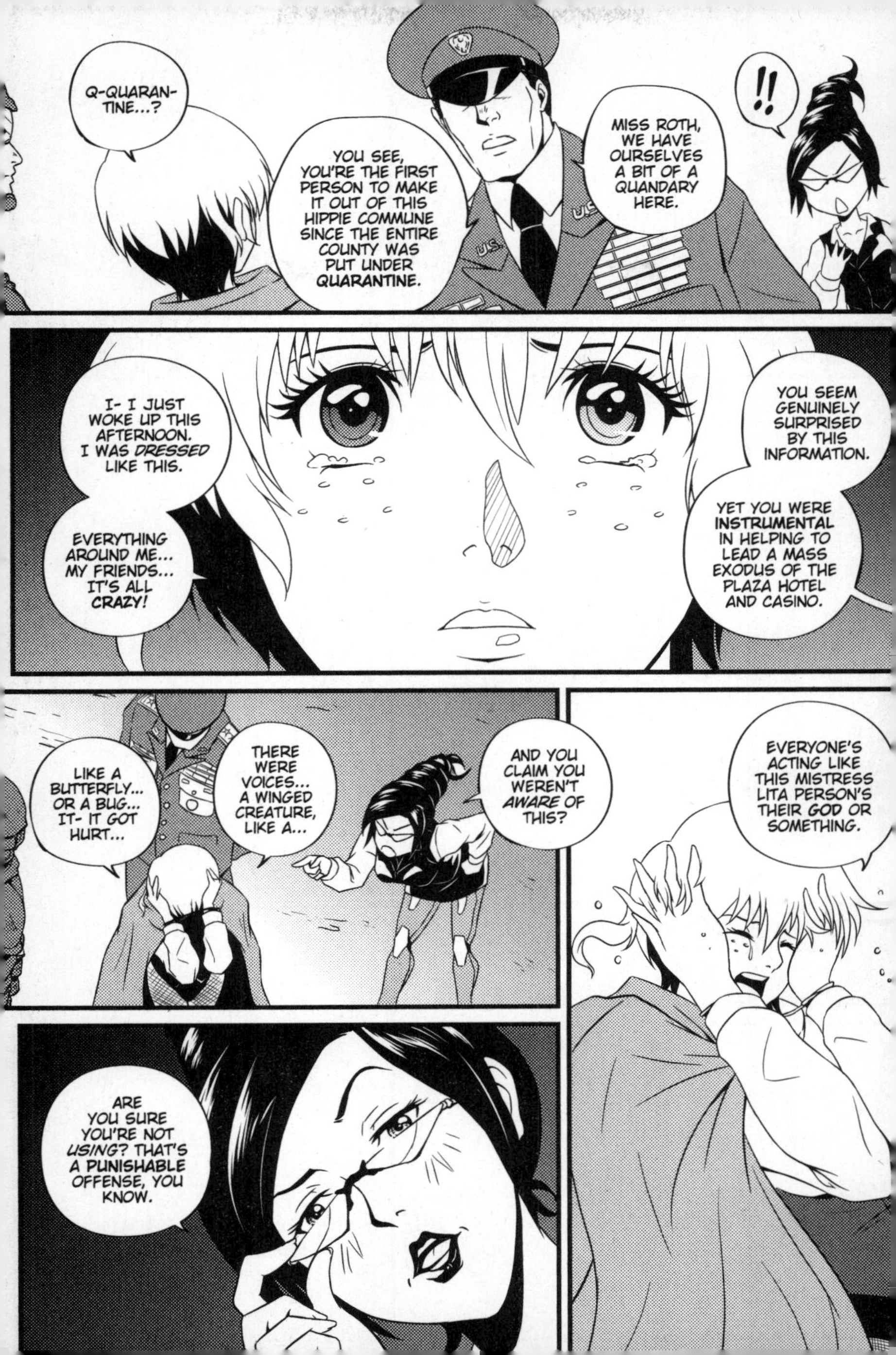
!!
MISS ROTH, WE HAVE OURSELVES A BIT OF A QUANDARY HERE.
YOU SEE, YOU'RE THE FIRST PERSON TO MAKE IT OUT OF THIS HIPPIE COMMUNE SINCE THE ENTIRE COUNTY WAS PUT UNDER **QUARANTINE**.
Q-QUARANTINE...?
YOU SEEM GENUINELY SURPRISED BY THIS INFORMATION.
YET YOU WERE **INSTRUMENTAL** IN HELPING TO LEAD A MASS EXODUS OF THE PLAZA HOTEL AND CASINO.
I- I JUST WOKE UP THIS AFTERNOON. I WAS *DRESSED* LIKE THIS.
EVERYTHING AROUND ME... MY FRIENDS... IT'S ALL **CRAZY!**
EVERYONE'S ACTING LIKE THIS MISTRESS LITA PERSON'S THEIR **GOD** OR SOMETHING.
AND YOU CLAIM YOU WEREN'T *AWARE* OF THIS?
THERE WERE VOICES... A WINGED CREATURE, LIKE A...
LIKE A BUTTERFLY... OR A BUG... IT- IT GOT HURT...
ARE YOU SURE YOU'RE NOT *USING*? THAT'S A PUNISHABLE OFFENSE, YOU KNOW.

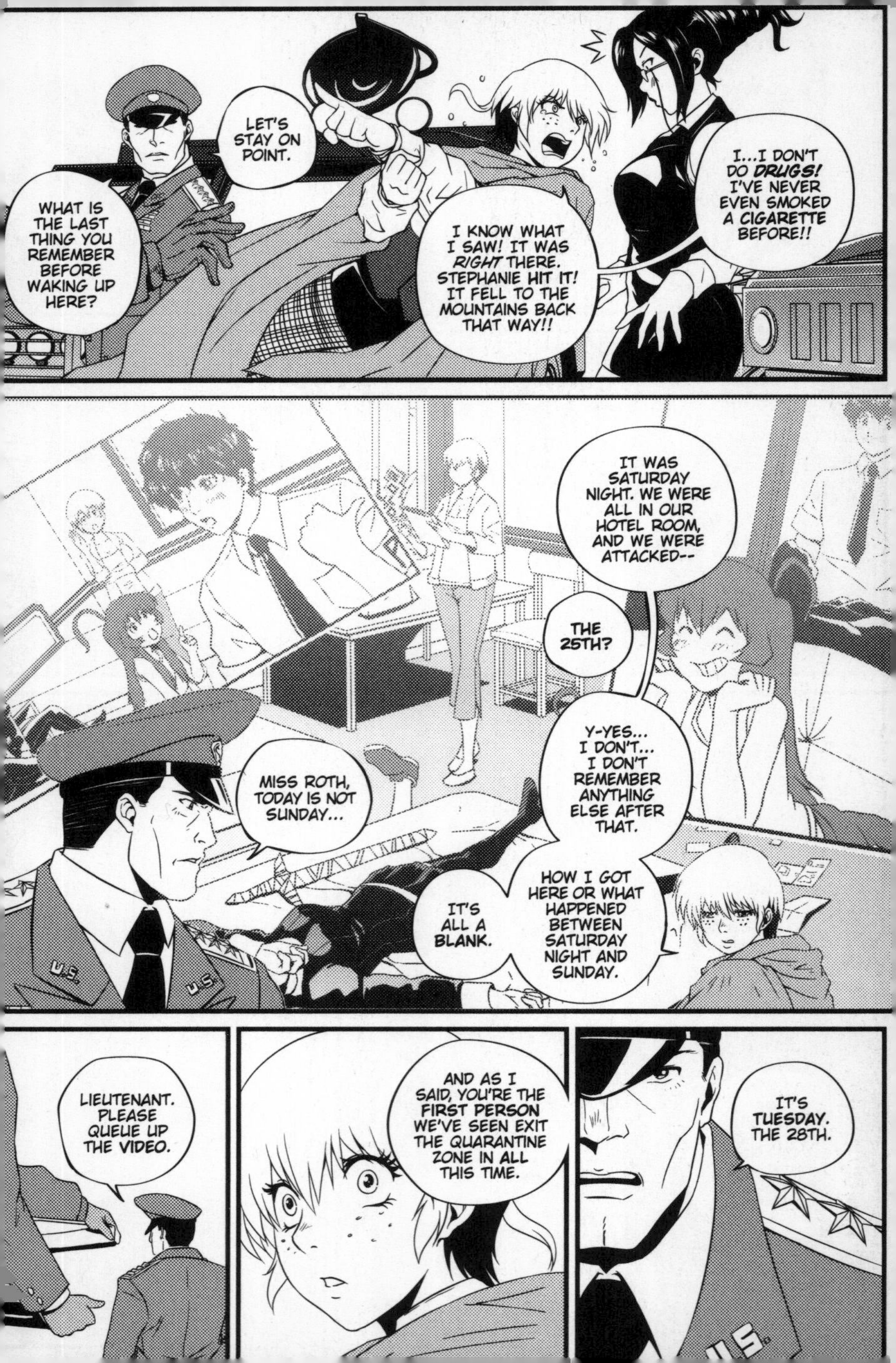
I...I DON'T DO **DRUGS!** I'VE NEVER EVEN SMOKED A **CIGARETTE** BEFORE!!
I KNOW WHAT I SAW! IT WAS *RIGHT* THERE. STEPHANIE HIT IT! IT FELL TO THE MOUNTAINS BACK THAT WAY!!
LET'S STAY ON POINT.
WHAT IS THE LAST THING YOU REMEMBER BEFORE WAKING UP HERE?
IT WAS SATURDAY NIGHT. WE WERE ALL IN OUR HOTEL ROOM, AND WE WERE ATTACKED--
THE 25TH?
Y-YES... I DON'T... I DON'T REMEMBER ANYTHING ELSE AFTER THAT.
HOW I GOT HERE OR WHAT HAPPENED BETWEEN SATURDAY NIGHT AND SUNDAY.
IT'S ALL A BLANK.
MISS ROTH, TODAY IS NOT SUNDAY...
U.S.
U.S.
IT'S TUESDAY. THE 28TH.
AND AS I SAID, YOU'RE THE FIRST PERSON WE'VE SEEN EXIT THE QUARANTINE ZONE IN ALL THIS TIME.
LIEUTENANT. PLEASE QUEUE UP THE VIDEO.
U.S.

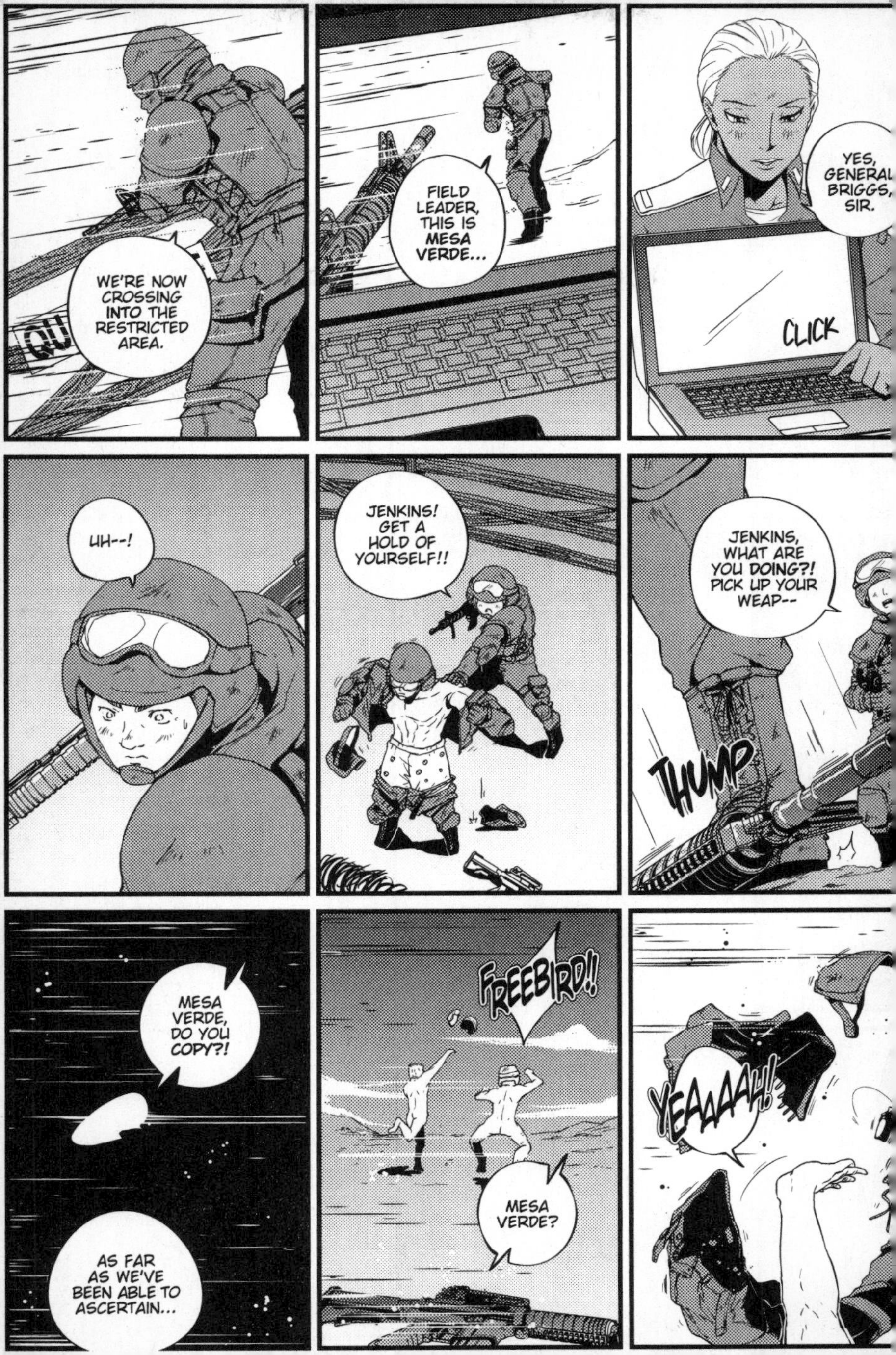
YES, GENERAL BRIGGS, SIR.
CLICK
FIELD LEADER, THIS IS MESA VERDE...
WE'RE NOW CROSSING INTO THE RESTRICTED AREA.
JENKINS, WHAT ARE YOU DOING?! PICK UP YOUR WEAP--
THUMP
JENKINS! GET A HOLD OF YOURSELF!!
UH--!
YEAAAAH!
FREEBIRD!!
MESA VERDE?
MESA VERDE, DO YOU COPY?!
AS FAR AS WE'VE BEEN ABLE TO ASCERTAIN...

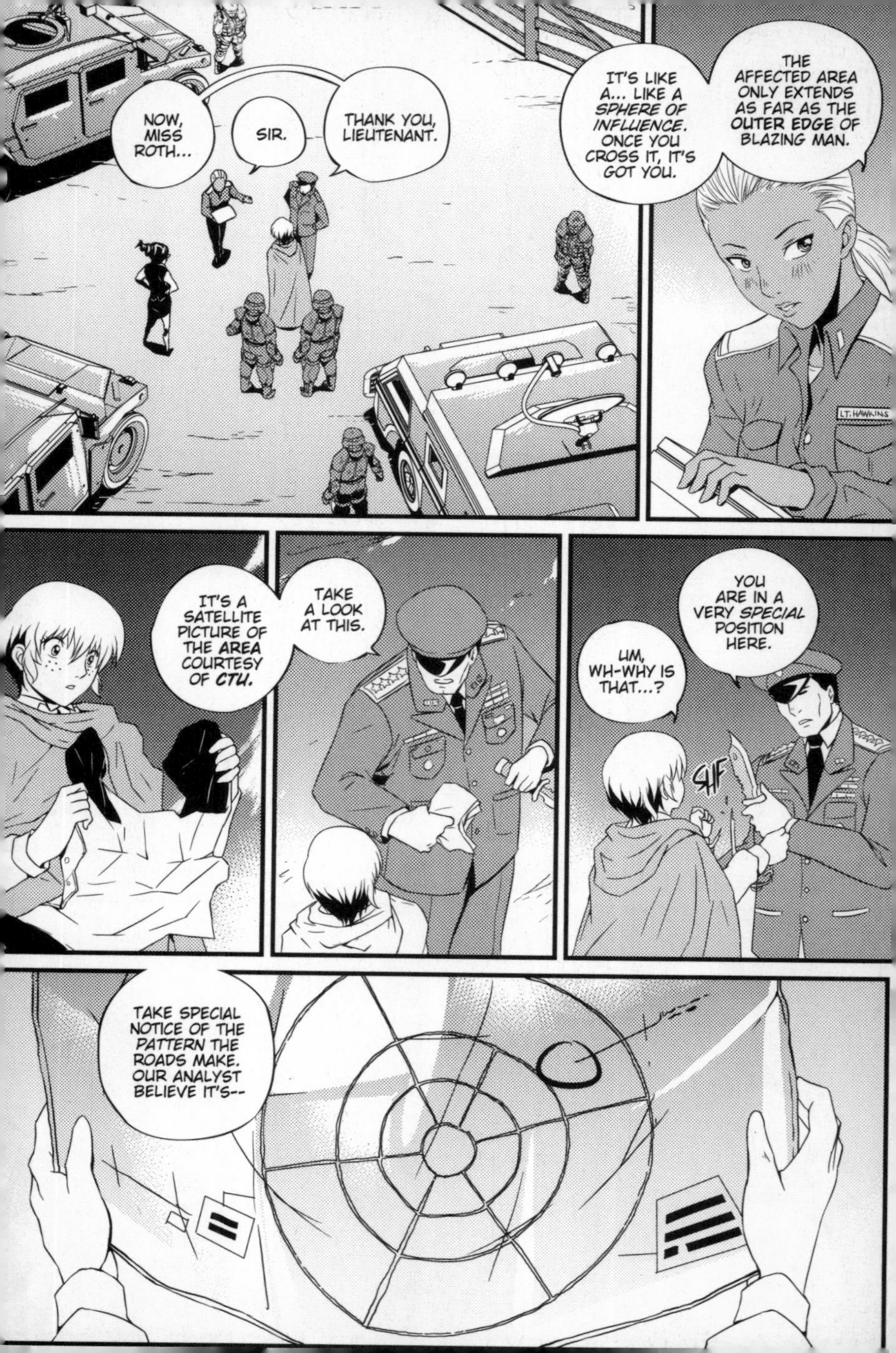

THE AFFECTED AREA ONLY EXTENDS AS FAR AS THE OUTER EDGE OF BLAZING MAN.
IT'S LIKE A... LIKE A *SPHERE OF INFLUENCE.* ONCE YOU CROSS IT, IT'S GOT YOU.
LT. HAWKINS
THANK YOU, LIEUTENANT.
SIR.
NOW, MISS ROTH...
YOU ARE IN A VERY *SPECIAL* POSITION HERE.
UM, WH-WHY IS THAT...?
SHF
TAKE A LOOK AT THIS.
IT'S A SATELLITE PICTURE OF THE AREA COURTESY OF **CTU.**
TAKE SPECIAL NOTICE OF THE PATTERN THE ROADS MAKE. OUR ANALYST BELIEVE IT'S--

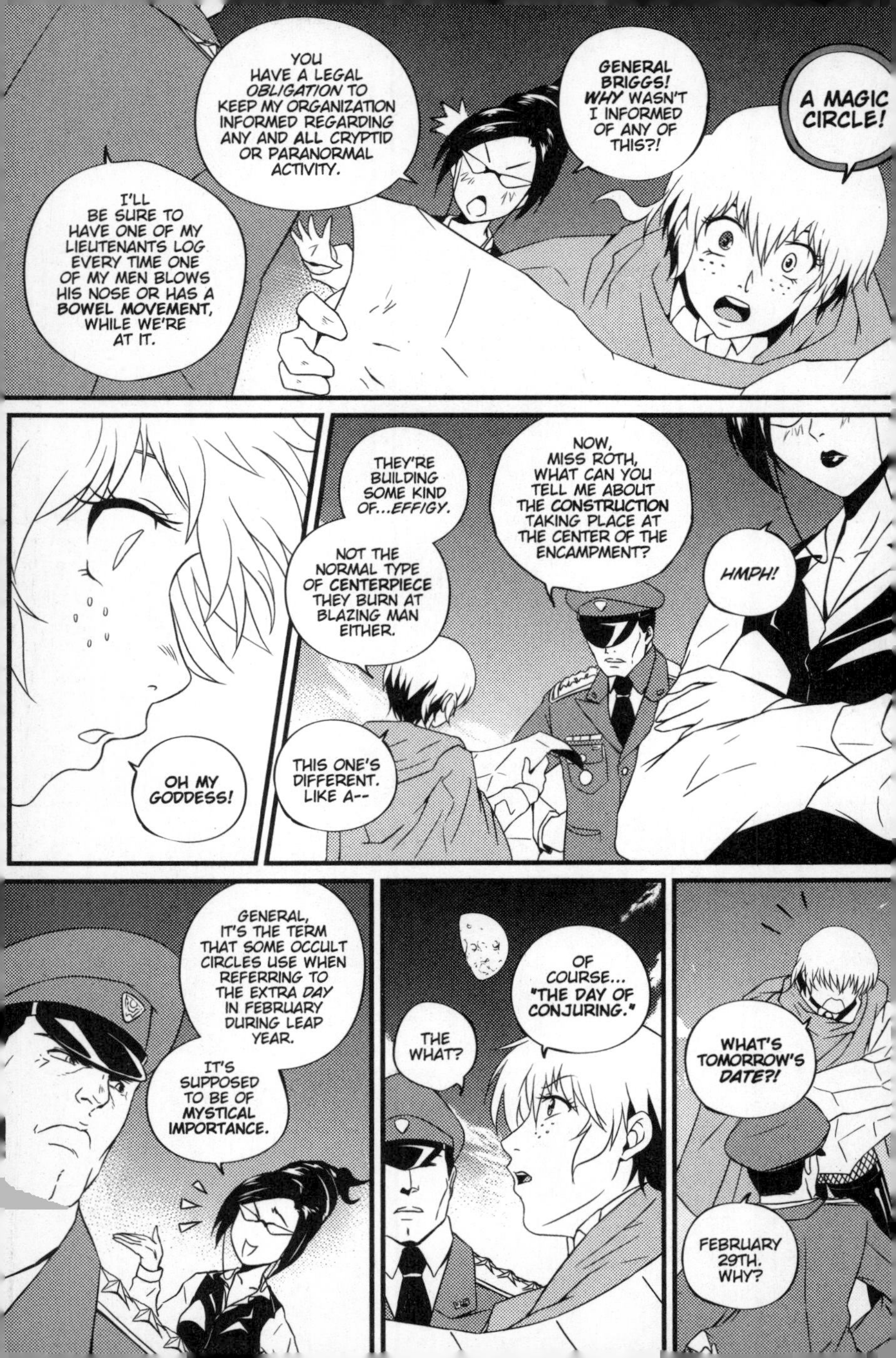
A MAGIC CIRCLE!
GENERAL BRIGGS! WHY WASN'T I INFORMED OF ANY OF THIS?!
YOU HAVE A LEGAL OBLIGATION TO KEEP MY ORGANIZATION INFORMED REGARDING ANY AND ALL CRYPTID OR PARANORMAL ACTIVITY.
I'LL BE SURE TO HAVE ONE OF MY LIEUTENANTS LOG EVERY TIME ONE OF MY MEN BLOWS HIS NOSE OR HAS A BOWEL MOVEMENT, WHILE WE'RE AT IT.
NOW, MISS ROTH, WHAT CAN YOU TELL ME ABOUT THE CONSTRUCTION TAKING PLACE AT THE CENTER OF THE ENCAMPMENT?
THEY'RE BUILDING SOME KIND OF...EFFIGY.
NOT THE NORMAL TYPE OF CENTERPIECE THEY BURN AT BLAZING MAN EITHER.
HMPH!
THIS ONE'S DIFFERENT. LIKE A--
OH MY GODDESS!
WHAT'S TOMORROW'S DATE?!
FEBRUARY 29TH. WHY?
OF COURSE... "THE DAY OF CONJURING."
THE WHAT?
GENERAL, IT'S THE TERM THAT SOME OCCULT CIRCLES USE WHEN REFERRING TO THE EXTRA DAY IN FEBRUARY DURING LEAP YEAR.
IT'S SUPPOSED TO BE OF MYSTICAL IMPORTANCE.

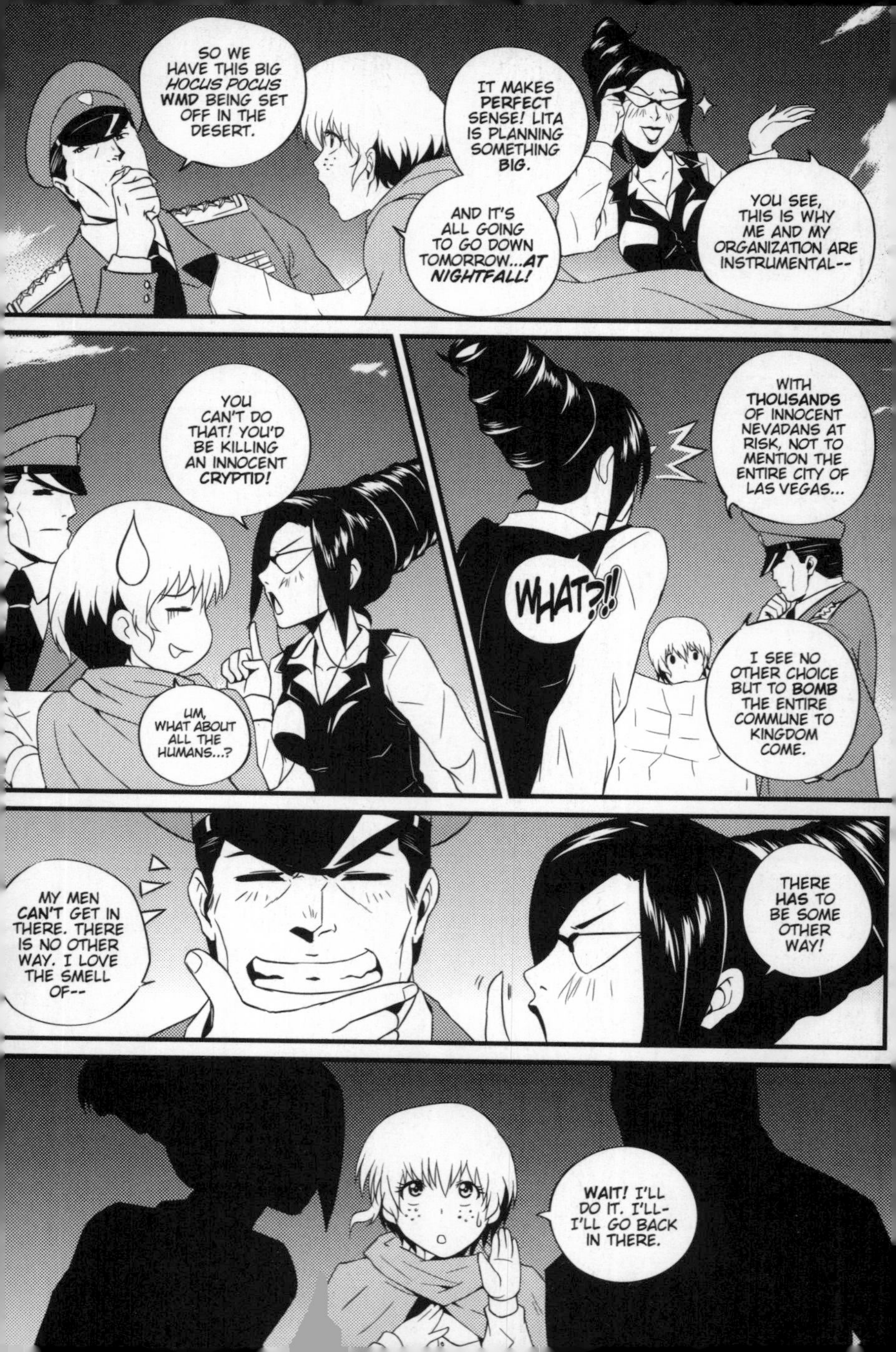
YOU SEE, THIS IS WHY ME AND MY ORGANIZATION ARE INSTRUMENTAL--
IT MAKES PERFECT SENSE! LITA IS PLANNING SOMETHING BIG.
AND IT'S ALL GOING TO GO DOWN TOMORROW...AT NIGHTFALL!
SO WE HAVE THIS BIG HOCUS POCUS WMD BEING SET OFF IN THE DESERT.
WITH THOUSANDS OF INNOCENT NEVADANS AT RISK, NOT TO MENTION THE ENTIRE CITY OF LAS VEGAS...
WHAT?!!
I SEE NO OTHER CHOICE BUT TO BOMB THE ENTIRE COMMUNE TO KINGDOM COME.
YOU CAN'T DO THAT! YOU'D BE KILLING AN INNOCENT CRYPTID!
UM, WHAT ABOUT ALL THE HUMANS...?
THERE HAS TO BE SOME OTHER WAY!
MY MEN CAN'T GET IN THERE. THERE IS NO OTHER WAY. I LOVE THE SMELL OF--
WAIT! I'LL DO IT. I'LL- I'LL GO BACK IN THERE.

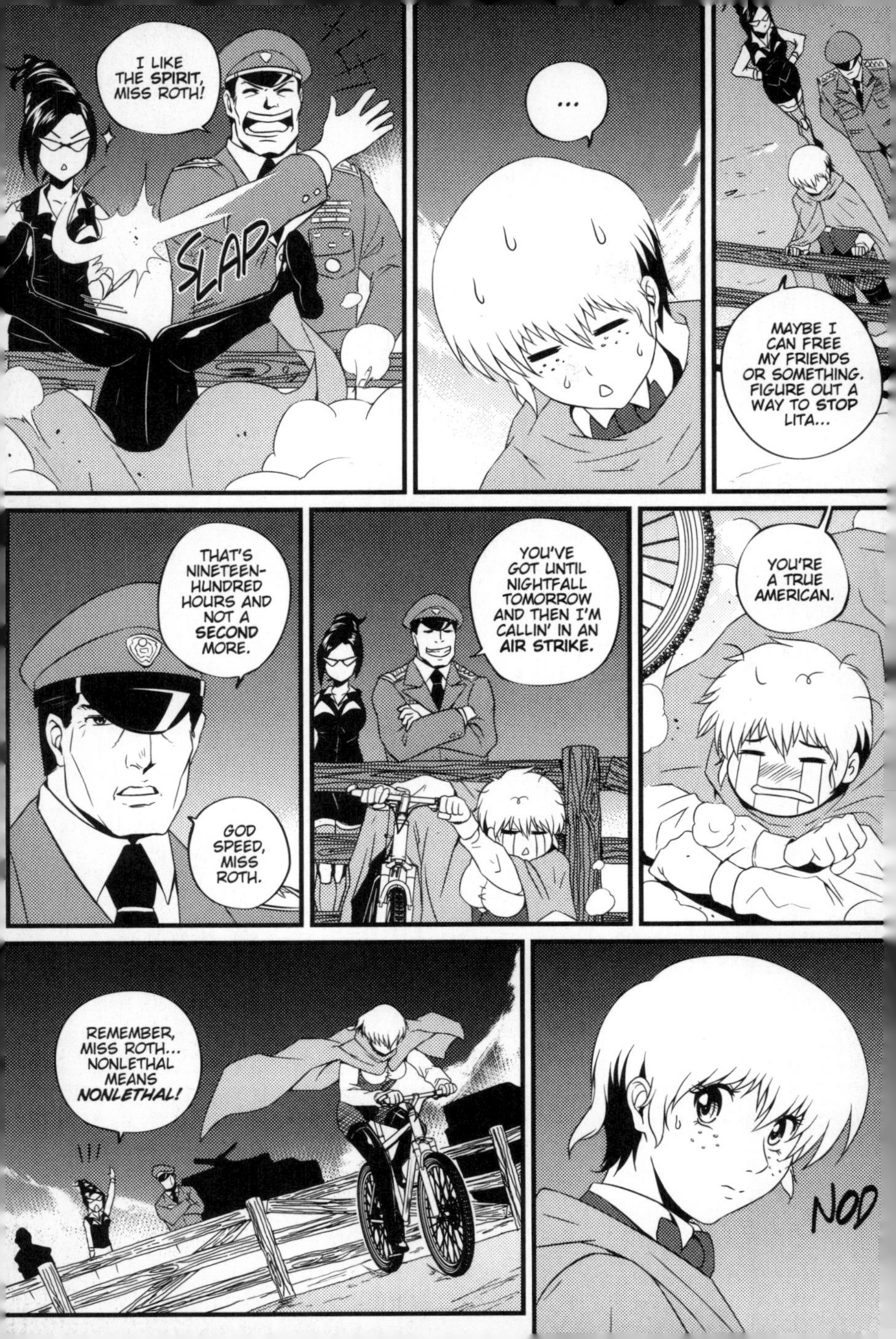
MAYBE I CAN FREE MY FRIENDS OR SOMETHING. FIGURE OUT A WAY TO STOP LITA...
...
I LIKE THE SPIRIT, MISS ROTH!
SLAP
YOU'RE A TRUE AMERICAN.
YOU'VE GOT UNTIL NIGHTFALL TOMORROW AND THEN I'M CALLIN' IN AN **AIR STRIKE**.
THAT'S NINETEEN-HUNDRED HOURS AND NOT A **SECOND** MORE.
GOD SPEED, MISS ROTH.
NOD
REMEMBER, MISS ROTH... NONLETHAL MEANS ***NONLETHAL!***
!!!

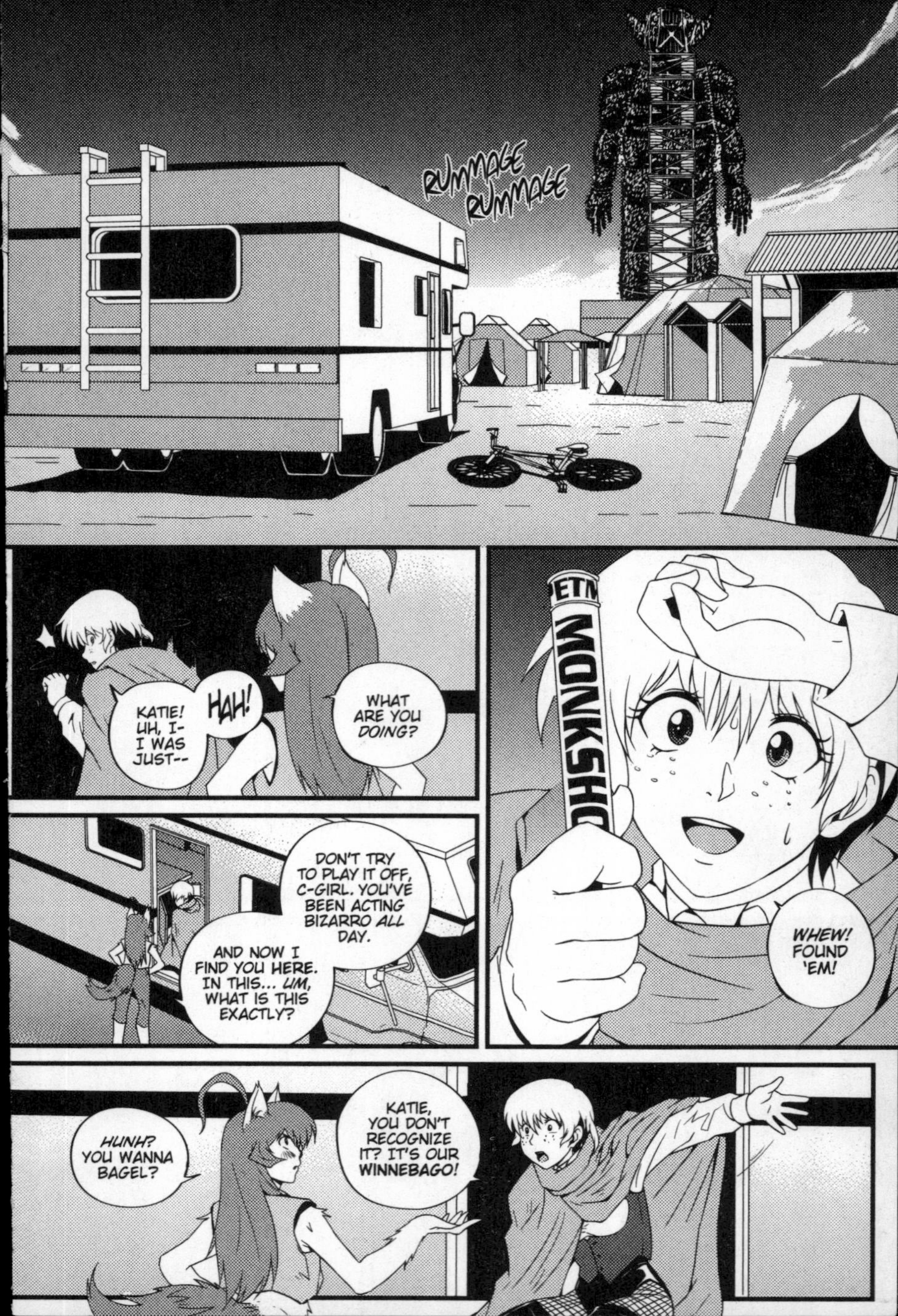
RUMMAGE RUMMAGE
MONKSHO
WHEW! FOUND 'EM!
WHAT ARE YOU DOING?
HAH!
KATIE! UH, I- I WAS JUST--
DON'T TRY TO PLAY IT OFF, C-GIRL. YOU'VE BEEN ACTING BIZARRO ALL DAY.
AND NOW I FIND YOU HERE. IN THIS... UM, WHAT IS THIS EXACTLY?
KATIE, YOU DON'T RECOGNIZE IT? IT'S OUR WINNEBAGO!
HUNH? YOU WANNA BAGEL?

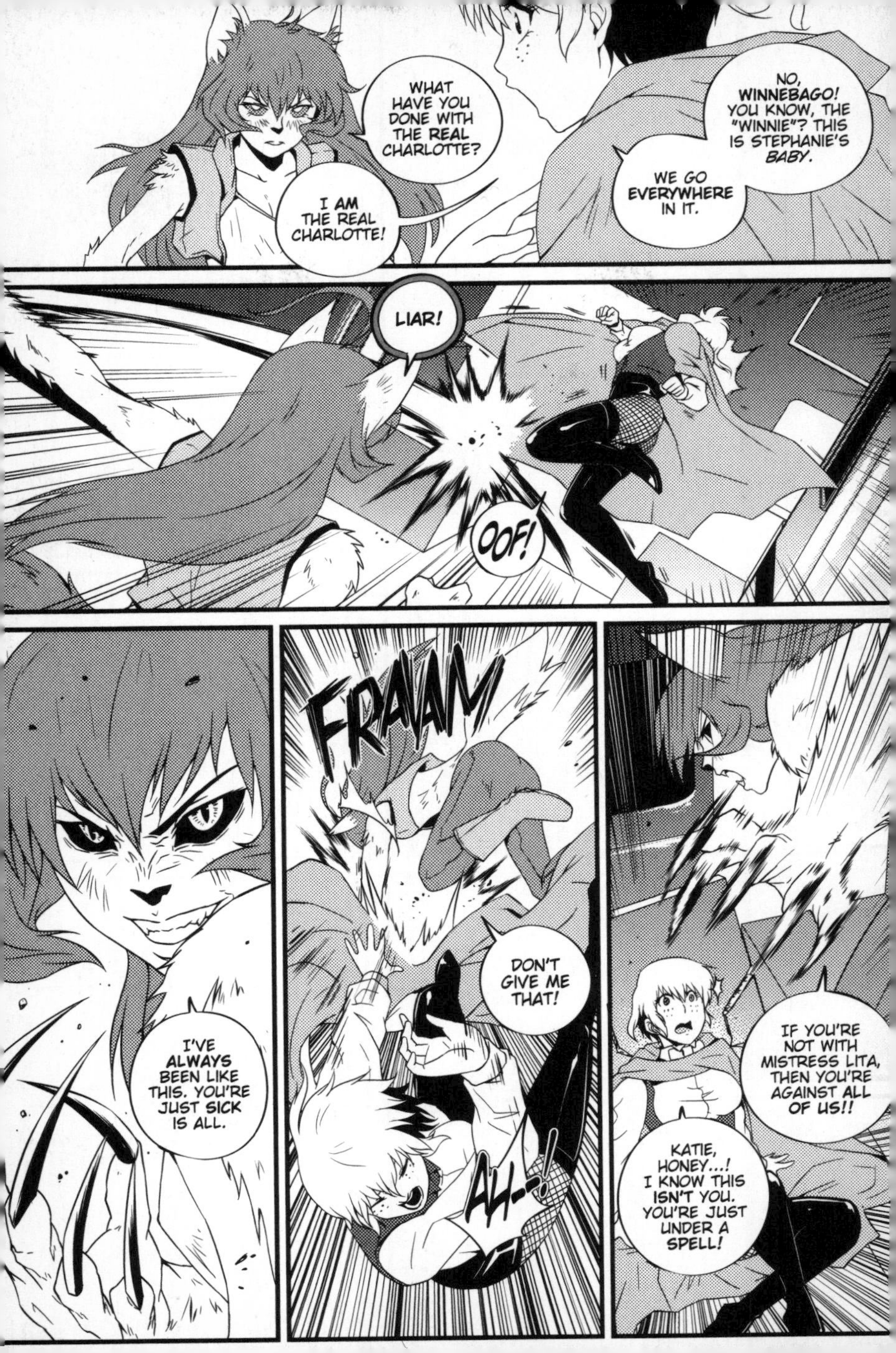
NO, *WINNEBAGO!* YOU KNOW, THE "WINNIE"? THIS IS STEPHANIE'S *BABY.*
WE GO EVERYWHERE IN IT.
WHAT HAVE YOU DONE WITH THE REAL CHARLOTTE?
I AM THE REAL CHARLOTTE!
LIAR!
OOF!
IF YOU'RE NOT WITH MISTRESS LITA, THEN YOU'RE AGAINST ALL OF US!!
KATIE, HONEY...! I KNOW THIS *ISN'T* YOU. YOU'RE JUST UNDER A SPELL!
FRAAM
DON'T GIVE ME THAT!
AH--!
I'VE *ALWAYS* BEEN LIKE THIS. YOU'RE JUST SICK IS ALL.

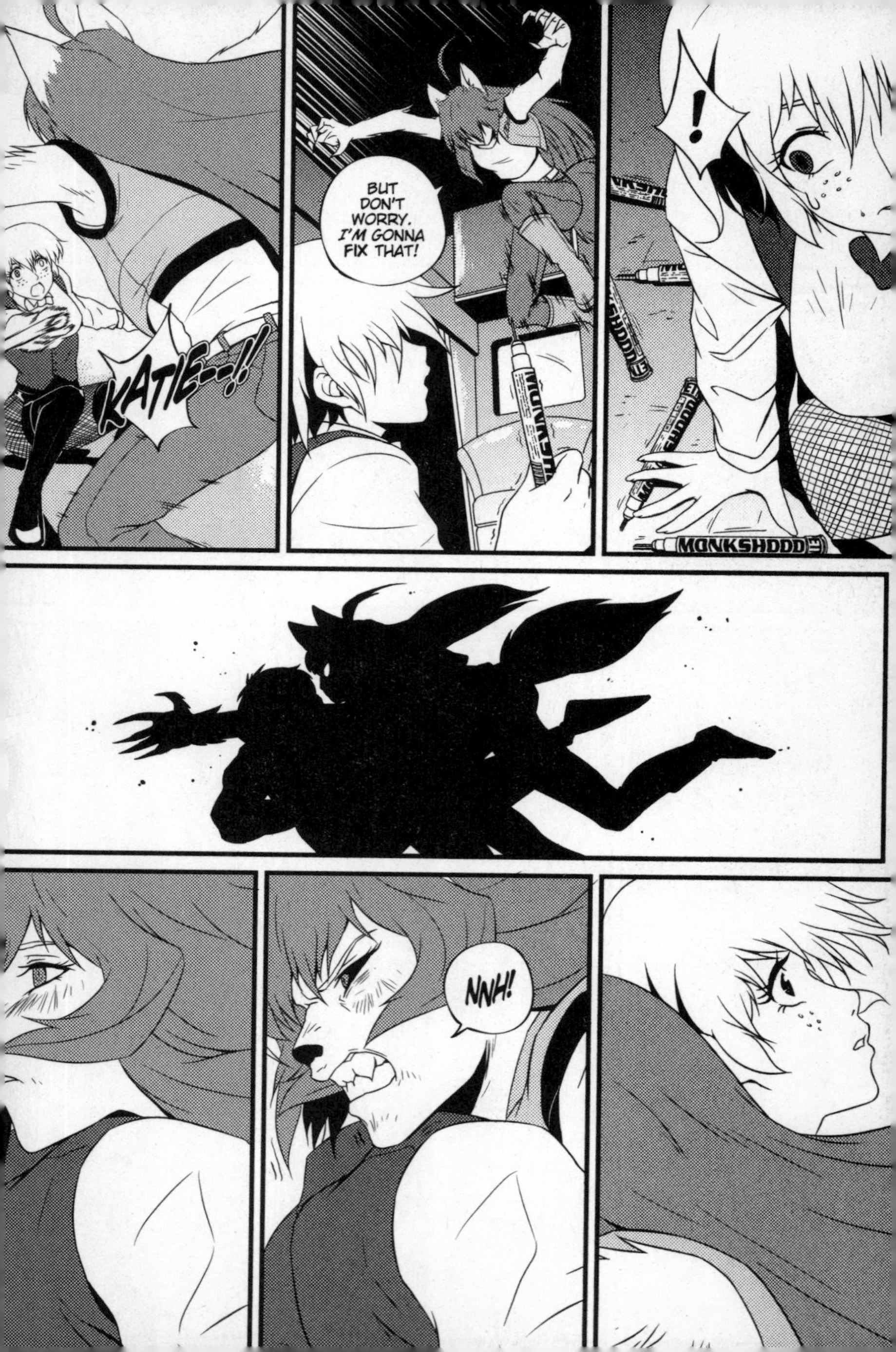
!
BUT DON'T WORRY. I'M GONNA FIX THAT!
KATIE--!!
NNH!

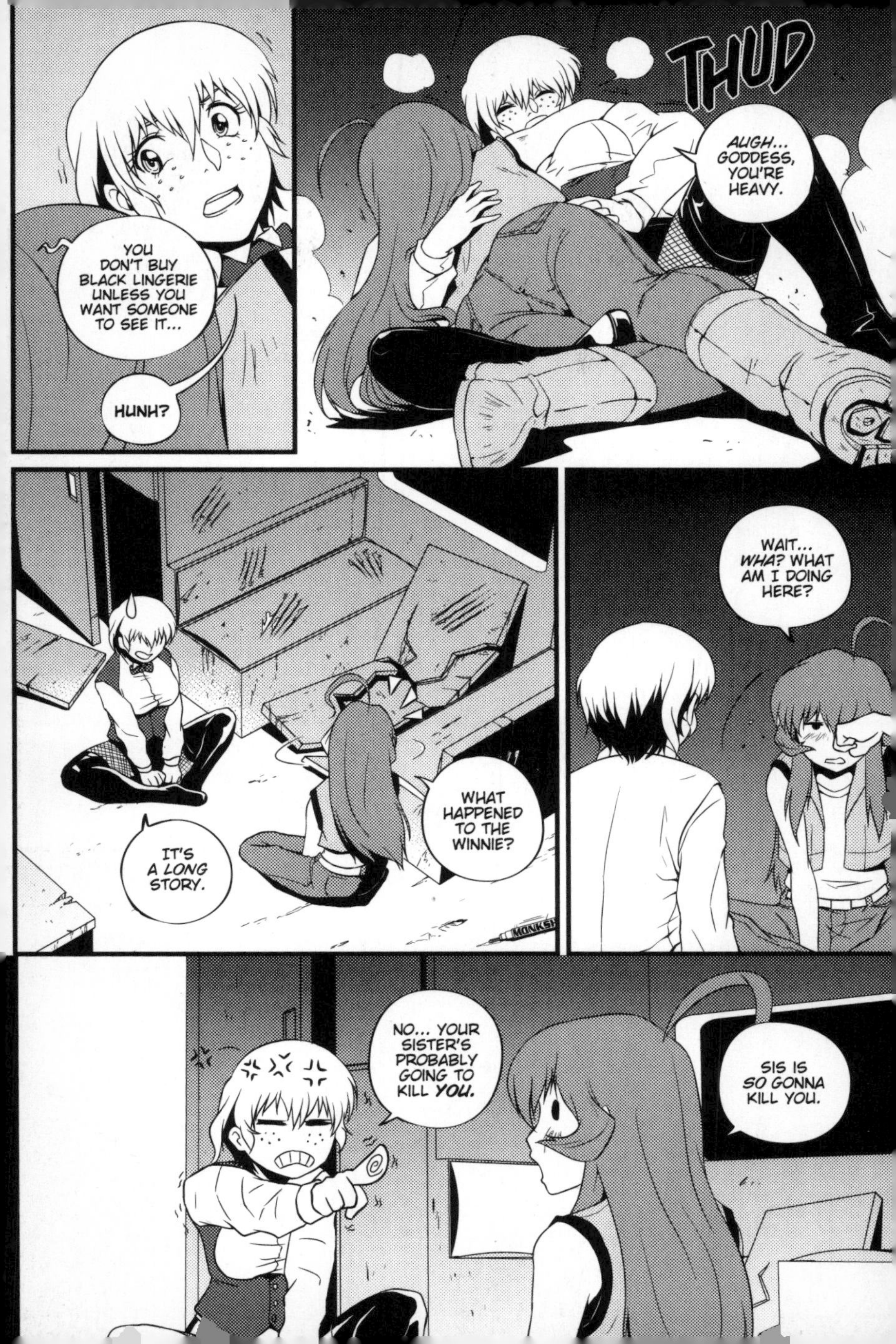
THUD
AUGH... GODDESS, YOU'RE HEAVY.
YOU DON'T BUY BLACK LINGERIE UNLESS YOU WANT SOMEONE TO SEE IT...
HUNH?
WAIT... *WHA?* WHAT AM I DOING HERE?
WHAT HAPPENED TO THE WINNIE?
IT'S A *LONG* STORY.
SIS IS SO GONNA KILL YOU.
NO... YOUR SISTER'S PROBABLY GOING TO KILL ***YOU.***

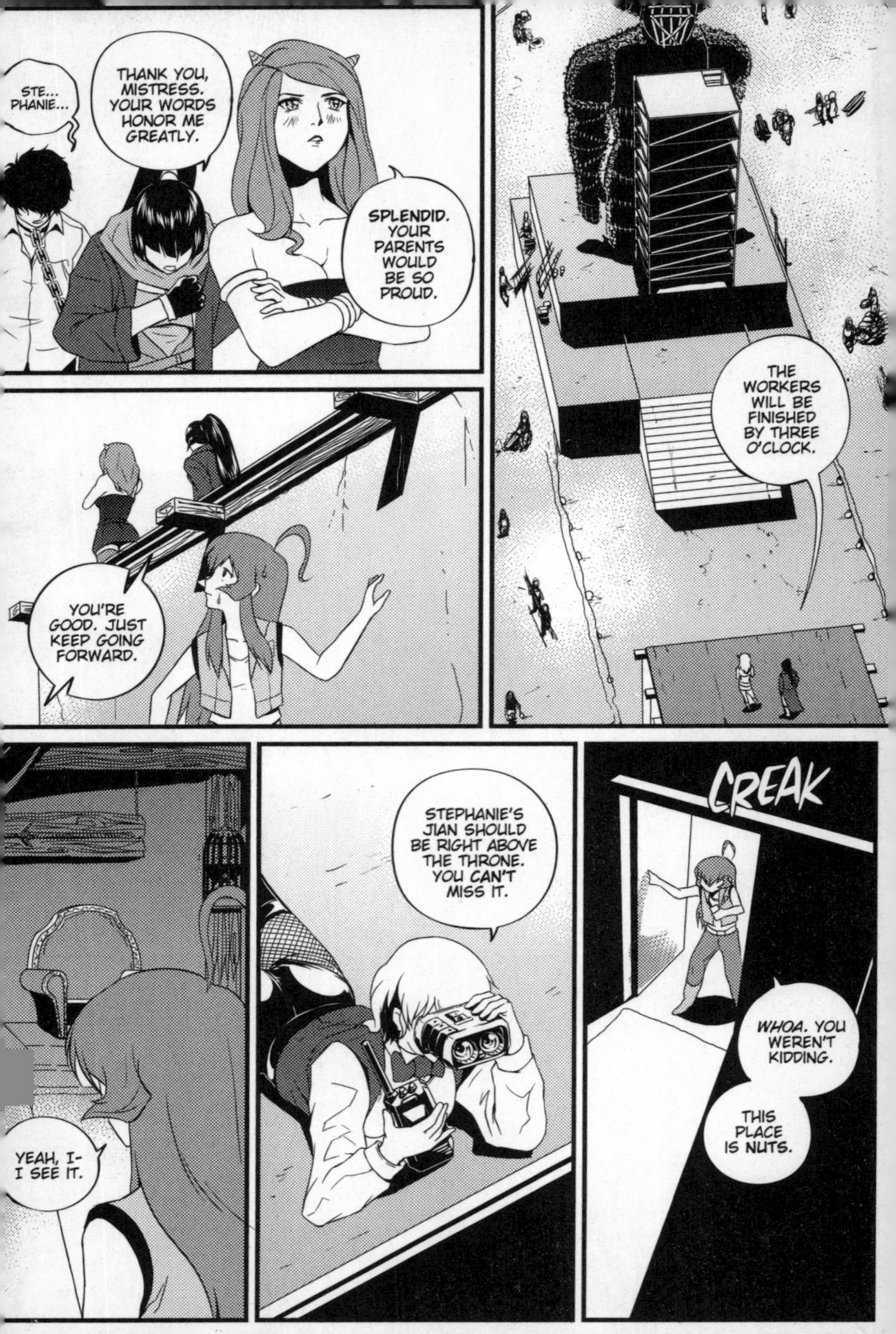
THE WORKERS WILL BE FINISHED BY THREE O'CLOCK.
SPLENDID. YOUR PARENTS WOULD BE SO PROUD.
THANK YOU, MISTRESS. YOUR WORDS HONOR ME GREATLY.
STE... PHANIE...
YOU'RE GOOD. JUST KEEP GOING FORWARD.
CREAK
WHOA. YOU WEREN'T KIDDING.
THIS PLACE IS NUTS.
STEPHANIE'S JIAN SHOULD BE RIGHT ABOVE THE THRONE. YOU CAN'T MISS IT.
YEAH, I- I SEE IT.

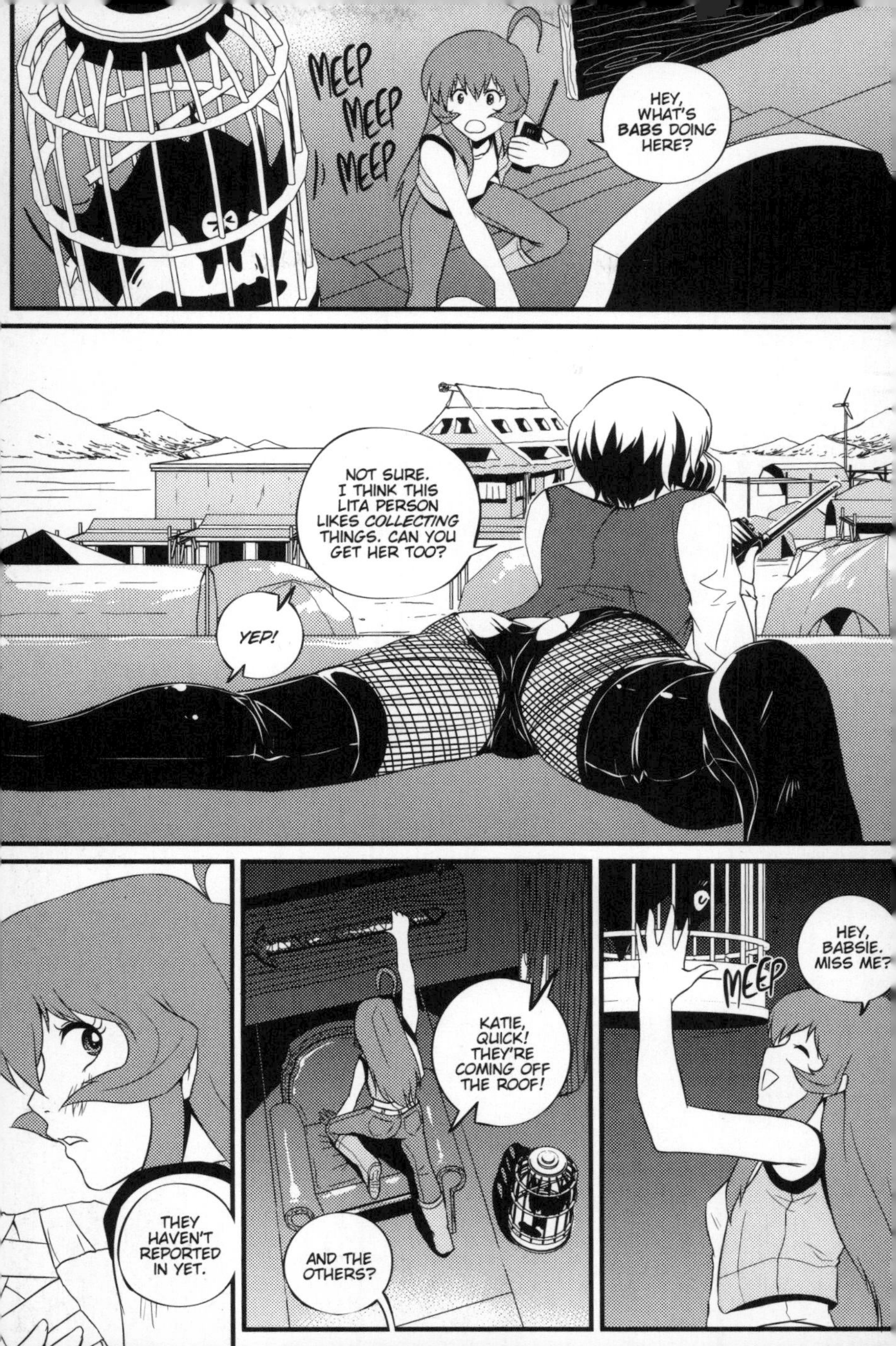
HEY, WHAT'S BABS DOING HERE?
MEEP MEEP MEEP
NOT SURE. I THINK THIS LITA PERSON LIKES *COLLECTING* THINGS. CAN YOU GET HER TOO?
YEP!
HEY, BABSIE. MISS ME?
MEEP
KATIE, QUICK! THEY'RE COMING OFF THE ROOF!
AND THE OTHERS?
THEY HAVEN'T REPORTED IN YET.

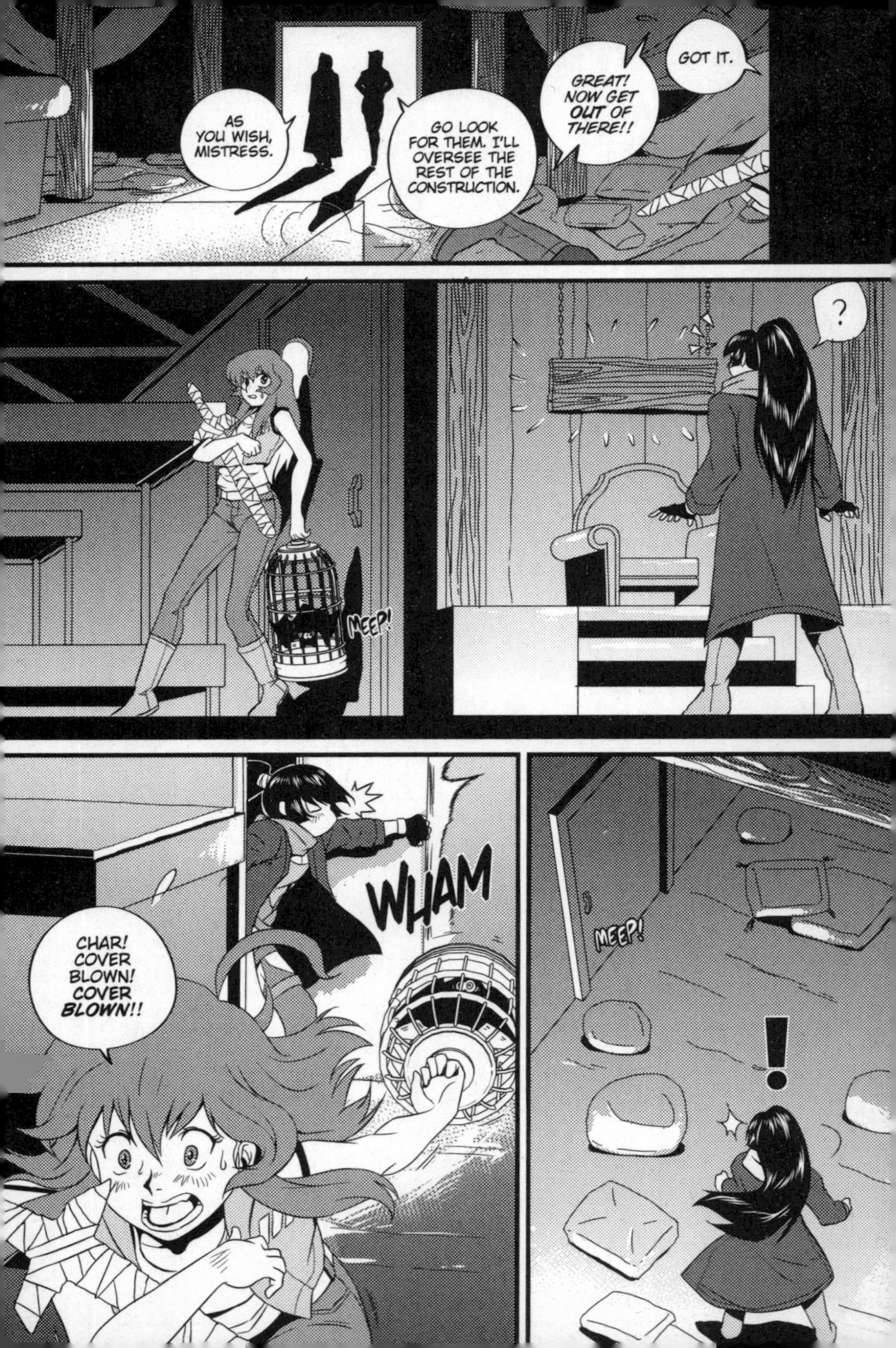
GOT IT.
GREAT! NOW GET OUT OF THERE!!
GO LOOK FOR THEM. I'LL OVERSEE THE REST OF THE CONSTRUCTION.
AS YOU WISH, MISTRESS.
?
MEEP!
MEEP!
!
WHAM
CHAR! COVER BLOWN! COVER BLOWN!!

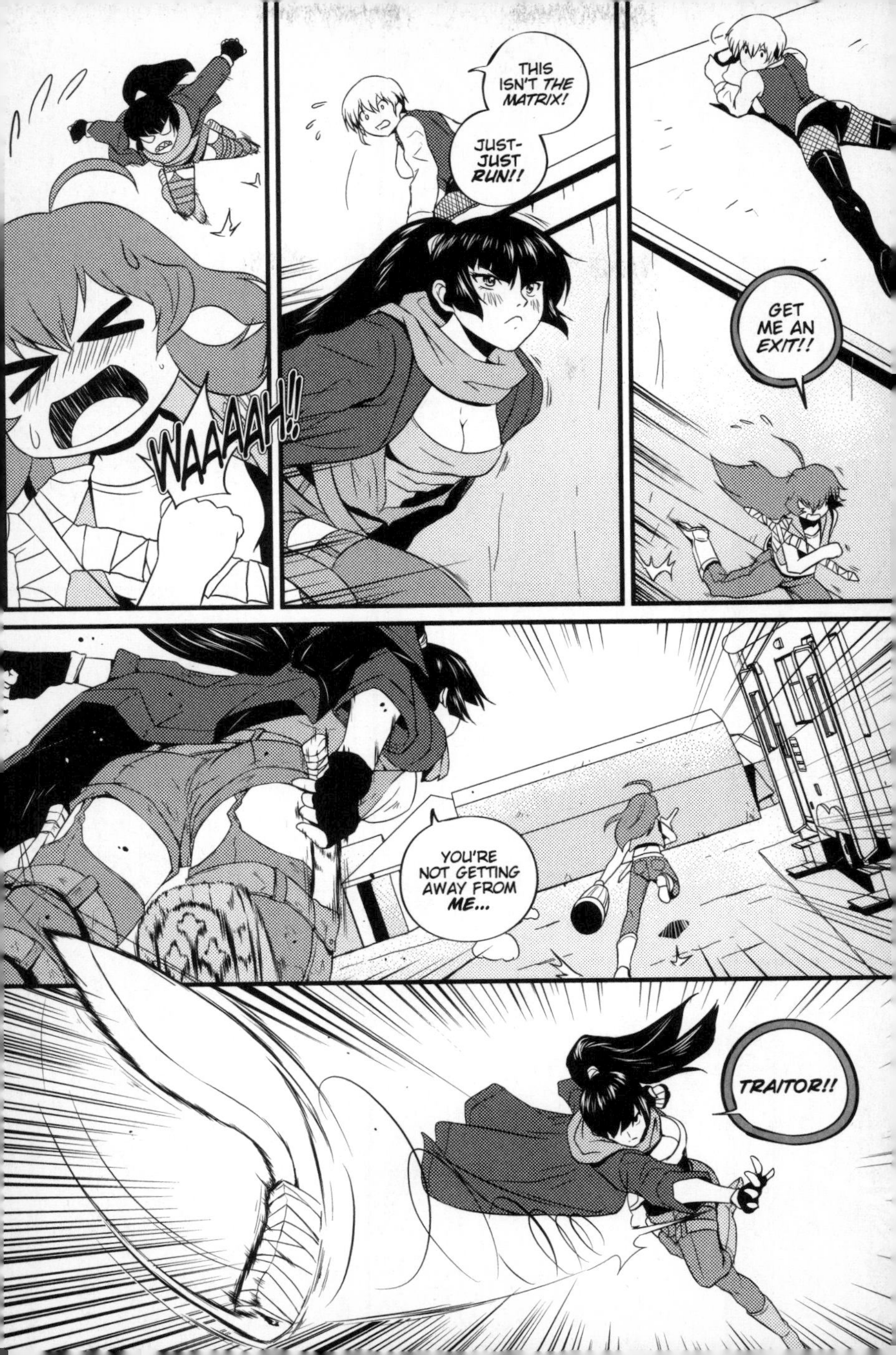
GET ME AN EXIT!!
THIS ISN'T THE MATRIX!
JUST-JUST RUN!!
WAAAAH!!
YOU'RE NOT GETTING AWAY FROM ME...
TRAITOR!!

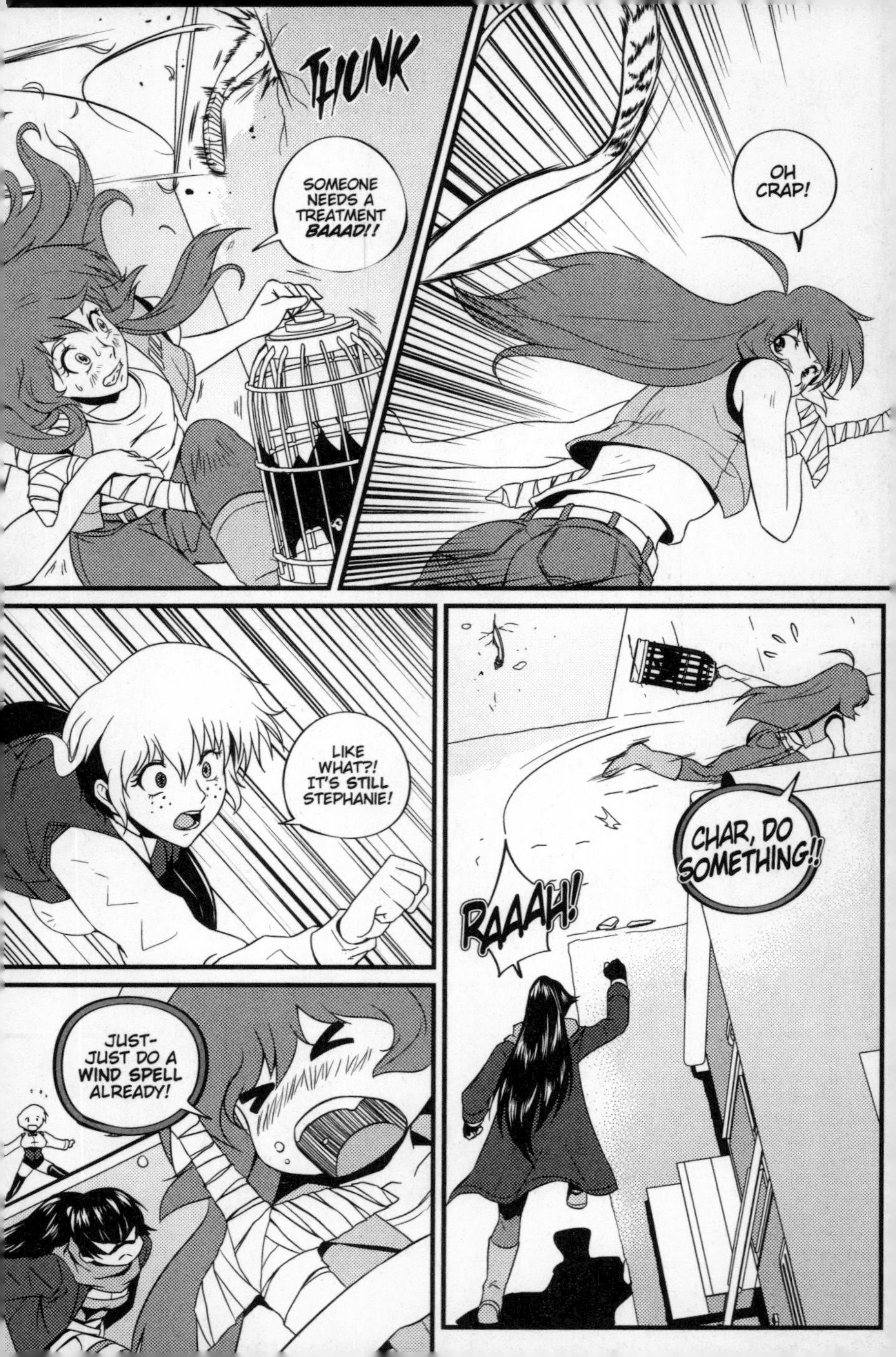
OH CRAP!
THUNK
SOMEONE NEEDS A TREATMENT BAAAD!!
CHAR, DO SOMETHING!!
RAAAH!
LIKE WHAT?! IT'S STILL STEPHANIE!
JUST- JUST DO A WIND SPELL ALREADY!

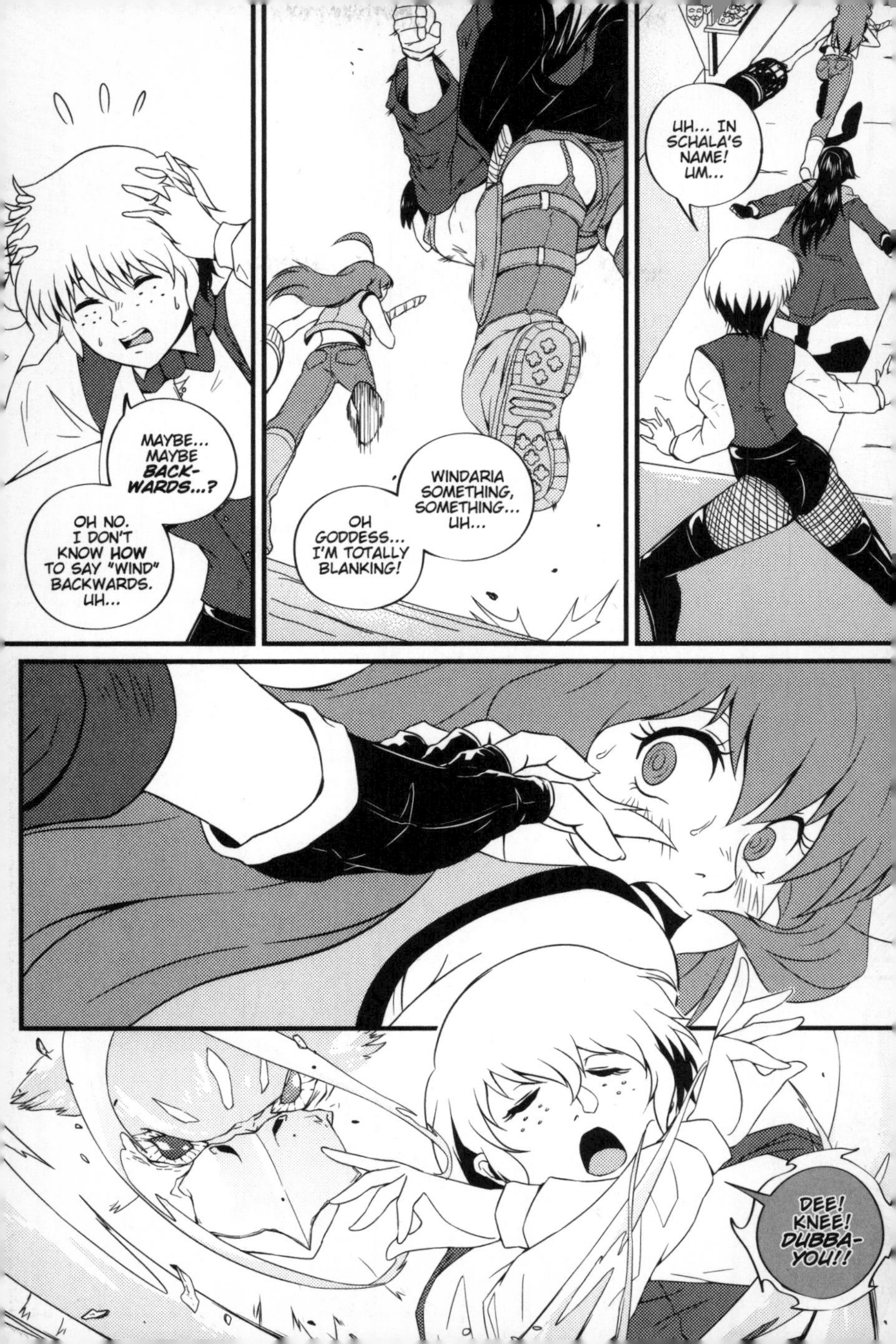
UH... IN SCHALA'S NAME! UM...
WINDARIA SOMETHING, SOMETHING... UH...
OH GODDESS... I'M TOTALLY BLANKING!
MAYBE... MAYBE *BACKWARDS*...?
OH NO. I DON'T KNOW HOW TO SAY "WIND" BACKWARDS. UH...
DEE! KNEE! *DUBBA-YOU!!*

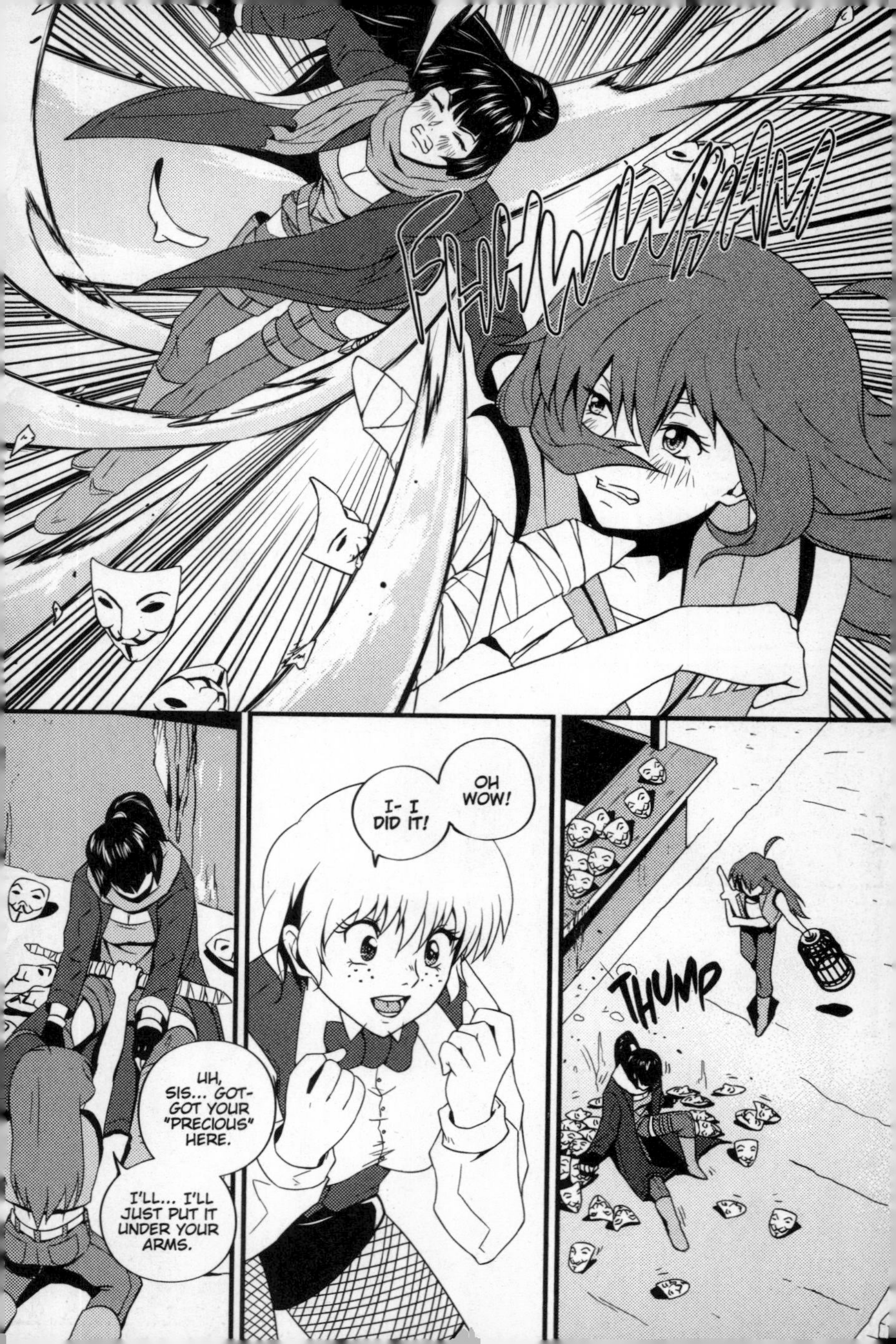
THUMP
OH WOW!
I- I DID IT!
UH, SIS... GOT- GOT YOUR "PRECIOUS" HERE.
I'LL... I'LL JUST PUT IT UNDER YOUR ARMS.

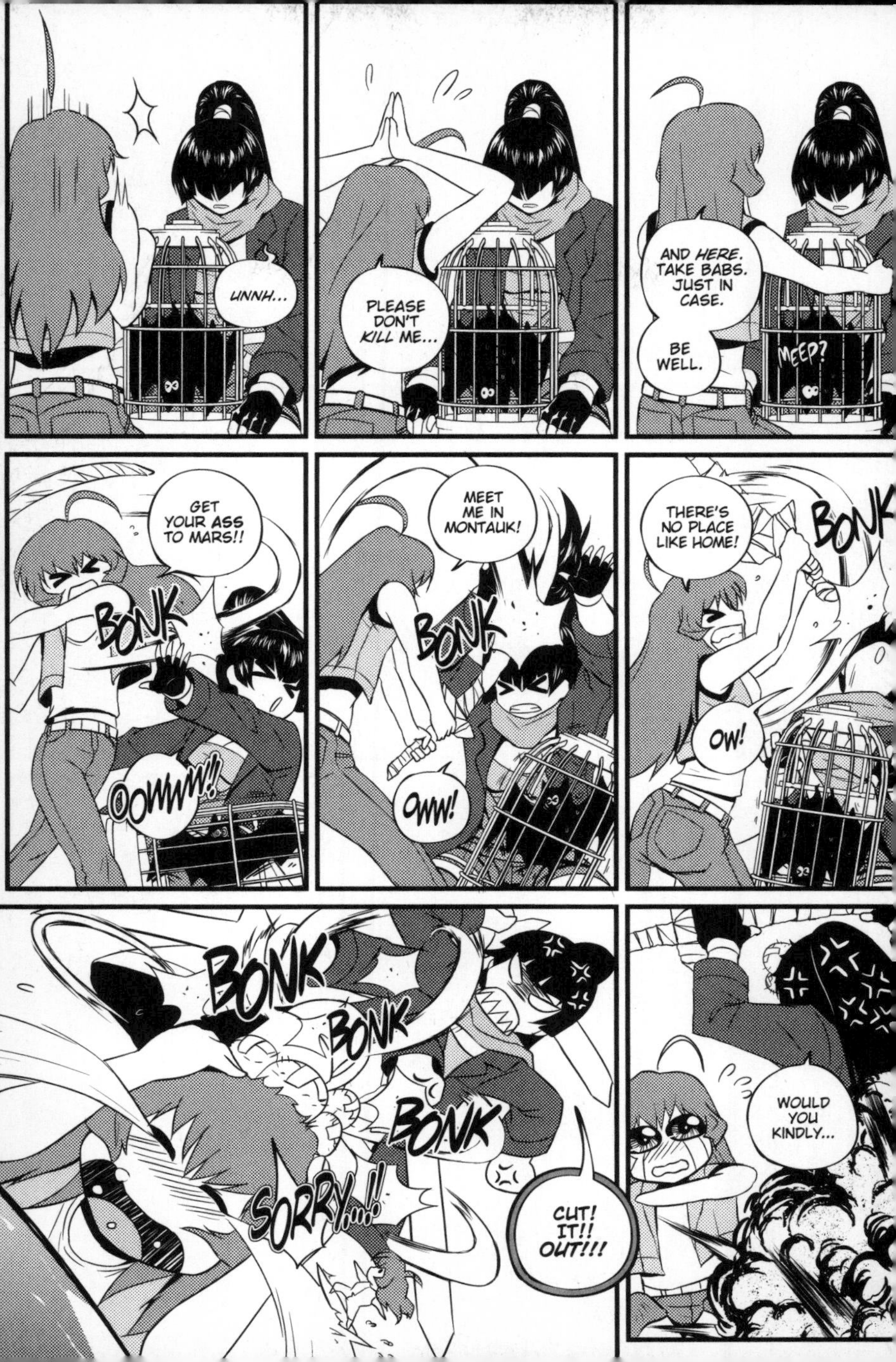
AND *HERE*. TAKE BABS. JUST IN CASE.
BE WELL.
MEEP?
PLEASE DON'T *KILL* ME...
UNNH...
THERE'S NO PLACE LIKE HOME!
BONK
OW!
MEET ME IN MONTAUK!
BONK
OWW!
GET YOUR ASS TO MARS!!
BONK
OOWWW!!
WOULD YOU KINDLY...
BONK
BONK
BONK
SORRY...!!
CUT! IT!! OUT!!!

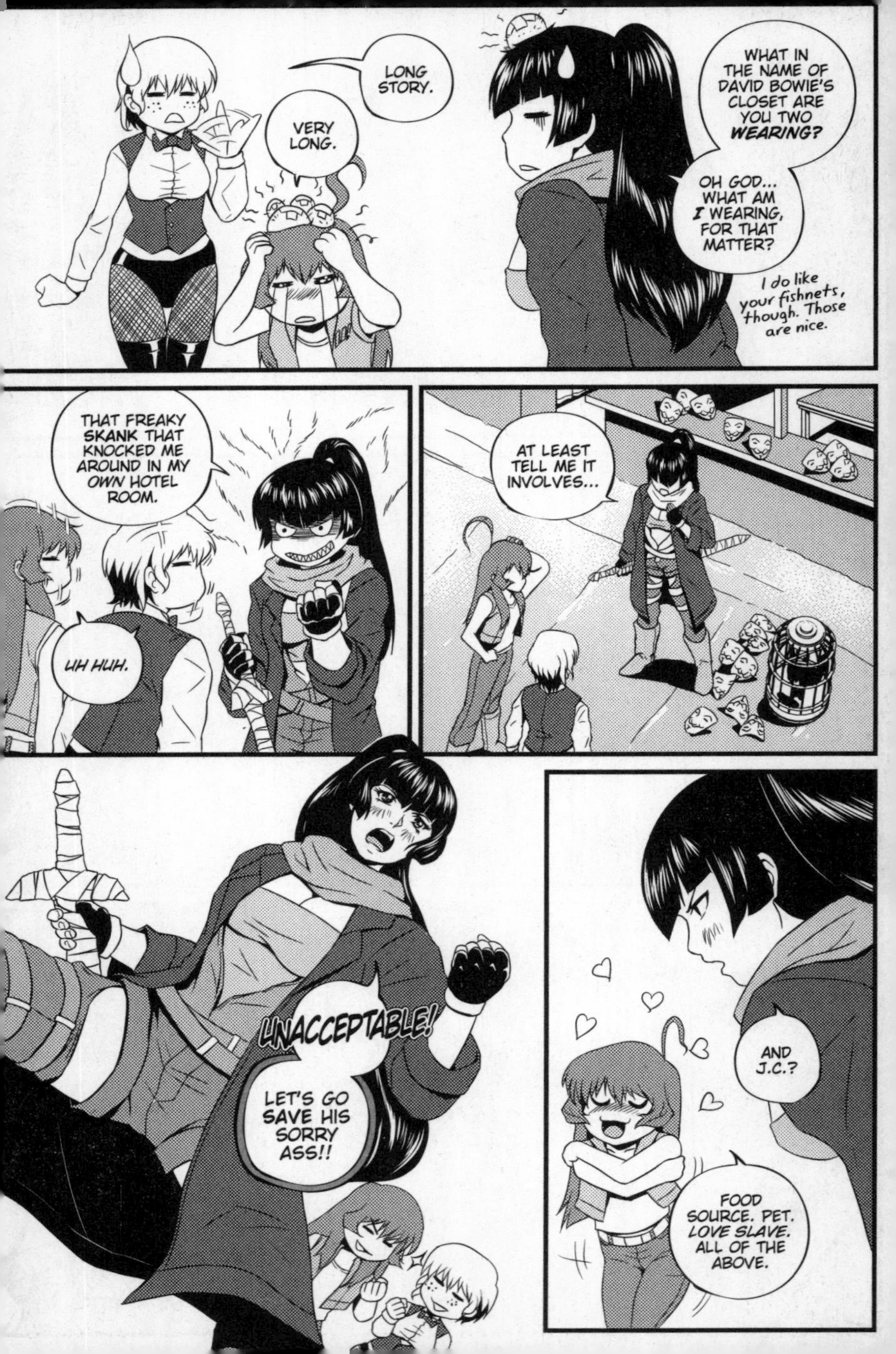
WHAT IN THE NAME OF DAVID BOWIE'S CLOSET ARE YOU TWO *WEARING?*
OH GOD... WHAT AM *I* WEARING, FOR THAT MATTER?
I do like your fishnets, though. Those are nice.
LONG STORY.
VERY LONG.
AT LEAST TELL ME IT INVOLVES...
THAT FREAKY SKANK THAT KNOCKED ME AROUND IN MY *OWN* HOTEL ROOM.
UH HUH.
AND J.C.?
FOOD SOURCE. PET. *LOVE SLAVE.* ALL OF THE ABOVE.
UNACCEPTABLE!
LET'S GO SAVE HIS SORRY ASS!!

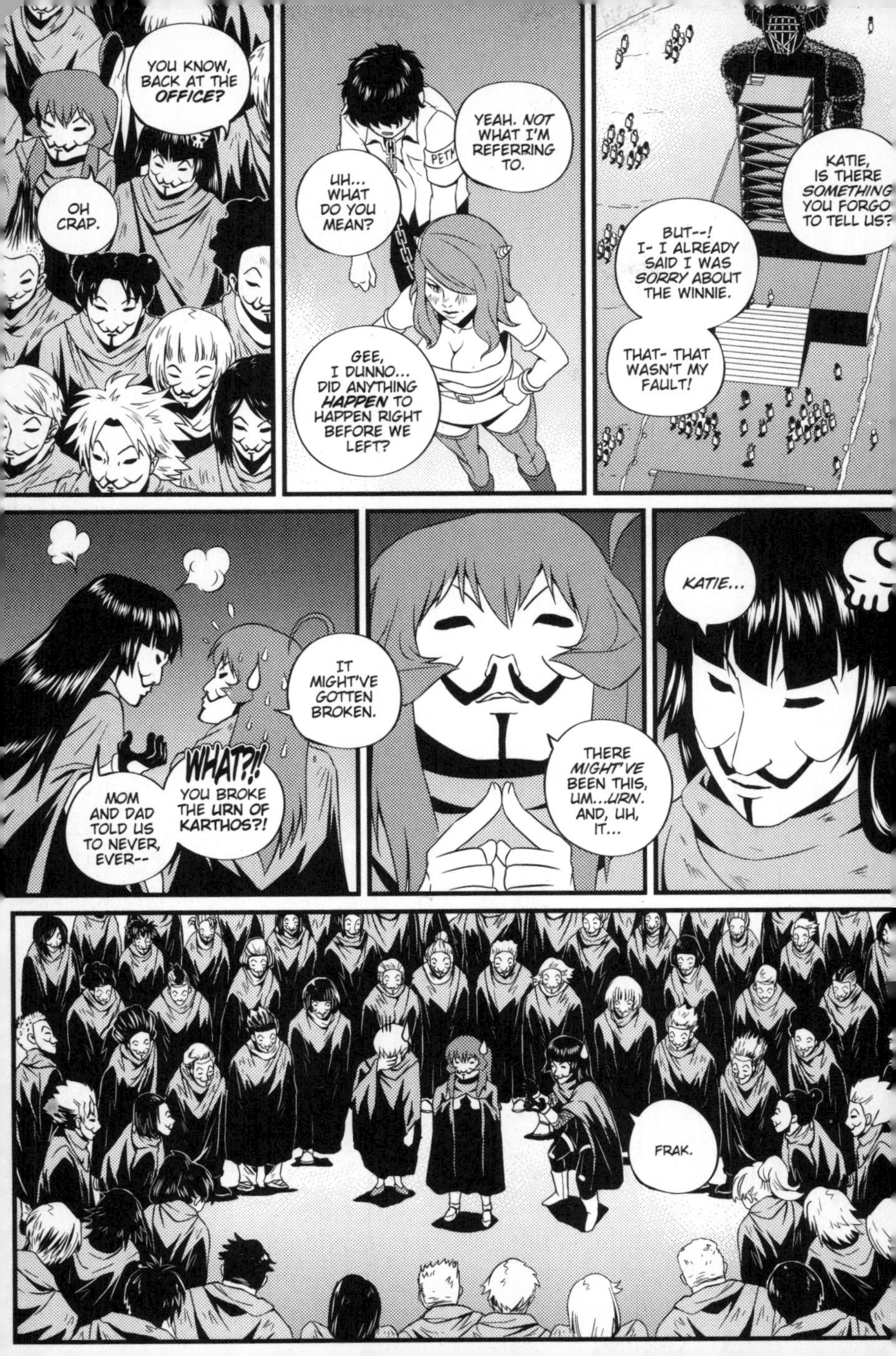
KATIE, IS THERE *SOMETHING* YOU FORGO TO TELL US?
BUT--! I- I ALREADY SAID I WAS *SORRY* ABOUT THE WINNIE.
THAT- THAT WASN'T MY FAULT!
YEAH. *NOT* WHAT I'M REFERRING TO.
UH... WHAT DO YOU MEAN?
GEE, I DUNNO... DID ANYTHING ***HAPPEN*** TO HAPPEN RIGHT BEFORE WE LEFT?
YOU KNOW, BACK AT THE ***OFFICE?***
OH CRAP.
KATIE...
THERE *MIGHT'VE* BEEN THIS, UM...*URN*. AND, UH, IT...
IT MIGHT'VE GOTTEN BROKEN.
WHAT?!!
YOU BROKE THE URN OF KARTHOS?!
MOM AND DAD TOLD US TO NEVER, EVER--
FRAK.

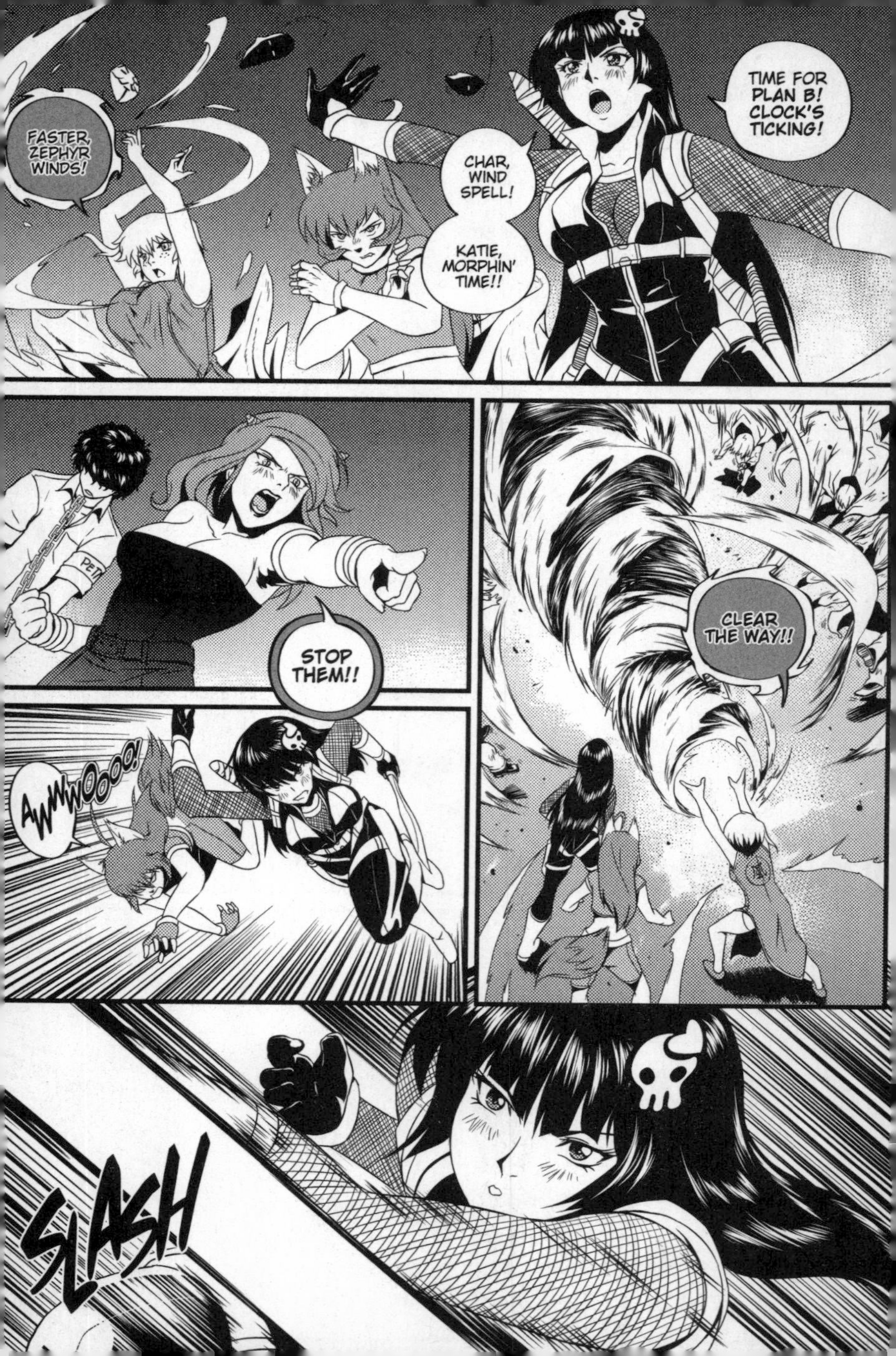
TIME FOR PLAN B! CLOCK'S TICKING!
CHAR, WIND SPELL!
KATIE, MORPHIN' TIME!!
FASTER, ZEPHYR WINDS!
CLEAR THE WAY!!
STOP THEM!!
AWWWOOOO!
SLASH

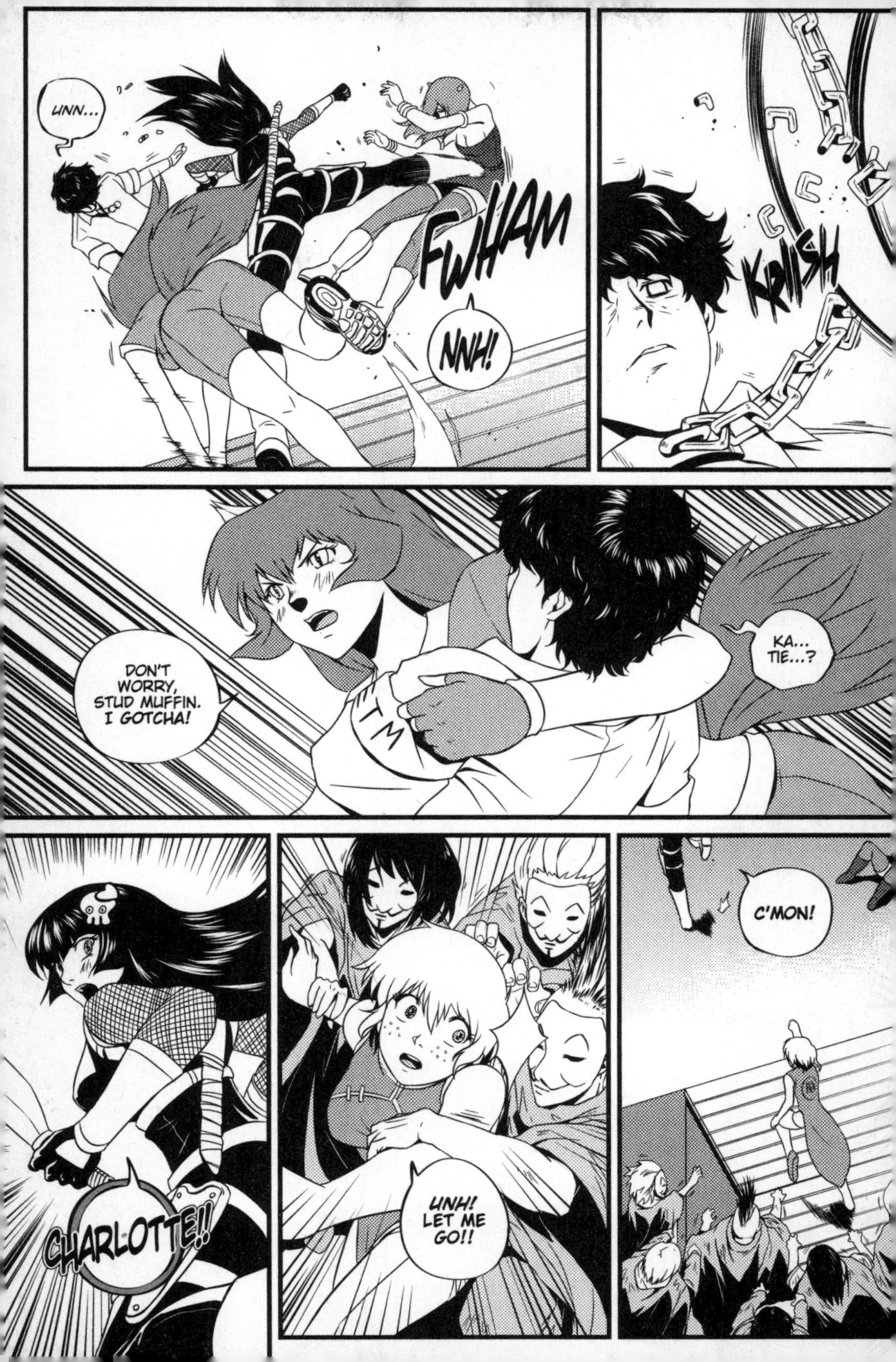
KRISH
FWHAM
NNH!
UNN...
KA... TIE...?
DON'T WORRY, STUD MUFFIN. I GOTCHA!
C'MON!
UNH! LET ME GO!!
CHARLOTTE!!

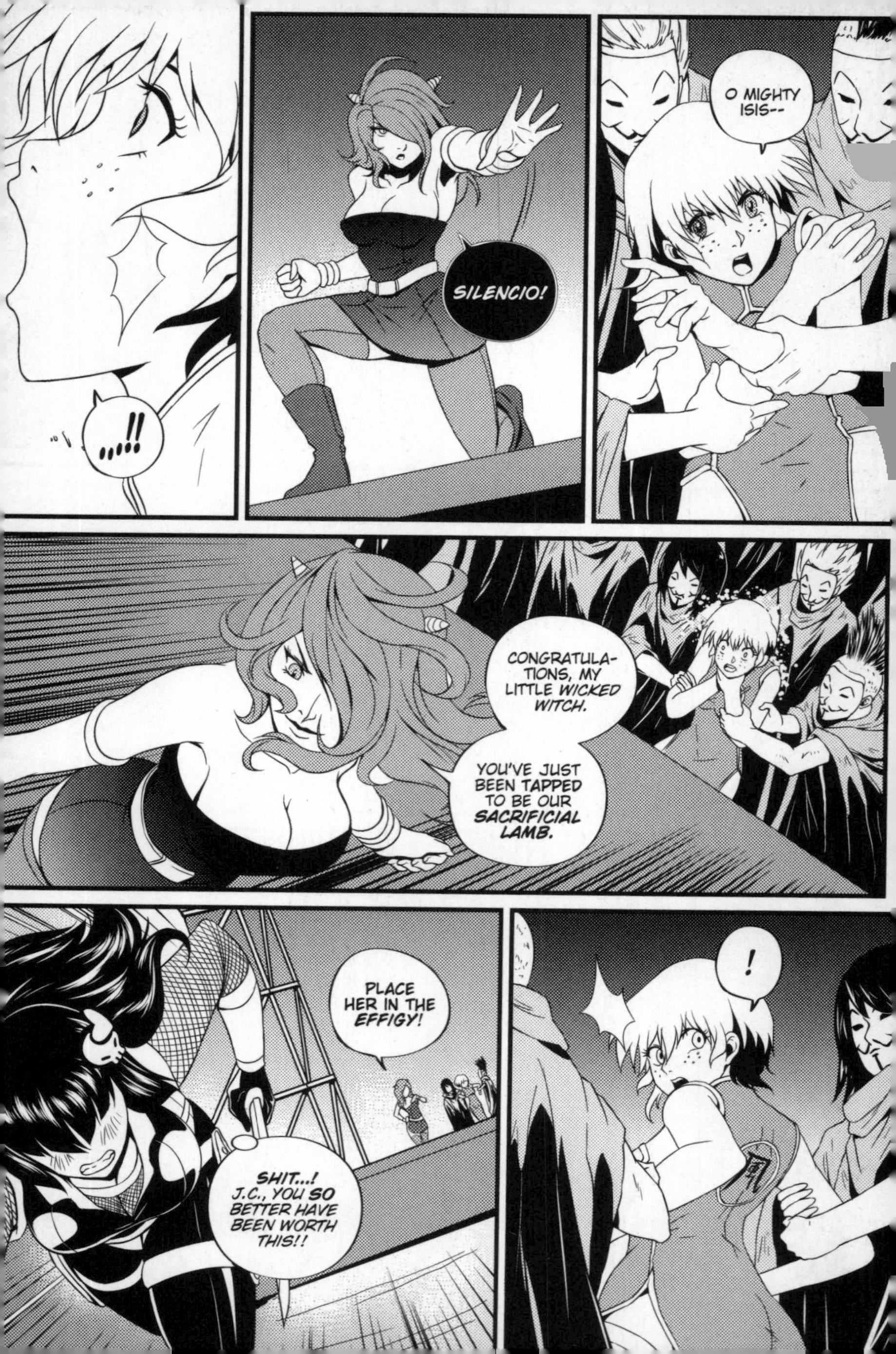
O MIGHTY ISIS--
SILENCIO!
...!!
CONGRATULA-TIONS, MY LITTLE *WICKED WITCH.*
YOU'VE JUST BEEN TAPPED TO BE OUR **SACRIFICIAL LAMB.**
!
PLACE HER IN THE *EFFIGY!*
SHIT...! J.C., YOU **SO** BETTER HAVE BEEN WORTH THIS!!

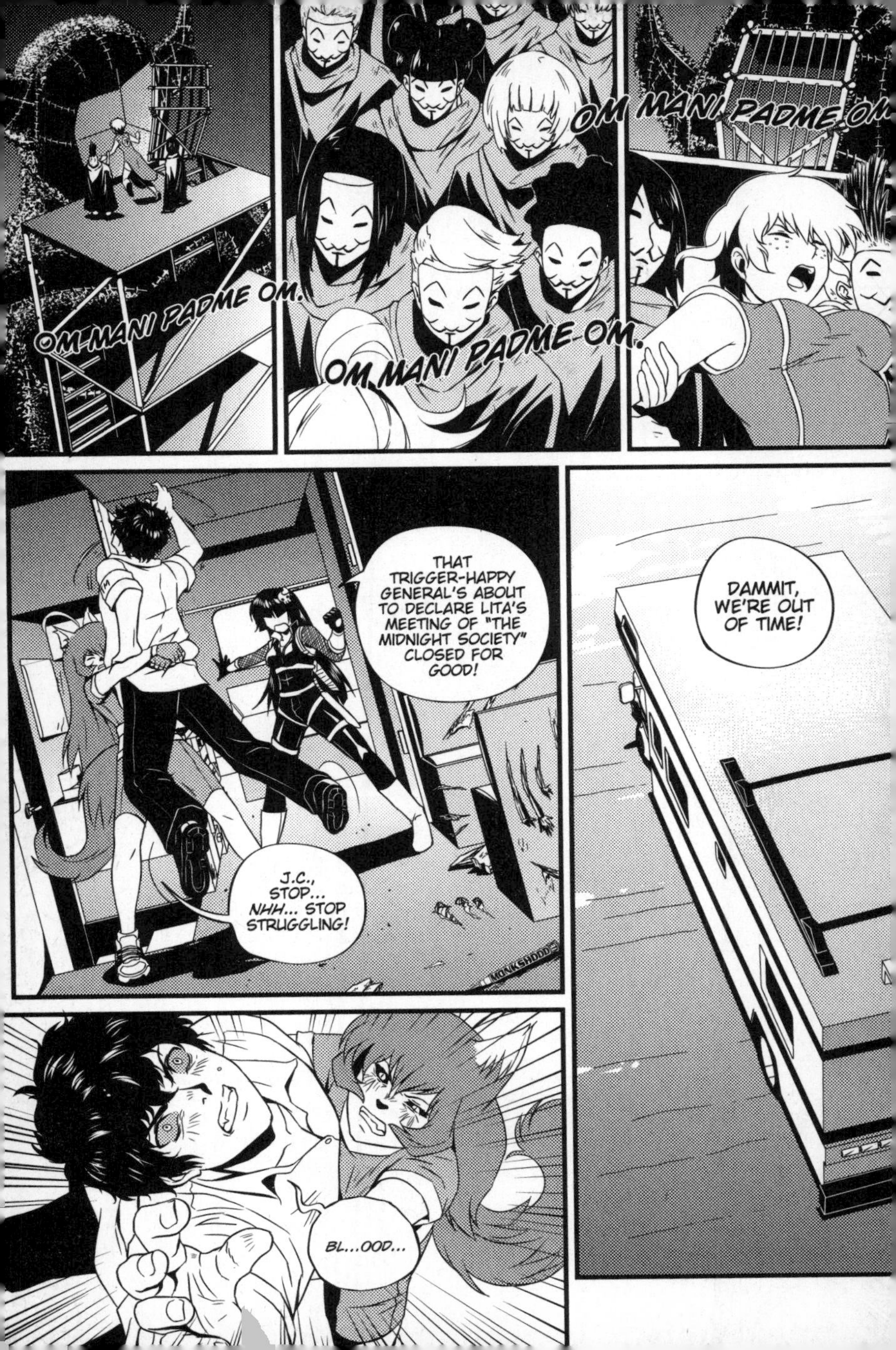

OM MANI PADME OM
OM MANI PADME OM.
OM MANI PADME OM.
DAMMIT, WE'RE OUT OF TIME!
THAT TRIGGER-HAPPY GENERAL'S ABOUT TO DECLARE LITA'S MEETING OF "THE MIDNIGHT SOCIETY" CLOSED FOR GOOD!
J.C., STOP... NHH... STOP STRUGGLING!
BL...OOD...

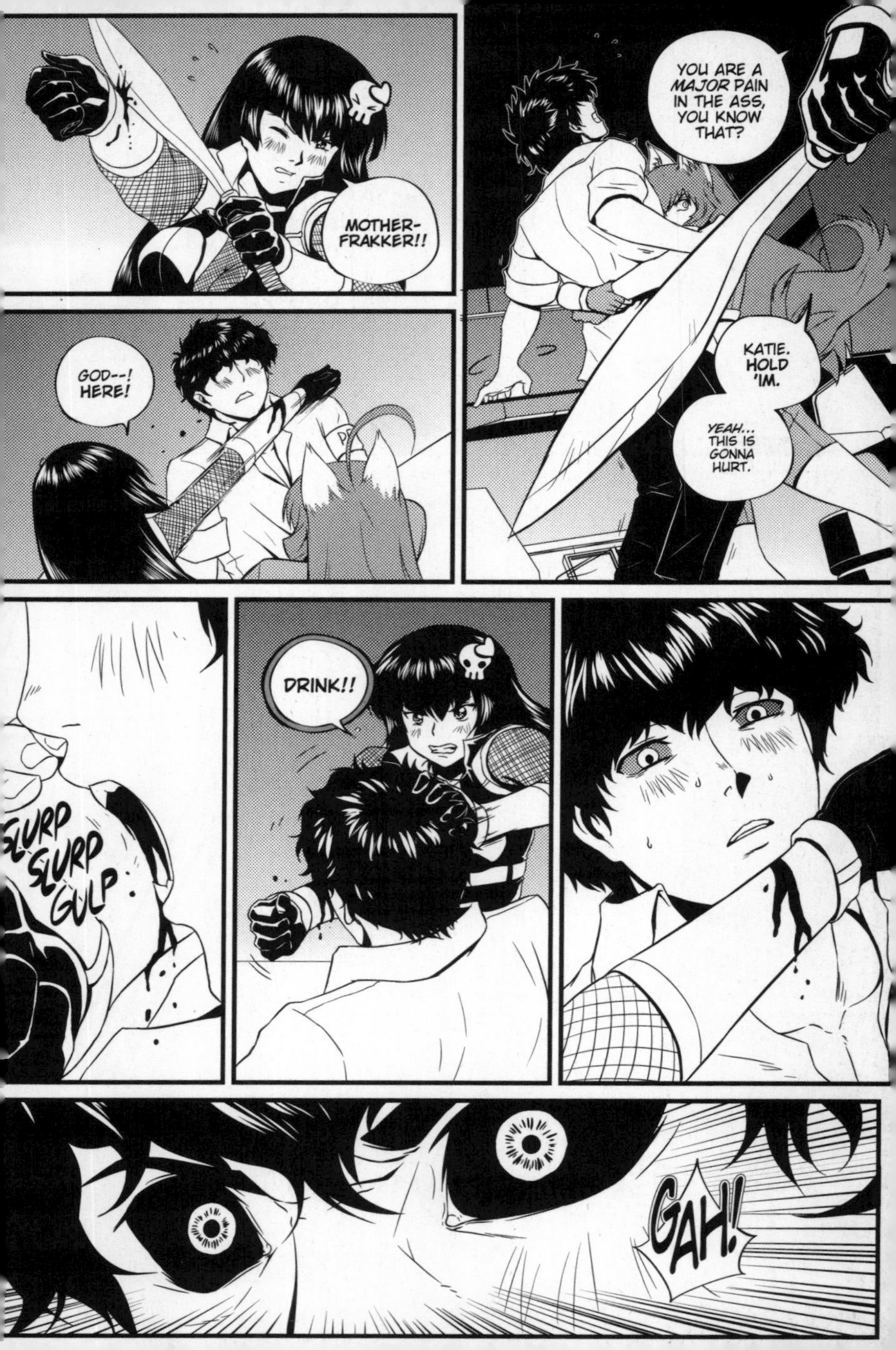
YOU ARE A MAJOR PAIN IN THE ASS, YOU KNOW THAT?
KATIE. HOLD 'IM.
YEAH... THIS IS GONNA HURT.
MOTHER-FRAKKER!!
GOD--! HERE!
DRINK!!
SLURP SLURP GULP
GAH!

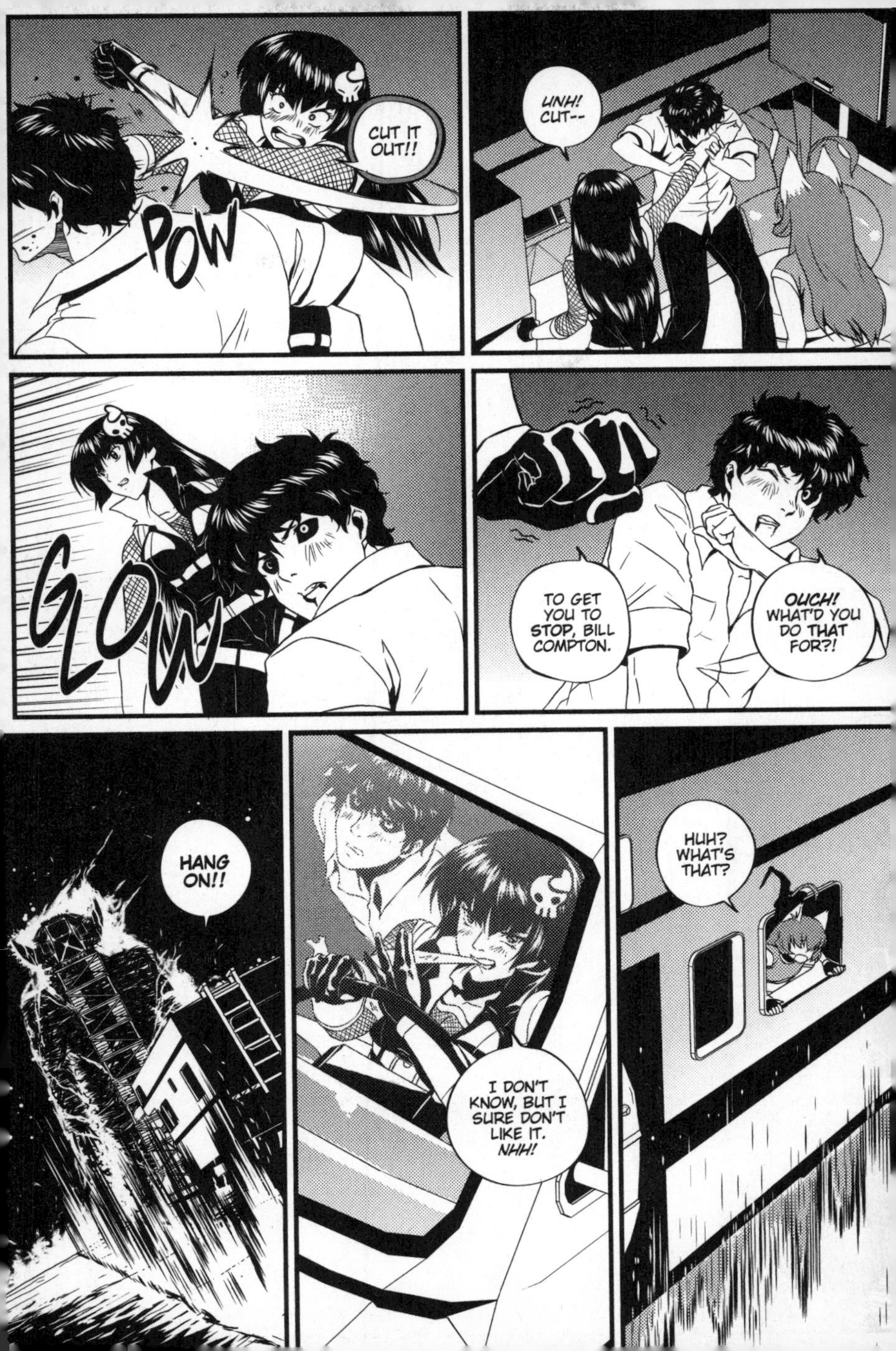
UNH! CUT--
CUT IT OUT!!
POW
OUCH! WHAT'D YOU DO THAT FOR?!
TO GET YOU TO STOP, BILL COMPTON.
GLOW
HUH? WHAT'S THAT?
I DON'T KNOW, BUT I SURE DON'T LIKE IT. *NHH!*
HANG ON!!

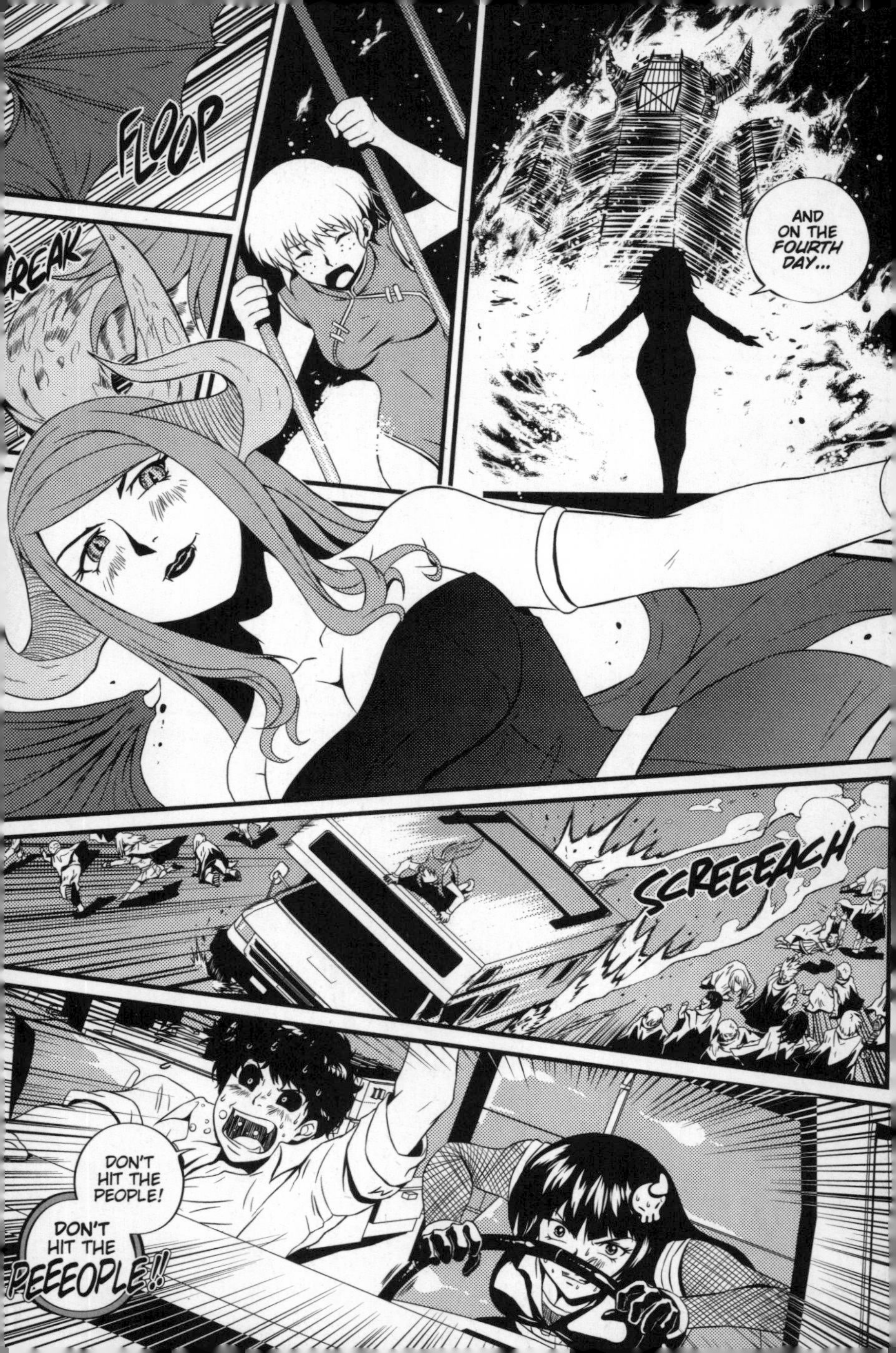
AND ON THE FOURTH DAY...
FLOOP
REAK
SCREEEACH
DON'T HIT THE PEOPLE!
DON'T HIT THE PEEEOPLE!!

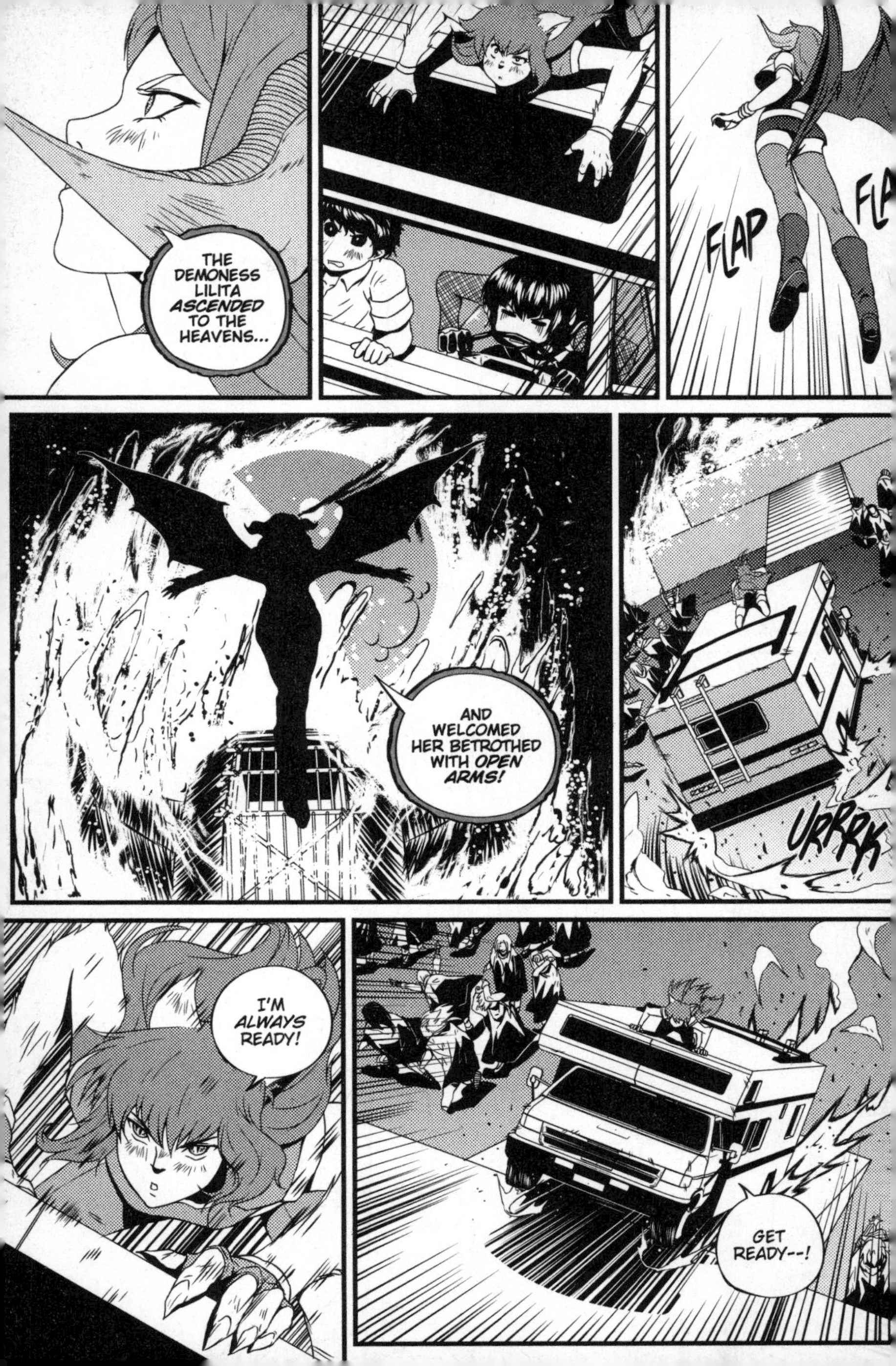
FLA
FLAP
THE DEMONESS LILITA *ASCENDED* TO THE HEAVENS...
URRRK
AND WELCOMED HER BETROTHED WITH *OPEN ARMS!*
GET READY--!
I'M *ALWAYS* READY!

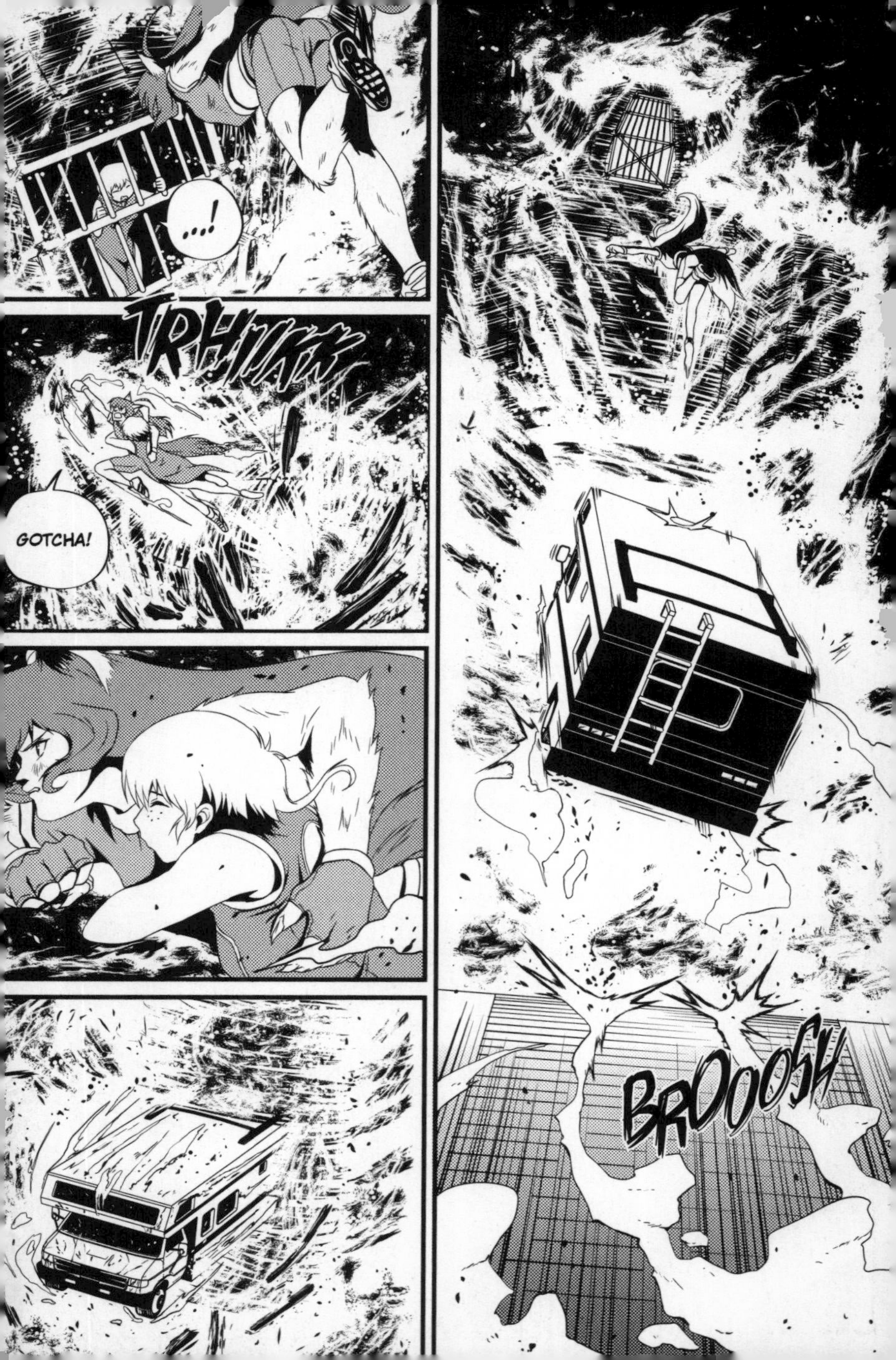
BROOOSH
...!
TRHIKK
GOTCHA!

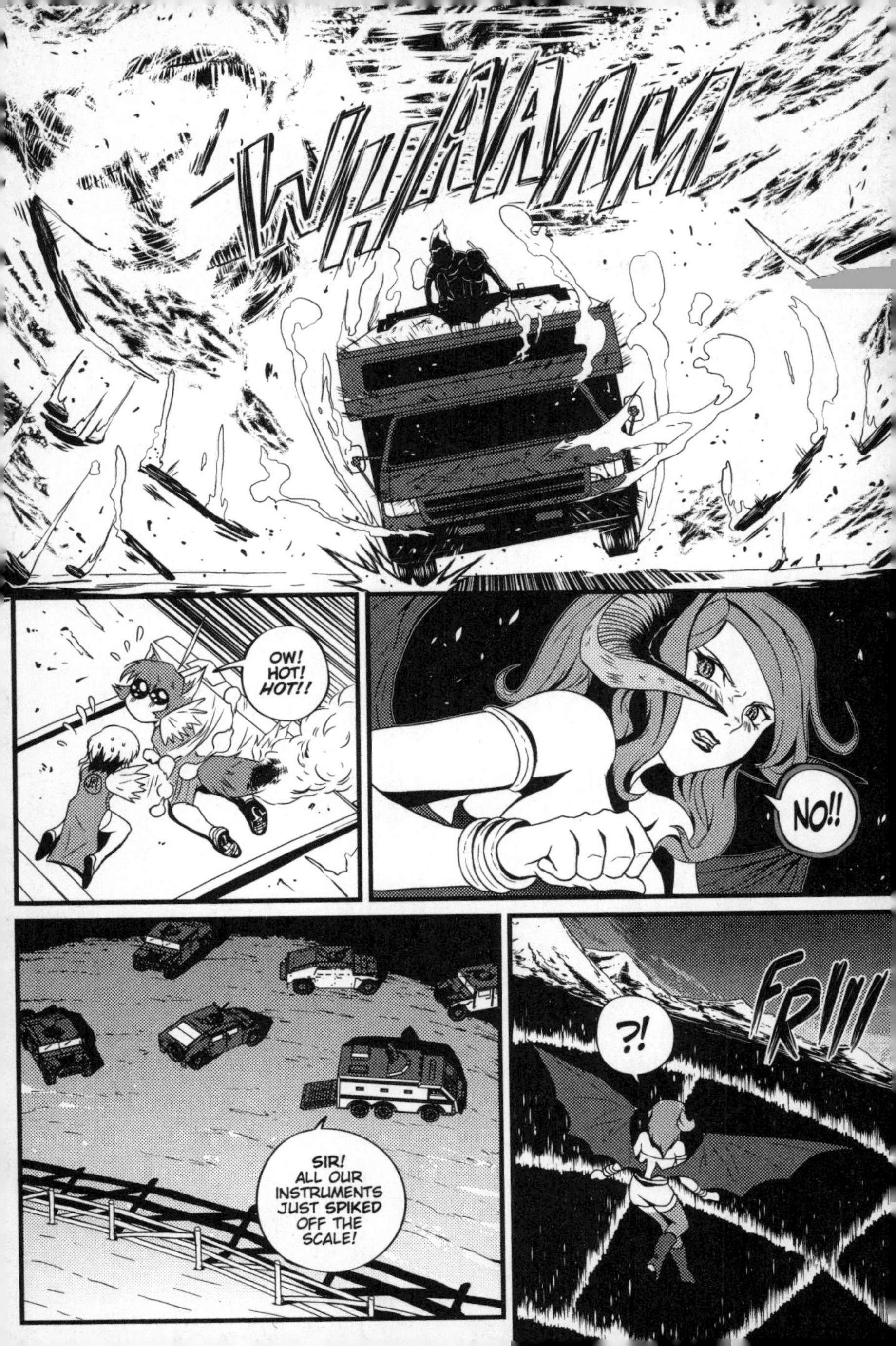
WHAAAAM
NO!!
OW! HOT! HOT!!
?!
FRIII
SIR! ALL OUR INSTRUMENTS JUST SPIKED OFF THE SCALE!

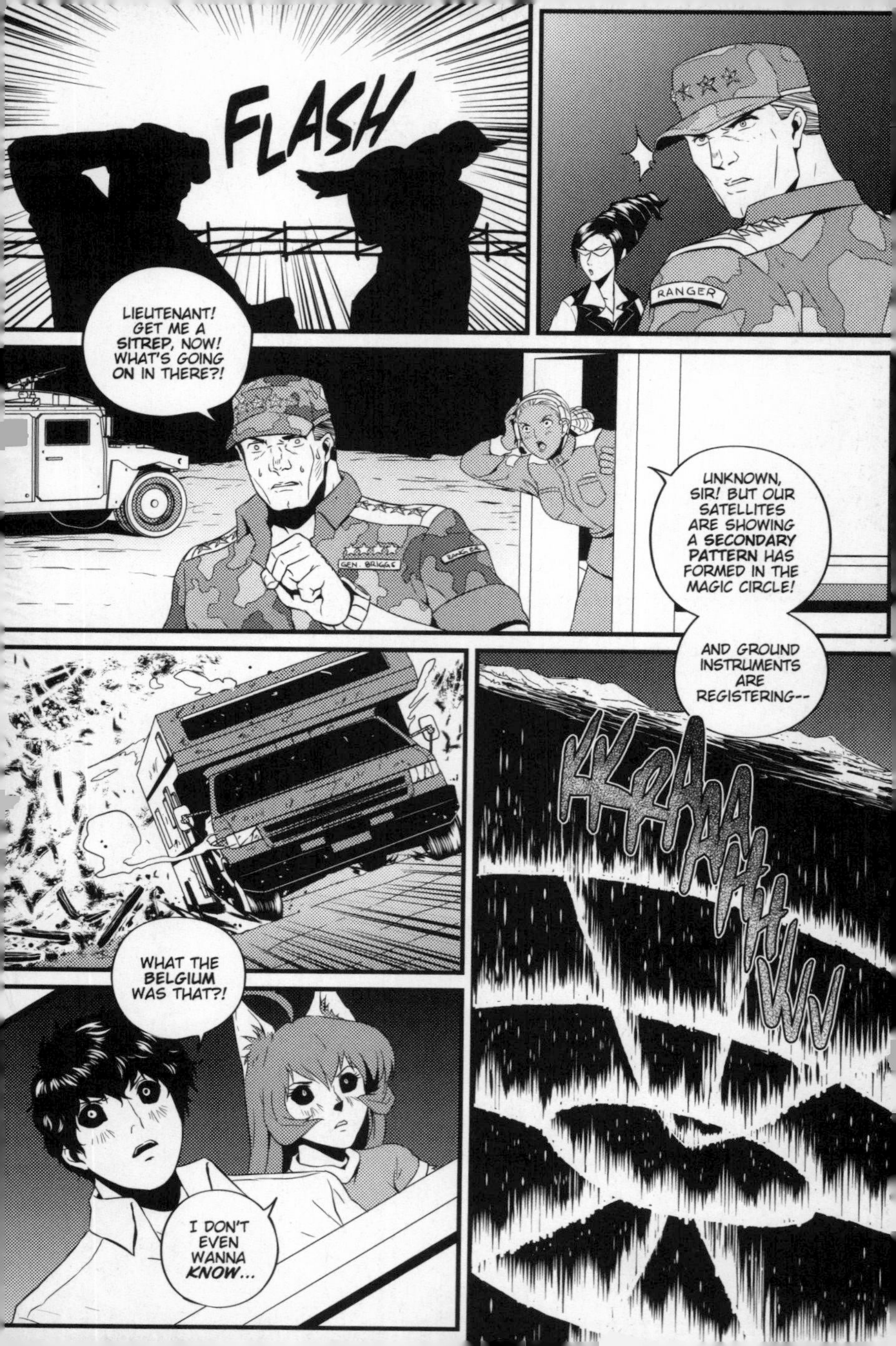
FLASH
LIEUTENANT! GET ME A SITREP, NOW! WHAT'S GOING ON IN THERE?!
RANGER
GEN. BRIGGS
UNKNOWN, SIR! BUT OUR SATELLITES ARE SHOWING A SECONDARY PATTERN HAS FORMED IN THE MAGIC CIRCLE!
AND GROUND INSTRUMENTS ARE REGISTERING--
KKRAAAHHWW
WHAT THE BELGIUM WAS THAT?!
I DON'T EVEN WANNA *KNOW*...

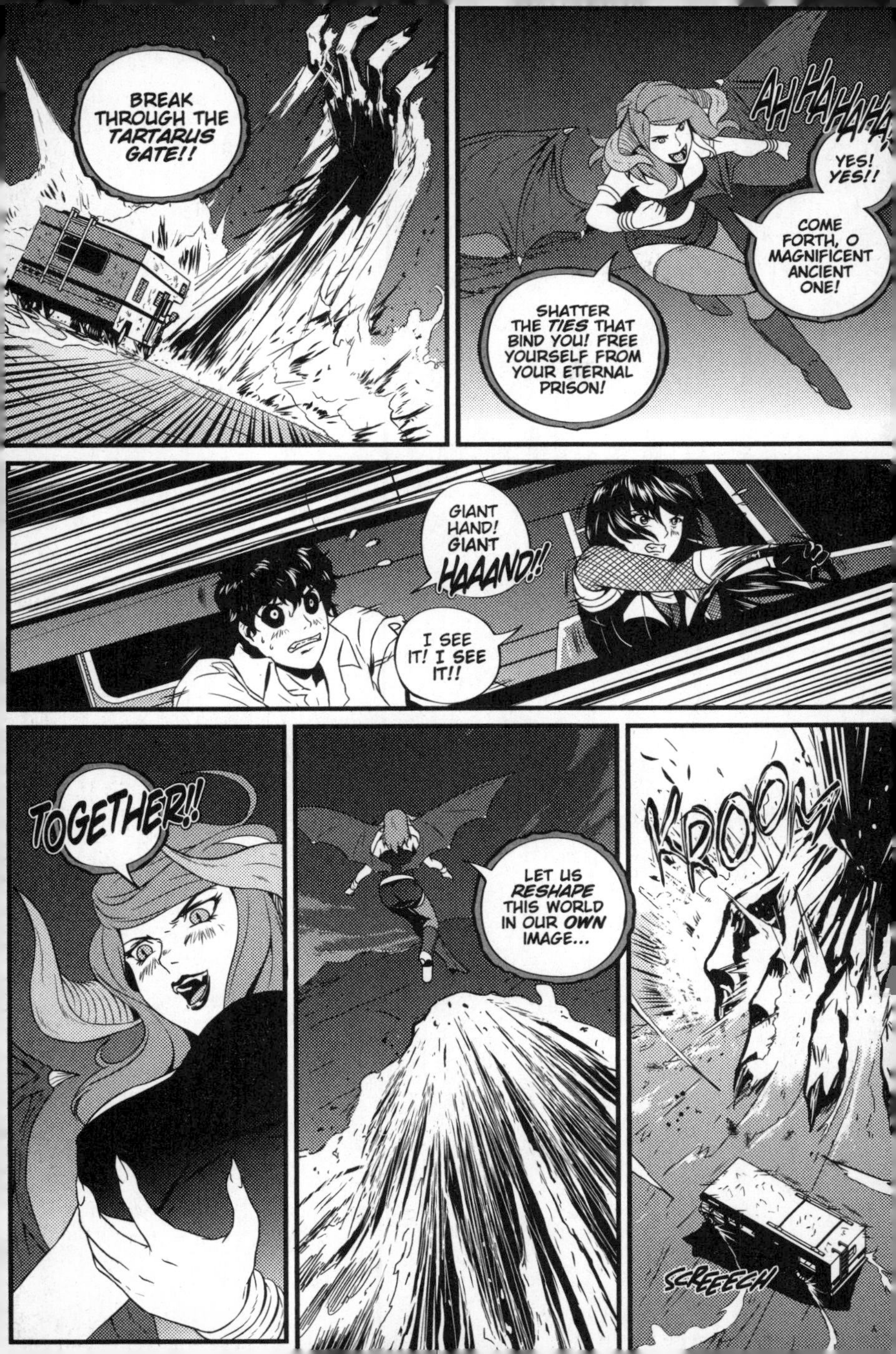
AHHAHAHAHA
YES! YES!!
COME FORTH, O MAGNIFICENT ANCIENT ONE!
SHATTER THE TIES THAT BIND YOU! FREE YOURSELF FROM YOUR ETERNAL PRISON!
BREAK THROUGH THE TARTARUS GATE!!
GIANT HAND! GIANT HAAAND!!
I SEE IT! I SEE IT!!
KROOM
SCREEECH
LET US RESHAPE THIS WORLD IN OUR OWN IMAGE...
TOGETHER!!

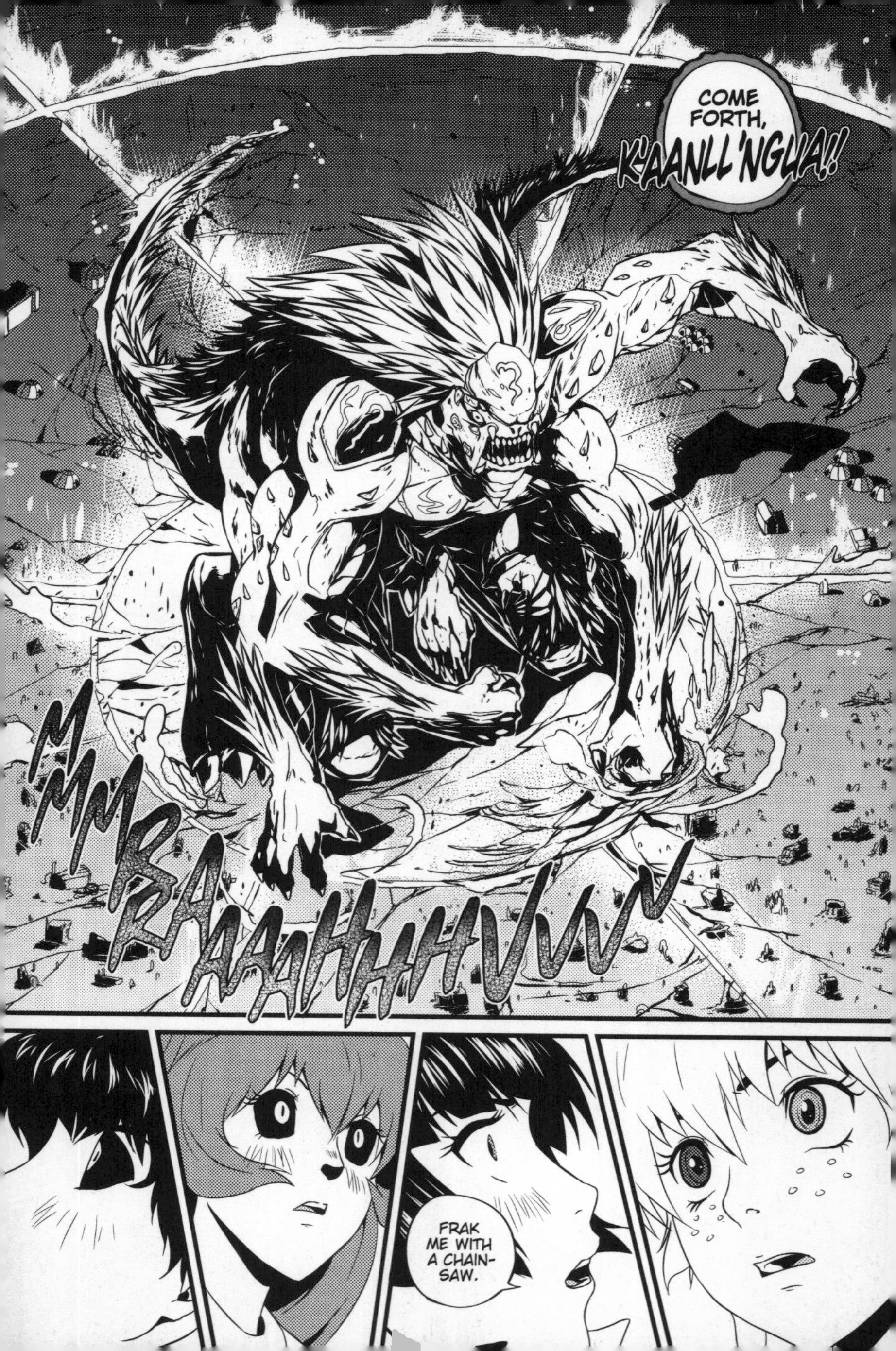
COME FORTH, K'AANLL'NGLIA!!
MMMBAAAHHHVVVN
FRAK ME WITH A CHAIN-SAW.

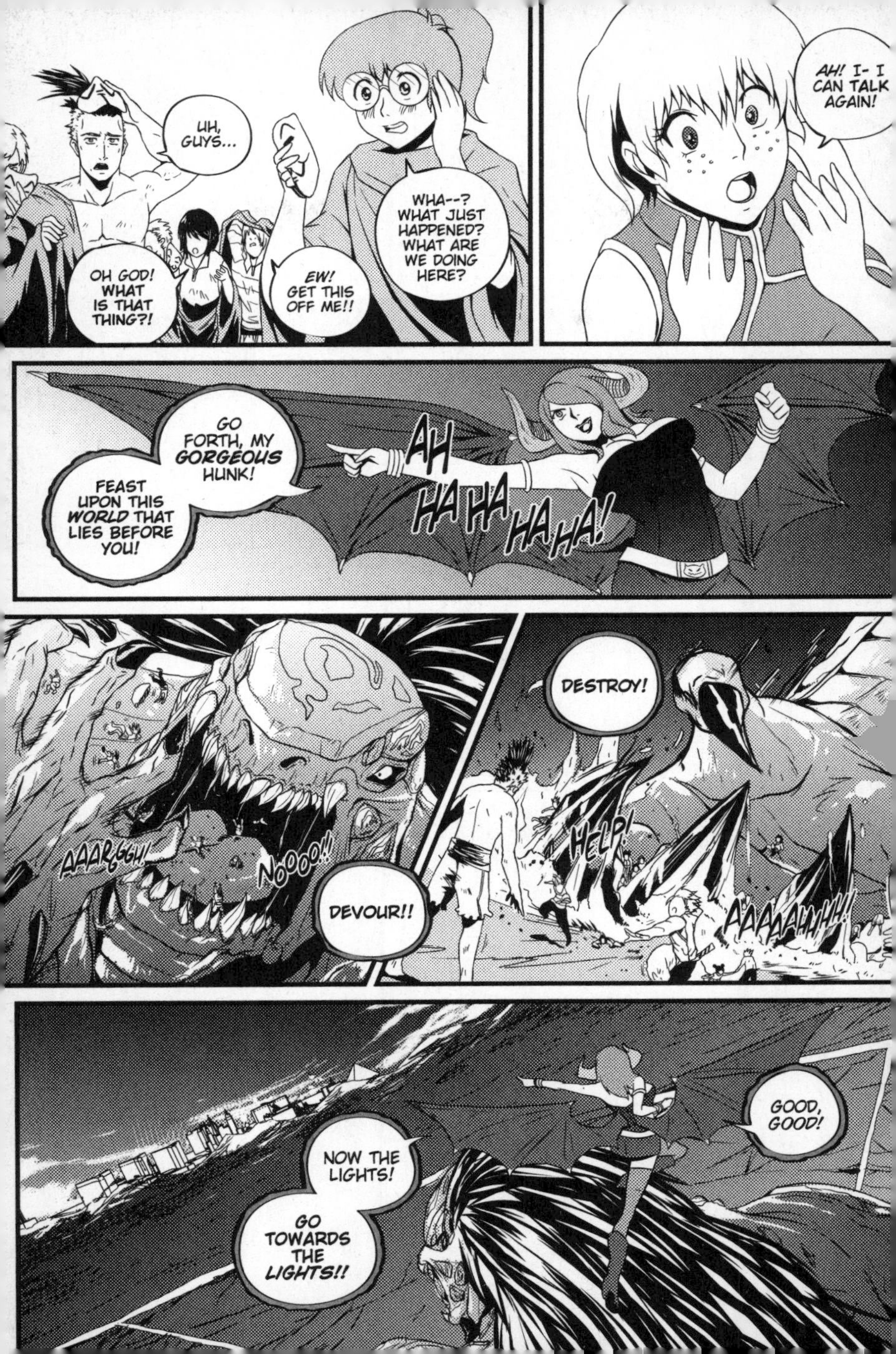
AH! I- I CAN TALK AGAIN!
WHA--? WHAT JUST HAPPENED? WHAT ARE WE DOING HERE?
UH, GUYS...
EW! GET THIS OFF ME!!
OH GOD! WHAT IS THAT THING?!
AH HA HA HA HA!
GO FORTH, MY *GORGEOUS* HUNK!
FEAST UPON THIS *WORLD* THAT LIES BEFORE YOU!
DESTROY!
HELP!
AAAAAHHH!
NOOOO!!
DEVOUR!!
AAARGGH!
GOOD, GOOD!
NOW THE LIGHTS!
GO TOWARDS THE *LIGHTS!!*

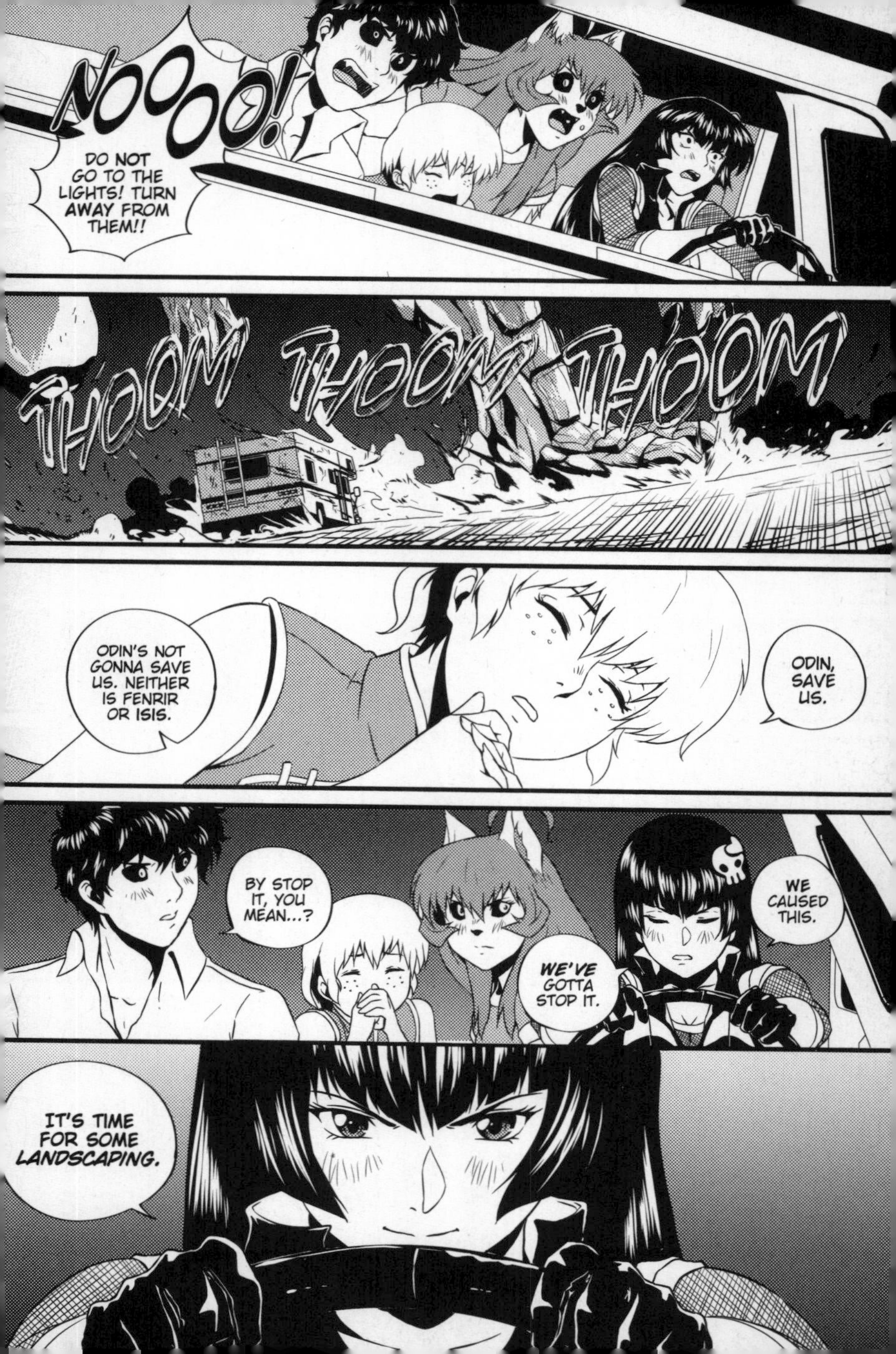
NOOOO!
DO NOT GO TO THE LIGHTS! TURN AWAY FROM THEM!!
THOOM THOOM THOOM
ODIN, SAVE US.
ODIN'S NOT GONNA SAVE US. NEITHER IS FENRIR OR ISIS.
WE CAUSED THIS.
WE'VE GOTTA STOP IT.
BY STOP IT, YOU MEAN...?
IT'S TIME FOR SOME *LANDSCAPING.*

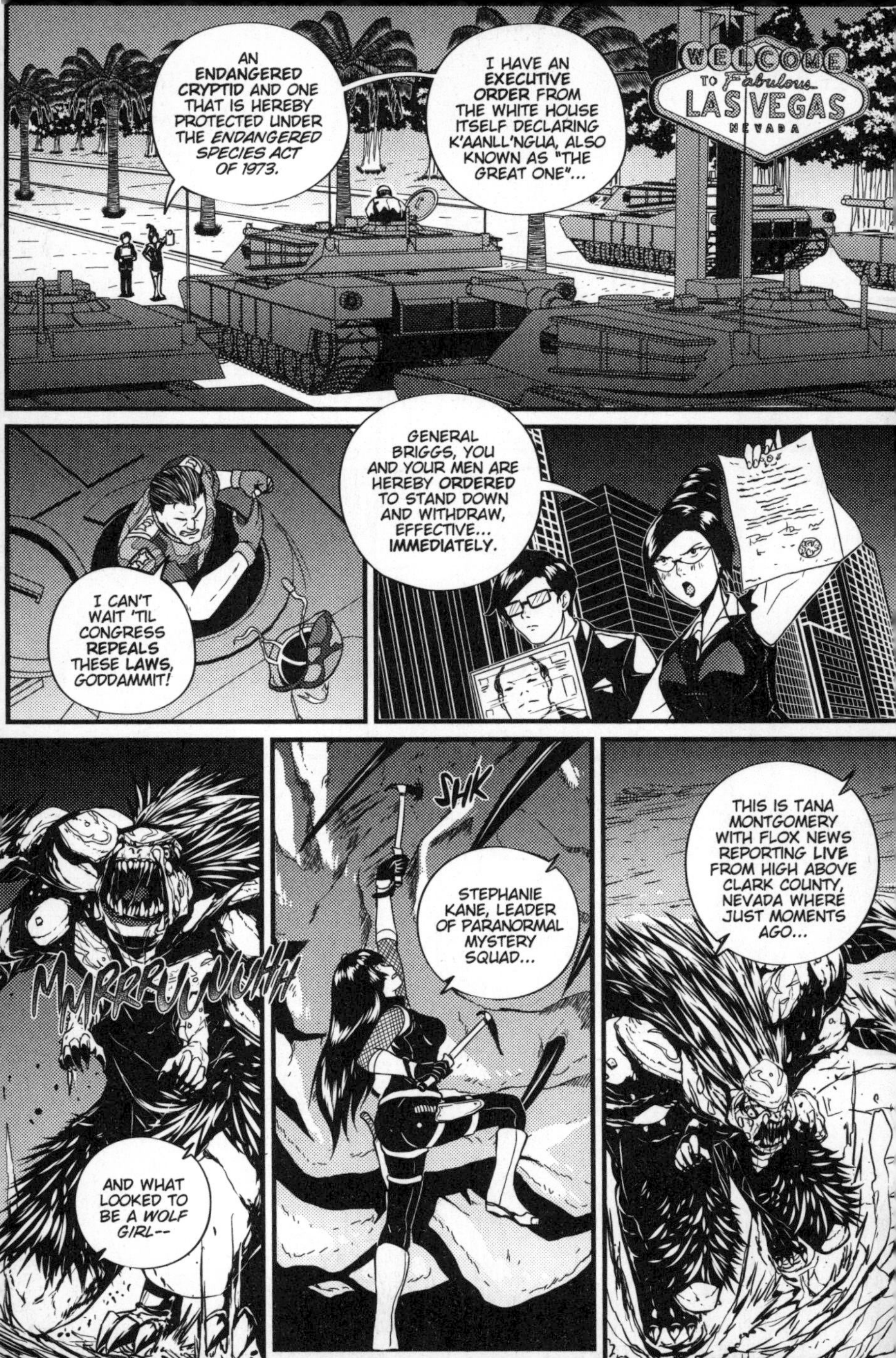
WELCOME TO Fabulous LAS VEGAS NEVADA
I HAVE AN EXECUTIVE ORDER FROM THE WHITE HOUSE ITSELF DECLARING K'AANLL'NGUA, ALSO KNOWN AS "THE GREAT ONE"...
AN ENDANGERED CRYPTID AND ONE THAT IS HEREBY PROTECTED UNDER THE ENDANGERED SPECIES ACT OF 1973.
GENERAL BRIGGS, YOU AND YOUR MEN ARE HEREBY ORDERED TO STAND DOWN AND WITHDRAW, EFFECTIVE... IMMEDIATELY.
I CAN'T WAIT 'TIL CONGRESS REPEALS THESE LAWS, GODDAMMIT!
THIS IS TANA MONTGOMERY WITH FLOX NEWS REPORTING LIVE FROM HIGH ABOVE CLARK COUNTY, NEVADA WHERE JUST MOMENTS AGO...
SHK
STEPHANIE KANE, LEADER OF PARANORMAL MYSTERY SQUAD...
MWRRRUUUHH
AND WHAT LOOKED TO BE A WOLF GIRL--

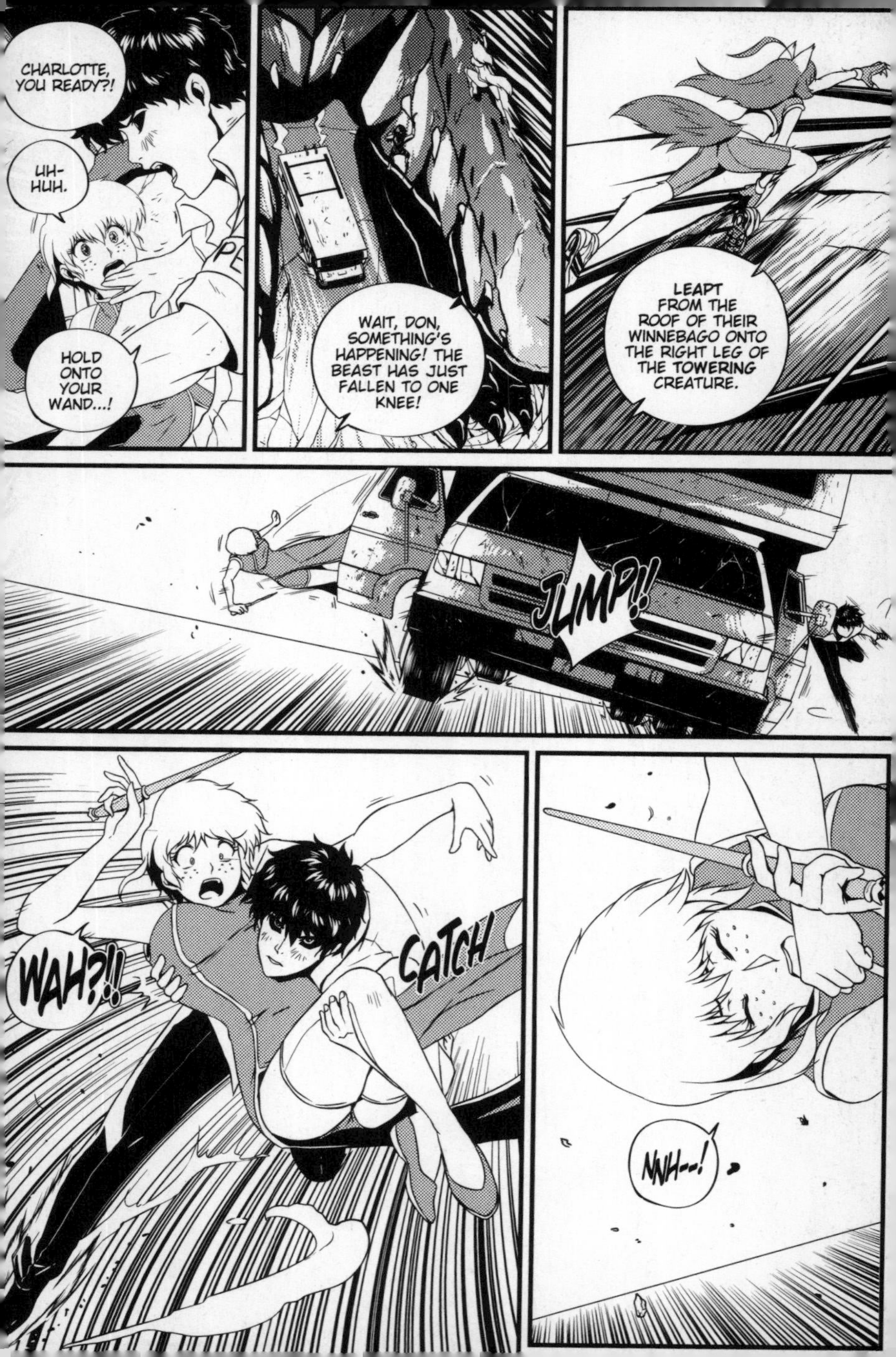
LEAPT FROM THE ROOF OF THEIR WINNEBAGO ONTO THE RIGHT LEG OF THE TOWERING CREATURE.
WAIT, DON, SOMETHING'S HAPPENING! THE BEAST HAS JUST FALLEN TO ONE KNEE!
CHARLOTTE, YOU READY?!
UH-HUH.
HOLD ONTO YOUR WAND...!
JUMP!!
NNH--!
CATCH
WAH?!!

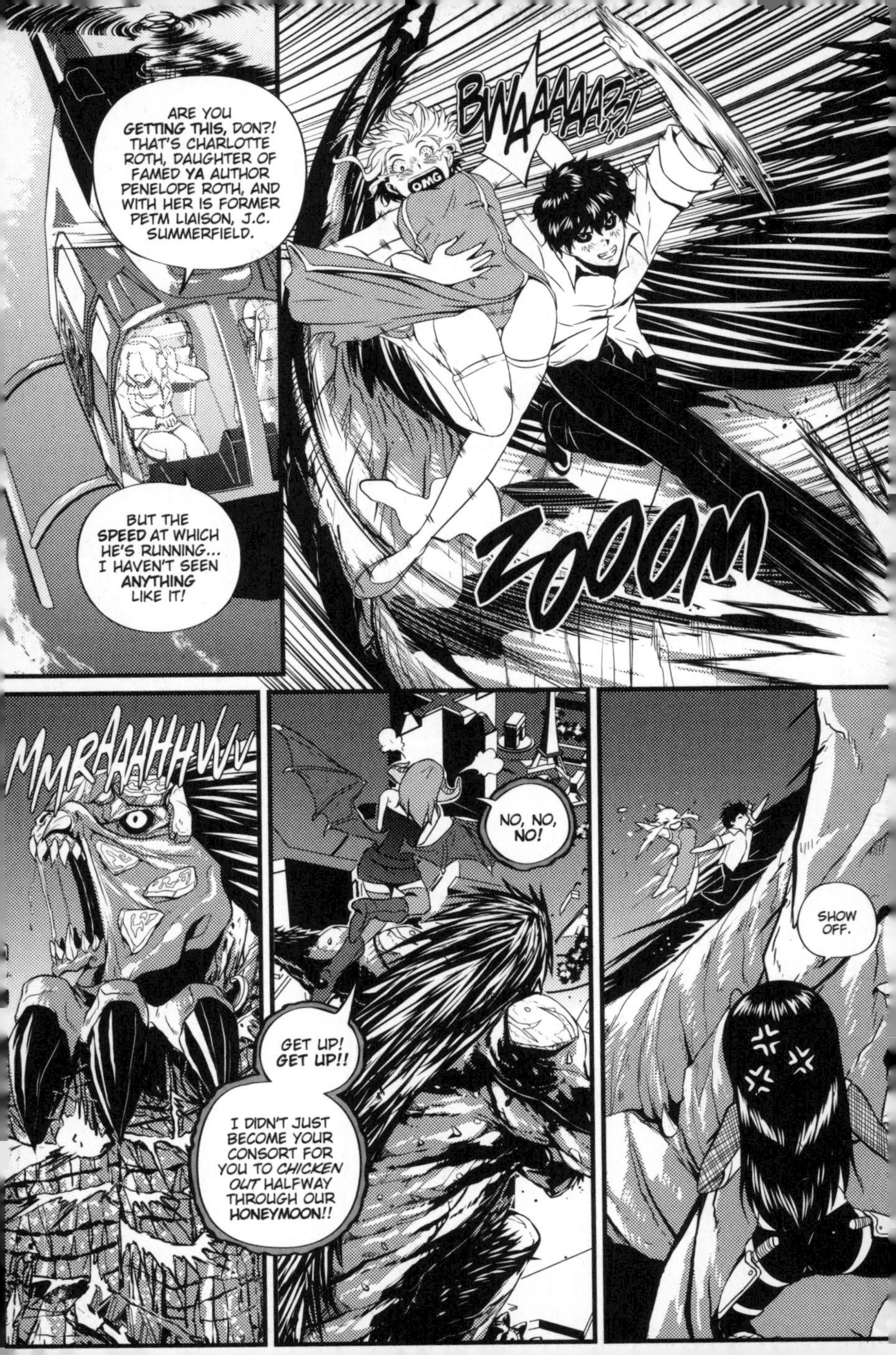
BWAAAAA?!
OMG
ZOOOM
ARE YOU GETTING THIS, DON?! THAT'S CHARLOTTE ROTH, DAUGHTER OF FAMED YA AUTHOR PENELOPE ROTH, AND WITH HER IS FORMER PETM LIAISON, J.C. SUMMERFIELD.
BUT THE SPEED AT WHICH HE'S RUNNING... I HAVEN'T SEEN ANYTHING LIKE IT!
SHOW OFF.
NO, NO, NO!
GET UP! GET UP!!
I DIDN'T JUST BECOME YOUR CONSORT FOR YOU TO CHICKEN OUT HALFWAY THROUGH OUR HONEYMOON!!
MMRAAAHHWW

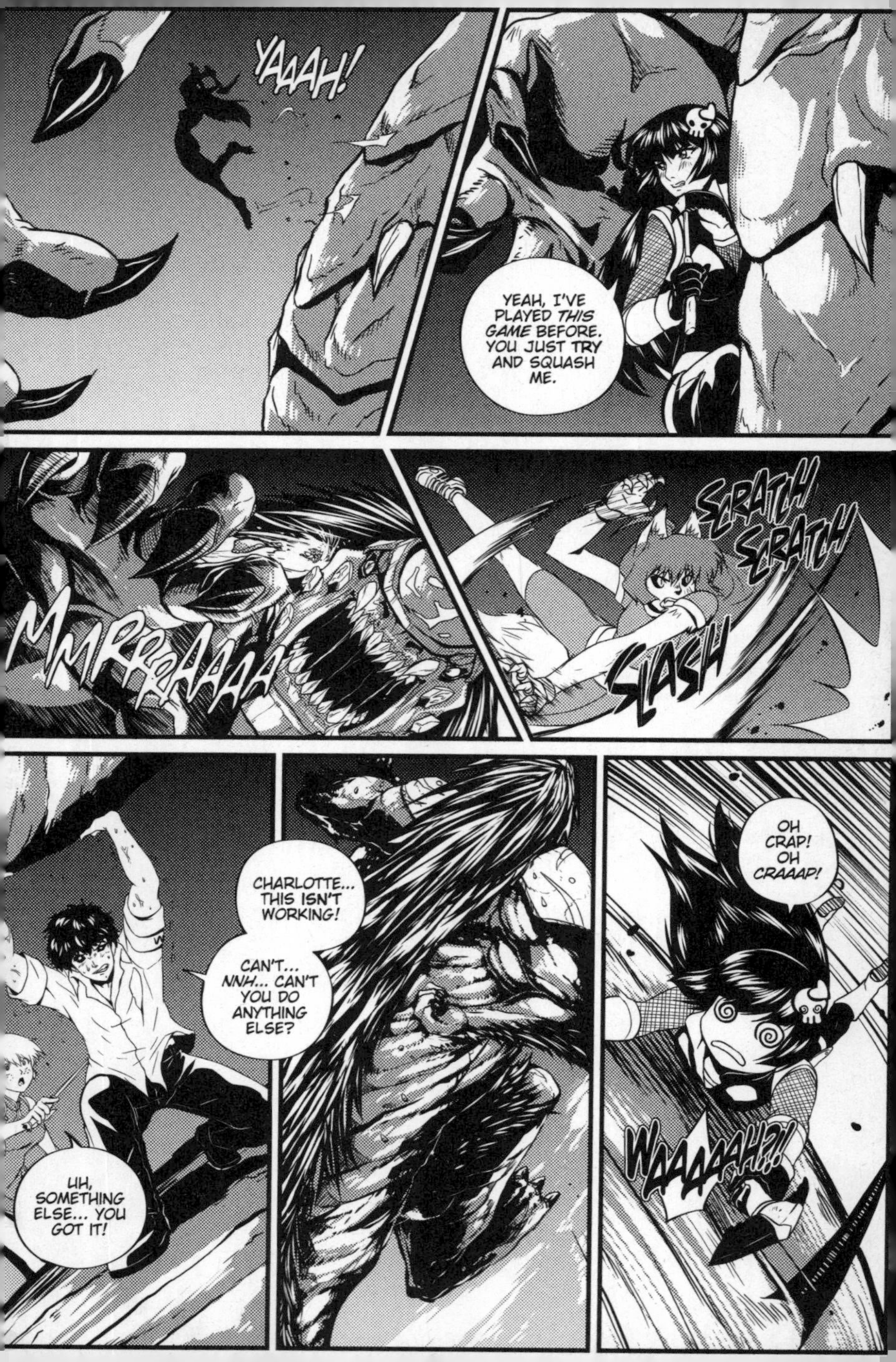
YEAH, I'VE PLAYED THIS GAME BEFORE. YOU JUST TRY AND SQUASH ME.
YAAAH!
SCRATCH SCRATCH
SLASH
MMRRRAAAAA
OH CRAP! OH CRAAAP!
WAAAAAH?!
CHARLOTTE... THIS ISN'T WORKING!
CAN'T... NNH... CAN'T YOU DO ANYTHING ELSE?
UH, SOMETHING ELSE... YOU GOT IT!

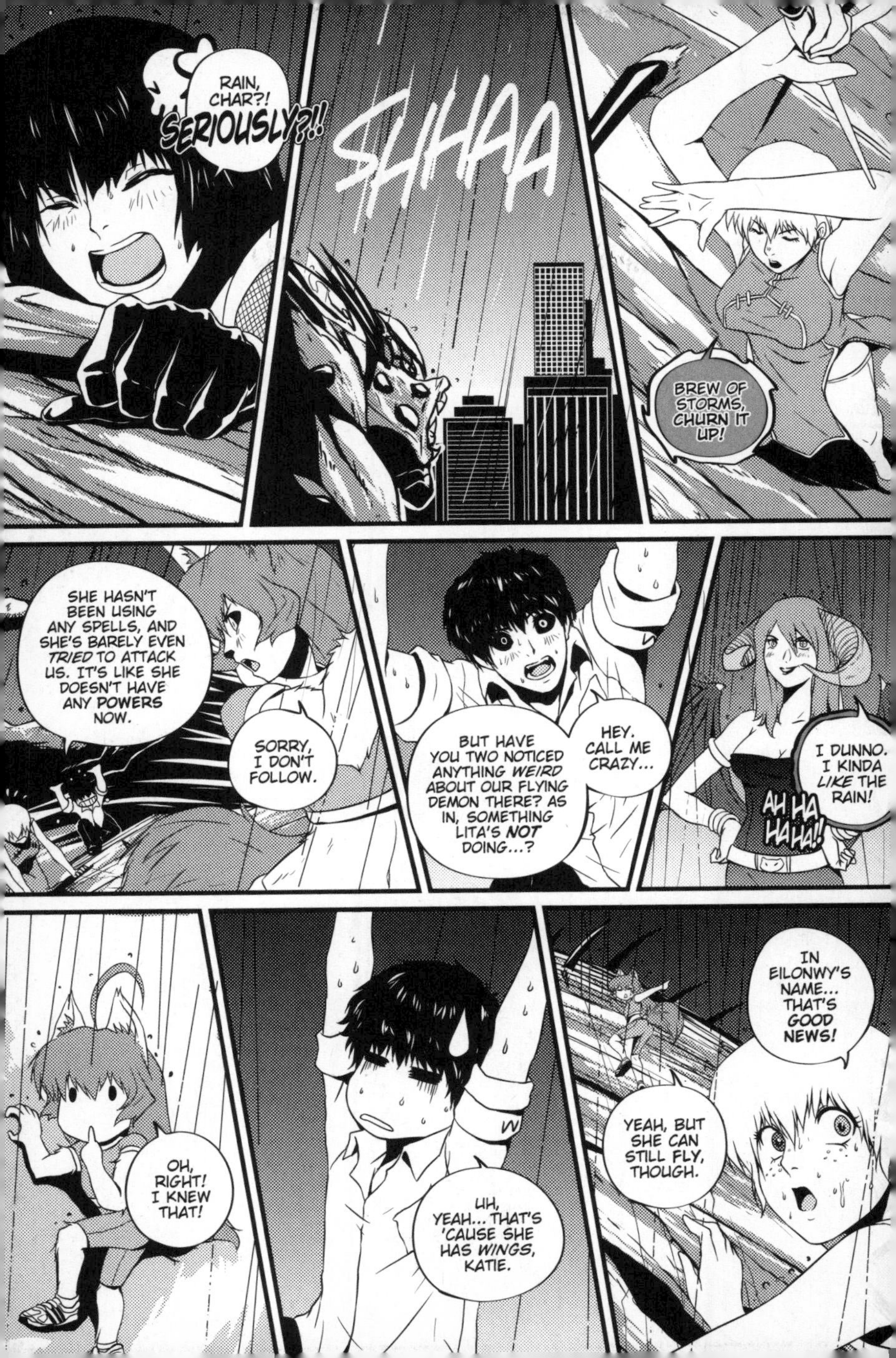
BREW OF STORMS, CHURN IT UP!
SHHAA
RAIN, CHAR?!
SERIOUSLY?!!
I DUNNO. I KINDA *LIKE* THE RAIN!
AH HA HA HA!!
HEY. CALL ME CRAZY...
BUT HAVE YOU TWO NOTICED ANYTHING *WEIRD* ABOUT OUR FLYING DEMON THERE? AS IN, SOMETHING LITA'S **NOT** DOING...?
SHE HASN'T BEEN USING ANY SPELLS, AND SHE'S BARELY EVEN *TRIED* TO ATTACK US. IT'S LIKE SHE DOESN'T HAVE ANY **POWERS** NOW.
SORRY, I DON'T FOLLOW.
IN EILONWY'S NAME... THAT'S **GOOD** NEWS!
YEAH, BUT SHE CAN STILL FLY, THOUGH.
UH, YEAH... THAT'S 'CAUSE SHE HAS *WINGS*, KATIE.
OH, RIGHT! I KNEW THAT!

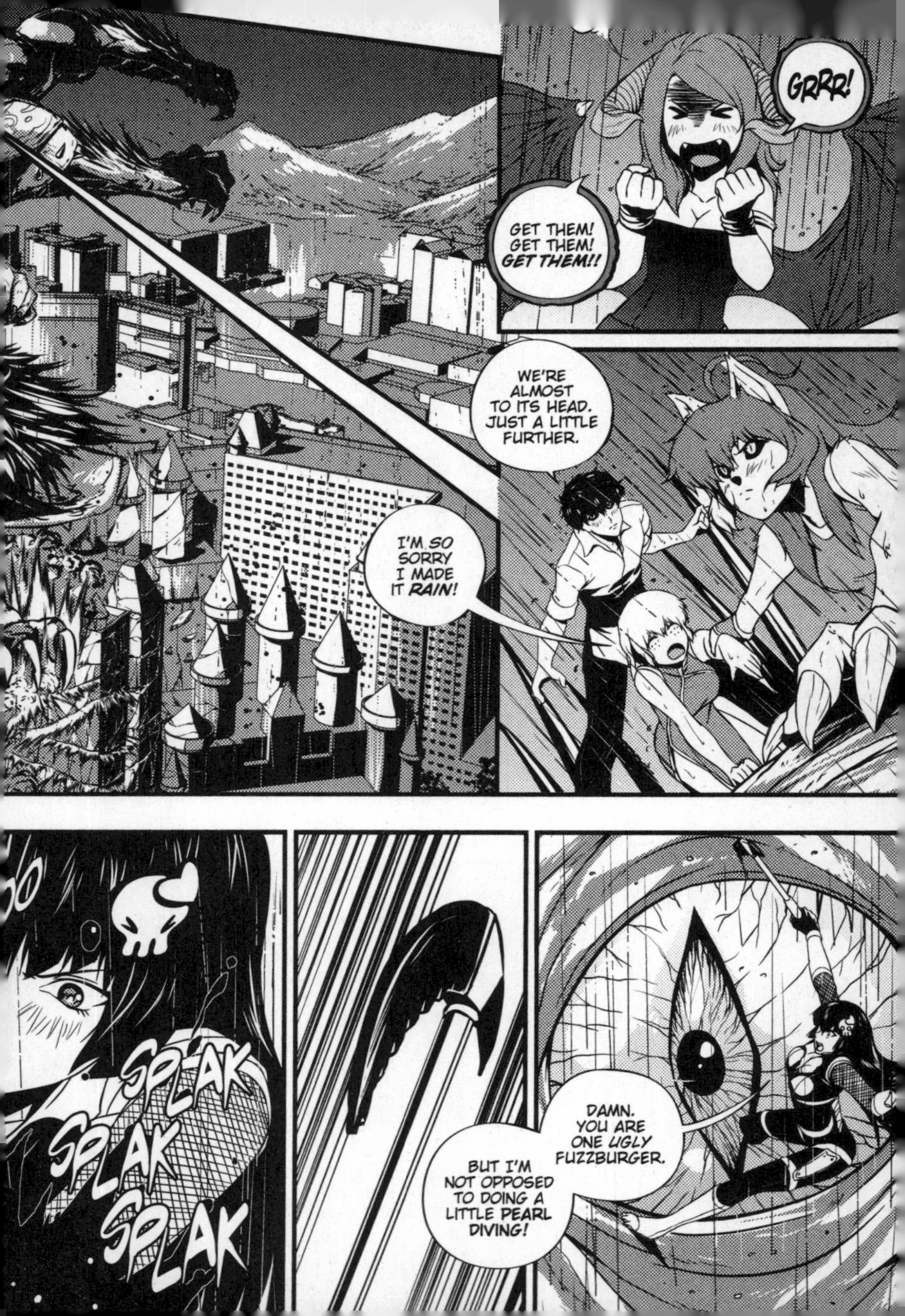
GRRR!
GET THEM! GET THEM! GET THEM!!
WE'RE ALMOST TO ITS HEAD. JUST A LITTLE FURTHER.
I'M SO SORRY I MADE IT RAIN!
DAMN. YOU ARE ONE UGLY FUZZBURGER.
BUT I'M NOT OPPOSED TO DOING A LITTLE PEARL DIVING!
SPLAK
SPLAK
SPLAK

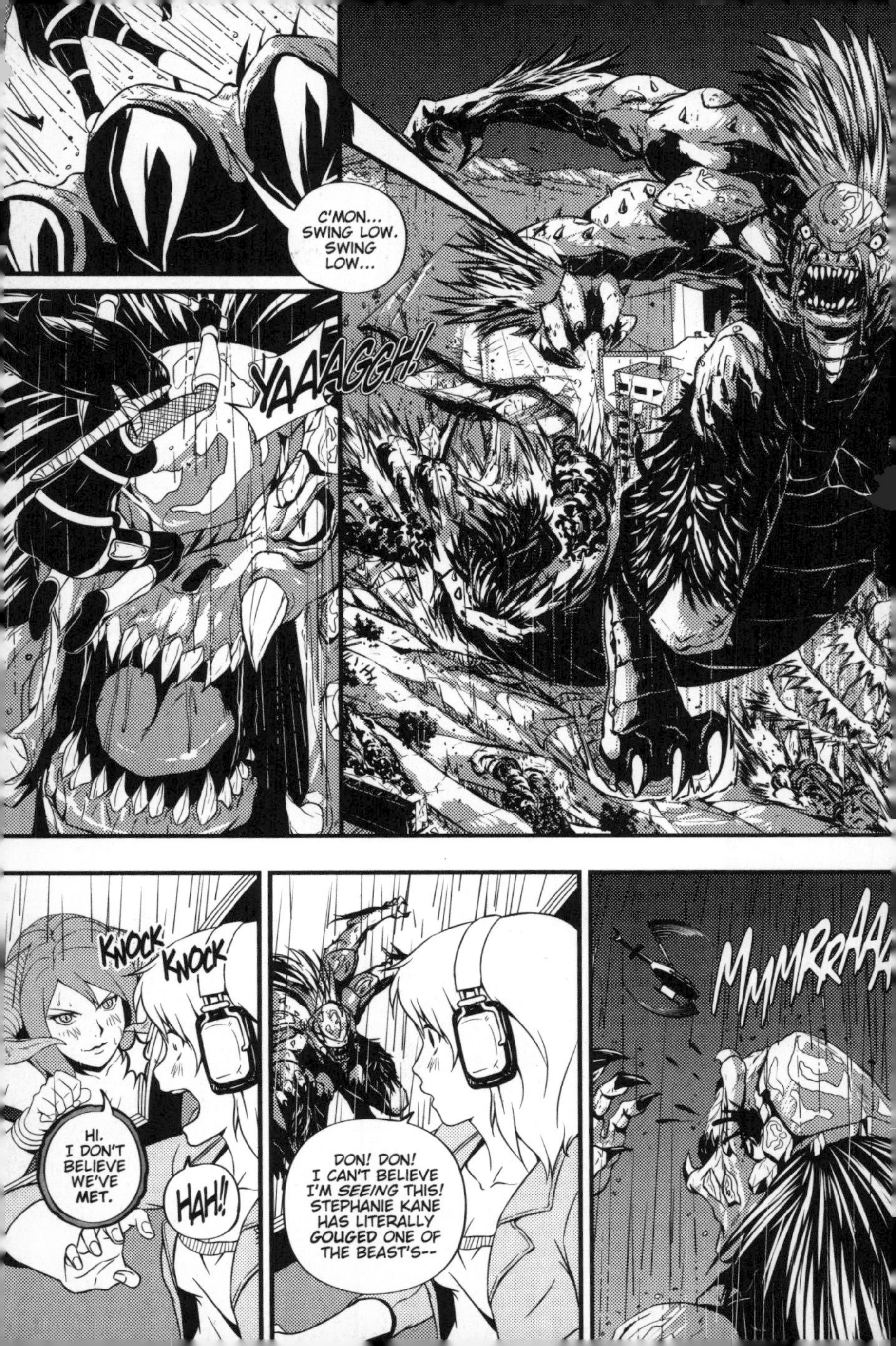
C'MON... SWING LOW. SWING LOW...
YAAAGGH!
MMMRRAAA
DON! DON! I CAN'T BELIEVE I'M *SEEING* THIS! STEPHANIE KANE HAS LITERALLY GOUGED ONE OF THE BEAST'S--
KNOCK KNOCK
HI. I DON'T BELIEVE WE'VE MET.
HAH!!

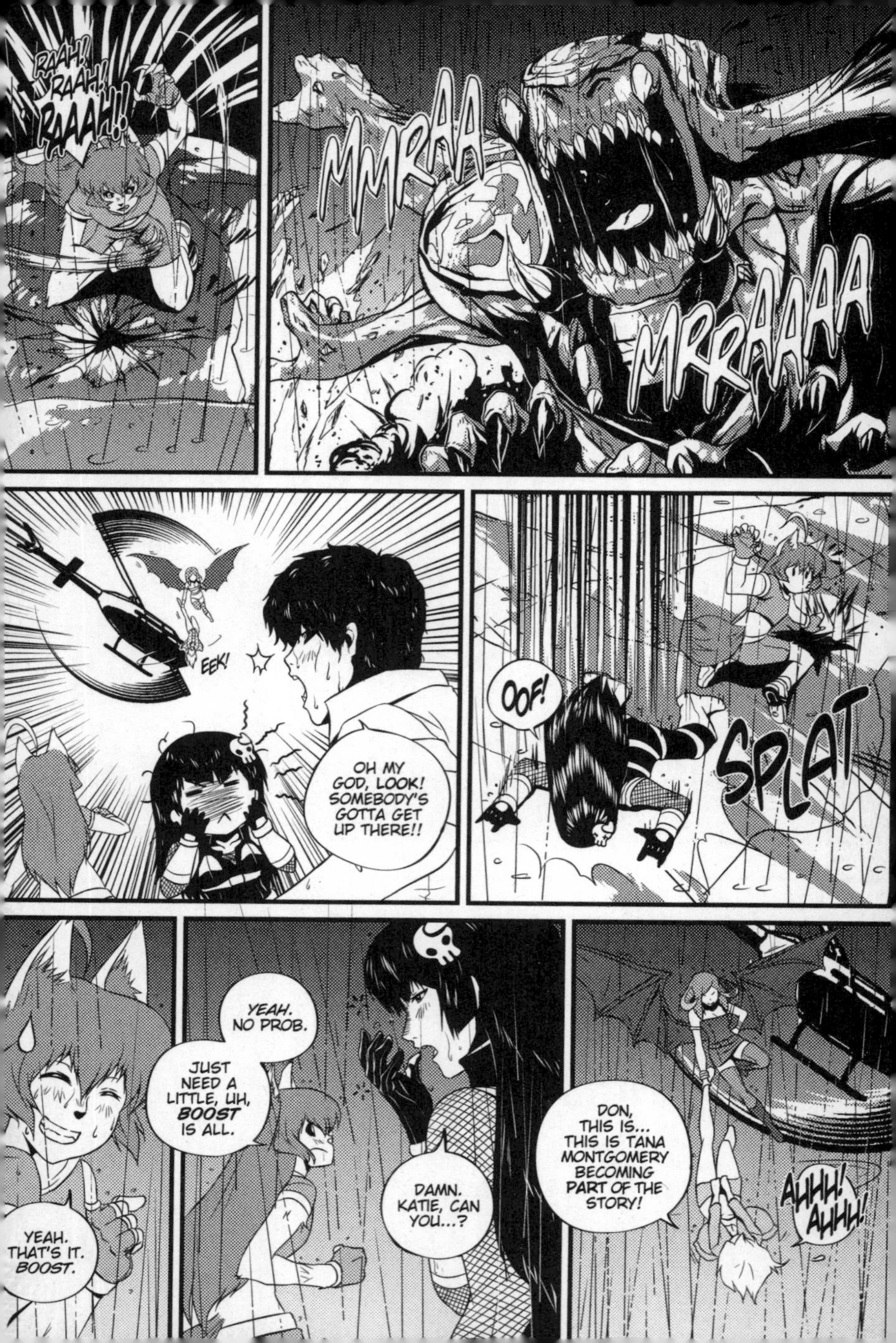
MMRAA
MRRAAAA
RAAH! RAAH! RAAAH!!
OOF!
SPLAT
EEK!
OH MY GOD, LOOK! SOMEBODY'S GOTTA GET UP THERE!!
DON, THIS IS... THIS IS TANA MONTGOMERY BECOMING PART OF THE STORY!
AHHH! AHHH!
DAMN. KATIE, CAN YOU...?
YEAH. NO PROB.
JUST NEED A LITTLE, UH, ***BOOST*** IS ALL.
YEAH. THAT'S IT. *BOOST.*

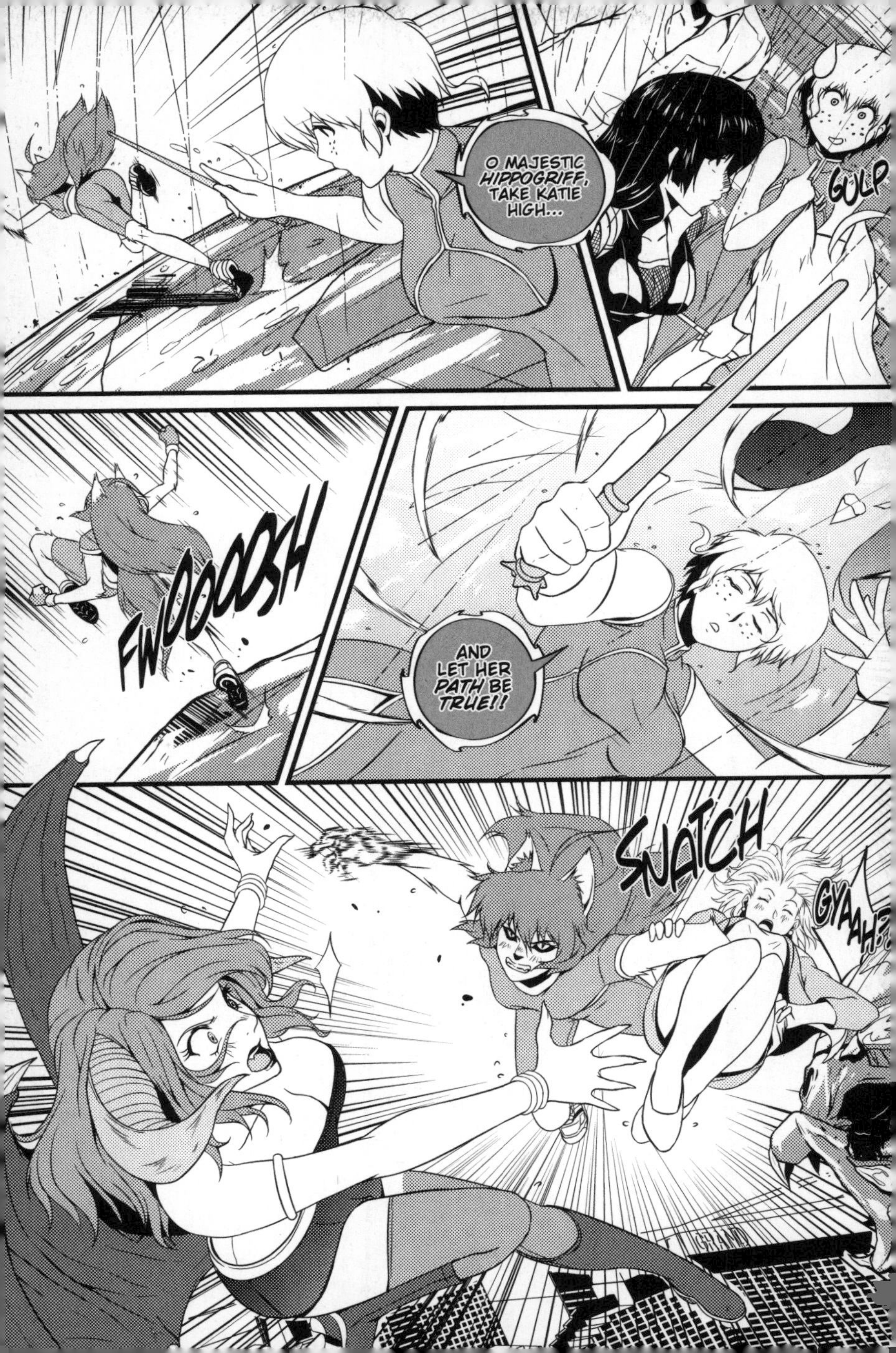
GULP
O MAJESTIC *HIPPOGRIFF*, TAKE KATIE HIGH...
AND LET HER *PATH* BE *TRUE*!!
FWOOOOSH
SNATCH
GYAAH?!
GRAND

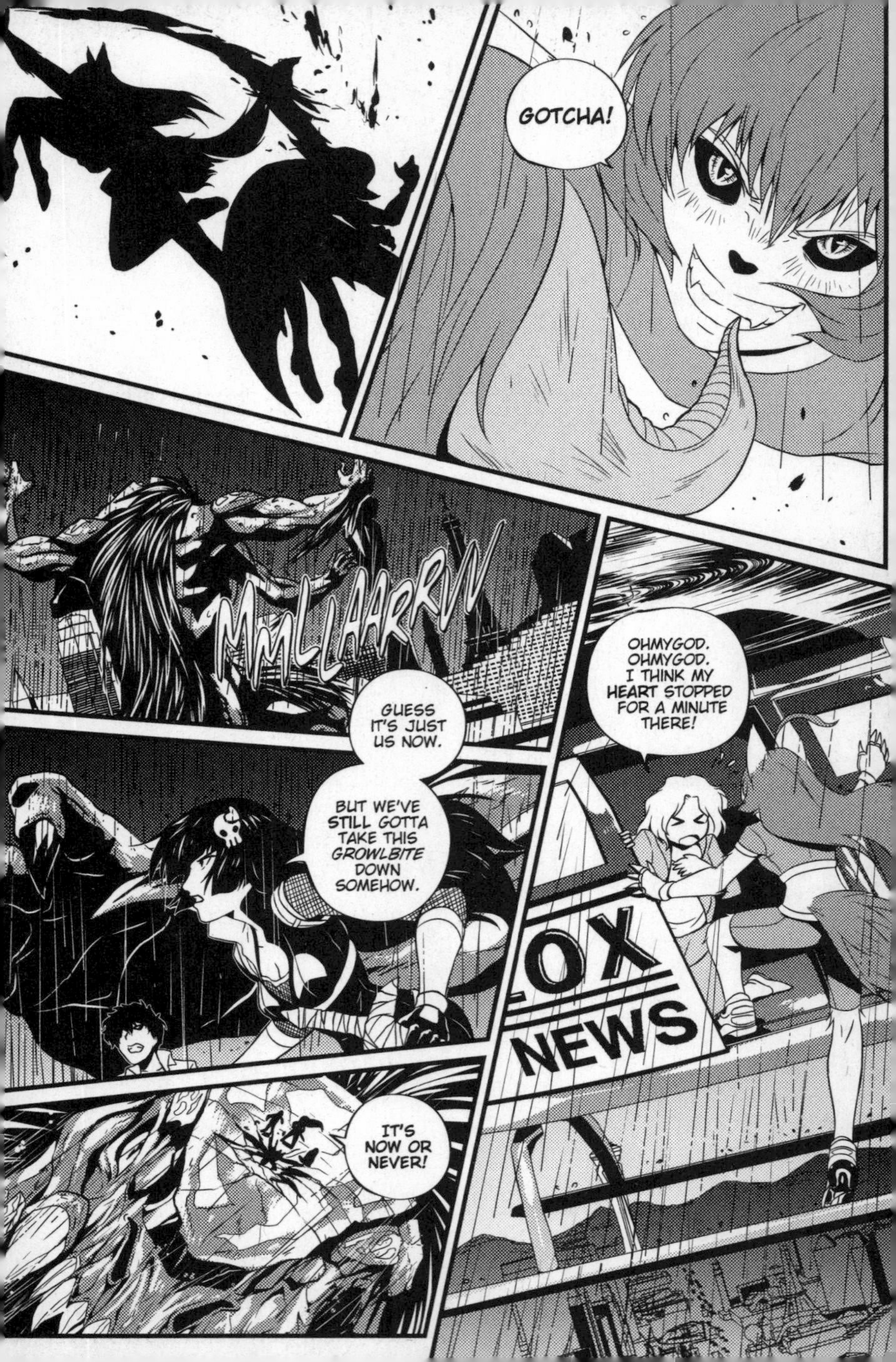
GOTCHA!
OHMYGOD. OHMYGOD. I THINK MY HEART STOPPED FOR A MINUTE THERE!
OX
NEWS
MMLLAARRVV
GUESS IT'S JUST US NOW.
BUT WE'VE STILL GOTTA TAKE THIS *GROWLBITE* DOWN SOMEHOW.
IT'S NOW OR NEVER!

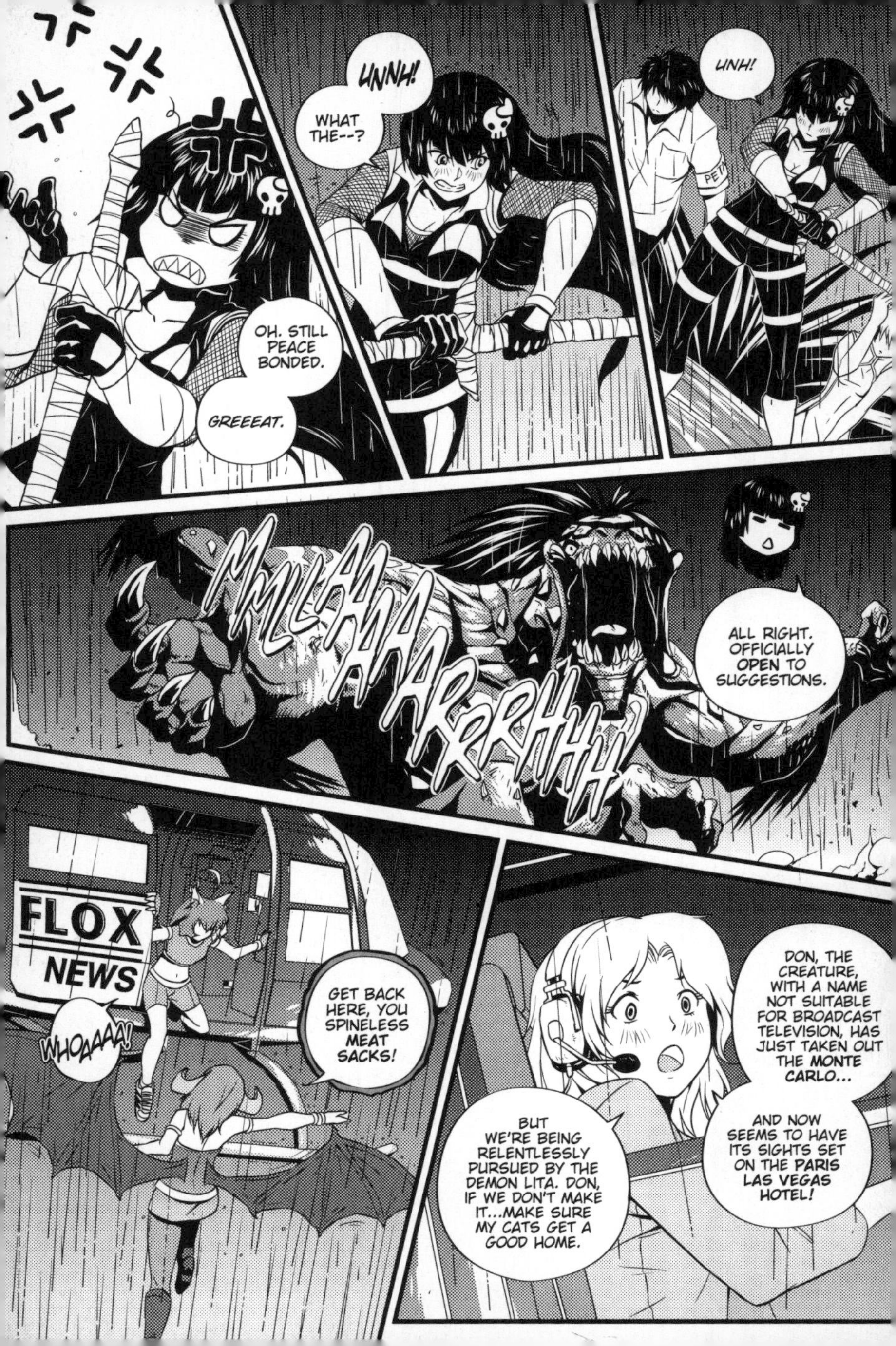
UNH!
UNNH!
WHAT THE--?
OH. STILL PEACE BONDED.
GREEEAT.
ALL RIGHT. OFFICIALLY OPEN TO SUGGESTIONS.
MMLLAAAAARRRHHHH
DON, THE CREATURE, WITH A NAME NOT SUITABLE FOR BROADCAST TELEVISION, HAS JUST TAKEN OUT THE MONTE CARLO...
AND NOW SEEMS TO HAVE ITS SIGHTS SET ON THE PARIS LAS VEGAS HOTEL!
BUT WE'RE BEING RELENTLESSLY PURSUED BY THE DEMON LITA. DON, IF WE DON'T MAKE IT...MAKE SURE MY CATS GET A GOOD HOME.
FLOX NEWS
GET BACK HERE, YOU SPINELESS MEAT SACKS!
WHOAAAA!

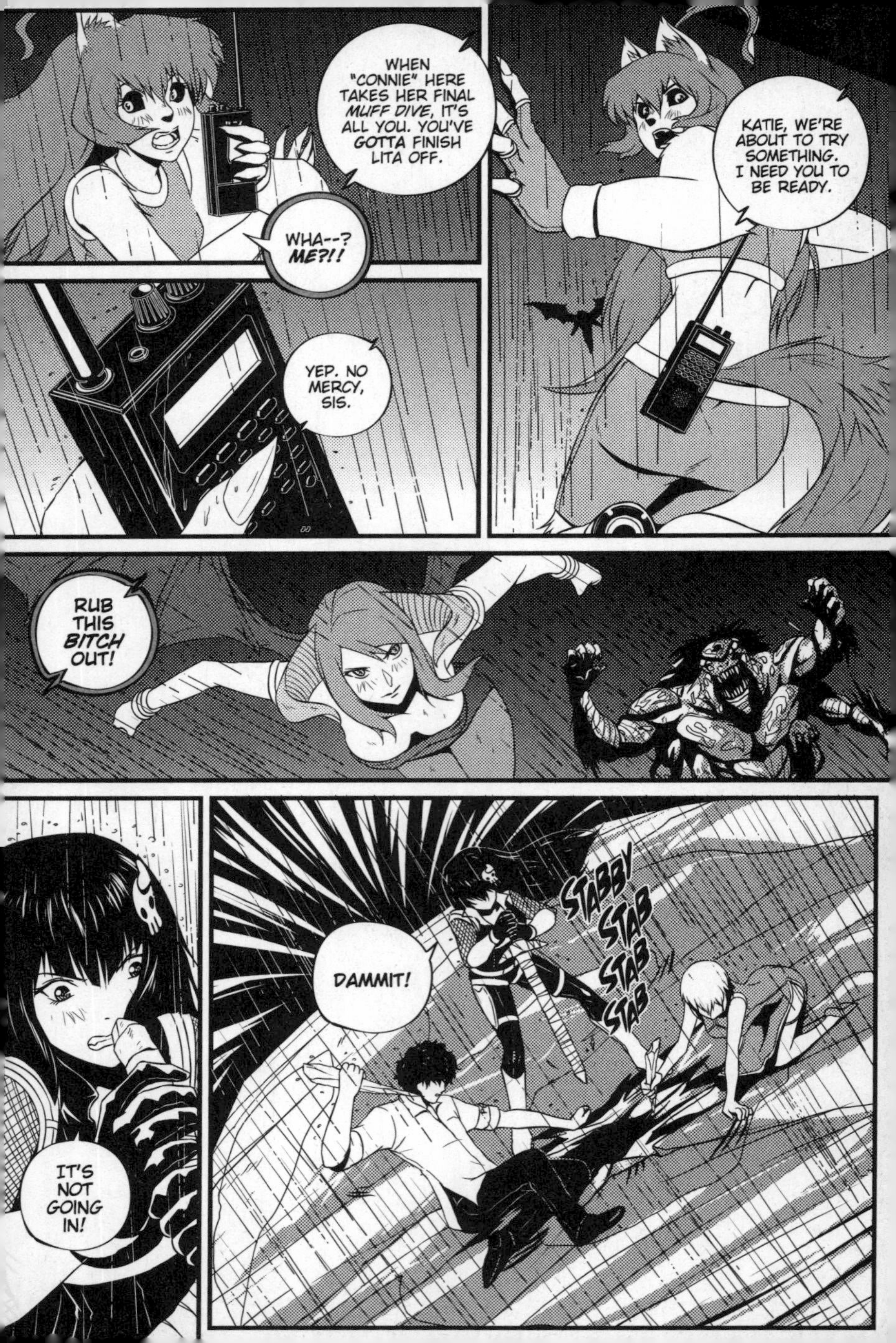
KATIE, WE'RE ABOUT TO TRY SOMETHING. I NEED YOU TO BE READY.
WHEN "CONNIE" HERE TAKES HER FINAL *MUFF DIVE*, IT'S ALL YOU. YOU'VE GOTTA FINISH LITA OFF.
WHA--? *ME?!!*
YEP. NO MERCY, SIS.
RUB THIS *BITCH* OUT!
DAMMIT!
STABBY STAB STAB STAB STAB
IT'S NOT GOING IN!

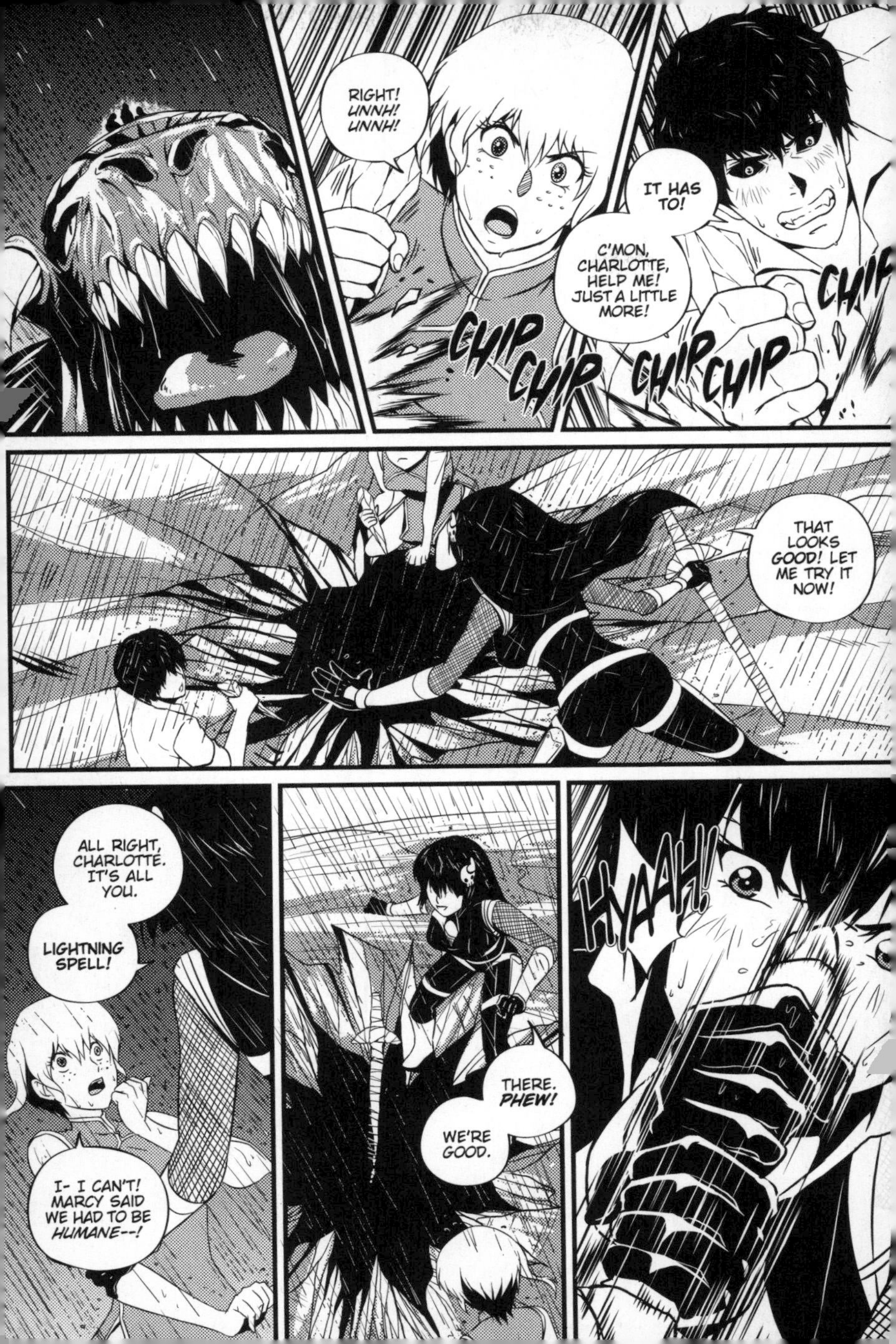
IT HAS TO!
C'MON, CHARLOTTE, HELP ME! JUST A LITTLE MORE!
CHIP CHIP CHIP
RIGHT! *UNNH! UNNH!*
CHIP CHIP
THAT LOOKS *GOOD!* LET ME TRY IT NOW!
HYAAH!
THERE. *PHEW!*
WE'RE GOOD.
ALL RIGHT, CHARLOTTE. IT'S ALL YOU.
LIGHTNING SPELL!
I- I CAN'T! MARCY SAID WE HAD TO BE *HUMANE*--!

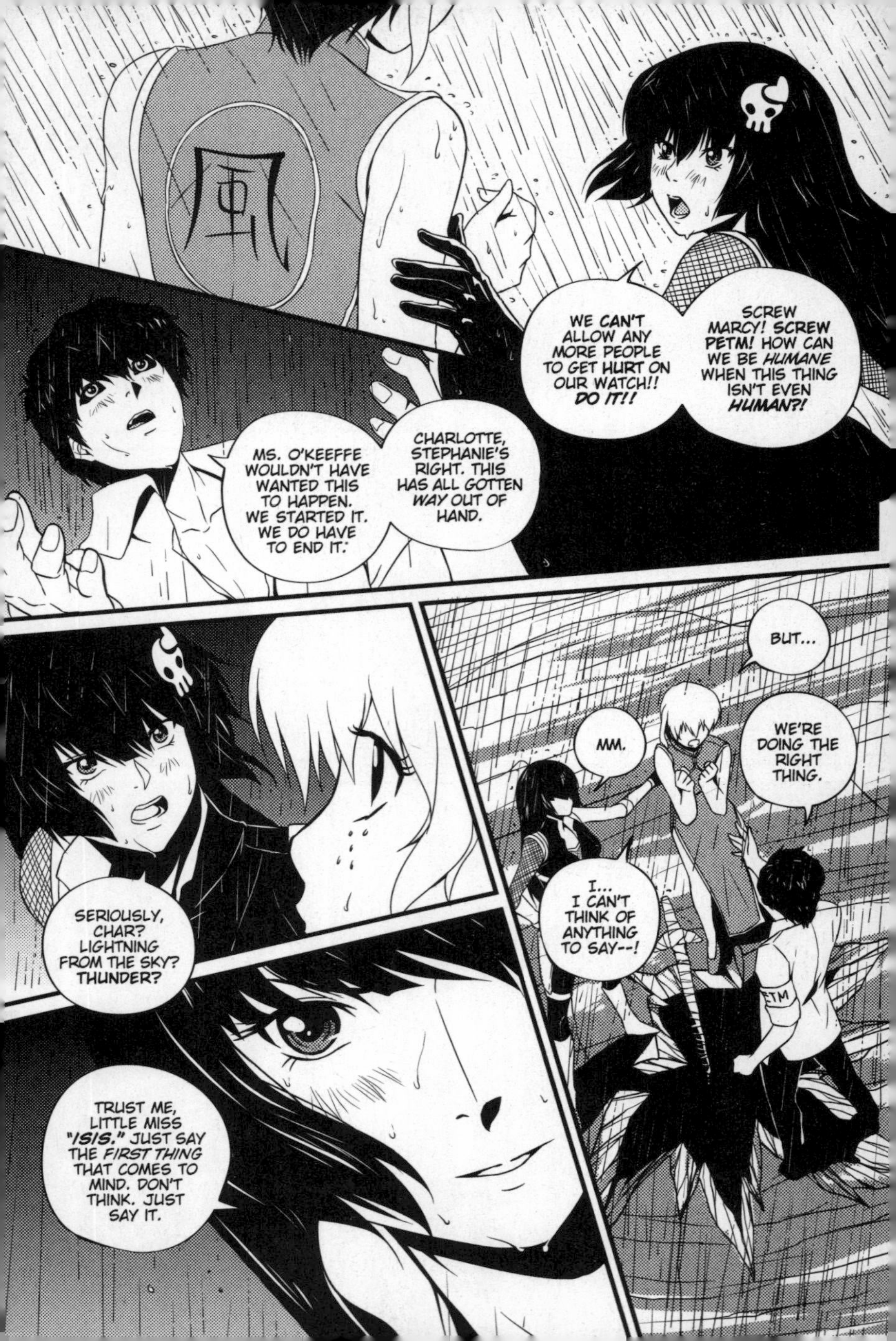

SCREW MARCY! SCREW PETM! HOW CAN WE BE *HUMANE* WHEN THIS THING ISN'T EVEN *HUMAN?!*
WE CAN'T ALLOW ANY MORE PEOPLE TO GET HURT ON OUR WATCH!! *DO IT!!*
CHARLOTTE, STEPHANIE'S RIGHT. THIS HAS ALL GOTTEN *WAY* OUT OF HAND.
MS. O'KEEFFE WOULDN'T HAVE WANTED THIS TO HAPPEN. WE STARTED IT. WE DO HAVE TO END IT.
BUT...
WE'RE DOING THE RIGHT THING.
MM.
I... I CAN'T THINK OF ANYTHING TO SAY--!
SERIOUSLY, CHAR? LIGHTNING FROM THE SKY? THUNDER?
TRUST ME, LITTLE MISS *"ISIS."* JUST SAY THE *FIRST THING* THAT COMES TO MIND. DON'T THINK. JUST SAY IT.

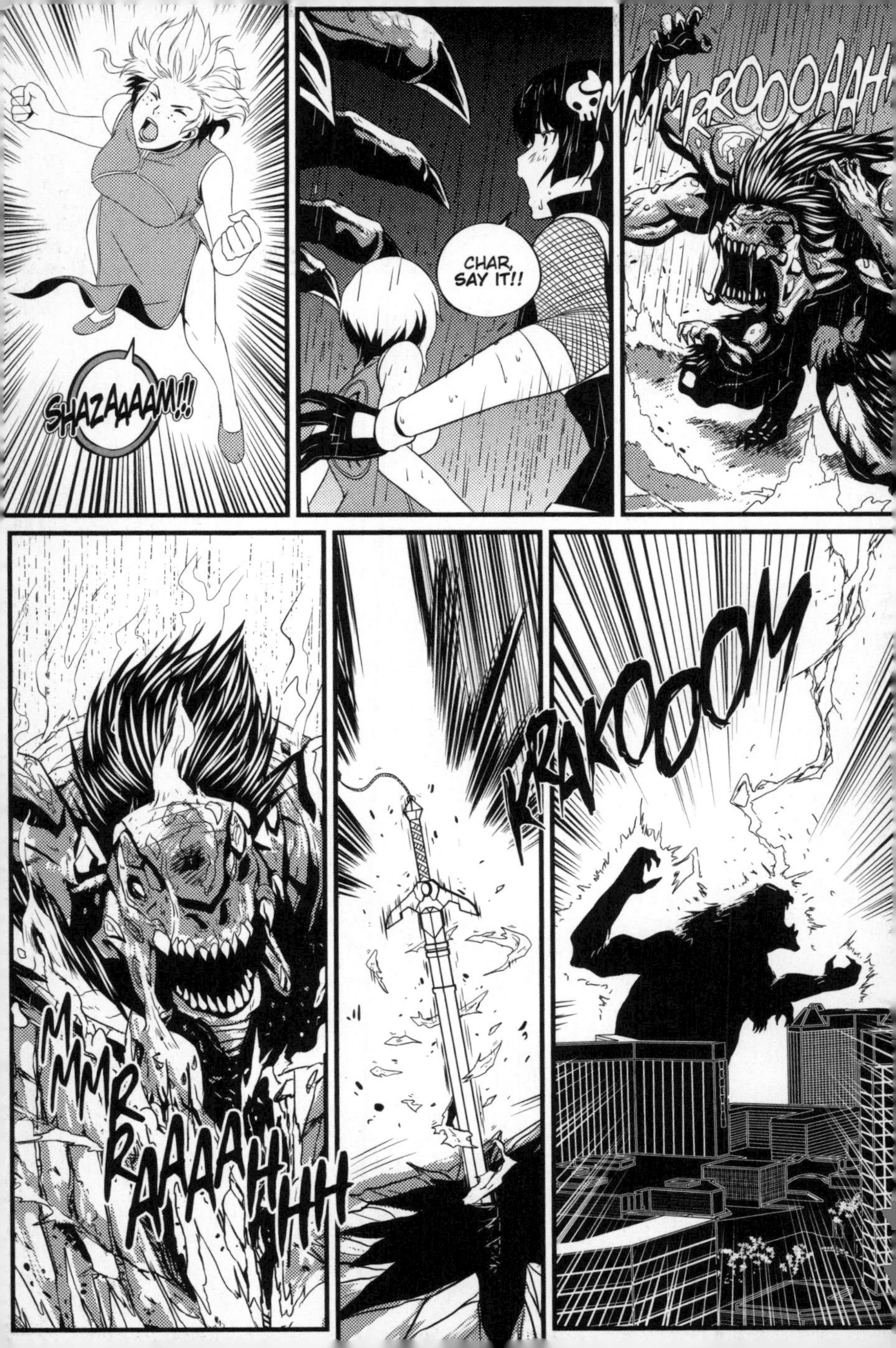
MMMRROOOAAHH
CHAR, SAY IT!!
SHAZAAAAM!!
KRAKOOOOM
MMMR RAAAAHHH

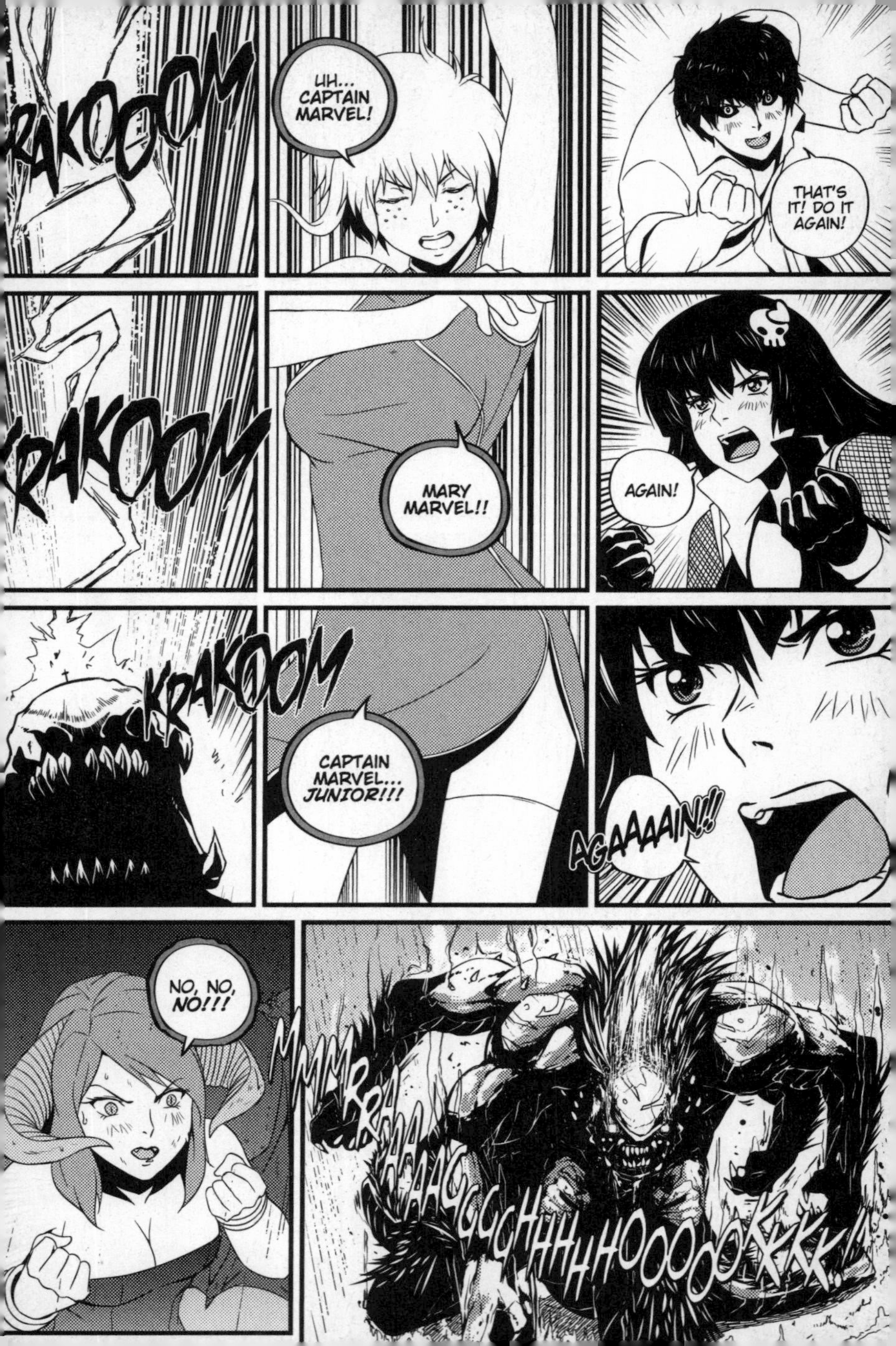
THAT'S IT! DO IT AGAIN!
UH... CAPTAIN MARVEL!
KRAKOOOM
AGAIN!
MARY MARVEL!!
KRAKOOM
AGAAAAIN!!
CAPTAIN MARVEL... JUNIOR!!!
KRAKOOM
MMMRRAAAAGGGHHHHHOOOOOKKK!!
NO, NO, NO!!!

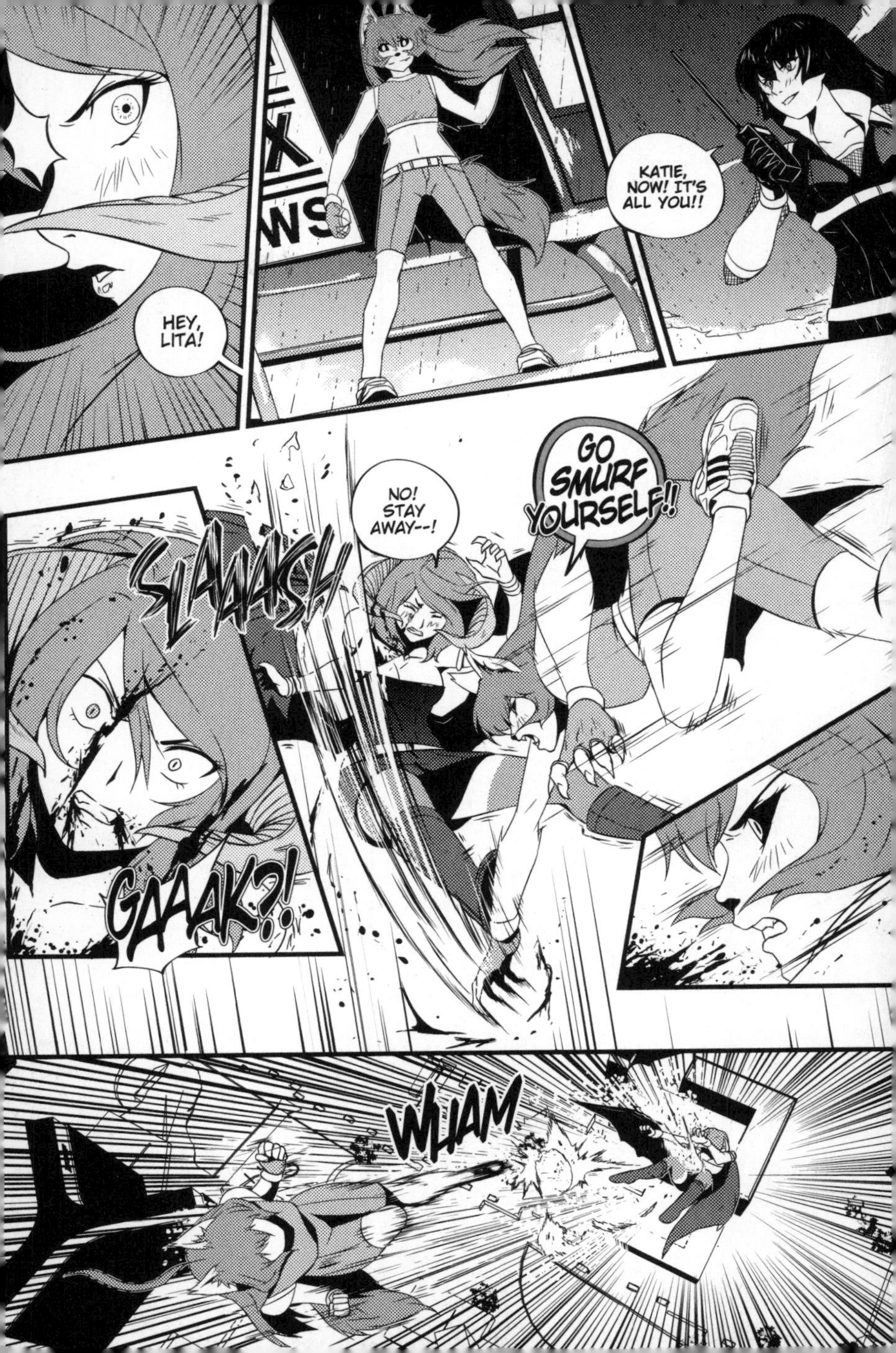
KATIE, NOW! IT'S ALL YOU!!
HEY, LITA!
GO SMURF YOURSELF!!
NO! STAY AWAY--!
SLAAASH
GAAAK?!
WHAM

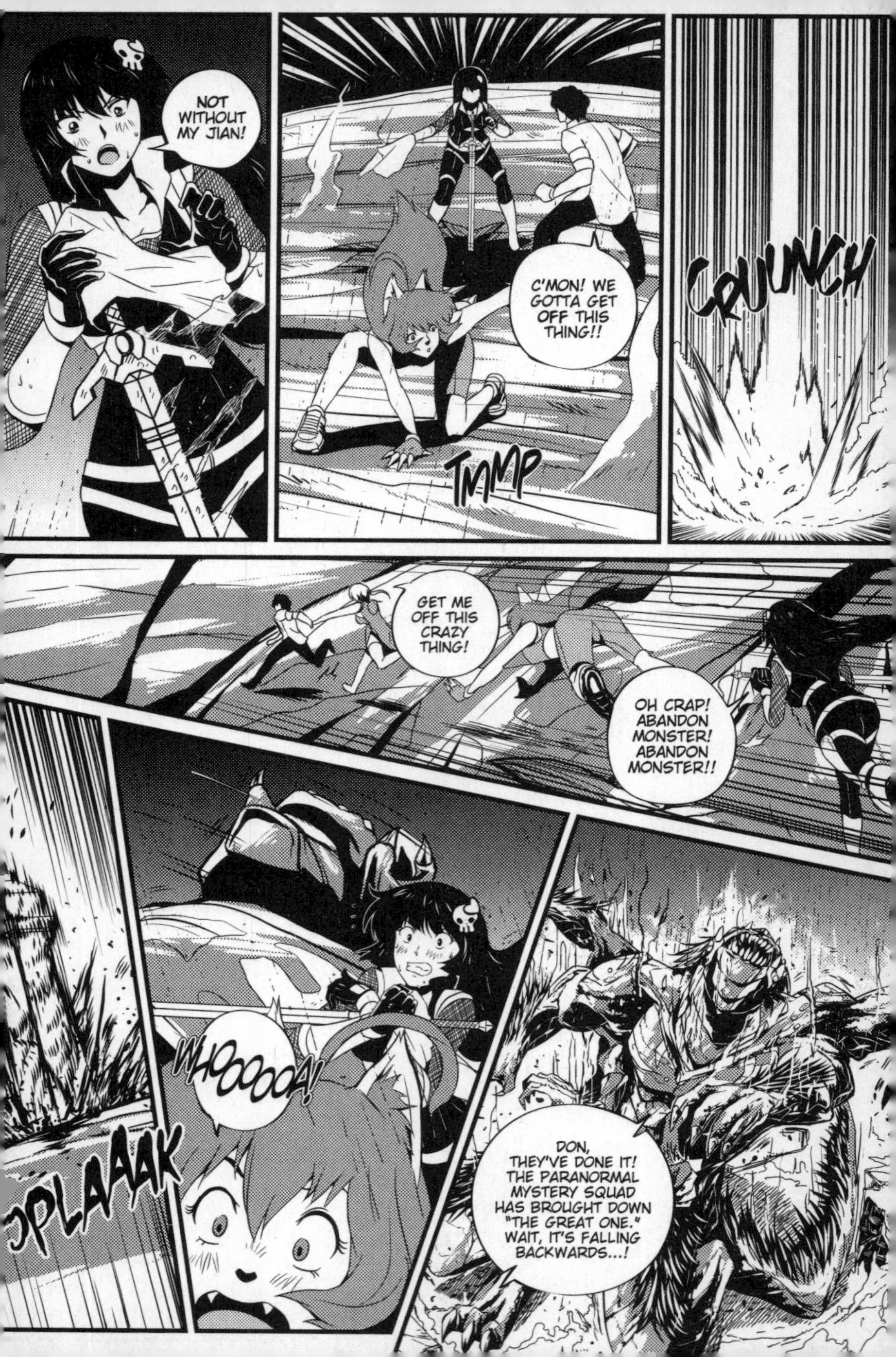
CRUNCH
C'MON! WE GOTTA GET OFF THIS THING!!
TMMP
NOT WITHOUT MY JIAN!
OH CRAP! ABANDON MONSTER! ABANDON MONSTER!!
GET ME OFF THIS CRAZY THING!
DON, THEY'VE DONE IT! THE PARANORMAL MYSTERY SQUAD HAS BROUGHT DOWN "THE GREAT ONE." WAIT, IT'S FALLING BACKWARDS...!
WHOOOOOA!
PLAAAK

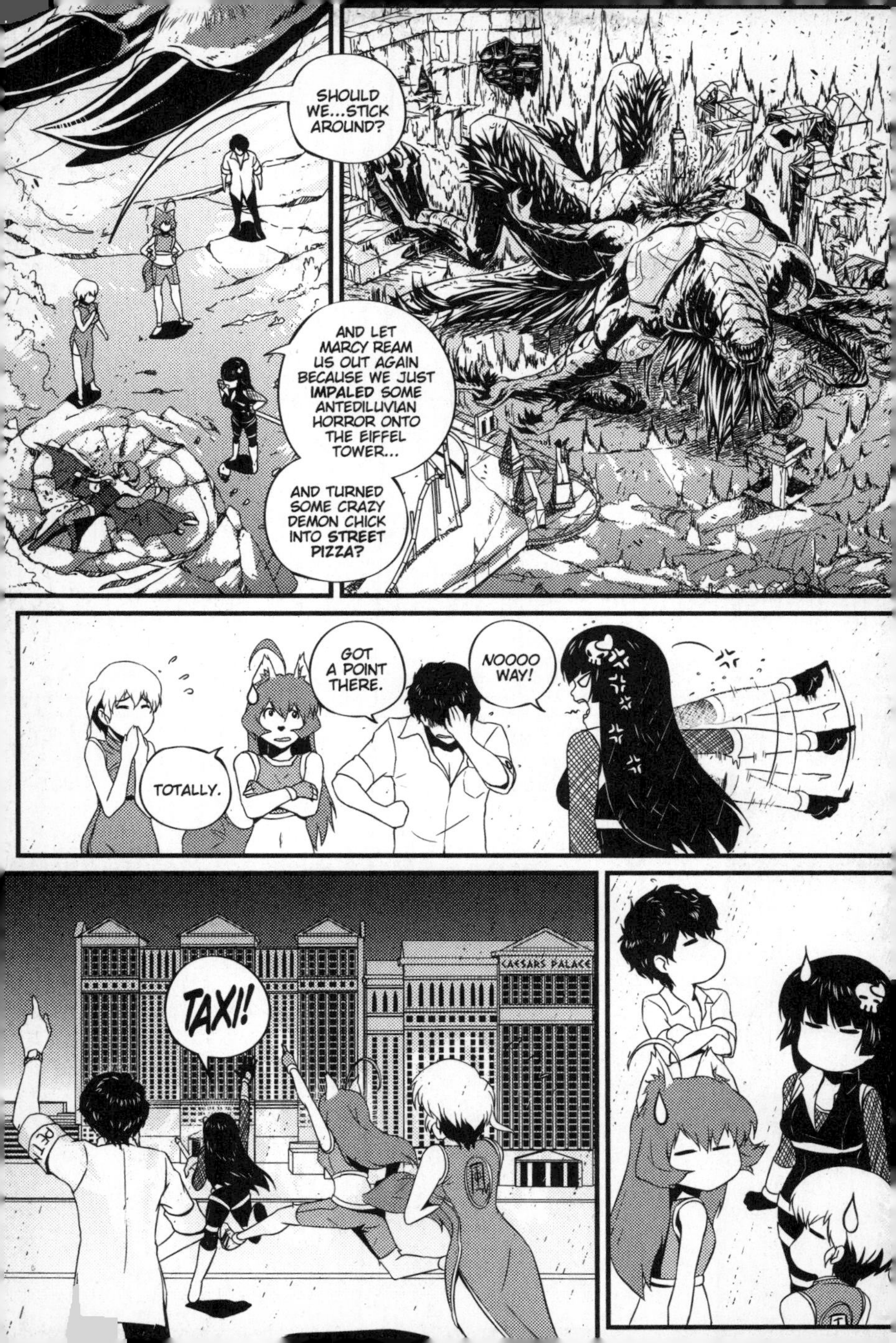
SHOULD WE...STICK AROUND?
AND LET MARCY REAM US OUT AGAIN BECAUSE WE JUST IMPALED SOME ANTEDILUVIAN HORROR ONTO THE EIFFEL TOWER...
AND TURNED SOME CRAZY DEMON CHICK INTO STREET PIZZA?
NOOOO WAY!
GOT A POINT THERE.
TOTALLY.
CAESARS PALACE
TAXI!

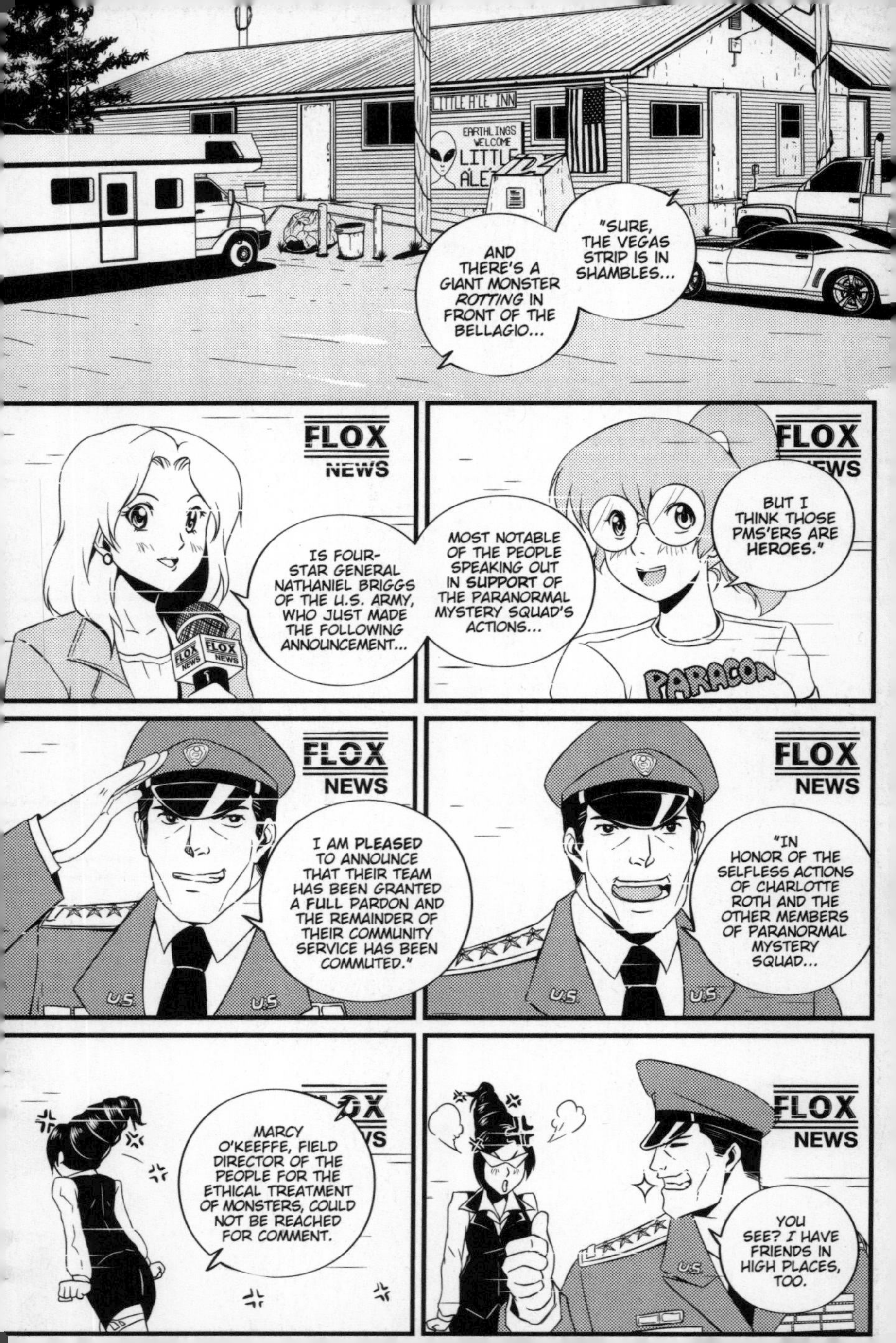
LITTLE A'LE' INN
EARTHLINGS WELCOME
"SURE, THE VEGAS STRIP IS IN SHAMBLES...
AND THERE'S A GIANT MONSTER *ROTTING* IN FRONT OF THE BELLAGIO...
FLOX NEWS
BUT I THINK THOSE PMS'ERS ARE HEROES."
PARACON
MOST NOTABLE OF THE PEOPLE SPEAKING OUT IN **SUPPORT** OF THE PARANORMAL MYSTERY SQUAD'S ACTIONS...
FLOX NEWS
IS FOUR-STAR GENERAL NATHANIEL BRIGGS OF THE U.S. ARMY, WHO JUST MADE THE FOLLOWING ANNOUNCEMENT...
FLOX NEWS
"IN HONOR OF THE SELFLESS ACTIONS OF CHARLOTTE ROTH AND THE OTHER MEMBERS OF PARANORMAL MYSTERY SQUAD...
FLOX NEWS
I AM PLEASED TO ANNOUNCE THAT THEIR TEAM HAS BEEN GRANTED A **FULL PARDON** AND THE REMAINDER OF THEIR COMMUNITY SERVICE HAS BEEN COMMUTED."
FLOX NEWS
YOU SEE? *I* HAVE FRIENDS IN HIGH PLACES, TOO.
MARCY O'KEEFFE, FIELD DIRECTOR OF THE PEOPLE FOR THE ETHICAL TREATMENT OF MONSTERS, COULD NOT BE REACHED FOR COMMENT.

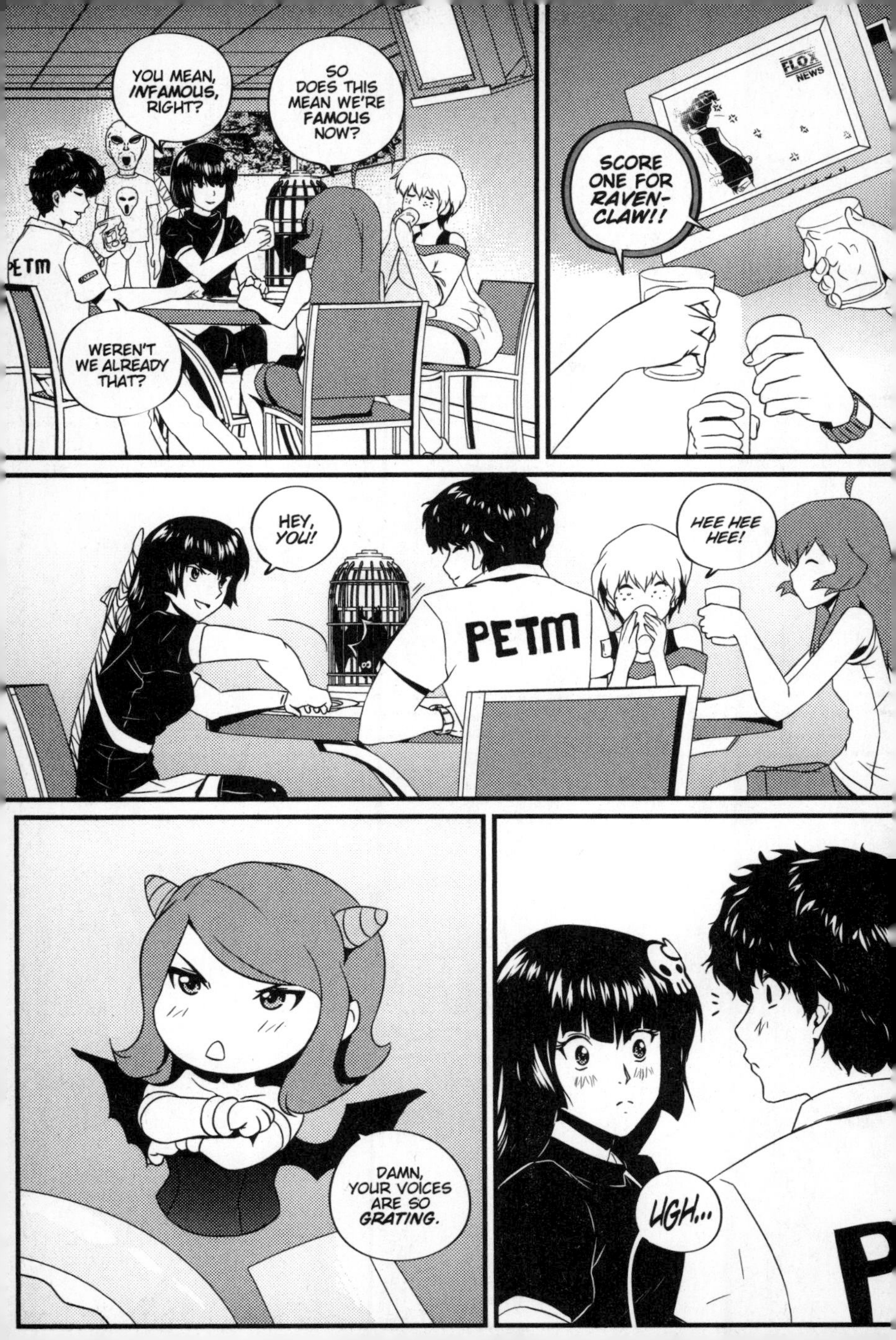

FLOX NEWS
SCORE ONE FOR RAVEN-CLAW!!
SO DOES THIS MEAN WE'RE FAMOUS NOW?
YOU MEAN, INFAMOUS, RIGHT?
PETM
WEREN'T WE ALREADY THAT?
HEE HEE HEE!
HEY, YOU!
PETM
UGH...
DAMN, YOUR VOICES ARE SO GRATING.

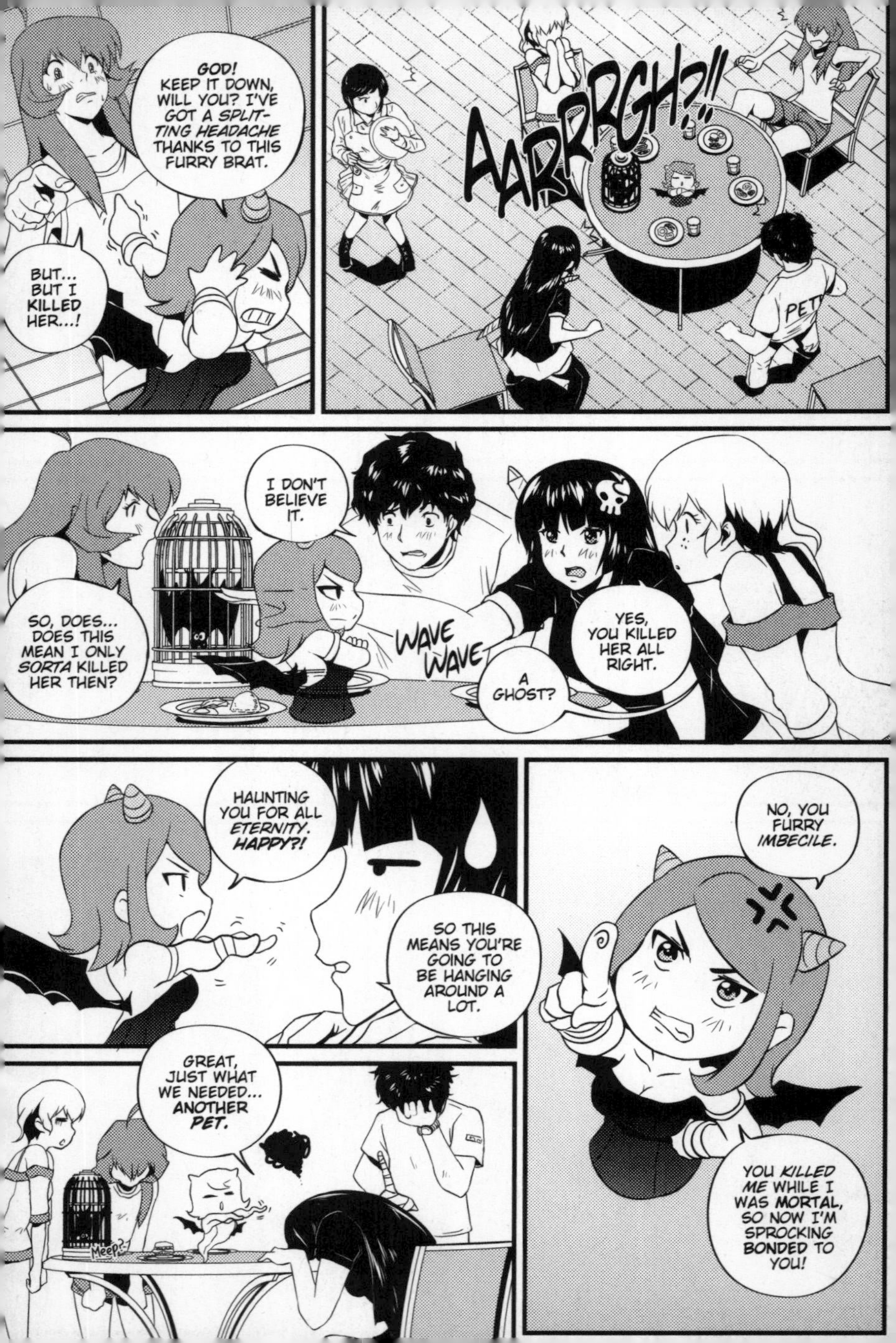
AARRRGH?!!
GOD! KEEP IT DOWN, WILL YOU? I'VE GOT A *SPLITTING HEADACHE* THANKS TO THIS FURRY BRAT.
BUT... BUT I KILLED HER...!
I DON'T BELIEVE IT.
A GHOST?
SO, DOES... DOES THIS MEAN I ONLY *SORTA* KILLED HER THEN?
YES, YOU KILLED HER ALL RIGHT.
WAVE WAVE
NO, YOU FURRY *IMBECILE.*
YOU *KILLED ME* WHILE I WAS **MORTAL**, SO NOW I'M SPROCKING **BONDED** TO YOU!
SO THIS MEANS YOU'RE GOING TO BE HANGING AROUND A LOT.
HAUNTING YOU FOR ALL *ETERNITY.* ***HAPPY?!***
GREAT, JUST WHAT WE NEEDED... **ANOTHER *PET.***
Meep?

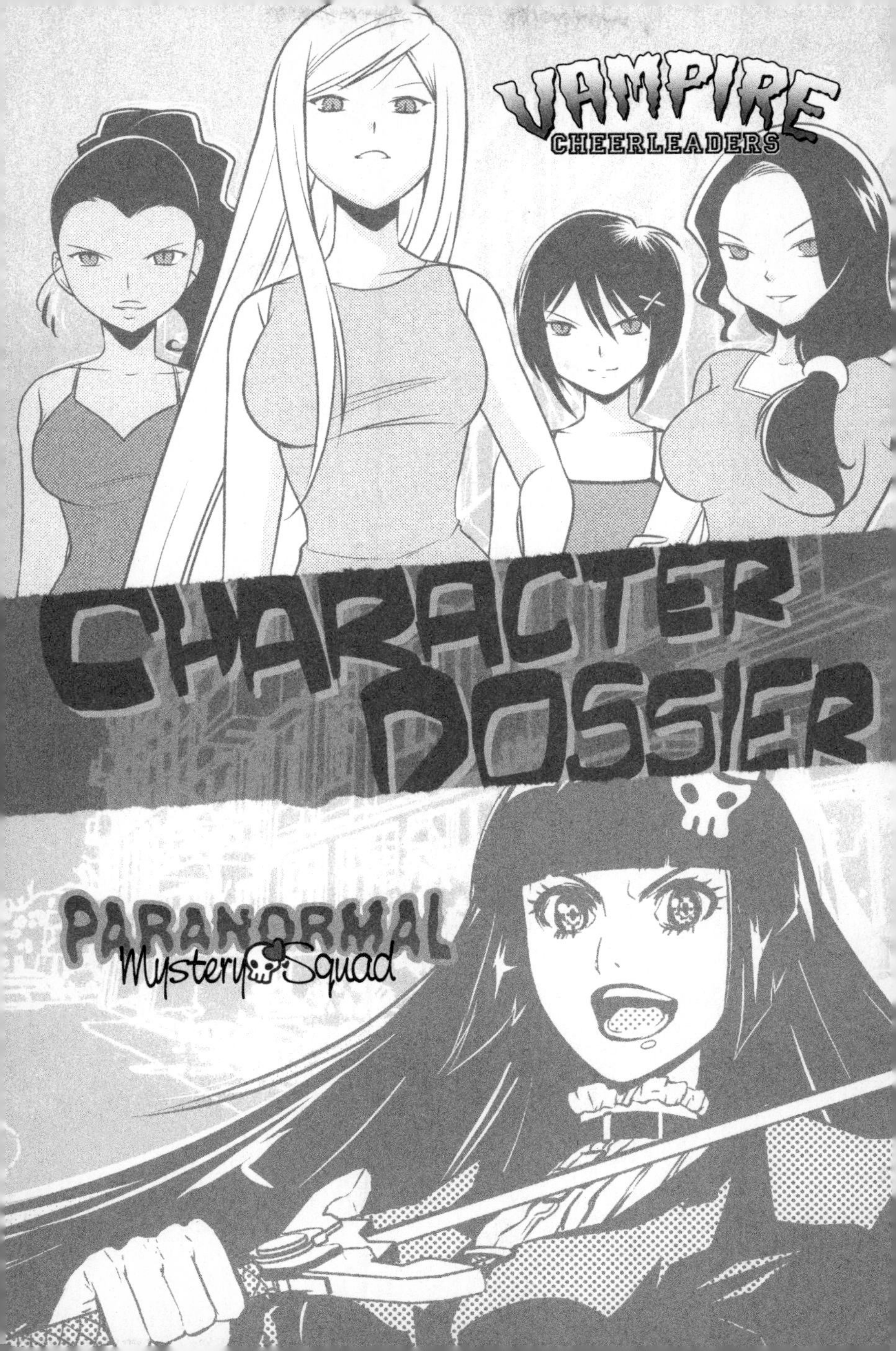
VAMPIRE
CHEERLEADERS
CHARACTER DOSSIER
PARANORMAL
Mystery Squad

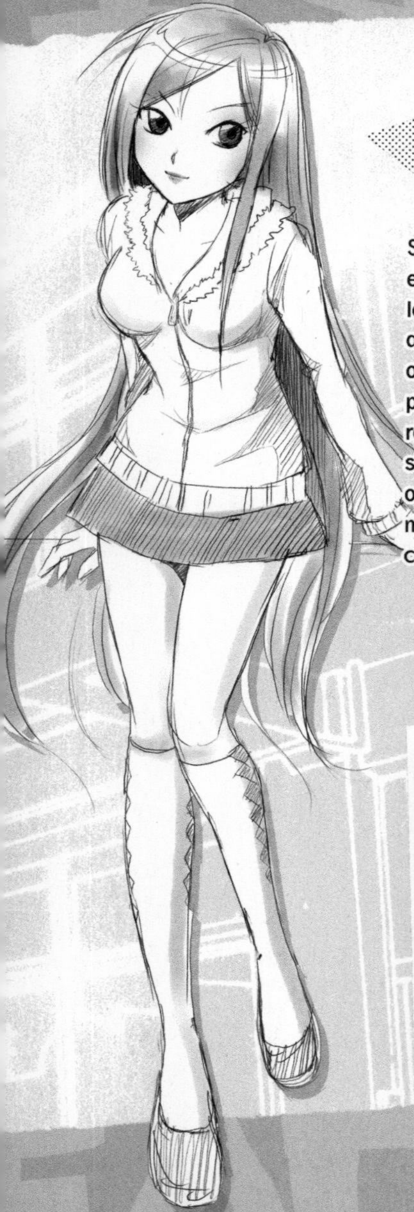

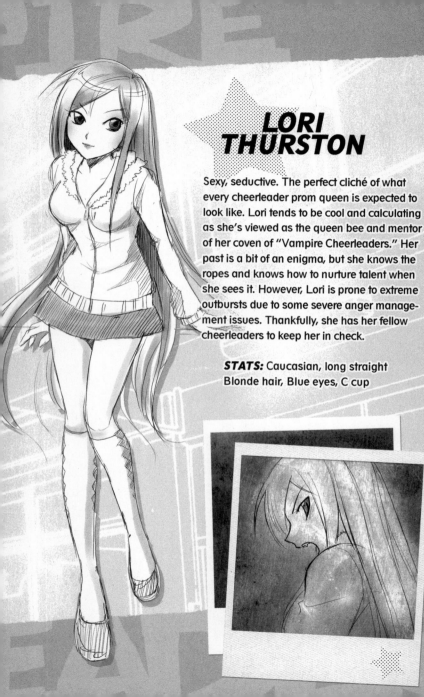

LORI THURSTON

Sexy, seductive. The perfect cliché of what every cheerleader prom queen is expected to look like. Lori tends to be cool and calculating as she's viewed as the queen bee and mentor of her coven of "Vampire Cheerleaders." Her past is a bit of an enigma, but she knows the ropes and knows how to nurture talent when she sees it. However, Lori is prone to extreme outbursts due to some severe anger management issues. Thankfully, she has her fellow cheerleaders to keep her in check.

STATS: Caucasian, long straight Blonde hair, Blue eyes, C cup

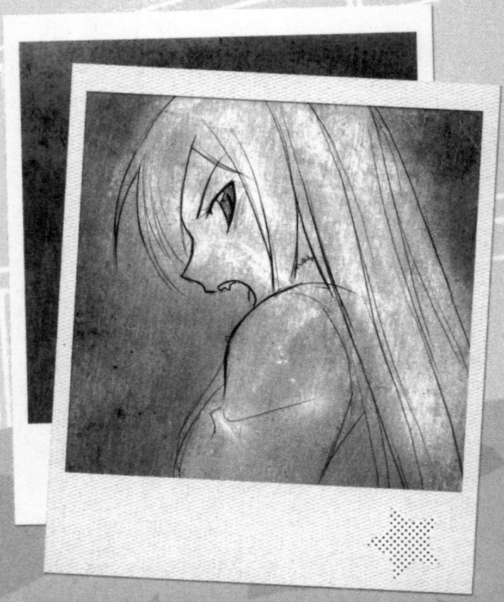

HEATHER HARTLEY

An eleventh grader on the B Squad who is seen as a goodie-two-shoes. Indeed, Heather's parents are overbearing and avid churchgoers, so Heather has lived a sheltered life. Once Heather gets turned into a vampire, however, a whole new world opens up for her.

STATS: Caucasian, Short (Petite), Brown hair done in a single pony tail in the back, Green eyes, B cup

ZOE WELLER
CO-CAPTAIN

Zoe has a good head on her shoulders and is Lori's right-hand woman. Unfortunately, Zoe seems to get rubbed the wrong way by Suki at every turn. The two always seem to be at each other's throats over the most trivial things. Playful rivalry? Or something else...?

STATS: African American, Brown/Black hair, Brown eyes, C cup

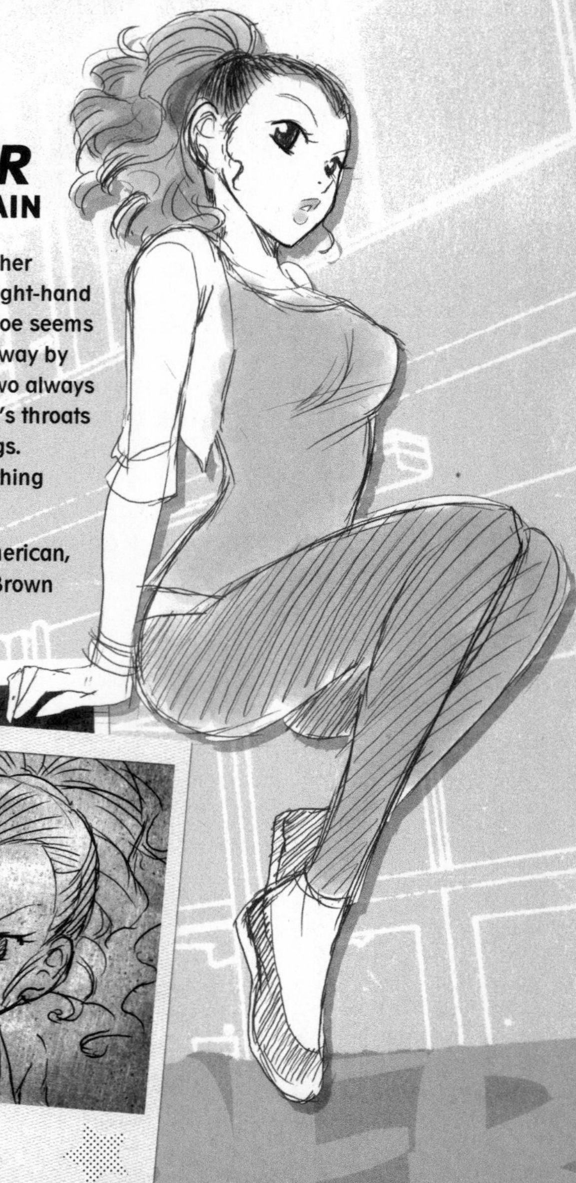

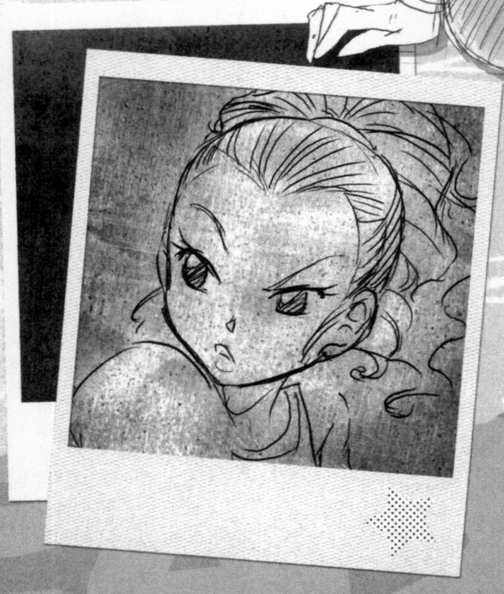

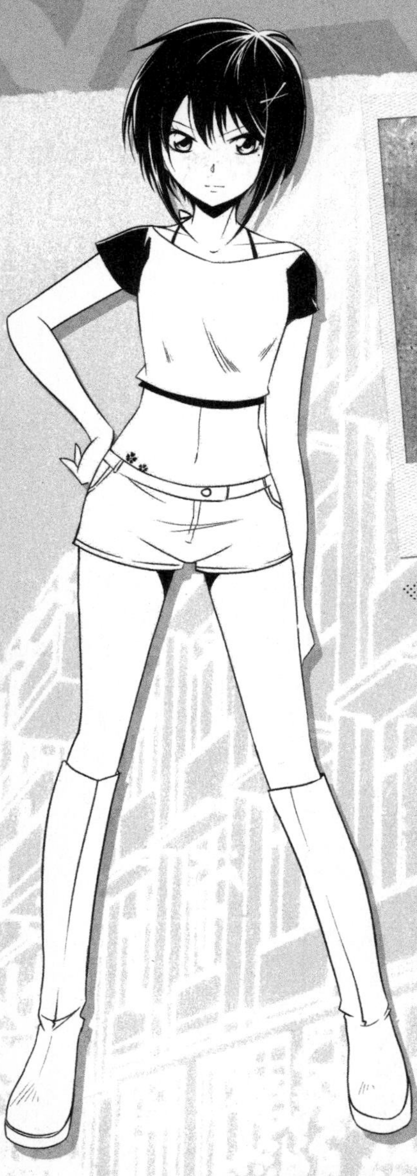

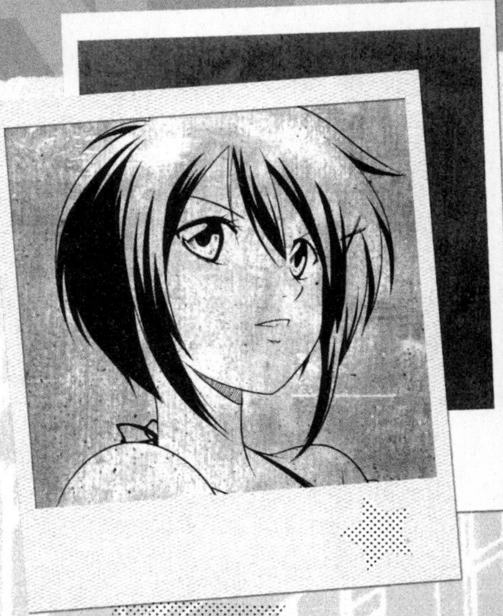

SUKI TAFT
CO-CAPTAIN

The bad seed. She knows guys dig Asian chicks and she knows just how to use her talents to bleed 'em dry (pun intended). Always saying whatever's on her mind...even when it's totally inappropriate and the wrong thing at the wrong time. Has a friendly(?) rivalry with Zoe.

STATS: Asian American, Black hair with highlights, Brown eyes but sometimes wears colored contacts, A cup

LESLEY CHANDRA
TEAM TREASURER

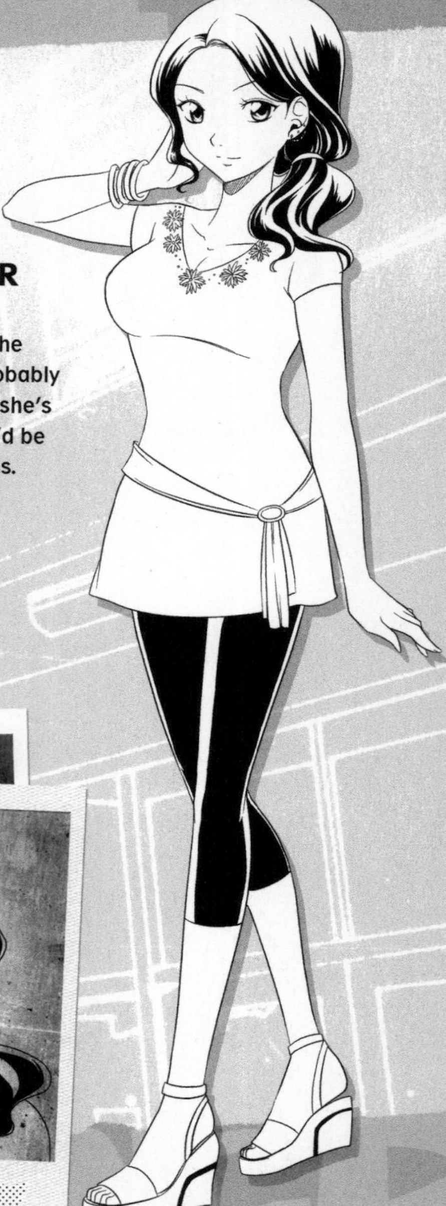

Pleasant personality, friendly. The voice of reason in the group. Probably the smartest of all the girls. But she's also got a wild side. In fact, you'd be surprised to know that she's "Ms. Kama Sutra" in a cheerleading costume.

STATS: East Indian American, Black/Brown hair, Brown eyes, D cup

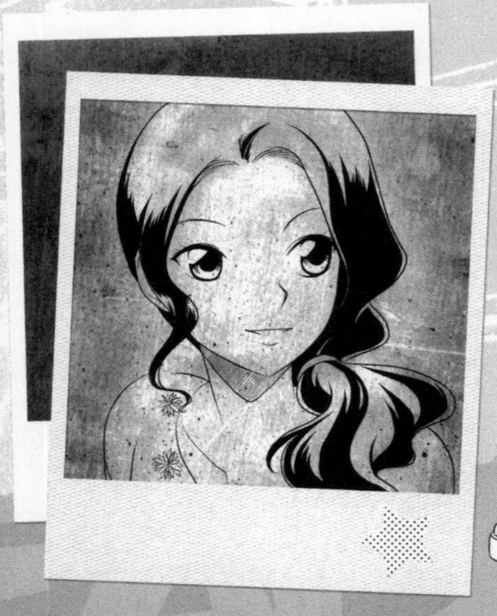

CANDICE

The team's former fifth member. She's up and disappeared without a trace. One of the rumors floating around school is that she got pregnant and her parents freaked and had her sent to a monastery. But the Vampire Cheerleaders know otherwise.

STATS: Caucasian, semi-curly/wavy hair, Brown eyes, C cup, Braces on her teeth.

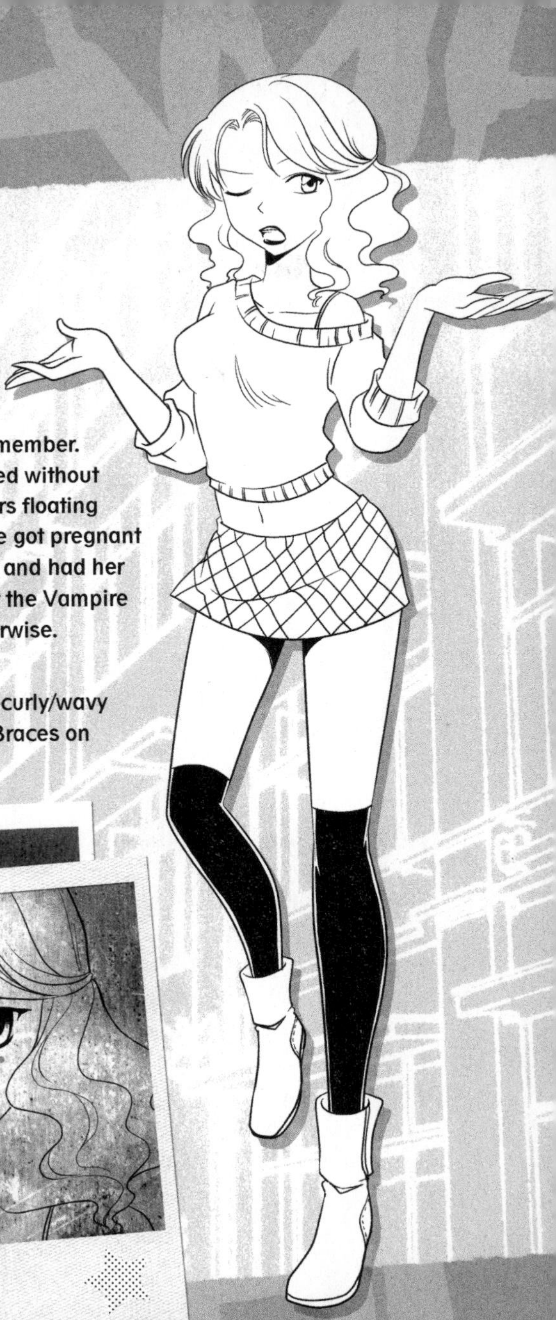

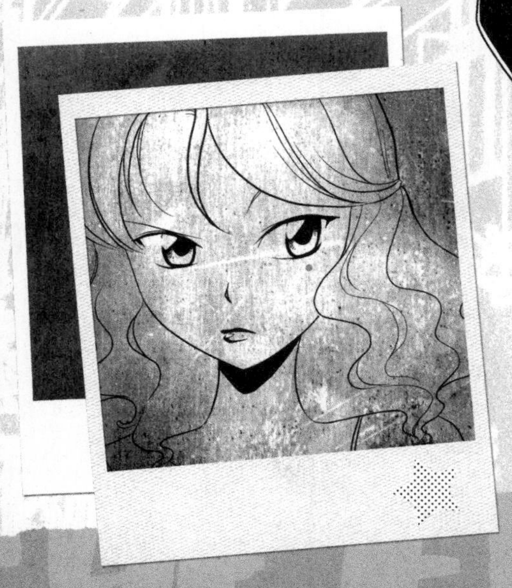

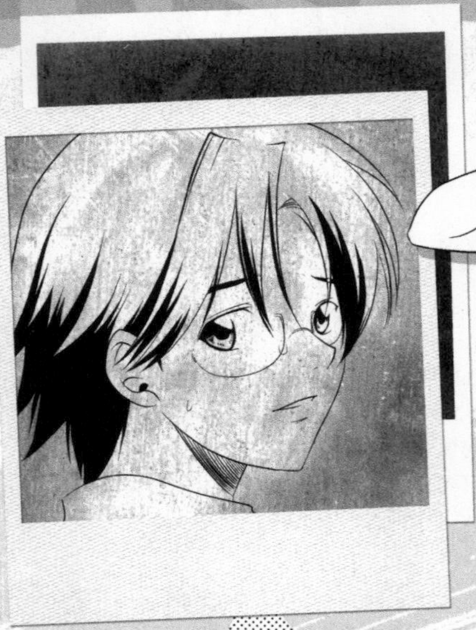

LEONARD DUVALL

Heather's best friend. A geek that dresses in fandom t-shirts and swears that he's discovered that the Bakertown cheerleaders are all vampires. Kinda shy/nervous. Has a crush on Heather, so it breaks his heart to see her go from the sweet girl he's crushed on for so long into a wild creature of the night with loose morals.

STATS: Caucasian, Brown hair, Blue eyes.

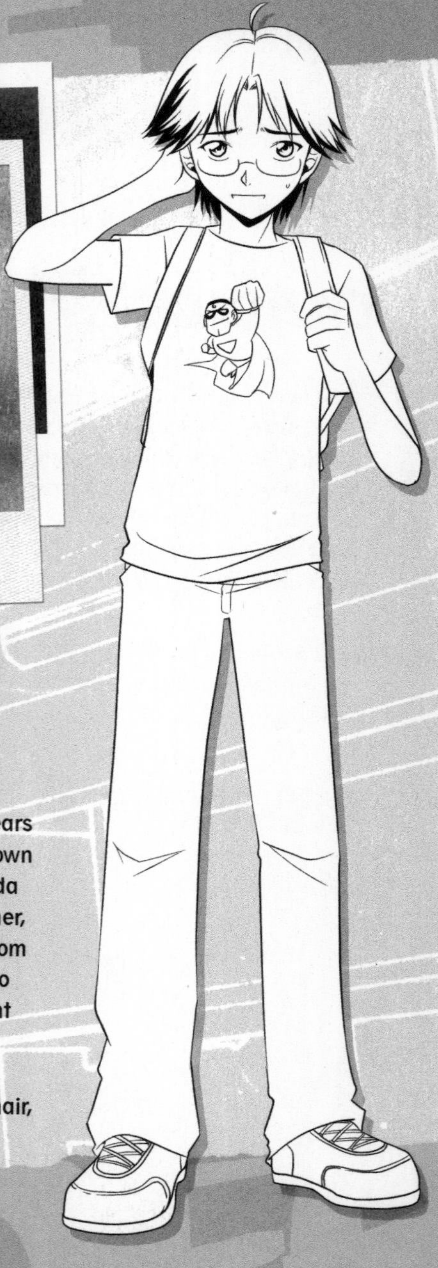

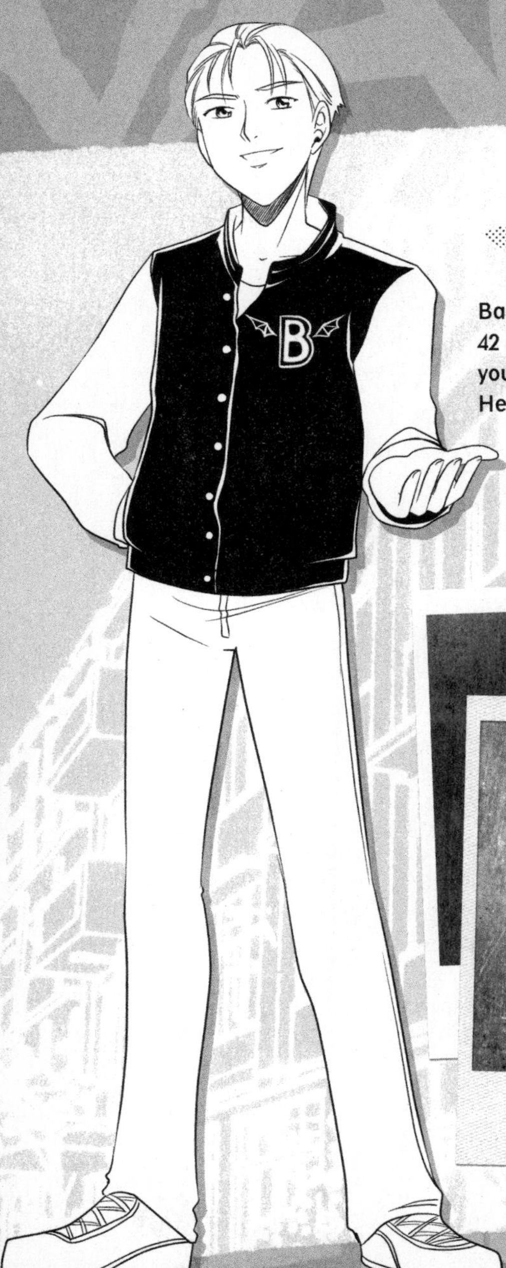

JULIAN

Bakertown's star kicker and number 42 on the team. Hunky guy, but not your typical jock meathead. Likes Heather and Heather likes him.

STATS: Caucasian, Blonde hair, Green eyes.

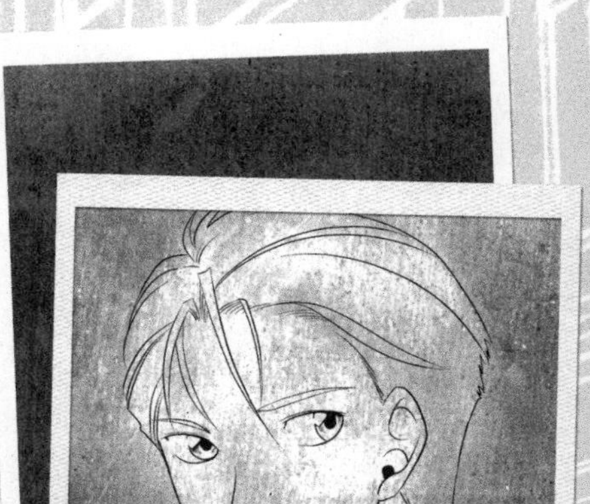

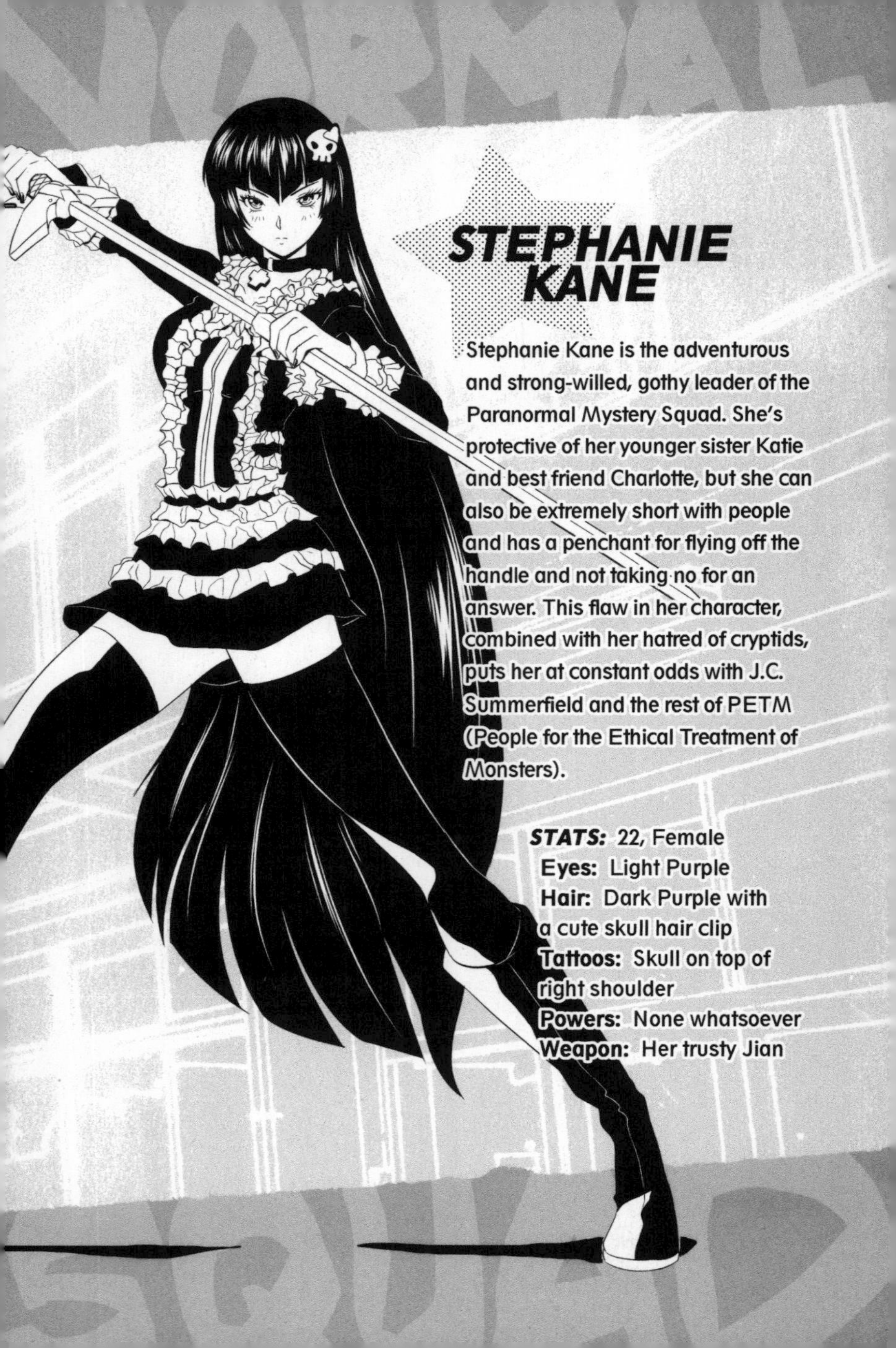

STEPHANIE KANE

Stephanie Kane is the adventurous and strong-willed, gothy leader of the Paranormal Mystery Squad. She's protective of her younger sister Katie and best friend Charlotte, but she can also be extremely short with people and has a penchant for flying off the handle and not taking no for an answer. This flaw in her character, combined with her hatred of cryptids, puts her at constant odds with J.C. Summerfield and the rest of PETM (People for the Ethical Treatment of Monsters).

STATS: 22, Female
Eyes: Light Purple
Hair: Dark Purple with a cute skull hair clip
Tattoos: Skull on top of right shoulder
Powers: None whatsoever
Weapon: Her trusty Jian

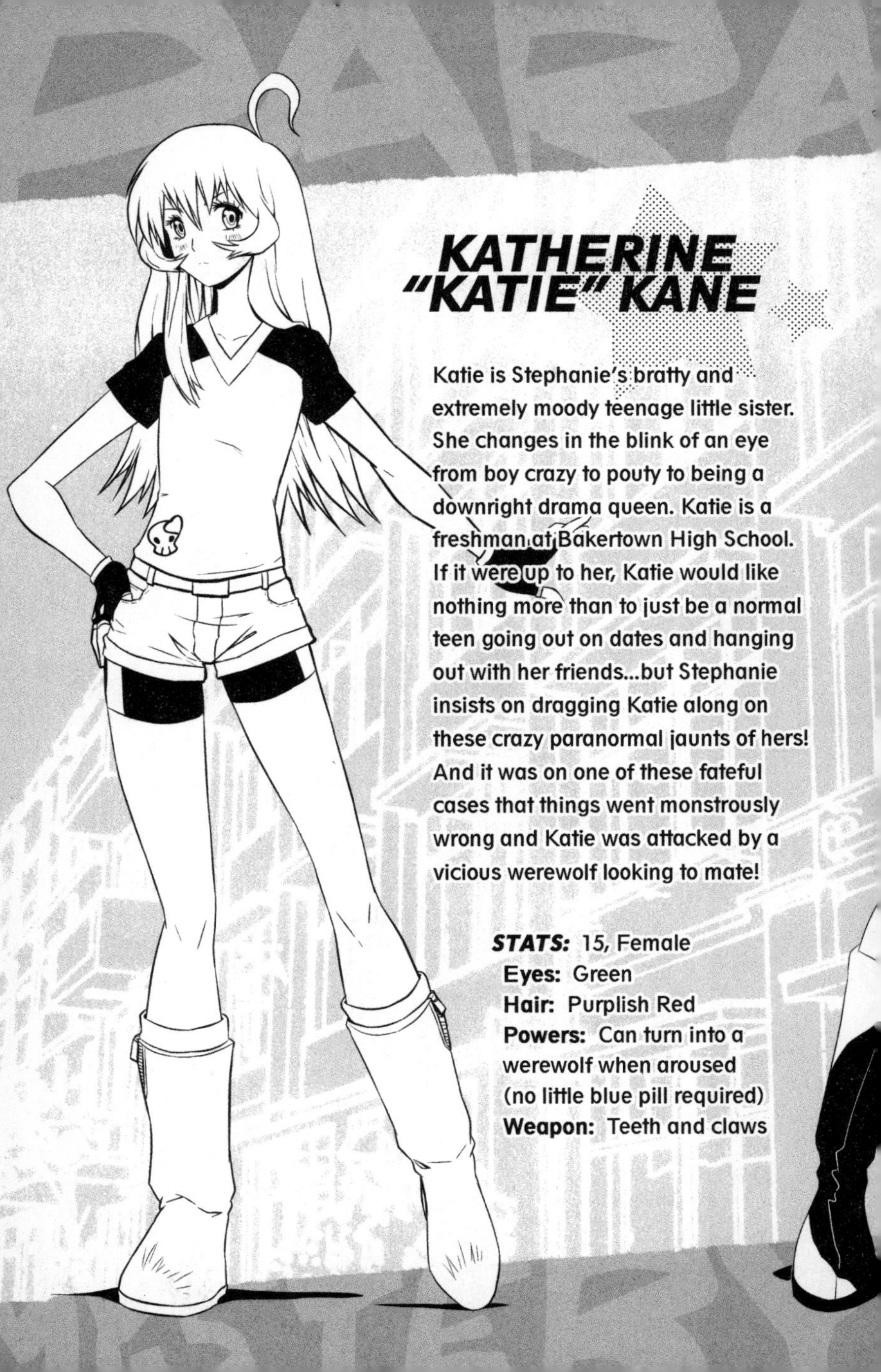

KATHERINE "KATIE" KANE

Katie is Stephanie's bratty and extremely moody teenage little sister. She changes in the blink of an eye from boy crazy to pouty to being a downright drama queen. Katie is a freshman at Bakertown High School. If it were up to her, Katie would like nothing more than to just be a normal teen going out on dates and hanging out with her friends...but Stephanie insists on dragging Katie along on these crazy paranormal jaunts of hers! And it was on one of these fateful cases that things went monstrously wrong and Katie was attacked by a vicious werewolf looking to mate!

STATS: 15, Female
Eyes: Green
Hair: Purplish Red
Powers: Can turn into a werewolf when aroused (no little blue pill required)
Weapon: Teeth and claws

CHARLOTTE ROTH

Charlotte and Stephanie have been thick as thieves since childhood due to their parents dragging them around the world on various paranormal and cryptid-hunting jaunts. Charlotte is a practicing Wiccan and has a special fondness for old TV shows...which oddly enough, seems to spill over into her spells. Charlotte is a very cheerful and warm person by nature, but she doesn't do well under pressure and can get quite flustered or freeze completely at the worst possible moment, much to the chagrin of her teammates.

STATS: 21, Female
Eyes: One Green, One Blue
Hair: Green and White
Powers: Wiccan with the power to see auras and cast elemental spells...if she can focus long enough, that is
Weapon: Magic staff and occasional wand (for easy portability)

J.C. SUMMERFIELD

J.C. Summerfield is a PETM employee who has been placed on Stephanie's team—over her protests—to observe and record Paranormal Mystery Squad's future cases. J.C.'s bleeding heart views towards cryptids often puts him in direct conflict with Stephanie, whose philosophy is "the only good cryptid is a dead cryptid." Unfortunately for J.C., his nervous demeanor and lanky, anemic build don't earn him any brownie points with the tough-as-nails P.M.S. team leader either.

STATS: 23, Male
Eyes: Brown
Hair: Brownish-Black, Curly
Powers: Spoilers...
Weapon: His bare hands...if you can get him to actually fight

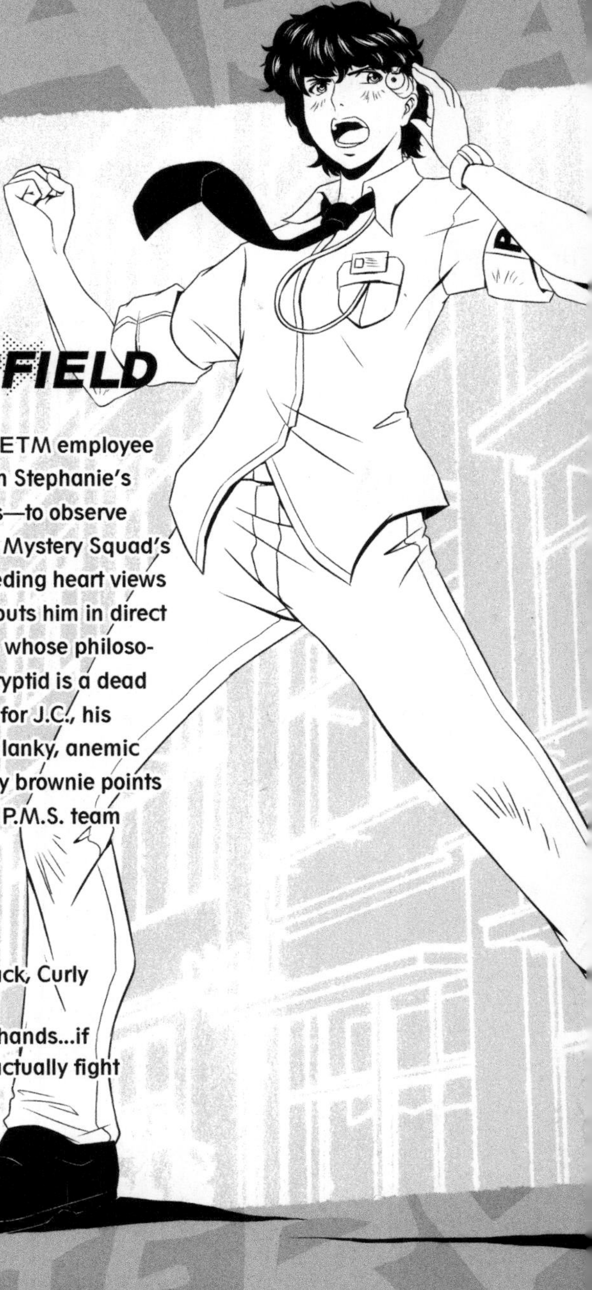

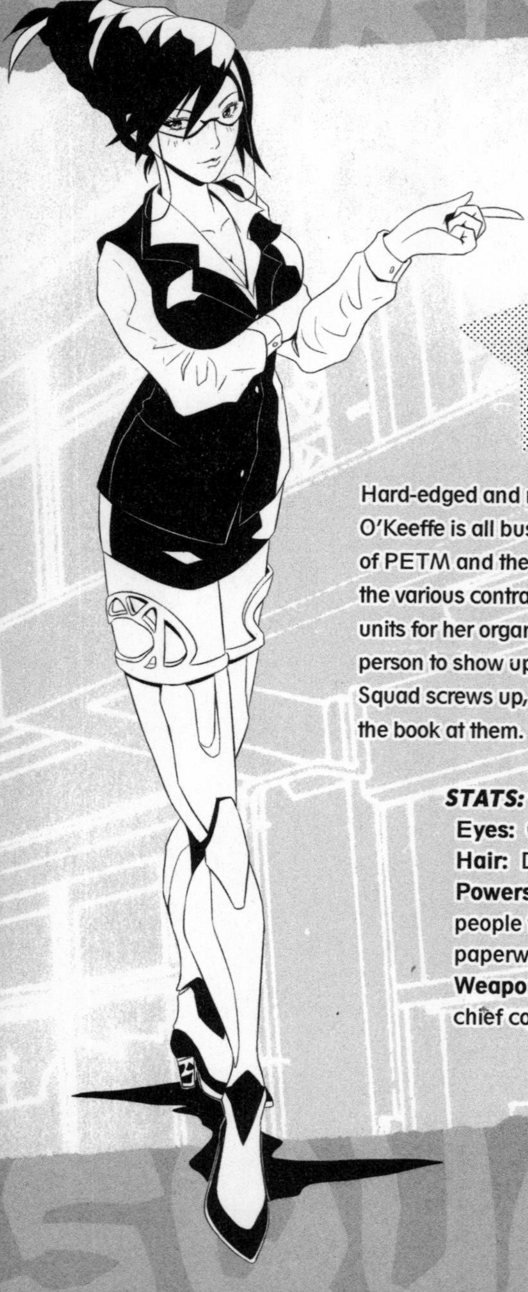

MARCY O'KEEFFE

Hard-edged and not to be messed with, Marcy O'Keeffe is all business. She is the Field Director of PETM and the person who directly oversees the various contractors and specimen retrieval units for her organization. She's also the first person to show up when Paranormal Mystery Squad screws up, and the first person to throw the book at them.

STATS: 42, Female
Eyes: Green, Wears Glasses
Hair: Dark Green
Powers: The ability to bury people that cross her in endless paperwork and litigation
Weapon: Mr. Lomax, PETM's chief counsel

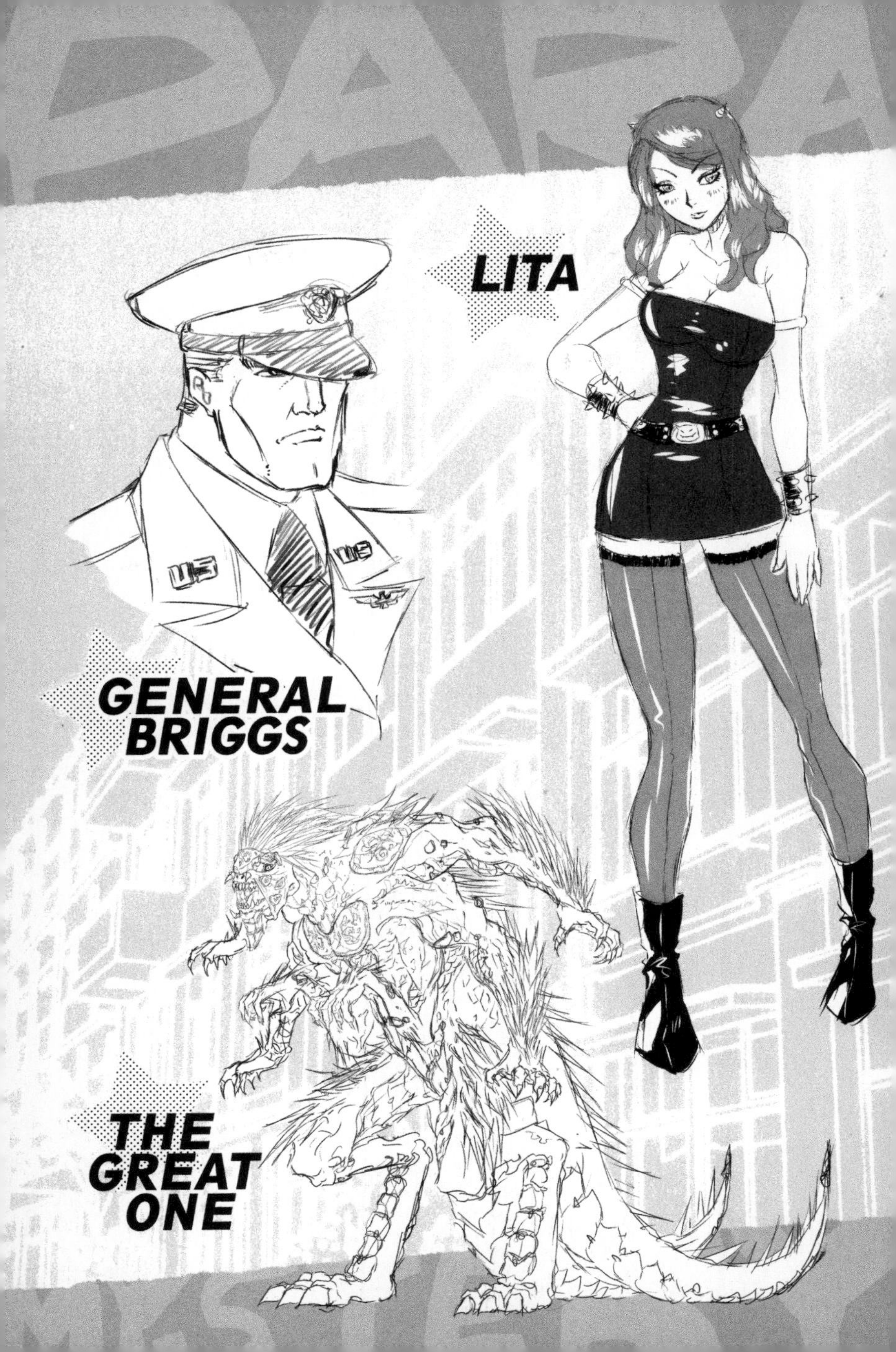
LITA
GENERAL BRIGGS
THE GREAT ONE

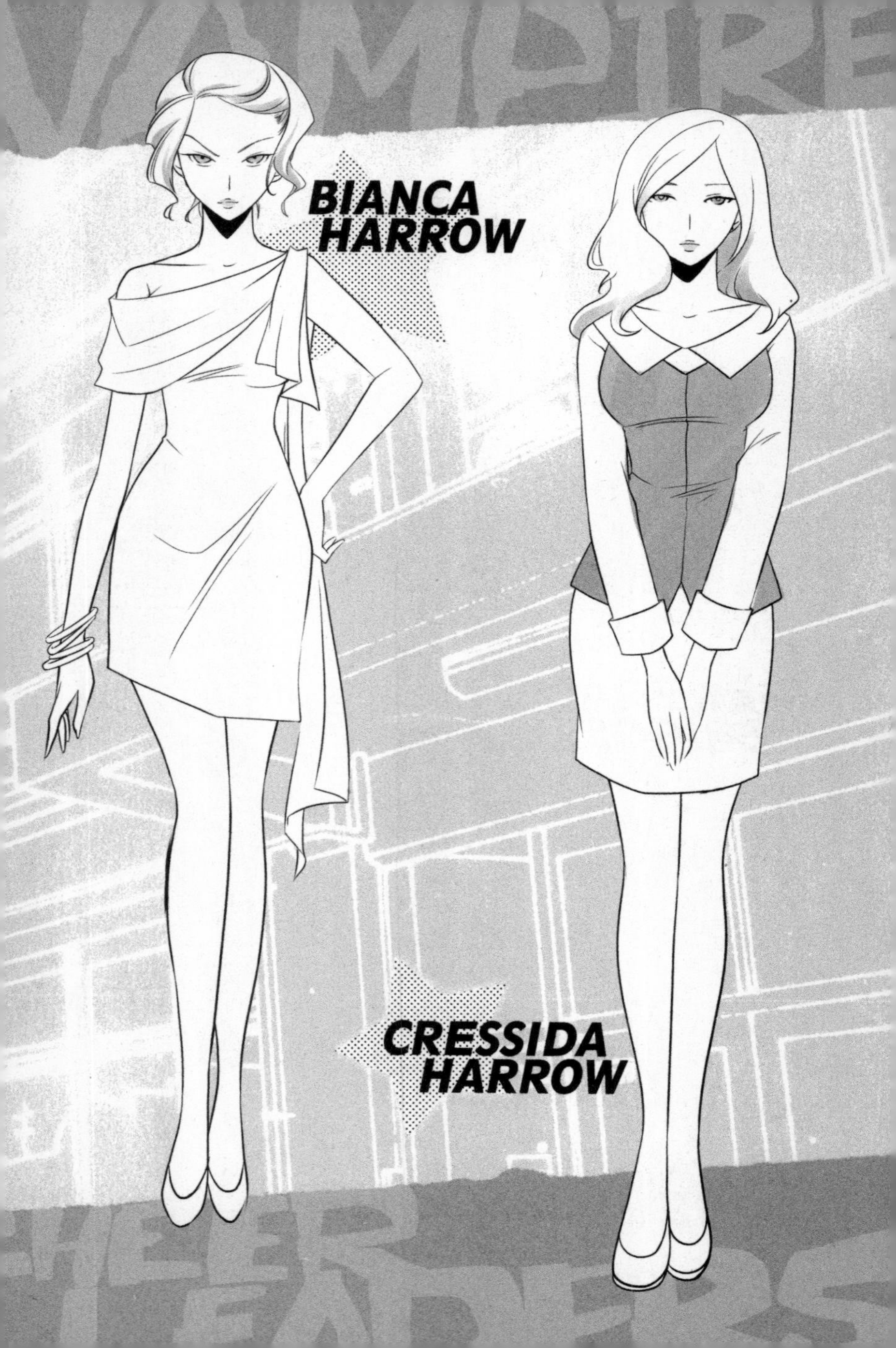
BIANCA HARROW
CRESSIDA HARROW

READ ME LEFT-TO-RIGHT →

Eerie Cuties / PARANORMAL Mystery Squad

LINGONBERRIES Guest Strip 1 (of 2)

written by Adam Arnold / artwork by Shouri

SOME YEARS AGO
THEY LOOK DONE TO ME.
JUST A LITTLE BIT LONGER, NINA... EH HEH...
YOU SURE THIS WON'T HURT?
NAH, IT'LL BE QUICK. YOU WON'T FEEL A THING. JUST A QUICK PRICK.
OKAY...
TOYS
CHOMP
HA HA! THAT TICKLES, LAYLA!
MMM. STEPHANIE, YOUR BLOOD IS SO SWEET.
TANGY EVEN. LIKE RASPBERRIES, NO... LINGONBERRIES.
REALLY? IT TASTES THAT GOOD?
YEAH! BLOOD TASTES DIFFERENT DEPENDING ON THE VINTAGE. AND YOU'RE A GOOD VINTAGE.
DON'T BELIEVE ME? GO ON, SEE FOR YOURSELF. GIVE IT A LITTLE TRY.
STEPHANIE, I DUNNO...
WELL, I DO LIKE LINGON-BERRY JAM...
OH, HECK... WHY NOT?
LICK
BLAAAH! IT TASTES LIKE TINFOIL!
PITOOWE! PITOOWE!!
AH HA HA HA HA!!
GOTCHA!!!

Eerie Cuties by David Lumsdon & Gisèle Lagacé (eeriecuties.com)

READ ME LEFT-TO-RIGHT →

Eerie Cuties / Paranormal Mystery Squad

TREASURE IT ALWAYS Guest Strip 2 (of 2)

written by Adam Arnold / artwork by Shouri

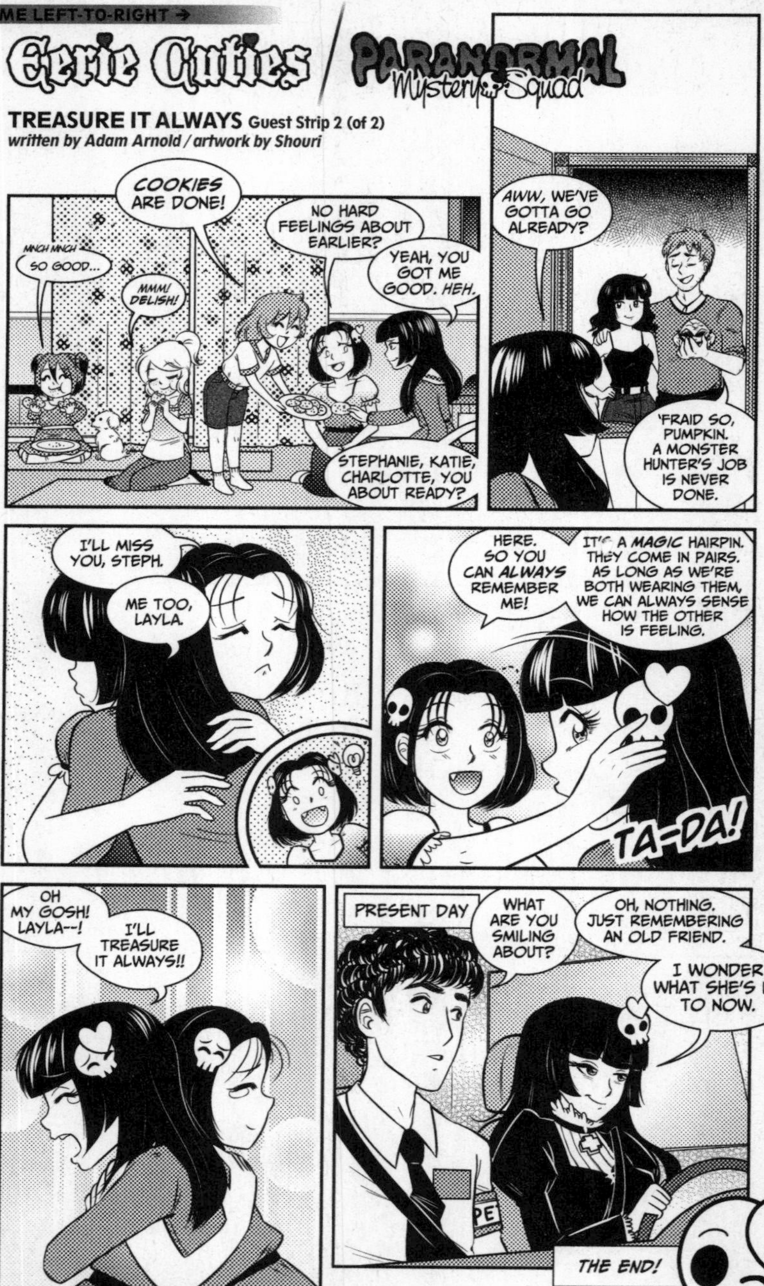
MNCH MNCH
SO GOOD...
COOKIES ARE DONE!
MMM! DELISH!
NO HARD FEELINGS ABOUT EARLIER?
YEAH, YOU GOT ME GOOD. HEH.
STEPHANIE, KATIE, CHARLOTTE, YOU ABOUT READY?
AWW, WE'VE GOTTA GO ALREADY?
'FRAID SO, PUMPKIN. A MONSTER HUNTER'S JOB IS NEVER DONE.
I'LL MISS YOU, STEPH.
ME TOO, LAYLA.
HERE. SO YOU CAN ALWAYS REMEMBER ME!
IT'S A MAGIC HAIRPIN. THEY COME IN PAIRS. AS LONG AS WE'RE BOTH WEARING THEM, WE CAN ALWAYS SENSE HOW THE OTHER IS FEELING.
TA-DA!
OH MY GOSH! LAYLA--!
I'LL TREASURE IT ALWAYS!!
PRESENT DAY
WHAT ARE YOU SMILING ABOUT?
OH, NOTHING. JUST REMEMBERING AN OLD FRIEND.
I WONDER WHAT SHE'S UP TO NOW.
THE END!

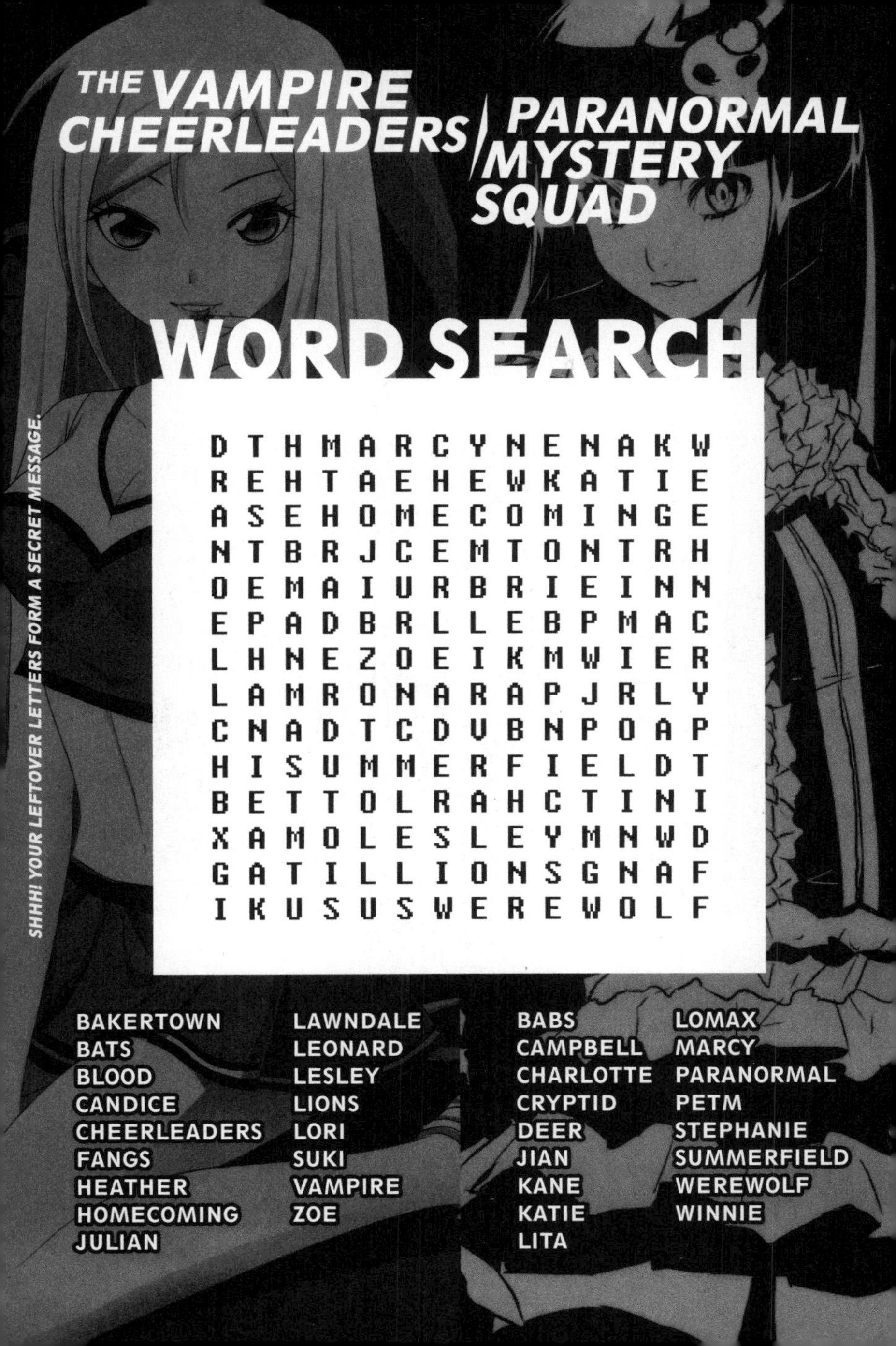

THE VAMPIRE CHEERLEADERS / PARANORMAL MYSTERY SQUAD

WORD SEARCH

D	T	H	M	A	R	C	Y	N	E	N	A	K	W
R	E	H	T	A	E	H	E	W	K	A	T	I	E
A	S	E	H	O	M	E	C	O	M	I	N	G	E
N	T	B	R	J	C	E	M	T	O	N	T	R	H
O	E	M	A	I	U	R	B	R	I	E	I	N	N
E	P	A	D	B	R	L	L	E	B	P	M	A	C
L	H	N	E	Z	O	E	I	K	M	W	I	E	R
L	A	M	R	O	N	A	R	A	P	J	R	L	Y
C	N	A	D	T	C	D	V	B	N	P	O	A	P
H	I	S	U	M	M	E	R	F	I	E	L	D	T
B	E	T	T	O	L	R	A	H	C	T	I	N	I
X	A	M	O	L	E	S	L	E	Y	M	N	W	D
G	A	T	I	L	L	I	O	N	S	G	N	A	F
I	K	U	S	U	S	W	E	R	E	W	O	L	F

SHHH! YOUR LEFTOVER LETTERS FORM A SECRET MESSAGE.

BAKERTOWN
BATS
BLOOD
CANDICE
CHEERLEADERS
FANGS
HEATHER
HOMECOMING
JULIAN

LAWNDALE
LEONARD
LESLEY
LIONS
LORI
SUKI
VAMPIRE
ZOE

BABS
CAMPBELL
CHARLOTTE
CRYPTID
DEER
JIAN
KANE
KATIE
LITA

LOMAX
MARCY
PARANORMAL
PETM
STEPHANIE
SUMMERFIELD
WEREWOLF
WINNIE

THE CHEERS OF
VAMPIRE CHEERLEADERS

Wanna cheer with the best of 'em?
Here's the full list of all the cheers from "Fang Service"
for easy reference! *GOOOO, BATS!*

**B SQUAD
PRACTICE CHEER:**
Front to back,
Left to right,
Come on, Bats,
Fight, fight, fight!

**DANIELLE'S
TRY-OUT CHEER:**
Let's go! Let-let-let's go!
C'mon, Bats! Let's go!
Let's go, let's go.
Bats, let's go!

**HEATHER'S
TRY-OUT CHEER:**
Bakertown Bats are here to fight!
And cowardly Lions meow with fright!
We're 6 and 0, and we've got flow...
So come on, team, let's go, go, GO!

BAKERTOWN'S HOMECOMING CHEER:
Bakertown, it's homecoming night! And the Bats are here...
To fight, fight, fight!
Now repeat after us, and lemme hear you yell it!
Purple & Black!
(PURPLE & BLACK!!)
Bats, let's fly!
(BATS, LET'S FLY!!)
Press the attack!
(PRESS THE ATTACK!!)
To victo-rye!!
(TO VICTO-RYEEE!!!)

LAWNDALE'S HOMECOMING CHEER:

Hey, Lions, are you there?
Raise your paws in the air!
Show your pride! Gold & Red!
Put these batsies right to bed!
Do it right! Roar! Roar! Rooooar!!

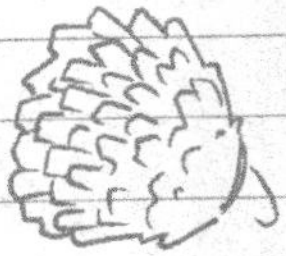

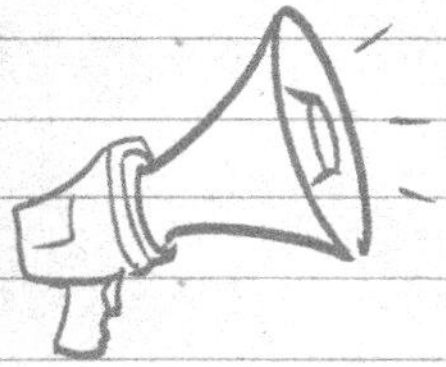

BAKERTOWN HOMECOMING RALLY CHEER:

Come on, Bats,
You'll be fine!
Just keep those cats
Way in Line!

UNUSED CHEERS

ALTERNATE DANIELLE TRY-OUT CHEER:

Come on, Bats, let's go!
Let-let-let's go!
C'mon, Bats, let's go!!

ALTERNATE HEATHER TRY-OUT CHEER (V.1):

Come on, fans! It's up to you!!
Stand up! Here's what to do!
Yell, "BHS!" Yes, "BHS!"
You got it!
"Purple & Black!" "Purple & Black!"
BHS, Purple & Black!

ALTERNATE HEATHER TRY-OUT CHEER (V.2):

Hey, hey, Bats, yell it loud and clap your hands!
PURPLE! BLACK! PURPLE! BLACK!
Hey, hey, let's do it again, this time yell, "BATS WIN!"
Purple! Black! Bats Win!!
Purple! Black! Bats Win!!

CUTTING ROOM FLOOR

Paranormal Mystery Squad
"So My Sister's a Bitch in Heat"
Deleted Scenes

SCENE 8-L - Katie Shedding

[Immediately following the Thunderbird cliff dive sequence, there would've been a quick gag back at the Paranormal Mystery Squad's offices. It was cut since there was already one couch gag earlier in the same scene. --AA]

THURSDAY NIGHT, NOVEMBER 3
The gang is vegging out in the living room watching TV ("*Fringe*" or "*CSI*") with their bowl of popcorn and snacks. Charlotte and Stephanie are on both sides of Were-Katie on the sofa/couch and J.C.'s in a separate chair. Katie's all furred out and taking up most of the couch, though. Stephanie then gets ticked off that Katie is SHEDDING.

> STEPHANIE
> Aw, Katie, get on the floor! You're
> **shedding** all over the couch!!

SCENE 11 - Normal Days Are Here At Last

[Once Katie is cured, three days pass before her furry symptoms rear their ugly head again. Originally, there was going to be a sequence where we get to see what Katie did those three days while a normal teen. This was cut purely for pacing reasons as it was so close to the finale. --AA]

1) MONDAY MORNING, NOVEMBER 7
Things are finally quiet today. No dogs. Just piece and quiet. And Katie can finally enjoy a walk somewhere and the nice sunny sky without having to worry about those darn dogs. (She should have her shake in her hand here. Maybe have head phones on with some music notes over her head.)

> KATIE (SMILING)
> *Ahh, that's better.*

Off in the distance, animal control is loading up the last of
the pound puppies. The poor guys are whimpering.

                    DOGS (SAD)
             Whimper Whimper

Next we have three (3) quick panels to show Katie's daily life
is all normal and happy happy now thanks to her miracle Monkshood
shakes.

2) **MONDAY AFTERNOON**
At school sitting in the bleachers drooling over the football
players practicing and the guys running track.

                    KATIE
             Look at all those *pork swords*...

3) **TUESDAY NIGHT**
Katie with her friends Gwen and Rani at the mall doing clothes
shopping and some cute guys pass by.

                    GWEN
             You should **totally** get that one!

                    GUYS
             Hey, ladies.

                    KATIE (HEARTS POUNDING IN HER EYES)
             Hubba hubba!

                    RANI (LOOKING AT HER WEIRD)
             Whoa, chill out, girl.

4) **WEDNESDAY NIGHT**
Katie at the movies watching some Romantic Comedy with Patrick
Dempsey or someone in it. And she's just mega-gaga in love.

                    MOVIE GUY
             "Nobody in the world makes me laugh
             the way you do. You're my best friend.
             I just wanna be with you."

                    KATIE
             Droool

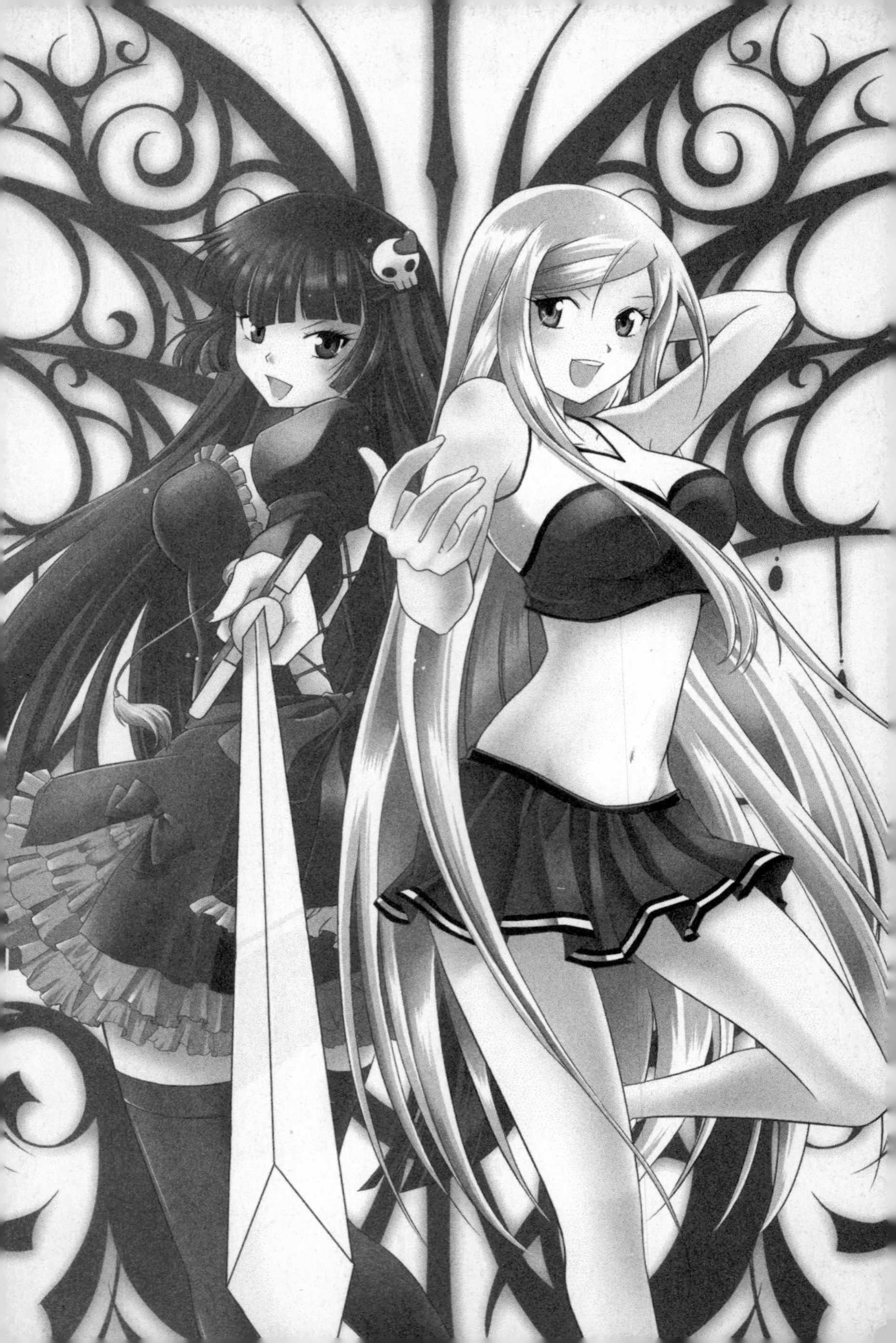

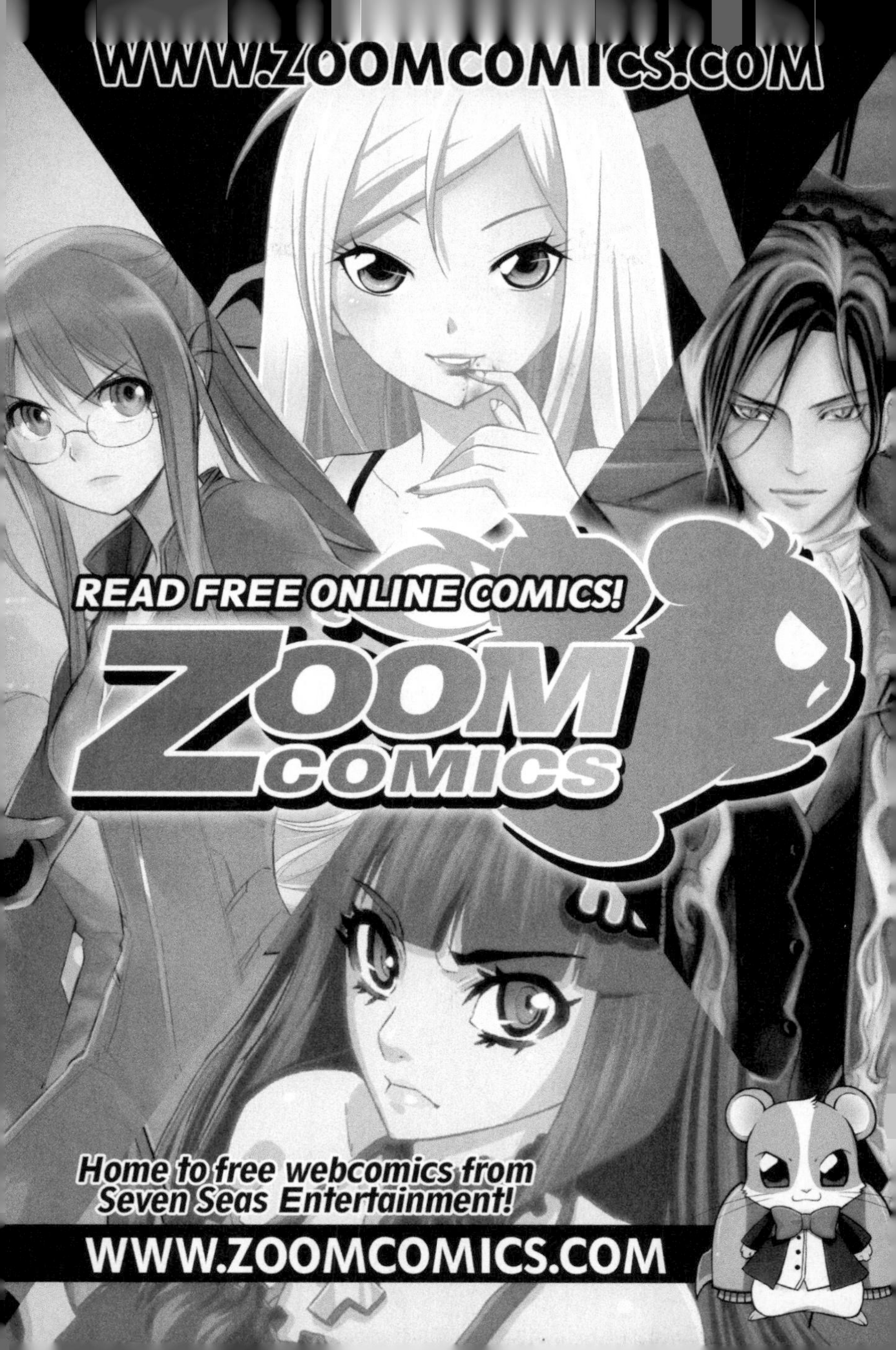

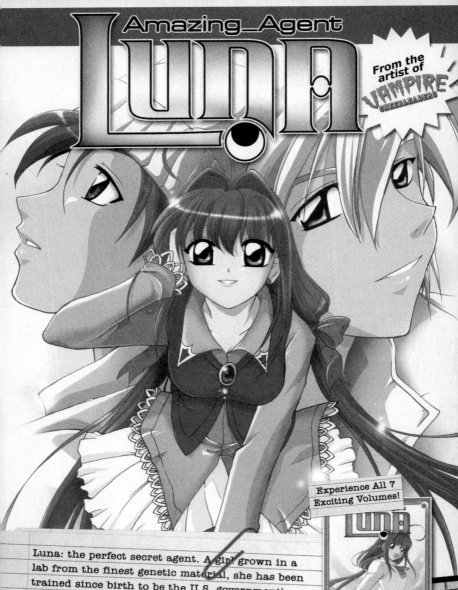

Amazing Agent LUNA

Experience All 7 Exciting Volumes!

Luna: the perfect secret agent. A girl grown in a lab from the finest genetic material, she has been trained since birth to be the U.S. government's ultimate espionage weapon. But now she is given an assignment that will test her abilities to the max - *high school!*

story Nunzio DeFilippis & Christina Weir • **art** Shiei